D1036822

THE JOURNALS

OURNALS

A Message from the Council of Ancients

THE JOURNALS

A Message from the Council of Ancients

R. T. Stone

DaScribe
Literary Marketing Services

DaScribe Literary Marketing Services
P.O. Box 541142
Cincinnati, OH 45254-1142

ISBN 0-9659-352-3-X

Publisher's Cataloging-In-Publication
(Provided by Quality Books, Inc.)

Stone, R. T.
     The journals : a message from the Council of Ancients. Book
I / R.T. Stone. -- 1st ed.
     p. cm.
     ISBN: 0-9659352-3-X

    1. Council of Ancients (Extraterrestrial beings)--Fiction.
2. Guides (Spiritualism)--Fiction. 3. Life on other planets--
Fiction.   I. Title. II. Title: Message from the Council of
Ancients

PS369.T66J64 1998   813'.54
                     QBI97-41382

Dedication

May the mysteries of this realm unfold before you.
May you become one with the Universe. May you
be filled with spirit and energy and light and love.
Namasté.

Acknowledgments

To my loving wife and family whose patience, support and understanding made this book possible. To the folks at DaScribe—Sherie, James, Ron, Mike, Craig, Jody, Brian, Keith and Cat—whoever said good help was hard to find? To John Kachuba, faithful editor and friend. To Jim and Brent for twenty-four hour days of great, dedicated effort. To Tammy and Rose, for their time and skill with a red pen. And to Boinger at Millennium for his excellent web work.

To anyone I ever hurt, I sincerely apologize. To anyone I ever helped, thank you for allowing me to serve. To everyone I have ever known, thanks for the lessons. Onward through the fog.

The Journals' Proceeds

It is the author's intent that *The Journals* should not only ease spiritual suffering but other heartaches as well. To achieve this goal, R.T. Stone has directed the publisher to donate a percentage of the net profits of this book to a local Cincinnati orphanage.

THE
JOURNALS
A Message from the Council of Ancients

Section

Who knows what the hand will do
What the mind will insist
What play upon man the act will become
What fortune holds for desperate self

I, Robert Thomas Stone, being of sound mind and body, do solemnly swear that I am innocent of all charges brought against me. I vehemently and categorically deny all wrongdoing in the matter of the United States versus Robert T. Stone. Specifically, I declare the following:

1. I am not guilty of arson related to the burning of the Cosmic Club of Covington, Kentucky.
2. I am not guilty of forty-seven counts of attempted aggravated murder.
3. I did not flee the scene of the crime as the police have alleged.
4. I did not resist arrest.
5. I have never attempted harm against anyone.

Further, I wish to convey in the strongest possible terms that I have been framed for these crimes by a power I cannot explain. A devious, extortionist force calling itself the Council of Ancients has set upon me a web of blackmail designed to conscript me into writing a book about the lives of Daniel Gilday and Allison Leslie Pippin, two people I have met only in passing. The Council, despite my profuse doubts, insists they have been chosen to herald the dawn of a new age of enlightenment on planet Earth.

For my part, I shall honor its request. I do this under duress. I do this to protect my freedom. I do this to save my life.

Once again, I emphatically protest my innocence. Signed and sworn before God and His witnesses in the great state of Ohio on this date, August 20, 1990.

Signed

R T Stone

Robert T. Stone

Witnesses

Rose Stone

Rose Stone

Parker Floyd

Parker Floyd

James Bennett

James Bennett

Chapter 1

August 5, 1990

Blackness. Deep. Dark. Ominous. Complete. An eclipse.

"Oh, Papa," a pained voice cried across the distant void. "Please, Papa . . . *wake up.*"

A raindrop splattered on my forehead. The voice approached. It was Twinkie calling. "Please, Papa," she sobbed. "Come back to us."

Another raindrop burned into me like hot tallow. I blinked to life, the brightness of the room blinding my eyes. The room was vague, unfamiliar, sterile. I struggled to wipe my forehead but couldn't move my arms.

"Papa!" Twinkie shouted, tears of joy in her eyes. "You're awake! Dear God, you're awake!"

I pulled my arms again—I was tethered to the bed rail, and my head spun like a drunken ballet dancer. I winced and tried desperately to adjust my eyes to the room.

Where was I? Brutal pain throbbed in my lungs. I attempted to sit up, and a fierce wave of agony tore through my spine. I fell to the bed, sucker-punched by fate.

A bandage was wrapped tightly around my torso, from sternum to navel, and I felt mummified. My right arm and right cheek, covered in gauze, stung.

What had happened? Something clipped to my nostrils delivered oxygen through a long, snake-like tube attached to the wall. A garden hose of a catheter was jammed into my penis. In the corner, a machine delivered faint blips like Morse code in harmony with my heartbeats. Opposite the bed, hanging as He had hung for nearly two thousand years, was a portrait of an immaculately-groomed Jesus, a golden aura silhouetting his head. Seems no matter how hard I try, religion won't leave me alone. I can't escape it.

I was too weak to move again, too afraid of the pain to try. "Where?" was all I could whisper.

"You're in the hospital, Daddy," Twinkie said as she squeezed my hand. "You've been shot."

"Who?"

Twinkie placed a cup of water to my lips. "A . . . a . . . a policeman." She struggled to hold her emotions together.

Shot by a cop?

I couldn't comprehend the startling words. "Why?"

"They say you burned down the C.C." Twinkie tore nervously at a shredded tissue.

"The Cosmic Club?" My heart pounded dull throbs of pain through my chest. The monitor beeped like a Geiger counter at Three Mile Island. "Arson. Me?" It was too hard to understand. Much too hard.

The C.C., as the family calls it, is the Cosmic Club, a restaurant and bar my son, Bobby, talked me into building for him a couple years ago. I spend most every evening there, tending the grounds, pulling weeds, watering flowers, before taking my nightly walk along the river. It's gone? Burned to the ground? And they accuse me? "How did it happen?" I asked.

"People saw you, Daddy!" Twinkie squealed in a high-pitched whine I'd often corrected her about when she was a child. "There are witnesses. People saw you near the dumpsters with a gas can."

I remembered being back there, but I was too groggy to piece my actions together.

"Oh, Daddy, it was terrible," Twinkie cried, turning toward the window. Behind her the tarnished copper dome of a church rose green streaked with black, like the rotting corpse of a watermelon. Forsaken to history, the spire stood jealously over the city, which had grown and changed while the church had not. The chipped, weathered cross on the bell tower, battered by lightning, was nothing more than a crap-varnished perch for pigeons. The bell hadn't rung in years.

"When did it happen?" I asked.

"Three days ago." Twinkie's sorrow spilled over like a kettle filled too full. "You've been unconscious for three days. The press has played this as a big mystery with you as some sort of criminal. Look—" She shoved *The Enquirer* in front of me.

I tried to focus on the newspaper. Damn. The condemning words scorched me.

CLUB BURNS TO GROUND

R.T. STONE—SUSPECTED ARSONIST—LEADS MYSTERIOUS DOUBLE LIFE

The story depicted me as a conniving master criminal, reporting the events of my life with total inaccuracy: my age was wrong, my wife's name was wrong, the number of children was wrong, and, worse, they accused me of being in bankruptcy proceedings. I've had some financial setbacks recently, but I'm nowhere near that drastic end.

"Where's your mother?" I struggled to free myself again, then studied the IV in my arm, amazed that modern medicine could keep a person alive with sugar water.

"Mom's in the cafeteria." Twinkie laid the newspaper on my lap, then dried her eyes. "She's been with you the entire time, Dad. Sitting in *that* chair." My daughter nodded and turned toward the abandoned church. "Praying for you for three whole days!"

That's my Rose, I thought. When crisis comes to call, she summons up the big guy. I've never subscribed to that faith. I've never subscribed much to any belief. Just a clever way of stealing your money, I figure.

But what the hell happened? How did I get here, bound and helpless? I frantically tried to recall the last three days. Nothing. Time had vanished on me, once again. My habit of forgetting my whereabouts for three or four days at a stretch frustrates the hell out of Rose. I'm used to it. She's a patient, understanding wife, though. Try as I might, I remembered nothing.

I stared at the cold headlines. Next to the disparaging article was a color photograph of the C.C., the once spectacular nightclub nothing but a blackened, burnt out shell. My stomach churned as I stared at the sickening picture. My club reduced to smoking ash. Bobby, the C.C.'s general manager, sat on the curb weeping. His military haircut was standing at attention above angry eyes, his face smudged, head propped on his left arm. I've never known a man to hold so many intense emotions as Bobby. Almost all negative. Almost all the time.

IMPARTIAL FATE AGAINST A FIERY BACKDROP.

Suddenly, an image of a book flashed in my head. "*The Journals,*" I said involuntarily.

"*The Journals?*" Twinkie said. "What's that?"

"A dark blue book with gold lettering, I think."

"*That* book!" She drew in her breath. "It's the prime piece of evidence against you. The cops say it's your diary."

"My diary?"

"Yeah." Her fear collapsed like a soggy waffle. "They say it traces your criminal career since you were a boy, Daddy—why?"

Twinkie hadn't cried like this since her divorce—actually her second divorce. Her first marriage at eighteen only lasted seventy-seven days. She smothered that one, too. Write it off to youthful experience. But the second divorce, away from Parker Floyd, that one mattered, and was very painful for Twinkie and for me. A man doesn't like to see his daughter hurt—for any reason.

"It's all right, Twinkie," I said, trying to console her.

My daughter's real name is Julie. She earned Twinkie after she and Parker split up, when she began treating her sadness with large amounts of junk food, most often Twinkies. She moved back home after the divorce. She was shattered, but instead of dealing with her depression over losing Parker, she retreated into some unrealistic emulation of the outdated American Dream of the nuclear family. She's since become an expert at making fancy Jell-O molds and is skilled at various ways of flavorizing and presenting noodle dishes as mundane as macaroni and cheese. Her assortment of pasta creations includes Spam rotini, asparagus-cucumber-parmesan casserole, and eggplant-pepperoni lasagna.

Oddly, I think Rose looks younger, and is much more spirited than our daughter. Twinkie's once girlish figure has morphed into a middle-aged *haus frau* with her wide girth and a lifeless, fifties-style hairdo. Twinkie's eyes, once bright with the wonder of the world, have dulled into a neutral dishwater color. She's afraid of being hurt again. She's afraid to try to live, to love. So she puts on her June Cleaver smile and pretends the world is a perfect place.

Twinkie's neurosis began many years ago, and she hasn't yet pulled herself out of her self-pity. Now, as she stood beside my hospital bed, I prayed that she wouldn't handle the stress of this current Stone family crisis the way she reacted the day the divorce was finalized—by cutting off all her hair with a pair of scissors.

To be fair, the day Twinkie was born the world changed—November 22, 1963—the day Kennedy was assassinated, the day the American Dream was murdered in the street. Gunned down. And the killing hasn't stopped since. What should have been a remarkable celebration of Twinkie's birth was marked by somber reflection on human mortality. Instead of passing out cigars, I sat numb with friends, too sick to believe the nation's leader was gone. In the midst of it all, my daughter was lost. That day seemed to set the tone for her life.

I often wondered if I hadn't overreacted to the president's death, if I hadn't spoiled Twinkie too much to compensate, made her expectations so great that she could never get enough attention from *any* man. I understand that a worldly person like Parker needs his space, that there is only so much affection one wants from a woman. Twinkie smothered their relationship. Parker was simply unable to give her the amount of devotion she sought. My conclusion—as fathers tend to think about how to get their twenty-seven-year-old daughters out of the house—is that Twinkie needs to find a man more needy than she. And that, I'm afraid, will be a very difficult task.

It wasn't clear to me, and possibly Twinkie, who had left whom at the corner of Desertion and Lonely Streets. It was clear only that the marriage had ended after three childless years. The disbanding of their union was a civil affair, Parker opted to do right by Twinkie, avoiding the unseemly scenes of former lovers exchanging their once heartfelt wedding vows for bitter words of scorn and resentment. No, Parker Floyd—some call him Pink, though I don't know why—is a discreet gentleman. I am intrigued by his profession: private detective. Parker is particularly good at his incognito trade. Unfortunately, it didn't jive with Twinkie's neurosis—but that's another tale. Despite the fact that he had broken my little girl's heart, I always liked Parker. I still do.

Funny how humans attempt to relate every issue to themselves. I felt Twinkie's divorce in my terms, *mine*. Sure, I was sad for her, but I was angry at Parker's rejection of me as well.

Today it seems silly. As Twinkie drips her Chinese water torture above me, I question whether they are truly tears of sadness for me or embarrassment that her father is a suspected arsonist.

"The book isn't mine," I said.

Twinkie didn't believe me. "It has a handwritten confession in it," she said, then dabbed her eyes, which flitted between me and the newspaper like a hamster on caffeine.

"A confession?"

"In your handwriting. Repenting all your sins to God, including the fire."

I hadn't seen the confession. I didn't start a fire. I hadn't done anything except take a walk. I'm innocent. I've been framed.

I needed time to think, time to figure out what this diary, *The Journals*, meant to me. My eyes grew heavy. "I'm so tired, honey," I said. "Let me rest while you get your mother."

"Okay, Papa." She kissed my forehead.

Twinkie calls me Papa only when things are going really well, or really wrong— most often when something is really wrong. I didn't have to guess which way to apply the usage this time.

My heartsick daughter left the room. I closed my eyes and a dream, real as daylight, hypnotized me, showing in precise detail how I came to be involved in this most unfortunate circumstance.

Chapter 2

July 1942

The man known as Sulphur slipped unnoticed past the German occupation force into the port of Tangier on a cloudless summer night. He met his Berber contact at the pre-arranged hour in the medina section of the city. He cautiously spoke the code word: "firefly." He was given new identification, traded his western clothing for Moroccan seraweel and kusam, and devoured a meal of pastilla pie.

Twenty-four hours after he arrived in the strategic seaport guarding the Strait of Gibraltar, Sulphur traveled by freight rail through the mountainous country to Meknes. There, he debarked into a drafty delivery truck filled with lambs for slaughter, and bumped his way along a rut-filled road to the city of Fez.

Sulphur practiced the French that had been relentlessly drilled into him back in Washington, distracting himself from the urine-soaked straw on which he sat. The pungent odor of lamb excrement assaulted his nostrils. He could scarcely believe his luck at being plucked from basic training as a raw recruit to serve in the OSS. It was his age, they said: no one would suspect a boy his age to be a spy.

The fact that he had excelled in every stage of his training had caught the drill sergeant's eye. As the truck's gears ground up a narrow pass of the Atlas Mountains, Sulphur thought of the other lessons he had learned. Morse code. Cryptography. How to win the support of the local population. How to incite rebellion. How to organize resistance against the Nazis. He learned which essential services to disrupt—electricity, rail, petroleum supplies, communications. He had learned how to kill a man with a crisp snap of the neck, although he had never done it, and prayed he would never have to.

Sulphur smiled at the expertise he had gleaned from his instructors in the art of arson. His talent far surpassed the rigid standards of his superiors. He knew how to make things burn. To explode—to disable a train, to render a building unusable, to destroy telephone switching stations—making it all look like an accident. No evidence. No trail. No trace.

Sulphur looked at the suspicious black-olive eyes of his Berber escort, whom he knew only as Mohammed. The unshaven man did not know that the stranger he had been sent to collect was the first member of America's response to Hitler's aggression in northern Africa. An advance scout for an invasion force.

Without notice, the American war against the Nazis had begun.

Chapter 3

August 5, 1990

I didn't ask for this job, and I'm certain I haven't the skill to complete it. I do not actually believe in the words I am writing. I merely function as a chronicler of events, but if they are true, they must surely change humankind. Since I've been unduly coerced into telling this tale—and I have no obvious way to get out of it—I may as well tell you the facts which led up to my conscription. I have no opinions one way or the other on the incredible subject the Council of Ancients wishes me to present. I am neutral. I am Switzerland. I just wish to do my job, save myself, and go back to living in obscurity once more.

My name is Stone—not a bad name for a man who builds foundations. I've always worked with my hands and I suppose that's what makes this impossible, unwelcome task even tougher; my callused digits are too big and clumsy to write with any semblance of decent penmanship.

In my early days, I was a mason by trade, working in the hard tradition of America. I'm an honest laborer. I've done my bit to build this country: shopping malls, office parks, power plants, restaurants, parking garages, anything that helps this country grow. I've paid my taxes, raised my kids, saluted the flag, made a good living. And with the exception of a few run-ins with some misguided environmental fanatics, my life has been pretty uneventful. Until now.

My wife says my ways are set firmer than the mortar securing the bricks in my sturdiest buildings. That's her definition of stubborn. She thinks that I should consider other points of view. I've gotten along fine until now. Why change? I have always been a solid man, logically thinking things through rather than jumping at the closest, most obvious answer.

However, I was never so bewildered as that first mystical night on the shores of the Ohio River. Since my semi-retirement two years ago, at the age of sixty-five, I've remained active by taking a stroll in the direction of the sunset each evening. I have an appreciation for architecture, and the sun's golden embers bouncing off monuments to man's achievements give me a special feeling of accomplishment. Cincinnati had all been wild forest and open hills once, but we conquered it. We shaped the land to our design, made it bow to our needs. I was part of that domination, proud and justified. And no radical, hug-a-tree environmental types can take that from me. People need a place to sleep, to shop, to park, to eat, that's what life's about. I won't apologize for it, just because the air gets a little hazy in the summer.

The Kentucky side of the river, where I walk, offers a striking view of Cincinnati. There is the concrete Serpentine Wall, with its picnickers and bicyclists and Frisbee throwers. Barges quietly chug up and down the gently flowing Ohio, carrying cargo to distant ports. The pleasure boats bob on the water beneath the city like worshippers come to pay homage to the good life. And floating restaurants fill the night with laughter and music and the smell of barbecue.

Newport and Covington are as much a part of Cincinnati as Cincinnati itself, and these cities come alive in the twilight as the day shift makes up for lost personal time with a night of revelry and partying. This town is vibrant and useful again. A great place to raise a family. That's America.

I love to walk along the grassy levy that holds back the vast Ohio. The blending of nature and civilization has a calming effect on me. Serenity. Watching day fade to night is one of the few pleasures I have to myself these days. The pressures of life dissipate with the warmth of the sun's rays and the slow, meandering current. Blue skies, golden sun, glistening water, perfect sunset.

But on this particular eve, the muggy night of August 2, I decided to walk east to spice up the old routine. A crowd had gathered at the Cosmic Club to watch the news about the Iraqi invasion of Kuwait. Press Secretary, Marlin Fitzwater, had commandeered the TV airwaves at 7:05 for a special announcement. President Bush would take the stage at 9:00 to address the nation. I chose to avoid all the spectators who secretly dreamed we'd get involved in a war and beat the turbans off some Arabs. I sensed a set-up by the Bush administration. The wimp was taking the gloves off for a hard-knuckle fight with Saddam Hussein. The Iraqis tried for months to reasonably settle their border dispute with Kuwait. Kuwait would have none of it—they seemed to be provoking Hussein, goading him into war. I'm not saying Saddam's a saint—he's not—but when it comes to oil, money, power, and greed, the Seven Sisters of the petroleum industry will stop at nothing for control and submission of the Middle East. I learned that lesson from Gilday.

How ironic that Iraq, the cradle of civilization, the home of the Sumerians, Mesopotamia, the land that gave rise to the great city of Babylon—the Gate of God— the place from which paternalistic religion sprang and from which the Jews and the Christians stole their myths and fables, the throne of the fair and masterful Hammaurabi, the womb of human law and the birthplace of the written word, was today a symbol of tyranny and injustice. Iraq again had its chance to participate in history. What would it teach us?

For two years I've been in the Western routine, and the first night I change the ritual, I'm suddenly thrust into one of the most incredible adventures, I believe, of the past century. Perhaps centuries! It was as if fate drew me east.

I'm not a writer of much art. I'm just a freelance warrior dueling with these words to make this epic come out properly. I don't tell this story for profit, nor self-esteem, but from obligation. If my writing seems awkward, forgive me; this narration only serves as a preface to the main tale. An extraordinary tale.

I'm an average guy. Why I was chosen, I'll never know. I've never been one for the spotlight, never one to get involved. Do your job, live quietly, and a have a little fun in between is my premise for life. It's odd that I should be selected since I have no formal education in English. Engineering is my forte.

A man shouldn't ask much of life, and I didn't. I put in my time, then retired—a decision I truly regretted. But I did it for my concerned family (the worriers), my "alleged" old age, and my failing health. Fifty years of the same grind is a long stretch, and it is extremely difficult to break off and start anew. Seniority doesn't agree with me. Listen closely . . . I have something to say . . . youth doesn't appreciate the wisdom of age.

As I said, I'm not an accomplished author, so if I drift a bit, please bear with me. Actually, I'm still perplexed as to how I came to grasp the talent I'm now expending, although I have a strong suspicion that my new ability can be traced to the mysterious writings I found lying on the shore.

I was a considerable distance from the C.C. when I decided to make my way to the shoreline, where the Licking River enters the Ohio. I took a tentative breath of the clinging, night air and gasped at the menacing chemical odor rising from the water's edge. I scurried down a steep incline, slipping on loose rocks as clumps of dirt gave way beneath my sneakers. A limb of thorns raked my arm as I hurtled out of control. I fought to regain my balance, but the momentum thrust me through a rough terrain of briars and scrub and driftwood. The river was approaching fast and I couldn't control my feet. The last thing I wanted was to land face-first in the Ohio. A crippled branch jutted upward to my left. I grabbed it, halting my perilous slide only inches from the drink.

I exhaled relief and plopped on the fallen red maple that had saved me. It was a mammoth tree—strong and proud once, I imagined—with a huge trunk three feet around. Its leaves were dried and withered. The maple had lost its anchor—its balance steadily eroded by the unforgiving current eating away at its footing until the tree tumbled over, a victim to its desire to grow so close to the water's edge.

The fallen tree rested on a sandy patch at the confluence of the two rivers which came together without fanfare. Murky brown mingled with murky brown in a swirling tan sludge. It was difficult to ascertain which was more polluted, the Licking or the Ohio, not that anyone cared. Both flowed toxic. It didn't stop restaurants and nightclubs from being built on the Ohio's shores, or keep black men from fishing its waters, and boaters from swimming and skiing. The next day's rashes or a week's worth of vomiting would be explained away to some other cause. Cancer in twenty years for those foolish enough to eat their catch. But the ones who chose to sit and watch the Ohio didn't know its dangers. They were too far away to smell it, and figured the liver-colored liquid between its banks was rich soil run-off from the fertile farms upstream rather than the industrial discharge of northern factories. I rather think that's what people choose to believe.

Still, I love rivers—the way they constantly run. Downstream they rush to a better place, a newer existence, adventure at every bend. Some may stay away from the Ohio for its poison, but it is a powerful stream. Much like life itself.

It was twilight, that exotic time between day and night, a changing of the guard, and I was a good distance from the nightclub when it happened: *Boom!* A loud explosion ripped the calm, startling me. The concussion of the blast whipped up a torrid current of heat, as if Zeus had waved an invisible hand in the stagnant haze. Instinctively, I turned in the direction of the detonation, the place I had just come from. Standing on tiptoes to see what had happened, I sunk down into the muck of the river bank. My view was blocked by the hill I had just ungraciously traversed. The enormous root ball of the red maple, my savior, its gnarled roots reaching like frantic arms and hands in prayer to the sky, its diseased head stuck in the brown goo of the river as if gulping life from a spring, further obscured my view.

With some maneuvering, I saw a billowing plume of black smoke rising into the muggy sky. Something was on fire. Had Prometheus come back to reclaim his gift, come to extinguish man, to stop him from his evil? I tried to pull my feet free from the muck without success. I pulled again, stuck like quicksand grabbing at my ankles.

The sky was dark now, the setting sun completely masked by the smoke. Sirens split the dense air. I turned my attention back to extricating myself from the mire. I hastened to get out of the slime and back to the disturbance.

That's when I saw it glittering just a few feet away. I might have missed it entirely had it not been for a single ray of eerie light penetrating the obscured sky as if the messenger Quicksilver were riding down on its beam. Was it a fishing lure? An earring? A gold coin? That lone sunbeam shone like a spotlight, illuminating the object. Instinctively, I moved toward it. My feet suddenly released with ease, as if hidden shackles had been unlocked. I approached the secret treasure. I stepped closer. There it was. A dark blue book with a strange golden star on the cover lay in the sand, looking as though it were placed there by the hand of God Himself, flawless in every way. I was transfixed by the title: *The Journals.*

"Jesus," I whispered. I paused a moment before daring to touch it. A curious, yet familiar feeling slowly embraced me. A force. My discovery seemed accidental, but I can now say with confidence that my find was not a twist of fate, but a deliberate and calculated move designed to install me as the spokesman for the fantastic adventures contained within the pages of the mysterious, blue book.

I slowly bent down and picked up the book with as much anticipation and tenderness as I had my first born, Bobby, from the crib. The finely-crafted cover smelled new, yet ancient. The gold lettering sparkled, giving it an otherworldly appearance. An aura emanated from the strange book, pulsing, beating with life. Or was that my heart?

Did someone misplace their sacred Bible? Did an apprentice monk contemplating by the waters decide his studies were at an end, and to hell with religion? I soon learned this was not the case. My brain was flooded with images as I read the first page.

> Whosoever shall find this truth will be forever blessed with gifts beyond this world of mortals. This book before you has found its way into your life. Welcome to your destiny.
>
> From this moment forward shall be known to you the secrets of this realm. You are a chosen one. You must seek the hidden answers. You must guard against injustice. You must reveal your story to the faithless.
>
> This book, as life, is both the message and the messenger. And so it shall be for you—you are both the message and the messenger.

"No chance," I said, not wishing to get involved. I was about to give this drivel an impromptu Ohio River baptism when, magically, before my incredulous eyes, these words scribbled themselves across the page.

"You think so, huh?"

"Jesus Christ," I gasped. Both awe and fear spread through me like a dangerous, hallucinogenic drug. I dropped the book. A tingling current ignited in the tips of my fingers and ran up my arms. Then, I hesitantly picked it up again. As if the book had a mind of its own, it wrote another message in royal blue ink across the page.

"Look around you, Stone, and tell me if you see any footprints, including your own, leading to where you are."

Prickly hairs stood up on my neck. "Wait a second," I protested. My eyes darted cautiously from side to side. What was going on?

"Look around," the words insisted, waiting patiently.

Sure enough, there wasn't a footprint anywhere. Even the deep mud holes from my shoes had vanished, and the sand was as smooth as a freshly poured driveway. I began to think I had retired just in the nick of time. I had to gather my senses before someone saw me talking to a book.

"Okay. Let's slooooow down here," I said aloud, grasping for reality, my breathing accelerated and shallow.

"You do not have much time."

"What do you mean?"

"You are only human."

"This is a joke, right? Some sort of prank? Okay, where's the camera?" A book, a self-writing book, can't be real.

"There is no camera. Only ether, earth, air, fire, and water."

"This is crazy. This isn't happening."

"Hey Stone, relax."

"How do you know my name?" I panicked. "I have to get back now, there's been an explosion of some sort."

"You are getting warmer."

"What's that supposed to mean?"

"You are in danger, Mr. Stone. Serious danger."

"From what? From whom? What's this about?"

"From the world. The Universe, to be more specific."

"How the hell can that be? I don't know what you're talking about. I haven't done anything wrong."

"Nor have you done enough, Mr. Stone. It is much more than a matter of right and wrong in this life you are given. It is a matter of learning versus ignorance. It is a matter of how much you have learned and how much you have ignored, unjust situations you could have corrected. It is a matter of who you helped and who you hurt."

"I haven't hurt a soul."

"Except maybe your own. Turn the page."

I thumbed it over and found myself looking at a poem: *Impartial Fate Against a Fiery Backdrop.* I read the first stanza aloud, my trembling voice seemingly the only sound in the Universe: "Who knows what the hand will do? What the mind will insist? What play upon man the act will become? What fortune holds for desperate self?"

My throat swelled to the size of a grapefruit. My mouth felt as if it was filled with river grit. I tried to swallow—acrid and empty. The poem was a disturbed tribute to fire, the confession of a tormented man who torches things in the name of the Almighty Lord, acting as a fatal redeemer. I was appalled at the twisted thought, the complete lunacy of a person who could commit such a crime, then justify it.

"Did you write this?" I asked.

"No, but it is up to you to prove you did not."

"I don't even like poetry. It's sissified crap that only ladies clubs and nerds read."

"Do not condemn what you do not understand."

"I can't believe this!" Now my anger was getting the best of me as the novelty of a conscious, thinking book wore off. "Let me tell *you* something. The day I start taking morals lessons from a lousy, stupid book is the day I hope to die."

"Precisely, Mr. Stone, precisely."

I was too stunned to respond. I'm going to die? Is that what this is: the final, incoherent ramblings of a dying man? But I felt fine, other than the twenty-gallon vat of sulfuric acid eating away at my stomach lining. I was unaccustomed to speaking with inanimate objects, let alone having one respond. These pieces of paper were everything but what they appeared to be. I felt weak at the knees and leaned back against the dying maple. Sweat beaded on my forehead. As Cincinnatians are fond of saying to rationalize the unpleasantness of their summer climate, "It isn't the heat, it's the humidity." Tonight—it is both.

I wiped my fidgeting palms against the tree trunk. I needed to think logically—if just for a moment—to sift through the previous entries in *The Journals*.

Relax, I told myself, calm down. I took deep breaths as I closed my eyes to ponder my present situation. So, here I am alone on this shore conversing with a book. Pretty bizarre, right? More than bizarre. This is absurd! What's going on here? More importantly, why is this happening to me? Most important of all, can this possibly be real?

One man's revelation is another man's insanity. God, that's it—I'm insane! All those years of working outside in hot weather have taken their toll on me in a demented combination of sunstroke and moon-madness. That's it, too much of the elements. My family was right—I had worked too long, too hard. America had done this to me, I thought. America with all its power had turned on me right when I was supposed to start enjoying myself. Where did I go wrong? I paid taxes. I never ran stop signs. I didn't abuse little girls. I didn't start any revolutionary party. I'm a Republican, for chrissakes. I never even . . . my God! I forgot to go to church. Shit! Shoot! Shucks! Who thinks of those things when you're out there working your tail off trying to survive? Religion—damn! All those years of slaving to get ahead and I forgot to toss a quarter in the basket every Sunday.

I opened my eyes, nestled the blue manuscript carefully in the Y of two limbs of the fallen tree, and looked into the white pages. "I'll go to church," I said, offering a pathetic olive branch.

"This is not about religion, Mr. Stone, far from it. It is about spirituality, true faith."

"Yeah . . . well . . ." My voice trailed off, deflated with the realization that any chance I had for salvation was blown a long time ago when I got into business with the unscrupulous Patrick Gilday. I pulled a piece of bark from the maple and nervously crunched it to bits in my hands before letting the fragments fall to the sand.

"It is not too late for you."

"It isn't?" I asked. "You mean I still have a chance to redeem myself?"

"Yes, you do. Your spirit knows."

"My spirit knows what?"

"It knows what it wants, what it needs."

"What's it need then?" I plunged headlong into the dialogue, dying to expunge myself from whatever the book was trying to do to me.

"*It needs what every spirit needs, Stone. A soul needs to be uplifted, it needs to learn, it needs to ascend to a higher state of existence.*"

"I don't get you." I've never been one to worry about spirituality and all that New Age nonsense. I figured I'd just scoot into heaven on my wife's faith. She's done enough good for the both of us.

"*Everyone, Stone—indeed, every thing—must grow. Your soul needs to expand.*"

"How do I do that?" I worked a large strip of bark off the trunk and twisted it slowly in my hands, careful not to take my beleaguered eyes off the otherworldly book. The pungent scent of burning tar reminded me that a fire raged down river. The fire seemed secondary. As large ashen flakes the size of leaves descended to Earth like a freak August snow, I knew this power would not release me. The white cinders fell all around like ghostly paratroopers invading my shore, taking my beachhead, a warning of the battles to come. I became more desperate. "So, how do I expand my soul?"

"*You must get involved. You have been quite the wallflower when it comes to helping others right injustice. Lots of suffering in the world that you have ignored. And, most importantly, you are letting the Earth die. Bad form, Stone. Extremely bad form.*"

"The Earth is dying because of me?" I was shocked. "I haven't done anything."

"*Precisely. There are many things you could have done, many things you did not.*"

"Like what?"

"*You built a shopping plaza in a wildlife area, Stone, even though those protesters told you what would happen.*"

"You can't expect me to ruin my business for the sake of a few squirrels, can you?"

"*Nineteen squirrels, five deer, three raccoons, forty-two rabbits, and three-thousand three-hundred seventy-one trees. You should have listened to them, Stone. The environmentalists have an important task at hand.*"

"But I couldn't make any money if I had to take all those crazy radicals into account."

"*That was just the devastation from one job. You built more than one shopping mall against the reasonable wishes of ecologists, Stone. You have destroyed much of nature. But worse, you also helped perpetuate the military-industrial complex. You made money from the ill-conceived American nuclear program, and now thousands of people will die painful, cancerous deaths.*"

"I didn't kill any one." Was this it? Was this Judgment Day? "I'm just a simple businessman." I inadvertently pulled at the skin of the dead tree, crumbling the flakes of broken bark in my moist hands.

"*A millionaire at one time, as my records indicate. But look what your capitalistic indifference has gotten you, Stone. Look where you are anyway. You are deep in debt.*"

Your investments have failed. Your former business partner cheated you, then hung you out to dry. I am not much of a business person myself, but I would say things are pretty much in ruins."

"What do you want?" I shouted. "What can I do? I'll do anything. *Please."*

"Get involved," it advised, *"like those protesters you scoff at. At least they are fighting for something they believe in. At least they are trying to right a wrong."*

"But . . . but . . ."

"You could do so much more."

The damn book was right, of course. I had never done much of anything except sit in my living room in front of the TV and complain about the world. I opposed the Vietnam War—in my mind. I was against tax breaks for the rich, even though I made out better from it. I didn't agree with the whole Iran-Contra mess, yet I voted for Reagan again. I was appalled at the savings and loan debacle, and I voted for Bush, even though he was responsible for the deregulation that precipitated the collapse. And I certainly don't want the United States involved in the current Iraq-Kuwait conflict. We have no business fighting over the price of gasoline. What was another ten cents a gallon compared to thousands of lives? The president had already frozen Iraq's U.S. assets and shut down all foreign trade. Saddam only invaded this morning; how could our usually inept, incompetent government have reacted so fast? Uncle Sam was scheming.

"Isn't there some other way I can save myself?" I asked. What good can a sixty-seven-year-old man do anyway?

"Well, we can flip a coin and see."

"Flip a coin? All my life amounts to is a flip of the coin? Chance, mere chance?"

"Chance gives us all a way out of this space. More on that later. It can be that simple or—"

"—Or what?"

"Or more complex, depending on whether you are willing to cooperate or not."

"Cooperate, how?"

"By working for us. Hell, do I have to spell everything out?"

I was astonished. My whole concept of religious people centered around whether or not a person used profanity. Granted, I did not consider one a Christian based on that criteria alone, but I did feel one had a better chance of being accepted into heaven if one exercised caution in using such language. "I didn't think . . ."

"Exactly." An invisible hand turned the page. *"You do not have to think at all. Leave that to me. If you will just listen to the offer I propose, I am sure we can reach an understanding."*

The book continued turning its own pages. I simply scanned its writing, spoke out loud, and it flipped over whenever appropriate. Phenomenal.

"Wait a minute!"

"I have time."

"I have a few questions I need answered before I go on with this charade," I said, trying to assert some authority.

"Stoney, Stoney, Stoney. What do I need to do to prove to you this is not a charade, not a dream, not a bad piece of fiction you read at the beach?"

"Tell me whose side you're on," I demanded, as if that knowledge would do me any good. Ozone and billowy, black smoke, mixed in a toxic haze, filling the sky.

"Side?"

"You know, good or bad, hero or villain?" I didn't wish to mention formal names for fear of a lightning bolt or heated pitchfork striking me dead.

"Tsk, tsk. You mortals are so hung up on this devil versus angel theory. Why do you always take things so literally? I mean, really."

"Well, the Bible talks about God versus Satan."

"Two sides of the same coin. There is no good without evil, no life without death, no joy without sorrow."

"What about the Bible?"

"What about it?"

"What about what it stands for?" Not that I would know. I've never read it. "Goodness, truth, honesty, virtue, helping old ladies across the street. The Bible—the book that stands for all that's decent on this planet. The book that holds this fragile egg together. The Bible—what about the Bible?"

"It is a good piece of writing, although I do think it gets a little boring at times. And confusing—what with all those 'and this person begat that person' et cetera, et cetera. Plus there is not one hint of humor in it at all. Did you ever hear of God laughing? No! All you hear is this eye-for-an-eye stuff, which does not make any damn sense. That is not love—that is not peace. Fire and brimstone, that concept is archaic. We are all pretty hip these days. Why, just the other night Luke threw a surprise party on Saturn. Talk about some heavy—"

"Cut the crap and answer my question! Whose side are you on?"

"Lighten up, Stoney," the book scribbled. *"I am getting to it."*

"Go faster." I tore at the white flesh of the tree with my fingernails. Sirens and engines roared in the distance, a sound circling the fire like fear. Ash paratroopers continued to drop from the blackened sky. I must get back! I thought. But the book held me prisoner.

"Okay, Stone, point blank, here it is: There are no sides. We are all part of a whole. People generally think in two ways—something is either right, or it is wrong— it is, or it is not. On or off, hot or cold, war or peace. Have you ever heard that opposites attract? You humans have missed the whole point. We provided a book a couple thousand years ago, hired some translators like yourself, but like the old rumor passed around the table, the crux of the matter got lost in the translation. The Bible

was meant as a guide—a road map. Sort of a general how-to book. It was never intended to be taken literally. Look what has happened. You have three thousand religions practicing everything from eating fish on Friday to sacrificing animals to killing each other over different translations of the same book. For what?

"The whole concept of the first book has been diluted, polluted, misconstrued, abused, and taken way too seriously. The point is that we know how people are going to act: some good, some bad. What the message really is, is to accept those actions and go from there.

"Anyhow, and I am going to get serious for a moment. Your mission, Stone, should you decide to accept it, is to commercialize this book. Translate the diaries contained in these pages and let the whole world know its message. Simplify it by adding a few comments here and there. Use pictures, music, hire an agent, whatever it takes, Stoney. Make it marketable. It is time to repay your Karmic debt."

I sat flabbergasted, reeling from the last entry. Karma? What the hell does some obscure Zen concept have to do with this? All my ideals of reality and life and death and everything I knew were crushed like so much brick under a wrecking ball. More questions raced through my mind at that moment than ever before in my entire meager existence.

"Let me get this straight," I said. "You're asking me to write a sequel to the Bible because the first time around the message got screwed up? I'm supposed to use some mystical insight to write parables and verse and—"

"No, no, no. Have some faith, Stone. This is going to be a contemporary piece taking place in modern times with real, documentable people. I will handle most of the plot. The events have already occurred. Do not be so skeptical. Have patience and all shall be revealed."

I was more than a bit skeptical. I was a true nonbeliever. As the sun disappeared beyond the horizon, hidden in dense, smoky drift, I felt my life slowly slipping away. All my illusions swept downstream in an ebbing cosmic tide, like so much silt from the river bed. My temples pounded. I could barely think anymore. Nothing I believed was real, and fantasy was becoming commonplace. I was scared and edgy, yet fascinated by what was taking place. I was determined to give one last shot at convincing the writing book that it had the wrong man for the job.

"What if I refuse?"

"Then you will never know."

"Know what?"

"The reasons."

"The reasons?"

"Who, what, where, when, how, and why, Stone. The reasons."

I raked my nails lengthwise along the rib of the tree. "Oh," I said, still unsure.

"Why do they always give me the tough ones? Surely you do not think I started one of the biggest fires in the history of Cincinnati just to wreak a little havoc and have some fun, do you, Stone? The reason, my son, the reason for the fire, the reason for you traveling east, the reason for the book, the reason for everything for God's sake!"

"All this for a crummy book?"

"It is slightly dramatic, but I had to emphasize a point."

"You're a damn lunatic!"

"Watch it, Stone, you are awfully close to the end."

"Can you, um, clarify what you mean by that?"

"Sure. All good things must come to an end—I borrowed that line. Civilizations, rivers, books, people. Everything comes to an end. There is a beginning, a middle, and an end. At least in human terms. Some are not as clearly defined as others, but, nonetheless, that is it in a nutshell."

"Are . . . are you talking about *my* end?"

"Only if you want it that way, Stone. We only ask your help to promote The Journals, and you will be saved."

"But why?" I pleaded. "Why me?"

"Because we have to get it right. The Bible has been corrupted and we need to set it straight."

"Then the Bible is true?" I said, in awe.

"There is truth in the Bible, yes, but its historical facts are false. And it is just a tad too complex and really quite harsh."

"How come you're making a joke of it?"

"Things must be put in perspective, Stone. The Bible was written over the course of a couple thousand years and a few billion people. Times change."

"Yeah, so what?"

"You have raised children, have you not?"

"Yes."

"So you know there were times when you had to exercise force to make a point. You know there were times when you had to summon up some of the deepest wisdom you could, right?"

"Yes."

"Did your children always listen? Did they always take your advice? Of course not. They ignored it. They made mistakes, bad ones, did they not?"

"Yes, they did." I thought about *The Journals'* point while carving my initials into the wounded tree trunk with the sharp edge of my thumbnail—RTS.

"And it got you pretty mad, right? Especially when they fought or stole or lied or got involved with any of the numerous corrupting forces on the Earthling market. Is this so, Stone?"

"Yes."

"But you still love them. You cannot turn your back on your own children, can you? Some people can, but the majority are good eggs. I mean, we all got our faults—"

"Yeah, like you don't use proper grammar. I thought all you angels and the like were supposed to be perfect."

"Perfection does not exist. But we do try to set a good example. As far as my grammar goes, you must remember that I just learned English this morning. It is tough translating one's thoughts into a strange language and then into print. Real tough, Stone, so do not be so quick to criticize."

"I just assumed you were American," I replied, stupidly.

"God is most definitely not an American. Get real. He does not play favorites. In fact, humans are not even His favorite species on this planet. But I am getting off track here, Stone. Your beliefs are based on what you want to believe, what you choose to see or not to see. We are really just trying to set a good example. We are not perfect either. If the head honcho was so perfect, why did He go and create venereal disease and liquor and atomic bombs and television talk shows?"

"I never thought of it that way."

"You know, Stone, humankind was God's one big mistake, and He is plenty ticked off at Himself for letting it go on so long. He is weary of all this corruption and violence and pollution and starvation. Yep. He has made a decision, and we all know what that means."

"I don't," I said.

"Yes, you do. You just do not want to know—like most humans—so you are not thinking about it. You have not thought about it since He gave you that construction company. You were doing all right until you got greedy. But like I said, you still have a chance to pay your Karmic debts."

"Okay, so what's the deal?"

"The deal is twenty years to life, Stone."

"I can't handle obscurities." I angrily pulled at a new piece of bark, splintering it to bits then letting them fall.

"Then, I will explain it simply. You have two options. As of this moment you are either in the worst trouble of your life—trouble so deep, even F. Lee Bailey wouldn't consider your case—or you are about to become internationally recognized as one of the greatest researchers to ever live. Decide!"

"I'll take the fame," I responded swiftly, hoping a fast answer would somehow hasten the end of my predicament.

"Excellent. But one should never make a hasty decision. After all, we are dealing with your life. Question. Probe. Do not accept things for what they are. Investigate."

"Fine. I'm not a dumb man. I read *The Cincinnati Enquirer* and watch *60 Minutes*. I'm reasonably informed. But you're just confusing me."

"Tools, Stoney, mere propaganda tools of the state, this 60 Minutes *and* Enquirer. *You need to look deeper than the surface. Do not just accept what is fed to you by the political apparatus. Question it."*

"Okay, fine! What's the scoop, the lowdown, the gist, the point, the bloody reason?" I shouted. "Just quit playing with me!"

"Fair enough," the book wrote. *"I am a messenger from a higher entity called the Council of Ancients. We have a strong interest in this endeavor you Earthlings call humankind. My purpose is to deliver the message. The message is a final warning contained in the contents of this manuscript. It is a true story beginning twenty-three years ago. It is continuing at this moment. It will be concluding in a short time."*

"How short?" I asked, fearfully.

"Ten years to infinity. That is ten years for most, infinity for some."

"For some?" My wife, Rose, was religious and forty years of her Christian torment had rubbed off on me, so I had a fair sprinkling of religion, accidental though it was. "Revelation!" I shouted.

"There you go, it is easy. And soon you will find the whole truth. It is all in front of you."

"In this book?"

"No, in your soul. It has always been there. Most people choose not to see. Some think they see, some pretend they see, some do not care to see, and others . . . well, they have seen it from the start. It will get clearer as we progress. Hopefully, all you have to do, Stone, is tell your story to the world."

"My story?"

"The story you will tell is about three very real individuals, their mistakes and misfortunes, as well as their triumphs. The tale is self-explanatory. However, getting the message across is going to take a great deal of understanding on your part. There can be no retreat. No way back. You are already committed."

Committed. Those words ran through me like a razor knife through a shingle.

"Well, okay. How commit—"

The book slammed itself shut. End of conversation.

"What the—" I exclaimed. Angry voices approached, shouting. A lynch mob. Disoriented, I panicked. Were they after me? The wrathful voices came closer.

"There he is!" someone shouted.

I leapt off the tree in a desperate jump to reach the underbrush. A thunderous sound lashed out through the smoky sky, echoing across the river through the concrete canyons of Cincinnati. My body lurched forward uncontrollably, as if an unseen bully gave me a mighty shove. I fell down into the water, my face half-submerged, facing west, as the brown goo filled my mouth.

Blackness. Deep. Dark. Ominous. Complete. A total eclipse.

"Oh, Papa," someone said as I awakened from a dream.

The stinging pain almost disappeared at the sight of Rose coming through the doorway, pursing her lips, spreading that pink lipstick of hers, making sure she looked her best for me. The sterile, white room came alive with color. Even Jesus' eyes seemed to twinkle in her presence—such is the grace she has. She strode to the side of the bed, making her way through the cords and cables and tubes plugged into me.

"Oh, R.T.," she whispered, hugging me lightly around the neck. "I knew God would bring you back to me."

Rose kissed my cheek, and my nostrils filled with her vanilla scent. God, how I love that aroma. It is Rose's and Rose's alone. I knew I'd be all right now that she was there. She stepped back and looked at me lovingly, faithfully, her mint-green eyes filled with compassion. Rose always looks at a person straight on, full of her own self-assurance. She placed her hand on mine, still strapped to the bed, and pushed the button for the nurse.

"Yes?" The voice was tinny, annoyed.

"R.T. is awake now," Rose said. "Would you mind loosening his restraints?"

"Sure thing, Mrs. Stone, be right in."

I could hear bubblegum pop on the other end of the speaker.

"And could you bring some medication?" Rose ordered politely. "He must be in terrible pain." Turning her attention back to me, she added, "We'll have you fixed up in no time." She produced a half-smile more sad than genuine.

That's the thing about forty years of marriage: we can read each other's minds. Rose was upset, but she would never let it show. No, she would be strong, as she had always been strong. Much more than I.

If there is one word that describes Rose, it's "poised." She is a rock. When Bobby had appendicitis, then strep throat, when he was drafted and sent to Vietnam, when he came home with a Purple Heart, then got busted for smoking pot and all through any disaster that befell that kid, she was there with her comforting words and her unshakable faith that, "God willing, everything will be just fine." Rose was no less the guiding light during Twinkie's personal disasters—and my own for that matter. Lately, she has had to play her most supportive role yet, what with me finding myself in one catastrophe after the next. How she bears it, I'll never know. She has the looks of an angel, the patience of a saint, the heart of a woman. I'm a fortunate man.

Twinkie cleared her throat. "Um . . . you two go ahead and talk . . . I guess . . . I'll clean the bathroom," she said, and reached into a grocery bag sitting on the spotless linoleum floor. If the Jesus on the wall could have, I'm sure He would have raised a curious eyebrow.

"How can it be dirty?" I asked, although I knew better than to question my obsessive daughter. "I haven't used it."

"Daddy, everyone knows hospitals are crawling with germs." Twinkie slid her hands into bright yellow rubber gloves that came up to her elbows. "Cleanliness is next to godliness." She pulled a sponge, a roll of paper towels, and a box of cleanser from the bag and disappeared into the bathroom, closing the door behind her.

"Twinkie is dealing with this the best she can," Rose said. She sat in the chair beside my bed and crossed her legs.

"And how's Bobby?" I asked, a twinge of pain rifling through my back. I hoped the nurse would arrive soon. Rose stared blankly across the room, out the window to the Church of the Holy Watermelon.

She didn't respond immediately but sat thinking. "You know how Bobby is," she finally said. "God willing, he'll come around."

"Rose?"

She furrowed her brow as she considered how to spare my feelings. "Bobby is being . . . Bobby," she said softly. Rose clasped her hands demurely, as if in prayer. "He's lost everything."

"We have insurance." I didn't know why she was so uncomfortable. "It's not like he built the club on his own. I gave him the damn thing."

"R.T., don't upset yourself. It'll be all right. After a couple days go by and he's able to see things in a better light, he'll be fine." She stared at her clenched hands, avoiding me. "Look at it from his perspective, R.T. You've been in the news a lot lately. First Fernald, then Zimmer, the lawsuits, the environmentalists, and now this—anyone would be a little embarrassed by it."

"So, he's ashamed of me." I felt a pit the size of Oklahoma in my stomach.

"Can you blame him?"

"I've given him a lot over the years, Rose. I would think he would support me in my time of need." Rose didn't reply. "You don't think I had anything to do with it, do you?"

She was silent. She pursed her lips again and twirled the gold cross she always wore, a nervous habit of hers. I looked at the expensive necklace that hung daintily from her neck as she fingered it, then to the pigeon-stained steeple. Where was her faith now?

"Rose?" I said, fearing the worst.

"Bobby said you had a terrible fight just before the fire." She didn't look at me but continued to stare at the dung-riddled church. "He said you threatened him."

I fought to regain that memory. Yes, there it was. I *had* argued with Bobby. But it was a ridiculous disagreement: he tried to blame his sagging business on the "no smoking" policy I recommended. The truth, which Bobby can't see because he doesn't want to see his own faults, is that the Rising Sun Seafood Emporium and Steak House, which had opened just upriver a few months earlier with much fanfare, was the culprit eating into Bobby's profits. That and the fact that his nasty disposition drove away customers looking for an evening's enjoyment.

When I had mentioned the competing restaurant, he scoffed and said, "Damn Japs, taking over everything." Then he insisted on my excusing his six thousand dollar rent payment. Permanently. He had demanded it as if I owed it to him.

I hadn't responded well. "Your rent is reasonable, very reasonable," I huffed. "The problem is your other expenses are out of line. You spent five times more than necessary on cutlery, Bobby. For what? Fancy, silver-plated, high-priced spoons? That's what's driving you out of business—bad decisions like that."

Mistake. Never attack a man about his addictions. Silverware to Bobby, Jr. was an addiction, though he'd never admit it. A habit. A blind spot. I've never understood it. He became belligerent. Hostile. Then he played his ace against me. Told me it was my fault that he lost his arm. Told me I was a shitty father. My temper flared. I yelled at the ingrate, told him I'd see the club in ashes before I let him slide out of his obligations. I stormed off to cut the grass and cool my anger.

"Rose, I wouldn't do anything to harm the family," I said. My face stung under the bandage like an albino in the Mojave basted with cooking oil. Again, no response. I looked out the window with a new appreciation for the forsaken church. Rose wasn't sure of me anymore. Why should she be? I thought. I've given her nothing but heartache these past few years.

Finally, Rose answered me. "I've stood by you throughout our marriage, R.T.," she began in a low voice, taking care Twinkie didn't hear.

Not that she would, as Twinkie was humming the theme from *Trapper John, M.D.* while she sudsed-up the lavatory. My daughter had picked up the annoying habit of humming or whistling theme songs from TV shows since the day her divorce from Parker became final. The exact day. It fits her modus operandi for dealing with his estrangement.

Rose continued over Twinkie's toilet bowl serenade. "I've put up with your indiscretions. I've been understanding of your unexplained absences. I've been there for you in your battles with the environmentalists, and I stuck with you through the Fernald indictments." She paused to compose herself. My heart began to quietly crumble—I had lost her belief in me. "It's a wife's place to support her husband," she said, as if reading the words off a wedding card. "So," she sighed, "I'll support you through this. God willing, everything will be fine."

Her words cut me deeply. My back throbbed, and each pulsing surge of blood oozed misery through my wounds as if the bullet hole stretched and tore with each breath due to Rose's admission that she didn't believe me. My blood flowed black. A foul taste was in my mouth, sour and disappointing. I was devastated. Without her faith, I was sunk, lost, destined to fail. She was always there beside me, giving me strength. "I didn't do it, Rose. You have to believe me."

She bit her lip and looked to Jesus. "It's not a matter of what I believe, R.T. I'll support you no matter what. In sickness and in health."

The nurse strolled in, chewing her gum maniacally, saving us from the conversation. "Up and around are we, Mr. Stone?" She spoke through her nose. Her hair was dull brown and pulled back in a ponytail clipped together by a Minnie Mouse barrette. She carried a small purple tray, faded from too many trips through the dishwasher. The tray held a syringe and a thermometer.

"I'm awake," I said, trying to be friendly, "but I'm not sure about the getting around part."

"That's nice," the nurse said. She held the syringe up to the light, squeezed it slightly until a few drops trickled from the tip. Then she injected it into the IV bag. "The pain will subside in no time." The nurse smacked her gum. She worked half-heartedly at the leather restraints, trying to keep from breaking off her inch-long, hot pink fingernails. I looked at her pale blue eyes, seeing her closely for the first time. Her pretty face was painted with make-up as if she were heading to the Friday night dance clubs on Pete Rose Way. She could be no older than twenty-five, I surmised.

"Mind if I help?" Rose said as she loosened the buckle of one of my restraints.

"Not at all," the nurse said. She sniffed the air. "Whew, we better get him a sponge bath."

Soon I was free. I rubbed my right wrist with my left hand, but my right hand was still bound. The gauze on my right arm bothered me. "When will this come off?" I asked.

"Doctor has to look at the burns." The nurse popped her gum. "He'll be making his rounds later today."

"Burns?" I said as the nurse slipped hurriedly toward the door.

"Yeah. You have some sort of chemical burn on your face, neck, and arm. Gasoline probably." She smiled as she exited, forgetting to take my temperature.

A policeman popped his head around the doorway, staring at me with resentful eyes, then pulled his head back out of sight.

"Who's that?" I asked.

Rose stood, her eyes fixed on mine. "Police protection."

"For what?"

"Death threats." She didn't flinch.

"Death threats?" Fear recoiled in me like a snake slithering down my spine. "Are those environmental nuts harassing me again?"

"No," she said. "A lot of people want revenge for what you did, R.T. There have been three or four letters."

"I don't get it. I didn't do anything. Whatever happened to innocent until proven guilty?" I shifted gingerly in my bed, trying to find a less painful position. The slow, warming drip of the narcotic made its way through my veins. I could feel the slightest trace of it working its magic.

The cop's walkie-talkie squawked in the hallway. "Dunn here, the patient is awake and coherent, sir . . . understand. The district attorney is on his way up. Over."

A muffled, static-filled reply shot back through the air: "Roger."

Twinkie continued her merry humming in the bathroom, breaking into the theme from *I Dream of Jeannie*. She is happiest when she's cleaning or baking something. It's strange, to be sure, but Rose asks me to be tolerant of the abnormality. I am patient, and I love Twinkie, I just don't think it's healthy for a woman of twenty-seven to pretend she's living in some perfect, pristine TV dream world.

Rose and I sat in silence for a few minutes, lost in the conflict between us—she thinking I'm guilty, and me knowing I've been framed. How do I tell her? How can I break this to her without it bludgeoning all her religious beliefs? I decided now wasn't the time and worried about the district attorney. I'd barely been awake an hour and already he was circling the waters, sniffing for blood.

I looked at Rose, her hands in her lap, turning her wedding ring around and around as she thought. She too was anxious about the D.A. We'd both been through so much with the Hamilton County Prosecutors Office that I'm sure she was most apprehensive with this latest impending encounter. I hoped the D.A. for northern Kentucky wasn't anything like his counterpart across the river, the tenacious Sylvester Rense.

The upper half of my right side flamed beneath the bandages. How did I get burned? Will I be scarred? Will I be a deformed freak that everyone will stare at? I tried to distract myself away from thoughts of the prosecutor's grill session. I chuckled at the absurdity of thinking permanent facial scars were a better diversion. Had my life sunk so low that that's the best I could hope for—to consider disfigurement better than talking to a lawyer?

It was during this drifting thought process, helped along by powerful pharmaceuticals, that it happened. Just as the D.A. tripped through the door, Twinkie burst out of the bathroom announcing, "All clean!"

Wham! The door slammed into the D.A., drilling him squarely on the nose. "Shit!" he yelled. Stacks of papers went flying. His glasses rocketed against the wall and fell to the floor. The D.A. grabbed his nose and dropped to his knees in pain, rocking back and forth on his haunches in agony.

"Oh, mercy!" said Twinkie. She knelt next to the man.

Officer Dunn, hand on his holster, made an imposing figure in the doorway. Did he think I had bushwhacked the D.A.? Once he evaluated the situation, though, Dunn's jaw unclenched, and he snapped his holster lock back in place. "You all right, Mr. McBain?" he asked. A quick, don't-ask-stupid-questions nod followed.

Rose swung into action. "Nurse," she said, pressing the intercom button. "There's been an accident in here. Could you please bring some ice and a bandage?"

Pop! The bubblegum response came through the speaker: "Sure thing."

"I'm so sorry!" Twinkie was almost in tears. "I'm really sorry."

"It's all right." The D.A. pinched his nostrils to stop the flow of blood, which made him sound like he had an early August head cold. "I should have looked where—I wasn't paying attention, I mean I'm always—well, pretty much always—it's my fault," he stammered.

The nurse arrived and mended the D.A., assuring him that his nose wasn't broken. Twinkie fussed over him like he was her son fallen off his bike. She retrieved his glasses from the floor, clumsily dropped them again, then unceremoniously stepped on them, twisting the wire frames into a distorted mess of tangled wire. The lenses had popped out of the frames, and she handed them to the D.A. separately, as if presenting a Christmas gift.

"Sorry." Twinkie shrugged her shoulders shyly. "I'm a bit awkward."

"That's okay." The D.A. pushed a smile through his pain. "I break them all the time."

I had never witnessed two such curious people bonding in all my life.

"Oh, beans," Twinkie whined, swiping at the D.A.'s chest. "Now you've got blood on your tie."

The prosecutor's boyish cheeks blossomed pink. "Well, ma'am," he said, sounding like he was sixteen instead of thirty-five.

Brian McBain was a twitching sparrow of a man, spilling over with anxious energy, eyes dashing about, his voice quivering, always trying to recapture his words the instant after he spoke them. "It's not actually—it's more like—well, I had lunch today—made it myself—and it's not blood, it's Dinty Moore Beef Stew."

"Dinty Moore!" Twinkie was alight with glee. "I love Dinty Moore. I always cut up extra carrots and put them in. It takes longer, but it's worth it."

"That would be good." McBain smiled as if he had found his high school sweetheart. "I like to eat mine—most of the time anyway—that is when I have time, which I don't because I'm so busy—with a big loaf of fresh-baked French bread. But mostly, like today—because I was preparing paperwork—I eat it straight from the can. Cold."

"I love that, too!" Twinkie said. "Just run it through the can opener and dish it out with a spoon."

McBain beamed, shaking his head covered in light brown, wispy curls to clear his ringing brain.

After he regained his senses and could see clearly again, Twinkie and McBain stared at each other in what can only be described as a smitten look of discovery. I looked at Rose, she at me, and we knew that something romantically cosmic was happening between the two. Twinkie's face was awash with a grin, as was the D.A.'s. They both looked away shyly, then giggled at the same time. It was weird.

Scientific studies have shown that people are attracted to one another by olfactory sense more than any other reason. This is the only possible explanation for the enamored looks on their faces, as it was most certainly not the clumsy circus introduction that attracted the two.

The bleeding stopped, his papers back in order, his dignity restored, the D.A. settled in for the purpose of his visit. "I'm Brian McBain. United States District Attorney, Mr. Stone. I am here to serve you with the following warrants—"

Twinkie, love-starved child that she is, stared at him admiringly as he read off the list of indictments. That done, McBain started to ask me questions.

It was difficult to take him seriously, especially with his prepubescent voice, a gravy stain the size of Africa on a God-awful tie, and a wrinkled suit with pant legs that stopped at his ankles. High waters we called them when I was young.

Rose took command. "Robert won't be answering any questions, Mr. McBain," she said with polite firmness, "until we have our attorney, Jim Bennett, present."

I'm so proud of her. I probably would have started talking away, answering his questions, digging myself a deeper hole, if she hadn't inserted herself in the drama.

"Okee dough." Brian McBain snapped his notepad shut, launching his pen cap into flight. It bounced off the floor several times before coming to rest under my bed. "It's an open-and-shut case, anyhow. I've got time."

McBain turned, trying hard to be suave for Twinkie, and stumbled into the table tray, knocking a plastic water pitcher to the floor. Some people are just clumsy that way. It's hereditary. "Sorry," he said. This was not his day.

And apparently, it was not mine, either.

So there you are, the whole sordid mess on how I stumbled my way into this predicament. I've been framed, shanghaied against my will. Engaged by the Council of Ancients to write a book. To tell a tale. One might wonder what I'm writing upon. It's hard to believe, but I'm writing in *The Journals*. I don't understand it, but just like on the shore, *The Journals* had mysteriously appeared, this time under the sheets of my hospital bed.

I have no idea what I am supposed to do. I've only recently recovered enough to even remember the incident on the shore. Most of my knowledge is derived from newspaper articles and stories I see on the six o'clock news. It is so disconcerting to see my trauma nudged against the crisis in Kuwait.

The United Nations passed a resolution today, number 661 to go along with number 660, freezing Iraq's worldwide foreign assets and imposing international sanctions. I wonder if people know what the U.N. is doing. Sanctions only hurt the general population, not their leaders. What the hell good will that do? I'm a card-carrying Republican, but I don't see the sense in this. To tell the truth, I'm having difficulties with both parties. The lesser of two evils perhaps.

War. Bush wants to beat the Middle East into submission. His old CIA director training is coming in handy. The propaganda has already started. All one has to do is read between the lines. It's reported that April Glaspie, the U.S. Ambassador to Iraq, informed Saddam Hussein in writing two days *before* he invaded Kuwait that we didn't have a position on regional conflicts in the gulf. Seems she was wrong.

I only hope I am, too.

What a wickedly cruel world we live in. So, there I am, plastered on the front page of *The Enquirer* along with Saddam Hussein, the scourge of the free world. Everybody loves to hate the villain, so the press invents one. Or two.

"How dramatic!"

Hey, did you see that? It wrote to me.

"Yes, I have returned. I will not abandon you. I have to help you, Stone. I have to get you out of here so you can promote The Journals.*"*

"Thanks a lot," I groaned. I had hoped it had been a nightmare, a psychotic figment of my imagination—but no, it was back, hounding me.

"One must be positive."

"I wouldn't be here if it weren't for you. Look at me, I'm talking to a goddamn book!"

Officer Dunn peaked around the corner. I waved to him, tangling my hand in my nose tubes. God, that hurt.

"That is just stupidity on your part, Stone."

"What is?"

"Getting tangled in your nose tubes."

"Why are you so critical of me?"

"I am sorry. It was inconsiderate of me to tease you."

"Apology accepted."

"Anyway, I think it best that we understand each other more clearly."

"What do you mean?"

"Simply put, I am here to guide you to the inevitable answers you seek. Until you have finished your task, no one will be able to see the entries I am making but you. The only writing anyone will be able to see will be your own. Ask me a question and I will answer. Pose a confusing thought and I will answer. Talk to me and I will answer. I will come and go as necessary. The time I spend hidden from your accusers will be used to assist you in attaining freedom.

"To release yourself from this dilemma you must completely and accurately tell the story of Danny Gilday (The Forger) and Allison Leslie Pippin (The Seed). You must do this under exceptionally demanding circumstances. No one will believe your story because everyone will think you are insane. Your friends and family will forsake you. You will be at odds with the world, yet there will be new champions come forth to support you.

"The quiet forces of truth, dormant in many of the chosen, will rise up from the public spectacle of your trial and gain strength through your adversity. Your voice will be the rallying cry for the last call of humanity. You, and several others like you, are the Second Coming."

"You make it sound as if *I'm* Jesus."

"You are Jesus."

"I'm not! I'm just a mason from Cincinnati."

"You are Jesus. I am Jesus. Every human, every creature, every living thing is Jesus. We have just forgotten that."

"I don't understand."

"Jesus is the physical representation of the spirit of Universal truth within all of us. He is a metaphor. His life on this plane was nothing more than a demonstration of each person's potential. His life and death are the symbolic cycle of the Universe. The creation begins because it must end. It must end so that it may begin again. You must have sorrow to experience joy. It must be. Jesus is in us all, if we look, but it has been displaced by physical distractions. Your job is to present the final warning. Your mission is to sound the alarm to a world that it is out of control. It is the last chance before we start over."

"Who the hell are you?"

The blue book paused a few seconds before answering. *"I am pure thought, Stone. I am pure consciousness. Pure being."*

"Whose thought?" I wiped a tear from my eye. My fear and anger and my complete frustration at being trapped by circumstance, as if all the world had conspired against me, welled up in a spring of emotion.

"I represent everyone's thoughts, Stone—all of humankind. I have come to answer a plea. A plea from the citizens of the world to end the cruelty of this place. And that I shall do."

My body began to shake. I couldn't stop. A river of sorrow brought on by complete helplessness rushed forth from me. I sobbed into the white linen pages of the book.

"Do not cry, Stone. I will not let serious harm befall you."

"I'm so mixed up. I don't know what to do. I'm not qualified for this. I'm a goddamn businessman for chrissakes! Please, let me go. Please, let me live in peace."

"Fulfill your obligation, Stone, and you will be free. Not until then."

"But, I—"

"Perhaps it is time to stop avoiding the task and start doing. Perhaps it is time to tell the tale."

"How am I supposed to know what to write?"

"Close your eyes and sit quietly. The Universe will present the gift to you."

"But, I—"

Poof! Like a magician's flash powder the nefarious book disappeared.

Chapter 4

July 5, 1967

Cara nervously fanned herself on the front porch swing, waiting for the right moment. She swayed like the rhythmic pendulum of a clock. Back and forth. Tick tock. The seconds evaporated slowly as she listened to the creaking strain of the swing, its chain rubbing against the metal hook in the ceiling, barely audible over the drone of the lawn mower humming powerfully in the backyard. She pulled out a moist, crumpled list hidden beneath her sweaty thigh as she rocked in the humidity of the early July evening. Cara studied it closely again, folded it neatly, and stuck it back in its fleshy hiding place. She had never seduced a man before. Certainly, she had never had an extramarital affair. Yet, here she was waiting for her gardener to finish as she brushed her brownish red curls, wilted in the heat, from her freckled neck.

She looked at his truck, bright green with white lettering: CELESTIAL GARDEN & LAWN SERVICE—THE GREENEST THUMB IN THE UNIVERSE. She secretly wished she would be leaving with him tonight, never to return. Cara smiled as she remembered the heart-stopping, breath-taking catch in her throat when she asked Matthew, over their weekly glass of iced tea, if he "would mind coming in the evening next week?" He agreed with a quiet nod. Then she had added those defining words that framed the moment with precise clarity and meaning, "Patrick will be out of town." The implication was clear. Matthew's magnificent brown Indian eyes sparkled. His gaze fell humbly to the flower bed, and he said nothing. Cara's heart turned with anxious anticipation, a feeling which had not subsided since she had made the daring comment. She was proud of her sudden boldness. It was liberating.

She insisted on calling him Matthew even though he preferred his spiritual name, McJic. Matthew is the 'M' in McJic. She believed the name Matthew to be more civilized, making his hiring easier for Patrick to accept. At the time it seemed important, but now she was embarrassed. Originally, she had misguided notions of bringing culture and breeding to a savage's life. She could not have known that neither she, nor anyone else on the planet, would ever meet another soul more civilized and ascended than McJic.

McJic was not of this world, a fact he learned as a six-year-old child. Near the town of Sedona his great aunt, Rising Moon, took him deep into the red mountains to a sacred energy center, where few humans entered. There she revealed to him, over the course of a three-day fasting ritual, his true purpose on the Earth. McJic was delivered to the planet by the Council of Ancients, guardians of Universal balance and harmony, guiding celestial events from another realm: Shanidar. From Shanidar his spirit descended to occupy the physical body of a human. His true origin was that of a light-being, an elite race of beings made of pure energy and light. He was sent to bring peace to all he touched, to teach all who sought his advice, and to alter Earthly events should they need such changing.

But McJic's greatest task, his primary mission, was to be fulfilled on this sweltering July night—to conceive a child greater than he—a child who would some day save humankind from self-destruction.

"When will he finish?" Cara said aloud, pulling the list out once more.

There was a stirring inside her, one that she felt whenever she had tea with Matthew, only this time much stronger. An unquenchable thirst. Is it his eyes, she wondered. His long, silky black hair? His muscular body? His melodic voice, so steady and smooth? What is it that attracts me so? What is it that draws me uncontrollably to him?

She thought of the fresh cut flowers from the garden he always left on the porch swing after he was finished for the day. Her mind drifted through all the long conversations they shared. His calm demeanor excited her. His gentle style. She adored the way he never passed judgment, always careful not to speak badly about anyone, always careful to respect another's point of view. She thought of his easy smile, white and perfect, and his proud, majestic cheekbones. Most of all, she loved the way he listened. Yes, that was the attraction—he listened. In that way, in that decidedly simple way, he was different from Patrick.

Cara played with the top button of her blue cotton blouse as she casually watched Tommy and Jimmy Hartley throwing a plastic coffee lid back and forth in the street like a Frisbee. Watching the boys reminded her of the modest desires she had in life—a few kids, a nice home, and a husband that loved her. She had one child (but longed for another) and a nice home, but the loving husband was an illusion. She doubted Patrick ever loved her.

Cara glanced at the chipped, white paint on the porch ceiling. Patrick should fix this, she thought, but knew he never would. He was rarely home, and when he was present, he was self-absorbed, doing only the things he wanted to do, which did not include house chores.

"How did I ever fall in love with him?" she said to herself, regretting the day they met at the roller rink. It was Patrick's first time out with friends, having always been preoccupied with taking care of his mother and sister and trying to run a business at eighteen. Patrick never had time for people, only making money, so he wasn't adept at dating. "How was I to know?" Cara said under the din of the mower.

Indeed, it was only later that she realized he was unable to love, unable to think of anyone but himself, and, by that time, they were married. "What have you done? How could you marry a man so wrapped up in his job?" she asked herself quietly. Patrick's obsession with his steel company, BG Industries, left her cold. Thank goodness for Calvin. She thought of their only child. He brought her so much joy.

Patrick's weekly business trips to Phoenix angrily reared up inside her. She thought of his infidelity and how it made her feel lonely and undesirable. But no one looking at Cara Gilday could ever say she was undesirable. She was a young, vibrant woman with an irresistible sensuality—evident in her stunning hair, her invitingly full lips, her magnetic, soft blue eyes, and a curvaceous form that turned heads at the supermarket. It was this sensuality that attracted her husband years earlier. Now, Patrick seldom acknowledged her existence, and so she sat on the porch planning to have sex with the hired help. A voice inside her asked, "How long has it been?" Five months. But there had been love once, she tried to convince herself. There must have been.

Cara smiled forlornly as she reminisced about the time when she and Patrick had been intense and passionate with each other. During one particularly memorable night of lovemaking, she had nicknamed Patrick's genitals. She loved that deliciously perverse thought. A naughty little secret born of lust.

"Such a long time ago," she thought, "before Calvin was born."

Cara first suspected her husband was having an affair four months into her pregnancy. It had temporarily stolen her self-esteem like a thief who had crept into her house. But she recovered and replaced her crushing unhappiness with contempt for a man with no morals. She became positive about his indiscretions two months before her child's birth, when the Phoenix business trips began. Patrick was guilty of having two mistresses: a woman of flesh, and his work. Between both lovers there was no time for his wife. Or for his son. Cara and Calvin were alone.

"But that was two and a half years ago," she said aloud, dismissing her sadness. "Screw him." Cara nervously fidgeted with her blouse, thought of her plan to seduce the gardener, and teasingly loosened another button. She had considered wearing no bra at all, like those women's libbers she saw on the news, but thought that too forward. "I'm from Indiana," she rationalized. She pulled the fabric wide, revealing her cleavage. "This ought to grab his attention," she said. "No man can resist these."

And no man could, not since junior high school anyway. Cara had developed early, and along with her womanhood came a keen sense of their power over men. By a little after 9:00 p.m. tonight, Matthew would be hers.

Removing her seduction plan once again, she examined every detail:

7:00 a.m.	Patrick leaves for Phoenix (hah!)
1:00 p.m.	Take Calvin to Mom's
2:00 p.m.	Hot bath, shave legs, perfume
7:00 p.m.	Matthew arrives, say hello
7:10 p.m.	Matthew unloads tools
7:15 p.m.	Matthew mows backyard
8:00 p.m.	He mows front yard
9:00 p.m.	Matthew takes a 10 minute break - offer him iced tea
9:10 p.m.	Seduce him

She waited a long time for this day. Planning, preparing, fantasizing until she couldn't wait any longer. She had considered seducing Matthew the moment he arrived, but decided to wait until he had done some work. She wanted him hot and sweaty, smelling of grass and perspiration. A primal man. She wanted his scent to linger long after he had left. All her genteel sensibilities were gone. Time and loneliness had evolved her simple daydream into a feverish, wildly delicious fantasy.

Cara stuffed the plan back under her leg and continued to methodically rock the swing. She stared at the truck again, unsure how much longer she would be able to contain her desires. GREENEST THUMB IN THE UNIVERSE. She thought it a strange saying, but acknowledged Matthew did have a tremendous green thumb. The Gilday yard was the lushest, most fertile and well-groomed lawn in the neighborhood. The vegetable garden Matthew kept was incredible, filled with huge, juicy red tomatoes, thick, long cucumbers, and succulent beets. His gardening skills were the talk of the entire subdivision, with many neighbors trying to hire his services. But Matthew was booked solid and could service no one else in the neighborhood but the Gildays.

Cara smiled and ran her pinkie through a wet curl as she looked at the gorgeous flower beds that adorned the front of the house—brightly splashed in purples, reds, pinks, yellows, oranges, and blues. The result of McJic's horticultural feat was a fantastic display of flowers. The results were all the more incredible because Matthew refused to use pesticides. After he had mowed, watered, and weeded, he would sit out back under an oak tree, cross-legged, chanting Navajo blessings to the spirit gods. This, he had said, was the essence of his success. Each blooming daffodil, tulip, iris, hyacinth, hosta, lavender, and black-eyed susan unfolded with Cara's blossoming yearning for an affair.

Patrick never commented on the flowers. He never seemed to notice. And that was the crux of her sadness—her needs, her feelings, her wants were ignored by the one to whom she had professed lifetime love. And he had rebuffed her. Now, she would give her affections to the groundskeeper.

His ancestry wasn't well known to the Gildays, but Matthew had confided in Cara that his grandfather was indeed a Navajo medicine man who had taken a white woman for his wife. Matthew didn't have the degraded, stereotypical television appearance of an American Indian, covered in headdress and speaking in halting English made up of "ughs" and "hows." He had the handsome fortune of inheriting the best genetics of both cultures.

Patrick, in one of his moods, had said it was just plain stupid that an Indian was a gardener. Cara agreed it wasn't common in Cincinnati, but Matthew was a damn good gardener. "What the hell is an Indian doing in Ohio in the first place?" Patrick said. She wanted to reply that Ohio is an Indian word for beautiful river, and that the land had originally belonged to them, but thought better of it. Another comment left unspoken. She had a mind full of unspoken replies, a mental treasure chest loaded with answers to Patrick's intolerances.

Cara checked the watch her father had given her two Christmases ago and wondered what he'd say if he knew what she was plotting. Her father didn't like Patrick either. Not since Patrick left for Phoenix when Cara was two weeks past due, and he had to drive her to the hospital himself. That was a husband's duty. Yeah, maybe Dad wouldn't object to this after all, she thought.

She glanced at the watch again. Shit! Another hour and a half, at least. Cara stopped the swing and got up, stuffing the note in the snug front pocket of her shorts. She took a deep breath and marched through the house, stopping only briefly to throw back an entire glass of wine in two big gulps. Then she went out the back door with a singular purpose.

"Matthew!" she called, waving her arms over her head. McJic silenced the engine and sauntered toward the back porch where she stood, her leg hiked up on the railing like a show girl in front of a saloon. She ran her hand slowly down her smooth leg. Her tight denim shorts rode high on her thigh. She squeezed her inner muscles, feeling a divine pressure. Her hormones controlled her now; there was no stopping her plan. The only question became whether she could hold out until the golden moment of ten minutes past nine. She could not. The time was now. "Would you like a glass of iced tea?"

"Yes ma'am," Matthew said shyly.

"Come in the house while I fix it." Cara's heart was pounding sweet exhilaration, a drumming that beat a wonderfully sinful rhythm. She would pay Patrick back for his infidelity, and receive her own pleasure in the bargain.

McJic had never been inside before, not even to use the bathroom. It simply wasn't done, allowing anyone but a white inside one's home. He bounded the steps with the quiet grace of a deer, and held the screen door open for Cara, who stood momentarily startled at the swift, athletic feat. He seated himself at the table as she poured herself another glass of wine then made the tea. McJic looked around curiously. Cara, her back to him, and getting ever braver, undid the third button of her blouse.

"Would you like a piece of pie?" she asked, her voice as shaky as the pitcher trembling in her hands. But she had second thoughts. It doesn't matter what Patrick has done to me, she reasoned, I shouldn't be doing this. She sucked in her lower lip, confused by what to do. I'm not an adulteress, she thought. I'm better than this. Her emotions became jumbled—lust and fear, excitement and shyness, promise and betrayal. She glanced at the refrigerator and spotted an Arizona postcard from Patrick, cactus and sagebrush, stuck with a pineapple-shaped magnet. *Fake!* her mind shouted at her. The son of a bitch sends me postcards to trick me when he's down at the river screwing some whore!

Truth was, Cara never knew when Patrick was in Arizona or on the river. She never knew when he told the truth or when he lied.

Cara drew courage from her anger and turned around to face McJic. "Do you find me attractive?" she said and took a sip of her wine.

"Cara," McJic said softly, sensing the difficulty she was having. "I find you the most attractive woman I have ever met."

Her heart melted. Her chest was warm, flushed with anticipation and wine. Heat, hotter than the July night, raged between her legs. She smiled. Smoldering and sensual. Finally, a man who appreciates her. Oh, Jesus, she thought, how long has it been? The words she had longed to hear, the emotion she begged for, was hers at last.

"There was a time," she said, her eyes wild with desire, "that a kind word would have satisfied me. Now . . ." She stalked across the short distance to McJic. "I need more than that. I've been so—" Her voice broke. The pain of Patrick's indifference overcame her. Cara crumpled into the chair next to McJic, deflated, and placed her head in her folded arms on the table.

"It's okay." McJic stroked her hair, breathing in its lilac scent, taking care to remember its exact fragrance. "You don't have to explain anything to me."

She raised her head. "How can you be so good and Patrick be so bad?"

McJic looked at her lovingly, feeling deep sympathy for this caring woman who had been so neglected by her unfaithful partner. "He's not here now, Cara. I am."

She turned sideways in her chair and reached needily for him. She hugged him tightly, as all her fears, the insecurities about the rights and wrongs of the affair dissipated as if they had never existed, banished from her life. Raw sexual energy took over her being. "I want you," she panted.

McJic smiled, a kind and genuine smile that Cara had never seen. "Let us take our time," he whispered.

He swept her up from the chair with a power and ease that took her breath away. "Let us enjoy the love we both so desperately need." He kissed her cheek and carried her up the steps to the master bedroom, and laid her down gently on the bed. Cara glanced over at the clock—7:25 p.m., as her heart thundered with expectation.

She pulled him down on top of her, working her tongue forcefully into his mouth.

McJic withdrew. She clawed at his shirt, her eyes glowing with sexual fever, reaching for him. "Give it to me," she demanded. A dangerous fire burned out of control inside her deprived body.

"Shh . . . patience." He touched his fingers to her lips. "There is much to share."

McJic laid down next to his lover. Slowly, he kissed her forehead, her eyelids, her ears, her neck. He ran his fingers down her arm as he nibbled gently at her ear. Then, as her desire rose to meet his embrace, he kissed her fully on the lips. An intoxicating rush filled her body as his warm tongue entered her mouth. She devoured his salty taste, wanting more. More, please more, her body begged.

On the bed where Patrick had ignored her so many times before, Cara at last received the pleasure she so longed for, the pleasure she so deserved. There, two willing bodies, two willing souls entwined in delirious ardor. As their beings melted together, like butter on warm toast flowing creamy, both, at the height of their discovery, at the climax of their union, cried out blissfully. Their souls surrendered to each other.

Hours passed as Cara and McJic caressed and played and explored. The sun had long since disappeared, taking Cara's sadness and replacing it with an awareness of McJic's special powers. He communicated to her without words, relying on the actions of his heartfelt love to speak for him. She was enraptured by the sex as swirling colors and erotic sensations swept over her in wave after wave of glorious ecstasy. Their energies finally spent, their spirits shared, they lay satiated on the bed, a tangle of fulfilled happiness.

"God," Cara moaned as she rubbed McJic's chest. "I never felt anything like that before!"

He didn't answer.

She looked at the clock—12:15. Then she turned back to her lover.

The two stared at each other, their eyes misting in the silence of their sacred moment, knowing they had experienced something miraculous. Not tears of sadness, nor tears of joy, but tears of quiet recognition of their eternal bond. They had shared a love that many never find in a lifetime. Cara was alive again. Warm and glowing inside, her soul set free from its marital dungeon.

"Who are you?" she whispered.

"I am McJic," he said simply. "Sent from the Council of Ancients, a light-being from Shanidar."

Cara, far from being astounded or afraid of his strange words, accepted them as if she had known it all her life. "Have you come for me?" she asked, hoping, dreaming momentarily of being swept away.

He knew his message would be difficult to deliver. "I have come to you to bring to you hope and faith, and to show you what destiny provides to those of tender heart."

She pulled the tousled sheet up around her breasts and sat attentively on her knees, fascinated by her lover. "You've made me so happy. I've never felt what I felt tonight. You pleased me so. When we made love, and I, you know," she said shyly, "when I came, I was in another world—hell, another galaxy. I was showered in light. I could see things in my mind, indescribable things, magnificent civilizations and beings and thought as pure as water. Only cleaner, purer." She wondered if he thought she was chattering. Patrick never liked to talk after sex, if he stayed in bed at all. Cara went on, not caring, unable to stop herself from expressing her emotions, confident that McJic was a listener. "Pure thought, that's it, I became pure thought. Able to do anything, able to see the Universe, to feel its emotion and understand its purpose. I saw things, Matthew. I did!"

"There are many wondrous things in this world, my flower," he replied, as he caressed her breast through the linen sheet.

She thought her heart would float away when he called her "my flower." She let the sheet drop from her breasts so she could feel the warm, gentle caress of his hands on her needful flesh. "Tell me about Shanidar, Matthew."

He looked into her eyes with a hypnotic stare. "Shanidar is a gathering of light and energy."

She could see Shanidar in McJic's brown spheres, as if there herself.

"It is the place where energy and light, what you may call the soul, come together. It is a dimension which governs the Universe. The strings of destiny are pulled from there," he said.

"Is it heaven?" she asked. Cara traced her index finger along a scar near his abdomen and imagined it a heroic war injury or a wound sustained in some secret Indian ritual.

"There is no such place, except in the heart," he answered. "But it is what many people spend their lives searching for. It is all emotion, all consequence in one place. Everything emanates from Shanidar."

"I knew there was more than this," she said, gently waving her arm through the air. Cara paused, puzzled, "What do you do there?"

"We play, we dance with the stars, we mix light with light. We live timeless, peaceful lives of thought. Time does not exist there. And without the existence of time, urgency, and the need to get things done, the need to conquer life does not exist. So spirit can be what it wants to be—free."

His explanation was incomprehensible to her, and he didn't have the time to explain away thousands of years of human religious dogma. Cara thought carefully about his words and asked, "But what do you do there?"

He paused. "I am a captain in the Council of Ancients, commissioned to carry out the directives of the great Council. To you, this would mean I am a sort of Universal ambassador."

"Kind of a cosmic diplomat?"

"Yes, Cara, a cosmic diplomat."

"What do you do for fun, Captain?"

McJic smiled broadly. "I write."

"Books? You write books?"

"Yes, I like to write books, Cara."

"Anything I've ever read?"

"Maybe someday," he answered.

"Very mysterious, Captain," Cara feigned, in a horrendous German spy accent: "So vie are you here?" She laughed, still euphoric from the sex. Anything Matthew told her, she would believe with a combination of inspired awe and giddiness.

McJic's eyes grew serious as he placed Cara's hand on her stomach and stroked her slowly. In an instant, the oft-ignored woman's eyes became wide. She knew immediately what his action said.

"You gave me a child!" she shouted. "You gave me a boy!"

McJic nodded his head proudly.

"My God," she gasped, then her voice fell away. "I have a son from the stars." She was overcome with happiness. She had wanted another child, but that prospect seemed distant with Patrick. Now, she would give birth to another boy after all. "But why? Why me? What does this mean?"

"His name shall be Daniel," McJic said. "And he shall be a born leader sent to help this world."

"What will he do? Will he be president?"

"No," McJic laughed. "Something much better than president. He will be a *true* leader, one who leads by example, one whose ideals people will understand and strive to emulate."

"Will he be famous?"

"He will be famous."

"How? How will he be famous?"

"He will be a writer and win the Pulitzer Prize," McJic said. "But more important than the Pulitzer is the message contained in Daniel's writing. He will be gifted and he will have fame. But his development, his nurturing, is up to you."

"You'll . . . um . . . you'll help out, won't you? I can leave Patrick," she said. Suddenly, her mouth was dry, her heart lightly tapping against her sternum: no, this was not meant to be. She hoped her heart was wrong, that the sick feeling ripping through her body was nerves, that somehow there would be more than one night of bliss with McJic. She had tasted immortality; she had seen the future; she had witnessed destiny; and she wanted to experience it over and over again.

He sat up in bed, his head bowed sadly, and said, "I cannot stay with you, Cara. As much as my heart would like to keep me here, it is not my place. I have come to give the world another son. Perhaps another chance." His lips trembled as he struggled to contain his sadness. He wanted with all his heart to stay with her, to love and care for her, to give her and Daniel all the love and happiness and life-knowledge he possessed. But he had another destiny waiting for him just a few short hours away. He regained his composure and said, "You have the seed of the Universe within your womb. It is a great honor to be chosen for such a deed. I would have cherished the right to live with you, Cara, but it is not to be."

She reluctantly accepted her position without further argument. She knew there could be no debate. She was torn between emotions, at once proud and terrified, honored and scared. "What . . . what will he look like?"

"He shall have your features," McJic said, and then added, to answer a question she had not asked, "Patrick will never be aware he is not the father." He laid back on the bed and pulled her to him. "Let us not talk for awhile. Let us revel in the night, for memories are powerful comfort."

The two lovers embraced and kissed deeply. To chase away the sadness, a trick she had perfected living with Patrick, Cara feigned playfulness. She sat up again, slapping McJic lightly on the stomach. "You've spoiled me, how can I ever enjoy sex again? There's nothing that can compare to this!" Cara reached for a cigarette. She smoked only when Patrick was away, her single act of defiance until tonight. Her hand shook. She tried to calm herself, but it was no use. The only man she would ever love was a one-night stand.

McJic reached over, grabbed the burning cigarette, and crumpled it in his fist. "You do not need this poison." He opened his hand and the cigarette was gone.

"How did you do that, Matthew? Are you magic or something?"

"No more than anyone else," he said. "But if you call me by my right name, McJic, I will show you a trick better than that. I will show you bliss in a word."

"What do you mean?"

"Say my name, Cara, and see if you do not feel bliss." He placed his warm palm against her cheek.

"Okay, okay . . . McJic."

Suddenly she began to feel a familiar warm stirring between her legs, which built rapidly within seconds as her entire body began to shudder and spasm. "Oh, God, God,

God . . . *Yeeesss!*" she screamed in delight. The climax lasted a full satisfying minute. She struggled to regain her senses, "Wha . . . what happened?"

He smiled. "The memory of our intimate bonding will always be with you. To relive the physical experience you need only whisper my name."

"No way, are you kidding me?" she laughed. "I just say McJic, and I get an . . . ooh, oh, no, not again—" As quickly as she had asked the question her pelvis grew hot and she was in the throes of yet another climax. "Jesus H. Christ on crutches!" she moaned, grabbing the headboard tightly. She arched her back in a sharp jerk, her knuckles white as she squeezed the mahogany with all her might. She let out a short gasp, then fell back on the bed, quivering.

After composing herself again, she said, "What a holy miracle! Thank you, Mc . . . Matthew." She loved sex, but two powerful orgasms in a row had left her drained. "I better save these up."

McJic leaned over, kissed Cara on the lips, then pulled her down to him so her head rested on his chest. He lightly stroked her beautiful hair, inhaled as deeply as he could to always remember her lilac fragrance, and said in a whisper, "Let us sleep now, love. It is time for quiet. Let our beating hearts speak awhile."

The first ray of morning sun shone through the bedroom window, waking Cara from her slumber. She moaned, gladdened by the new day, and felt the other side of the bed for Matthew. He was gone.

Her heart broke that instant, never to be wholly mended.

She wondered if it had all been a dream, just one of her lonely fantasies. The earthy scent of sex lingering in the room told her it had been real. Panicked, hoping she could change time, she hurriedly threw on a robe and raced downstairs to the front porch.

"Matthew! Matthew!" she called across the perfectly trimmed lawn.

There was no answer. The driveway was empty. The bright green truck with white letters was gone. An empty nausea set in as she stumbled weakly to the swing. She sat down, numbed by reality. There, glowing brightly next to her, sat a spectacular golden orchid emanating a surreal brilliant light.

Never has there been an orchid of this magnificence. A creation of McJic's love, a gentle weaving of botany, beauty, and romantic flame. A rare gift, precious and symbolic, bestowed upon a deserving lover. A golden companion to always remind Cara of their time, a comfort in her loneliness, a remembrance of their bliss. *Magicka carallus.*

Cara leaned into it, admiring its beautiful blooms. She inhaled its luscious aroma.

The scent from the miraculous orchid entered her, spreading welcome comfort. It had been real. All of it. Every sigh. Every word. Every emotion. Every kiss. Every touch. Every wondrous moment. She spotted a note.

> Dearest Cara,
>
> Our one night together held more love than most of humanity will experience in a lifetime. Let us be grateful for our time of bliss and thankful that together we have formed a bond which can never be broken: that of a child. I shall never love another, emotionally or physically. Our night was, for me, the purpose and reward of my existence on this Earth. I will always love your spirit. I leave this golden orchid as a reminder of the beauty of our union. Take care of our son.
>
> Yours in Spirit,
> McJic

Cara let the letter fall. She placed her hand on her stomach to feel for signs of the promise which lay inside her as delicate tears made their way down her face.

She had made love to an officer from the Council of Ancients. She had experienced an intense night of romance few will ever know. The sexual adventures she once thought so wicked left her bathed in the memory of glorious rapture. Moments she would never forget. Her life had meaning again, she would have a son with magic in his eyes. She found solace, content that her lonely life without her husband's love was not for nothing. The gardener had planted his seeds.

"Thank you, McJic," she said aloud. She picked up the note, kissed it, then pressed it to her bosom. "Oh . . . oh, sh—sh—shit . . ." she stuttered. A tidal wave of erotic want crashed upon her. She gripped the chains of the swing tightly, holding on as she bit her lip hard to keep from calling out her carnal experience to the sleepy neighborhood. She squeezed her legs together tightly and closed her eyes to bask in the enveloping glow. "Oh, my," she said after she had recovered, "I—I—must be more careful."

Chapter 5

July 6, 1967

The events I am about to relate are not for the meek. For never have I seen evil so dark as what McJic experienced after leaving Cara pregnant with her star-child, Daniel. She lay in peaceful slumber as he said goodbye with a light kiss upon her forehead placed in the first hours of morning. He returned the Celestial Gardening truck to its garage and set out on foot with no more than a guitar and a few possessions packed into a duffel bag thrown across his back.

He was acutely aware of his destiny, having always known that he would have to perform his conceptual duty with Cara, then leave her to raise Daniel alone. But knowing that did not make his departure any easier. He thought of her as he hitched a ride south on a desolate Interstate 75 into northern Kentucky. He stared blankly out the window, engrossed by the sad nature of his job, as the truck sped down the highway past the potholes and pollution. The choking, dirty, factory grime was of no concern to him this morning, as it might have been under different circumstances.

"Whew! Pretty strong odor, don't ya think, partner?" the truck driver said.

"Yes," McJic said dully. "The Earth is dying."

"Huh?" the trucker mumbled, then changed the subject. "Say, where you goin' feller?"

"Trying to catch up with my destiny," McJic said.

As an officer in the Council, McJic knew events before they occurred. He had the road map of life's many paths most of us don't even know exists. Yes, he had it all right—he charted the course of countless lives of unknown, unsuspecting souls who were guided toward this decision or that without so much as a second thought. Some would scoff at that notion that there are those among us who shape our fate—light-beings sent here to assist, spirit guides some call them. Yet, as I think of my particular dilemma—charged with attempted murder and arson—I must admit that if it weren't for one lousy night, a fire and a writing book, I wouldn't have ever known. So who is to say what is real? Not me. I'm a believer now—a true believer that nothing is as it seems.

The driver, who picked up hitchhikers as much for conversation to help break the boredom of the long haul, was disappointed at McJic's quietness and shot him a queer glance. He sensed the troubled loner didn't want conversation. The droning cadence of the tires was the only sound between the two.

McJic had other things on his mind as the rig took him to the Walton-Verona truck stop. He thanked the kind trucker and began to walk the deserted, dusty backroads, taking him ever further from his lover. "Cara will be all right," he reminded himself.

He found the road he needed parallel to the railroad tracks. He would hop a freight car after the next phase of his mission was completed.

The night was cool, with the sun hidden, just as McJic liked it. The air was only slightly cleaner here away from the city. "People like to think that it's only industry that causes pollution, but in truth cars account for most of it," he said. He loved to talk aloud as he walked. It kept him sane. Again, Cara came to mind as he breathed in her lilac memory. He closed his eyes and saw her smile.

He glided down the road, his feet seeming to float above the ground like a fabled Zen master in no need of the earth beneath his feet. Earth and air and water were all the same to him; he could control them at will, but he did so sparingly. Are there others of his kind in this world? Are there others with his gift among us? Are there others with his presence?

The light-being cut across a passive field of knee-high grass heavy with seed, each willowy stalk thanking him for walking among them. He worked his way down a long slope, down into Waterloo, his feet marching to the riddled beat of a distant battle drum. He stood at ease at the foot of the hill admiring the meadow before him.

"This is a good place to suffer," he said to the fuzzy yellow moon varnished by man-made haze. Across a clearing of short grass, sprinkled with a perimeter of cattails and wild roses, a trickling stream tripped over a ten-foot drop, forming a waterfall. An ancient weeping willow offered her compassion to him. A stand of tall green pines flooded the meadow with their healing scent, assuring McJic he would be cared for. An elm, soon to be his Calvary, smoothed its bark to reduce any chance of injury to him. The sympathetic elm, chosen for its transcendent properties, emanated strength and spirit in unbridled support to the martyr.

The water dove headlong over the falls, clean and rejuvenating, landing in a quiet pool, then continued its journey to the far end of the pond. "Featherbed Bank," McJic said aloud as he tossed his duffel bag to the grass near the elm. He gathered twigs and a few dead branches lying alongside rutted tractor tracks, the only sign of mankind's intrusion in the meadow. He bunched the debris in a pile, then struck a match to light a fire.

He sat melancholy, reflecting on his evening with Cara as the flames danced before him. The silent landscape around him prepared for war. McJic reached for his guitar and tuned it carefully. He looked to the sky, closed his eyes in prayer, and bowed his head. From his sorrow, he strummed the guitar and began to work on a song to lament the loss of Cara and his impending Passion. He loved the blues but not the emotion that came with them. He called the song "Crittenden."

Suddenly, a wild screech of rubber sliced the night. Rocks and dust sprayed painfully beneath the wheels of a battered pickup truck. Gravel shot from the tires like gunfire. A bevy of mourning doves cooed and scattered from the trees. The truck appeared from nowhere, sped across the clearing, then skidded to a halt inches from McJic.

He sat calm, unruffled, the headlights shining in his eyes. He made no move to shade himself from the blinding light.

Three men staggered out of the truck, drunken and hostile, shouting obscenities to the sky.

"Doggity boy. What we got here, Jesse?" snarled a bare-chested man. A gold cross, stolen from a sleeping cellmate in the county jail three years earlier, hung around his grimy neck. He wore a torn pair of baggy jeans, one of only two pairs of pants he owned, and grease-stained gym shoes he had found in a dumpster.

"Looks like we got us a Injun from the reservation, Grub," Jesse snorted, and tipped a flask of whiskey to his lips. The burning liquid poured down his angry throat, cutting at the tissue. He relished the painful sensation he'd known since he was thirteen. The flask empty, he smashed it into the fire like a meteor hurled from heaven. A soul cast out.

Jesse wore unwashed blue jeans, blackened by months of dirt, and a black muscle shirt that exposed his massive arms. He flexed his right bicep. A green, fire-breathing dragon tattoo, which clung to his arm like a menacing demon, expanded its chest as if ready to scorch anyone who dared come near. More foreboding than the dragon, however, was the word HATE stenciled on his hand in India ink, one letter of the vicious word spread across each finger. Jesse had scornfully stitched on the explosive warning one night after his girlfriend, whom he had beaten regularly, committed suicide, leaving him nothing but a letter blaming him for her misery. Jesse didn't see it that way. "Harlan, what you think of this red man?" he asked, spitting on the ground.

"I think it's an Indian broke the law and escaped from the reservation," Harlan answered. He ran his hand along the jagged scar, marking the ridge of his jaw bone. He tried unsuccessfully to cover the scar up with a pathetic patch of scruffy beard. Harlan had been rubbing it for years, each time a reminder of the alcoholic father who had smashed his face with a beer bottle when he was twelve. Harlan didn't wait on him fast enough. Twenty-three stitches it cost him. His father was dead now—but not the history. That would never die. Never. He had been exiled to the custody of a sadistic aunt, more drill sergeant than guardian, more tyrant than relative. He hated her, too. Harlan's past unleashed itself on anything and everyone in his path. He loved to watch things suffer—worms, butterflies, birds, cats (especially cats), dogs and people, it was what he had been taught. And, in that respect, the three men were perfect friends.

"Is that right, boy?" Jesse asked. "You escape from the reservation?"

McJic did not speak. He looked up at them with a calm that could have taken the breath from a tornado. The headlights shone directly on him, but he did not squint. The powerful beams magnified his shadow larger than the trees surrounding him. His silhouette, forty feet tall, seemed to be laughing. McJic lowered his head modestly. His shadow, somehow separate from him, looked back at him from the woods, defying the laws of physics. He and his shadow were two distinct separate beings, two distinct spirits. McJic would let his physical body take whatever abuse the rednecks intended on meting out, but his mind and spirit would watch it from a distance, detached.

"Answer me, boy!" Jesse yelled as he struck McJic across the face with the back of his hand.

McJic did not move, nor did he answer. He knew the kind of hatred that grew in men raised as these three were, and he knew he could not change their minds.

"I think he's an escaped lunatic rapist out here to screw our women," cried Harlan. He roughly pulled McJic to his feet and slammed his face into the hood of the truck. Blood trickled from the torn corner of the light-being's lip.

Jesse hooted his approval, ran to the other side of the cab, then reemerged with another bottle of whiskey. "Maybe the Injun likes to drink," he howled, his sinister eyes reflecting the insanity within his mind.

"Yeah," Grub said. He pulled the bottle away from Jesse and twisted off the lid. "Here, Injun, drink!" He laughed and pulled McJic's head up by his long black hair. He forced McJic's mouth open and poured the vile liquid down his throat, causing him to choke and spit.

"He spit on me, boys. The rapist spit on me!" Grub yelled. "You know what we do to rapists down here in the woods, Tonto?"

"We hurts them," Harlan squealed in delight. "We cuts and we hurts them."

In an instant, the three men began tearing at McJic's jeans, stripping them down to his ankles. They dragged him over to the elm tree, slammed him up against it with a thud, and bound him with jumper cables from the back of the truck, sadistically attaching the cable ends to his nipples. The hard, metal teeth of the clamps ripped into McJic's flesh.

He stood silently, unresisting, bound to the tree, as blood dripped from his aching chest. He let the pain run through his body, accepting its intensity. The campfire gave sufficient light for the men to see their captive. Jesse pulled down McJic's underwear, exposing his genitals.

The three stood in the forest dumfounded for a moment as a golden light from McJic's groin shone through the woods, the brightness of the amber glow illuminating the entire area.

"Shee-it. What's this?" cried Harlan. "Is he some sort of alien?"

"Na, he ain't no alien. Watch this." Grub ran to the fire and pulled out a short, burning branch. "He ain't no alien." He rammed the red embers into McJic's privates.

"Nooo!" McJic called out, unable to contain the horror. His hurt voice echoed through the empty forest, which strove mightily to give him all the energy it had. No human could hear his agonized plea, except those inflicting the punishment. No one could help McJic as the rednecks took turns burning his testicles with the fiery stick.

Harlan picked up the guitar, clumsily stroked a few miserable chords, then flung the instrument into the fire. "Kindlin'!" he bellowed proudly. The guitar popped and crackled, the strings snapping from the neck, a final wailing song of death. It burned away.

The drunks hooted, hollered, drank whiskey, and poked at their captive for twenty minutes more before they grew tired of the sordid entertainment.

McJic retreated into a deep mental reserve, an area of the brain where shock takes over to shield the body from the seriousness of an affliction. His tortured body was limp in the flickering light of the fire, strung to a tree, helpless and alone like Jesus on the cross.

"I *know*," shouted Harlan. He ran to the truck while Grub passed the bottle to Jesse. Harlan returned with his toolbox and grabbed a pair of tin snips. "Let's castrate the escaped, lunatic, rapist, alien, Injun."

McJic cried out in agony to the oblivious heavens as the chrome-plated instrument was put to him.

Disoriented from the early morning terror, McJic awoke in the stifling noonday sun. The brutal memories of the previous hours were a nightmare of anguish painted in horrific color on his physical being. His bloody pelvis was covered with dirt and grass. Carnivorous flies buzzed around his naked, vilified body. He struggled to prop himself up on his elbows but fell back weakly to the ground, a sword of burning torment slicing through his body. He tried again with a desperate grunt of exertion, and collapsed helplessly to the grass. Again, McJic lurched up on his elbows; again, he fell. Each time, he lunged forward an inch, perhaps two. Each time, the sword cut him deeper, more severe, with hellish delight. He could hear his punishers chiding him—a memory so evil it was now wedged inside his psyche to be carried forever.

Halfway to the stream, McJic found his charred testicles covered by legions of insects devouring its flesh. He clutched the withered remains in his hand and continued his arduous journey to the grassy bank. Exhausted, wrenched in pain, he reached the water's edge on his stomach and dipped his weary head into the cool wetness. His aching arms hung numb in the pond. McJic slowly opened the hand holding his severed testicles and released them to the water. They disappeared in the current.

51

McJic contemplated the hatred that was unleashed against him as he began to gather his senses. He understood it. It had been created in the same breath by the same life force that formed love. He didn't like that it was that way, but he knew it to be so. He sat up slowly and splashed water against his trembling body.

Then he spoke, "I am One with the Universe. I am Spirit and Energy and Light and Love. We are One." He lightly touched the torn pelvic region of his castration, concentrating his energy—the remaining particles of it—on his lacerated crotch. Suddenly, the meadow of Featherbed Bank came alive for its fallen warrior. Every stalk, every stem, every branch, every trunk, every leaf, every seed, every cone, every weed, every willow, every shrub, every flower, every plant, every creature transferred its own life force, its own nature to the ailing light-being. All the aromatic scents with their wondrous healing powers were released into the atmosphere by the muted foliage. The woodland was vibrant with a swirling spectrum of light directed at the brave captain. It danced and hovered around him like embracing tentacles wrapping him in safety and compassion.

McJic prayed and gave thanks. After several minutes his body began to spasm and jerk, contorting on the ground as if possessed by a demonic entity. The plant energy entered his body, unlocking his chakras like keys to a hidden treasure of soul, strengthening his aura. Power poured into him. He became stronger. Ever stronger. The energy increased, pulsated, vibrating faster and faster. The meadow was bright now, brilliant with a golden hue that seemed to dim the sun, as if a supernova had exploded in Crittenden.

Then, miraculously, the bloody ooze that was his crotch began to heal. The mangled flesh of his pelvis wove itself together, fusing in place to close the wound and make it whole. But now he was a eunuch. McJic would never make love again, not in a physical sense anyway. He had fulfilled the splendor of his mission with Cara and given the world his child. In this life, he would offer only one son to humankind.

He was not angry toward the men who had taken his manhood. He had only pity and sorrow—pity that the world had evolved to such a state, and sorrow that people were forced to endure such pathetic atrocities. He accepted his new burden without acrimony.

As I witnessed the castration of McJic in my mind, horrified by the brutality of the experience and the pain he must have suffered, I questioned why he had not resisted. Why didn't he wave his hand and strike them down, or use some mystical power to render them helpless? Instead, he bore the trauma and humiliation of being tortured by ignorant animals posing as humans. And then I thought of his name as given to me by *The Journals*: James Ignominy Cincinnatus Matthew Crittenden— McJic. The "I" stands for Ignominy, meaning shameful, disgraceful action.

The Journals asked me to share the tale of Danny Gilday and Allison Leslie Pippin, but McJic, on this planet acting out his role too, is a major part of the story. The shame he bore was but a cost paid in life for being here, the charge of admission to our putrid civilization, the high-priced ticket for a seat so close to the stage.

The morning of his defeat in Crittenden was the beginning of a test for McJic. The ignominy he felt on an immoral July morning was the shame borne by all humankind. He had endured it with honor.

But the question is . . . can we do the same?

Chapter 6

July 5, 1967

Patrick Gilday always parked his car, rented under the alias, Albert Speer, several blocks away to avoid suspicion. He grinned, pleased with himself (as he often was) and thinking how clever he'd been to use the name Albert Speer, the great master architect for the Third Reich. He had long admired Speer for his efficiency, for his clean, unsentimental understanding of physics, the way he designed and erected steel structures. Gilday conveniently overlooked the fact that Speer was spending the remaining years of his life in prison for Nazi crimes against humanity.

Gilday donned a pair of dark sunglasses, a Reds baseball cap, and a wrinkled overcoat to mask his identity. It wouldn't do to be discovered visiting his mistress, although he wasn't averse to letting it slip to the appropriate man of position who would appreciate such an extravagance. He grabbed the box of Esther Price chocolates from the seat next to him and left the parking garage. Blazing sun heated the top of his baseball cap like a laser beam through a magnifying glass, causing his bald spot to burn. He thought of the time when, as a child of ten, he ignited an old mattress in a condemned building with nothing but a magnifying glass and the sun. Gilday smiled. The building had burned to the ground. That was the day he realized how much power he had, how much power anyone could have if they took it.

He glanced about cautiously, as was his habit, to see if he was being followed. He walked past a disheveled collection of thrift shops, strip joints, all-night bars, used-furniture and appliance stores no one ever frequented—each doorway like a broken tooth in the decayed smile of an aging stripper overdone in lipstick and paint to hide the blemishes and wrinkles. People looked the other way when Newport was discussed.

Cara'd take everything I own if she found out, he thought. Patrick Gilday trusted no one, a policy he established as a streetwise kid, and one he kept as he amassed his personal fortune. He looked across the street to the park and saw the pigeons fluttering about for scraps of food. They competed with the winos and bums for bench space. A raggedy man approached him.

"Spare a dime for a cup of coffee, sir?" the man asked, stretching out a hand.

"Get a job," Gilday scoffed. He walked on, sparing no sympathy. He viewed these people as weak, mindless animals, too ashamed to apply themselves and make a go of life. He despised the needy for their symbolism. He didn't understand them.

"Never again," he said to himself. "Never again will a Gilday beg and grovel to survive."

Memories of his late father, Benjamin Gilday, trounced his disturbed mind as he strutted past forlorn buildings and dilapidated homes like a peacock in the ghetto. Gilday thought of how his father had come to America hoping to make his fortune. Another poor immigrant, spending it all for a ticket across the rainbow. Benjamin had arrived in New York City to low wages and a shabby tenement shared with another disillusioned family. But he worked hard in a steel factory, saving his money, and eventually found himself in Cincinnati working in a steel mill. It was difficult, demanding work but provided better living conditions. Patrick was five when they had moved from New York, and he had no recollection of that place. Cincinnati was his home.

At thirty-two, Benjamin, having acquired a keen knowledge of steel, struck out on his own. His small business, BG Industries, specialized in sheet metal work, yielding a modest income for the Gildays. Patrick was brought into the business at the age of twelve, not so much out of desire as necessity. He learned the trade well from his father, but Benjamin Gilday wasn't a great businessman. He knew steel, not finance. Patrick remembered the tragic day when John Ogilvey, an official from the First Kentucky Bank, came to visit.

Patrick watched in spiteful silence as Benjamin pleaded with Ogilvey for a little more time on the loan. Ogilvey, singular in task, was deaf to the proposal and informed Benjamin that he had no choice but to foreclose on BG Industries. Patrick remembered the pitiful sight of his father rising from his chair, his face white and moist, patting his head with a sweat-stained handkerchief; Benjamin Gilday paused for a moment, looked at Ogilvey, and said, "If that's the way you want it, John, then so be it," then dropped dead.

Patrick stood horrified as he watched his father's fiery energy dissipate like the orange-red heat of molten steel hardening.

Patrick, his mother, and two sisters were penniless. He would never forgive John Ogilvey, the First Kentucky Bank, or his father for the heart attack. At fourteen, he was working the streets doing odd jobs to make ends meet for his family. His mother, Elizabeth, worked nights as a washer woman in the Carew Tower, scrubbing floors and emptying wastepaper baskets, which humiliated him. As the man of the family, he should have been able to provide.

It was an experience Patrick couldn't let go of no matter how lavishly he surrounded himself with luxuries. He had ably learned the fast double-talk of con men, gaining insight into the way the world really works. Forget the American Dream, he thought, it's only propaganda. He took care of his two sisters, Maggy and Claire, as best he could for three and a half years, until his mother announced they were returning to Ireland. He rebelled against the decision. He would not let America defeat him. He joined the service.

Patrick Gilday mistakenly took his family's departure as a rejection of himself and his ability to provide. He thought of his abandonment as he walked beneath the archway marking the exclusive entrance to the marina. The perfectly kept yachts and pleasure boats of the wealthy were hidden just a few feet and a right turn away from the boarded-up pride that once was Newport. The message was lost on him. As an adult, he no longer felt any compassion for the class of people he had grown up with. If he had made it, why couldn't they?

"I've killed that miserable time," he said aloud as he stepped on the squeaky, wooden dock toward the houseboat. "Dead. Gone. Buried."

Indeed, Patrick would always remember the lesson of his dead father, so much so he named his company BG Industries after his father's failed one. This constant reminder, so visible on company stationery, business cards, signage, and trucks, would burn in his psyche daily, never allowing Patrick a moment's rest. But he had not destroyed his past. Instead, he simply dealt-out cruelty rather than received it.

"Skye, I'm here," he called, as he entered through the sliding glass door. "Skye?" He tossed the box of chocolates on the counter and cased the room. "More damn plants," he said as he took off his disguise. "Why does she keep filling this place up with so many goddamn plants?" The houseboat was alive with ferns and ivies and greenery of all sorts, every available corner teeming with extravagant plants. It was Skye's way of masking Patrick's Spartan decorating style—plain as vanilla pudding in a dessert contest.

"Hello, Patrick," Skye said. She stood in the bedroom doorway, her slim, tanned body covered in only his favorite starched dress shirt—unbuttoned—and white cotton panties. Her fine, black hair twisted and curved its way past her breasts to her exposed navel.

But Patrick didn't notice. "Have you been buying more plants? It looks like a damn jungle in here. I thought I told you not to buy any more green stuff."

Skye smiled, refusing to let Patrick upset her. She knew him, knew his quirks, his peculiarities, his shortcomings. She had to: he was her special assignment, the reason she had been sent to Earth by the Council of Ancients. She turned and walked to the bar.

"Where's my drink?" he said.

"I'll get it for you, Patty," she replied sweetly, tossing her hair over her shoulder.

"I told you I'd be here at four o'clock. Why can't you have my drink ready when I get here? I don't ask much."

She didn't hear him. She had learned to tune out his demands as a means of maintaining her sanity during this most difficult of tasks. Skye was particularly suited for a temperament like Patrick's. She had earned a well-deserved reputation on Shanidar for having tamed the most insensitive of Earthlings. As Patrick continued his childish tirade she focused on her spiritual mentor, McJic, envying his lifelong mission.

"Are you listening to me?"

"Yes, Patty, I'm listening," she lied as she wrestled with the ice for his drink. Exactly four cubes, not three, not five—four. She didn't count them anymore, her inner ear knowing through repetition the sound of four clinks in the tumbler.

McJic had worked with Skye for years, teaching her how to maintain humility and balance, how to accept the harshness of Earth, how to weather the unbearable sadness while on the planet. Her assignment was a brief one, twenty-four years in all, but long enough to bear a child and raise it to the age of five. Unlike McJic, who could change shapes and forms to suit his plans, Skye was stuck with mostly human traits. Like all light-beings, though, she could read minds and see the future. But, oh, if she could master energy and thought the way McJic could, to travel through time, she would feel so blessed. "I hope he's all right," she said to herself, knowing McJic's fate this day.

"It sure doesn't seem like it," Patrick complained, breaking her concentration. "Doesn't seem like you're listening at all."

Skye poured the gin into the glass, added a splash of tonic, then squeezed the lime. She looked at him as little as possible, disdaining the man, yet trying to accept him.

He stood at the huge picture window staring out at the city which sat in a valley, a large ashtray of a town, the buildings sticking their smoking, crumpled butts into the air, a hazy film covering everything within its choking grasp. A rusty barge worked its way down river, carrying coal to a factory or power plant which would produce even more pollution.

"It's beautiful isn't it?" Skye said. She handed him his gin and tonic.

"What's beautiful?"

"The skyline, silly boy."

"You know what I see?"

She already knew what he would say. She saw deeper into his soul than he would ever know. She knew of his need to express life in cold terms. It sheltered him from life itself, kept him from being bothered by it.

"I see so many girders and I-beams, so many pounds of steel. I see profit."

"Oh, Patty, there is much more to the world than money, so much more to life than steel."

His eyes narrowed, "No, there isn't. There is money and steel, two hard objects you can touch. You can't buy shit with that skyline. I'll leave the beauty of it to the poets as they starve trying to gain recognition for their thoughts. They can keep their damn emotion; it only hurts you. Emotion is for people who have nothing else in life."

"You know what I see?"

"A filthy city swimming in smog?"

"I see a marvelous city of magicians and sages, of Wiccans and healers cast under the spell of an evil master who came one day and shrouded the people in a paralyzing mist so their eyes couldn't see truth any longer. He fogged their minds so they couldn't think clearly. But one day soon, the sleepy townsfolk will awaken and the evil will be dispelled."

Patrick snorted his disapproval. "Have you been reading those damn occult books of yours again? I swear you do everything the opposite of what I want."

"I like to tell stories, Patty, that's all," she said softly.

"You and Cara are the same," he said. "You think the world is a romantic place full of love and friendship, when all the while the movers and shakers make the rules and take everything you've got. Then, when it's all gone, you sit and wonder what the hell happened."

"Dear Patty," Skye said, stroking his hair like a child. "How misguided you are. How tormented you must be to despise anything different from you. How completely sad you are."

Her direct nature infuriated him, but at the same time he found it most comforting. He couldn't control his mistress like he did his wife. He couldn't weld Skye to his will—she was too free-spirited, too independent. This caused great confusion in him as he bent to Skye's desires. He acted tough in the relationship, lord of the manor, king of the castle, and let this show in his anger, but they both knew she was in charge.

His face turned red. Patrick clenched his jaw and made a fist. "I don't like it when you talk to me that way!" he yelled.

"Don't raise your voice to me, little boy."

"Don't talk to me that way," he insisted in a voice suddenly twenty years younger than his age.

"Patty, I told you not to talk back to your mistress."

"I hate you."

"You're to get a spanking for that." Skye pretended to be forceful. "Get to your room, little boy, and take your pants down!" Being a peaceful Shanidarian made it difficult for her to be aggressive, but in Patrick's case, due to his hateful attitude, she actually liked dishing out discipline on his bare bottom. But not too much.

Patrick, his head down like a sobbing five year old, shuffled to the bedroom where he undressed. She remained in the living room, making him wait, while she thought of Cara. Skye felt sorry for her. "I could be such a good friend to her," she said. "I could show her love."

Skye stroked her long black hair over and over to soothe herself, building up the courage to go into the bedroom, discipline her paramour, and receive his affections. She looked at the pottery wheel sitting idle in the corner, and longed for Friday, when Patrick would again be gone, so she could make a vase for a friend of hers in Pleasant Ridge. She stared through the white sheet of smog to the rotating Western Southern Life clock—4:17. It turned, 87°. "This will be over by four-thirty," she said, taking a deep breath as she strolled to the bedroom and an anxious, adolescent Patrick Gilday.

It was over in minutes. As always. During the four or so minutes that the copulation took place, Skye thought of watering the plants. The outdoor plants were especially dry and the ferns always needed attention. Skye, being deliciously human, wanted sex in a longer, more sustained fashion, to simmer and sizzle until the sweat dripped from her dark skin, splatting like rain upon her lover. She often thought of McJic when Patrick was between her legs, envisioning what it would be like to make love to the captain in human form, to mix spirits, to taste each other and revel in the experience of physicality. But this was never to be, as she well knew. Still, she could dream of McJic as Patrick clumsily, unskillfully tried his best to be a Valentino. The deed done, her thoughts on botanical issues, she was satisfied and smiled.

"What are you so happy about?" Patrick asked. He pulled his underwear up over his flushed, red buttocks.

"I'm just glad you came, Patty," she said, her mind off in a distant galaxy.

"I don't suppose I'm ever going to understand you."

She wasn't listening again. She was thinking contentedly of her completion of phase one of her mission on Earth. She couldn't contain her happiness. "Patrick, why don't we go out tonight and celebrate?"

"Celebrate what? What is there to celebrate?"

"Oh, I don't know, the next two days together, I guess."

"I don't like going out, Skye. You know that. I'm well-known around here. What if someone sees us?"

She pouted, rolled out of bed and stood at the closet door, searching for something to put on.

"Why don't you just wear my shirt?" he suggested.

Skye said nothing as she reached for a sleeveless sundress and slid it over her smooth body. Patrick craved her, always in awe of her perfect shape, but quickly became perturbed that she ignored him again. Skye didn't care. She had no respect for him; he lacked the emotional sensitivity necessary for people to become close to him. He was hard and callused and unforgiving of the world.

Skye Pippin did all she could to overcome Patrick's dark nature. She zipped up the back of her dress, turned toward her lover, and forced a smile. Nothing would dampen her glorious moment. Her finely-tuned body could feel the sperm furiously swimming their way to her egg. The sensation enveloped her abdomen with light tingles of divine warmth. She would conceive this day.

"Okay, Patty, let's stay in tonight and I'll make us a nice dinner."

"How about pork chops?" he suggested. "They're my favorite. Let's celebrate whatever it is we're celebrating by having pork chops!"

"Pork chops it is. Grilled or baked?" Skye resented the coming answer. Grilled pork chops again. *And how about some mashed potatoes and gravy with biscuits,* she knew he would respond. She needn't use her psychic ability; it was simply his dull pattern. She doubted Patrick had ever noticed that she never ate meat. A vegetarian in Cincinnati was decidedly uncommon, and Patrick was most unobservant of anyone but himself.

"Grilled. And how about some mashed potatoes and gravy with biscuits?" he said on cue.

It's just like him to take my celebration and ask for something he wants, she thought to herself. Why are men like that? Can't they consider a woman's feelings for a change? After all, this is the sixties.

"I'll make supper." Skye grinned at the unsuspecting father. She left him in the bedroom where his attentions would soon turn to business. She thought of Shanidar, where such vast disparities between men and women didn't exist. True, on Shanidar gender didn't exist, but light-beings respected each other, and their desires, for what they were—without judgment, without control, without the human need to possess. Today, with Patrick's seed racing through her uterus, Skye knew she only had five more years to endure his immaturities. And that gave her solace.

She took the chops from the refrigerator and set them next to the chocolates, thinking that she'd stack them later, next to all the other boxes of candy in the pantry that would go uneaten. Skye didn't fancy chocolate either. She determined that phase two of her mission would center around her changing Patrick's close-minded view of the world. "I'll get him to respect women," she told herself as he began his round of business calls to his broker, his accountant, and his attorney. "I'll get him to love Cara."

For now, she would grill the pork chops and mash the potatoes and bake the biscuits and mix the gravy and spend two days with a sorry, misguided little boy. Nothing he said or did from that point on would bother her. She would accept her fate and bask in the knowledge of her secret. She found honor in her pregnancy. She had conceived a child. She would bear the girl who would dance with the muses—the woman who would love all life, the spirit who would walk with the gods and offer undying hope to humankind.

Skye had forged the future with a man of steel.

Skye sat on the deck of the houseboat, slumped in a lawn chair, a bulky winter sweater draped over her knees. Sobbing, she stared at the washed-out heavens. Her palms were wedged firmly between her legs as she shivered. In the early morning darkness she looked at the digital clock spinning on the roof of the heliport across the river—3:57 . . . 74°. She thought of her teacher, McJic, and the horrid ordeal he was suffering at that exact moment. The two, she and McJic, were bound by their light-being consciousness, feeling human elation and tragedy together—connected.

"I am with you," she said to the air, knowing her thoughts would make it to him. She wanted to buffer him somehow, to reduce his painful burden. It is the way of light-beings. "Give me your sorrow," she offered. "Let me bear it for you." She closed her eyes and prayed.

Chapter 7

August 1942

The shipment had arrived, the crate landing within two kilometers of the drop-off point. The freedom fighters Sulphur had organized moved fast in a truck with its headlights dimmed, sweeping across a rocky scrub of desert near the foothills to collect the cargo. The drone of the plane had barely dissipated in the dark Mediterranean night before the Resistance had the crate aboard the ground transport.

Sulphur grinned at the efficiency of his men as they bounced their way to Central Intelligence Command. He was pleased the operation had gone so smoothly. In the two weeks since he reached Morocco, he'd had much success. The country, held by the Vichy French under German control, was ripe for revolution. Nobody liked the Germans—not the French, the Moors, the Riffs, the Berbers, or the expatriates from Europe. Surprisingly, he had discovered only passing Nazi interest in Morocco. Intelligence analysts viewed the North African front as the most likely place for an American invasion force to land. The passageway for all ships entering the Mediterranean Sea and the doorway to Middle Eastern oil was crucial to German victory. Yet only Casablanca was heavily fortified by the puppet Vichys. The rest of the country was openly resentful of the Germans and their French traitors, willing to expel them at any cost.

Sulphur stared out the gritty window, thinking of his orders as the truck shook its way down a seldom-used mountain road. He remembered the words of Colonel Eddy, the English professor turned spy: "Intelligence will win this war, not guns." Indeed, Sulphur knew this to be true. Aiming heavy weapons at an empty town while the enemy outflanks you would surely result in defeat. Air raids on civilian targets accomplished nothing. But properly directed attacks, using good data and analysis, he'd been taught, would ensure victory. If only General Donovan could convince those eggheads in Washington.

Sulphur thought of the politics being played at the highest levels in the States— turf wars among bickering military leaders with so much disregard for the lives at stake. General Donovan, head of the Office of Strategic Services, had convincingly won over FDR to establish an intelligence network. The navy, army, and FBI protested, placing obstacles in the way to protect their own power.

Donovan himself had taken Sulphur aside the night before he flew to Lisbon. "You're the first," the soft-spoken man said, sitting sideways on the front edge of a desk stacked high with top-secret documents.

Sulphur looked into the quiet, blue eyes of the enigmatic general. There was an intensity there, an energy more dynamic than that of two dozen tired generals lounging about the Pentagon.

"We need a win here," Donovan said, "if we're going to establish ourselves as an intelligence force." The chubby man picked up a manila folder and slipped a memo from it. His eyes hardened as he studied the correspondence. "A victory will keep Admiral Leahy from shutting us down. It will also keep unnecessary tragedies like Pearl Harbor from happening again."

It was well known within the OSS and throughout the top brass that Pearl Harbor was a major military blunder. The codes had been broken by the genius William Friedman, who had sent the messages on to all responsible authorities, including Roosevelt. Some said it was a calculated move by the president to ignore the evidence of imminent Japanese attack in order to push the United States into the war, against heavy antiwar protests at home. If it was true, FDR had reasoned correctly.

"We're counting on you." Donovan slapped Sulphur lightly on the back. "Maybe we can stick it to that faggot Hoover, too."

"Sir?"

Donovan slid off the desk, standing before the one-man Moroccan invasion force. "The Popov Affair," he said, his voice a light, feminine wisp. "Hoover completely botched it. Popov was a double agent professing to work for the Germans when he was actually in British control. The Krauts sent him to the States to spy for them, and British MI-5 asked the FBI for the proper cover. Hoover refused, despite high-level briefings, believing that Popov was a German spy and not a double agent. Hoover compromised Popov's position with his inquiries and sent Popov back to his death in Germany. Hoover was too busy cross-dressing and calling himself Mary to be concerned over national security issues. I wish I'd never selected him to run the FBI. Worst mistake I ever made."

"Yes, sir."

Sulphur was jolted back to the present by a gaping pothole in the road. The truck rumbled its way into Fez with its covert cargo. The real work was about to begin.

Who is this stranger come to visit?
A fiery heretic in the temple with eyes of desire
Who ordained the species to deface the altar?
A guest whom Chance invited to the feast

Chapter 8

August 7, 1990

"Will it be war?" Rose asked, distracting me from the front page headline—HOSPITAL BOMB SCARE.

She tried to shield me from it, as if I didn't already know I was a pariah, as if I was oblivious to the death threats. Some lunatic vows to blow up the building, and I'm to blame. Even the other patients were calling me, telling me to recuperate elsewhere. I understood why people were hacked off: German shepherds sniffing the halls, all noncritical patients forced outside in the blistering heat. It was like a bad day at Auschwitz.

The scare was a false alarm instigated by a maniac getting his jollies at my expense. Secretly, I hoped it wasn't *The Journals* fabricating more mayhem.

The crisis in the Gulf being the only other news item of interest—besides my lynching—Rose's question was a suitable enough diversion. I stared at the scuffed outline where Jesus used to hang. I couldn't take his repentant eyes staring at me any longer, trying to peer into my soul. Lest any decent Christian take offense, I would have stuffed images of Buddha, Mohammed, Krishnamurti, Vishnu, or any other religious icon into my night stand, too. Neither Rose nor the gum-smacking nurse appreciated my scorn for religion. "Yes," I said, "war is inevitable. The government's made up its mind. Christ, Rose, they've even gotten King Fahd to let our troops into Saudi Arabia."

"Don't you think they should? To protect us?"

"Holy smokes, honey." I crumpled the newspaper in my lap. "We don't have anything to fear from Iraq. They got the crap kicked out of them for eight years when they fought Iran. Their economy is in shambles and their army is exhausted. They'd be insane to go to war now." I reached for a glass of water to get rid of the pasty taste in my mouth. It tasted like something crawled inside me and died, like disease was farming forty acres in the soil of my bowels. "Something's not right, though. The Saudis would never let us in there unless we exerted heavy pressure on them. American troops on Arab sand, that's taboo in the Middle East."

"But don't you think we need to protect our oil?" Rose was standing at the window. She looked out at the decrepit church tower. The steeple was surrounded in translucent ozone, the ghosts of past parishioners come to cough. The sun was shrouded in cloud, the sky and the surrounding hills of Greater Cincinnati draped in gray-white mist. The town, like me, was diseased. She glanced back at the spot where Jesus had been, no doubt finding some sign, some divine message in it all.

I tried to read her thoughts while the pigeons cooed their secret language to each other and shit on the already splattered roof. I've seen much religious architecture in my time—red tile roofs hunched over Greek Orthodox stone and brick, the intricate mandapa at the Shore Temple in India, the impressive vimanas of the Hindus, the Seven Horses of the Sun carved into the Black Pagoda of Konarak, simple Buddhist supas, the columned porticos and terraces of Angkor Wat, the ornate torana at Sanchi, and the Bodh Gaya pyramidal tower, where Siddhartha found enlightenment. I've seen the evergreen-reminiscent pagoda of the Horyuji Temple, the bell-shaped Shwe Dagon in Rangoon, the nature-inspired shoden and honden of the Shinto shrine of Ise—set in nature worshipping the sun goddess—and the torii on the sacred island of Miyajima. My eyes have taken in the cruciform plan of naves and transepts of the Chartres Cathedral, the unassuming dome of Rachel's Tomb rising like a solitary breast toward God on the road between Jerusalem and Bethlehem, the wooden synagogues of Poland, the onion spires of Prebrazhebnye Church, and the majesty of St. Peter's Basilica.

Yes, I've seen holy centers fashioned in Baroque, Persian, Islamic, Georgian, Byzantine, Moorish, Greco-Roman, Sephardic, Gothic, Romanesque, Renaissance, Quaker, Spanish, Victorian styles, and Frank Lloyd Wright contemporary. I've seen them all. I've seen churches with balustrades, pilasters, arches, towers, cupolas, domes, steeply pitched roofs, basilicas, bots, cellas, gables, cornices, flying buttresses, chattris, chedis, chigis, rococo, sikharas, piers, and mihrabs.

I've seen churches crumble under the thumb of time. I've seen them collapse, give glory, christen and baptize, bury and resurrect. I've seen them betroth and divorce. I've seen them raise and praise. I've seen them honored. I've seen them abandoned. I've seen them in hope and in despair. I've seen them burn. But in all the ways that I have seen churches, I have never seen one as forlorn and forgotten as the tarnished one outside my hospital window.

"War is never a good idea," I said. "Except in self-defense."

"We need oil for our cars, R.T.," Rose said.

"Rose, it's not our oil." Harsh memories crawled in on their bellies, a sixty-pound military backpack of dark recollections strapped to my brain. A sneak attack. "I've seen the work of war back in the forties, Rose. It's indescribable what it does to people."

"But that was necessary," she said, turning away from the window. "You helped fight the Nazis. You helped stop their tyranny."

"Did I? Seems like we ended up in the same place. All I did was replace bridges for the engineering corps, honey. I didn't stop anything."

"But you did your part."

A flock of pigeons lifted from the shit-lacquered church, reminding me of the battle-scarred steeples of Europe. If she only knew. The memory commandos crept closer. It's not something one talks about—all the dead, the dismembered, the homeless, those missing limbs, or eyes, or burned so badly they didn't look human anymore, the shattered and mourning survivors wishing they hadn't made it through. I can still hear their shouts as they beg to die. I see mile after mile of destruction, everything gone, nothing left but rubble. And that's why I chose to be a developer—to undo all that devastation.

"I could have done more," I said. My eyes fixed upon the forsaken church, tiles missing from its slate roof. "And I should have done more to stop Vietnam."

Rose's eyes reassured me. "You couldn't do anything, R.T."

"Okay, I know I couldn't have stopped the war, but I could've tried to get Bobby out. I could have used my influence. Then maybe he wouldn't have—"

"Don't blame yourself for that. Bobby volunteered. He joined the service on his own. It's not your fault he lost his arm."

But maybe it was. Maybe *The Journals* was right. Maybe if I had done more it wouldn't have happened. Maybe if we all did more, there would be less violence.

But before I could reply, Jim Bennett came in.

"Well, isn't this a cushy place to take a vacation?" he joked, a typical flamboyant entrance. He often said that lawyering was ninety-nine percent showmanship and one percent facts. "You really must give me the name of your travel agent," Jim chuckled as he set a gorgeous red orchid on the night stand—*Laelia* zip—and I wondered if he recognized the irony of its common name: Fireball. That would be just like Jim to punctuate the ironic. I smiled as images of Cara Gilday's breathtaking, celestial gold *Magicka carallus* shimmered in my mind. Ah, the power of dreams.

"Present," Bennett laughed. "For Rose."

Jim Bennett is a large man with a gregarious personality that could have set the Spanish Inquisition into knee-slapping hysterics. He has a rare persuasiveness that allows him to change adversaries into pussycats.

"I know your passion for orchids, R.T.," Bennett said. "Thought it might cheer you up."

He was right, orchids are my love, a peaceful hobby unlike any other. "Hi, Jim." I grinned, relieved to see him. "Thanks for the gift."

Next to Rose, Jim Bennett was the most supportive confidant I had. He stepped next to the bed and patted my hand firmly with his oversized mitt as he shifted a large manila envelope under his right arm.

"So good to see you," Rose said.

"Same here." He smiled mischievously, his resonant voice reminiscent of a deejay on a classical radio station. The late night sounds of Jim Bennett bringing you the mellow strains of Rachmaninoff. "R.T., I'm seeing you so much that my wife is starting to get suspicious," Jim teased. That's one of the pleasures of working with him, he always has a positive attitude no matter how glum the circumstance. Bennett tossed the package on the night stand. "Special delivery," he said and looked at the newspaper. "I didn't know you were into Middle Eastern affairs, R.T. Your friends in Washington keeping you current? So many secrets for such a young man." He winked.

Bennett and I were anything but young, he being two years my senior, although he kept himself in fine shape through exercise and lots of laughter. The man was unflappable. He appeared twenty years younger—late forties, tops. We'd been together for forty-five years. I was his first client; I had him incorporate me. He was just twenty-six, right out of law school, and begging to get into the action. He hasn't lost a step, though, hasn't missed a point of law, hasn't lost a drop of enthusiasm since.

The envelope had been opened. "Do you read my mail now, too?" I kidded.

Jim framed his jaw with his hand and rubbed his chin. "No," he hesitated. "The cops gave it to me."

Rose was indignant. "So, they're reading R.T.'s *mail?*"

"It arrived during the hullabaloo about the bomb," Bennett said. "They were suspicious that it may have been an explosive."

Rose gritted her teeth. She believed Bennett, but not the police. "Which came first, the opened mail or the bomb threat?"

"That's the least of our problems—" Bennett glanced out the window. "Boy, that's an ugly church. Anyway, R.T., are you well enough to travel?"

"Travel?"

"Yeah," Bennett said sheepishly. He pulled a folded letter from his pocket. "I tried to fight it, R.T., but the hospital has influence, too. You're getting the boot."

"What!" I exclaimed.

"It's awful, I know." He shook his head. "But they say the safety of their patients is their primary concern."

I was furious. How dare they kick me out before I recuperated. "It's not fair. They can't do this, can they?"

Bennett subpoenaed me with a wide grin. "Can and did," he said. "Don't sweat it, though. We'll get you home and sue them later, if you want. This isn't the right battle just now." His voice turned solemn, but his grin stayed put. "You're in serious trouble, R.T."

"Tell me about it." I rolled my eyes. I've heard him say that before.

"I've arranged your bail, had to put your house up for collateral," Bennett said. "This case isn't good. They have witnesses, corroborating evidence and a whole lot of public pressure."

Rose stroked my arm reassuringly. "That may be, Jim," she said, looking him straight on, "but R.T. didn't do it."

Privately, she had her doubts, too—rightfully so—but no one would know it except me. Thank God for her.

Bennett winced. "They have a sworn statement from your own son," he said. "If they put Bobby on the stand, and they *will,* he'll bury you." His grin sequestered itself in chambers. "R.T., I've always stood by you, and I always will, that's my job. But if there's any chance that you did this, you need to tell me now. We can plea bargain this thing down."

"I'm innocent. I've been framed." Straining, I reached under the sheets for *The Journals,* which lay against my left thigh. "Look, I can show you. I have it right here, the book that framed me. See?" I said as I pulled out the manuscript. I held it up proudly, then gaped at the disappointed faces of my wife and lawyer.

"The Bible can't help you," Bennett said with the seriousness of a Baptist minister sermonizing against the evils of alcohol.

"What!" I turned the book around, examining the cover—*The Holy Name Bible.* Damn, it had shape-shifted on me. "Son of a bitching book is screwing with me."

Rose and Bennett shot each other concerned glances.

"Look, R.T.," Bennett whispered, his eyes moving back and forth, checking to see if anyone was listening. "They've overheard you talking to yourself, claiming you're Jesus." His eyes shifted again. "You can't do that. Unless, of course, you want to use insanity as your defense. But I'd advise against it." He slapped me lightly on the arm. "But, if that's what you want, keep talking to yourself."

"I'm telling you two . . ." I tried to keep my voice low. "I've been framed by a higher power."

Rose's eyes immediately went to the smudge where the missing Messiah had hung.

"Well," Bennett said, straightening up, "if it decides to take the stand in your behalf, give it my number."

He and Rose burst out laughing.

"Jim," I protested. "It's true."

"We'll get through this, don't you worry," he said, a tad too condescendingly.

Am I losing my mind? I wondered. If Rose and Bennett don't believe me, then who will?

"For now," Bennett said, "we'll have to make arrangements to get you home later this afternoon." He observed my facial bandages. "Say, I thought you got shot in the back. What happened to your face?"

"I'm not sure, but it stings like hell. Doctor Finkleday said it was a chemical burn."

"Ouch." Bennett clenched his jaw and glanced at Rose as he drew a breath. Then he looked at me. "R.T., I'd advise against filing for bankruptcy just now. I don't know what it does to your financial picture or how long you can keep the wolves at bay, but bad impressions won't help the case."

Rose twisted her necklace. I fidgeted in bed, acting like I was trying to get comfortable, but there was no way—the discomfort was in my heart. Why did Jim have to bring up our money problems?

"Okay," I said.

"Oh, shoot." Rose stamped her foot lightly, changing the subject intentionally, trying to protect my ego. "I just remembered: Julie was going to bring you a home-cooked meal, but now you're going home."

"What's she making?" I shuddered to think of Twinkie showing up with a casserole.

"Fresh fennel and sardines over linguini," Rose said without flinching. "And sautéed Vienna sausages in a white wine sauce on the side."

Bennett chuckled. "That little girl of yours sure is creative. Well, sorry I won't be able to enjoy it with you. I'm due in court—*God*, that's an ugly church."

Then we said our goodbyes.

Rose was out of the room, taking care of my move, when *The Journals* reappeared. I was livid about it abandoning me.

"*I must reveal myself at the proper time.*"

"Goddamn it, where the hell have you been?"

"*Busy making preparations, Stone.*"

"I don't care what you've been doing, you've been no help to me. None!" I said, slamming the book shut.

The book opened itself up, writing to me.

"*You are upset. Quite understandable, given the circumstance. What you must do is get healthy and begin researching the lives of Daniel and Allison.*"

"Look, I mean no disrespect, but you really have the wrong guy. I'm just a simple bricklayer turned developer. I'm a man with no religious outlook, no real interest, I'm simply the wrong guy. The Council made a mistake!"

"*No, no, no. We have the right man. Robert Thomas Stone of Cincinnati, Ohio: You have a wife named Rosetta, a daughter named Julie, whom you like to call Twinkie, and a son, Bobby, Jr. Plus, we have your DNA profile and a complete dossier of your life. If you do not believe me, Stoney—although by now I should think you would—ask me any question about yourself, your family, friends. Anything. Go ahead, ask.*"

I was having none of it. I believed. It was a writing book after all, which came and went as it pleased. The best proof of its power was the fact that I was in trouble because of it. "I don't need any more proof," I said. "I'm just overwhelmed by the insanity of it all. I can't take any more. I'm not strong enough for a task of this magnitude. I'm sinking like a stone into a bottomless well."

"*Personally, I have tremendous faith in you. Are you not the one who financed and built the Millennium Tower at Seventh and Vine?*"

"Yes."

"*Are you not the one who worked behind the scenes to organize the largest amateur tennis charity tournament in a five-state area?*"

"Yes," I answered modestly.

"So, Stoney, you really have some remarkable talents, do you not?"

"Building a skyscraper and organizing a tennis tournament are not the same as researching, writing, and promoting a book to replace the Bible—especially while facing charges of attempted, aggravated murder and arson," I huffed.

"Yes, but life is adversity, and adversity teaches life's lessons. The lessons teach strength, and through that strength comes success.

"You will be fine, Stoney. Besides, you are not replacing the Bible, you are providing an alternative, a complementary source of evidence, much in the same manner as the Koran, the Cabala, the Book of Zen, the Egyptian Book of the Dead, the I Ching, and the ancient Vedic texts, to name a few."

"So those other books are true, too?"

"Of course. Is there only one way to do anything? No! There are always many, many alternatives. The trouble begins when individuals refuse to accept and tolerate any belief but their own. Trouble, trouble, trouble, I say. More people killed in the name of religion than by Adolf Hitler, by God. Think about it. Anyway, Stoney, I have nothing but confidence in you. You, my good man, can do it!"

"Well, it's not like I have a choice," I said. "I suppose you may be right."

"There is no doubt about it, Stoney, I am right. Now, you must put this self-deprecating manner of yours behind you and get to work. We need you positive, Stoney, motivated and committed. It is essential that you get in the spirit here!"

Of course, *The Journals* is right. As long as I'm committed, I might as well get a positive attitude and dig myself out of the hole, even if I only have a spoon. No one else is going to help.

"Okay," I agreed, "but I have no idea where to begin."

"Start with that envelope that just arrived."

"What does that have to do with anything?"

"One cannot know until one looks. Many signs are given, few are seen. It is time for you to awaken and search for the answers you seek. They are always there."

I reluctantly set *The Journals* aside and slipped several editions of a newspaper-style periodical called *Eastern Crescent Review* out of the envelope. A yellow sticky-note was attached:

> Mr. Stone,
> Thought you could use some help.
>
> M

The note was written in a fanciful, woman's script complete with curly Q's on her ascenders and descenders. Not that I'm a handwriting expert. Why would someone send me headline stories about the Gulf Crisis? The *Eastern Crescent* story didn't match the facts in *The Enquirer* or what I was seeing on the tube. Curious.

I picked up *The Journals*, flipped its pages, and asked, "How is reading about the Iraqi-Kuwait conflict going to save me? How does this help you get the story published?"

"There are many invisible threads woven in the fabric. Read."

As instructed, I read further. There was an article about how a July 31 meeting between Iraq and Kuwait, which was sponsored by King Fahd, Hosni Mubarek, and King Hussein of Jordan, had suddenly collapsed at the intransigence of the Kuwaitis. The article was well-researched, citing numerous credible resources, one of which compared the Kuwaiti attitude to that of "small-time grocery store owners." The paper reported that in Arab circles, Iraq's claims were well-founded, and Kuwait was encouraged by the Arab leaders to accept the Iraqi request. All the while, the CIA was telling the Kuwaitis to stand firm against Saddam. Bad advice, I'd say.

And what were the Iraqi demands? First, Saddam wanted Kuwait to stop flooding the world's oil market in violation of their OPEC agreement. Prices had dropped from $20.50 a barrel last January to $13 by June, costing Iraq $12 billion in revenue. That was enough to steam anybody's turban. Saddam wanted the money paid back. Second, he demanded that Kuwait stop stealing oil from Iraqi reserves in the Rumaila oil field located on the border; he demanded $2.4 billion in restitution for the stolen crude. A reasonable compensation, I'd say. Third, Saddam wanted Kuwait to renounce its claims to the disputed oil field. The fourth demand called for Kuwait to waive Iraq's $10 billion war debt. Finally, Saddam demanded that Kuwait cede Bubiyan Island to Iraq.

Most of the Arab world sided with Saddam Hussein on the issues. Iraq had defended Kuwait against Iran just a few years ago, but now Kuwait was smacking the Baathist nose of the Iraqi president. Reputable Middle East experts in Washington and London concluded that the CIA was manipulating the crisis.

There was good evidence to support that theory. The U.S. had constructed secret state-of-the-art air bases in Saudi Arabia ten years earlier. Kuwait was violating Arab tradition by responding to Iraq with insults, knowing that Saddam was easily angered and volatile. Having served in the region briefly during World War II, I knew that insults are not easily ignored in that part of the world.

My military training had taught me the historical facts of that unstable region. I recalled that Kuwait had been stolen from Iraq under British directive from Sir Percy Cox in 1921 and was set up as an independent country, thereby cutting off Iraq's access to the much needed Persian Gulf waterway. In 1963, the allegedly peace-loving United States helped overthrow President Abdel Kassem, the popularly-elected Iraqi leader who nationalized Western holdings in 1958. Why did the U.S. back tortuous regimes instead of a democracy? I know why. My buddies at the CIA, acting on behalf of the oil companies, couldn't afford to allow freedom to get in the way of their profits.

Aghast, I lay in bed as the conspiracy in the Gulf region unveiled itself layer by layer like an exotic dancer in a Moroccan kasbah. I thumbed through another edition, my fingers smudged from the chalky, black ink. Feeling like I'd been fingerprinted, I wiped them on the sheets and read on. Turkish sources had confirmed that the U.S. ambassador to Iraq, April Glaspie, had set up Saddam on August 1 by telling him that the United States had no interest in regional Arab-Arab conflicts. At the same time, the CIA was telling Kuwait to play hardball.

Before most Americans were up pouring milk on their Wheaties, Bush had already frozen Iraq's assets. We strong-armed Saudi Arabia to allow our troops in, mobilizing 125,000 soldiers before they had agreed. I was sickened. We were creating a war. But why?

I picked up *The Journals* again. "What does this have to do with me?"

The reply was cryptic. *"To know and not to act is not to know."*

"What?"

"Knowledge without action is a sin."

"What are you saying? That I'm responsible for what happens in the Persian Gulf?"

"Ignorance is no excuse for crimes against humanity. Learn what you will. It is all important. Read the signs, Stone, they will show you the way."

"What way?" I said desperately. "What do I have to do with the damn Gulf Crisis?"

"We are all responsible. Whether we wish to be or not. Hundreds-of-thousands may die. What will you do to stop it?"

"Wait a minute." My palms were sweating, my heart rate soaring. "You said all I had to do was get the book published. You're changing the rules. You can't do that!" The book was deceptive, double-crossing.

"I am changing nothing. Sometimes, Stone, the path we choose is hard to see, sometimes difficult to follow. There are many routes, many detours, many intersecting crossroads. That which you say is unrelated is, in fact, necessary to complete the journey."

"You're lying to me, you son of a bitch," I shouted. "You're using me to—"

"Hello, dear." The tentative voice of Rose entering the room broke up the conversation.

"Oh . . . um . . . *hello*, Rose." I blushed, reading the worry in her face.

"Talking to yourself again, dear?" she asked quietly. She patted my hand, trying to act like nothing was wrong. "Officer Dunn is taking a coffee break, so you don't have to pretend anymore."

Oh, Rose, I thought, if you only knew.

"You were just talking to yourself because of Jim's instructions, *weren't* you, R.T.? You *were* just pretending, right?"

"Yes, of course I was, honey," I lied. "Nobody talks to a book that doesn't exist." But I knew I would have to tell her the truth soon, to convince her somehow, in some irrefutable way.

"I've made all the arrangements," she said, trying to sound enthusiastic. "You'll be eating linguini and sardines in your own bed tonight. Won't it be grand to get home to your solarium? I'll bet the orchids miss you."

My eyes lit up. Ah yes, my orchids, those exquisite flowers of temperament. How I love my girls. Rose turned her cross around and around, focusing her eyes on the forlorn house of worship. Lord knows what she must be thinking, I thought to myself. "My husband's a loony bird!" she must want to shout.

Rose spun gracefully toward me, like a ballerina in a command performance before the king. She leaned in, smelling of succulent vanilla, kissed my cheek, and said, "God willing, everything will be just fine."

Rose is like that, always there for me with a kind word or a cup of tea or a gentle massage to soothe me. To me, that's true love. Love that transcends words. Love that moves in silent emotion. To me, love is my Rosetta.

August 8, 1990

I am convinced—and an elite team of Harvard debaters and network executives can't convince me otherwise—that television is a sinister device. America is in ruins because of the evil box. The current decay of society can be directly traced to the origins of television. I have had my fill of distasteful TV over the last three days of my stay in the hospital—a steady feeding of degenerate soap operas with unscrupulous women and two-faced men; talk shows with midget, transvestite bowlers in full regalia; and trance-channels from the Sirian galaxy declaring the End Time is coming; and insipid political commercials for my accuser, Brian McBain, who plans to take the office of mayor in Covington come election day. To top all that, one can't hide from the incessant coverage of the Gulf Crisis—the press dramatizing it for the sake of increased advertising revenues. Doesn't anyone else see the duplicity? Reporters and network anchors are acting like cheerleaders for war, egging it on. President Bush is on TV tonight; perhaps he'll make some sense of this thing.

Has my perspective of the world changed since that fateful night of August 2, when *The Journals* came into my life? I feel more aware, somehow. The TV drains me. It takes my energy and makes me numb. Void. An automaton being told what to do, what to think. Programmed.

And what of my dilemma? I've been home for less than twenty-four hours, yet I feel a sense of urgency that I must get cracking or *The Journals* may up the ante on me. My one hope is that the Council of Ancients allows me sufficient time to heal. Certainly they don't expect me to make great progress with an oozing flesh wound on my back and riveting pain shooting through my body. That damned, persistent cough I had before the fire is also back. I can't shake it nor the nasty taste in my mouth. Gargling twenty times a day doesn't help.

How does one start an investigation? I've no experience. I'm not a professional detective. I can't use the cops—ah-ha, that's it! It was there before me all the while, and maybe I can help Twinkie by playing Cupid in the process. The obvious solution—hire

Parker Floyd to do some initial legwork. He's an odd mix of a man. Never met anyone like him. A master's degree in theology and a bachelor's in ancient civilizations, yet he chooses to be a detective. He told me once that he was a searcher, a guy who was always looking for answers.

It's good to be home in my own bed. Except for the charred front door, courtesy of an arsonist trying to send me a message with lighter fluid, my arrival was pretty much without incident. The paramedics did their best to reduce the bumps and jolts on the journey, inflicting only a dozen or so shards of cutting misery on me. As I was wheeled through the foyer, eye-level with the antiquities Rose so loves I was treated to a horizontal view of the house (Rose is right, the ceiling needs painting). The bronze plates, copper jewelry, porcelain vases, pewter statues, urns and earthen pots, the tributes to past civilizations reached out to me: Babylonian, Sumerian, Persian, Egyptian, and Mayan; relics from Susa and Nineveh and Rosetta and Troy; cultural items from Palenque and Altamira and Luxor and Knossos. Each ancient piece tells a tale of the artisan who made it come alive in high reliefs of deities and nymphs, dances and deaths, princesses and caliphs, warlords and slaves, priests and prostitutes, sacrifices and symbols, stars and animal gods, aliens and astronomers, queens and concubines, lovers and demigods. Each piece tried to touch me in a way I've never known, speaking to me from the past.

Over the years, I had allowed Rose to indulge her fancy in the extravagant collection, taking only a mild interest in it myself, seldom raising an eyebrow at the exorbitant costs. It was the fee I paid for her tolerance of my indulgences. I can see now why she thinks my matchbook collection, sitting in a giant brandy snifter, is inappropriate among her antiquities.

This morning in bed, over buttered boysenberry toast, I tried to tell Rose the whole incredible tale of *The Journals*. Her worrisome eyes betrayed her doubt, like a French Resistance freedom fighter caught in the glare of a Gestapo flashlight. I explained the details from the beginning through today. Rose looked at me, smiled politely, and said, "If the Lord is working through you, dear, then we must do as He asks." Then she hesitated, fingering that cross, and added in her oh-so-polite manner, "It *is* the Lord calling, isn't it, R.T.?"

I did my best to appease her Methodist underpinnings, to convince her of *The Journals'* divinity, although I am not convinced the Council would call itself God; it would probably call itself an entity more than anything else.

I feel my conversation with Rose did little to appease her fears. Given my past legal troubles and my disappearances, it's totally understandable if she has her doubts. Hell, I have my doubts. Could they have chosen a less spiritual, less religious champion for their cause than me?

It's funny how each family member treats me now. Rose is unsure. Bobby, Jr. is hostile. And Twinkie is ambivalent, except for the fact that she gets to attend to me, which she somehow seems to love. I can't say why: I'm not an easy man, especially with a bullet wound and a perpetually nauseous stomach.

Twinkie, dear girl, took a week off from work to dote over me. She comes in twice daily, can of disinfectant at the ready, rubber gloves up to the elbow, white gauze mask covering her mouth, workman goggles on her eyes, and begins the extermination of every single germ known to the epidemiological world. In between sterilizations, she checks my bandages and doles out my medicine with admirable efficiency. She does so at the precise minute of its prescription, not one minute before or after. I've made her this way. It's my fault. I should have been a better father. If I had shown up at some school plays or taken time to read with her or helped her with her homework, perhaps she wouldn't have such a need to please me. Her actions are a manifestation of her constant need for attention. I love her. I do. But how does a father undo years of neglect?

Twinkie, obsessive lass that she is, had prepared an experimental list of culinary delights for me. Sometimes I wonder if she didn't work secretly for a major food company and diabolically used me as her test subject.

"I have lunch," she smiled, holding a silver serving tray. "Guess what it is?" She sounded like a commercial. I should have paid more attention to her when she was young, kept her away from the tube, been more of a dad. I studied the tray, her washed-out eyes, her June Cleaver hairdo and the 1960s housedress Rose had mothballed almost three decades ago. "Now, come on mister sick man," Twinkie said. "Take a guess."

"Hmm, Twinkie," I said, "I don't know."

"It's peanut butter and jelly," she crowed. "I made them into jumbo peanut shapes."

Twinkie set the glimmering tray on my lap and pulled a white paper from her pocket. "Guess what else, Daddy." She unfolded a neatly written list.

I picked up a jumbo peanut and took a bite. It was delicious. Boysenberry jam.

"I'm going to personally nurse you back to health by cooking you great meals every night until you're better," Twinkie announced proudly. "Tonight, it's squid-ink fettuccini with mussels, clams, and squid. Tomorrow night, it's lobster ravioli with fresh tarragon garnished with nasturtium blossoms." She hardly paused to breathe. "And Friday night, instead of that bad old pizza you love so much, we're having codfish cakes with pineapple salsa and an anchovy kale side salad."

"But—"

Twinkie smacked her lips, savoring the idea of the meals, then held up a chafed dishpan hand to silence me. She insists on doing the dishes in the sink before putting them in the dishwasher, she says they get cleaner that way. A psychiatrist friend of mine said to leave her with her idiosyncrasies, but I'm not so sure. I think that shrink is a bit off his nut himself.

"Now, I already know how much you appreciate what I'm doing for you, Daddy, but gosh, you've taken such good care of me my whole life. It's the least I can do. Now,

Daddy," she said, "Saturday night is salmon mousse marshmallow pâté on crisp dark rye crackers lightly dusted with powdered sugar. How does that sound?"

I groped for the right words, hoping my eyes didn't spill my true emotion. "Um, it sounds like you're getting away from your Spam fetish—"

"I am," she said gleefully. "Seeing you in that hospital made me realize life is too short. I need to broaden my horizons. Sure Spam and Jell-O have their place, and I still love them, but I need to try new things, explore new regions of taste-bud temptations."

"Sounds like you're getting into seafood."

"Yes!" Twinkie shouted ecstatically. "Seafood is good for you, Daddy. It'll help you heal quicker. It has so much nutrition and, gosh—"

Before she could finish, Bennett called, saving me from the madness. He informed me we have a deposition in three weeks and a trial in three months, which he would try to delay through continuances and other legal maneuvers. I stayed on the phone as long as I could, flashing Twinkie a thumbs up in deceitful approval of her menu. I must talk to Rose and put a halt to this, I thought.

To be fair, the sardine linguini was tasty, if not a bit overpowering in smell. I can stomach one of Twinkie's meals a couple times a month, but not every night. My stomach is too sensitive for that.

Bennett left me with a joke so funny it aggravated my wound. I wish Rose would get back. I want to see how she's taken our conversation, now that she's had some time to think about it. Blessed Christian girl that she is, my wife marched right into the storage room and pulled out a dusty, old typewriter for me to use after hearing my *Journals* story. That's Rose, supportive no matter what.

I must confess that I type at a much slower rate than I write. However, if I am to tell the story properly I need to present the tale in a professional manner. I'm confident that I will master typing in a few weeks. Rose went to the bookstore to buy a typing book. I could use the help.

The Journals was right, I need to take a proactive approach. I'm going to diligently work at this until all the details are firmly hammered into place. But I best be careful not to get overconfident. Arrogance can destroy a man. My biggest problem is a serious lack of information. I need clues. Signs. Assistance. Help!

"*I knew you would come around,*" The Journals suddenly wrote.

"Welcome back, wayward script," I proudly typed. "Pretty good huh?"

"*Not bad, Stoney. I am encouraged by your attitude, but you may want to wait till your wife gets home. You seem to be a little slow on the draw. We need to finish this before the next millennia.*"

"I'll get the hang of this, just you watch."

"*I have no doubt you will. I have no doubt.*"

"Me either. It's going to be a challenge, but I can do it. This could turn out to be fun!"

"I am afraid, Stoney, things will get worse before they get better."

"What do you mean? Things are already getting better."

"Like all life, there are peaks and valleys. It is a great cycle. But not to worry—in the long run, you will be fine."

"First I'm down, and you tell me to get up. Now I'm up, and you bring me down. What's going on?"

There was a long pause as the pages sat blank. I wondered if *The Journals* would answer me.

"Stone, what you and I are dealing with here is a delicately complex and serious situation. Through the process of illuminating the truth about Danny and Allison there will be heartache and triumph, there will be golden moments of insight and deep days of uncertainty. It is the purpose of our days here to live these lessons and learn from the experience. Danny and Allison are two very special people, yet they are flawed as all humans. You will need to stay with them through their trials, as I will stay with you through yours. It will not be easy, but it will be the greatest experience you shall ever have. I guarantee this."

I understood what it was saying, and I had figured on ups and downs. That is the grand exercise, I suppose, but *The Journals* seemed to be forewarning a gloomy future. That's all right, I thought, I can take it. It can't get that much worse. "Understood," I replied confidently. "So when do I get to see the rest of the story?"

"Whenever you wish."

"Great, that'll be great," I typed, then thought of something. "Hey, now that I'm such a whiz at the typewriter, do I have to go back and retype all my handwritten notes from the hospital?"

"No, Stoney, you do not."

"Why not? You can't write a book with different type, different paper, different handwriting—nobody will read it."

"True, but I will collect all entries, dialogue between us, handwritten pages, typewritten pages, and whatever else the story may be documented on and record it upon the correct master," The Journals confided.

"But then what do you need me for?"

"I need you to write, research and interact, and ultimately take the master and have it published."

"How many copies?"

"A few thousand at first. More if it catches on."

"So I can write this on anything and you will take care of putting it in a single document?"

"Yes. My consciousness is harmonized with the speed of thought, so no matter where you are, no matter what inspiration you are having, no matter what you write your thoughts on, I will feel them. You can even write on a cocktail napkin should you have a revelation in a bar."

"A cocktail napkin? Why would I write on that?"

"*Inspiration, dear Stone, cannot be controlled. Despite what the church with its antiquated dogma, the school system with its false history, and television with its mindless programming might want you to believe.*"

"Whatever." I dismissed the sermon. "I want to get started."

"*Read Danny and Allison's words. Bring their lives into your being. Do this and you will find a most pleasant experience awaits.*"

"Good, I'm ready."

"*This is their story, don't forget that. Yours is to fill in the gaps when necessary.*"

"How do I do that?"

"*Use your intuition. Use your psychic ability to see the story in your mind.*"

"How do I do that?"

"*Simply think. Each of us has the ability, one merely needs to tap into it. Use your mind. Every human has psychic talent if he or she chooses to develop it. Close your eyes and listen to your soul. The images will come clear and bright. You shall see.*"

"I'll try," I said, my hands twitching to get at it.

"*My spirit will be leaving for a few days, but the diaries will remain. I will not be in communication with you, although physically, the book will be at your disposal.*"

"Where are you going?"

"*To Arizona to clean up some business.*"

"You can be in two places at once?" I was astounded, even though I'd believe almost anything these days.

"*We all can, Stoney. Think of it as an out-of-body experience. Anything I do can be mastered by any human living in balance with a pure heart and proper intent.*"

"So what do I do while you're gone?"

"*Read the entries. Learn about Danny and Allison. Goodbye.*"

"Wait!"

"Did you need something, Daddy?" Twinkie called down the hall.

"No, no thanks," I replied.

Once more, I was left alone by the traveling manuscript. Twinkie was humming the tune to *The Andy Griffith Show* in the kitchen as dozens of questions saturated my brain.

Who sent me the *Eastern Crescent Review*? What does it mean? How does it relate to me, to my dilemma? Am I supposed to stop a war? Me? Who is this 'M'? Is it McJic? Is he still alive? If so, is he still on the planet? Can trees and plants really heal like they did at Featherbed Bank? Do they have spirits and energy like people? How do I find Danny and Allison? Should I find them? What do I do once I find them? What if I translate the story wrong? What if I hear something wrong? See it wrong? Should I go back and review the first part of the story and change it if I notice a discrepancy? When will I be well enough to get up and about? When will my chest stop burning? When will Rose get back? I need her. What the hell am I doing here anyway?

"Tough it out, Stone," I told myself. Buck up. Focus. Concentrate. Breathe deep. Breathe slow. That's it, man. That's it. If I remain calm, I may be able to unravel this Gordian knot I've bound myself in. In the meantime, I have a lot of reading to do.

August 8, 1990 (10:20 p.m.)

The president spoke: "Iraq has amassed an enormous war machine on the Saudi border, capable of initiating hostilities with little or no additional preparation. Given the Iraqi government's history of aggression against its own citizens, as well as its neighbors, to assume that Iraq will not attack again would be unwise and unrealistic. And, therefore, after consulting with King Fahd, I sent Secretary of Defense, Dick Cheney, to discuss cooperative measures we could take. Following those meetings, the Saudi government has requested our help, and I have responded to that request by ordering U.S. ground and air forces to deploy in the Kingdom of Saudi Arabia."

"He seems nervous," Rose commented. "His eyes are blinking and he's choking on his words."

"I'd like to know what my friends at the CIA think about Saddam invading Saudi Arabia."

Rose turned toward me in the bed and handed me a cough drop to quell my irritated throat. "Looks like the president is going to protect our oil whether we own it or not."

"It doesn't add up," I said. "The president said he's sending troops to help King Fahd, yet his four-point plan to remove the troops is all related to liberating Kuwait. Isn't that strange?"

I wondered if anyone else in America caught Bush's subtle bait and switch. I wondered if anyone in America cared.

"When it comes to American foreign policy," I said, "things aren't always what they seem."

Chapter 9

August 9, 1990

I slumped into my favorite recliner like a sack of potatoes on the pantry floor, *Journals* in hand. Today, I was finally able to get out of bed. Small steps with assistance from a walker—damn aluminum contraption. I made it from bedroom to bathroom. My solarium will await another day, once I have more strength, less pain. My orchids call me, my paintings, too. Ah, it's good to be home, modest as it may be, among my art, among familiar surroundings.

Rose had gone to bed during the eleven o'clock news, switching it off indignantly as the pompous newscaster restoked the remnants of the Cosmic Club fire, squeezing in one last pathetic interview with a psychologist at the university who fabricated theories about the inner thoughts of arsonists, of which I am allegedly one. Twinkie was last seen heading to her room to plan next week's menu, blissfully humming the theme to *The Patti Duke Show*. A root beer bubbled on my end table, applauding like the faint roar of a crowd, dividing the silence with the meter of the clock announcing the past.

I love that clock—it's a masterpiece. A one-of-a-kind work I picked up in Turkey several years ago, made of fourteen-karat gold. The three-feet-high clock sits on four legs, each a tribute to the other four elements that make up life—earth, air, fire, and ether. The base is intricately carved in high relief, depicting various scenes of ancient, merry-making water gods. It is said that it took the skilled Iraqi clock maker, Zurvan, two years to perfect this jewel. The internationally renowned artisan died twenty years ago, taking her secret understanding of physics to her grave. The clock is a marvel of engineering. For years, I have tried to grasp the science that went into its mechanism, but I have yet to figure out how it functions. The Arabic face of the clock, eleven inches in diameter, displays numerals like a dance of veils. It is driven by a waterwheel powered by water flowing through a series of plumbing-like channels in an elaborately, simple design. Why didn't the water evaporate? How could it flow and keep perfect time? It defies all who view it. The waterwheel powers the minute hand to the top of the hour, then a trap door opens and an exact measure of pebbles fall into the basin, announcing the time by the number of splashes: one o'clock, one pebble plops; ten o'clock, ten pebbles plop. Once they land in their lagoon, the stones are scooped out and ride to the top again. The clock's machinery is precise, its sound omnipresent. There is always a trickle of water, always a reminder that life is flowing by like a current, a stream unstoppable, always going somewhere—time.

I love that clock, but tonight it's Chinese water torture. I much prefer silence this night. I glanced toward the mantle at a disturbing portrait of me and my family, including myself, who stared back angrily, as if wishing they were somewhere else. I thought of the day we sat for it, all the Stones, moments after Bobby threatened to sue me over my refusal to give him the presidency of Stone's Construction Company when I retired. He wasn't capable and far too unstable to run an operation of that size. His childish tirades and the complaints from employees proved my point. Bobby had come back from Vietnam a troubled man. Unwilling to turn my company over to an unqualified son, I built him a nightclub instead.

Bobby's silver spoon collection, a reminder of him in a friendlier, less tormented time (pre-Vietnam) reflected distorted images of objects in the room. Bobby's spoons weren't forged for the act of human consumption; no, they were collectibles, acquired by Bobby since he was seven. Everyone in the family would bring him back a spoon from their travels. To be honest, the collection looked out of place among the antiquities and sculptures and paintings. Like a plastic McDonald's Fun Meal cup amongst the porcelain in the china cabinet. But Rose kept the collection in the room, hoping it might spark some miraculous return to innocence lost during his tour of Southeast Asia. Bobby never collected spoons after Vietnam. Some of us, even with the war over, are still prisoners.

I pulled the chain on the reading lamp, inspected the fresh notepad and felt-tip pen in my lap, and settled in for a night of *The Journals*. I was immediately sucked into the world of Daniel Oliver Gilday, experiencing life through his words, silently witnessing his early years.

What follows is an abridged version of his lengthy entries, edited to reduce the size of the manuscript for the reader's sake. The summary of my observations, coupled with entries by Danny and Allison, could easily swell the manuscript to two thousand pages in length. Danny's entire, unedited text might be obtainable from my publisher, upon request. Or, if you prefer, you could ask the Council of Ancients for a copy—though my experience says this is not without its price.

The Book of Daniel
The Forger

May 1, 1978

Dr. Muse asked me to keep a diary. She isn't really a doctor; she's a psychologist. Father says she's a high-priced shrink, but I think she's nice. At first, I thought it might hurt to go to the doctor. I took a lot of tests in the beginning, but now we just talk. Heck, I can talk to anybody, but Father wants to pay for me to talk to her. Oh well, it's his money.

Dr. Muse said I could call her Gina, but I haven't done that yet. She has curly brown hair that smells like lemons and real white teeth. Like I said, she's nice. Don't get me wrong—I don't go for that mushy stuff. Besides, she's not my type.

Her office is kind of empty. Just a couple of big green cushy chairs, the kind I can sit way back in and stretch my legs all the way out. There's a coffee table, stained with rings, set between the green chairs. The table is oak, and a clear crystal candy dish filled with orange toffee creams sits on it. I love toffees.

There's also a big wooden bookcase with hardly anything on the shelves. *Science and Human Behavior,* by B.F. Skinner, and *Psychological Types,* by Jung. Junk like that. Oh yeah, a book by Pavlov. I hope Dr. Muse doesn't ask me to salivate for her.

The best part of her office is the framed black and white poster of Einstein hanging on the beige wall just above Dr. Muse's head. I can look at her and see Einstein. Sometimes if she changes position, she blocks the caption under him: "I WANT TO KNOW THE THOUGHTS OF GOD, THE REST ARE DETAILS." Now that's deep.

There are two reasons why I have to see Dr. Muse. There is the real reason and the pretend one. The real reason is to get Mom off the hook with Father. The pretend reason (the one they're saying is the real reason) is to test me to see how smart I am. Dr. Muse says I have a high I.Q.—144. Father calls it my ticket to Harvard, and he couldn't be happier about that. Dr. Muse says I could be a child prodigy. I don't see what difference it makes. I'm just a kid. I just turned ten one month ago today.

I'm supposed to keep my diary secret until the doc can analyze it. I'm good at keeping secrets most of the time. I know lots of them—especially about Mom. The other night I accidentally blabbed one from a long time ago at the dinner table. I knew I said something wrong when the vein in Father's forehead bulged out and his face turned red. Mom started talking real fast, saying I had an overactive imagination. Mom—her real name is Cara—was really working to explain that secret away. She said maybe I should be looked at by a professional to determine the extent of my intelligence. I overheard them talking when they thought I was upstairs. Parents should be more careful.

"You know how smart he is," Mom said, in that syrupy voice she uses to weasel out of trouble with Father. "He's been writing his own books since he was seven."

"That doesn't explain his Uncle John comment," Father said.

"He's a genius, you know that. He's a naturally gifted writer with a lot of creativity bottled up inside his mind."

"He *is* smart, I'll give you that." Father softened, then boasted, "He's been reading the goddamn encyclopedia since he was five for chrissakes."

"And the dictionary," Mom reminded Father, changing the tone of the whole conversation.

I breathed a great sigh of relief that Mom wasn't going to get hit because I slipped up and spilled a secret.

"I just wish Calvin had half his brains," Father said.

My mouth turned sour. I wished they wouldn't compare me with Cal.

"Danny got all the smarts and Cal, well . . ." Father didn't finish.

I hoped Cal wasn't listening from his favorite spy spot with his ear against the heat duct. It would hurt his feelings bad.

"Cal is a good child," Mom said. "With a heart of gold." She was always defending Cal to Father, who was always tearing him down.

"A good heart doesn't get you far in this world, Cara. Not far at all," Father said. "You'd better be right about Danny. That story better be a product of his imagination."

I wished more than anything to see Mom's face, to know how she reacted to Father's tough talk.

She played him perfectly, as I'd seen so many times in my short ten years.

"Oh, Pat, you know how kids are, especially one as bright as Danny. You'll see, a boy with his mind gets all sorts of crazy things in his head," Mom said. "I think he has a hard time telling fantasy from reality."

That hurt my feelings, but I know why Mom said it. I know more than she thinks I know. I always have. I know what's real, too. It's parents who have a hard time telling the truth from lies. Grown-ups always underestimate their children. I remember the whole secret like it was yesterday. It was March 18, 1973. It was sunshining. We all took the Caddy into Cincinnati to see The St. Patrick's Day parade. Me and Calvin rode in the backseat, turned around so we could make faces at the cars behind us. We shared a big pack of grape bubblegum that Calvin bought with money he stole from Mom's purse. But that's another secret.

I set *The Journals* in my lap, took a slug of the silent root beer (the cheering had died down), cleared my tear ducts of sleep, and thought of Cara. The soda fizzed in my stomach like a chemistry experiment. I stared at the lifeless portrait over the fireplace, unhappy faces peering at me across time. Not much had changed. Bobby hasn't spoken to me since the fire.

The delicate scent of orchid tickled me. *Magicka carallus.* The beauty had sashayed in and out of my mind since I first saw her. What was it *The Journals* said? Use my intuition? My psychic mind? Anybody can do it, but how does one begin? Then, without effort, and with probable assistance from the Council, a faded image appeared. Grew clearer. More focused. Vivid as a dream.

The smell of earthy, fresh-cut grass delighted Cara as she turned down the page of her slim book, more short story than novel, and looked at Danny. She rocked gently on the front-porch swing. The sweet smell of spring reminded her of the anniversary coming soon—July 5, the day she had conceived. She spotted Mrs. Smitch looking like she'd stepped from a horror movie, her hand holding merciless, pink curlers wound tightly to her head, secure against the prevailing wind. Mrs. Smitch patiently stood next to her mailbox in a gown the color of lemon meringue. Mozart, her wispy, piano-playing dog, took his time doing his business against a maple tree. No one had ever seen Mozart play the piano, but Mrs. Smitch insisted he could. She spent a few hours each day with the dog, between lessons for human students, showing him how to tickle the ivories. Cara told herself not to be judgmental of Mrs. Smitch, who was widowed by cancer. Cara waved, then turned her attention back to Danny.

"Writing in your journal, my star-child?"

"No, Ma," Danny said. He set the pencil he borrowed from his father's desk down, and breathed in the moist scent of coming rain. He considered it one of life's better smells. Rain, starched clothes, buttered popcorn, all-day vegetable soup, and artists' paint. "I'm sketching the flower bed."

"Can I see?"

"Not yet," Danny said, sticking his tongue into the side of his cheek. "It needs work. Maybe tomorrow." He scrunched his forehead, thinking. "Hey, Mom, what're you reading?"

Cara's eyes darted to the cover of the book. She held it up to him.

"*Jonathan Livingston Seagull.* It's pretty good," she said. THE GLORIOUS #1 BESTSELLER was printed over the white silhouette of a seagull.

Danny stopped the glider and peered at it across the porch. "What's it about?"

"A seagull who believes he can do anything, even though everyone tells him he can't. He learns to break the laws of physics and travel by thought."

"Neat. Maybe I could write a bestseller, Mom."

Cara pulled her sweater tight against the cooling wind and smiled. "I'm sure you will," she said confidently.

"You think so?" Danny beamed.

"I'm sure of it." Cara Gilday looked at the white, chipped ceiling that she had painted eight years ago and remembered the passionate affair with McJic. Warmth stirred between her legs. She shut out the thought. Not here, not now. She could always call the memory up later, with much more reward, by simply speaking his name. She had mastered her self-induced orgasms since that night, changing the inflection to make it milder or stronger, short or lasting. Sometimes, in moments of utter wanton desire, she said his name quickly in succession and fell back to the bed as wave after wave of pleasure washed over her body like a warm Malibu surf. Other times, she would say "McJic" forcefully and be instantly engulfed in blazing climax. Still, she longed for a man to take her.

Cara ran her tongue slowly across her lips, thinking how much she loved sex. She reveled in the thought of repaying Patrick his wickedness. The breeze teased her as she thought of all the lovers she had taken since then, more out of companionship and spite than love. Twenty-two in all. Each one pleasing her far more than Patrick. But none coming close to the bliss of McJic. She shook her reddish hair to break the delirious spell. "How's your book coming?" she asked.

Danny looked down at the enamel coated slats of the glider. "Which one?" he half-whispered as he rubbed a grass-stained gym shoe on the floor.

"Any of them."

He shrugged. "Okay, I guess. The Case of the Poison Hamburger is almost done."

Sensing that he needed encouragement to relieve his shyness about writing, Cara said, "A man from a long time ago told me you'd be a writer."

"Was it another uncle?" Danny asked, his innocence barely distinguishable over his mischievous grin.

Cara's smile was carried off by the wind. "No," she said softly. "He was a very wise man. A magical man. He told me before you were born that you would do great things in this world."

Danny's angel-blue eyes shimmered with excitement. "Mom, how long do I have to see Dr. Muse?"

She stared at her son, trying to judge just how smart he was: Does he know more than he lets on? Does he see through me? He must. He's a gifted child with powers I couldn't begin to comprehend, she told herself.

"You'll go until your father forgets about our dinner conversation," Cara said, recalling how she'd barely avoided getting beaten that night.

"I'm sorry, Ma." Danny's voice broke. "I didn't mean to tell."

"I know, honey," she said.

Cara went to him, wrapping her arms around the heartsick boy. It wasn't Danny's fault, she realized. He was only ten and going to make mistakes. Her vibrant eyes dimmed, her freckles hid behind flushed skin. I hate Patrick for his violence, she thought. Cara remembered the night he choked her for burning the City Chicken in the skillet. She was left gasping on the kitchen floor as Calvin sat trembling and Danny wailed from his highchair. She feared her husband and made plans to leave him as soon as the kids were grown.

I opened my eyes, in awe of the psychic grant bestowed upon me, pleased to have experienced the sheer wonderment of seeing in another dimension. Kinetic energy surged through me, jolting my body with exquisite discovery. The Council was urging me on. I read another journal entry.

May 6, 1978

"That's an interesting story you told about your mother," Dr. Muse said. She laid my journal on the coffee table next to the candy dish filled with red-striped peppermints twisted in plastic wrappers. "Do you like telling stories?"

"Yeah," I answered, a little shy about someone reading what I'd written. I looked away to a brand-new statue on her bookshelves, hoping to avoid her eyes. The office wasn't as empty as before. It was beginning to fill up with decorations, as if a real person worked there. Not even Mom and Father got to read my made-up stories, and here is Dr. Muse reading my personal thoughts.

"I love to write. Rodin's *The Thinker*, right?" I said, pointing. "Is it bronze?"

I have to look away from Dr. Gina Muse. Her brown eyes stare at me, constantly trying to get inside my mind. It's like she's picking the lock on my personality. She never breaks her focus. She draws me in until I have to tell her what she wants to know. In a way, Gina is a lot like Rodin's sculpture, serious and brooding, lifeless and thoughtful, never revealing anything about herself. I have a secret, too—I'm keeping two sets of journals, the one she can read, and this one—my private one. I can't have her knowing too much about me.

"You *are* bright," Dr. Muse said, cocking an eyebrow. "Most boys your age would have no idea what that statue is."

"Thanks."

"You write well for a child of ten," she said, as if she was dictating into a tape recorder. "How long did you say you've been writing?" She full-well knew the answer. Dr. Muse does that a lot, asking the same question a different way to see if I'm telling the truth.

"Since I was five or six, I guess."

"And how many books have you written?"

"They're more like short stories," I said. "About fifteen or so."

Dr. Muse tapped the well-chewed tip of a pen against her forehead. "What are some of the titles?"

I thought a minute, scooched around in the cushy green chair, and said, "The Case of the Poison Hamburger, Monkey See Monkey Do, The Elephant Wears Pink Pajamas, The Alien in the Pantry, stuff like that."

Dr. Muse tapped the mangled pen against her head. "Interesting choice of titles," she commented, and scribbled a note on a yellow pad. I tried to see what she wrote but couldn't make it out upside down. "How did you learn to write so well?"

"I don't know," I admitted with a shrug. "A gift, I guess. Mom says I'm blessed. I practice a lot, writing every day if I can. Oh, and I learn tons from my writer's magazine. It's just for aspiring authors, and it's loaded with all kinds of neat advice from experts. Writing is all technique; learn the rules, practice, and the better you become. It's probably not much different than studying to be a therapist." I grinned.

Dr. Muse stared, eyes unblinking. "What kinds of things have you learned?"

"Oh geez and crackers, there's so much!" I exclaimed. "Backstory, advanced backstory, plot, pace, descriptions, how to write indoor scenes, outdoor scenes, characterization, how to edit, how to create architectural suspense, all kinds of neat stuff. I'm actually not that good at it yet, because I'm so young." I rambled on, happy at being able to describe what I love. "Someday I hope to be as good as Vonnegut, Dickens, Twain, or even Tom Robbins. The magazine comes every month, so I pick up new tidbits all the time. Mom got me a subscription for my eighth birthday."

Dr. Muse changed the subject abruptly. "Do you watch much television?"

"Some."

"What programs do you like?"

"A lot of science fiction junk, you know, *Project UFO, Man from Atlantis*, that kind of stuff. Plus I like old reruns of *Star Trek, My Favorite Martian* and *Bewitched.*"

Not a muscle moved in Dr. Muse's pretty but stern face. "Would you say you have an interest in aliens and extraterrestrials?"

"Maybe, I don't know. I don't really watch too much TV. It's bad for you. I like to read much better."

"How often do you read?" Her eyes locked on me like a tractor beam.

"Every day," I said. "Usually a couple books a week, sometimes more, depending on the length of the books."

"What's your favorite book?"

That's an easy one. "The thesaurus," I said.

"And your second favorite?"

"The dictionary."

She scribbled a note. Einstein was proud.

"I try to learn twenty new words a day. They're so interesting, don't you think? They take you to whole new worlds. I love them."

"You certainly are an active learner."

"Do you read, Gina?" I asked.

Her stoic face crumbled, her brow wrinkled like she wanted to say something. She glanced about the room, looking for a way out of answering. She was uncomfortable talking about herself.

Medical training, I thought. Take the personality out of the doctor so she can give better, unbiased, unemotional treatment. Something seems wrong with that.

Dr. Muse found the gold watch on her wrist, staring at its neutral face ticking toward her reprieve, and said. "I'm sorry, time's up for today, Daniel. Perhaps we can talk more next week."

"Sure," I said, not fooled by her changing the topic.

"And Daniel," Dr. Muse said as she rose from her chair. "Would you like to bring in some of your short stories?"

"Sure," I said, as if it was the last day of school. "You bet."

"Daniel." Dr. Muse stopped me before I got to the door, her great, brown eyes searing me like a brand on a reluctant steer. "The St. Patrick's Day story about your mother, was it true?"

"No," I lied, knowing who was paying the bill. "I made it up."

And that, as they say, was that.

I took another sip of root beer, shutting my eyes to consider this brilliant child, Daniel Gilday, whom I had perceived as an average kid. Why wasn't it obvious? How many other children are there with genius inside waiting to be loosed upon the world? Images of his next passage floated across my cerebral cinema.

Cara set the first bag of groceries on the counter when the phone rang. Was it the boys calling for her to pick them up from the paper drive? So soon?

"Mrs. Gilday?"

"Yes."

"My name is Alice Chalmers, from Good Samaritan Hospital."

Crap, Cara thought to herself, not another solicitation. Can't these people leave me alone? "Yes?"

"We need you to come down here," the sympathetic voice said. "Now, there's nothing to worry about. It looks like he's going to be okay."

Cara Gilday's motherly instincts kicked in. "Who? Who's going to be okay?"

"Danny," the voice said. "He's been hit by a car."

Silence. Numb fear.

"Mrs. Gilday?"

"I'll . . . I'll be right there."

She ran from the house, leaving the Popsicles she bought for the boys thawing on the counter, her heart shivering in dread. I should have stayed with him, she thought as she gunned the engine. Cara barreled out of the driveway, gripping the wheel tightly, leaning into it, ignoring all traffic signals and hostile shouts of "you crazy woman driver," making the trip to the hospital in what she thought to be some sort of record, even for paramedics.

She wheeled into the emergency entrance, slammed the car into park behind the ambulance she knew must have carried Danny, and ran inside.

"Danny—oh Jesus, Danny," she said after being hurriedly escorted to his room. "Are you all right?" Resolve gave way to worry. Her legs wobbled at the knees as she looked down at his scratched face. A large abrasion covered his left cheek, a smaller but deeper one reddened his stitched chin.

"I'm okay, Ma," Danny smiled. "But I feel like a bruised banana."

Cara laughed uneasily, looking at the nurse for confirmation. The nurse nodded, and Cara's jangled emotions yielded to relief. She leaned over and held her son tightly, making up for every time she felt too tired to do so, giving him as much love as possible in one tender embrace. Suddenly, she panicked again. "Where's Cal?"

"Right here, Mom," Cal said from a chair in the corner of the room. Cara rushed toward him, sweeping him into her body, mashing his face against her chest. "Thank God you're all right, too."

"Course I am," the child said nonchalantly. He was smudged from newsprint, and his shirttail hung out. "Why wouldn't I be?"

"If anything happened to either of you, I'd . . ." Cara Gilday let the words evaporate. Guilt overtook her.

"Oh, he's all right," Cal said. "It's his own fault. Should have looked both ways before he crossed the street."

Cara ignored the comment and turned back to Danny, her sapphire eyes shining love. "Are you really okay?" she asked, holding his hand.

"Sure, Ma," Danny grinned. "It was pretty cool. I don't remember much except floating in the sky way up to the stars toward this light. It felt so warm. Next thing I know, I'm in the ambulance and a guy named Christopher is giving me gum. Cal and me got to ride in an ambulance!"

"How did it happen?"

"I was in the back of the trailer reading this cool book I found, *The Principles of Forgery*, when I realized Cal and Mitch were gone. I went looking for them. After that, I woke up on my way to the hospital."

Cara glared at Cal, telling him without words to take better care of his little brother, even though she knew that it was Danny who always took care of Cal.

"Excuse me, Mrs. Gilday," the nurse interrupted. "The doctor would like to see you in the hallway."

The two women stepped out.

"Mrs. Gilday, I'm Dr. Jenkins."

They shook hands, Cara slightly warmed by his grip. His eyes were the color of wheat bread.

"What is it, doctor?"

Jenkins pretended to evaluate Danny's chart. "We'd like to . . . um . . . keep Daniel here for a day or two for observation."

Cara tried to determine if it was a ploy to inflate the hospital charges. She'd read a recent article that documented such practices and was determined they would not make extra profit from Danny.

"Why?" she asked, crossing her arms.

Jenkins placed his hand on her shoulder in reassurance. He took a half-step toward her and lowered his voice. "Because of his description of what happened while he was knocked out."

"What do you mean?"

Jenkins glanced at the chart, paused, then lifted his eyes to her. "It took the paramedics three minutes to get a heartbeat."

Cara gasped and leaned back against the wall to steady herself. "No, not my star-child," she told herself. "Not Danny."

"We're not sure why it happened. The car wasn't going that fast. The contusions don't appear too serious; however, his description of floating, of being surrounded by light, suggests a near-death experience." The doctor cocked his head. "We don't like to take chances with things like this."

Cara struggled for breath, placing her hand on her chest. "Are you . . . are you saying . . . that he almost died?"

"I'm saying technically, his life-support systems weren't functioning for at least three minutes. Perhaps longer. So, yes," Jenkins said. "Daniel almost left us."

Danny was admitted to the hospital. He was amused by the attention, particularly the next morning's newspaper article about his accident. The young man was enthralled by the irony of his story appearing next to one about a Mr. C.J. Teasdale, who had been arrested for counterfeiting that same day after trying to sell a hundred thousand dollars in twenties to the FBI.

Even more ironic, perhaps providential, was the thoughtfulness of Chris, the paramedic, who returned to Danny a book he'd found in the ambulance, *The Principles of Forgery.*

After he learned of Danny's accident, Patrick Gilday searched for a way to cleanse his guilty conscience, which weighed upon him. This burden was further emphasized by the act being committed at the moment of the phone call—he was between the legs of his latest mistress.

On the flight back from Arizona, he racked his mind thinking of the perfect gift, something which Danny would love so much that he would forget that his father was seldom home. The obese lady next to him, her nails chewed to the nub, perused a *National Geographic* as the plane tossed about in the turbulence. The FASTEN SEAT BELT sign flashed on with a beep and an announcement from the stewardess. The frightened woman laid the magazine on her lap and clutched both arm rests, her ravaged fingertips digging into the vinyl. Patrick glanced over, saw the magazine, and hit upon the idea of a pet.

Patrick Gilday hid the surprise behind his back as best he could as he walked slowly into Danny's room. The present was covered by a white towel. Patrick was proud of himself; he knew he could be a good father. Maybe this gift would ease the unspoken distance between him and Danny, he thought. He unveiled the surprise to his son's delight.

"A dove!" Danny said. He admired the snow-white bird. "It's so pretty."

"It *is* pretty, isn't it Daniel? But it's not a dove; it's a pigeon."

"A pigeon, great!"

Patrick laughed. "We'll have to build a cage for it tomorrow."

"Wow, my own pigeon. What does it do?"

"This is a special pigeon, called a homer. They're popular in New York. You can teach it to fly places and come back to you," his father said. "The clerk at the store said he's extremely rare, an albino."

"Cool. Does he have a name?"

"No, I don't think he does."

"Then I'm going to call him Homer. Thanks, Dad." Danny got up and hobbled to his father for a hug, his heart soaring.

"You're welcome, Daniel." Patrick stepped back, avoiding Danny's outstretched arms, a queer look on his face. "Daniel, would you please call me Father?"

Danny stared at him for a second. "Sure, Father, thank you," he said, as his heart plummeted to Earth without a parachute.

Danny scoured the library for books, settling on two, determined to find out how to train Homer. He read the books fervently, with Homer at his side. Danny took notes, and at times read aloud so the pigeon could learn along with him. He studied and read, then reread the chapters he found most important until the big day came.

The amber sun was just up like a pat of butter on a plate of Kentucky flapjacks. It was a gorgeous summer's morning in Lake Cumberland, Danny's favorite spot on Earth. The family was there for the annual Gilday Memorial Day weekend. Danny loved the fresh forest air, the jade-colored lake, and the cedar smell in the family cabin.

Carefully, Danny followed the instructions to the letter as Patrick stood by, his mandatory cup of coffee in his hand. With a thin rope tied around Homer's neck, Danny whispered final instructions into the white bird's ear and tossed him into the air. On cue, just as the books said, the bird flew to the length of the rope, circled, then landed. Danny gave his aeronautical student a sunflower seed and laughed. Then he tossed Homer into the air again. Around in a circle the bird went, then landed. Again, he did it. And again. Each time, Danny gave his friend a seed of congratulations.

Danny's face was aglow with pride in his noble pigeon. The boy sat on a stump, which functioned as the launch pad, to rest and looked at a stand of evergreens guarding the hill that sloped to the water's edge. Homer cooed softly in his lap, looking for gentle rubs on his crown.

"Okay, boy, one more time," Danny said.

His father tilted his empty coffee cup, a cold drip finding his lips as the great, white bird was tossed into the air. The rope, secure for the previous flights, slipped from Homer's neck. Up he rose on his fluttering wings. Up, up into the azure Cumberland sky, over the evergreens, and out of sight.

Danny's heart snapped like a frail twig under a hunter's boot. "Daddy, he's gone," the boy cried.

"Goddamn it, Daniel, you didn't tie it good enough," Patrick rumbled. His fists tightened, deep-red anger pulsing in the vein in his forehead like a poisonous viper.

"Yes, I did." Danny's face was a torrent of tears.

"Then you didn't check it to see that it stayed tight."

"I'm sorry, Daddy. He just flew away. He's gone."

Gilday exploded. He grabbed Danny by the shoulders, his fingers bruising his startled son's skin. "Call me *Father!*" he shouted, shaking the terrified boy. "Call me Father. Do you understand me? Father, not Daddy. *Father!*" Furious, Patrick pushed his quivering son away and stomped off to the house, unable to admit he had lost his cool, blaming his son for his anger.

Unknown to Patrick Gilday and the rest of the family, and maybe even Danny himself, it was a moment that Danny would never forgive.

The next couple of days, Danny spoke to his father as little as possible, avoiding him by taking long walks, going fishing with Cal, or canoeing by himself. Anything to stay away from the man he had hatefully nicknamed "The Dick."

Nothing could change his animosity. Danny's anger ran so deeply that not even the miraculous appearance of Homer, puff-chested on his perch, greeting the Gildays as they returned from the lake, could calm him. His elation at Homer's triumphant two-hundred-mile journey home, and his own proud accomplishment at having trained Homer so expertly, did not mean forgiveness for his father. Patrick's ire would not go unpunished.

I opened my eyes, wondering if I had made some of the same mistakes as Patrick Gilday. Is that why Bobby never called? Had I been blaming it on Vietnam, when actually it was me? I retrieved some antacid tablets from the bathroom, poured another slug of root beer, and resumed my position. The clock dripped midnight as I continued reading. Another day surrendered to time.

May 31, 1978

Boy, what a lousy meal we had tonight. Not just the food—liver and onions (*yuck*)—the whole dinner was awful. I don't know why Mom keeps making liver and onions; she knows me and Cal hate the stuff. If liver was all I had to deal with, that would be one thing, but Father got mad at me again. I'm not sure what I do to make him get so angry—it just happens.

"Oh, God, Ma, not liver and onions," I said, making a disgusted face.

"It's the grossest junk," Cal chimed in.

Mom wasn't fazed, she'd heard it all before. "Now boys, it's a great source of vitamins and iron. Eat up while it's still warm."

"Gosh, Mom, do I have to eat this?" I said.

"Eat your damn liver," Father ordered. "And quit your complaining. There are kids starving in Africa."

That line was older than grandma's false teeth. "Maybe we could send them my liver, Dad," I said.

"Maybe you would like the belt," he warned.

I had learned long ago not to push any further when Father mentions The Belt. He always says it with a dramatic pause, like a radio announcer. I'm sure he does it for effect. The Belt. Whenever Father whipped me with The Belt, it hurt bad for hours. He goes wild when he has The Belt in his hand. "And I've told you a thousand goddamn times not to call me Dad. Call me Father."

"Now Patrick," Mom said. "Let's not swear at the dinner table."

"It's my goddamn house, and I'll swear where I goddamn want to."

"Yes, dear," Mom replied, but her blue eyes narrowed and her face said, "Screw you." She always gave in to Father at the table, but lately I can tell she resents him more and more.

I decided to change the subject. The way this dinner was headed someone would end up in a fight for sure. "Hey, Da—uh, Father, I've been reading this book about printing, it's really interesting."

"That's nice, Daniel," he said with a big wad of liver in his mouth. He ate that crap like he was starving.

"I was wondering if you knew someone down at *The Cincinnati Enquirer* who could give me a tour."

"A tour? Of what?"

"Of their paper. I think it'd be neat to see how they make the newspaper."

"That would be cool," Cal agreed.

"It would be a nice thing for the children to learn, Patrick," Mom said. "That's how Joseph Pulitzer made his fortune."

"Why in the hell would you kids want to see them print the newspaper?" Father scoffed as he shoveled a forkful of sautéed onions in his mouth. "And who the hell cares about Joseph Pulitzer?"

Calvin sank a wad of liver to the bottom of his milk glass, kind of a beef-organ depth charge. The milk didn't hide it well enough, though, the dark brown edges of the liver showing through. I told Cal on liver nights we should always ask for grape Kool-Aid—you can't see the liver as well when you spit it in your glass.

95

Mom knew the score. "Drink your milk, Calvin," she smiled. When Mom got that smile of hers, we knew she knew.

Calvin turned paler than his cow juice as he picked up the now whitish-brown liquid and took a sip. Gross!

"Well Daniel," Father said. "Why do you want to see a crappy old newspaper operation?"

"I just think it would be neat, Father," I shrugged. "Besides, I've been reading this book, like I said."

"What book?"

"*The Principles of Forgery*. It's great. It tells how to make fake money and everything."

"Forgery!" Father shouted, throwing his hands in the air in disgust. "Now, I've heard it all. Do you believe this, Cara? Your ten-year-old son wants to be a forger. Jesus H. Christ. What next? Bank robbery? Murder?"

"It's only a book, Father," I said.

He wasn't taking this well. Maybe Father didn't like liver either. Maybe nobody really likes liver. Maybe liver makes people tense. Maybe liver is one of those foods people pretend to like because it's supposed to be good for them, but really everybody hates it. They can't say so, though, so everybody gets tense and irritable. I can see why. I mean, the encyclopedia says the liver processes all the toxins and pollutants in the human body. A cow's liver must be there for the same reason. So when people eat liver aren't they eating a cow's septic tank? The thought is just putrid-gross—I mean, really. "Did I say something wrong?"

"No, you didn't say anything wrong, dear," Mom said. "But a book on forgery is not the type of reading material you should be studying."

She had a point. Did she know what I was thinking about doing? Did she figure out my secret plans to become a master forger? Did Dr. Muse tell her that? I've seen the doc four times so far. She's not bad. I wonder if she's telling stories on me, though.

"Christ, Daniel," Father moaned as he stabbed another piece of nasty meat. "I've been trying to get you to come with me to the steel plant for ages. Now, instead of coming to see what your father does for a living, you want to visit some goddamn newspaper." His red face huffed, getting worked up again.

"Joseph Pulitzer was a famous newspaperman who changed the way the world got its news. His estate established the Pulitzer Prize," Mom said out of the blue.

"Get off Pulitzer, Cara, nobody cares," Father said.

"Magic," Mom whispered, grabbing the edge of the table hard. She closed her eyes tight, and smiled peculiarly like she was in a dream, pleased about something.

I love Mom, but at the strangest times, especially when Father is being a jerk, she says magic and goes off into another world. Maybe it's her way of counting to ten to calm down. Weird stuff.

"It's not that I don't want to see . . ."

"Bullshit!" Father shouted. "If you don't want to follow in your father's footsteps, that's fine. But I'll be damned if I'm going to contribute to you becoming a little criminal. If you're going to forge anything, it's going to be steel." He hammered his knife into the table. The force of the blow knocked over Calvin's glass, sending milk and liver oozing onto Mom's tablecloth. "Goddamn it, see what you made me do," Father yelled as he stalked from the room.

He's mental. Really. What did I make him do? Mom sat there fanning her flushed face with a napkin. Cal caught a break, he made it through the liver ordeal without any real punishment.

Maybe forgery isn't the sort of thing a parent can be proud of, but I didn't make Father do anything. I'll bet he's still mad about Homer coming back after having screamed at me. Well, now it's for certain—he's an official dick. USDA Government-inspected, Grade-A Dick. At least now I know not to talk about sensitive topics during liver meals. Liver is a bad omen. Oh, Lord, de-liver me.

July 2, 1978

We've been at the cabin since late Friday night. Yesterday me and Cal played in the woods and took a long hike. Grasshoppers were flying everywhere. Cal caught a few for bait, crunched them, stuffed them in his pocket, and wiped the guts on his shorts.

It's a scorcher. On past vacations it always rained, which makes it muggy and miserable, but so far it hasn't dripped a single drop. This afternoon, I let Homer free to sweep above the trees and swoop down to the water. He looks so smooth as he plays the wind.

I had a major scare when two hawks attacked him. It was like *The Battle of Britain* with Homer the underdog as he tucked and rolled and maneuvered to get away. Me throwing rocks at the hawks and shouting frantically did no good at all. Cal got out his BB gun but, like the rocks, they fell way short of the aerial combat. I don't know what I'd do if I lost Homer, he's such a good friend.

He took care of himself pretty well, the scrapper, only getting a slight graze on one wing. My heart beat a jillion miles an hour. Hawks are natural enemies of pigeons. I wonder why. I guess people aren't the only ones who treat their species bad. A hawk looks serene as it soars on the breeze, rising and falling with the currents, but underneath that sleek exterior is a vicious predator just waiting to rip other birds like Homer apart. I have to think of a way to train Homer to fight back or get out of town fast when hawks are on the wing.

I'm down at the dock, journaling by lantern light, thinking about last night, which was real special. I can't write in the cabin 'cause everybody asks to see. Snoops! Cal tries to steal my journal and read it out loud. If he ever did, I'd kill him. Dead. Anyway, I want to write about last night because it was so cool.

I was down at the dock, lying on my back under the stars with a life jacket as a pillow, looking up at the bright quarter-moon surrounded by jillions of stars in heaven. Just me and the Milky Way.

"Is anybody out there?" I asked the big empty space. Only the crickets answered. "Can anybody hear me?"

No answer: just the lake lapping at the posts of the dock and the chirps of thousands of bugs. My question seemed fair. Not much different than how people pray. I'm not a true believer in God. Mom is. Father isn't. But I'm still a kid, so I really don't know for sure. I do kind of favor an intelligent life form. Maybe aliens brought us here to colonize Earth. There's an awful lot of questions in life that no one has answers to. Does Dr. Muse believe in God? Do you, Dr. Muse?

I thought about painting the Cumberland sky with its shimmering stars. What a magical piece it would be if I could capture it. Maybe I can be the first to do it best— to capture the light.

A lantern fired in the garage, someone was coming to see me. Please not Father, I hoped. No, the lantern was swinging too low; it had to be Mom or Cal, I thought, disappointed that my quiet was interrupted. It was Mom. Turns out she brought me secret presents: a telescope, which was so cool, and a book about Joseph Pulitzer.

"To encourage you." Mom smiled as the lantern illuminated her happy face. "Somebody told me once you'd win a Pulitzer Prize."

"Who told you that?"

She swatted a mosquito. "A friend, a dear friend from a long time ago, when you were still in my belly." Her smile glowed in the night.

Mom was pretty all of the time, but last night, her face radiant in the darkness, she was extra beautiful. I could tell she was really happy.

"How could anybody know what I'll become?"

"Some people live among us with exceptional gifts, Danny."

"What do you mean? What kind of gifts?"

She thought for awhile, looking at the ceiling of stars. "Gifts of insight and knowledge, unique gifts available only to a select few. And this person, the one who said you'd win the Pulitzer, had psychic insight into your future."

"Yeah, right, Ma. Okay."

She swatted another mosquito, the big kind with a tail about the size of a B-52.

I like it when Mom talks to me. She treats me like I have a brain and not like I'm some dumb ten year old with no thoughts at all.

"Maybe I could write something magical about pigeons and people, Mom," I said as I hugged her tight, smelling her orchid perfume. She makes it herself with the blooms of that wild orchid in her bedroom. The scent is so familiar to me. She's always worn it. I took a big whiff of the humid Cumberland night air, the scent of orchid pleasant in the heat. "It's such amazing perfume," I said. "It gives me memories."

"It *is* magical, isn't it?" she said, her voice far off.

There's that word—magic. I decided to ask her something that's puzzled me for awhile: "Mom, why do you always say the word magic?"

"Oh, that," she laughed, brushing her auburn hair lightly with her fingers. "That's just what I do when I can't take your father's temper."

"Why is he like that?"

She hesitated. "I'm not sure, probably born an asshole." She giggled.

Geez and crackers! Mom confessed she thinks Father's an asshole! She even used a cuss word! Once, she made me eat a piece of soap for calling Tommy Hartley that. The lanterns hissed as dozens of bugs scorched themselves, insect Joan of Arcs martyred trying to get to the light.

"You know what I call him, Mom?"

She chuckled and rubbed my peach fuzz. "I'm not sure I want to know, but okay."

"Dick!" I said proudly.

"That fits." She smiled and tickled my stomach. I laughed my guts out. Mom is like a friend. That's when she asked me to keep the scope and the book a secret. She said Father is a tightwad and wouldn't understand the Pulitzer thing—especially since he wants me to follow in his steel-toed footsteps. No way. I'm not going into the steel business.

"We'll just tell him Gramps gave it to you, okay, my star-child?" She rubbed her hand briskly through my hair again. She always calls me her star-child. I like it a lot. It makes me feel close to her.

"Sure, Ma, I can keep a secret." I put the telescope to my eye. "A falling star!" I shouted. "Look!" Shooting silently across the sky was a bright white star, then— *Poof!*

Mom leaned in and whispered, "I've heard falling stars are chariots of light carrying ancient gods to their destination."

What a cool thought. "Really? Like who?"

"Like McJic," she said. Then she lost it. "Oh, shit!" Mom threw herself backwards on the dock, her limbs rigid, her legs swaying from side to side. She lay there rocking back and forth on the hard wood, moaning, her fingernails digging into the boards. "Ohh . . . ohh . . . Jesus H . . . ohh . . . God!" she shouted loud enough to silence the crickets.

"Mom! Mom, are you okay?" I freaked out. "Should I get Father?"

She had a strange smile on her face, glassy, but her body was twisting and turning all weird. I hoped she wouldn't get splinters. She didn't say anything for a long time, she just lay there dreamy-like. Finally, she sat up, throwing her head back as she leaned on her arms.

"I'm okay, Danny. It's just my condition."

I've seen Mom's *condition* plenty of times, but it still scares me some. She recovered pretty quickly from this one.

"Who's McJic?" I asked. I had never heard of him in mythology before.

"Oh, he's a special god who brings light to the world, a very special god."

"Is he Greek or Roman?"

"Well, Danny," Mom said. "I think he was around before either the Greeks or the Romans. I think he belongs to The Ancients."

The Ancients. How cool. Mysterious. The Ancients, I like it. "His name kind of sounds like magic doesn't it? McJic—magic."

"Yeah, I suppose it does," Mom said, pulling me to her. She held me tightly, as only a mom can, making me warm inside and letting me know she loved me. She gave me a hard squeeze and let go.

"Thanks for the presents, Ma," I said. "Maybe I'll find McJic—or maybe a UFO!"

Mom laughed.

"Would you like to look for McJic, Ma?" I handed her the telescope.

"Yes, Danny. Yes, I would."

July 9, 1978 (Actually, early July 10)

I'm at a loss for words. How can I describe it? I'm still shaky from the experience, feverish and numb to be exact. We just saw the most incredible sight ever on our way back from Cumberland. It was near Crittenden.

"Cara, look! What the hell is that?" Father called, waking me and Cal.

"What?" we both said.

"Jesus H. Christ on crutches," Mom gasped.

"Look boys," Father said, pointing. The car slowed. "To the east. See the light?"

There it was: a brilliant arch of light in the distance, golden and eerie.

"Wow!" was the best I could do.

"Cool," was Cal's response.

"Patrick, what is it?" Mom's voice shook. "I've never seen anything like it."

It radiated above the darkened treetops, rising up a couple hundred feet in a giant half-circle like a single-colored rainbow. Everything beneath the ellipse was golden, too, awash in the supernatural phenomenon.

"Is it a forest fire?" Mom asked.

"Is it stadium lights?" Cal asked. "Maybe there's a game."

Father hesitated. "I don't think it's either. I'm not sure what it is, but I'm pulling over."

He skidded the station wagon to the emergency lane behind several other cars that had stopped to investigate the strange light. We jumped out. Twenty people stood pointing at the light. No one spoke. The light reflected off people's skin and shone on the nearby objects, like a hundred jillion lightning bugs all captured in one giant jar. The silence was scary. People, standing silently by the side of the highway, glowed in the light. No cars passed. Everyone on I-75 stopped to witness the curious glow that fell like a star from the sky and lodged itself in the Kentucky farmland. Soon there were fifty people.

"Is it a meteor?" I asked Father.

Mom pulled me close and held me tightly against her hip. "It's magic, Danny. Magic," she whispered. "Don't ever forget this spot. Crittenden."

A strong vibration swept through me. My arms and legs tingled. I could feel the light pulsating, throbbing like a huge electric grid inside me. It was like being in a science-fiction movie. My body buzzed at the same rate as the sensational glow filling the horizon. Did others feel it, too? I became dizzy, disoriented. My head spun. I tried hard to keep my eyes fixed on the light, watching it shine like a cosmic flare, a fantastic illuminating force field. I felt drawn to it, like I knew what it was but couldn't remember. I could feel its heat being absorbed by my body, soaking into me like a sponge. "Mom, I don't feel so good."

She put her hand on my head. "You're burning with fever," she said, alarmed.

"It's a spaceship!" I heard myself shout, but it wasn't me. I mean, I said it, but I didn't do it on my own.

The crowd stepped back a few yards, forming a half-circle behind me and faced the light. They stared, as if whatever I had said shouldn't have been spoken. Suddenly, five state troopers pulled in, lights flashing, dust flying everywhere.

"Okay, let's break it up. Let's go," they said, doing their best to hurry people along.

"Wait a minute, officer," Father said. "What is that?"

The trooper in charge looked at Father. "Probably tractor lights. Locals doing some night farming, nothing to get excited about. C'mon let's go. There's a real traffic hazard here with all you folks pulled off the highway like this."

"Hold on there, bubba," protested another man, half-drunk.

"No, you hold on," the trooper said. "Anyone not in their cars in thirty seconds will be arrested for obstructing justice, illegal parking, and anything else I can think of."

And just like that, everyone hustled to their cars and went on their way.

I sat up front between Mom and Father, turning my head to watch the light vanish in the distance as the highway dipped into a valley.

"Danny, are you all right?" she asked, her voice faint. Everything was muffled and blurry.

"Huh . . . what . . . Ma?"

"Are you okay, son?" Father said, concerned.

I put my foggy head on Mom's lap, feeling the fever take control, sending me into a dream, floating on a cloud surrounded by the light of Crittenden, warm and protected. It was so darn weird. "It's the color of your orchid, Ma. The lights of Crittenden are the same as your orchid."

"They do look similar, Cara," Father said.

"It's the same light I saw when I got hit by that car." I sighed, imagining both Father and Mom sharing a shocked look of worry between them.

I must have passed out. I woke up in my sweaty bed a few minutes ago. It's twelve-thirty a.m. I'm writing by flashlight under my covers so I don't get caught. My head is on fire. I must have the flu. I haven't told anybody this, and I probably shouldn't put it in my journal, 'cause Dr. Muse will read it, but while we all stood by the roadside like sheep, staring at the magnificent light, I heard voices talking to me, filling my head with strange words in a language I couldn't understand. And I saw symbols, like math problems, so complex I couldn't figure them out.

I can't explain it. I don't know how to put it on paper, but this I know: on the 9th of July, 1978, I, Daniel Oliver Gilday, witnessed a UFO or some extraterrestrial experience near Crittenden, Kentucky. To this, I swear before any god who will listen.

July 20, 1978

Another tension-filled meal. Dinners at our house have become something of an event. Father had some unbelievable news to tell, but even he didn't seem to believe his own words. No matter, I know it isn't true. Father called home at lunch and asked Mom for pork chops and gravy—the good stuff—for dinner.

It's generally understood around the Gilday house that anytime we have chops it means Father is in a good mood, which is difficult for anyone outside the family to tell, but it's true Father is happy when he's munching on pig. So tonight being pork chop night and all, no one would have expected any fireworks.

"Good meal, honey," Father slobbered, sucking the last strip of fat off his chop with the force of a vacuum cleaner. He wiped his greasy chin with a cloth napkin. He uses cloth, the rest of us use paper. I always use three or four. "Guess what I found out today?" he said.

"What?" Cal said.

"I found out what made those lights over Crittenden on the ninth."

"You did?" Mom said, sitting straighter.

Boy this was cool, we were going to find out the scoop on the whole thing. I scooched forward in my chair.

"Sure did." Father smiled like he had made some great discovery. "I went down there and talked to the police and some of the locals. Turns out it was all caused by night farming, planting soybeans I think they said."

No way. No possible way. "What? That ain't right, Dad!" I said.

He ignored my calling him Dad, hesitated, then said, "I'm convinced. I talked to a couple of farmers. They were out planting that night. They showed me their equipment. Huge tractors, eight of them altogether running along a thousand acre farm. You should see those big things. Huge, huge tractors. I believe the light could have come from those machines."

I looked at Mom, then Cal. No one was buying it.

"No way, Dad," I said, dropping my fork.

"Call me Father, dammit! And it's true. That's all there is to it." He picked another chop up with his fingers and stuffed half the thing in his mouth like an anaconda swallowing a rat. His voice was sure, but I don't think he really believed it.

"I'm sorry, dear, but that just can't be," Mom said. "The light was a perfect, symmetrical arc. There was no sound of heavy machinery. No sound at all. And what about Danny's fever? It couldn't have been farmers plowing fields."

"Sounds like another government cover-up to me," Cal said.

Father looked flustered. "Think what you want. I say it's tractor lights. It doesn't matter." He sucked on his teeth to dislodge a piece of pig flesh. "Because that isn't the best news. While I was down in Crittenden snooping around, I found out something even better."

"What?" asked Cal, hardly able to contain himself.

"John Ogilvey." Father's face turned angry. "The banker who killed my father owns a farm down there. He owns an old plantation, several hundred acres, he probably got by foreclosing on some poor sap like my father. That thief made his fortune on other people's grief, and I can't let that stand."

"What do you mean, Patrick?" Mom asked. She studied him with worry.

"I'm going to ruin that son of a bitch just like he did my father. I don't know how yet, but I'm going to pay Ogilvey back for murdering my father."

An evil glare distorted Father's face. Revenge—if that's what the look was—is ugly. "I thought Grandpa died of a heart attack," I said. "Pass the spuds, please, Ma."

"Ogilvey killed him!" Father raised his voice. "Plain and simple. Now, he'll get his."

"I'm not sure that's a good idea, Patrick," Mom said.

"Why the hell not? Shit, is everyone against me around here?"

"No one is against you, dear," Mom said calmly, as she slid me the mashed potatoes. "I just hate to see you get worked up over something that happened so long ago."

"You weren't there. You didn't see him die before your eyes. I did. It was horrible. Ogilvey killed him. He'll pay."

"Gravy please, Father," I said, doing my best not to smirk. I knew Father was enraged now, lit up by the past. I couldn't let it go without pushing his buttons (just to see if I could get away with it). "I never met Grandfather, but he must have had a heart condition, high cholesterol or something that caused—"

"Ogilvey murdered him. That's it!" Father asserted, handing me the gravy boat.

"Thanks, Father."

Mom looked coolly toward a pile of green beans, her face pale, her eyes drooping sadly.

"Well, I think the lights were from an alien spaceship," I said, changing the subject. I try to do that when Mom gets that sad look.

"Me too," agreed Cal.

"I'm with you, boys." Mom smiled, recovering nicely.

"You're all wrong," Father said. He slathered margarine on a biscuit. "Aliens, hah!" But he wasn't convinced. I could tell.

July 31, 1978

Sparks again at dinner. We're heading for a Gilday family record. It seems like it's the only time the whole family is together, Father being gone so much. This time he lost it over some guy named Stone. Fried chicken, too—should have been a peaceful meal.

"The son of a bitch has no right buying my art!" Father banged his fist so hard the crystal in the good china cabinet shook. I almost swallowed a whole drumstick. Mom makes great fried chicken, better than that stuff you get at a fast food joint. The Colonel should take a cooking lesson from her.

"What son of a bitch is that, Father?" I said, trying to cough up a chunk of chicken.

"Don't talk like that, Daniel," Father corrected.

"I said Father, Father." I grinned innocently.

"Don't say son of a bitch, Daniel," he said. "You did well to call me Father."

"But you said son of a bitch," Cal challenged.

"What is this, a goddamn conspiracy? I said don't say son of a bitch, and now both of you boys are saying it."

"I think the boys are wondering why you can say son of a bitch, but they can't say son of a bitch, dear." Mom said joining in the fun.

"It's hypocritical," I added.

"Forget it," Father said. "The subject isn't swearing, it's R.T. Stone. He's trying to buy my art."

"I didn't know you made art, Father." I worked on being clever. I've convinced myself a boy needs to be clever to make his way in the world.

"I mean he outbid me on a piece I really wanted for my office at work." Father was exasperated. "The son of . . . the guy drove the price up and stole it from me for two thousand dollars more than it was worth. It's outrageous. He paid over twelve grand for it."

"Maybe, he just liked it more than you," I said.

"The man stole it from me, Daniel, plain and simple. Just overpaid for it is all. No other explanation."

"I've met Mr. Stone before, dear, and he seems like a nice fellow. He and his wife are good people," Mom told Father.

"I know him, too, I've done jobs with Stone before. None of that matters. He

104

outbid me on purpose, probably trying to make me look like a fool." Father seethed as he ripped a hunk of white meat from a chicken breast, doing his best to look like a ravenous Viking.

"I'm sure he didn't do anything malicious, dear. He probably just wanted the piece more than you did," Mom said.

"No, I'm convinced he wanted to show me up. How do you know so much about him? Where did you say you met him?"

"Oh, Patrick." Mom blushed. "He and his wife, Rose, belong to the same fine-arts committee. Rose even gave me a delicious potato soup recipe. We had it last week, remember?"

Father didn't know what to say. "Yes, well, then don't make it anymore. And if you do, I won't eat it."

If I acted like that, he'd smack me one. Father has his own rules, though.

"People actually pay thousands of dollars for paint on canvas?" I asked, an idea forming in the back of my noodle.

"People buy art as an investment," Father said.

"I thought people bought art because it was pretty or inspiring," I replied.

"That's for amateurs. I'm going to become a serious collector. That way I will be accepted in the right circles."

"What circles?" I asked.

"The wealthy, Daniel, the Indian Hill set, the millionaires. I want to be accepted in the elite circles of Cincinnati society," Father said.

"Why? Are we millionaires?" Cal asked, looking around the table.

Mom silently squished gravy into her spuds, making them a gloppy mess.

"Not yet, but soon we will be. It's never too early to plan one's rise to social prominence. It is an important thing indeed." Father sounded like he had been born a Rockefeller. "By the way, boys, one bit of advice—it's as easy to fall in love with a rich girl as a poor one, so pick a rich one."

"Patrick!" Mom said.

"Geez—" Cal said.

"And crackers," I added. Like we care about girls at all. Who has time?

"Why don't you just buy pictures you like and tell people you paid a lot for them?" I asked.

"One doesn't do such things, Daniel. There are experts in the field who know the difference between a good work of art and a bad one."

"Can they tell a fake one?" I asked.

"Yes," Father said curtly. "You're not bringing up this forgery business again, are you?"

"No, sir. Hey, I did a painting called *The Lights of Crittenden*. Do you want to hang that in your office, Father? You could put it behind your desk."

He didn't hesitate. His eyes rolled, disgusted, as if my idea was the worst, most ridiculous idea ever made in the entire history of the entire planet. "My office is *not* the kind of place for children's doodles. I need art with sophistication and reputation to give me the image and place in the community I'm looking for. I need art to give me status."

My heart hurt, as though Father had reached inside and squeezed it dead himself. My eyes watered up. Mom and Cal were a blur, I looked at my plate, ashamed.

"Patrick, Danny paints some nice works, maybe you could at least take one into the office," Mom suggested.

"No. I will not have anything but respectable work by established artists. That's final."

Mom stood up. "Patrick, he's your son, for chrissakes. How can you be . . . how can you be such a . . . a . . . dick!"

Silence. Dead silence. Father said nothing. Mom glared at him. She told him that if he spoke she would shred him to bits. He was pink as a medium rare T-bone, but I'm not sure whether it was shock or embarrassment or fear that turned him that color. One thing I know is it's the maddest I ever saw Mom get. She was an atomic bomb waiting to explode.

Then, out of nowhere, Cal, who usually keeps quiet when things go this far, said, "Practice, practice, practice."

"What?" Mom said, baffled.

I don't know if it was utter bravery or sheer stupidity, but Cal with a gigantic smile said, "Practice, practice, practice—that's all it takes to be a dick."

I spewed my cherry drink across the table, splashing Father in the face.

His vein popped out on his forehead as red droplets fell from his cheek. Mom gave him a forbidding *don't you dare* look. I handed Father a paper napkin, which he tossed to the table with a scowl. Cal sat there acting innocent but we all knew it was intentional. This was a big moment in the Gilday family: honesty at the table. Mom had said it, Cal confirmed it, I had written it, and now Father knew it. The secret was out— we all knew—Father *is* a dick.

Father picked up his cloth napkin, wiped his face slowly, looked at me, then Cal, then Mom standing beside her chair poised to kill, and said weakly, "I'm going to Arizona."

I've come to a major conclusion about Father and art. First, he wants art for the wrong reasons, and because of this he does not appreciate true artistic effort. Second, he has shunned me for the last time. Third, since he doesn't appreciate art, no matter what he buys I'm going to forge and replace it without him ever knowing. I'll get him to hang my work in his office whether he knows it or not, whether he likes it or not. And that is something I can appreciate.

Oblivious. That's the best word to describe my life. R.T. Stone—oblivious. Tattoo it on my body. Put it on my headstone. I had no idea Gilday was ticked about my purchase at that auction. I scarcely remembered it. If Gilday wanted the art, why didn't he bid more? Is the Council binding me closer to its plot in some inexplicable way? How long have these plans been made? What's my connection? How committed am I?

I chewed another antacid and listened to the single splash of the clock announcing one a.m. and I thought about the infinite connections that weave into one's life. I shuffled to the bathroom to pee, my mind dominated by Danny's fascinating story. I stared at my pupils, big as pennies, adrenaline spiking my system as I rinsed my putrid mouth with Listerine. I was high with the power of the Council's message. Drunk with vision. I leaned closer to examine the lines around my eyes, convinced that I appeared younger. But *The Journals* wouldn't allow my ego to distract me. The image in the mirror wasn't me. It was Danny. He had taken over my subconscious. A voice told me to return to the family room and listen to my mind. I obeyed.

Something had happened to Danny that mysterious night in Crittenden. Something otherworldly—extraterrestrial. To the average observer, it was an unexplained phenomenon, conveniently explained away by the state police to the satisfaction of Patrick Gilday. To this narrator, with Shanidarian glimpses flooding my increasingly psychic mind, Danny's experience with the unearthly Crittenden light was the beginning of an orientation for our hero. A telepathic learning regimen grooming him for future service. An unfamiliar language of symbols and scientific formula poured into Danny. It was neither frightening nor puzzling to the young student. He suspected what it was and enjoyed it.

Mesmerized, I watched as the beautiful Dr. Muse, upon reading Danny's startling account in his diary and seeing his skillful rendering of the fantastic vision on canvas, did her best in therapy sessions to coax out all that he knew about the lights of Crittenden. The painting was a masterpiece. A brilliant work at any age. She promised secrecy and meant it. "Don't tell a soul about this." She leaned forward. "We don't want government scientists probing you." Dr. Muse hoped to shield the young genius from the invasive microscope of government bureaucrats bent on keeping knowledge from the public, under a mistaken belief that its power was too dangerous for the common man.

Throughout the summer and into early fall, the light visited Danny in intervals anywhere from one week to two apart, the duration sometimes lasting as long as three days. The celestial student relayed these events to an information-addicted Dr. Muse only in terms of the physical and emotional sensations which occurred: the light-headedness, the ever-present feeling of being watched, and the euphoria of discovery. But he did not describe any spiritual manifestations.

Like a student at the feet of a yogi she asked, "If you had to describe it in one sentence, what would it be?"

"It was like the beginning of time," Danny said. "The start of the Big Bang."

It was at this point that Dr. Muse's professional mask shattered, and she became hopelessly enamored with the boy. The patient was more a comfort to the doctor than the doctor to the patient. She knew he was special, gifted beyond anyone she'd ever known.

Danny, maturing at an extremely fast rate, noticed Dr. Muse's attentions and took every advantage possible to peak down her blouse, as curious boys are wont to do.

The doctor rationalized her sensual treats as good for Danny's sexual development and self-esteem; however, her real motive was her own carnal fantasy. She had repressed a healthy sexual appetite in order to pursue her medical career. Women had to work twice as hard to get half as much, she told herself. After twelve years of deprivation, the doctor's desires were often more deviant than her patients'.

With the cute *wunderkind* sitting before her week after week, with Mediterranean-blue eyes and a mischievous smile, she delighted in teasing him, knowing that would be as far as it went. For his part, Danny had a major crush on Dr. Muse.

The light kept pouring into him, flashing brightly with special knowledge of this strange sphere we occupy. It sparked in his subconscious like a welder's torch fusing together the skeleton of a building. The wisdom gained wasn't overt in the manner of instructing Danny how to be a subatomic physicist or a brain surgeon, although the principles of physics and mathematics were certainly imbedded in his mind. No, the wisdom provided was subtle, but far more valuable. He was being trained how to be a Messiah.

The welder's arc connected vital neural pathways of intuition. It bonded his being with a compassion for others. The work established a direct connection with Shanidar. As the construction continued, Danny was given the powerful ability to see the intent of a person's words, to understand what lay beneath the surface, inside the soul. He was given the talent to see one's emotions, to understand all sides of an issue, and empathize with each. The Council also saw fit to install the mastery of seeing through the superficial aspects of everyday life—the pleasantries said but not meant, the social graces designed more for ego than need, the hypocritical nature of people in general. Danny's mind filled with the potential to find the flaws in any social system or human logic. To find true reality, but this reality, as I have dramatically learned, is never what it seems.

Sometimes in the early hours of the morning, when the moon cast its healing glow upon the Earth, Danny asked questions. "What are you telling me?" he'd whisper as he lay flat on his back, his hands crossed over his chest. "Am I doing good? Am I doing what I'm supposed to?" The flow continued, Danny's mind awash in enchanted wonder. "Couldn't you do this in English?"

For months, the exercise went on as knowledge poured into him. Danny was aware of its presence but ignorant as to its purpose. It flashed inside him like heat lightning under his eyelids. The perimeter of his sockets sparked internally. It was life force coming into him. Prana. Celestial Morse Code. A subtle, asynchronous cosmic communication like a modem transmitting bits and bytes and hexadecimal.

Don't for a minute doubt that this can occur. It can. It did. Each of us may be programmed from afar. Call it God. Call it a return message for our prayers. Danny called it *talking light.*

The mission of the talking light was not to make him a superhuman with perfect traits and godlike potential. Far from it. Daniel Oliver Gilday was given tools for life, destiny gifts, but they were worthless unless he knew how to use them. And to do that, he had to discover their existence within his soul. He had to work at life like everyone else. Danny knew he was unique, as most of us do, but he didn't have a *true* appreciation for the knowledge so carefully forged in his being. After all, he was a boy of ten, more fascinated by the fleshy contents of Dr. Muse's brassiere than the contents of his mind.

Concurrent with the teachings of the Council, Danny did the things a normal child would do—with one exception. He carefully plotted revenge against his father for refusing to hang Danny's paintings in his office. It was an insult. A snub.

The embarrassment festered in Danny's young mind. "I'll pay him back."

He called his plot Operation Snow Job. He didn't tell a soul, unless of course one counts the ever-faithful Homer, Danny's feathery confidant.

Danny spent all his available time when his parents were away or asleep forging the first piece, a Mamet, in his bedroom. A child of natural talent, he meticulously duplicated Mamet's elemental style, a style Danny didn't care for. The boy stood in his darkened room, his easel illuminated by a flashlight laid at just the right angle atop a math book and two magazines on his desk, a towel stuffed under the door to keep Cara and Patrick from seeing his clandestine activities. The room was rich with the oily odor of paint, a delicious smell which inspired him as he applied his strokes like an Old World craftsman. His efforts to paint *Pansies in Crystal* were remarkable considering he had to work from a Polaroid hastily taken while Patrick was using the toilet at BG Industries. Danny had convinced his father that having a picture of the Mamets was a sound insurance measure. But Patrick didn't know that Danny shot an extra set while he was in the can.

Throughout the fall, the boy worked hour upon hour, revenge driving him on, sometimes working exhausted with only one eye open, pressing forward. The talking light came and went, and Danny's talents for living in the world and in painting grew dramatically.

On November 2, 1978, Danny proudly put the finishing touches on his first forgery, and immediately turned his attention to the next as he began to plot how to exchange the paintings without Patrick's knowledge. Good fortune lent a hand as Patrick announced he was bringing the Mamet collection home to hang in his den, making room for more expensive, more accepted elitist art in his office.

It wasn't until the snows of early January, with his parents at a dinner party and a preoccupied babysitter wrestling in his parents' bedroom with her boyfriend, that Danny was able to make the switch. The forger had completed two of three works, and was satisfied. Operation Snow Job was a success. Somewhere during the process, a repentant Daniel Gilday had lost his desire for retribution against Patrick, as Dr. Muse had predicted, and replaced revenge with an impulse to see how far he could get without being caught.

It was at this time that Danny became interested in environmental issues, motivated, no doubt, by the defining influence of the talking light. He read the paper daily, clipping stories of blatant, wide-scale pollution and government inaction at places like Love Canal. He followed legislation, trying as best he could to make sense of the rhetoric between the Democrats and Republicans. His inquisitive nature brought him an excellent grasp of world events and the more he learned, the more he yearned for. The Council had welded a bright talent determined to master both the wisdom and stupidity of the planet.

By late winter, in March of 1979, Danny was positive that aliens lived among the human population. He played elaborate fantasies in his mind about being from an advanced civilization. He studied his father's traits, and Cal's, and Cara's, watching them at dinner and during TV time, knowing that he was different from them, ultimately concluding it wasn't possible that he was Patrick's son. He wondered regularly if his presence in this world was the result of his Mom's visitation with an unknown "uncle." Little did he know, despite his wild imagination and the tutelage of subliminal Shanidarian education, that he actually was a light-being from a distant galaxy. Still, he'd stare at the cool night sky, bright with autumn stars, and dream.

I finished the last of the root beer, the ice rattling in the bottom of the glass. People are like ice cubes, I believe—hopelessly trying to remain separate, yet constantly giving off their energy until they mix into society without notice. Just another nondescript human living a dull life. Watered down. Nonexistent.

One forty-four a.m. Another antacid. I picked up the blue-sleeved book.

March 10, 1979

Dinnertime again—the only time we ever see Father, really. He's too busy. Turns out Father knows all about the new nuclear plant being built east of Cincinnati.

"Yes, Daniel, that would be Zimmer. Big job." Placing a folded slice of bread in his mouth, Father mumbled, "I have a contract to supply some steel piping there. Highly profitable, these government subsidized programs." Then he laughed.

"Why's that?" I asked.

"Because the Feds don't know what they're doing. The Nuclear Regulatory Commission gives a blank check to the companies building the reactors."

"How come?"

"Because it's the government, and the people working for it don't make enough money on their own, so the contractors pay them to look the other way."

"Bribes?" I was shocked.

"Sure." Father laughed again as he mopped up gravy with another slice of white bread.

"But . . . but how do you know they are building it right?"

Father slowly looked at the ashen faces around the table, then smiled. "I suppose you don't. Pass the beans, Cara."

I was sick. I pushed my plate away. "But if they don't build it right, there could be an accident, and we could all be exposed to radiation. That stuff is deadly."

Cal grabbed his throat, gasping, choking himself as he pretended he was dying.

"No, that won't happen. Even if they miss a few welds here and there, and use some cheap materials, it'll still hold up. Besides the real problem is up there at Fernald," Father said.

"What's Fernald?"

"It's actually the Feed Materials Production Center, but everybody calls it Fernald. That's where they enrich the uranium for the nuclear warheads," Father said, half whispering.

"What!"

"Don't get so excited." Father chuckled.

Mom looked distressed, and Cal wasn't joking around anymore.

"Nuclear bombs? Where?" I couldn't help myself.

"Oh, about fifteen miles or so north of Cincinnati; five, maybe six miles from here. I heard they've been doing some top-secret work there."

"Like what?"

"I'm not sure exactly." Father licked his finger clean, completely unconcerned. "But it's not what they're making that's the problem. It's how they're disposing of the by-products that's scary."

"What do they do?"

"Oh, you know, standard stuff to get around the EPA, nighttime emissions, dumping contaminated water into open ponds, things like that," Father said.

My stomach turned over. I sat back in my chair, my energy gone. I didn't realize how strong my feelings about pollution were, but as Father told what was going on I couldn't control myself. *"Things like that*, what do you mean?"

"Yes, Patrick, what's going on?" Mom asked.

"Everybody does it. You can't run a business profitably by following the regulations of those left-wing fanatics at the EPA. Besides, a little money and they lose their righteous attitude pretty quick."

"You bribe people?" Cal asked, drawing a menacing stare from Father.

"No, I don't bribe people. I have politicians take care of the concerns of BGI. It's all above board, all legal. What's everyone getting so upset about? We have a nice home, don't we? Nobody is dying because of this. It's just a little waste. It can't hurt us. There are hundreds of families living near Fernald, and they're all fine."

"How do you know?" I said. "It takes years for tumors to develop. And genetic birth defects can happen over time. Has anybody studied these families? Does anybody really know?"

Father looked at Mom, me, and Cal as if he knew he were in a losing battle. "All I know is they have some problems up there, and I put a bid in on building some double-hull, titanium reinforced, lead-lined containment silos."

"Jesus!" the three of us exclaimed at once. Cal's jaw hung open, Mom looked worried, and I was upset.

"That sounds really bad," I said, my appetite completely gone.

"It's not so bad," Father said. "The government knows how to clean it up. The Department of Energy will straighten it out. In the meantime, guess who I got the subcontracting job with?"

"Who?" Mom asked.

I was too mad to speak.

"Stone. Your friend on the arts council. His company and mine are teaming up to do the work. It's big money, folks, big money. This could make us millionaires."

"That's nice, dear," Mom said softly.

"Stone isn't such a bad guy after all. And he does know his business, and does good masonry work."

"He knows art, too," I said, trying to piss Father off.

"That he does." Father smiled. "And he knows how to bid a job. Now Stone and I are going to be rich."

I left the table. How can it be that they are making enriched uranium for nuclear warheads in Cincinnati? How can it be? And now I'm part of it because Father is making titanium something or other for it. Is this what money does to people? A few months ago, Father was so mad at Mr. Stone he wouldn't even let Mom make Mrs. Stone's potato soup recipe. Now, they're in bed together, bribing politicians to get jobs at nuclear sites. Strange bedfellows. Does greed override everything? It isn't right. I have to learn more.

April 6, 1979

I had to do something to show I was serious. I had to do something to get Father to reconsider his Zimmer contract, especially after Three Mile Island. Geez and crackers, how could anybody support the nuclear industry after *that*?

"Wipe that shit off," Father growled after a good stare at the glow juice I had smeared on my face in protest. I had decided the dinner table was the perfect place to stage my protest.

"If greedy businessmen, with no real experience or understanding of nuclear power are building these plants," I said, "then what makes us believe they are safe?"

No one could answer that.

Father sent me to my room. The dick. I don't care. I'd rather spend my time reading the truth about Three Mile Island and nuclear energy than sitting around the dinner table listening to Father boast of his involvement. I'm convinced there's a government conspiracy with big business covering up the flaws of America's nuclear plants. I'm right. I know it. Being sent to my room is a blessing. It's where I write and read and paint. After Father cools off, I'm going outside to watch Homer fly in the blue sky.

May 26, 1979

I'm bummed. We usually go to Cumberland on Memorial Weekend, but this year we can't. Father has business in Arizona, and he wants me and Cal to help Mom around the house. House chores—what a drag. I was looking forward to stargazing with my telescope away from the lights of the city. In Cumberland, there are a jillion stars.

I had a good idea today, though I actually got it from an old Mac Davis song I heard on AM radio. He sings about leaving a letter for someone hoping they write back. So my idea is to attach a note to Homer's leg and see if someone replies. I know he goes to all kinds of places. He disappears for hours at a time. So anyway, I wrote a note and stuck it on his leg with a rubber band and sent him off. My first experiment didn't work, he came back about two hours later with the same note.

I'm going to send him out everyday until I get a reply. It's kind of like a message in a bottle.

> To Whom It May Concern:
> Anybody out there? My name is Danny, my pigeon is Homer. If you get this note please write back. I am looking for a friend.
>
> Sincerely,
> Danny
>
> p.s.—Please be careful not to snap the rubber band on Homer's leg. It hurts.

May 28, 1979

I have good news, bad news and major-bummer-terrible news. The bad news is I'm not going to see Dr. Muse anymore. Father doesn't think I need it and that it's a waste of money. I don't think I ever needed to see her—Mom and Father are the ones who need the help. Something isn't right between them. It's hard to tell they're in love, and if people are married, it shouldn't be hard to tell that.

I do kind of like talking to Dr. Muse. It was nice of her not to tell my parents about the forged Mamets. We've become so close. I'll never forget our last visit. Gina Muse was choked up.

She hugged me and sniffed, "I'll miss you, Danny. Keep our secret, okay? Don't tell anyone, not even your parents, about the talking light."

I hugged her, winked at Einstein and left. That was that. Goodbye, good doctor. Our secret is safe.

The major-bummer-terrible news, which is also part of the good news, is that Father has invited the assistant curator of the Cincinnati Art Museum over for dinner next Saturday to look at his Mamets. Of course, the major-bummer-terrible part of this is that they aren't Mamets—they're Gildays! I know I can fool Father, but a professional curator? I'm in big trouble. I'm good, but not that good. Crap! Crime never pays.

The possible good news is that Father is going to ask the curator to give me an apprenticeship in the Young Artists Program at the art museum. That would be really cool. I have to be accepted first. The apprentice classes take place all day every Saturday, so I wouldn't be able to see Dr. Muse anymore anyway. Father says getting me in is a done deal.

Well, wait until he finds out I forged his Mamets; it may not be such a done deal. I have to figure out a way to switch it all back before next Saturday, or I'm going to be in deep, deep toenails. I have to think. When can I make the switch? How can I get my parents out of the house? Should I get Cal to help me? Would he tell on me? How could I have been so stupid? Can I be arrested for this?

May 30, 1979

Homer went out on another mission yesterday, and he hasn't come back yet. I hope he's okay and hasn't fallen prey to a hawk. Maybe he landed somewhere. It'd be great if I got a message back. I bet he found himself a girlfriend. Probably shacking up in some loft somewhere.

I haven't solved my forgery problem yet. No sign of help either. I may just have to face the music and take whatever punishment the evil lord of the manor dishes out. Things are looking bleak—Homer is gone and Father is going to kill me. Summer vacation is next week, but it doesn't look like I'm going to live to see it. Even if I do, it won't be pretty.

If I survive, I've decided to listen to the talking light, to decipher it. Inside me, I can hear it transmitting. I have a greater purpose. There must be a reason for my life, a reason the light chose me. I think it's telling me to become an environmental activist. I'm beginning to understand it. Either that or I'm growing up. The light makes no mention of my forging activities, but I think I can sell my paintings and donate the money to Greenpeace or Superfund or some worthwhile cause and make it all right. Make up for past sins.

But first I have to make it through Saturday's dinner with the curator.

Ah, the perilous life of a master forger.

Chapter 10

September 1942

His encoded transmission finished for the night, Sulphur fell back on his bed, exhausted. The transmitter, key and code book sat dangerously exposed on the anemic rolltop desk, left unvarnished and knicked by its previous owner. He rubbed his sore finger joints, crimped from pressing Morse code for the past half-hour, as he thought of the progress made.

Throughout Morocco and Algiers, dozens of operatives, solicited in the previous two months by a widening network of spies under Sulphur's guidance, recorded invaluable information. His eager agents astutely picked up the finer nuances of intelligence gathering. Cargoes coming and going. The morale of the French army. The discontent of the local population. Amounts and locations of munitions stockpiles. Defense installations. Local maps. The capacity of the railways. The condition of roads and tracks. Charts of reefs and beachheads up and down twelve hundred miles of coastline. Tidal tables. Wind conditions. Telegraph lines. Switching stations. Electric grids. All came in to the American spy who only months before worked anonymously in an obscure midwestern city.

The information was collected, processed, and sent by encrypted radio transmission to Lisbon, eventually finding its way to London and Washington. What they did with it back there, Sulphur didn't know. Argued about it, he guessed. He only hoped he was being of use.

In the months since his arrival, he'd accomplished much; many French officers had assured him personally they'd offer no resistance to an American invasion. Even more volunteered to join the cause. All this was aided by the large amounts of cash he and his team spread around Fez, Tangier, and Casablanca. It was counterfeit, of course, and meant to destabilize the government. But nobody seemed to care.

Sulphur, upon first arriving in this land of odd custom, was cautious and unsure. But success makes even a timid man brazen, and he spent his money freely, like a New York millionaire. His cover had changed to that of an American businessman sent to purchase bulk phosphate for his company's soap production. That was Sulphur's profession by day. At night, he slipped into his role of OSS operative, holding secret meetings, meticulously planning which acts of sabotage and interdiction to perform when he finally got the word.

He knew orders would come. But when? If there had been one disappointing issue in the whole of his Moroccan assignment, it was that he hadn't had a chance to burn anything yet. Sulphur knew he needed to follow orders—for discipline—but he also knew himself. He wouldn't remain amused by setting small fields ablaze in the lowlands of the Atlas mountains much longer. Sniffing the inspiring scent of matchheads before he went to bed couldn't hold back his burning desire. Only one thing could quell his lust—fire.

Chapter 11

August 10, 1990

"R.T.," Rose shook me awake. "It's five a.m., dear, come to bed."

"Huh?"

"You'll hurt your back sleeping in that chair." She took my hand. "Come on, let's go to bed."

"Rose, Rose," I said excitedly, remembering all that had happened in my visions and readings. "You won't believe it."

An insistent light invaded my eyes, blinding me. Rose clicked off the lamp and we sat in the predawn light.

"Won't believe what?"

"*The Journals*," I said, reaching for the book. I found its smooth, stellar surface and handed it to her. "Look. It's all there."

I blinked, white pixels firing across my corneas like sparklers, as Rose leafed through the book.

Her forehead wrinkled, her lips pursed. "This is the Koran," she said. "Are you studying Islam?"

Goddamn *Journals*. Benedict Arnold.

"It's playing with me," I said. "Don't you see? Until I prove that I'm making progress in getting the story told, it won't reveal itself."

Rose feigned interest in the pattern on the sofa, her eyes unable to meet mine. She traced her hands along its lines, her composure shaken. "Dear," she said, touching the gold cross hanging above her bosom. "Jim already recommended we drop the insanity ploy."

"I'm not insane, Rose." My mouth was ripe with morning breath. "I'm hopeful. I've been reading about Danny Gilday all night. The most incredible thing happened."

Rose's eyes drooped like balloons the day after a party, the happiness gone, the celebration over. My stomach felt as if a wrecking ball had crashed through it. I was determined to reveal what I knew.

"Rose," I said, smiling. "I'm psychic. The spirits have given me a gift."

She stood motionless. "Would you like me to put on some coffee?"

"Rose, please," I said. "Listen. I can see the story in my mind, like I'm watching a movie or a TV show. It's incredible! Danny's been sent here by aliens to help the world. He's a light-being. He's the next Messiah, Rose. He's the Second Coming."

"R.T., stop! Don't blaspheme this way."

"I'm not. It's true. Totally true. You'll see."

Rose looked down with a scolding glower. "R.T., I'll support you in any way I can. I'll stand by you. I'll come to your trial every day. I'll never say a cross word about you to our kids or friends or anyone. I'll be a good wife and help you heal. But I won't allow this . . . this . . . *Journals* business of yours to mock the word of God. I forbid you to desecrate His holy name." She stalked off to the kitchen to make a pot of coffee.

I decided I needed rest, being completely zapped from all my mental work. Using an unknown part of my brain, learning a new cerebral technique, was most taxing. I glanced at the dripping clock and stumbled off to bed, planning to catch a few hours sleep before beginning Allison's entries. I passed Rose in the kitchen. She measured out heaping scoops of java with agitated determination. Her parting words filled me with resolve of my own. I'll prove I'm right.

"I'm going to find you a good therapist, R.T.," Rose said without looking at me. "You need help."

Chapter 12

December 24, 1977

This is the official and most secret diary of Yvonne Allison Leslie Pippin, written because there are so many things a nine-and-a-half-year-old orphan has to tell. I'm not absotively sure what just yet, but Sister Dena assures me I'm a precocious child who always has something to say. I don't talk all that much unless of course I have an opinion, which may be why everybody thinks I'm so wordy—I always have an opinion. I can't help it if I'm constantly coming up with great ideas.

I've lived at the St. Alexandria (St. Als) orphanage in Cincinnati since I was five. It's a giant, brooding place, the kind one reads about in Victorian literature, the kind where each room has a story, and every corner knows the dark past of the residents, the kind of place where everyone has secrets—the caregivers and takers alike.

Everyone calls me Allison; I sort of insist on it. Mother Peculiar resists as much as possible, but mostly I'm known as Allison. It sounds so much prettier than Yvonne. Lucy Carver nicknamed me Woodpecker once, on account of my bright red hair, but she stopped after I nicknamed her Juicy. I have a nickname for everyone; it makes life more interesting here, breaks up the boredom. Here's part of the list:

- St. Alexandria is St. Als
- Mother Superior is Mother Peculiar (fits like a glove)
- Sister Dena is Sister D
- Mary Overby is Ovaries (she's my roommate, and the name makes her blush)
- Sister Claudia is Clod (I prefer the nickname Parrot because she has an annoying habit of repeating other peoples' last sentences, but Clod is the obvious choice of St. Als' kids)
- Sister Bernadette is Barney Rubble (on account that she looks like Barney Rubble from *The Flintstones*—stubby with a pickle nose)

I've made up several more names, but it would take up more space in my journal than I can spare.

Unlike most of the other kids, and nuns too, I don't mind being here so much, but I miss my mom. She had the most beautiful name—Skye. Why did she have to go away? I was brought here on the saddest of days. It's all fuzzy now, but I know it was cold and my aunt was crying. I cried too. I haven't seen her since. She said she'd come back when she could, but now I know she was lying. Sister Dena was at the door to greet me, her eyes sparkling blue. Her eyes are always bright, much brighter than the other prune-faced nuns around here. Sister D is the youngest of them all by far, maybe thirty years old, and the prettiest, too, with her dark brown hair. She keeps it styled and beautiful. The other nuns are wrinkled and frumpy, their hair tied back in buns or cropped real short, and they're way too serious about things. Get out of line around here and—whack! No questions asked, just, whack!

Evenwise, ever since that first day here when Sister D took me in sobbing and gave me a glass of milk and told me I could have as many chocolate chippers as I wanted, ever since then she has taken care of me. She's like a mother. For some reason, she took a liking to me right away. She comforted me and took away my fears. The other nuns, Clod and Barney Rubble and Mother Peculiar, acted like I was a bother, an unwelcome interruption. Not Sister D. She spent most of that first day showing me around, getting me settled in my room, taking time to explain things. She even read me a book good-night. And she's read to me every night since that first night, which she doesn't do for all the kids, there's too many. Over fifty, I think. She also tutors me every day after school for an hour or two so that I'm always prepared for my lessons. It makes me feel so special that she goes out of her way for me. The other kids are jealous, but I absotively love her.

The thing that bugs me most about St. Als is that everything is the same. All the girls wear the same clothes, the same shoes, the same hand-me-downs. A lot of the girls wear lipstick and eye shadow at night, after we're supposed to be in bed. Perfume, too. Most of it is stolen from the people who invite us on field trips. There's a thriving band of thieves inside St. Als. I call them The 88s (a name they like) after the character on *The Flintstones* named 88 Fingers Louie, who stole pianos for a living. I just love the line by the cop in that show when he says to Fred, who had bought a stolen piano for their anniversary, "Just remember, if you play with a hot piano, you'll get your fingers burned."

Evenwise, the burglary ring has been in operation inside St. Als for over twenty years, passed down from generation to generation of outcasts. I'm not a member of the gang, but I was the first one to name it. A hit list of stuff to steal is always drawn up and assignments given out as soon as a field trip is announced. I never stole anything and never will. God wouldn't allow it.

We have the same routine every day. Monday is beans and weenies. Tuesday is beef barbecue. Wednesday is egg-salad sandwiches. Thursday is fried chicken and apple sauce. Friday is always fried fish with macaroni and cheese. Cheesecake, I wish they would change it a little. Sister D says it's because we're an institution, and that's the best way to feed all the boys and girls.

The thing Mary hates the most (she's my absotively best friend) is the white soap.

We get donations from a local soap company, but it makes Mary's skin dry and flaky. Once, I snuck into Mother Superior's quarters and "borrowed" a moisturizing bar for Mary. I didn't use any—the soap doesn't bother me.

Mary wasn't my first roommate, she was my third. I had Kathy, then Michelle before her. They were both placed in foster homes. I pray at the side of my bed each night to be picked. I'm good at praying. Most everybody agrees I should have been chosen by now. Sister D can't figure it out. Someday soon God will hear my prayers, and I'll find a nice family. I know it. I have faith. Undeniable faith.

Evenwise, Mary and I have been roommates for the last three years. Her parents died in a plane crash and nobody else in her family could look after her. My mom drowned in the river. I never knew my dad; he left before I was born. I had an Uncle Patrick, though, but he quit coming around after Mom died. I guess he didn't love me enough to care for me.

Mary and I became friends real quick as I showed her around St. Als on her first day; not the nuns' tour, the real tour. The ins and outs of the place: the stairwells and closets, the boiler room, the fire escape, the unused places like the east wing. All the areas we aren't supposed to be in. I like sneaking around finding new adventures to explore. Sometimes I pretend I'm a spy. I know every squeaky floorboard and stair, every creaking door. I know when each sister goes to bed and who gets up in the middle of the night. I know what girls are sneaking to see the boys and what boys are spending the night with which priests. The priests never take girls on sleep-overs, only boys. There are a few nuns who invite girls on a sleep-over once in awhile, but never me.

You grow up fast in St. Als—street wise. You have to. It's a tough place. Lots of the kids are mean and throw tantrums. Some, like the Cutters, need more attention. I could never be a Cutter. Being an orphan might not be easy, but slitting your wrists isn't the answer. I prefer to get lost in books, a habit I picked up from Sister D, and when times get too hard to bear, I cry. We all cry. Every one of us. Even the boys who act tough during the day. I see them in their rooms at night, when I sneak out the fire escape, crying into their pillows. It's truly sad.

I'm not ashamed to admit I cry. The ones who can't cry, the ones who are so hard they cover it up, those are the ones in trouble. They're usually Cutters. Cutters are mostly teenagers, although they don't always slice a vein to end their misery. Some overdose or try to hang themselves with sheets. We call them Cutters evenwise. We can all relate to their sadness, but I can't see killing myself over being abandoned. Cutters haven't learned to accept being a reject, a recyclable can, a disposable diaper, a forgotten soul—we kids talk about it a lot when we're alone. We have our own language in here. The Cutters seem to take the conditions worse than the rest. The Church does its best to provide counseling, but some kids are beyond repair. Three Cutters have succeeded since I've been here. Twenty-six have tried. According to Sister D, the bulk of the Cutters don't really want to die, they're just looking for attention, a form of expression she calls it.

The first time Mary heard me crying she came over and climbed into my bed and held me. Now, whenever either of us are sad, Mary comes into my bed. I think she's as scared as me. It feels so good having her next to me when I'm afraid. She's a good friend. We've been comforting each other for a long time. Sometimes when we fall asleep together the nuns wake us in the morning and they're mad. I don't know why. Mary is like my sister. I really love her.

I don't mean to make St. Als sound like a bad place, it's not. But it isn't like a real home either. And I don't mean to be ungrateful. My life has been so blessed. Miracles abound here. It's always been that way. I have visions in my dreams sometimes. Of angels and God and Heaven. I never told anybody, but the night my mom died I had a vision. She came to me in my sleep and told me she was leaving. Then I saw her drowning. She came to me afterwards and told me everything would be all right, that she was living in a city of light, that she would always watch over me. I can still hear her voice saying, "Don't let anyone take your spirit, Allison. You must always shine. Shine brightly for the world. Shine. I love you so very much, Allison," she whispered as she vanished. I never told anybody because I thought maybe it was my fault. That maybe my dream caused Mom to die.

If anything ever happened to Sister D, I'd be lost. I couldn't bear to lose another close friend. She's my guardian angel. Sometimes I wonder if my mom's spirit entered Sister D's body when she died. The Church wouldn't hear of such heresy, but a girl can dream, can't she? Souls have to go somewhere, don't they?

I won't ever forget how Sister Dena brightened my first St. Als Christmas. That was the night of the first true miracle. I was so sad because Christmas was coming and I didn't have any family. I think all little girls should have a family, somebody to talk to and be friends with. I still don't have any family, but I do have lots and lots of friends. I tried to be happy, I tried to smile, but all I wanted was to be home with Mom and a Christmas tree and presents and home cooking. I wasn't home, though, I was in an old, beat-up orphanage with a bunch of old, beat-up looking nuns. Oops, that's not fair— this is a good place, and the nuns do their best.

Sister D must have known I was down because on Christmas Eve, after everyone else was asleep, she brought me into the main room by the Christmas tree and read me stories. We bundled up in a warm blanket on the sofa. She read a book called *Silent Seraph.*

"This is a little book I found in the library, Allison," she began softly, her arms tight around me. Usually when she speaks, her arms fly about like a Dutch windmill, but that night I was nestled up snug against her in my pajamas and robe. There was a cozy fire crackling in the fireplace, which made the whole room glow. Outside the frosty windows, the wind blew cold.

She read me the story as the fire popped: "In a land so very near, in a life so very close to your own, there was an angel. Her name was Silent Seraph. She had descended from heaven to help the unfortunate." Sister gently turned the page. "Silent Seraph had taken a human form so that she could live and work among those needing the most help. She was a lovely angel with beautiful auburn red hair like a sunset in a foreign land."

"Hey, I have red hair. I have pretty red hair!" I shouted.

"Shh . . . yes, you do, Allison, gorgeous red hair and darling freckles, but we must be quiet," she cautioned, turning back to the book. "Her beauty was matched only by the kindness of her tender heart. For she was in this world to help those who could not help themselves. And the angel worked night and day. She worked in soup kitchens, she made warm clothes for people who needed them, she offered assistance to anyone who asked. Silent Seraph often neglected her own health in her enthusiasm to help others."

"But if she's an angel, she doesn't need to worry about her health," I said.

"Well, I think if an angel comes to Earth, then she becomes human and probably has the same problems as we all do," Sister D answered.

"Oh," I said, acting like I knew what she meant, but I didn't understand it then.

"The angel was loving and giving, and she did her best for mankind for many months. But one day Silent Seraph began to feel that no matter how much she did there was still much more to do. The angel became sad at all the suffering and began to doubt that she was really any help at all."

Sister D looked at me, then kissed the top of my head. "Silent Seraph prayed, asking for an answer to all the heartache. She cried to the Lord to help her understand. But He did not answer. And then, when she thought that all her work was for nothing, the Lord gave her a sign to bring her out of her sadness."

She flipped another page. I couldn't read at the time, so Sister D's voice was like magic to me. Now I think her voice sounds like music, sweet flute music.

"As she finished a day of caring for the homeless," Sister read, "she slowly climbed the stairs to her room. It was snowing outside. It was Christmas Eve, the night before the birth of baby Jesus, as the quiet angel walked to her room in sadness. Slowly, she opened the door, sure that her efforts had been wasted. She made herself some tea and looked to the bitter wind howling outside her window. And in that moment she saw something sitting outside on the ledge. Her heart leapt with joy. She quickly opened the window to find a bright purple orchid sitting in a pot."

I was electrified by the story. An angel come to Earth. Sister D continued as the fire crackled and popped.

"Silent Seraph brought the chilled flower into her room and dusted the snow from its beautiful petals. She set the orchid next to her bed and fell to her knees. For the orchid on her windowsill, in the harshness of winter, had survived. And she prayed to her Father, thanking Him for such a precious gift and such a certain sign. And she

124

smiled, as she knew that her work had been noticed. And she drifted off to sleep, making plans for the morning to help as many people as she could."

"Is that the end?" I asked. "Can you read it again? I really like that story."

"It is a nice story, isn't it, Allison?" Sister D said quietly. "But I think it's time for all little girls to be in bed."

"You know what?" I said, forgetting my sadness.

"What's that, Allison?" she asked, as she gently rubbed my arms.

"It's Christmas Eve and it's snowing and I have red hair."

Just then Sister Dena looked at me with a strange face and said, "Sometimes I think you are a little angel come to help the world. You are my quiet, little angel," she said as she stroked my hair. "Now it's time for bed."

She carried me upstairs. I just knew what I would find. As soon as she let me down, I ran to my window and lifted it up. And there, sitting in a tiny little pot, with tiny snowflakes clinging to it, was my beautiful purple orchid.

"Thank you, thank you, Sister Dena," I shouted as I jumped up to hug her.

Thump! She fell to the ground. She fainted.

"Sister Dena, Sister Dena," I said in a whisper as I shook her to wake her up. "Wake up."

"I . . . I . . . must have blacked out," she said after a few minutes.

"Look Sister, look at my beautiful orchid. It's just like the one in the book. Isn't it the most extra special flower in the whole world? Where did you find it for me?" I asked, thinking that she had planned the whole thing to cheer me up.

"Allison, sweet, sweet Allison." Her voice trembled softly, tears running down her cheeks. "I didn't buy this flower. It must truly be a sign from God," she whispered as she made the sign of the cross, then pulled me close. (Sister D is a hugger by nature. Always hugging me.) She rocked me back and forth in her arms until I fell asleep.

That was both the best and the worst Christmas I ever had. Since then, every Christmas Eve Sister Dena and I sneak down to the main room and build a fire, and she reads me the book, *Silent Seraph*. And in the saddest of moments or the coldness of the winter I look at my orchid and thank the Lord for taking care of me.

August 11, 1990

Stone here. I slept all that day into the next morning, apparently more fatigued than I realized. I was so zonked that I slept right through the racket of Rose having a couple of the boys from the construction company come replace the door. She was pleased that the previously charred door had been removed. It was an embarrassing reminder to her and the rest of the neighborhood that a suspected arsonist is amongst them.

I awoke refreshed, aching to get at *The Journals* again, with only mild discomfort burning in my gut. I assumed the irritation was due to the pain medication taken on an empty stomach. Still, the bitter taste in my mouth grew stronger, more odiferous. With the aid of my walker, and loaded up on Pepto Bismol and a handful of antacid tablets, I managed to navigate my way to the solarium. My beautiful orchids welcomed me with open blooms. Their petals stretched sensually to greet me in the opaque summer sun, which wheezed its way through the whitish ozone slathered upon the suburbs of Cincinnati like some pervasive insect repellent. Someone take their finger off the Raid Fogger, would you? Another pollution advisory today, I guess. Keep your children and your grandparents indoors.

Defiantly rising beyond the solarium windows stood the triumph of the Stone backyard—Prometheus. The great Titan statue ascended fourteen feet into the air, a symbol of man's persistence in the face of adversity. Prometheus dominated the flower gardens and the accompanying eight acres of grounds.

Prometheus was my inspiration. I had the statue commissioned on my fiftieth birthday. It took a student from the university, Dwight Appello, nineteen months to fashion the god out of clay and rock. The sculptor did well for himself after that. He changed his name to Johnny Chisel and went to New York, where he established a following. His works sold in the tens of thousands before he succumbed to AIDS—hundreds of thousands after. It was an exhaustive, artistic, and constructive feat to have Prometheus come to life in our backyard.

Allison's next entry told of an angelic affirmation on New Year's Day, 1978. Bundled up against winter in a donated coat, she and the other orphans made the pilgrimage to the Krohn Conservatory in Eden Park to see the annual Nativity.

January 1, 1978
What an absotively strange experience greeted my new year. I was standing in the cold, my cheeks frosted pink, staring at the likeness of baby Jesus. I was holding hands with Mary.

"I can feel your heat through my mittens," Mary said. She looked at me strangely, her front teeth all bunched together like three old women at the communion altar. "You feel like an electric blanket. Feels good."

"It's God's light," I said. I stared at the Nativity. "I'm just so happy to be in His presence." I figured the warmth was my happiness at being at one of my favorite Christmas activities. I look forward to coming to the Nativity each year.

We went inside the musky, gray building for a tour of the exotic plants. We walked through all the flower exhibits. Somehow I got separated from the group and ended up at the orchid display. It was so beautiful. That's when the heat returned to me. I became dizzy, like I had a fever.

"Look at that girl," a worker said, pointing at me.

"Oh, my God," a young girl exclaimed. The room seemed brighter. A light surrounded me. God's light. I know it was.

Sister Dena was summoned. I just stared at the orchids in a trance, amazed at His grace. I don't know how much time went by before Sister Dena showed up. At first, she stood away from me and stared, not directly at me, but above me.

"Allison," she said, finally putting her arm around me. "Are you okay, angel?" The fever broke. The heat dissipated. The light vanished. It was absotively heavenly.

February 8, 1978

Today was a good day. I was in the library this afternoon with Sister D, her hands whirling about like a blender, emphasizing this point or that, having our usual tutoring lesson, studying advanced writing techniques. She's the one who encouraged me to start this journal. Smart woman. Evenwise, during the whole lesson she had this grin that wouldn't go away. It curls at the end of her lips in the cutest way, her nose perks a bit, and her eyes sparkle like sapphires in moonlight. (Sister told me I should work more on descriptive writing.)

"What are you so happy about?" I asked finally.

"I have a surprise for you," she said, her arms extended excitedly. "The final grades for the first semester. And guess who got straight A's again, for the tenth semester in a row?" She smiled so wide I thought her silk face would crinkle.

"Me?" I jumped up. "Again?" I raised my arms in victory as Sister D nodded proudly. "Yes!" I shouted, and received some nasty glares from disturbed readers. "What's in the box?" I asked, knowing it had to be a present for me.

"A reward for all your hard work," Sister beamed. She tossed her thick brown hair over her shoulder. She handed me a wrapped box, which I tore open. My hands shook. Inside the wrapping paper was a felt box. A gleaming gold pen and pencil set shone back at me. I was overjoyed. I plopped next to Sister D, elated at her generosity.

"Oh, Sister, I love it!" I said. "I really *do*."

Sister Dena patted my back in congratulations. "There's talk that you should skip a grade and go to school with the sixth graders, Allison. Would you like that?"

I scribbled blue ink on a scratch sheet of paper. (I'm writing this journal entry with my new pen now.) "I'm not sure I want to skip ahead," I admitted.

"Well, you're much too smart for the class you're in now, angel," she said. "You're at least a year, maybe two, beyond the lessons as it is."

I didn't like the idea of being in class with people I didn't know, so I told Sister D I'd like to think about it. She asked what I wanted to be when I grew up and scrunched her face, disapproving, when I said a nun, like her.

"Like me?" she pointed at herself in exaggeration. "Whatever for?"

"Because you're such a good person," I said, "I want to help people the way you do. Plus, I think the Lord wants me to."

Sister Dena shifted in her chair, then moved again, then scooted it so that her back was to the rest of the room. "Allison." She lowered her voice and wrung her hands together. "You're the most gifted child St. Als has ever had. I think you'd be wise to explore all your options before settling on the Catholic Church."

Whoa, that's a shocker. "How come?"

Sister glanced about to make sure no one was listening. "A life of religious service isn't for everyone," she said. "You're a free-spirited girl. I'm not sure how easily you could conform to the rigid life of a nun."

"But you're a nun," I protested.

Sister Dena's face turned sour, her happiness gone. "Not by choice," she said, in a voice I could barely hear.

"What?" I whispered. "You're a great nun. What do you mean? You don't want to be a nun?"

"I do now," she said. "It's my vocation. I've become good at it, but it wasn't my first choice. I wanted to be an athlete. A track star," she said.

"Really?"

"Yes," she said, her blue eyes pale, her voice disappointed, her hands gripping themselves as if squeezing the last tear drop out of well-used hanky. "I was pretty good. I won the Indiana state championship in the 400 meter. And a host of other races. It gave me courage and self-esteem. Winning a race was the one thing I knew I was good at. It meant a lot."

"Jesus winning the long jump on the road to Galilee, I didn't know that."

"Everyone has an interesting story to tell if they can find someone to listen," Sister D said, downhearted.

"So, how come you didn't become a track star then?"

"Even the saints had to change careers every once in awhile," she kidded without laughing.

"No, really," I giggled.

"It was the family way." She lowered her head. "Being a Catholic in Fort Wayne, it was understood that one of the family members was required to go into the church."

"What do you mean, *required?*"

"Just that. It's a long standing Church policy that Catholic families are to have lots of children, and one of those children is meant to serve the Church. Just like tithing."

"Cheesecake," I exhaled. "And you were the one chosen?"

"Not at first." She hesitated. Her index finger picked at the initials, P.C., carved in the table. "My brother, Wendel, was the one selected by the priest."

"So how did he get out of it?"

Sister Dena's blue eyes misted over, her hands clasped together. "He killed himself."

A shiver rocked my spine. I couldn't speak. Why? Why did he do that? I was too full of pity for Sister D to say anything. She continued to pick at the initials. "I was twelve at the time; Wendel was twenty-one. They put so much pressure on him," she sighed. "Even though he told Mom and Dad over and over he didn't want to, the priest didn't let up. Dad said he'd disown him if he didn't join the priesthood. Wendel gave in. He went to seminary school, but didn't like it and quit. But the priest still insisted."

"Oh, God," I barely whispered, my stomach in knots.

"Dad and Wendel argued. I watched the whole thing. After it was over, Wendel went out in the barn and blew his brains out." The words slowly dropped from her lips. "My mother was decimated, never the same, her spirit knocked out of her. Somewhere in the midst of years of grief and mourning, somewhere in the twisted emotions, I offered to go in his place. I don't know if it was guilt or fear or a desire to get out of Fort Wayne, but I became a nun. Maybe I was hoping to avoid another catastrophe. Maybe I knew the diocese wasn't going to count Wendel's death as fulfilling the bargain."

I placed my hand on Sister D's. What a strong woman. How incredibly brave to do what she did. Most would have run away. I would have. I searched for the right words to say. I needed just the exactly perfect ones to pay her back for all the times she comforted me. "Well," I offered in my most upbeat voice, "you became the best darned nun I ever met."

Sister D laughed. Her blue eyes shimmered slightly as she pulled me toward her. She hugged me tight, her heart thumping against my chest. I love her hugs, absotively love them. That's one great thing about Sister—she always hugs me. And, in turn, I hug lots of people.

"Be anything you want in life," she said, kissing the top of my head. "Don't let anybody force you into something you don't want to do."

She kissed my cheek. It was heaven.

"Don't worry," I said strongly. "They won't take my spirit. I'm going to shine."

Sister D chuckled. Her sadness left her as she ruffled my crimson hair with her hand. "I'm sure you will," she said. "If anyone on this Earth will shine . . . it'll be you."

I placed *The Journals* on the bench next to me as the sun elbowed its way through the gray atmosphere into the solarium. Why orchids? What is their meaning? Their purpose in this tale? I looked at my orchids (my children) and the newest addition to the family, Fireball. Were the others jealous? Sibling rivalry perhaps? Orchids are a temperamental lot. They need the proper mixture of sun and light, humidity and temperature, moisture and dryness, to survive. They also need the right attention. They crave it. Being the aristocracy of flowers, the sensual belles of the fauna ball, they need constant care and tenderness to thrive. Failure to give these rare nobility their just homage inevitably results in a holding back of their blooms. Without the perfect cultivation and devotion from their masters, orchids simply refuse to reveal their bright faces, their loveliness forever hidden inside skinny naked stalks of green. Alas, much care must be taken if their true meaning is to be discovered.

I thought about the giddy nature of Allison, the unbreakable orphan, and her single, purple miniature dendrobium. Then I thought of *Magicka carallus*, a truly mystical siren that has seduced my mind. Soon, my newfound talent for telepathy had switched on, and I witnessed Allison's world firsthand.

Allison's irrepressible spirit infected most everyone she came to know. In early spring, she came up with the idea of growing a vegetable garden so that the kids at St. Als could eat fresh produce. She had an ally in Sister Dena, whose own penchant for flower gardens could be seen blossoming throughout spring, summer, and fall. To the amusement of the staff and the other kids, Allison began collecting fruit seeds at meal time from the cores of eaten apples, peaches, watermelons, and tomatoes.

During the first week of May, Allison, accompanied by Mary and Sister D, spent the entire weekend plotting out, tilling, planting, and fertilizing a spacious garden. The delight on her face made even the stoic Mother Superior smile. Allison dug her hands in the fresh earth, bringing a handful of soil to her nose. She inhaled with a sigh. "Ahh, heaven on Earth."

I laughed at her sweet outlook, her uncorrupted perception of the beauty of life. She loved living. In watching her, my heart lifted, and I realized I should use some of that magic myself. I went in the kitchen and held Rose. We hugged, without words, telling each other in a phrase Rose has used all her life—God willing, everything will be just fine. I hoped so. I returned to the pleasant but formidable task of documenting *The Journals*.

May 9, 1978

Jesus biting into a jalapeño at the last supper, what a surprise today! I was working in the garden after school when a green truck from Celestial Garden & Lawn pulled up. Two men in brown coveralls got out, unloaded a big wooden shed painted white, and set it about twenty feet from the back row of corn. Mother Peculiar was outside instructing them. After they placed the shed, they unloaded new shovels and spades and hoses and every kind of garden tool ever invented!

I smiled from ear to ear. Mary came out to do some gardening and was totally amazed. After the delivery guys left, another truck from a garden store drove in with all sorts of top soil, fertilizer, and plants. It was so neat. They even delivered gardening gloves for me and Mary—just our size, too! I asked Mother Superior where all this stuff came from, and she said it was an endowment from a caring patron.

I looked up endowment and patron in the dictionary to make sure I knew what she meant. Whoever the patron is, he sure is generous. He must be the kindest person on Earth. Of course, it could be a woman, too. I'm so happy. I have everything I need to have the bestest garden in Cincinnati.

May 18, 1978

The nuns are in an uproar over the vote in Italy today. The sisters have been gossiping, saying Hail Marys, and carrying on like the end of the world is coming. The Italian legislature voted for abortion rights for women. The nuns call it heresy that the home of the Catholic faith, the Vatican, is smack dab in the middle of a country where abortion is legal.

I don't understand too much about abortion or why a person would need to have one, but if the Church says it's wrong to legalize it, then I agree. I overheard Clod (the Parrot) mimicking Mother Peculiar's words that adoption is better than abortion. I agree with that, too, but there are an awful lot of orphans here at St. Als who can't find homes, and this is just one orphanage in one city. Just think how many other unwanted kids there are. And how many unwanted kids who aren't in orphanages. What a depressing thought.

It's a shame more adults don't like children. I've been here so long. I miss my mom, even though I can't remember her so well anymore. I can still hear her voice telling me to shine. Evenwise, Sister Dena is like a mother to me now. She takes care of me. And I'm just sure, any day now, the perfect family will adopt me.

May 20, 1978

Another glorious day in the fields. Until Mother P showed up. I love my garden. It's so peaceful. It makes me feel important to know I can grow things, to care for my plants every day. I talk to each one of them. Mary says I'm crazy, but I know it helps. Sister Dena smiles, and Mother Peculiar . . . well, we have our differences.

Mother Superior and I had a *big* argument in the garden. She doesn't like me evenwise, so it was inevitable. I'm still waiting to hear if my punishment will stand. I've never described Mother P in my journal before, and Sister Dena keeps encouraging me to write more descriptively. She thinks I should be an author, so here goes.

"Yvonne," Mother P said, standing above me in the spring heat, blocking the sun like a slab from Stonehenge. I didn't know she was in the garden, and she startled me. I looked up, shielding my eyes from the sun. Mother P's large mass blocked the brightness. All I could see was black swallowed by a burst of light. I couldn't see her black, menacing eyes or bushy eyebrows. But it was her all right, there's no mistaking her commanding height and her wide girth. She is, by far, by way-way far, the biggest women I've ever met. She's a big-boned woman with crinkled skin drawn tight over jagged cheeks, like a dried mud puddle. If the bulk of her presence wasn't enough to give her away, the fact she called me the Y word (Yvonne) was. "Child, your vegetables are getting eaten up by bugs."

"Yes, Mother Superior." I squinted.

"We have a shed full of pesticide over there. Don't you think we should spray and get rid of the little heathens?"

"Spray!" I shouted, jumping up. "We can't spray. That's like . . ." I stuttered. She was to the side of the sun now, but the white skunk stripe in her black bird's-nest hair reflected into my eyes. I moved back a little to see her better. "That's . . . that's . . . murder!"

"Now, child," she frowned. "It's not murder of any kind. They are bugs. Pests. Nothing more."

Nothing more my big toenail, I thought to myself. I smelled pesticide before. I've read the labels; the words I understood evenwise, it's dangerous. "We are all blessed creatures on God's green Earth." I tried my best to put it on her level.

"Fiddle sticks," she huffed.

"But, Mother Superior," I protested. "Have you seen what is in that stuff? It's poison."

"Now, dear," she said, gritting her teeth. "It's only poison for the insects, not for humans."

"How do you know? Read the bottle. It can't be good to spray plants and then eat the vegetables. It can't be," I pleaded. I knew I was right about this. If poison kills things, anything, then it has to be harmful. "We don't know what's in there. We don't know it's safe."

Mother Peculiar bristled, straightened herself, narrowed her beady black eyes, and firmly said, "You are just being silly, Yvonne. I want you to spray this garden to keep it from getting ruined." She was stubborn. But so am I.

"It's Allison, ma'am," I insisted. "I'll spray it for you, Mother Superior, but it's the last thing I'll have to do with the garden. And I won't eat any of the vegetables, either."

"Don't give me ultimatums, child, I'm the law around here," she reminded me sternly. Her face, red as Georgia clay, was ready to crack.

"Fine. I'll just spray poison all over the place and kill everyone. Don't blame me when all the kids start coughing up lungs after they eat their salads. It's on your head, Mother Peculiar." I slipped. Jesus admitting he was just a kid from Judea, why do I always do that? Say the wrong thing at the wrong time?

Mother P pursed her skinny lips, no thicker than dental floss. "What did you call me?"

I was in trouble big time. It just slipped. I didn't mean it. "Nothing, ma'am, Mother Superior, ma'am," I said, looking at a row of beans, shuffling my right foot in black velvet mulch.

"You called me, Mother *Peculiar*, didn't you? So that's where the nickname came from. Yvonne Pippin, you troublemaker, you have one month kitchen duty for this."

Cheesecake! Why did I say that? Why do I let her get me so mad?

"Get to your room this instant! I'll spray the blessed garden myself."

So here I am in my room after a fight with Mother P. I didn't go looking for a fight, it just happened. Evenwise, I don't want a month of kitchen duty, but a girl has to stand up for her principles. Working in the kitchen is such a drag. I hate the heat and the greasy, grimy dishes. I asked Sister Dena for leniency, but it isn't all that likely. I suppose I shall just have to bear the unfair sentence of my sadistic warden, Mother Superior.

May 21, 1978

Poor Mother Superior. She should have listened. I may be ten but I have brains enough. She had to be taken to the hospital. She couldn't breath and a rash covered both her arms. Pesticides. I'm the toast of St Als, the kids evenwise. My punishment never came to be. But the absotively best news is that the garden was declared pesticide-free.

July 13, 1978

I don't mean to complain or anything, but sometimes I think people are terribly mean. I figured this out because of everything that happened over the last week. It all started Friday when we went to the Cincinnati Zoo. I don't like the zoo. And I don't mean just the Cincinnati Zoo—I don't like any zoo. I never want to go there again. I live in one.

I'm so sad. I can't believe it, Lord, won't You help me? I try and be good. I try to be a proper Catholic. I try to shine. I try. But You aren't listening. Won't You talk to me?

It was a gray day, which should have told me right away the zoo was going to be boring. But really, it was more than boring. It made me think. I was already pretty down when we were let off the bus at the main gate. Our zoo is supposed to be one of the best in the world. It was neat at first, seeing all the animals: the monkeys, the reptiles, the elephants, and giraffes. Because we're orphans, we got a preview of a place with insects that opens in August, which was really creepy. Mary didn't like it at all. She's squeamish. She's afraid of spiders and bugs. Me, too, but I don't scream when I see them like Mary does, with her gray little mouse-eyes popping out of her head in fear, like a cartoon character.

We walked around looking at the animals, listening to the tour guide tell us about each one. The guide described how the zoo created a natural habitat for animals to feel at home away from their native land, which got me to thinking—these animals aren't happy. They were all kind of lazy, just hanging about. The tigers were sleeping and could barely hold their heads up, if they looked up at all. The tigress didn't hunt for her food like she would in the wild; she just strolled over to a bucket inside her *natural habitat* and casually ate. It wasn't natural at all. They had lost their spirit. They were

133

depressed. The monkeys sat staring back at me like I was on display, like they were watching us, like *we* were the strange animals.

Maybe we are.

Even the picnic lunch and cotton candy couldn't keep me from thinking how absotively heart-breaking it was to see these nice, beautiful creatures locked away like pets. I couldn't wait to leave. Eventually we did, but not before visiting the temple of the last known carrier pigeon. They have a building at the zoo that houses a stuffed pigeon named Martha, which was the last carrier in the world. She's sitting there, gray and lifeless, with marble eyeballs.

"A trophy to man's lust for hunting and for killing things innocent," Sister Dena said, putting her arm around me as we stood inside the musty rotunda. "A symbol of man's guilt."

"I could never ever, even ever, consider killing anything," I said to her as I stared at Martha. "How many species have we made extinct that we don't know about?"

"Far too many, angel," she said. "So many that they have an extensive endangered species list."

That was all we said as we both stood quietly, staring at a dusty, stuffed bird. That's it—the only one left—stuck away in a crumbling zoo, barely remembered. How dismal.

But that was a picnic compared to what happened the next day. It was Saturday, a good sleeping-in day because it was still gray, but I couldn't sleep in because a couple looking to adopt came to visit. I woke up tangled in my sheets, the blanket and bedspread thrown to the floor. My eyes looked like a bag-worm camp in an apple tree. I didn't sleep much the night before, thinking how glorious it would be if I was chosen. I did my hair in pretty, red curls. I showered and scrubbed under my nails. I even ironed my dress so that I would be the absotively most beautiful girl anybody could ever want. I practiced my answers and told myself to be polite and respectful.

We were trained, drilled to be precise, to be on our best behavior when they arrived. Usually potential foster parents look at lots of papers and junk before they select one of us. After it all looks good in writing, then the child being picked is brought to Mother Superior's office for an interview. But this time was terribly unusual. So unusual it was sick, and of course, I said so.

We were all lined up in the great hall in our school uniforms like we were at one of Mother Peculiar's military inspections. The white glove kind. All of us girls were there, close to thirty, when the Adlers came in. My throat shrank to the size of a bobby pin, my stomach felt like a water balloon loaded with vinegar, my knees locked in place, my body tight as guitar string. Bunny Adler, that's the lady, was decked out in a full-length fur of some helpless mammal (in summer, no less), complete with gaudy jewelry and long fingernails the color of pearls. Her nose turned up naturally, like she was born better than everyone. Myles, the husband, thought he was going yachting, dressed in white pants, deck shoes, a captain's hat tilted just so over his drifting left eye, a navy blue blazer adorned in half the gold braid from Annapolis, and an unlit pipe hanging perfectly from his mouth. I doubt he even smoked. Dirty habit, that.

They walked the length of the line of girls, looking us up and down carefully. Inspecting us. Measuring us, not saying a word to us, to the sisters, or to each other. Bunny's olive high-heels clicked with each judgmental step. Myles was barely present. Finally, after ten minutes of this, they started at the head of the line asking questions. Sheila was first. Then Linda and Ann and Mary and Joyce Wilkerson, then me. With each person there was a nasty comment about this flaw or that. Too skinny, too fat, and on and on, until they came to me. I was not in the best of moods.

"Well, Buns, look at this one would you?" Myles Adler droned in his best stiff-upper-lip accent. I bet he was raised rich and taught to sound rich, too.

"Yeesss, she does have a certain, *charm* about her," Bunny drawled, as if she couldn't decide whether she wanted to talk or sleep. She was bored. "But, Myles, dawling, that red hair of hers. I don't approve. Do you?"

"I see what you mean, Buns. Do you think we could dye her hair? You know I'm partial to blondes." He almost laughed but decided it was too much work.

"I suppose we could do that. But then what can be done with those freckles? You simply won't be able to fool anybody . . . those freckles scream red hair," she said in such a way that I wanted to elbow her ribs. Instead, I made a suggestion of my own.

"Excuse me, ma'am," I said quietly. "But did you know that red-haired girls are noted for their caring and intelligence?"

Her eyes opened wide, as if she had just woken up. "Well, no child. I didn't know that," she said, leaning closer to inspect me. She put her hand on my cheek and stroked me like a cat.

"Did you know, ma'am, that freckles are God's little kisses, and my red hair is the fire of the sun caught by the angels?" I said sweetly, batting my eyes.

"Well, no child," she cooed.

It was very disturbing.

"Do you like that one, Buns? Should we wrap her up and take her home?" Myles offered. It was that comment and Bunny's stroking me like a kitten that set me off. I snapped. Bad. I couldn't help it.

"Did you know, ma'am, that the idle rich are considered generally impotent?"

Smack! Her hand lashed my face. I gritted my teeth as the sting burned its way across my skin. I wouldn't cry. She'd never see that from me. Her eyes flashed daggers, her caked, made-up face drew tight. She raised her hand as if to strike me again. I wouldn't show fear. Never. Not to someone like this. Not to someone who gets their thrills from other's pain. I puffed out my lips, narrowed my eyes like laser beams to burn through her. "Did you know, Buns, that if you used less make-up and lost forty pounds, you'd still be uglier than Mussolini?" I mused, kicking her hard in the shins.

A big commotion erupted. Kids and nuns gasped, astonished. Sisters were everywhere, apologizing, pulling me out of line, dragging me off. I let my feet go limp across the dingy tile like a demonstrator at a peace rally. One more slur. I couldn't resist.

"Did you know, ma'am," I shouted, "that you can't shop for kids like you shop for a puppy?"

"Quiet, Allison!" Clod admonished me with her trademark frown. She is one of those people who has to work hard at not looking mean. A frown is always there. Must be because her boobs droop to her navel. My blood spewed hot lava. One more slam.

"Did you know it's ninety degrees out? It's hot, Buns, hot!" A hand slid over my mouth to gag me. I bit it. Hard. The hand flinched and drew away. "Hey, Myles, did you know that Cincinnati doesn't have a navy?" I was pushed around the corner, laughter from the girls cheering me on.

That was all I could get in as I was hauled into Mother P's office, Clod's hand smothering me. She pushed me along, her boobs flopping into me like prods. I didn't bite her again. The damage was done. My point made. Mother Peculiar wasn't there, of course, she was in the great hall licking the boots of the admiral. I waited a long time for her to come scold me. I expected to get in lots of trouble. I didn't care. Why should I? I'm not a pet store display. I'm not an animal in a zoo. And that's when it hit me like a shovel in the head. I *am* an animal in a zoo. All us kids are on display for anyone who cares to see. Come and look at human children in captivity. Come see the misfits, the ones no one wants.

Mother P never did come to her office. Sister D came instead, worried.

"Allison, are you all right?" she asked as she sat behind Mother Superior's huge mahogany desk. I like Mother's office, it's rich and smells of leather. I stared at a portrait of Pope Paul VI, which hung in a gold frame above a table that held a silver chalice. He was so regal in his vestments. I love his eminence. I thought about drinking Kool-Aid from that chalice once, to sneak it to my room and have my own Holy Communion. I chickened out.

"Yes, ma'am," I said, sitting on my hands nervously like Mary always does. "I'm fine."

"What happened, Allison?" Sister D asked.

Maybe it was the way she asked the question, maybe it was the whole day, but I burst into tears. "I don't know."

"Angel," she said as she stood up and came around to the front of the desk. "Let's sit on the couch." She pointed to the burgundy leather sofa in the corner. "Let's talk about this. What's upsetting you?"

What was going on? I expected to be in major trouble, kitchen duty for life. Instead, she's asking me what's wrong. I didn't understand the kindness. Not that I didn't expect Sister D to be nice, she's always nice, but this was a job for Mother

Superior. She had a reputation for liking these kinds of things. Fringe benefit of the job—disciplining children.

"I don't think it was fair to be treated that way. Didn't you see how fake they were?" I wept.

"Yes I did, but that doesn't mean you should be disrespectful."

"But they acted like I was a pet."

"Sometimes people act a certain way that we may not like or agree with, but that doesn't mean we have to act the same way," she explained, holding my hand. Her blue eyes shone compassionately. "And sometimes people have problems so deep that they don't know how to be good people."

"I don't get it," I said, sniffing.

"Allison, maybe the Adlers have grown up in wealth, in a lifestyle that gave them everything they wanted without having to work for it. And now these unfortunate people discover that there is one thing they cannot have: children. And that's the only thing they want. But they can't have it. They haven't learned how the rest of the world works. They don't know how to treat people, so they treated you badly. But instead of getting mad, you should feel pity because they will never know the happiness you have."

"What happiness?" I cried loudly.

"Oh, child, the happiness of finding your orchid, of planting a garden, or talking to a caterpillar," she said, smiling, referring to the time I was caught daydreaming in class, staring at a callipitar inching across the window. That was a day when a power came over me, like a vision. Mary said the whole room was amazed when I calmed Barney Rubble down. She was screaming at me, but I placed my hand on her shoulder and told her that we are all God's children. I don't remember it exactly, but Mary and some of the others have told the story so often that sometimes I feel like I do.

"I guess I *am* happy most of the time," I said. I looked at the pope, wondering if I had disappointed him, let him down and all Catholics everywhere.

"You're an angel," Sister D said as she patted my leg, "because you understand that simple pleasures are the greatest treasures."

I like Sister Dena. She always talks to me like I'm a mature person and not two years old. Most of the nuns act like we're little kids. But Sister D and I have grown close through the years of extra tutoring and our special Christmases and things. Still, I couldn't get Myles and Bunny Adler off my mind. "She wanted to dye my hair like I was her fur coat, like I was something she could own."

"Yes, she did. But most people aren't like her, are they?" Sister asked.

"No."

"So that should tell you that she isn't normal, that she has a problem."

"But they inspected us like we were livestock, like we weren't people," I whined.

"Yes, they did, and what does *that* tell you, angel?" she asked, her voice as quiet as a spring breeze.

"That something is wrong with them. But it isn't right. People like that should be shown they're wrong, not be allowed to get away with it. And St. Als let them line us up and treat us like animals. They aren't right and neither is Mother Superior," I said, getting bolder.

"Now, Allison, you should learn to show some understanding."

"If I make a mistake like talking in class, I get in trouble. I get disciplined. If adults make mistakes, nothing happens. It's not fair. Is it because the Adlers have money? Is that it?"

"I'm not sure why the adoption was handled this way, angel," Sister D said, running her fingers through my hair. "I'm sorry. Unfortunately, money can cause people to disgrace themselves. It gives those with money a power over people who don't have it. But it doesn't make them any happier, only richer. Sometimes it leaves them hollow."

"It's so sad," I said. "That rich people can't share all their money and poor people can't share all their wisdom."

"What a sweet thought, Allison," she said. Her fingers combed through my hair. "But in reality there are both good and bad, smart and ignorant people in all walks of life; rich or poor, we're all on the same ship, sailing toward God's shore."

I knew religion would enter into it. God is always there. I just forgot He has a plan for me. He must have. I know it. I stared at the blurry, unsmiling pope radiating his divinity at me. Mom said to always shine. Sister hugged me tight and kissed my cheek. Then we walked back to my room, where Mary was waiting with juicy comments from the kids about my bravery. Even Joyce Wilkerson, who hates me, thought it was pretty cool. I wasn't brave; I was mad.

Evenwise, tomorrow will be a brighter day. Tomorrow, I will shine.

August 10, 1978

It's been the saddest of all days since the sixth. The saddest of all times. Pope Paul VI passed away. The nuns were upset. I was able to comfort Sister Dena and a few others. I retreated to my garden for comfort. I must have watered a dozen heads of lettuce with my tears.

I've been so busy this summer taking care of the garden. I weeded it daily and watered in the evening just so Mother Superior couldn't change her edict on pesticides.

My garden makes me so happy. I've given away lots of lettuce and tomato sandwiches. The girls love them. The 88s gave me some lipstick as a thank-you, but I don't dare wear it.

I also went to the library to find a book to take my mind off Pope Paul VI's passing. It was the most special experience. I accidentally found a book called the *Sign of the Twisted Candles*. It's absotively amazing how similar the character in the story is to me—trapped in a home. Evenwise, the Nancy Drew mysteries are a godsend. We only have three or four of them. I want to read them all. Someday, I'll be a real-life Nancy Drew detective.

September 30, 1978

Tragedy strikes the Catholic Church again! The new pontiff, John Paul I, died of a heart attack last night. He wasn't on the job long. I didn't have enough time to get attached to the new pope, so I'm not as grief-stricken as I was when Pope Paul passed on.

Many of the nuns are whispering in dim rooms. I don't understand why. Maybe they think it's a bad omen. Was it foul play? Was it murder? My keen private-eye instinct tells me something is amiss in the Vatican. What dark forces are at play here? Allison Leslie Pippin will discover the truth.

I didn't tell anyone, and never will, that I had a dream three days ago about Pope John Paul I. He was in bed in his nightgown. I watched him from the corner of the room. I could hear him breathing, snoring every other breath. The door creaked open and two men in black crept in. They stood above the sleeping pope, snickering, then one put his hands over the pontiff's mouth to keep him quiet. The other man grabbed a pillow and pushed it into John Paul's face. He smothered him. The pope kicked weakly, trying to escape, but he was overpowered. The kicking stopped. John Paul was dead. Murdered.

Was it a premonition? I don't dare tell anyone—ever. What if they came after me? Farewell Albino Luciani, alias John Paul I. I shall miss you.

October 13, 1978

Jesus eating a snowcone at the circus, Journal, you won't believe what happened today! I went to the library to return *The Thirteenth Pearl*, and there were twenty new Nancy Drew books on the shelf. I asked the librarian, Sister Margaret, where they came from, and she just looked at me behind those round, wire-rimmed glasses of hers that make her look like Ben Franklin in drag and smiled. Smiling is not an art she is skilled at. I stared at her, expecting a recitation from *Poor Richard's Almanac*, but she said, "Providence, child, providence. The Lord blesses us all."

That was her answer. The Lord blesses us all, for cheesecake. That's no answer. If anything it's another question. What does Nancy Drew have to do with the Lord's blessing? Couldn't she just say, "We bought them with the money from our bingo receipts." Evenwise, she smiled, and that was that. I shouldn't complain, there are now tons of Drews for me to read. Isn't it great? I certainly, absotively, most positively must have a guardian angel watching over me.

October 23, 1978

We have a new pope. John Paul II, the first non-Italian pope in 455 years. Cheesecake, that's a long time. He's from Poland. He has a gentle face, one you can trust. I'm just positive he will be a great pontiff. Oh, I can just imagine the pageantry of his coronation. The cardinals dressed in their finest scarlet robes, the Vatican bedecked in thousands of flowers and crosses of gold, millions of people jammed into St. Peter's Square. The ceremony performed in Latin, the noble language of God. What I wouldn't do to be there. I love the splendor and goodness of the Church.

November 29, 1978

It's been a month since I last wrote—I've been busy with school work and Thanksgiving and studying hard to become the world's greatest detective. But I just simply had to write in my journal today.

A horrible act occurred in South America. It's all over the news. It's a nightmare. California Congressman Leo Ryan traveled to Guyana to investigate an American religious cult. A few days ago, the news reported Congressman Ryan and his party had disappeared. Turns out he was murdered when his plane landed near Jonestown. He came with a news team from NBC to check out rumors that the Reverend Jim Jones was brainwashing his followers, forcing them to sign over their possessions, and making them perform sex rituals. I don't get how anybody could follow a cult religion like that.

Evenwise, it gets worse. Not only did the religious fanatics murder the congressman and the four people in his group, but the reverend and his followers committed mass suicide. Nine hundred and nine people killed themselves for the Reverend Jim Jones by drinking Kool-Aid laced with cyanide.

God, that's scary. What would make people become so devoted to a religion that they would give up everything they had to live in the jungle? What faith must a person have to sign over one's money to a cult? What evil power must Reverend Jones have had for people to die for him?

They showed pictures on the national news of hundreds of people lying dead next to a big vat of Kool-Aid. It was sick. Very, very sick. People need help. They said the cameraman, Robert Brown, recorded the murders of the congressman and his fellow journalists until the moment Mr. Brown took a bullet in the head. Why? Save yourself— the news can wait. Don't become part of the statistics on behalf of NBC. Was the cameraman as blindly devoted to his company as the cult members were to Jonestown?

How does something like this happen? Why don't people question their beliefs and rely on themselves? One thing I know for sure, I'm not drinking any Kool-Aid for a long time.

I looked through the grit-stained panes of the solarium into the dull August sky. Dried splotches of rain had left their dirty marks like magnified bacteria on a microscope slide. I told myself I'd clean them when I healed, realizing I was telling myself that a lot lately. Prometheus looked toward the house in anguish as the eagle loosed upon him by Zeus tore at his abdomen. My own entrails weren't feeling too good. I chewed a few antacids.

The sun was directly above me. Lunch time, I guessed. High noon. Twinkie was at work, so I had good assurance I'd be eating no hauté cuisine. I'd been sitting in the sunroom for over two hours, reading Allison's journal and seeing it play out in my mind. Whether the messages came via diary or psychic transmission, I was totally spellbound, which seems a near constant state for me since the book forced its way into my life. My belly growled, but I couldn't tear myself away. Rose was at the store buying me a typing book so I can complete this job before I die. Even with her doubt, she supports me. What powerful faith it must take.

Allison lured me in, calling me back to her.

She made it through winter by honing her detective skills (training provided by mystery books) and a strong interest in the new pope, John Paul II. She followed his journeys. She listened to his words, trying her best to believe in them. Allison also became wrapped up in the affairs of Iran, which crumbled under the tortuous regime of the shah. She was appalled at the harsh treatment of women under the Islamic fundamentalists by "some guy nobody ever heard of," the Ayatollah Khomeni. Everyday she read in the paper of the arrest and execution of Iranian citizens who opposed the new revolution. "Why doesn't the pope just call him up and straighten him out?" she asked a surprised Sister Dena.

Her birthday came. Number eleven. April Fools' Day. She chose as her present a subscription to *Detective* magazine. From there, she launched her latest career. That of a gumshoe.

April 26, 1979

It didn't take long to crack my first case. I call it, "The Honeysuckle Affair." I fell into it right away. Here's the skinny (that's detective talk for scoop):

I was skimming the latest Nancy Drew mystery, checking the plotline for validity, per Carolyn Keene's request (she's the author), on a warm spring evening. A light scent of honeysuckle from the garden below hung lazily on the breeze as I edited Carolyn's book, perched in the window of my tiny bedroom, flashlight in hand. I was practicing night surveillance by reading Nancy under cover of darkness. My partner, Mary, lay crashed in her bed. She could sleep through a quadruple chainsaw homicide the way she saws logs. Though she has difficulty making it through stakeouts, Mary is valuable to me anyway.

Evenwise, I'm sitting in the window, carefully scanning the text, when I heard a giggle coming from the garden below. I quickly jumped back into my room and peered over the ledge, careful not to be seen.

"Not yet," a female voice teased as I watched two suspects enter the garden. It was Rita Starks, a fourteen-year-old resident of St. Als, and an unidentified male. "Right here under the lattice of honeysuckle is fine," she said in a sickly sweet voice.

"Are you sure it's okay?" asked the male suspect. He looked to be 5' 4" tall, 125 pounds, brownish hair, wearing a light yellow Windbreaker, jeans, and dirty gym shoes. One untied.

"Mary, Mary wake up," I whispered across the room, but to no avail. She was gone. Stewed tomatoes. Sleepy Gonzales. Jesus on sleeping pills, she was conked out.

I looked back to the action below. They reached for each other, Rita pulling him close to her. "It's just fine, Jason," she said coyly as she kissed him on the lips.

Jason, hmm . . . no Jasons in the orphanage, must be a local boy. How did Rita find him? How did they arrange their meeting? What secret desires brought them together under the half moon in the garden below my window? I lost my thoughts for a minute as I stared at them groping each other. I've never seen two people actually kissing like that before. Yeah sure, I've watched it on TV, but not lip to lip, tongue to tongue stuff. They were really going at it.

"Jason?" Rita moaned as she kissed him madly.

"Hmm?"

"Do you want to feel my breasts?" She pulled up her top. God! I couldn't believe it, Rita was going to second base with a local! Oh my God, I thought I would pee my pants.

"Mary, wake up!" She was out cold, her jaw wide open, giving her teeth some breathing room. She needs braces. But the way things run around St. Als she'll never get them—too expensive they say.

"Do you like my breasts, Jason?" Rita teased as she lifted her bra so he could feel her skin. My mouth dropped open as she put Jason's hand on her breast. I was impressed, she actually had something to feel. They were a nice size to have. Not too big.

"Yes, honey," he exhaled. "Yes, honey. Yes, yes," he said again.

"Then taste them. Suck me," she said. She guided his lips to her breasts.

Cheesecake! He was sucking her tit in the middle of St. Als' garden!

Rita leaned against the lattice as Jason's tongue licked her. She moaned and threw her head back, smiling as she pulled him harder into her. "Suckle it honey, suck—" she said in heat.

Crack! The sound of splintering wood split the night. Rita and Jason went flying backward into the flower bed as the lattice broke from their weight. The broken wood also broke their passion as they hit the ground. Jason was on top of Rita among the mums and petunias and tulips crunched by their weight.

"Shit!" Rita yelled.

"Ouch," Jason said, quickly getting up. He pulled Rita to her feet, lifting smashed flowers from her hair. Her breast hung exposed in the moonlight; its nipple upturned like a perfect banana from a tree. They both stood there for a moment, looking at the crumpled flowers. Their foreplay ruined the garden.

"Shit. Sister Dena is going to kill me," Rita said as she tucked her boob back into her bra and pulled her blouse down.

"I . . . I . . . I gotta go," Jason said. He pecked Rita's lips. "I'll meet you at the usual spot on Monday at ten. Okay?" Then, he disappeared into the night.

Rita tried to pick the lattice up from the flowers, but it was mashed into the dirt pretty well. She pulled on it but couldn't get it free. She looked around cautiously, let go of it, then ran off. A few minutes later, with my ear to the door, I heard her sneak down the hall to her room.

The crime was discovered the next morning. Mother Peculiar stood like an aged granite tombstone on the sidewalk, unmoving and solemn, her hands knotted together behind her gray, college sweatshirt. On Saturdays, by dawn's early light, one can always count on Mother P to wear the football colors of her alma mater. Usually, she walked around with a football under her arm, ready for a day of watching NCAA football, a hobby she shared with Barney and Clod (though they probably watched more out of trying to score points with Mother P than a genuine interest in the sport). Me, I hate football. It's too violent. What's the point? Most Saturdays, while the sound of football matchups droned out of Mother P's office, St. Als security was lax, and The 88s used it as a means of distributing the previous weeks pilferings to the underground network of customers (kids). Others used the lapse in authority to visit the east wing, where a number of secret hideouts were established.

I imagined as Mother P stood there with clenched fists behind her brick back that if she undid her iron clasp, she would punch a hole clean through the first person who walked by. Her temper could not allow a breach of discipline, and it was clear she wanted to accuse, convict, and punish the guilty party before kickoff.

A curious sneer grew on Mother Peculiar's dour face. She was planning revenge.

Sinister and decisive. A look of death. Death for the perpetrator of this heinous crime (I got that line from my *Detective* magazine). I couldn't tell whether she was upset more by the destroyed garden or that she didn't get to catch and punish the criminals. She personally spanks a half-dozen kids a week.

With uncommon courage and daring, I walked over to her and offered the services of Big Al's Detective Agency.

"I am not amused," Mother P said like Queen Victoria.

"We're the eyes and ears of the orphanage. I could break this case wide open." I smiled.

She wasn't impressed. She rolled her eyes, and turned her back, dismissing me. Her gray shadow blotted the sun.

If that's the way she wants it, fine, I told myself. I won't help in her investigation. I'll keep my eye-witness account as privileged information. I'll show her how to snub somebody.

I looked back at Mother P. She was half-heartedly assessing the damage. I could see her mind twirling, the plan taking shape. The corner of her mouth twitched. Peculiar. That's when I realized my nickname for her *was* perfect. Mother Peculiar—it fits. It wasn't a mere fluke when I came up with it, the name *is* dead on target. Providence. I didn't realize when I invented it that her name would catch on so well, just like the nickname of St. Als. I'm still paying the price for both of those creations. Too late, I can't change it now.

I went to my room to get into some work clothes so I could help Sister D clean up her flowers. As I changed, I glanced down at the flower bed and saw her wiping a tear as she sat in the grass opposite her pride and joy. I cried, too. She loves those flowers. I dressed quickly so I could go cheer her up.

When I arrived at the lattice, Sister D greeted me with a smile. "Good morning, Allison. What brings you down here?"

"I'm here to help you replant the flowers," I said cheerfully.

"We best get started then," she said. She pulled out the goners. The goners are the ones that had no chance of surviving, the totally mashed or broken-in-half ones, which turned out to be most of them.

Sister D and I worked silently in the garden for a long time, neither of us speaking, lost in deep thoughts about what had happened. It meant a lot to be the only one out there with her. Without words, just momentary glances, becoming closer.

After a while, we began to talk. She wasn't as upset as I thought. She admitted her disappointment that her flowers had been harmed, but she kept her anger inside. I asked why.

"Even the saints had a bit of bad luck every once in awhile."

"No, really," I replied.

She stopped digging and turned her brightening blue eyes toward me. "God has forgiven me many things. As a child of His Word, I should always emulate Him."

"What's emulate mean?"

"It means that I should try and live by His example. To live in peace and not harbor anger for things that cannot be undone."

"But your flowers are ruined," I said.

"Yes, they are. But they are not my flowers—they are yours and mine and God's. I simply water them for Him and admire His beauty in their petals."

"Well, that's awfully nice of you to not get mad. I wouldn't be so understanding."

"To be truthful, Allison, I was upset. That's human nature, but to transcend that anger to see the grander lesson is more beautiful than the lost flowers."

What lesson could there be in Rita falling into the flower bed during hormonal overload, I thought. "What possible lesson could there be in this?" is what I actually said.

Sister D looked at me, her round face radiant again, thinking of her answer, trying to find the answer in my eyes. "What lesson could there be, Allison?"

"I . . . I don't know," I stammered. She had turned it around. I felt guilty, as if she knew I knew what happened. I was uneasy. My throat tightened. Should I tell her? Should I keep the secret? I couldn't tell on Rita—that would be like betrayal. A death wish inside St. Als. I stared at the destroyed flowers.

"God teaches us daily to respect many principles," Sister D began, clearing dirt around a broken stem. "I'm learning tolerance and understanding for this senseless act. I could have thought that someone had wrecked the garden to spite me, but that would be selfish. I could have looked to punish whomever it was that caused this destruction, but that would be vengeful." She tried vainly to prop up a broken mum. It fell over, lifeless, its spine snapped. "Instead, I look at the cycle of life and realize that broken flowers are like broken hearts; we may find many of each in our lifetime. I choose to mend flowers and hearts rather than dwell in the sorrow they represent."

Wow! That's so beautiful, so deep! She was calm about the one thing, as far as I knew, that really mattered to her—her flowers. The most precious thing in her life lay destroyed around her, and Sister D showed no hatred, no anger. She understood. I wouldn't be understanding if it had happened to my vegetables, I can tell you that.

If she knew Rita was out here panting in heat, getting her honey suckled when the lattice broke, would Sister D be so understanding? I wonder if she would change her mind about the lessons she learned. It's funny, but I know more about what happened than she does, and I see it differently. I don't see God's lesson in this. I see a horny accident that was over in seconds. Sister D saw God's message, as if some heavenly

145

mystery had taken place. I wanted to tell her about it. I wanted to tell the truth. I honestly thought if I told her, maybe she would like me more, or would give me some kind of reward for cracking The Honeysuckle Affair.

But I couldn't spill my guts. The words wouldn't come. Rita didn't mean to ruin the flowers. It just happened, and telling on her would only cause more problems. It wouldn't be right to tell.

We worked quietly until lunch. Sister D must have sensed my hunger. "Allison," she said. "Why don't we go in and have a sandwich and a nice glass of lemonade?"

"Okay," I agreed. "I'm absotively starving."

"Maybe after lunch, Rita would like to help us reset the lattice," she said. My mouth must have dropped to my kneecaps. I looked at her, amazed. Did she know? How did she know? She must know. Why else would she choose Rita out of all the other girls? Is she trying to get me to tell? She must know. She chose Rita.

As we walked toward the kitchen, the sun was just above Sister Dena's head, shining like a halo through her hair. I thought how she always called me her angel and wondered if she wasn't the one who was the angel. I looked at her again, seeing a knowing smile.

April 27, 1979 (8:17 p.m.)

It's Monday night and that means Big Al's Detective Agency is on the case. Being the great detective I am, I can't let tonight's rendezvous between Rita and Jason go by without yours truly observing the dangerous meeting. I'll be there, undercover, to bring back all the dirt, all the sordid details of the honeysuckle lovers' secret encounter.

Mary will stay back at the office to cover for me. Besides, she goes to bed at 8:30. What a sleeper, that girl.

April 27, 1979 (11:42 p.m.)

I shadowed Rita as she snuck down the dormitory hallway, passed the hall monitor's room, down the steps, through the kitchen, and out the back door. It's not the route I would have chosen, but hey, I'm a professional. Evenwise, the suspect proceeded toward the St. Christopher gazebo. It's called that because it's a place to go and pray before the statue of the protector saint. The gazebo is away from the main building by about fifty yards, near the edge of the grounds. Not a bad spot to have sex, actually. Not that I would know, but it's great for surveillance.

I hid myself near the corner of the bell tower, invisible between the wall of the tower and some shrubs. I estimated my distance from the suspect to be approximately twenty to twenty-five feet. The night was dark with the moon peeking in and out of heavy cloud cover. Not a good night for field work, but great for lovers in heat. I had a good vantage point.

The suspect peered about nervously, obviously trying to determine if she was being followed. She was, by the best in the business, but I was no threat to her. I wasn't there to expose her affairs. I was there to find out more about this local boy who had fallen with Rita into the flora and then deserted her. I wanted to know what she saw in this guy that she would risk it all for a couple of hours of exchanging saliva. Sure, I tailed her, but I was no threat.

Rita paced inside the darkened gazebo. There was a light switch on the wall. I doubted she would use it. My watch read six minutes past ten. He was late. Was she mad? Was she afraid? What would the two of them do? Rita had gotten off for trashing the flowers, would it be the same hot romance as before, since their part in The Honeysuckle Affair lay undiscovered? What would happen?

I didn't have to wait long in my position in the bushes.

"Hey, Rita," Jason whispered. The chain-link jangled as he climbed into the orphanage. "How ya doing?" He was out of breath. He must have run to get to her on time.

"You're late."

"I'm sorry, my mom was talking to me in my bedroom, and I couldn't get out any sooner."

"That's okay, honey." Rita sighed as she pulled him close to her.

Yep, that was it, no wasting time for Rita—her sex drive was in high gear. She kissed him deeply on the mouth, their tongues wrestling each other.

Whoosh! Bright lights! Cheesecake, it was a bust by the nun squad! I dropped to the ground behind the bushes, my heart pounding, bits of mulch stuck to my lips. Mother Superior, Barney Rubble, and Clod rushed toward the gazebo like John Wayne in *Sands of Iwo Jima.*

"Stay where you are," Mother Superior called out with a bullhorn.

Cheesecake, how dramatic, a bullhorn to catch two teenage lovers.

"Yeah," Clod echoed. "Stay where you are."

God! It *was* effective, though. For a moment, I was frozen, wondering if they knew I was hidden next to the bell tower. I wasn't taking any chances. I crawled on my stomach to the door of the tower, my hands scratched by dirt and rocks. I carefully reached up to try the handle. Unlocked—great. I turned it slowly, careful not to make a sound, pushed the door open slightly, and slid inside. It was pitch black. I leaned my back against the door and breathed a sigh of relief. I wiped my sweaty palms on my jeans. My heart still raced, but I was safe. Nancy would have been proud of me.

I gathered myself together, slowed my breathing after a few moments, and decided to crack the door open to see the action. Mother Superior, giant stone Amazon, scolded the suspects as the sisters nodded their approval of her reprimand. Rita's face was flushed, tears running down her cheeks. Jason was scared, his face bowed toward the ground, arms crossed. They were in big trouble.

147

I couldn't hear what Mother Superior was dishing out, so I opened the door a bit wider. No better. The light from the floods poured into the bell tower. I didn't feel safe with the floodlights covering the grounds, but I had no choice. I had to know when it would be safe to sneak back in.

Just when would that be? Obviously, they had to take Rita back to her room. That would be after a long conversation, which I hoped would take place in Mother Peculiar's office. That would mean I could climb to my room via the fire escape. If they went to the main room, I'd have to take the same route I used before. No good. I'd get caught for sure. Please, God, help me, I prayed.

The chastising ended as the soldiers escorted their prisoners toward the main building. All the rooms were lit like a hotel during Mardi Gras, the windows occupied by curious kids watching the public arrest of Rita and her lover boy. The whole orphanage was awake, and the sisters would probably go room to room to quiet the children and make sure they went back to sleep. I looked to my room; it was dark. God bless Mary, she slept through it all. Maybe the nuns would pass by our room and I would be safe. Maybe.

I peered from my hiding spot behind the door as Mother Peculiar and her troops brought Jason and Rita up the path toward the house. Her giant stature towered over the infidels as she railed about the virtues of a young woman and the responsibilities of the Church and the like. Just as they passed the door, Rita turned her tearful head sideways, smiled coyly at me, and winked.

Jesus getting his picture taken at a peep show, I was discovered. Did anyone else know I was hidden in the tower? No. No way, they would have nabbed me, too. I would've been listening to the same sermon from Mother Peculiar as Rita if they knew. Cheesecake, Rita took chances, but I was cool for now.

They walked on and soon disappeared inside the big house. The faces of the other kids quickly left the windows and the curtains fell back in place.

I waited two or three minutes and made my way to the fire escape. I climbed the ladder like a cat (hey, I'm a professional), and made it back to my room without being noticed. God, it was great. What a thrill to be so close to danger but not getting in it. My panties were wet, I'm not sure if I peed them or not. What a feeling, though. God! I can't wait for my next case.

May 9, 1979

I've decided. After careful consideration and long deliberation (I read that in the paper), I am hanging up my gumshoes for the world of international intrigue. That's right, I'm Special Agent Pippin, international spy. Member of the CIA and the NSA, arch enemy of the KGB.

I've had my successes on the domestic scene, now I need the danger and jet-set action of foreign shores. I'm ready to be a supersleuth. My code name is Red Angel, and

I've been assigned a dangerous mission. I have special instructions to meet my contact in the bell tower on the sixteenth of May at four p.m.

I'm skilled in seven languages, am a practicing black belt in taekwondo, and can kill a man from twenty yards with a hairbrush. I'm not a bad cook, either.

Of course, I'm just kidding about all this, but I do like to pretend. Keeps the wit sharp, the senses crisp, the mind clear. Until the sixteenth, mon ami, adieu.

Chapter 13

May 16, 1979

I found the most absotively perfect spot today. A place where I can be alone, see the world, and it can't see me. Such an enchanting place of mystery. Such history. A place to explore and imagine. The bell tower.

I was a spy on a secret mission. The Red Angel drawn to a clandestine rendezvous by a mysterious note from the director of the CIA himself. The intrigue was thick as I tiptoed silently toward the meeting place. Was I alone? Or were agents of the KGB waiting in ambush for me? I had my lipstick laser and eye shadow nerve gas dispenser in my superspy purse.

The Soviets are clever, so I best be cautious. I quietly edged to the end of the hall leading to the door of the bell tower. I peeked around the corner looking for signs of another human presence: nothing. Good. The mission seemed secure. I took the lid off my laser lipstick and clutched it securely, ready for a quick blast just in case I had underestimated my adversary. My finger twitched nervously on the trigger.

In the spy biz, you trust no one but yourself. You can't trust your friends, your relatives, or your country. Life is too fickle, the stakes too high. It's just you, your weapon, and your wits. That's all.

I snuck across the hall to the olive door and cracked it open. I peered into the darkness through the narrow slit. Something moved behind me in the hallway. Who was it? I had no time to react. Instinct and years of espionage training took over.

"Hi yea!" I shouted as I let go with the full force of my lipstick.

"Yvonne!" shrieked Mother Superior as she put her arms up in self-defense. It was too late though; her habit was already stained by the attack.

"Oh, I'm so sorry, Mother Superior, ma'am," I apologized.

She stood there, formidable in her drab gray smock loose enough to accommodate her bulk, looking like a slab of unforgiving cement, tempted to assign me kitchen duty or swats for my misdeed. Oddly, her temper flared, then left her. She gauged the damage to her ugly outfit, not much more than a feedbag.

"Yvonne, I understand you have an active imagination, and that sometimes you get carried away in a make-believe world. But if you could please restrain yourself from getting too involved in your characters I would very much appreciate it."

Well, all I could do was stand there in shock. Normally, I would have been severely disciplined to the point of tears. She was being nice to me. Too nice. Polite even. I had marked up her clothes with red lipstick. Girls aren't even supposed to have lipstick at St. Als. What was up? Was this really Mother Superior or a KGB agent in a clever disguise? The thought crossed my mind, but I didn't question the suspect. I decided to mentally file this incident for future reference and possible reconnaissance.

"Yes, Mother Superior," I said quietly.

She stalked off down the hall, muttering, the floor shaking under her footsteps.

Alone again. I opened the door to the tower and quietly crept up the steps, one by one, careful to step on the edges to prevent them from creaking. It's an old spy trick, and great for sneaking around St. Alexandria when you need to get to the kitchen for some munchies at midnight. As I reached the top of the stairs, I breathed the dusty wood smell of fifty years. I opened the door into bright sunshine, which poured in, dousing me in glorious light. Sweet air filled my lungs. There, hanging in the center of the tower, was a large bell, rusted and lonely, taller than me. It was surrounded by a walkway so it could ring free. The iron was chipped, flaking off from years of weather. The old girl was tarnished and faded. She was absotively beautiful.

I looked out from the tower beyond the grounds and saw a new world. There was the usual neighborhood scene of Reading Road and the Twin Drive-In and the Norwood Lateral, but at a completely different way-up-high angle. What a view! I saw spring green trees, the tops of downtown skyscrapers, and birds flying by, carrying straw as they busily built nests. I sucked in the fresh spring air as if I had never smelled it before, my heart leaping in wondrous discovery. This is my place. I claim this in the name of Allison Leslie Pippin—the Red Angel.

This will be my special spot, where I can read my books and write in my journal. It is so absotively beautiful up above everything, as if St. Als and the kids in it are very, very small. As if I am bigger than my problems. This is a place to shine. The bell tower, secluded and deserted, rising high above the city, shall be my place of freedom until I am released unto the world.

From her perch high above the world Allison was free. Immediately, whenever weather permitted, she made daily visits to her secret place, bringing with her an armful of books, the day's newspaper, and her journal. This became her spot, a sacred realm that only she knew of. The other kids could have their den of thieves and their cubby holes in the east wing, but this, oh, this was where Allison belonged.

On bright days, when the wind was blowing, she'd lean over the railing, face to the sun, feeling the exquisite ecstasy of her wild hair floating like a red kite. She pretended to be carried away by the breeze, a crimson ribbon loosed from a princess's bow. From her bell tower, she was the queen of the city; its citizens were her patrons. She could see the clouds and almost touch them. She could flap her arms and pretend to fly. Twirl about like Julie Andrews on a mountain top. Up above it all, she was more than an orphan—she was a woman of the world. She fantasized a hundred cherished thoughts. She dreamed of meeting the pope. And of meeting her father, although she was sure she wouldn't know what to say to either. But they were her dreams—and hers alone. No one could touch them. No one could interrupt them. No one would laugh at them. And Allison, the Red Angel of the bell tower, came to adore this most secret of places.

May 30, 1979

The most absotively incredible thing just happened. Another miracle. I was up in the bell tower around 7 o'clock tonight, reading the newspaper, making notes in my journal, when a magical pure white bird appeared. It was a sign from God. He has heard me. He has come.

The bird's name is Homer, and he is a beautiful white dove owned by a guy named Danny. He had a note on his leg from his owner. It was so cute. The sun was cooling down a little, but it was still bright and warm. I was just getting ready to pack up my things to go jump rope with Mary when he fluttered in, landing gracefully on the railing. He cocked his head at me, cooing softly, almost like he was asking me to take the note.

My hands were shaking as I removed it. I've never been that close to a bird before.

"It's okay, pretty boy, I won't hurt you."

Homer cooed.

I stroked the feathers behind his head as he rubbed against me. Such a soft bird. I read the short note as my heart thumped. I ripped a page out of my journal and wrote back.

> Dear Danny,
>
> Homer has landed in my special reading place. My name is Allison. I'm looking for a friend too. I'd love to write and get to know you. I hope Homer remembers how he got here and knows how to make it back. He seems like a really smart bird.
>
> I'm a damsel locked in a tower, waiting for my knight to rescue me. Will you save me?
> Sincerely,
> Allison
>
> p.s.—I was real careful with the rubber band.

I finished my note, rolled it tight, held it to my bosom for a moment and said a prayer. Then I placed it back on Homer's leg.

"Fly, boy," I said, tossing him into the air. His bright wings flapped wildly, and he swooped out a few feet, then came back to the railing. "Now, Homer, you sweet bird, how can I get a message back to your master if you don't fly home?" His head bobbed up and down playfully, begging me to rub him.

He's a happy fellow, not at all like the birds I've seen hanging about, pecking at scraps. He's dignified. Majestic. Evenwise, Homer wasn't about to go anywhere, so I stayed and talked to him for awhile. It was like he was trying to keep me company. I told him all about life at St. Als and how I felt about living here so terribly long without being adopted. I couldn't help myself, I cried a little, more like a whimper. He hopped onto my shoulder and pecked my cheek with little bird kisses. That made me laugh. But, as much as I try and be upbeat, I'm sad about being stuck here. Why haven't I been adopted? Doesn't anybody want me?

After an hour or so, I told Homer I had to go in because the sisters would be looking for me. Just like that, he flew off. I watched him climb high into the sky, flapping his wings as they carried him north toward his master, Danny.

I know his arrival was a sign, a message from God Himself. He is a symbol of peace, of love. My days of being stuffed away in an orphanage are almost over. A pure white bird has landed—an omen from God of His providence has come.

I'm here, Danny. Come save me. Please.

Chapter 14

November 7, 1942

Sulphur pressed his heels against the dark corner of the balcony, his sweaty hand gripping the cold revolver to his chest. He closed his eyes, praying he wouldn't have to use it. He wedged his tightened back and shoulders into the sandstone wall. He scarcely breathed. His tense abdomen was sucked into his ribs, for fear of being discovered outside the suite of General Nogues, commander of the French Vichy forces in Morocco.

The fateful words which placed him on the balcony, inches from the enemy, rang in his ears.

"Allo, Robert," the BBC broadcast had signaled. "Franklin arrive."

These were the words he had waited four months to hear. All his covert training, all his activities depended on those words for his deadly talents to be unleashed. Sirens shrieked throughout the besieged city. Gunfire could be heard near the docks. Explosions ripped the sleep off Casablanca. Fireballs from the oil terminal mushroomed into the sky, bringing daylight at one a.m.

Sulphur grinned satisfaction, knowing it was his network of saboteurs creating the destruction. Operation Torch had begun.

He wished he could watch. Quickly peek his head around the corner and stare at the beauty of the devastation. He dare not. It would mean certain death. From his vantage point, the only thing he could see was the shadowy Mohammed standing in an alley smoking a cigarette, waiting patiently to speed him away from the crime scene. An assassin needs a getaway driver.

He adjusted the gun in his palm as his resentment grew. It isn't fair, he told himself of Colonel Eddy's decision that Sulphur be the one. I should be out there blowing up trains, detonating plastique, having fun, he thought. He reconciled himself to his orders. He knew he was the best operative to neutralize the leader of an Axis counterattack.

Light emanated from the suite. Sulphur brought his attention back to the voices planning strategy inside. Frenzied words exchanged in French. General Nogues was meeting with his staff, poring over maps, arguing whether to fight or assist. Heatedly, they discussed defensive options for repelling the American invasion. Two of the officers were informants. A third would comply with anything the others agreed upon. That left General Nogues as the only obstacle to the U.S. victory in North Africa.

Sulphur fidgeted, his mouth dry as Moroccan sand. When will the phone ring? Please. Please ring. He stretched his numb fingers, wrapped around the weapon, careful to keep his index finger on the trigger. Welcome blood rushed into his joints. Come on phone, ring. He wanted off the balcony, preferably without putting a bullet through the commander's temple. If the call came soon, there would still be time for him to make the three a.m. detonation of the railyard fuel supply. His eyes widened as he envisioned the wreckage of twisted metal caused by his handiwork. He could almost smell the smoke and diesel. He could almost smell the inviting, thick cloud of combustion.

The phone ringing split his daydream.

Sulphur quietly cocked the gun. He leaned ever so slightly forward to listen. Dear God, he thought, make the right choice. He swallowed hard, his throat like tangled barbed wire, as he waited for the general's reply. The call came from Admiral Darlan, commander of French forces in North Africa, at the insistence of Bob Murphy, American diplomat extraordinaire, with explicit instructions to assist the United States in its efforts to take North Africa. The general hedged. There were jack-booted Nazis to deal with, he argued.

Sulphur imagined the French admiral, with information from Murphy, detailing the strength of the American invasion force to the shocked general—110,000 troops would be coming ashore within two hours. The general, his face ashen from the intelligence report, adjusted his collar, summoned that infamous French dignity in the midst of defeat, and agreed to offer no resistance.

Sulphur exhaled deeply, relieved. He would execute no one this night. He secured the cocked revolver, heard the catch of the safety and relaxed the finger off the trigger. The spy turned would-be assassin turned arsonist smiled as he shimmied down the tile drainpipe to the street. He would make his three o'clock appointment.

Section

The intruder bids welcome in false sincerity
And proceeds to devour all the fruits before him
Who licensed the forger to gorge at will from the hostess
Leaving her weak and barren with nothing but seed

Chapter 15

August 12, 1990

Homer landing upon Allison's bell tower was a conscious act of fate, a divine intervention. It cannot be disputed. Invisible forces of compassionate destiny were at work. From Danny's backyard in Colerain to Allison's lonely orphanage would be too far a stretch of coincidence. No. The gods, the Council of Ancients in God's clothing, facilitated the bird's arrival. I am certain of this. For what purpose, I, like you, do not yet know. Perhaps this shall be revealed as we venture further into the text.

The fact that Rose, acting entirely on her own, came home from the store with a surprise gift to aid my conscripted endeavors was also the result of strings being pulled by the Council. Yes, the gods stepped in again to arm me, manifesting an act of predestiny. It cannot be denied. A sign, Rose calls it. A whim, I might have said, if all the remarkable circumstances of the last ten days hadn't presented themselves in dramatic, unmistakable fashion. A bullet in the back, a live, thinking book, my sudden psychic vision, and incessant death threats tend to open one's eyes. A new paradigm, as trendy business types might say, and with one's eyes so wide open, the signs are as prominent as neon on the Vegas strip.

"R.T.," Rose said, crinkling her nose. She detected the stench of disease in the solarium, strode to the glass door and slid it open. She glanced at the pan at my feet. "Are you still vomiting?"

I nodded, embarrassed.

"Maybe Dr. Finkleday can do something about that when he takes the bandages off Monday," Rose said. Her mint green eyes twinkled. "And that darn cough, too."

I'm not so much worried about the cough as I am the pain in my groin. It hurts to pee—I've written that off to having a catheter shoved up my urethra for three days—but it should have subsided by now.

"Did you get the typing book?" I asked, feeling a bit cranky.

"No," she said smugly. "Better than that. I bought you a computer." I was shocked. Speechless. Elated. "Now don't you let that conservative nature of yours dismiss it," Rose said, "before I have a chance to explain its virtues."

I started to mention our impending bankruptcy but decided against it. We've become good at avoiding unpleasant conversation. Neither of us wants to talk about selling off the antiquities, the art, or worse. I couldn't bare to see Rose lose her home.

There would be no talk of bankruptcy. I nodded instead, and listened intently, knowing I had no choice in the matter. Rose was on a roll, pleased that even though she had doubts about *The Journals*, as well as my innocence, she was determined to support me.

"A carpenter needs a hammer," she said happily. "A gardener needs a hoe, and a writer needs a word processor."

And with that pronouncement I became the proud owner of an Apple Macintosh. I'm typing on it now. Rose is a godsend.

I must confess.

I know Danny and Allison. Personally. Not in the way their journals describe, but as acquaintances whose lives briefly crossed my path a few years ago. I knew their father well. Far too well, God rest his soul. Patrick was a man I wish I'd never met—a dangerous manipulator who stopped at nothing to attain his goals. The worst possible business partner. It's hard to believe he was their father.

Reading their journals has changed me, humbled me. From what I knew, I couldn't have guessed, couldn't have imagined their past. They were kids. Innocent and likable. Nothing special. Nothing extraordinary. Certainly nothing celestial about them.

My head is humming with a thousand questions. I am awestruck by the complexity of human connections. What does it mean? How does their history entwine with mine? Why is my present entangled in their past? Should I go to St. Als? I've had the strongest urge to see it. There's something there I'm meant to find. Something about Allison. Should I go? Parker sure picked a helluva time to be out of town. The seventeenth will have to do. I pray it's soon enough.

Where is *The Journals* when I need it? Arizona. Doing reconnaissance work. Hah! Lounging about on vacation no doubt, hanging me out to dry. Or wrecking someone else's peaceful existence. There's so much work to be done and no one around to do it. I need help. I can't do this on my own.

Rose is in the kitchen, talking Twinkie out of making peanut-butter, pumpkin soup for dinner. She's been on a peanut-butter recipe kick ever since my plain PJ request. I've lost my appetite lately, which is odd because I'm a big eater. Bland soup is all I want, standard fare. Chicken noodle. Vegetable. Rose's famous potato soup. Anything but one of Twinkie's concoctions. Some of the smells from the Stone kitchen are reminiscent of a Hoffman-Laroche chemistry experiment. I've had a spot of trouble holding food down. There's a battle going on inside, and I'm not sure who's winning.

Speaking of war, Hussein, lunatic that he is, made an interesting proposal today. He'll withdraw from Kuwait if Israel withdraws from the occupied territories. That guy has balls. I'm not sure he recognizes the full might of the U.S. military. We have the strongest, best equipped fighting force in history. The U.S. military outspends the top twenty-five nations combined on defense. Almost three-hundred billion a year. We have weapons so secret even the president doesn't know about them. Bush isn't going to back off this one. I can feel it. He smells oil. The government treated Iraq's proposal as a joke. God, I hope we don't go to war. I've seen too much of it, been too near it. No one wins.

What is this world coming to? It's all topsy-turvy. Here I am, R.T. Stone, new computer owner, official icon of the nonbeliever, born-again human being, writing of angels and officers from remote galaxies. I had no idea they existed two weeks ago. My entire life has been spent *not* thinking of philosophical things. I was grounded firmly in the physical world. This was my credo: you can keep all that New Age crap. But that was before. I've been transformed.

August 17, 1990

A day of surprises. (What's new, huh?) Parker was scheduled to come for lunch to discuss the case. I had cleverly arranged for Twinkie to take a day off work to prepare the meal, a sacrifice I was willing to make in the interest of playing Cupid. Maybe they could make amends. One can always hope.

Rose had to make an emergency dash to the market because Twinkie had forgotten the Gruyère for the asparagus-arugula frittata. Who could blame her? She had remembered everything else. She completely outdid herself for the occasion. The menu consisted (and I do not embellish) of the aforementioned asparagus-arugula frittata as an appetizer, winter squash sticks, deep fried in cornbread batter, smothered in peach glaze as the vegetable, and Beefaroni sesame-seed fajitas served cold with dill sauce as the main course. I almost called Parker to cancel.

Twinkie, dear hamster that she is, was harried during the preparations and had to jump in the shower just prior to Parker's scheduled arrival. We would talk and have lunch later. I hoped that Parker would once again be smitten by my Twinkie. Once I heard the luncheon menu, I knew this was not to be.

The bell rang. I hobbled as best I could to answer it, prepared to greet Parker with a robust handshake and welcome grin. Instead, there on the stoop, in a wrinkled brown polyester leisure suit with wide lapels stitched in yellow, and a thin orange and mango tie that hung from his neck like a suicide victim's bed sheet, stood a twitching sparrow of a man. Brian McBain stared at me behind a twisted pair of wire framed glasses. Behind him was a more unwelcome site—the buzz cut, bad attitude, bulldog face of the Hamilton County Prosecutor—Sylvester Rense. Behind him stood two burly gentlemen

161

with mustaches, sunglasses, closely cropped hair, and mismatched sport coats and trousers. Plain clothes detectives, I assumed. Behind them, across the street, my next door neighbor, Mr. Bing, stared, no doubt wondering what I had done now.

I've never gotten to know Bing all that well. He's Asian, I think. Made his fortune in collapsible lawn furniture. Bing Chair-Ease he called them, and, amused at his own wit, laughed all the way to the bank. He waved. I pretended not to notice and turned my attention to the four intruders on my porch.

"Mister . . . um . . . Mister Stone, sir, I'm here with these gentlemen—unless, of course—well that doesn't matter—well, you see, sir, I'm here to—that is—I have a search warrant." He pushed the writ at me. Sylvester Rense and his buffoons smirked. McBain's pupils buzzed around the perimeter of the porch to avoid direct eye contact, but failed to find a safe place to land.

I didn't know how to react. "Come on in," I said. Sucker punched by life again. They entered the foyer.

"I see you collect—oh, those are nice, never seen anything like—these must be worth a—how long have you been, oh goodness," McBain stammered. "You collect antiquities. How interesting."

"And matchbooks," Rense added.

"Not really," I said. "I just pick them up wherever I travel. After fifty years you get quite a few."

"Curious, most curious hobby for a man, who—well, a man accused of arson," McBain said.

"Who is it, Daddy?" Twinkie called from the top of the stairs, dripping wet in a towel wrapped around her body. She rubbed her hair dry with the other. "Oh my God!" she squealed and scampered off.

"Shit," I said, under my breath. I took the warrant from McBain and inspected it. "You guys wait here while I phone my attorney."

"Sorry, Stone," Rense insisted as he pushed through. "That ain't the way it works."

I stalked to the kitchen and plugged in the phone, which I've kept unplugged to limit the crank calls and death threats from friends and family of the *alleged* victims of my arsonist plot. Behind me I could hear Rense utter, "Did you see that scar on his face?"

I dialed Bennett's office and thought of the irritating Rense standing in my foyer. I'd had my run-ins with him before, thanks to Gilday, over Zimmer and Fernald. He pursued me with a vengeance. He made it personal. There was no doubt in my mind, as Rense and his goons examined my antiquities with an uneducated yet discerning eye, that he was accompanying McBain as part of his ongoing vendetta. He resented his embarrassment in the press, having previously boasted of my imminent conviction, when he was forced to drop the charges against me. Rense had been occupying his time as of late with making Cincinnati a national joke with his pious moral crusades against smut. A campaign which most Cincinnatians, if asked, would call mean-spirited censorship by a lonely man with a sick fetish for prosecuting those with tastes dissimilar to his own.

Bennett wasn't in. A junior associate advised me to sit tight until he could locate Jim. Twinkie bounded down the steps humming the *Dragnet* theme just as I rejoined the interrogation squad, one of whom was videotaping the articles in my foyer.

"Expensive pieces, Mr. Stone," Rense said.

"Why, Mr. McBain," Twinkie blushed, "what are you doing here? Papa, you shouldn't keep these gentlemen here in the hall. Let's go to the kitchen."

Before I could say a word, Twinkie led the entourage into the kitchen. Rense, who couldn't wait to uncover some diabolical evidence against me, followed her, the two goons trailing him. McBain lingered behind, examining the Nabu.

The doorbell rang. I hoped it was Parker. I was feeling outnumbered. Twinkie was offering morsels of home-cooked delicacies to the law enforcement members who had invaded my house. McBain looked at me pensively.

"Want me to get—I mean I could—what with your back, I—"the D.A. stuttered.

"Yeah," I interrupted him. "That'd be nice."

"Pink!" McBain said.

"Hel . . . low Swami. Brian, I didn't expect you to answer the door," Parker said. "Small damn world, eh fella?"

"Come on in," McBain said. "What's with the—that is . . . um—what's with the carrot?"

"Better vice than smoking," Parker said. He took a bite out of the carrot he was holding in his left hand and swallowed. "Healthier. Habit I picked up in India. Say, fella, I saw your commercial on TV. Pretty snazzy."

"Aw," McBain said shyly. "You know how it is when you run for office."

"Mayor of Covington, that's big doings, Brian."

Jesus, I thought to myself, so that's it, McBain is running for mayor. He's going to make this a high profile, winner-take-all case so he can win the election. Parker was thinking the same.

"Awful risky, fella, taking a case like R.T.'s in an election year," he warned, nibbling on his carrot.

Parker always had a carrot in his mouth, not a carrot stick, but the whole enchilada with the exception of the nubby end. It's a peculiar habit. He nibbles on the edges of the thing like an anorexic guinea pig. He stares as he nibbles, thinking, his eyes fixed on objects, looking through them, like x-ray vision, only he's not looking through to see what's on the other side; he's looking inside to find the truth of the object. As if he can see its energy, some hidden spectrum unattainable by normal human eyes. Ever since his pilgrimage to the Middle East, he's eaten well. Sometimes he gnaws on celery.

"Lose the case, lose the election," he warned McBain, with a healthy chomp of the orange root.

That's another thing about Parker. He usually just sucks or nibbles on his carrot, cajoles it like a lollipop, but when he has a definitive comment, or some illuminating idea he's just discovered through those sonar eyes and clear mind of his, he takes a loud, crunching bite of carrot for emphasis. The bite is an exclamation mark of inspiration. When Parker bites down, some truth is to be told.

"Open and shut," McBain smirked, the firmest three words I ever heard him speak. "The election is near, and the trial isn't for awhile, so the case isn't even coming—well, Stone won't be in court until this is—that is to say—I'll be mayor before Stone is convicted."

"Don't be too sure." Parker chuckled. I love his laugh, genuine and rich, deep within his body. "Still have Reds season tickets?"

"Fourth row blue," McBain said proudly. "They're in first, that is they've been playing—you know, they could go all the—Pinella's got a good team."

"I see you two know each other." I interrupted the reunion while I worried about the Hamilton County detectives rummaging through my possessions.

"No sense getting jealous, R.T." Parker grinned, holding the carrot in his hand like a fine Cuban cigar. "I still love you." He sauntered over and embraced me, careful to hug my upper body and avoid my stitches.

"Good to see you," I said.

"We haven't hooked up since the winter solstice of `88," Parker said, sniffing. "Twinkie been cooking again?"

"Afraid so," I whispered, then coughed.

"Man, R.T., you sound worse than a leukemia patient on a Tobacco Institute test panel! You should see a doctor." He smiled easily, his boyishness surprising me, as it always does. He tossed his head to the right, flipping his chestnut ponytail over his back, exposing a diamond earring. His tan skin showed no trace of whiskers on a smooth face that refused to grow up. Parker's Pacific-blue eyes scanned the room, taking everything in, capturing all the light, all the features, sucking in detail like a visual vacuum. Thin brows hovered delicately over his inquisitive eyes and long dark lashes, like a Venus Fly Trap. Parker is a man who takes in the essence of the situation in vivid color and a sense of wonder, but projects back only what he doesn't need. He keeps the truth to himself. One gets the impression that there's a special reality that only Parker sees.

We entered the kitchen. Parker nibbled as he studied the food on the countertop. "Boys," he nodded to Rense and his crew of professional ransackers who lurked about, inspecting every inch of the kitchen, family room, and solarium.

"Parker," Rense acknowledged gruffly while the others mumbled.

"Got your hands full busting up art exhibits?" Parker chided the prosecutor, referring to the ill-fated Mapplethorpe exhibit that Rense and his Puritans had closed back in April.

Rense had arrested the director of the Contemporary Arts Center on pandering obscenity charges and tried to shut down the show despite protests from thousands of demonstrators in the streets. It was the first time an art museum had ever been brought up on such charges. His action had earned Cincinnati negative national publicity and the dubious title of Censornati. The trial takes place in a few weeks. I took it by Parker's remarks that he didn't agree with Rense's decision to impose his personal moral standards on the general population.

Rense snarled like a dog deciding whether to bite a leg or lick himself. "I'm just upholding family values," he growled. "Community standards are important."

Parker grinned, the carrot wedged tight in his teeth, and chomped down hard as he stared directly into the eyes of the D.A. A lump appeared in Parker's right cheek like a large wad of baseball player's chaw. "You can't legislate morality, Rense." Parker's eyes mocked him. "There's this little document called the Constitution that protects society from zealots like you and your wealthy elitist backers."

Rense's bodyguards stepped closer to their fearful leader and huddled in a defensive posture. "You freaking liberals make me sick," Rense said. He turned away to avoid further confrontation.

Parker laughed and winked at me. "When you going to stop making Cincinnati the laughingstock of the nation?"

Rense walked into the family room, seething I'm sure, but unable to defend his position to anyone in America except Christian Coalition fanatics.

McBain examined the hors d'oeuvres, as if deciding whether to interrogate them. Twinkie, brimming with unexplained happiness, picked up a tray and pushed it toward him. "Want one?" she asked with a teen crush.

"Sure looks delicious." He licked his lips. "If you don't—that is if you're not expecting—maybe just—sure, I'll have one." The others begged off, too busy videotaping and searching for clues to my devious past.

"So, how do you guys know each other?" I asked as I kept a watchful eye on the detectives.

McBain had his mouth full of peach-oozing squash so Parker answered. "I did a sub-job for the D.A.'s office in northern Kentucky. Forgery, wasn't it, Brian?"

The D.A. nodded, vainly trying to keep the peach syrup off his sticky chin. No luck. He reached for another. "You ought to try these, Pink. They're terrific."

"No thanks," Parker said, patting his carrot, much to Twinkie's pouting chagrin. "I'm good for now."

"Okee dough," McBain said, gobbling up another. "That was a good case, we really locked—well it was mostly you—I mean I had to try the—but you did all the hard stuff, busted them good. Insurance fraud, wasn't it, Pink?"

"That it was," the detective said. "Man, was that fun. They actually tried to pull a double switch by selling their paintings in Europe, then having the forgeries stolen from themselves here. Double-dipped. Pretty tricky, that one." He ended in a British accent.

Rense and his people sequestered themselves together near the step to the family room and talked in whispers.

"What brings you out to see Mr. Stone?" McBain asked as I took a seat. They remained standing at the island counter. McBain, doing his utmost to appear suave in front of Twinkie, leaned against the counter *à la* Cary Grant.

Parker wrinkled his brow curiously, took the carrot from his mouth and examined it with eyes like a sealed indictment. The question would not be answered. He never divulged his client's reasons. "What brings you?"

McBain's eyes found Twinkie's frittata. "I—well, it's kind of like—we are actually looking—it's all part of the—me and the Hamilton County—"

"We're here on a search warrant!" Rense barked from the family room.

I never liked that guy.

The awkward D.A. pecked at another squash stick, smearing it in extra peach glaze, avoiding eye contact at all costs. Twinkie blinked bashfully at him while snubbing Parker.

Suddenly, pandemonium broke loose. Twinkie, ever the klutz, bounded to the refrigerator and somehow managed to trip over nothing. Simultaneously, McBain's arm slipped on the counter, slid across the slick surface, and smashed with surprising force into the covered serving tray of Beefaroni fajitas that had taken all morning to prepare. Twinkie was on her butt as the fajitas launched into mid-air. The fajitas jettisoned their aluminum-tray booster rocket and flew into orbit with a trajectory that splattered a half-dozen Beefaroni-laden flour tortillas squarely on her knee caps. The remaining fajitas ejected and crashed in various linoleum locations. The eagle had landed.

Parker helped Twinkie to her feet. She slipped on a slimy piece of noodle. He kept hold to keep her from landing on her rump again.

"Didn't you two meet this way?" I tried a weak attempt at match-making, referring to the night at a local restaurant when Twinkie (somewhat attractive then) managed to break the switch on the soft-serve ice-cream dispenser. A steady flow of creamy vanilla-chocolate swirl relieved itself on the floor like an unending pile of dog doo. Twinkie, frantic, yelled across the restaurant, "Papa. Please help!"

Parker, who was eating a cheeseburger and fries in a nearby booth, jumped to the rescue, but not before she stepped on the sugary glop and landed on her keister. I wanted to sue. Bennett said no. It wasn't the most romantic of ways to meet one's future spouse, and it may have been a foreboding of things to come, but that is indeed how Twinkie and Parker met.

Twinkie, Beefaroni running down her legs, gave me a glare as ominous as a Titan missile.

"You all right?" Parker asked, holding her upright.

"Still playing cops and robbers, Parker?" she said tersely.

"Sort of set the stage for our marriage, didn't it, that first night?"

McBain gulped. "You two were—I mean, lived together, in holy—actually were—when did this—how long—you're divorced now, right?"

"Righto," Parker said, nibbling away a little too smugly for Twinkie's liking.

"Thank goodness," she simmered, red from the incident. She wiped the disgusting entree off with a paper towel. "*Papa,*" she stressed, "you take the company into the family room while I deal with this? Okay?"

There was no saying no. I started to inform Twinkie that these intruders were not company, but it would have done no good.

We adjourned to the family room. Me and Parker took the beige-striped sofa Rose absolutely had to buy during a Moonlight Madness sale six years ago, and McBain selected my favorite recliner. The three musketeers from Hamilton County stood and inspected the backyard, with the bulldog, Rense, looking anxious to gnaw into something. My stomach was queasy. My penis felt like a number two pencil had been crammed in sideways.

"Something to drink?" I said nervously, thinking civility may lessen their vigilance and hasten their departure.

"Coffee would be good," Parker said. McBain agreed. The defenders of justice shook their firm heads no as they filmed away.

"Twinkie!" I shouted. "Would you bring some coffee?"

No response. I could hear her nerves percolating from the kitchen.

"I'll get it," Parker said.

He left the room, carrot in tow. Knowing him, I'm sure he went to assuage Twinkie's hurt feelings. He's kind that way.

McBain fidgeted, stuffed an errant shirt tail back in his pants, eyed the portraits over the fireplace, then let his eyes wander about the place.

"Whew . . . eee," McBain said. "This is an expensive—I mean it's a large—I couldn't begin to afford—how many square feet is this place?"

"About seven thousand," I said. "Why?"

"No reason, just curious, always found it interesting to—that is, what wealth can—holy cow!" He rose to his feet and pointed. "Look at that. What is it?"

Rense stepped back from the sliding glass door and meandered around the family room, his eyes floating from object to object, looking for clues to my guilt.

"I call it the Path of Prometheus," I said.

"Sensational backyard," Rense said, a hint of resentment present in his voice as he inspected the spoon collection. He stuck his face close to the spoons, examining his pug nose in the reflection, which I'm sure did the ugly man no favors. "Flowers, stone path, extremely cultured."

McBain whistled his amazement. "And look at that statue." You would have thought he was at Disney World. "Prometheus, you say? Wasn't he—well, in Greek mythology, wasn't he the guy—oh my, now there's a revelation."

"Spit it out, McBain," Rense snapped. As the D.A. gushed about my lodgings, I wondered if Rense wasn't concocting some hare-brained charge of obscenity against me for Prometheus's exposed loins hanging free before God, his testicles as big as softballs.

"Isn't Prometheus the god who brought fire to Earth?"

McBain surprised me with his knowledge of myth. "Yes," I said.

"Curious for a man accused of arson," Rense said. He studied the unhappy family picture above the fireplace. "Nice portrait."

"Indeed," I replied. Figures a man as cold as he would like it. "Good family values."

"Exotic clock," he said curtly, with neither admiration nor disdain. "Never seen anything like it."

"Yes," I said, "One of a kind."

"Real gold?"

I nodded, then glanced at Parker's eyes, which seemed to say, *No, R.T., don't give him anything.*

I decided to clam up. A man like Rense looks for reasons to hate people like me. That clock, rare and expensive, would set him off. It was one of five in a series. The only five ever made, fashioned using the five elements of existence. This one used water. The ornate piece had been meticulously hand-crafted by a renowned artisan near the Euphrates River. Zurvan was her name, and she was the most acclaimed clock maker of this century. I first discovered her art in the bazaars of Istanbul during the war. I bought the water clock—so intricately designed—and managed to find three of the other four. The fifth, the fire clock, I tracked to a Jewish broker in Amsterdam just prior to World War II. It was said to have landed in the hands of Goebbels himself, the chief Nazi propagandist, when Germany invaded the Netherlands. I haven't been able to complete the collection, despite my best efforts. The earth, air, and ether clocks occupied my den, Rose's study, and our bedroom, respectively.

I felt it best, based on Parker's subtle signals, not to divulge anything further regarding these priceless pieces. Rense wouldn't have been able to stomach it.

"You're an avid collector, Mr. Stone," Rense said. He turned to face me. "Spoons, art, orchids, antiquities, clocks, matchbooks. The boys in psychological profiles might say you have a need to control. Did you buy this with the money you and Gilday fleeced from the American taxpayers?"

My ears went pink. "Those charges were dropped, Rense. Insufficient evidence."

"More like a plea bargain and heavy pressure from Washington," he complained. His mongrel mug contorted with anger. "I don't know if it was your connections or sheer luck that the Feds didn't want the nuclear controversy in the press. If it wasn't for that, you'd be in jail. Funny thing about people like you, Stone: you think you're immune to the law so you get more and more brazen. It's the typical criminal pattern—keep flaunting the law till you get caught. Well, this time, Stone, you're caught."

McBain, perhaps sensing an opportunity, perhaps just extremely naive, said, "So, if you don't mind my—if doesn't seem too forward—I can save this for the deposition—but since I'm—what were you doing the evening of August 2, 1990?"

My stomach boiled like a pregnant volcano. The whole painted Stone clan, well-groomed and stiff, smiled at me. Why don't I like that picture? It eludes me.

"I was taking a walk," I said, adjusting my legs to bring relief to my stomach.

"Why would you be—I mean, why then, why that night—could it be—just why were you taking a walk on that particular night? Why August 2?"

"I walk every night."

"So, Mr. Stone, not to sound—that is to say, not to accuse you—but really, it doesn't appear as if you—well frankly, you don't have an alibi." The man who is every fashion designer's nightmare shook his head.

My abdomen burned, my stomach raged an acid bath. Was I getting an ulcer? No, I reasoned, I shouldn't have taken my medication on an empty stomach.

"Why do you walk alone?" McBain asked.

"I like the quiet. I like to think."

He scratched the spongy crown of his head. "Would you—now don't take offense, I'm not implying anything—well, maybe I am, but it's not personal—so you're saying you're a loner, a drifter, a man of few friends."

"No!" I said. "I wouldn't say that at all!"

Rense raised his eyebrows.

"Have you always had a quick temper, Stone?" McBain continued. "Have you always lashed out at people who disagree with you?" He posed his questions directly, dropping his scattered-thinker gimmick.

"What? What are you saying?"

"Do you have arguments like this with your son?"

"No," I answered, my abdomen on fire.

He peered at me down the run of his nose, past the bent frame of his glasses, and said, "Your son, Bobby, runs the Cosmic Club, doesn't he, Mr. Stone?"

"Yeah, but what does that have to—"

"Wasn't Bobby grateful enough, Stone? Is that why you torched the place?"

"What? Are you nuts?" My intestines writhed like slithering snakes.

Parker stepped back into the room. "Coffee's on," he announced with a firm crunch of his carrot as he sized up the situation. "Be done in just a minute. R.T., you don't look so good. Are you all right?"

169

"I'm fine," I said. "This idiot here is interrogating me, which I'm sure is illegal. And if it isn't, it's unethical. You got anything to say about that, Rense?"

"Nope," he smirked, like a sly bulldog just done chewing up his master's slippers.

Parker raised those fine lines above his piercing eyes. "You wouldn't be doing that, would you, Brian?"

"No—oh, no," he lied, falling back into that routine of his. "I'm just—I was trying to—anyway, make a little conversation—it's just curious is all, the way that Mr. Stone has—without notice, for long periods—disappeared for days at a time. Gone. No trace."

"Hmm." Parker mulled over his words as he chewed his vegetable to mush. "Fella," he advised, "that's probably best saved for the deposition. When is that anyway?"

"August 30," McBain replied. "Eleven a.m. I think, should be—that's what I've been—that's what my secretary said. Curious to see how much insurance there was on the place. Not that I'm asking now, I'm not, I'm simply a curious sort, but with bankruptcy looming and—well that's your affair—finances in tatters—oh well, I see your point. You're right, Parker, better to wait for the official inquiry."

My stomach gurgled and foamed. "You moron," I said. "You're totally incompetent. I didn't set fire to the C.C. It's not arson, you'll see that. I was framed."

"If it's not arson," McBain rebutted, "then how could you have been framed?"

"By an over-zealous, office-seeking, fashion-deficient, imbecilic district attorney who'll do anything to get elected mayor!"

"Now, R.T.," Parker interjected as he sat next to me. He took the gnarled carrot from his mouth and pointed the remains at McBain. "Let's be fair. I'm sure Brian didn't mean to break the law here today." He stared at Brian, warning him.

McBain tinkered with the twisted spectacles on his amber face, blinking rapidly.

"Did you, Brian?" Parker said.

"No." The D.A. squirmed. He got up from the recliner as Twinkie entered the room, *Dragnet* tune riding shotgun, but no catastrophe looming.

The phone rang. I listened.

"Leave me the hell alone," I fumed at the caller, who warned he was going to roast me like a marshmallow. I slammed the phone in the cradle. "Why don't you do something about that, Rense, instead of busting convenience stores for selling *Playboy* or hassling innocent citizens like me? Why don't you go after the real kooks?" Of course, he's one of the kooks.

The phone rang again. This time it was Bennett informing me the duplicitous D.A.s—McBain and Rense—could search to their hearts' content. Which they did. Box after box of records were hauled from my den. I don't even know everything they took. I do know that when they were done, not a scrap of paper remained in any drawer or filing cabinet of either Rose's or my office. They even copied everything off my hard drive! Twinkie, for all her previous shyness of the past few years, followed McBain around like an affectionate puppy, bordering closely on aiding and abetting the enemy.

After about a half-hour they were finished.

"Once Bennett gets a hold of this warrant," I warned, "I'm sure he'll find you fellas stepped over the line."

McBain frowned. "Remember when the Reds were in the playoffs against the Pirates, Mr. Stone?"

"Yeah, I attended a couple of games."

McBain gathered some confidence. "All around me were bigger men, taller men, people with gloves, everybody waiting for that one chance to snag a foul ball. And the chance came off the bat of Johnny Bench—fourth row blue—in the bottom of the fifth. A pop foul. Everybody, I mean everyone, pushing and shoving for position, gloves up, elbows flying. It was the playoffs, the Reds were going to the World Series, and everyone wanted that ball. I watched it as I was jostled and stepped in front of. It climbed into the stadium lights. Then it dropped. And the pushing got worse, people shouting, 'I got it! I got it!' Someone knocked me to the ground. More shouts, more shoving, hands flying everywhere. I heard the ball hit. It bounced high as people lunged for it in the seats. I sat on the ground, my pants soaked in spilled beer and peanut shells, as the ball rolled right to me. I picked it up, grabbed it tight, and jumped to my feet, holding it high like a trophy. I had the ball. Me. I won out over all those others. The crowd cheered. And you know what, Mr. Stone?"

"What?"

"That's how my life is." He walked toward Twinkie. "I get pushed around, abused, take a lot of crap from people like you, but in the end, as incompetent as I may seem, I win. And that," he said with uncharacteristic confidence, "is what I'm going to do with this case. Win."

McBain accentuated his grand exit by tripping slightly on the step from the family room to the kitchen. Rense and his storm troopers chuckled as they followed him out. I was in too much pain to laugh. As a humming Twinkie showed them the door then went back to her room, I lurched forward, grabbing the garbage can under the end table. A firecracker exploded in my gut. I threw up.

"R.T., are you okay, fella?" Parker came to my aid.

I dry heaved. Then again. Involuntary tears formed at the edges of my eyes. My forehead dripped sweat. A sour bile stayed in my mouth. I excused myself.

In the bathroom, I splashed cold water on my face, then gargled. The taste wouldn't leave. I spit into the sink. Rinsed with mouthwash. Spit. Rinsed. The rancid flavor lingered.

When I returned to the family room, Parker was examining the garbage can and Rose, who had just returned from the grocery, sat next to him. They both looked grim.

"There's blood," Parker said, his oral veggie sidekick nowhere around. "You need to see a doctor."

As Rose played with her cross, I played down the incident. "Oh, that's just from the medication. I shouldn't have taken it on an empty stomach. Says so right on the bottle. I'm sure I'll be fine." And I *was* feeling better.

"Parker's right, dear," Rose said, her eyes bearing in on me, leaving no room for escape. "You haven't been eating. You have that awful cough. It's the middle of August. You can't have a summer cold for three weeks. Something's wrong."

"Okay, okay." I raised my hands in defeat. "I tried to talk to the doctor about it when the bandages came off, but he had some emergency come up. He only had enough time to snip the tape, snip the gauze, glance at the scar and say, *Looks like the 13th hole at Pebble Beach,* before he scooted out the door. It all took sixty seconds. I didn't have a chance to ask a question, nothing. I'll call Finkleday on Monday and see if I can get in. How's that?"

Rose's expression relaxed. Parker seemed satisfied.

"Now, can we get down to business? Rose, you missed an exciting show a few minutes ago." I said.

"You sure did, Mom," Parker chuckled.

She smiled. Rose loved it when Parker called her Mom. She ate it up. He'd continued speaking with her after the divorce, always checking in every six months or so to see that Rose was all right.

"The food was flying, people were falling. Just like old times," Parker joked.

"Twinkie?" Rose guessed.

"Yep," we said in unison.

My stomach gurgled again. Not a good sign. I turned the subject to the main event. "Parker, I was wondering if you'd handle a case for me?"

"Of course, R.T., no problem. Why wouldn't I?"

I wished I could smile as easily as him, as naturally. I stared at the portrait above the mantel, frowned, then returned to Parker, who was so full of life as he celebrated its oddities, finding intrigue in the most mundane places. That's it! I hate that picture because all us Stones are faking smiles, pretending to enjoy life, but we weren't. Nobody in the family wanted to be there.

"R.T.?" Parker broke my thoughts. "Why wouldn't I?"

"Oh, um . . . you refused the tree-hugger case, so I wasn't sure that you wanted to help me."

"Are you kidding?" He punched my arm lightly. "You're family."

"So, why didn't you help me with those enviromaniacs?"

He glanced at my facial burn, trying to be discreet. It had healed fairly well, leaving a pinkish blotch reminiscent of the Nagasaki atomic explosion as a farewell gift. Rose puts cream on it daily. She says it looks like St. Peter's Basilica. Twinkie says it's like a Hostess Snowball.

"It was the principle. You wanted me to dig up some personal dirt so you could intimidate them into backing off. I don't do that kind of work," Parker said. "And honestly, R.T., I think they were right."

"You do?"

"Yeah, the world doesn't need another strip mall. It needs trees and flowers and animals. Overdevelopment is killing this planet. And I'm really not into destroying people just because I can. It's really bad karma."

"There's that word again, karma," I said as an idea struck me. With all the crisis of the last few weeks and all the confusing details, and the Council of Ancients shifting things about on me, perhaps I should draw up a Declaration of Innocence. "Say Parker, would you mind coming over in a couple of days, say the twentieth, to witness a document for me?"

"No problem, R.T." He shrugged as he scooted close, looked at Rose as if to apologize in advance, and said, "What about Twinkie? She could make things uncomfortable."

Parker referred to the final incident that forced him to leave my daughter, the one that sent her back home in shreds. Twinkie blew one of his biggest cases. She can be extremely possessive in an unhealthy way. She called Parker's office every hour. Checked on him when he went out with the boys, making sure he was where he said he was—the bowling alley, a bar, wherever. He endured that pretty well until the night he was at a dinner meeting with a senior executive for the Diamond Trust Bank who was about to recruit him to set up a phony business. The executive would approve loans to Parker's fake company, the loan would default, the company would vanish, then he and Parker would split the amount of the loan. The senior executive didn't realize that his dinnermate, whom he knew as Kevin Price, was on retainer by the board of directors at Diamond to ferret out the corruption. The executive was in the midst of making the offer when Twinkie unexpectedly showed up, demanding to know "just when, Parker Floyd, are you coming home for dinner?"

That was it. His cover was blown, the job was lost. She had been warned before, many times. He had been patient. It was the last straw. The marriage was over. A detective's life isn't conducive to marriage or relationships, and if Twinkie is the wife, forget it.

"We don't want her leaking facts out of jealousy, revenge, or just plain compulsiveness," Parker said. "Perhaps you should use someone else."

"No," Rose said firmly. "Parker, you're our man. We won't trust R.T.'s fate to anyone but you." She stood. Parker joined her, playing the consummate gentleman. I stayed put, having a valid excuse. They hugged.

173

"I'm glad to be on the team," he said. He looked at me, vibrant enthusiasm pulsing from him. "This is exciting stuff, fella." He retook a seat. "Now," he said, self-assured. "Tell me how you came to be charged with attempted aggravated murder."

Chapter 16

August 21, 1990

I told Rose there wasn't anything to worry about. Finkleday agreed. He gave me a routine exam with about as much thoroughness and twice the speed of a USDA chicken inspector trying to make his quota in an Arkansas poultry plant. I shivered when he put his cold hands on my back while he listened to my heartbeat. The stethoscope was only slightly warmer.

After I'd dressed, the nurse ushered me into his expansive office. Rose was seated in one of two black leather chairs set in front of his walnut desk. On the blue wall nearest him was an impressive, albeit crooked, array of diplomas and honorus emeritus and other such stuff. On the opposite wall hung a framed thousand dollar bill. No doubt the receipt from the first checkup he administered. A hideous black iron statue of a golfer in mid-swing stood in the corner.

Finkleday came in, drying his hands. A distinct whiff of pharmaceuticals followed him. It smelled like my medicine cabinet.

"Well, Robert," he said, tossing a thin file on top of his desk. I could see my reflection in its sheen. "Ironic, isn't it? I don't see you for ten years, and now I'm treating you for gunshots and ulcers and . . ."

"I have an ulcer?"

"No, no." He shook his head. "I didn't mean to imply anything of the kind."

"What is it, then?"

The doctor was an expert at detachment. Rose scrutinized the doctor's face, searching for clues to my health. She evaluated his cropped, white hair, his deep 18-holes-a-day tan. "Is R.T. all right, Dr. Finkleday?" She sat forward, back stiff.

"Please," he half-smiled, encouraging Rose, "Call me George." He blinked. "Robert is fine." He swiveled around in his chair in a giant swooping motion and brought back a book more worn than Doc Holiday's medicine bag. "Side effects from the medication, I'd say." He placed a big thumb into the book and leafed it open. His eyes searched for the data that would prove his theory. He spoke as his eyes skipped down the entries on the page, as if scanning for the number of the local pizzeria. "Wouldn't hurt if you took better care of yourself. You're twenty pounds overweight. Maybe it's time you got back on a walking routine, three, maybe four miles a day at a brisk pace."

I didn't tell him I'd already tried that. I couldn't walk the levy anymore. With my reputation I'd be shot or stabbed or pummeled to death by some lunatic who believes in guilty until proven innocent. Too many crazies want a piece of me. Still, walking in the wealthy confines of the well-bred village of Indian Hill was no better. People I've known for years look the other way when they see me out, or cross the street, ignore my hello's and generally shun me with complete contempt. It's painful. I never told Rose. The only guy who ever acknowledges me now is Bing, of Chair-Ease fame, which is odd because I haven't been all that friendly to him.

"George," Rose said as Finkleday continued to pore through his book of witchcraft and sorcery. "He's lost sixteen pounds in the last two weeks. And he threw up blood the other day."

"It's a miracle diet!" I joked. Nobody laughed.

"Ah, yes!" he said, triumphantly putting his index finger on the magic answer. "It's all here in black and white. Side effects include nausea, cramping, dizziness, blood in mucous. If vomiting occurs, discontinue use. Well, that's it then," he announced, slamming the book shut. "I'll change the prescription."

Rose wasn't placated. "And what side effects will this new drug have?"

"This one is much milder. Been giving it for years. Wouldn't hurt if you laid off spicy foods," he said, which I immediately translated into a plan to dissuade Twinkie from preparing any outlandish dishes for awhile.

"And if R.T.'s symptoms don't subside?"

Finkleday scratched his wrist, then his scalp. "I'd better order you up some tests to be safe," he said as an afterthought.

Thank God for Rose. I'd have just sat there agreeing to whatever he said.

The doctor quickly scribbled some unintelligible lines across a prescription pad and tore it off. "The nurse will arrange with the clinic for the tests," he said, rising from his chair. "We'll call you when the results are in—about ten days or so."

"Ten days, George," Rose said. "Does it take that long?"

Finkleday blushed like a cherry tomato after the first frost. "No, but I'll be in the Cayman Islands until then."

Rose wasn't pleased. "Can't someone else read the results?"

"Rose," Finkleday looked down his nose at her. "I'm your doctor."

August 25, 1990

"Hello, R.T." Parker greeted me with his trademark carrot dangling from his mouth. It was carefully shaved clean and glistened orange. "Sorry I'm late, yoga class ran a bit long."

"Hey, Parker," I said, eyeing the knicked vegetable. "No problem."

Over Parker's shoulder, Bing waved to me as he slalomed between cherry trees on his Toro riding mower. I waved back. It's all we do, wave; I haven't said ten words to him in twenty years. "Don't you get tired of those things?"

"Carrots? Nah. Good brain food. Helps me think." He nibbled like a rabbit at the edges of his reddish-yellow root. He was modestly dressed in faded blue denims and a bright floral print from the Caribbean. His hair hung freely to his shoulders, like a renegade hippie from the early seventies. I thought the country was going to hell then. "You know the private-eye biz, R.T.—the stress, pressure, too much time on my hands, that kind of thing. Carrots relax me, man. Plus they're a great source of beta carotene and Vitamin A. How's the stomach?"

"Ugh. I've been chugging gallons of Kaopectate. My doctor says I'll be fine."

"Your rash looks better." He nodded at my cheek. "Kind of looks like Sirius Major, the Dog star, near the Orion constellation. You ought to put some Aloe vera juice on it. Heal it right up. Much better than whatever chemical-laden salve they've got you slopping on."

"Oh?"

"Did you have your skin tested to see what caused it?" Parker asked as we walked past the fourth-century B.C. Egyptian urn Rose had purchased at a New York auction. We'd seen a play that weekend, too.

"Never thought of it, but I bet the hospital did. Mc*Brain* will probably claim it's gasoline."

"You should cut that guy some slack," he said.

I headed toward the solarium. Parker stopped, clamped the carrot firmly between his teeth, laid his briefcase on the table, and snapped open the locks.

"This will do," he said. "Hel . . . low Swami, what's this?" He pointed to a freshly delivered FedEx packet. I'd just opened it before he arrived.

"Oh, it's crap about the Middle East. Someone's been sending me copies of the *Eastern Crescent Review*."

"May I?" He reached for the envelope. "Local address, female handwriting . . ." He twirled the carrot with his tongue. "Hmm . . . Dear Mr. Stone." Parker brought the Post-it note to his nose and sniffed. "Interesting woman. I'd say she is well-read, with Eastern-Indian ancestry, loves both her parents deeply, and is into aromatherapy. Very New Age woman. I'd much like to meet her."

"You're guessing," I laughed, but his eyes told me he wasn't. He was practicing his craft. An appreciable talent. A gift perhaps.

With much humility and no fanfare he stated, "The ascenders and descenders of her handwriting have equal sized loops in her j's, g's, b's, f's, and such, indicating a strong affection for her parents. The Post-it note has a distinct trace of sandalwood oil used primarily for massage and aromatherapy. Sandalwood is an Indian mainstay as aromas go. And," he concluded, "if she were not well-read, you would not be receiving these periodicals. Expensive way to send a letter—FedEx." He bit his ever-present carrot with crisp authority. The guy is amazing.

"At least they'll deliver," I complained. "The damn mailman has refused to bring our mail—says it's too risky with the death threats and all. Rose has to go to the post office every day."

"Is that why your phone's off the hook?"

"Yes, how'd you know?"

"Elementary, my dear Watson. I couldn't get through for hours." *Chomp.* A novel thought came from the great detective. "Why don't you just get it changed and unlisted? Aren't you worried about getting a real letter bomb?"

"Good thought," I said before dismissing his concern. "I'll get it changed. And no, I'm not worried about getting blown to smithereens. I've seen enough of this type of fear in my time. People like to act indignant and pretend to seek revenge, but that's just chest thumping. Nobody really wants to blow up a bricklayer from Indian Hill."

"So what do you think of this Gulf situation?" He sat back to chew. That's the one thing about Parker, he's a student of life; he asks people's thoughts and listens to their replies.

"I'm not sure I have an opinion yet. Although *The Journals* seems to think I should."

"*The Journals?*"

"Yeah, it thinks we're all responsible for every little thing that goes on in this world, including Kuwait. It thinks I should do something about it."

"I agree," Parker said. "We *are* all responsible. If we look at the facts of this thing, there's no logical reason for Bush to be so adamant. As president, what does he care? As founder of the Zapata Offshore Oil Company, Bush cares a great deal, being as how Zapata sank the first well drilled off Kuwait."

"How do you know that?" I was impressed by his information, though I shouldn't have been. Parker has always been historically and politically astute. The carrot was placed gently inside his briefcase for future contemplation.

"I study these things, R.T." His eyes danced as his fingers played with the yellow Post-it note from the mysterious 'M.' "I'm fascinated by the manipulations of the power elite, the Trilateral Commission, Bechtel, the entire Reagan-Bush connection. So if you look at Bush's financial interest—he being an oil man—then consider his domestic problems—Reaganomics being exposed for the sham that it is, the U.S. economy is in the shitter, Congressional elections are coming up, *and*," he stressed as the yellow note turned over and over in his hands, "last but not least—the Savings and Loan debacle is getting deeper and wider. It's easy to see he needs to make a move. Bush was the guy who deregulated the S&Ls under Reagan, you know. And George's son, Neil, not so coincidentally, is up to his eyeballs in bad loans in a billion-dollar fiasco at his

Silverado Savings & Loan. I'd say Bush could use a good war right about now. It may be the only way to save his presidency."

"So you don't think the U.S. should get involved?"

"Hell no." Parker played with the yellow Post-it, blowing on it, watching it flicker. "The Kuwaiti Emir runs a completely hostile country with few human rights, no women's rights, no democracy, and has imposed strict censorship. The Emir, the fat cat Bush wants to defend, even exiled fifty prominent Kuwaiti writers and editors out of the country. And Bush says we're protecting their freedom? Hah! He's protecting his own ass—and those of the oil barons." He stared at the note from 'M.' "I have a feeling about this 'M' person," he said dreamily. "She plays a part somehow."

"You have news?"

"Hel . . . low Swami," he exclaimed, his vacuous pupils absorbing the room. "You're going to love this."

"I could use some good news. What did you find?"

He pulled a neat manila folder from his case as he spoke and reinserted the carrot between his lips like an old-style mob boss smoking a stogie. "I've been doing a little digging over at the Catholic archives trying to track down Yvonne Pippin, I mean Allison. Interesting the records they keep. Interesting indeed," he mused, relishing his success.

"What? What is it?" I licked my lips, foreseeing my salvation.

"It was tough. The Catholic Church takes secrecy with pronounced seriousness." He read my impatient expression. "I gained access to Allison's orphanage records," he beamed, patting the stack of papers like a good child. "I reviewed them during the period of Allison's stay. There were some strange entries referring to something called Opus Dei, which bears looking into. But the interesting part is that St. Alexandria ledgers show ten thousand dollars a month began pouring in, coinciding with Allison's arrival."

"What does that mean?"

"It means we have a paper trail to the Diamond Trust Bank and to Allison's father!" Parker slapped his hand on the table triumphantly. "Payments of that size to the orphanage can only mean one thing."

"What's that?"

"The father of the child bought the Church's silence to cleanse his guilt by giving such huge contributions. Don't you see?" Parker was thrilled enough to bite a hunk of hard carrot root.

"That's good work," I said happily. "It's Patrick Gilday, right?"

Parker bit a chunk of the carrot in half, his blue eyes quizzical. "How did you know?"

"It's in *The Journals.*"

His eyebrows raised in disbelief. "Right. Well then, what do you need me for?"

"You just keep on doing what your doing. I need physical evidence."

"No problem." He grinned.

"How did you manage to get all these records?"

A smile crept across his face like a sly cat. "The second best tool a detective has is his ability to lie—convincingly. There are some things you don't want to know, R.T."

"What's the best tool then?"

"Instinct. We've got a good start on the evidence—receipts, ledgers, even notes written on the sides of invoices—from P.G."

"Patrick Gilday," I said in a low voice.

"Private-eye heaven." Parker's eyes glimmered. "My next step is to visit Mr. Winston Held III at Diamond Trust and see if he'll spill anything useful. If not, I'll work around him."

"Great," I said, chipper about the progress. "Have you found anything on Danny? Any luck there?"

Parker shook his head, his long hair shimmying on his shoulders. Nibble. Nibble. Nibble. "He's disappeared. Changed his name a couple years ago and dropped out of life. Hard to believe he walked away from all that money."

"Blood money," I said, absently, referring to Patrick's unethical tactics of obtaining wealth. I thought back to when Parker did the same thing as Danny, dropped out of life. He quit the business after he and Twinkie divorced and went to India. Traveled to Tibet, Sri Lanka, China. Studied with sages and rishis and gurus and yogis for five years. He sent postcards to us occasionally, always from an exotic locale. I didn't understand his leaving then, running away like that, but I do now. Some people are on a perpetual search for knowledge. I admire him for it. Under my current duress, I've considered doing the same. When he came back, he was a vegetarian and a New Age private-eye.

"I have his school records, nothing exciting there," my ex-son-in-law, private detective, truth seeker, vegetable lover, said. "Good grades. A run in with his Biology teacher. Nothing unusual. He's almost as hard to find as this McJic fellow. I haven't been able to find anything on him. That trail's pretty cold. You say he was in Cincinnati back in '67?"

"That's what the book says," I replied.

"Finding some mystical guy from twenty-three years ago, that's a tall order, fella," he said, casually glancing at 'M's Post-it note.

"Try the Celestial Garden & Lawn Service."

"Tried that. They don't exist."

"What? You have a receipt right here."

"That may be, R.T., but there are no business records at City Hall, the County Commissioners Office, or the State Department of Taxation."

"No records? That can't be. Did you try Kentucky?"

"I tried Ohio, Kentucky and Indiana. Nothing." His royal crescent eyes bounced from object to object in the kitchen, taking their energy. Nibble. Nibble. Nibble. "This is one cosmic case, fella."

"How so?"

"The slam dunk evidence is tough to corroborate, yet hard to crack information is coming our way. It's weird man, like some force is pushing me where it wants me to go." He closed his eyes for a second, having gathered up a reservoir of stimulation. "R.T., I want to help any way I can, but I'm not sure what good I'm doing here. So you gather the information, so what?"

I saw his point. It didn't make sense to me either. "I'm to write a book," I explained. "*The Journals* won't clear my name unless I write their stories."

"Yeah, I know all that." His face showed worry. "But why?"

"I'm not clear on that," I admitted. "I just know I have no choice. Do you believe me?"

Parker's concern changed to enthusiasm. "Sure, I believe you, R.T. One thing I learned in the Far East is not to question fate. And fate is what brought us back together, pure and simple."

"You're an amazing person."

His baby bottom face turned cotton candy pink. "Thanks. But like you, I feel I have no choice. This is a great mystery. You're about as likely to torch your own club as I am to have a sex-change operation and move to Sweden."

"I appreciate it, Parker. I really do. It has to be hard for you—"

"Not really." He shrugged, and fiddled with the yellow sticky from 'M.' "People put their faith in unseen forces every day. The least I can do is believe you, even though I can't see it just yet. But I have a feeling, a strong one, that I will."

My eyes watered. Finally, compassion from someone. No one else believed me. Not Rose or the kids or the pious religious bigots at church or my next door neighbors who have shunned me. I'm a pariah. Now, my former son-in-law, for no reason at all, looks me in the eyes and says he believes me. Hope comes from the oddest places.

"Thank you." I choked on the words.

"It's all right, R.T. We'll beat this thing. I think it would be a good idea if you let me borrow the manuscript you're working on. It's probably loaded with clues. Help me get inside their heads, too."

His words thrilled me like an acceptance letter from a publisher. "It's in there," I nodded toward my study.

"Say, I haven't told you another interesting bit of news." Parker handed me a copy of a Concord, New Hampshire obituary dated June 1970.

My blood ran cold as I read the clipping.

"It's incredible, isn't it?" he said as he picked up 'M' again.

"Amazing."

"And sad," Parker almost whispered.

"I didn't know McBain had a brother."

Chomp. "So there's more to the D.A.'s interest in justice than we thought," he said, his carrot a mere nub of what it had been when he arrived at my door some forty-five minutes earlier. "There may be psychological motives at play in addition to political ones."

My breath was stolen. I felt pity for McBain. "His brother died in a house fire."

"While under Brian's care."

Chapter 17

August 28, 1990

I performed the most daring deed today. Parker inspired me. Made me quit feeling sorry for myself and get off my butt. I went to St. Alexandria. Allison wouldn't leave me alone. Something pushed me there. A hidden hand. My subconscious, maybe. Guilt. A desire to know more. Whatever it was, I'm glad I did it.

What a day! It was four a.m. when I convinced myself of the necessity of the adventure to the orphanage. I called at nine, saying I was interested in making a large donation. I stashed a bottle of antacids in my suit coat and drove myself to St. Als, the first time I've driven since the fateful night of August 2. My wound had healed sufficiently enough for me to walk without a limp. The nuclear mushroom scar on my face had faded but was still conspicuous. Allison's invisible, yet unmistakable presence, greeted me as I entered the circular drive to the front entrance. Triple somersaults of anxiety bounded off my trampoline stomach. I chewed a handful of antacids, checked my face in the mirror, wiped the chalky powder from my lips, and headed for the front door. A heavy curtain fell back into place. Someone had been watching.

The nuns were polite, dressed more as social workers than nuns, as they escorted me around the grounds. I was shown the garden where the spirited Allison grew her seeds and nurtured her plants, now overgrown with weeds, and the gazebo where the infamous "Honeysuckle Affair" bust took place. I took the standard tour through the main room, where Allison and Dena shared so many wonderful Christmases, to the dorm where the children stayed. All so dull. So uniform. So institutional.

The nuns took me through the kitchen to the mess hall where the children were eating. This was Friday—what did Allison say they'd be having? Fish. Many hopeful yet suspicious children's faces peered at me. Pleading. Innocent. Hardened. Broken dishes, they are. White porcelain faces chipped from a battered life. Black glazed faces taken from the kiln too early. Imperfections that nobody wants. I wanted to bring as many kids home with me as I could, but this was not the time. An alleged felon wouldn't be at the top of any adoption waiting list.

A voice whispered inside me. A woman's voice. No, a girl's. Allison. "The bell tower," she said. "The bell tower."

"So, Mr. Stone," a molted sister said. "Will you be able to see your way clear to bless us with a donation?"

"I wonder if I might be allowed to wander alone about the place to form my own impressions?"

"Yes, Mr. Stone, sir, whatever you wish," the craggy-voiced nun replied. She was used to this type of second thought. Buyer's remorse, I suppose. Did they know I was the reviled and detested R.T. Stone of *Cincinnati Enquirer* fame? Did they care?

"The bell tower," Allison whispered.

Alone, I strolled about St. Als seeing visions of the Red Angel playing here and there, watching her creeping cautiously through the orphanage in her superspy role. I walked down the hall, where Allison nailed Mother Superior with her laser lipstick. It was just as *The Journals* had shown me in my mind. The details of R.T. Stone's newly opened cerebral cinema (psychic vision) were exact. My heart skipped a beat upon seeing the door to the bell tower. I checked the hallway, my body in a mixed state of anxiety and euphoria. I was a kid again, playing detective just like Allison. Just like Parker. I was alive. The door creaked a welcome as I entered the darkened tower.

Slowly, I navigated the stairs, my stomach a tempest of activity, my back twanging sharply, reminding me of my peril. Winded, I reached the last step. There was a time, several decades ago, when I could have bounded to the top. I was in heaven. I don't know why. A tremendous elation overwhelmed me as I stepped out onto the platform and saw the great rusty bell. I imagined Allison discovering this place for the first time. It was beautiful. I clinked the bell lightly with my index finger. A slight tinny sound just hinted of its grand potential loosed when it strikes the hour.

I'm not a man of much emotion, but as I looked out from Allison's world from the bell tower of her imprisonment, something touched me. Something angelic. Something harmonious struck a hidden chord within. An angel's wing brushed a celestial harp string. The string, the purest sound ever heard, was attached to my heart. I cried:

Tears of joy.

Tears of sorrow.

Tears of recognition.

Tears of anger.

Tears of pain.

Weary, I rested on the weathered floorboards. I hadn't cried this hard in years. Not since Bobby blew his arm off in Nam. Not real tears anyway. I'd been taught a man doesn't do that. I believed the lie.

"If only I could have helped you, Allison," I sobbed to the wind. "If I only had known."

I cried for a long time. More tears than I had cried in my lifetime. I was Noah standing atop his ark, feeling the tears of humanity rain down from God. Only they were my tears. The emotion passed slowly. Strangely, in the middle of the deluge, I was both happy and sad, feeling somehow that Allison and I would meet again. Wishful thinking, perhaps.

Gradually, I composed myself. Opening my eyes, I spotted a slip of paper, just a ribbon's edge, lodged behind a splintered slat of the tower wall. I pulled at the paper, tearing it. Something was hidden behind it. I pulled hard on the board, hoping to pry it open just enough to free the paper.

Crack! The board snapped in half. There it was! Sitting there like a dusty miracle behind the broken slat, like Cinderella's grand invitation to the ball, was a neatly bundled stack of notes wrapped twice, length-by-width, with red rubber bands. I carefully removed the bands and read a note.

"Dear Allison," it read. I began to quiver. My God! My hands shook. Instantly, I knew what I had discovered—Danny's letters to Allison! Elated and panicked, afraid the nuns would discover me with the notes and confiscate them, I stuffed them down my pants and secured the packet in my Jockeys. Lots of room down there since my weight has plummeted.

I reset the board in place and hurried down the steps of the bell tower. This was evidence. Real evidence of their existence! I rushed passed the nuns, barely aware of my rudeness.

"Will you see fit to make your donation, Mr. Stone?" one asked.

"I'll call you," I shouted back as I walked briskly to my car, aggravating my stomach further. It burned acid, but my heart sang with promise.

At home, jubilant with my discovery, I anxiously dove into the letters. I hadn't been this excited since I won the Zimmer bid (that one was worth ten million dollars to me).

"Congratulations, Stone, you have made progress," the AWOL entity suddenly typed across my computer screen. A less informed man would have been shocked at the electronic intrusion, but me, I've seen its theatrics before.

"You're back," I shouted. "Welcome back! Do you see what I found?" I felt sixteen again. "Danny's letters to Allison. She must have saved them."

"She must have. Congratulations again, Stone. Splendid work."

"I'm not sure if I should be mad or grateful."

"What do you mean?" it typed in a font I didn't recognize.

"No one believes me, especially Rose. And that hurts."

"Certain things cannot be helped. Rose and the others will come to believe in you in their own time."

"Why not now?"

"Allow me to explain. Rose is a kind-hearted woman who has spent her entire life believing in certain fundamental values. She is a devoted wife, a good mother, a housekeeper, a Christian. Her world is made up of daily rituals which shape her views. If you try to change the belief system she has taken sixty years to cultivate she will not be able to handle it. She will need to adopt slowly to a new reality. Her mind, while strong and active, cannot handle such shocking change in such a short period of time."

"So you're saying she can't cope with reality?"

"Precisely. But only because her current reality is so different from the real one. However, over time she will come to accept and understand. And so it is with the rest of the world. People cannot be expected to just throw out their faith willy-nilly."

"Willy-nilly? C'mon, where'd you hear that?"

"I saw it on Mr. Ed, *I think. Now that is a funny show. A talking horse. Ha ha, the things you Americans come up with."*

"Yeah, yeah, *Mr. Ed* is funny—stick to the subject, my life is in jeopardy here. I can't take this lightly. When will she believe me?"

"After you come to believe in yourself."

"You know, I've been thinking, and—"

"Always dangerous, Stone, this thinking."

"Cut it out. I *have* been thinking, and I don't understand why you need me to begin with?"

The Macintosh sat blank, staring at me in shades of gray.

"Stone, I am not just here to save the planet, I am here to save individuals as well," it finally explained. *"You spoke to Rose of Revelation and the hundred and forty-four thousand or so."*

"Yeah, so?" I remembered that conversation. It had not gone too well—Rose recommended I see a therapist.

"Well, Stone, since you have not figured it out yet, I will tell you—you are one of the chosen!"

Chills shot through me. "Me? Chosen? Why? I'm not deserving of this."

"Yes, you are. You may not be aware of your life's path yet, but you will fulfill the requirements to make it to the next world."

"The next world? Where's that?"

"Shanidar, of course."

Holy smokes, a hundred conflicting thoughts bombarded me. Why me? What about Rose? How about my kids? What about the orphans in St. Als? What about the innocent children starving by the millions in Africa? How come they got such a bad deal? They're not all bad people. What about the five billion other people who are trying? Why should anyone have to suffer?

"All will be revealed before The Journals *reaches its final conclusion. As an ancient Chinese proverb says, 'the journey is the reward.' You shall evolve and learn and question and grow. I am sure of it."*

"Well, the journey may be the reward, but you've placed a bounty on my head. What kind of reward is that? I don't know why you have to extort my services by threatening my life."

"Extortion is a bit strong, Stoney. I prefer the term forceful persuasion. Now, the reasoning for the forceful persuasion is that you ignored all the signs and omens sent

to you during your lifetime. You simply chose not to listen, chose not to see. In modern day vernacular—we sent a wake-up call."

"A fire that almost kills forty-five people is more than a wake-up call. What did they do to deserve that?"

"Everyone—and I mean everyone, Stone, has a price to pay. The patrons of your nightclub have each learned some lesson from that horrible tragedy. Something brought them there that evening."

"But why? Why a fire?"

"Symbolism, Stone. Lots of symbolism in fire. As your citizens worry about the people almost burned to death while drinking and merry-making in a club—very little thought is being given by your society to the hundreds of thousands of people about to be bombed out of their homes in Iraq."

"This is about Operation Desert Shield?"

"No, it is about an endless chain of circumstance. It is about responsibility, accountability, karma, involvement, and the need for people to realize that while one enjoys the good life, billions are in agony. It is about the undeniable link between us all."

"But why burn down my club and traumatize forty-five innocent people?"

"First of all, no one is innocent. And I told you—you ignored the signs. Secondly, there is a greater purpose here which you cannot grasp yet. And the final reason is impartial fate. Sometimes in life, whether on this plane or another, there is no reason. Sometimes things happen just because. It is a chaotic Universe. We are merely spirits trying to reduce the chaos. We cannot control every aspect of life. We cannot do away with the ugliness of the world: the evil, starvation, greed, war, and all that. For if it were not for the ugliness of chaos, there would not be the beauty of the great cycle."

"The great cycle?" I asked, trying to keep up with the glowing gray screen.

"Yes. The great cycle is a Universal law that says everything has an elliptical cycle (or pattern) to it. On the outer extremes of this cycle are the opposites which make up the ends. These ends are also beginnings, for they are like a huge circular path of mass and space, thought and light, in all their positive and negative iterations. You cannot have one without the other. No happiness without sorrow. No life without death. It is basic religious and philosophical doctrine. You humans are close to the answers in your beliefs—some of you anyway—not all."

"I'm confused," I said. "Are you saying I'm going through this crap because of chaos, or the great cycle, or because you feel like putting me through it, or . . . what the hell are you doing this for?"

"Because you are chosen."

"But I'm just a bricklayer."

"And Jesus was just a carpenter. You understate yourself. Either way, bricklayer or developer, one's profession has little to do with it. What is in one's soul determines

the real path of destiny. You may step off at any time, Stone. But you must be prepared for the pain and suffering like the rest."

"Why is it that I can handle this knowledge, this change, and Rose can't? What makes me different?"

"You do not have the same delusions of religious indoctrination as Rose. You have a clear mind, free of institutional programming. You have remained free from the grip of misguided mind-control."

"I'm still confused."

"No matter, Stone. When this is finished you will understand—as will your readers."

"My readers?"

"Precisely. The Journals *shall have your name on it. You are the author."*

"But it's not me," I protested. "It's you and Danny and Allison. It's not my life at all."

"Ah, but it is you, you see. It is exactly your life. You are The Journals.*"*

Gulp! The Council of Ancients has bound my fate to that of *The Journals.* This reaffirmation slammed me hard once again. It gets clearer by the second. I know what I need to do. I must press on and get the job done. I've made progress—hired Parker, improved my typing, learned how to use a word processor, and faithfully recorded the story. And I just found the letters from Danny!

"As a reward for your great find, Stone, and your initiative, I would like to give you a present."

Boom! An explosion rumbled across my desk, scattering papers, knocking over the *Addams Family* "Lurch" paper-clip holder Twinkie bought for me on spring break in Florida several years ago. I can't stand the thing but don't want to break my daughter's egg-shell self-esteem by pitching it.

"What the—"

A shoe box had fallen from the ceiling, materializing from nowhere. "What's this?"

"Open it and see."

I tore the lid off. "Another stack of letters. Allison!" I shouted. The letters from Allison to Danny. Jesus! "Holy smoke, now I'm cooking!" I was exuberant.

"Are you all right, dear?" Rose called from the kitchen.

"I'm fine," I laughed out loud.

I can't believe my good fortune. Proof! Proof of both Danny and Allison. Real evidence to clear my name. Life was getting brighter. Everything will turn out fine. It may take some work but I'll succeed. I've had great challenges all my life, (true, none as intense as this) but challenges nonetheless. "Where did you get these?"

"Mulciber."

"Where?"

"I have to go, Stone. People to save and all that. Bye."

"Bye," I said stupidly before I realized it was leaving without answering me. It's incredible. It just zips into a book, into my sleep, into my consciousness, and now into my computer. What kind of being can do that? I have to learn these tricks.

It's gone, leaving me a huge guilt complex about the world and the great cycle in its vapor trail. No one is innocent it says. Is that true? Are we all guilty?

For me, life is getting brighter. I have my first real clues to prove my innocence. Hope is shining upon me. Before I read the letters, I'd better send a check to St. Alexandria. As Rose would say, can I afford not to?

"Good show!"

Chapter 18

January 16, 1943

Mohammed steered the difficult truck with both hands, his dark face a jolted half-grin. He no longer distrusted his passenger of the last six months; the man had proven himself again and again. The Germans had been thrown out of North Africa, in large part due to the efforts of Sulphur. The truck jiggled and ground and bounced its way through the narrow streets of Casablanca, out of the medina section into the French, where the wealth of the city lay.

Mohammed thought his cargo strange, his fascination with fire bizarre, but he liked him anyway. Sulphur knew this. He could read it in the brown eyes of his Berber guide. The truck slowed in front of the hotel. American soldiers sitting in jeeps mounted with machine guns held the perimeter secure. Sulphur didn't know why he was being brought to the hotel. The orders had come from Colonel Eddy, along with instructions to shower, shave, and dress in his best suit.

He was quickly ushered past the sentries through a side door and down a hallway. He marched briskly three steps behind his military escorts. He eyed an earthen bowl filled with matchbooks from the hotel. With the quickness of a fly, he reached out and grabbed a pack of matches without a pause in his stride. He dropped the matchbook into his coat pocket and entered a large room. The air was pungent with cigar smoke cut by cigarettes. Sulphur, despite his appreciation for matches, flame throwers, all things combustible, and dynamite, detested cigars. He considered the stench an affront to the crisp, undeniably primal scent of ignited sulphur. He inhaled the repugnant air, trying to discern its sulfurous roots.

A door on the opposite end of the room slid open, exposing another much larger chamber. A voice he recognized as Bill Donovan's spilled out into the space he occupied. The general strode in, hand outstretched in generous welcome.

"Come join me for a few moments," the OSS chief said casually, as if they were at a pub. "There are two gentlemen who would like to meet you."

Sulphur's eyes burned through the fog of nicotine hanging in the air like a musty Persian rug. Who was he to meet? Why all the secrecy? He saw the cigarette holder first, an unlit cigarette attached, held at a forty-five degree angle toward the ceiling, then the wheelchair, then the tired eyes trying to sparkle behind years of tedious burden. Then he saw the man, frail but holding on, determined to see his mission through.

Sulphur snapped to attention. His dutiful salute brought howls of laughter from another face obscured by a nimbus of cigar smoke. A grumpy voice gurgled a lazy English drawl. "You have your boys well trained, Franklin. I'm impressed."

Franklin's eyes dropped with disdain to the half-empty cognac glass barely held from the floor by the drunken fingers of his chubby friend.

"At ease, Lieutenant," General Donovan ordered.

"Laugh if you must, Winston. This man almost single-handedly assured our victory here."

Sulphur blinked his eyes sharply in succession, partly from the stagnant air, partly in disbelief. He stood, hands folded properly behind his back, legs spread apart precisely as he had been taught in intelligence school. He swallowed a brick of fossilized nicotine, or so it seemed.

"Mr. President, sir," General Donovan announced, "Mr. Prime Minister. May I present Special Agent Sulphur."

"Yes, yes, quite right then, lad," snorted Winston Churchill. "Saved the bloody lot of us, did he?" It was obvious to everyone that the Prime Minister was drunk.

"Pleased to meet you, son." President Roosevelt extended a warm hand. His eyes gained a measure of spark. Even through the cloudiness, Sulphur had noticed it. "Our nations owe a debt of gratitude for your work, son. Who would have thought one so young as you could have pulled this off? We took a risk and you came up aces. Congratulations." FDR clasped his other hand on top of the handshake and shook firmly. Genuinely.

"Waiter," Churchill croaked like a bloated bullfrog. The waiter was a British MI-6 officer. "Where's my drink?" The snifter lay toppled over at his feet. The leader of Great Britain leaned his head forward like snarling drunkards do, tripling his blubbery chin as he inhaled a huge gulp of his insidious cigar, the tip glowing like the fuse on a keg of powder. The officer snapped to and began pouring another glass. FDR cocked his eyebrow, telling the officer to water it down. He did.

Donovan slapped Sulphur on the back. "You've done an excellent job, Lieutenant."

The president fumbled lazily at his pockets. "Got a light, son?" he looked into Sulphur's incendiary eyes.

"No, sir," he lied, without knowing why. "Sorry, sir."

"Know how many men we expected to lose in the invasion, son?" Roosevelt asked as Donovan flicked a lighter for the president.

"No, sir." He did his best to act like a soldier. He wasn't a soldier. A spy maybe, a Midwestern businessman, perhaps, an arsonist, definitely. But he had never considered himself a soldier.

"Ten thousand." The president grinned, his eyes glowing brighter. "Know how many soldiers we expected it would take to invade Africa?"

"No, sir."

"Half a million." The president bit the tip of his cigarette holder, keeping it firmly in place as his smile grew larger.

FDR was thinner than Sulphur had expected. Less healthy. He hadn't known him to be a cripple and was shocked to see him confined to a wheelchair like a convalescent.

The president, his blue eyes afire, stared directly into his face. "Now here's the crux of it all, Sulphur—we only needed a total invasion force of a hundred-ten thousand men. Of those, we expected to lose ten thousand lives. And we lost less than two hundred. That's great work. You saved a lot of innocent people."

"Thank you, sir," the spy barked in his best soldier's cadence.

"No, son." FDR's voice softened. "Thank you. And for your contribution to the North African campaign, I hereby promote you to the rank of captain in the OSS."

"Thank you, sir," said Sulphur, his eyes straight ahead. Had he looked at the president at that moment, his proud smile would have exploded like a hand grenade.

Roosevelt's eyes radiated the glory of America, its undying allegiance to freedom, its patriotic call to honor. "The world will never know its debt to you."

Chapter 19

August 29, 1990

I have labored to present the correspondence between Daniel Oliver Gilday (Danny) and Yvonne Allison Leslie Pippin (Allison) in as true a form as possible, given the unique method through which they exchanged letters. I was up all night keying their letters into the computer, fascinated by their relationship. Improbable as it appears, I am personally convinced the two did begin their longstanding relationship via air mail. That is to say—a homing pigeon circumvented the U.S. Postal Service, providing direct communication between the two young friends.

Homer, the pigeon of record, carried out his duties flawlessly for more than a year. His incredible skill enabled Danny and Allison to share their feelings and experiences, forever binding them in devotion to each other. Soulmates.

Those unfamiliar with the attributes of the homing pigeon may view this entry with a skeptical eye. However, those who have studied, owned, raced, or bred pigeons know of the remarkable abilities of this noble bird. I for one, having researched Racing Homers, am convinced of their uncanny instincts and dedication to their masters.

And again, no doubt, the Council of Ancients had an unseen hand guiding the great bird back and forth between our two stars.

May 31, 1979

Allison,

It worked! The experiment really worked. I'm so glad you wrote. Tell me everything. Your name, age, phone number—all the good stuff. Especially why you're locked in a tower.

I'll tell you about me. My name is Daniel Oliver Gilday. Call me Danny. I'm eleven, born an April Fool, and proud of it. I live in Colerain, near Northgate Mall. It used to be a field where we could ride bikes and build forts, but now it's a place where people buy stuff they don't need.

I'll save you, my damsel, but first I need a horse. Knights in shining armor ride horses. Until then, my trusty bird will watch over you.

Your friend,

Danny

June 5, 1979

Dear Danny,

I don't believe it—it's a sign—we have the exact same birthday! Exact same! Isn't that absotively wondrous? I'm eleven, too, born April 1, 1968! I hope you can read my teeny writing, there isn't much space on these notes. Evenwise, my whole name is Yvonne Allison Leslie Pippin. I hate the name Yvonne, so I insist the nuns call me Allison. Everybody does, except Mother Superior. Oops, I should have told you earlier I live in a Catholic orphanage called St. Als, so I don't have a phone number.

That's also why I'm a damsel in distress. I've been stuck here six whole years. I'm not complaining, though. The sisters are good to me, especially Sister Dena. It's just that I want to live in a real home. Sorry, out of room. Write soon.

Your Pen Pal,
Allison

June 6, 1979

Dear Allison,

I rigged an old shotgun shell around Homer's neck to carry bigger notes, two notebook pages in all. Now we can write all we want. Sorry you're stuck there. Somebody will adopt you soon. When that happens, be sure and tell me where you moved. I don't wanna lose touch now that we got this cool pen pal system going.

I've been thinking about you ever since the first note. It's so cool we have the same B-day! It must be fate. Do you believe in fate? I do. I want to tell you lots of things about me and learn lots of things about you. What do you look like? Are you pretty? Are you tall? What do you do for fun?

I paint, study the stars, read and write stories. I was supposed to be accepted into the Young Artists program at the Art Museum but they said I was too young. It's for fifteen-year-olds and up. That made my father mad, so he canceled a dinner with the curator (lucky for me). I could have been in major trouble if that curator came over.

I play outside a lot, but I like to be alone, too. I'm teaching myself how to copy paintings. Mom says I'm a pretty good painter. Well, I'm not so good at writing long letters yet, so I guess I should end now.

Your Friend of Fate,
Danny

July 2, 1979

Dear Danny,

I *do* believe in fate! Don't laugh, I believe God sent you to me. Homer landed in my bell tower as a sign of hope. God protects me. I'm His angel. And you, no matter what, are going to save me, right?

I love reading, just like you, especially the newspaper (I've been reading it every day since I was eight), and Nancy Drew mysteries. Did you read that the Supreme Court ruled minors don't need their parents' permission for an abortion? Cheesecake, the nuns had a cow over that! I can't ever imagine having to make that choice. The nuns act like Armageddon is coming because of it. I don't know what's right. I only know there are too many unwanted kids in here and not enough parents willing to adopt.

I love, absotively love, gardening. I have a whole garden full of vegetables. I especially love beets. I collect seeds in a small canvas bag I found in the abandoned east wing. And Sister Dena—she's my best adult friend and the only sane one around here—let me send away for a wildflower catalogue. But, of all the things in the world, I love my orchid most of all. It came as a miracle on my first Christmas Eve here. Her name is Seraph.

I love my roommate Mary, too. She's sweet, and Sister Dena. Sister D tutors me afternoons three days a week. I like to learn, unlike some of the other kids in here who don't read or do their work at all. I don't blame them. Everyone here has been left behind. We're all unwanted. For some, I think it's hard to care. Not for me, though. I'm a bright-sider. I do my best to shine.

I blabbed for too long now. Write soon and tell me about you.

Your Friend of Fate,
Allison

July 16, 1979

Dear Allison,

Now you have two miracles: Homer and your miracle orchid. Geez and crackers, my mom has an orchid, too! Isn't that weird? Hers is golden, a color so rare I've never seen it in any other flower. I've only seen that color twice before—once when I got hit by a car and knocked unconscious—and another time when I saw a flying saucer. That makes me think Mom's orchid is some sort of outer-space flower.

Do you believe in UFOs? I do. I saw one. It was the freakiest thing, and ever since that night I get messages in my head. Talking light I call it. I consider it an honor to receive their transmissions even if I can't translate everything they're saying. Now only you and my ex-therapist Dr. Muse know about talking light. Messages from the Cosmos.

Something freaky is going on here—I keep a journal, too! I tell ya, fate is working on us. Don't you think? Homer, orchids, reading, journals—pretty dang freaky! Hey, I have a great idea! Why don't we make a top-secret pact? We can tell each other our darkest, most private stories, and no one else will know. What do you think?

Your Friend of Fate,
Danny

July 29, 1979

Dear Danny,

I would love, absotively love, to form a pact with you. I have no experience at this except when I tried to put together my detectives club, which bombed despite the fact

195

that I single-handedly cracked numerous high-profile orphanage cases. Why don't we start a club called The Friends of Fate and have a pact the members swear to? It will be absotively splendid!

Jesus with a twin brother, we're so much alike I feel like I know you. Does that make sense? There's lots more miracles than just orchids and pigeons and journals, I'm surrounded by miracles! My life is filled with them. It's like I just think of what I want and it appears for me. Most of the time. The only thing that hasn't come true for me is finding a home with people who love me. But I will! I'm absotively sure of it! Too many miracles flying around here for it not to happen.

I suppose UFOs could exist. Sister D said humans are God's chosen species and mankind is pretty much it as intelligence goes. I don't see why there can't be both aliens and God. Why not? If you say you saw a spaceship, then I believe you. I never saw one, but I'd like to. As long as they didn't abduct me and perform all kinds of gross experiments on my paralyzed body. From your account, it sounds like you have friendly aliens speaking to you.

Did you see in the paper where the Ayatollah banned broadcast music? I don't think I could bear it if I couldn't hear "Instant Karma" by John Lennon occasionally. It's my favorite. Especially the chorus—the part about shining on. I love it! When I was younger, I used to think it was Instant Carmel. Now I know better.

Evenwise, I think the Ayatollah (if he doesn't like music) must be anti-talking light, too. Stay out of Iran. I don't have talking light exactly. But I do have visions, realistic dreams where angels and spirits talk to me. They tell me things in my sleep. The scenes in my dreams sometimes come true. Usually, I dream strange, heavenly thoughts of magical places and celestial beings. I barely remember a place called Shanidar. There have been times during the day when light has visited, surrounding me with warm peace. Sister D advised me, just like your doctor did you, to be quiet about it. Only she and Mary know. I love it when the light comes to visit. It fills me with bliss.

I weeded my garden today—cheesecake, was it hot! I was sweating buckets. I picked some scrumptious tomatoes and a cucumber and made a salad. Fresh vegetables. Mmm. The fruit trees I planted from seed last year, that nobody believed would survive, are growing pretty good. They won't bear fruit for a long, long time, and with the grace of the Almighty, I'll be gone by then.

Evenwise, I think it's neat you like to paint. I don't know what you mean when you say you copy paintings. Is that legal? Gotta go, the bell is due to ring on the hour—it's almost four. This is not the place to be when the clapper strikes. I made that mistake once, scared the Lucifer out of me. Vibrations echoed through my whole body. Boing! I couldn't hear for two days, either. So, I absotively must be going.

Your Freaky Friend of Fate,

Allison

August 4, 1979

Dear Freaky,

Just kidding (ha-ha). I took a stab at writing our pact. I made two copies—sign and spit in the lower right corner on both and send one back to me. That way we each have one. I spit in the corner already, so try and spit on top of my hocker.

Friends of Fate

Super Secret Pact

(tell no one or die!)

We, Danny and Allison, do swear on our most highest honor on this 7th day of August in the year of our Lord, 1979, that we will share our most deepest secrets with each other and no one else.

We are bound by fate and miracles to trust and take care of each other no matter what, for as long as we both shall live. It is our sworn duty and fate to seek out and find miracles to help the world. Should either person break this pact, may a squadron of pigeons poop on their head. (trust me, Allison, it's ugly).

Friend of Fate,   Friend of Fate,

Danny   Allison

I thought the miracle part was a nice touch; we should help the world. I dated the pact the 7th to give Homer time to get to you, just in case. I never know if he stops along the way to play with other pigeons or visits a girlfriend or what.

Cal (he's my brother) and me just got back from Lake Cumberland. We bum around together all the time and have lots of fun. I like going to the lake. We fish and tell jokes and goof off. I take Homer there all the time, except this trip because he was flying a secret mission to St. Als.

Father asked me where he was. I had to fib, told him I didn't know, which is close to true. Sometimes any answer to Father is a bad one. I've worked hard to figure him out, what to say and not. But Father is so unpredictable, it's best to avoid him. That's the plan Cal and I devised to keep from getting spanked.

As far as painting goes, I have a super-duper absolute secret you can't tell anyone, no matter what. Are you ready? Promise? Cross your heart and swear on the Friends of

Fate? Here it is: I'm going to become a master forger. I've already forged two of my father's paintings. I'm planning my next forgery now. I can make tons of money at this and make a great career. Danny Gilday—master forger. Sounds cool, doesn't it?

Forging things is as easy as drinking a pop. I see things in my mind, like I can with my eyes. It's cool. I've always been able to see. Mom says I have vision, calls me her star-child. I don't think it's the same kind of visions that you have—you sound psychic to me. Mine's more memory than anything.

Did you know my initials backwards spell GOD? How about that? Isn't that cool? I wonder if my folks thought of that when they named me. Nah. Your's spelled backwards is PLAY. Neat, huh?

I'd love to see what you look like. Do you want to exchange pictures? Let me know.

Well, it's time to go catch fireflies with Cal. We had a bedroom full of a hundred, once, flying all over. Cal likes to squish the glow part off and smear it on stuff. He's weird that way. He swore he wouldn't kill any this time. If he squishes any I'm gonna punch him. Send a picture.

> Your Friend of Fate,
> Danny

August 7, 1979

Dear Future Convict,

I have so much to write. Where to start? I signed the pact, it's perfect. Now we are bound, you and I, forever. Since we're official Friends of Fate, I have some advice for you—give up your plan of becoming a master forger. A life of crime isn't like TV, where criminals are heroes. Lots of St. Als kids are here because their fathers or mothers broke the law doing drugs or robbing banks or worse, are either in jail or dead. It's not right. You're too smart to waste yourself. Why do you want to ruin your gift? You've been blessed by God. Can't you see that?

Also, your father is the only one you'll ever have. You should try and be good to him. I wish I had a dad. Alas, my father is the Lord. He protects me. He sent Homer to me. I'm such a fortunate girl.

Exchanging pictures is an absotively splendid idea! I didn't send one yet because I have to sneak it from the St. Als photo album. Next flight, I'm yours, at least on film. Please send me yours air mail real soon. Did you hear that Iran closed its leading newspaper today? Cheesecake, talk about censorship. Thank God we live in America, where the news is reported accurately. Although Barney, in her sisterly duties, takes a Magic Marker and blackens out the daily horoscope in *The Enquirer* every morning (she calls it evil), but not before she reads what Jean Dixon says about *her* sign.

Do you ever think of Homer when he's visiting me? He's so graceful and pretty zipping through the sky. I feed him old bread the nuns throw out. He likes his head scratched while he's eating. I'm still amazed at God's grace for bringing you to me. You're my true Friend of Fate.

That's why I wrote those things earlier. I care about you. You need to stay out of jail long enough to save me. After that, you can steal the crown jewels, if you like. Then I can spring you from the slammer. Evenwise, kidding aside, you are my friend and I do care.

Okay, no more boring lectures. I get enough from the nuns, and I'm sure you do from your parents and teachers.

Oh, no, it's starting to rain. Must go. Bye. Write.

Your Savior of Fate,

The Red Angel

August 18, 1979

Dear Red Angel,

Geez and crackers, I didn't know I needed saving. Your letter miffed me at first, but I can't be mad at you for caring. Don't worry about me, Red Angel. I have a guardian angel of my own sitting on my shoulder. He's always here. Just like you with your God, it's the same thing.

Besides, forgery is harmless fun. Who really cares about a bunch of rich people being tricked by a fake? Since I'm only eleven, the cops wouldn't touch me. Besides, I only forge stuff to see if I can get away with it. So far I've been lucky. It's not like I'm in the Mafia.

Don't forget, I have talking light on my side. It sends the right stuff into my noggin. I can't go wrong with space-age code from the Cosmos keeping me straight. Sometimes, it feels like I'm being programmed like a computer. It's not painful or anything, just freaky. My brain learns more and more all the time. It's like a force field of knowledge protecting me. They aren't about to let anything happen to their star-child.

I *always* think of you when Homer is visiting. I pretend I'm there in the bell tower with you. I can see you petting him. I daydream about flying like Homer, up above the Earth on the wind, sweeping you away from there. You and I would travel the world, helping people. We'd fly like Peter Pan and Wendy. Cool, huh?

Have you ever wondered what it would be like to be a bird? To fly around the world? Someday, I'm going to fly to space. Not by myself—in a rocket. I bet by the year 2010 (we'll be 42), people will fly to space as easy as flying to New York. I hope so. The talking light says so. So does *Omni* magazine.

I have to go. I need to put this note on Homer, then clean his loft. Father's orders.

Then I have to cut the grass. What a drag. Hope you like my picture. It was taken at my birthday party. That's Grandma planting a big kiss on me.

Your Reformed Criminal,
Danny

August 23, 1979

Dear Danny,

Thanks for the picture! You're cute. I'll keep it forever. I looked at your blue eyes a hundred times already. You could be a hypnotist. I can't tell from your letter if you listened to me and quit forgery or if you're just explaining why you will still do it. Evenwise, I think it's wrong. I've started praying for your soul every night! I am also most skeptical that your cosmic trainers, talking light as you call it, would recommend forgery as a career. Methinks thou needs a translator. That's my opinion on the matter.

I smuggled Homer to my room in my book bag. After the rain the last time, I decided I need a better place to write from. I took him out and put crust on the windowsill so he'll know where to come next time. I gave him careful instructions, too. Besides, once winter gets here it would be nice if I didn't have to freeze getting your letters. The nuns will also think it awful peculiar for me slip off to the bell tower in mid-winter; they're a suspicious bunch, these nuns. Not that we don't give them reason. Somebody is always scheming. But they like catching us. It's like a game. Mother Peculiar enjoys blistering a fanny or two per week.

I found a picture for you. It's not very flattering, and I almost didn't send it. But I promised, and I can't break my word. Evenwise, it must have taken lots of guts for you to send one with your grandma smooching you. I think it's absotively sweet. My red hair and freckles (which I like to call God's kisses) really stick out in this one. I think it was taken at the zoo on a very bad day for me. There isn't a better picture, evenwise; the nuns don't take many. Too much work maybe.

I've blabbed enough already. Ask Homer to remember my windowsill. I hope you like my picture.

Your Friend of Fate,
Allison

Sept 4, 1979

Dear Allison,

I love your red hair! Geez and crackers, whose the woman behind you? She looks like a giant cinder block! Is she part of the building (ha-ha)? Mother Superior, right? I really do like your picture. A lot. It's so cool to see your face. I love your smile. Don't get the wrong idea here, I'm not trying to get mushy. And just because we signed the Friends of Fate pact doesn't mean you're my girlfriend or anything.

I put all your letters in a shoe box for safe keeping. Mom got me new gymmies for school. They're red with green shoestrings. Wild, man. School starts tomorrow. I have bus number twenty-nine. I have to be at the corner at 6:50 a.m. That's too early for a kid.

Sorry I didn't write sooner. We just got back from the lake yesterday. I couldn't send Homer on a mission because Father would get mad. Things aren't much better with him. Mom made her award-winning meatloaf Saturday. Father got upset because Cal lost a fishing pole. His face turned red. He tried to say something, couldn't, and smashed the meatloaf against the wall instead.

Mom yelled. Father stormed out. I scraped a good hunk of clean loaf off the floor, and Father hadn't flipped the mashed potatoes, so we had a good meal anyway. Nobody said much; we were in shock. Mom looked sad, as usual, when it comes to Father. I can't tell you how many meals end up that way.

After he leaves, the meal is actually a lot better. Maybe we need to get him mad before dinner, then he wouldn't show up at all, and we wouldn't have to serve our meals from the floor. It's a thought. But, as requested, Allison, I am trying to get along with him.

Enough about Father. I missed you. I want to write you everyday. I don't think Homer's wings could take it, though. Do you miss me? Do you think about me? Have you started school yet? What are your classes? Write soon.

Your Friend of Fate,
Danny

Sept. 6, 1979

Dear Danny,

Homer made it to my window! I got back from class and he was sitting on my ledge sunning himself. I gave him some bread. He ate it up. Birds don't smile, but if they did, I think he was.

To answer your question, I think about you all the time. I look at your picture a hundred times a day. I showed Mary (swore her to secrecy, of course): she thinks you're a doll. I know you probably don't like that word, being a boy, but Mary does think you're cute.

School is in for me, too. I love it! I absotively love it! There is no place like a classroom with books and activities and assignments. It's great! There's only a few things I'd rather do. I made a list. Maybe you could make one, too.

Allison's Things To Do

1. Leave St. Als
2. Meet Daniel Oliver Gilday
3. Meet the pope
4. Read in the library

201

5. Stop the civil war in El Salvador
6. Go to Lake Cumberland
7. Work in my garden
8. Help the homeless
9. Fly like Homer
10. Restore democracy to Iran

There it is, my top things. What do you think? I can't write much today, tons of homework. See ya.

Your Friend of Fate,
Allison

Sept. 16, 1979

Dear Allison,

I know what you mean about schoolwork—I'm buried, too. The sixth grade is tougher than fifth. It's not the assignments that are hard—it's the number of them. School has always been easy for me, but this year there is so much more to do.

Sorry my note is so short, I have to write a 500 word essay. I chose the environment as my topic. I've been worried about it for awhile. My father thinks I'm being eccentric. He would. Nobody ever takes things seriously until it's a disaster, then everybody says "I told you so." Adults are weird that way. They shut their eyes to what's going on, don't do anything about it until it's too late, then look for somebody to blame. Not me. I'm doing something about pollution. With all the environmental problems in the world it should be easy to write an essay. Top 10 list coming soon to an orphanage near you. Write me.

Your Friend of Fate,
Danny

Oct. 6, 1979

Dear Danny,

Any note from you brightens me up. I run to my room after class each day to see if Homer is on my sill. Today he was. I have a great big smile right now. I'm looking at your picture while I write.

Jesus landing a 747 at the airport, the pope is in America! Isn't that absotively fabulous? He's the greatest, most spiritual pope ever! He said mass for two million people in Ireland. Two million, can you imagine!

He visited the United Nations on the second, and he will be at the White House today. The news commented about how his message condemning birth control, abortion, and liberal sex (whatever that is) is out of date. They're just jealous. They hardly mentioned his call for world peace and human rights. He's such a peaceful man.

How come they pick on him? I think he is the greatest person alive. Oh, were I to be worthy of his grace, he might bless me, and I would find a home.

Mother Superior flew to New York to hear him say Mass at Yankee Stadium. Wouldn't that be glorious? To see the pope, oh Lord, it would be absotively glorious! St. Als is all adorned for his visit. No, he's not visiting us, but it's decorated just the same, in honor of his being in America.

Wouldn't you like to see the pope, Danny? Me and you flying to New York (like Homer of course) to visit the pontiff? Wouldn't that be absotively splendid? I'm just bursting with happiness. Mary doesn't share my enthusiasm; she says if he was so great, we wouldn't be stuck here in the first place. I don't understand her logic, but she does admit he's a decent guy. She just doesn't care to see him. She says he's just a man in a funny white hat.

I have to go. He's going to be on TV later, and we are having special Mass tonight. Bye. Write soon. God bless.

> Your Friend of Fate,
> Allison

Oct. 20, 1979

Dear Allison,

It's good to hear from you. I love getting your letters. Mother Superior at Yankee Stadium? Do you think she wore a Yankees cap to see the pope? Now batting, number seventeen, His Holiness, Pope John Paul II. Wouldn't that be a kick?

Geez and crackers, you *are* into the pope, huh? I admit he's a decent guy who's done a lot of good for the Catholic Church. Lots of people follow him. I don't agree on some of his views, though. Under the terms of the Friends of Fate pact, I'm allowed to share my opinion on this. So don't get mad at me! Here goes.

Why doesn't the pope spend a few hundred million on the starving poor? I know the Catholics are rich. Father says they own more real estate than anybody. And the Vatican Bank is one of the largest in the world. Can't they do something?

How can the pope be against birth control when there is so much tragedy in the world? People are dying by the thousands. Birth control might help. I don't mean to preach, Allison, but how can a church, which should be helping mankind, turn its back on it? Don't be mad.

How can a guy (the pope) and a bunch of crusty old bishops know what it's like to be pregnant? Don't they watch the news? Don't they read *The Enquirer?* Don't they live in the real world? I say it's wrong for the pope to be against abortion when he doesn't know what it's really like. He lives in luxury with no problems at all. Let him get pregnant and see how he feels.

Well, that's my view. Please don't be mad. Sometimes when I get going I just can't help myself. I thought about whether I should send this letter at all, or tear it up and write a new one. But we're such good friends, I should be able to say what I feel. Please write soon.

Your Friend of Fate,
Danny

October 31, 1979

Dear Danny,

I almost didn't write back—you atheist PIG! There, I got it out of me. I read your letter over and over looking for something positive. Then I told Mary about it (without violating our pact), who claims I'm over-reacting out of some sort of mental illness called PFS—Papal Father Syndrome. She said I've projected my need for a male parent into a fixation on the pope. Says I'm in love with a Polish celibate because I know I can never have him. It's all so very complex. She made it up, of course, but the thought of it made me laugh (hysterically), and I'm not mad at you anymore. You should thank Mary.

I didn't write for a long time just to teach you a lesson. Now behave! No more trashing the Holy Father. You did say in your letter that you thought he did a lot of good, so I suppose you made a weak attempt at giving him his due. I'll give you credit for recognizing his greatness. Since I lectured you about forgery, and you lectured me on the pope, we're even now. Okay?

Are you going out for Halloween? It's tonight. The orphanage is having a party. Everybody gets costumes and stuff. I'm not a big Halloweener. It's a devil's night. I'm not sure why the Church allows it. It's Satanic if you ask me. Sister D says it's harmless. Maybe so. I'll save my joy for Christmas and Easter, two days of the Lord.

Don't get me wrong, I'm dressing up, and I'm going to get my share of candy. I'm just going to only half enjoy it. I like getting candy bars and those little peanut butter chews that come in black or orange wax paper. I like those. Mary complains about people that give apples. I always eat hers. Fruit is nature's candy.

Did you see all those antinuke protesters arrested on Wall Street two days ago? They hauled over a thousand people to jail. I only bring it up because of how interested you are in such things. I can't believe they arrested them. This is America, not Iran. This is America, right? Aren't we allowed to protest? Isn't that our right?

Evenwise, I've been thinking (when I'm not mad at you) how great it would be to meet you in person, to hear your voice. I've been thinking a lot about it. Wouldn't that be absotively splendid?

I have to sign off, time to dress up for Fright Night. I'm wearing a white angels outfit with gold lamé trim, it's very pretty.

Your Friend of Fate,
Allison

p.s.—You owe me a Top 10 list!

204

Nov. 4, 1979

Dear Allison,

Can you believe the Iranians seized the U.S. embassy today? Jimmy Carter is going to kick the crap out of those guys. Why do foreigners hate America so much? They call us the Great Satan over there. No way! It's not just the Iranians: the Europeans and Libyans and Cubans and lots of other people hate our guts. How come? I thought we were loved all over. That's what they taught us in school anyway. Oh well, they've probably just been brainwashed against us.

By the way, Saint Allison, it's amazing to me you have any faith in the Catholic Church at all, seeing as how you've been in that place for over six years. I guess if you still believe in the church and the pope after the stuff you've been through, I should, too.

Official List of Daniel Oliver Gilday
1. Meet Saint Allison
2. Win the Pulitzer Prize
3. Use goofy words like Saint Allison
4. Forge the Mona Lisa
5. Travel to outer space
6. Lake Cumberland
7. Stop nuclear waste
8. Make friends with Father
9. Talk to the talking light
10. Learn to play an instrument

Now that's a great list! You see who's at the top don't you? In fact, you hold two spots in the Top 10. I must be getting soft, letting a girl influence me like that. I almost put another thing on there but couldn't.

I really want to meet you badly. Maybe someday we will. We should make that our goal, to meet real soon. I have to see that red hair for myself.

Have to go feed Homer and send him off with a message to my best friend.

Your Friend of Fate,

Danny

Nov. 15, 1979

Dear Danny,

Am I really your best friend? My heart skipped a beat when I read that. I kissed your letter and squeezed it tight. It's wrinkled now. I never knew you felt the same way as me. I've wanted to tell you for so long that you're my best friend, but I was scared. Silly me.

Mary's over there on her bed puckering up, making smoochy sounds with her lips.

205

Gross! "Grow up, Mary!" I shouted. She's laughing now. She says you're not my best friend—she is—but she says you *are* my best *boy*friend. She says I'm in love. Can a 6th grader be in love? All I know is hearing from you makes me smile, smile, smile. If that makes you my boyfriend, so be it.

I have a confession. I looked up your phone number. I almost called you after school. I had the dime in the phone and everything. I hung up before I dialed. Nerves. I had to sneak to do it. Would it be okay to call you? Just to hear your voice? The more we write, the more I want to meet you. My chest hurts to think about it, not a bad hurt, a good hurt. I feel funny all over. All tingly.

I've been daydreaming about having Thanksgiving dinner with you and your family. To smell the turkey cooking. Meeting your parents and Cal. I'm absotively sure I could sweet talk your dad. He'd love me like a daughter if he just met me. It would be so glorious. We have good Thanksgivings here, but turkey day reminds everybody of our situation, having no parents and all that. Some kids take it bad. Lock themselves in their room. Or disrupt dinner by throwing food. I say it's caused by feeling unwanted. The nuns try real hard. And we always have a delicious meal. Still, it's tough on some kids, especially the Cutters.

Evenwise, I love my Gilday Thanksgiving fantasy. Maybe I should put that on my list. Then I'd have two entries with you. Actually, if you look at my number 6 (go to Lake Cumberland) I really meant to go there with you, so I now have three things on my list with you included.

About your Official List. I have some questions—especially about numbers 3, 4, and 9.

3) Use goofy words like Saint Allison. What's that supposed to mean? You owe me an answer, bub!

4) Forge the Mona Lisa. We talked about this—GROW UP!

9) Talk to the talking light. I need to understand this more. I don't think I paid as much attention as I should have.

Evenwise, write and tell me what you mean by numbers 3, 4, and 9 so I can sleep at night. I think I need a stronger prayer for you, Daniel Oliver Gilday! Plus you have to tell me the thing you almost put on the list—it's part of our pact. We must share our deepest secrets. I have it in writing, so spill your guts.

Write me soon. I can't wait.

Love,

Saint Al

p.s.—Can you believe what's happening in Iran? President Carter just froze their assets. They must be nuts to challenge the United States.

Nov. 22, 1979

Dear Allison,

Thanksgiving Day. I timed my letter so Homer delivers it on Thanksgiving to cheer you up. I want you to smile, smile, smile. We just ate dinner. It was DE-LICIOUS! It's only 2:30 in the afternoon and the meal's over already. Kind of weird how we eat a great big dinner at 1:30 when we usually eat around 6 o'clock. I'm stuffed. Ugh!

I'm so full I couldn't eat my pumpkin pie. I'll eat it later. Mom tried to cram some cranberry crud down me. Disgusting. She finally gave up after I took a bite and pretended to choke. Grandpa laughed. Father told me to behave. "Daniel, behave!" he ordered. "Yes, *mein capitan*," I wanted to say. But I shut up. Didn't matter, though—I got out of eating cranberry sauce. I asked for extra beets instead. Father hates beets; he insists they're for peasants. That sure came out of left field.

I thought about you all through dinner. Imagining you at the table with your smile, smile, smile and your beautiful red hair. Freckles, too. I have to meet you, I have to. Let's make plans right away.

Me and Cal are going to play touch football in awhile, then we're going to hear Mrs. Smitch's dog Mozart play chopsticks on the piano. No one actually believes he can do it, but it does make Mrs. Smitch feel good when we come over. To answer your questions about my *Official List*—especially numbers 3, 4, and 9, here is my best explanation.

3) Use goofy words like Saint Allison. You use some really cool words no one else says, like evenwise and absotively and cheesecake. Nobody says those words—well, people say cheesecake, but only when they're ordering dessert. It's cute. If I made up some words, people would think I was cool, too. So I figure I could make up a word like posilutely, which is a cross between positively and absolutely. You say absotively which is the same thing, only different. Do you get it? You should be flattered at my number 3 thing. It's a compliment.

4) Forge the Mona Lisa. A boy has a right to dream, doesn't he? It isn't like I already bought the supplies and sketched it out. But I have made a list of what it would take to pull it off. Don't worry, Saint Al, it's just a dream, not a plan. Although I wouldn't stop praying for me just yet.

9) Talk to the talking light. Well, I need to take lots of time to explain that one— and I can't do that today. Maybe I could save that for when we meet. Who knows, maybe the light will be talking when we see each other and you can put your head next to mine and see if you hear anything. Wouldn't that be cool? Excuse me, wouldn't that be posilutely cool?

I made up my mind to tell you what I almost put on the list. It's tough to write. It's kind of personal, so don't laugh at me. And don't think I'm getting all mushy either. And don't make a big deal out of it 'cause it's hard enough already. And you can't tell

anyone under the terms of our pact. If you do, the Friends of Fate will send a jillion pigeons to poop on you!

Okay, I'm ready now. Cross your heart and swear on the Friends of Fate. Ready?

I want to kiss you.

Satisfied? I confessed my biggest, most difficult secret to you. Is it okay to want that? Actually, I kiss your picture every time I send you Air Mail. I figure we already spit on our pact together, so we pretty much shared saliva anyhow. Have you ever kissed my picture, or thought about it? Would you let me kiss you?

My stomach feels funny, must be too much food. I have to go. Bye.

> Your Friend of Fate,
> Danny

Nov. 25, 1979

Dear Danny,

I'm the happiest girl ever! I kiss your picture everyday (right after I pray for your soul). It's sort of the finishing touch for God, you know? It's my own personal blessing so He knows I really mean it. I stare at your crystal blue eyes and dream about us being together. It might not be too normal for a girl my age to be in love, but I am. I love you! Of course you may kiss me.

Mary says I'm on my way to being a slut. Like she would know. There are a few girls here, like Rita and Rachel, who are really loose and talk about boys all the time. Not me. The nuns lecture us weekly on the value of abstinence. They talk about boys and how they will do and say anything to sleep with a girl. Like nuns would know. I simply can't imagine the last time any man hit on one of the aged sisters from St. Als.

Evenwise, I'm too young for sex, real sex that is. A little kiss with you is okay. I'm not sure how people even do sex. It must be one of those things that comes when you get breasts. I heard Joyce and Rita talking about it.

I'm not sure why, but Joyce has never liked me. She picks on me sometimes and tells on me. She might be jealous because Sister Dena treats me special. Joyce seems like an okay person. Other girls say she's friendly, she just doesn't like me. She calls me Allison Appleseed. Oh well, no point worrying about it.

Evenwise, I can't wait to meet you. I have a confession, too—I wanted to kiss you for a long time, too. I've thought about it a lot. That's probably why Mary thinks I'm being promiscuous (that's a word Sister Claudia uses in her sex lectures—I had to look it up). Don't you think adults should use words kids understand, especially if they're trying to teach you something? Cheesecake, I sat through the whole class on sex with Clod using that word, and I didn't know what she meant. Looking around the room, neither did anyone else.

Finally, I raised my hand and asked her. She got all flusterated and stuttered and closed her book and dismissed the class. Clod couldn't handle describing sex with any other word than promiscuous. Now Clod is a woman with a boob problem—they hang to her belly button. No kidding. Goofy, huh?

By the way, I thought about your Official List answers. You use plenty of goofy words already like geez and crackers, freaky, weird, cool, jillion. Those words are all yours. When I hear someone else say them, I think of you. If you absotively think it will help your vocabulary, go ahead.

I talked with Sister D about what the strongest, most potent prayer possible for a person's soul (short of a full exorcism) might be. She's consulting with a higher authority. But not before she raised her eyebrows and almost asked me why. I'm not too sure how I would have explained it. "You see, I know this boy who is determined to become a criminal." It just won't do.

Stay out of jail long enough for us to kiss!

Your Friend of Fate,
Saint Al

Dec 4, 1979

Dear Saint Al,

I love you, too! I never had a real girlfriend before. It feels neat.

Did you hear about The Who concert? God. Eleven people trampled to death at Riverfront Coliseum. I don't get it. What's so great about a rock concert that people should die over it? The Who is a good band, but people getting killed to see them play? It's crazy.

I talked to my mom about it because it's been bothering me. She said people got in a panic and didn't realize they were crushing other people. I don't know, it doesn't seem right. People should respect each other more. They should pay attention better. I'm bummed.

Your Friend of Fate,
Danny

Dec 5, 1979

Dear Danny,

Me, too. The sisters say it's Satan who rules rock 'n' roll. They blame everything bad on Satan and give God credit for everything good. I believe in good and evil, but people are to blame for most of it. I cried when I saw the bodies covered in sheets on TV. Why do innocent people have to die? How could this happen in Cincinnati? I can't understand how someone could step on another person and not stop to help them. It's so absotively sad. I'm wearing black all week, in mourning for the victims.

Your Friend of Fate,
Allison

Dec 7, 1979

Dear Allison,

Winter sure is here. Brutally cold, man! I don't know if Homer should fly when it's this cold out. He might get sick. Father and I moved his loft to the garage to protect him till spring. It's hard to send him out on missions when he can't make it back inside the garage. He can't knock on the door—his claws are too small—plus, I wouldn't hear him.

I don't know what to do. One thing I know is I can't let a little cold weather stop us from writing. Any ideas? Can you call me? Can I call you? We have to work this out!

Christmas break is coming soon. That will be nice. We need to figure it out by then. Can I write you normally, use the post office and stamps and envelopes? Do you get mail there? I'm worried we won't find a way, and I'll be lonely all winter long. Help!

Your Friend of Fate,

Danny

Dec 11, 1979

Dear Danny,

I don't have an answer. Phone calls are tough, even for a superspy like me. Letters will raise suspicion, and I don't trust the sisters to *not* read my mail. Can Homer stay with me? Maybe I could hide him in my closet. I've been saying a great prayer for you, thanks to Sister D, who came through with what she calls the granddaddy of all Catholic soul-saving prayers.

I might be able to call you once in awhile, but you can't call me. If the nuns ever found out about us they would go crazy. We have to lay low (that's detective talk). I used to pretend I was a detective. I could mail letters to you, but that doesn't help much since you can't write back. Are you sure Homer can't fly in winter? I'll have to really, really think about this. Maybe Mary has an idea.

Did you see in the paper that Mother Theresa won the Nobel Peace Prize? Isn't that great? What a wonderful woman she is. She inspires me. Oh, to work alongside her in the streets of Calcutta helping the unfortunate ones. I would absotively love to do missionary work and help the poor. Who wouldn't though, right?

Someday I will be just like Mother Theresa—helping anyone who needs it. Without question. I want to be just like her. She is so humble and kind. She is a woman all women can look up to—and all men can, too! God has blessed her life.

Do you think maybe God is punishing us, keeping us from writing, because you insist on breaking the law? Because you're determined to be a forger? Maybe He is trying to send us a message about goodness and doing what's right. What do you think? He may have heard my prayers and decided He needed to step in directly and straighten you out. (Even if it is painful for me.) It's possible. You better listen, Daniel Oliver Gilday.

Your Friend of Fate,

Allison

Dec 15, 1979

Dear Allison,

I think Father Winter is the one to blame for keeping us apart. Funny how winter comes every year. I really don't think God invented the seasons so He could use them as a way to keep us from writing. Nice try, though. It's getting mighty cold out. We have to think of something quick.

Christmas is coming and I have a great surprise for you. You're gonna love it! I've been working on it since Thanksgiving. I have to think of a way to get it to you.

Why do you keep bugging me about forgery? I haven't forged anything since we met. All I did was admit I was thinking about it. Is that so bad? Lots of boys get into trouble. Cal steals twenties from Mom all the time to buy cigarettes and bubblegum. He smokes them on the side of the house, and he's only thirteen! Maybe you should pray for him, too.

There's a lot worse people to worry about than me. Every day somebody is murdered, somebody else is thrown out in the cold. And look at those Iranians holding all those hostages. They need a prayer or two. So do the hostages! I suppose I shouldn't complain if you want to make me your life's project. It can't be all that bad if you pray for me. Something good should come of it. Maybe you will win the Nobel Peace Prize for saving my soul and leading me away from a life of crime.

Hey, did you know the Nobel Peace Prize was started by the guys who invented dynamite? I looked it up. They were arms dealers. They got filthy rich selling weapons to anybody looking to fight a war. And they sold to both sides. Very ironic. Peace prizes from the guys who create wars. Adults sure behave weird. I might write a story about it.

We still haven't worked out getting together. I'd love to meet you over Christmas break. That would be posilutely cool. Wouldn't it? Can we arrange it? Can you get out? Can we meet at a mall or something? I can't stand it. I need to see you! Let me know what you think. Try real hard to work it out. I have to go—Father is yelling at Mom in the kitchen. I have to see if I can distract him. I hate it when he does that. When I grow up I'm not ever going to lose my temper—ever!

Your Friend of Fate,
Danny

Dec 16, 1979

Dear Danny,

I want to meet you so bad I could burst. But I don't think it's going to work out over Christmas. Even though we're on break, Christmas is the time of year when folks who forget about us the other fifty-one weeks begin to feel guilty. So we get all kinds of attention from people and businesses and charities. The Masons throw a party. The Magellan Company has us sing Christmas carols. All kinds of barren people begin thinking of adopting, so we have lots of tours and junk. It's so busy the sisters tack a calendar of events on the bulletin boards around St. Als and give us each one in home

211

room. I've seen the calendar so much I could recite it from memory. That's not a big deal to you, of course, being a genius and all that, but to me it's amazing. I'm sick of seeing those red construction paper calendars everywhere. Enough!

Evenwise, the schedule during Christmas break is packed. There's only a few two-to-three hour periods when something isn't planned. It's impossible to squeeze anything in between. That doesn't mean I don't want to see you. You owe me a kiss. And sooner or later I'm going to collect.

I made a present for you, too. I'm going to mail it to you in a box on Monday. I won't put my return address on there so your parents won't be suspicious. It's pretty neat to sneak with you. It's like we have this giant secret only you and I share—and Mary, of course. She thinks we're nuts, by the way. I've told her my intimate desire to kiss you and other things. She thinks it's completely gross. What does she know?

Your Friend of Fate,

Allison

p.s.—I never told her anything you wrote—that's absotively top secret!

Dec. 17, 1979

Dear Danny,

Merry Christmas! I hope this note and gift find their way to you in time for Christmas. I saw a commercial on TV from the post office which said it's important to mail early. I couldn't mail it any earlier. Evenwise, I wish you the most merriest, happiest Christmas ever!

I hope you like my present. I made it myself. Do you like the wrapping paper? It was donated by Gibson Greetings. Open it up now before you read any more, or it will ruin the moment. Go ahead, open it up.

What do you think? I'll just bet you're wondering what it is, aren't you?

It's a Christmas ornament. I made it out of Queen Anne's lace. Every summer, we girls go out and pick Queen Anne's lace. We dry them out, flatten them in a book, and paint them just before Christmas. I painted yours gold and sprinkled it with shimmering silver sparkles. It's the best one I ever made. Do you like it?

If you look real close on the back near the bottom, I wrote "I love U." See it? You can't read it very well, but it's there. Hang it on your tree so you think of me on Christmas. Just tell your parents it was a school project. I'm not one to lie, unless it's for a good cause.

I wish I could be at your house Christmas morning. The brightly lit tree. The presents scattered about underneath. The decorations around the house. It would be so glorious. I think about you all the time. I'm not joking. All the time. It must be those blue eyes in your photo. Or maybe it's your criminal nature. I read somewhere that certain women are attracted to bad men. Maybe I'm one of them. Have you given up your plans to forge the Mona Lisa? Why don't you work on winning the Pulitzer Prize, instead? It was number two on your list. That's a great goal. Maybe you should start writing a book. Evenwise, consider it.

Don't think I won't have a good Christmas, I will! I love, absotively love Christmas. I love all the ceremony of the church. We pray and go to midnight mass. We're putting on a play Wednesday night, the nineteenth. I don't have much of a part, despite my best efforts to land the starring role. I wanted to play Mary, mother of Jesus, but they gave it to Joyce Wilkerson. Probably because of her breasts. The nuns look at those things. Mine haven't grown at all. Mosquito bites. Evenwise, I have a bit part as the North Star. Still, it's a part, and I know my lines. It'll be fun.

Baby Jesus brings hope to our world. Doesn't Christmas just make you want to cry with joy? Doesn't it? I can't wait. Oops! Sister Clod is calling—time for rehearsal. I hope you like your ornament. Merry Christmas, Daniel Oliver Gilday! Happy New Year!

I Love You.

> Your Friend of Fate,
> Allison

p.s.—Kiss this spot—

> Dec 24, 1979

Dear Allison,

Merry Christmas, Saint Allison! I timed Homer's arrival for Christmas Eve day. Here's your present! I couldn't wrap it. It was tough enough figuring a way for Homer to carry it. As you can see, I used a film canister and scrunched it in to make it fit. I had tons of fun sketching it. Let me know what you think. Anyways, I hope you like it.

Thanks for the ornament. It's posilutely cool! It's hanging by my window so I can look at it more often. I'm always in my room when Father is home—hoping to avoid him. I hooked it on the curtain rod. It spins and glistens when the light hits it. It's perfect. It shines little speckles of light all over my walls like magic. I'll keep it forever.

I wish you were here. I want to see your smile, smile, smile on Christmas Day, and maybe kiss you, too! Ever since we spilled the beans to each other, I've been thinking about it nonstop. I can't get you out of my head, Allison.

How did the play come out? I'll bet you were the best North Star in history! I could never be in a school play. I can't stand up in front of all those people and remember lines. I'd freak. I'd probably stutter and say the wrong thing and turn a serious play into a comedy somehow. I'm destined *not* to be an actor. I know that for sure.

About us writing through winter, your plan using the post office should work. I suppose Homer could do fewer flights and come back right away. He would only be gone a couple hours that way. I looked on a map of the city—you're only 9.3 miles from me, as the pigeon flies. Homer could fly that far in a half-hour on a bad day. I thought it took a lot longer. I could write you, Homer could warm up with some Cracker Jacks and a little water while you write me, then come back. We could write the same day! It could work. We could send notes every two to three weeks and save up all our news. It's a good plan.

Merry Christmas, Saint Allison. I'm dreaming of you. Write back. I can't wait to hear if you like your gift.

Your Merry Friend of Fate,
Danny

Dec 24, 1979

Dearest Danny,

Jesus getting his portrait done by Michelangelo, this is the most precious gift ever! I like it even better than the present Rita Starks ordered from The 88s (they're a band of St. Als thieves). She asked them to steal "Instant Karma" for me, which they did, and Rita gave it to me this morning. Why she likes me so much, I don't know. Evenwise, we snuck over to the east wing and played it several times on a stolen turntable heisted a few years back from a local appliance store. Me and Rita danced and sang in whispers, to keep the nuns from hearing us. It was a blast.

But not even John Lennon can beat the present you made for me. I'm crying great big tears of happiness. Your drawing is the most beautiful, romantic thing I've ever seen. You can't imagine how surprised I was to see Homer shivering on my windowsill with the canister tied around his neck. He reminded me of one of those St. Bernards in the Swiss Alps with the beer kegs. How clever you are.

My hands trembled when I slid your present from it. I couldn't help but cry when I saw the pencil sketch of us with Homer in the bell tower. It's so beautiful. How did you do it? It's absotively perfect. You're so good. I knew you painted, but I didn't know you were this talented. I'm smiling and crying at the same time. Mostly, I have a smile, smile, smile. I love it so much. It's so special. Thank you. Thank you. Thank you.

Each day that goes by becomes better and better for me. Just knowing you are thinking of me makes me so happy. You are a very good person, Daniel Oliver Gilday. I'm touched that you used your great skill for something legal. There is hope for you after all, I'm absotively sure of it.

I have to find the perfect hiding place for our picture. I like the title you gave it, the Friends of Fate. You're so clever. Gosh, I'm happy. I'm bursting! I'm shining with joy.

I have an idea. With New Year's coming up, maybe we could write a new pact to always be friends. What do you think?

Homer is gorging himself on Cracker Jacks and eggnog—a little Christmas cheer for him, too. He loves it! I hope he doesn't get fat from all this sweet junk food. He's so cute next to Seraph, pecking away at his Christmas snacks.

Well, much as I hate to, I better finish up this letter. Mother Peculiar and the rest of the Catholic Crusaders will be calling us to dinner soon. Later, Sister D and I are going to read together. It's a tradition. I absotively love Sister D. She is the bestest grown up I know. She calls me her angel.

Merry, Merry, Merry Christmas, Danny! You've made this the best Christmas ever. I'm going to sleep with your picture tonight. I love you. I'll be thinking of you.

Your Friend of Fate,

Saint Allison

p.s.—Kiss this spot—

Dec 31, 1979

Dear Allison,

I'm really glad you liked the Friends of Fate sketch. I worked hard to make it right. It's New Year's Eve (like you didn't know). Cal is at a friend's, and Mom and Father are at a dinner party. I'm in my room. There's a baby-sitter downstairs. She'll be sneaking her boyfriend in anytime now, so I won't be bothered. I was planning on creeping down later to watch them make-out and get some tips on how to kiss you properly. I've been practicing on your picture. Sometimes I feel like I'm kissing St. Als' masonry, I mean Mother Superior, when I kiss your picture. It's a weird thought, I know.

Your photograph is wrinkled from my lips. I'm going to need another one soon. I made a copy of the Friends of Fate for myself, too, but I can't kiss it `cause you'll smear. Anyways, send me a new photo, if you can.

I like your pact idea. I have another one to go along with it. We should make a New Year's resolution to meet on our birthdays. We could meet on April 1 someplace really neat, like the planetarium or the Museum of Natural History. Wouldn't that be posilutely cool?

I thought about the pact. I gave it a shot.

Friends of Fate

Super Secret Pact #2

We, Danny and Allison, do swear on our most highest honor on this 31st day of December in the year of our Lord, 1979, that we will remain the truest of friends for our entire lifetimes. Forever and ever. If by chance, through no fault of our own, we become separated by an act of God, natural disaster, one of us moving, the Bubonic Plague, or any other bizarre occurrence, we will

meet at midnight on New Year's Eve 1989 (10 years from now).

Ever who shall break this pact will be subject to the evils as spelled out in Pact #1.

Friend of Fate,   Friend of Fate,
Danny   Allison

Sign and spit just like before, okay? If you want to change anything, just scribble in what you want.

Did you get any good presents for Christmas? I got some neat stuff: a bike, a Supertramp album, clothes, money from my uncle, the game of Life, and a few other things, but nothing as good as my ornament. It's the best! Oh, and I got a StarGazers glow-in-the-dark kit. It's a stencil of the Northern Hemisphere night sky and a bottle of glow juice. You paint it on the wall or ceiling, and it glows at night just like the stars in the sky. Is that cool or what?

What are you going to do with your new year? I gave this a lot of thought. You will be pleased to hear that I have given up my goal of forging the *Mona Lisa*. It's too risky. Everybody knows that painting. I have a much better idea. I actually got it from the paper.

I read that somebody forged Hitler's diaries and sold them for a million dollars before they were discovered to be fakes. Here's my new plan. Mom gave me a book last summer about Joseph Pulitzer, which I started but didn't finish. The part I did read was pretty ugly. He was not a nice guy, Joseph Pulitzer, decidedly mean, in fact. Anyways, here's my idea—I'm going to forge the diary of Joseph Pulitzer! Wouldn't that be a feat?

Now, I know you're going to lecture me about this, but think how exciting it would be to pull off such a grand hoax. I could make a million bucks! I could take the money and buy us a house to share when we both turn eighteen. It will take me that long, anyway, to research Pulitzer, study his handwriting, detail his life and make up events in his past. Not to mention the forgery part. I'll have to hand write a couple hundred pages in different inks and age the paper somehow. I know I can do it.

Just think, we could live together like rich people. You could leave the orphanage. You'd be free. We would have fun all the time. We could have a swimming pool with a slide, and a closet full of bubblegum, and a big circular driveway, and hire a butler named Jeeves to wait on us. "Jeeves, would you be so kind as to freshen Lady Allison's Kool-Aid, please?" Wouldn't that be posilutely cool?

I'm going to work on it next week. At least I'll finish the book on him and plot my scheme from there. Now don't be mad, Allison, it's only an idea. If you just think about the good parts and forget the illegal piece, I'm sure you'll see how brilliant it is.

I have other plans for 1980 by the way. I plan on becoming as good a fisherman as Cal. I'm not sure what his secret is, but this is the year I learn it. Also, I'm going to study astronomy more. Mom gave me a telescope last summer, which I love. And I decided, or the talking light told me, that I need to look at the stars. I love star-watching on dark summer nights with a jillion shiny lights in the sky. Doesn't it make you wonder? Did you ever think you were from outer space? I look at my family and don't think I belong here. I can't relate to my relatives at all. I look like my mom, but sometimes (and I know this sounds weird), sometimes I think I'm adopted. I don't know why, but I wonder if I was sent here from another planet. Not like I'm a green Martian or anything, but from an advanced civilization. Is it weird to think that?

Do you think I could be from outer space? Maybe I just want to be from outer space. I imagine it all the time. The talking light makes me believe it. How many people do you know who hear talking light? How many have seen flying saucers?

Anyways, I'm going to study astronomy and figure out where I'm from. I'm not normal. How come I'm so much smarter than the rest of my family? My father had me tested for Mensa by the way (like I care), so he could brag about me. I'm a prize for him. He doesn't even know me, or try to, and he talks to his buddies like I'm a trophy he won, which bugs me immensely.

I'm also making a New Year's resolution to start writing in my journal again. I haven't written since you and me started writing each other. I'm not too good at making daily entries. I always forgot even when I was writing in it regularly. Now I don't write at all. Instead, I tell you everything.

God, I really want to meet you! Well, I think this is one of my longest letters yet. I better go. Send Homer back tonight—I want to hear from you.

Your Friend of Fate,
Danny

Dec 31, 1979

Danny,

Jesus shoplifting Christmas presents, Daniel Oliver Gilday, are you completely INSANE? Forging the diaries of Joseph Pulitzer? You're a melon head! Do you actually think you can *ever* win the Pulitzer Prize by forging documents of the founder? I can't believe you even thought of it. Cheesecake, are your paint vapors killing your brain cells?

I know one thing, if the talking light suggested this, you better find another source of advice. Forge Joseph Pulitzer's diary and you'll be arrested for sure. Even if you did pull it off, which you won't, I wouldn't live with a hardened criminal. So you'll have to spend your million bucks alone.

I would never break the law. Or be with somebody who did. No way, padre. Forget it. Hasn't anything I've been writing sunk in? Why, Danny? Why do you have this need to be a con man?

I've been using a really big prayer on you. For what? So you can switch to a different crime? Obviously, my prayers aren't working. Or maybe you are just so bad that nothing will work. I'm so mad I could spit.

Speaking of spitting, I will not sign this pact until you change your mind about this crazy forgery idea. How could you even tell me this? You know what I think? You're nuts! You should be committed to an institute for the criminally insane. But they'd probably throw you out. That's all I have to say.

Allison

Jan 1, 1980

Dear Allison,

I'm sorry. I didn't mean to make you mad. Please forgive me. I can't help myself sometimes. I just thought it was a good idea for us to be together. I don't see what's wrong with it. Forgery doesn't hurt anybody. It's not like murder or rape or robbery. Nobody really gets hurt. In fact, lots of forgers are considered heroes. They have a following. Even the police respect them.

I'm sorry, Allison. Can you forgive me? Please?

Your Friend of Fate,
Danny

Jan 12, 1980

Dear Allison,

How come you didn't write back? Are you that mad? I said I was sorry. What more can I do? Friends are supposed to be understanding. And we're supposed to be best friends. Can't we forget all about the Pulitzer forgeries?

A funny thing happened at dinner last night. It was slimy-meat night (pot roast), so it was destined to be weird. Me and Father got into a discussion about the Japanese building a plant in Ohio. Actually, it's Honda who is going to build a factory in Marysville. You probably saw it in the paper.

"Goddamn Japs are building a plant in Marysville. You believe that, Cara?" Father said.

"So?" Mom said.

"So the Japs are taking over the whole goddamn car industry. Next thing you know they'll own the whole damn country."

"What's wrong with the Japanese building in Marysville, Father?" I asked.

"Son, the Japs are undermining our whole economy. So many people are buying those damn rice-burning cars that the Big Three are hurting." He was ripping at the disgusting beef.

"What's the Big Three, Father?" Cal asked.

"GM, Ford, Chrysler."

"So, that's just competition, ain't it?" I said.

"Isn't it, dear," Mom corrected me. "Isn't it."

"That ain't competition. They're subsidized by the Japanese government. It's not fair," Father said.

"Why not?" I said. "Didn't Chrysler get a billion dollar loan from Uncle Sam last July?"

"Because it's not American!" Father bellowed. He refused to listen to the facts. "They're taking the profits out of the country."

"Well, at least they're going to build them here," I said, washing a hunk of slimy meat down with a swig of milk.

"That's not the point!" Father said. Mom was glaring at him.

"What is, then?" I asked.

"The point is those Japs are outselling the Big Three, and that's not good for America."

"But aren't people buying them because they're better cars, Father?"

"They can't be better cars. Damn Japs."

"Why else would people buy them?"

"Because they're traitors!" Father yelled like some World War II call-to-arms.

"The news said Honda is hiring five thousand American workers. That's a lot of jobs. Plus, in Marysville, they think it's great," I said.

"Greed is behind it. They're going to let those yellow devils in because of greed."

"But if it gives people jobs, and they make good cars, and people have a choice of what to buy, what does it matter if they're from Japan?" I asked.

"It matters, goddamn it. It matters!" he said.

"You weren't upset when Volkswagen built a plant in Pennsylvania last year. How come?"

"It's different," Father said.

"How? Because they're German?"

"It just is. Look, I don't want to talk about it anymore. Pass the gravy, Cal," Father said. But I wasn't finished.

"If it were me, I'd call Honda and see if they need local steel suppliers." I smiled.

After dinner, around eight o'clock last night, I heard Father call his vice president at home and tell him to call Honda first thing in the morning. "Eight a.m., sharp! Don't be a second late. Got it?"

Isn't that cool? Father listened to me. He actually took my suggestion. Anyways, I thought it was neat, even if Father couldn't admit he was wrong. Didn't I do good?

Write me. Please.

Your Friend of Fate,

Danny

Jan 17, 1980

Dear Allison,

You're breaking my heart. Saints aren't allowed to break hearts. They're supposed to heal them. I guess you don't love me anymore. Am I right? Please forgive me, Allison. I'm sorry. I really am. What do I have to do? Beg? Okay, I'll beg. Please, please, please, please, on my hands and knees, please forgive me.

Are you okay? Are you sick? Did you get caught with Homer? Did the Catholic Gestapo discover you? Are you under house arrest? Should I come and bust you out? What?

Please write!

Your Friend of Fate,
Danny

Jan 20, 1980

Dear Allison,

Okay, you win! I swear on the Friends of Fate that I will not forge the diary of Joseph Pulitzer. Happy? C'mon Allison, it's been three whole weeks. Please write me back.

I miss you. I need you. I love you.

Your Friend of Fate,
Danny

Jan 20, 1980

Dear Danny,

It's great to hear you've given up your master plan to become a career criminal. I love you, too. It was so hard not writing. Sorry I had to ignore you. I missed you so. I can't tell you. Evenwise, that's over, so now we should make plans to meet. April Fools' Day is perfect. But where?

I'm not sure how to do it. It's on a Tuesday. We would have to sneak after school. It's so exciting, just the thought of being able to look at you up close. How absotively thrilling! School gets out at 2:50 for me. I might be able to grab a bus out front and meet you somewhere close. Maybe you could catch a ride over near St. Als, and I could walk and meet you. That way we might have more time. It's fun to think about, evenwise.

It's good your dad listened to you about the Honda plant. From what I can see, adults need lots of help from us kids. Lots of times, a sister will make a mistake about some obvious world issue, and it's up to us to change her mind. Isn't it supposed to be the other way round?

As you can tell, I signed and spit on pact number two so we are most definitely going to be friends for life. There's no getting out of it now. You're stuck with me forever, Danny. It's for the best; I'll keep you on the right track. I'm getting quite a collection of stuff from you. Lots of letters, a drawing, and two Friends of Fate pacts. When we weren't speaking (writing), I reread every letter from you. An amazing feeling came over me, and I smiled and smiled. I cried a little. And laughed. Mostly, though, I realized again that God brought you to me. I'm absotively the most fortunate girl to have a best friend like you.

I confess, I haven't written in my journal since we met, either. Isn't that funny? We both do the same things, we both like the same things—it's like we're related or something. Except I don't think I'm an alien. I am perfectly willing to believe you're an alien (ha-ha). An angel in love with a space creature. Our love story could be a science-fiction movie. Hey, you're not one of those guys that peels his skin back and reveals a locust face, are you?

Mass was beautiful today. It's always beautiful, but today was better, maybe because I knew we would be writing again. I had a dream about it. Homer flew to my window. I opened the shotgun shell, took out your note, and read your apology. Cried happy tears. That was my dream last night. Now, I'm writing you this letter. The date on your letter even matched the one in my dream. Spooky, huh? Evenwise, I was so happy in Mass because I knew you were going to wake up and do what's right. My prayers worked.

There's not much going on here. I'm bored. January is always a slow month. Post-Christmas let down. Mostly the kids just sit and watch TV, which I try to avoid, or play board games. A couple girls have a weekly poker game going with some boys, strip poker. If the nuns ever found out—*Wham!* Swats for everyone courtesy of Mother Peculiar. I don't like to play cards, and certainly not strip poker. Evenwise, at first I thought it was only a rumor, that the suspects were probably just betting their desserts and chore assignments, but the Red Angel slipped into action and discovered the truth firsthand. The rumors were true—they are playing cards and getting naked. They looked like they were having a lot of fun. Evenwise, there's always rumors inside St. Als. Not very holy for a place like this. One would think only the truth would do. Oh well.

Write me soon, Danny. I miss you.

> Your Friend of Fate,
> Allison

> Feb 1, 1980

Dear Allison,

Two months from today we meet! Isn't that great? Two months isn't so long. At the same time, it's like forever. I can't wait. Can you try and call me on the phone? I'd love to hear your voice. I never felt this way before. It hurts my heart but it feels good, too. Weird. It must be love. I can't believe you're my girlfriend, and I'm dreaming of kissing you. It's all I think about. Just two years ago, when I was nine, I would cover my eyes and look away when people kissed on TV. It made me squirm. Now, I can't wait to smack lips with you. I must be growing up.

Speaking of growing up, what are you going to be when you grow up? I'm going to be a scientist, a philosopher, an artist, or a writer. Maybe all four things! Why not? I'm smart.

Father says I'm going to Harvard. That's in Boston. Bean Town. I'm not sure being a lawyer is in my blood. Whenever relatives visit, he makes a point of telling them I'm going to be a lawyer. I go along with it. They all ask serious questions about fields of practice and tell me how much money I'll make. I just sit and agree, trying to look cute. Now, after three years of it, everyone, I mean everyone, thinks I'm gonna be Perry Mason. I can't get out of it.

I mentioned at dinner one night how neat it would be to be a published author. Father said, "Yeah, if you like starving to death in some unheated flat somewhere." It was obvious he didn't share my dream. Mom encourages me, though. She buys me books and reads the stuff I write. I don't think I ever told you, but I wrote a short story called "The Case of the Poisoned Hamburger." It was about the President of the United States being assassinated by a bad batch of beef. Mom liked it. Father wouldn't read it. I turned it in for extra credit and got an A+. Then the teacher read five to six pages aloud to the class each day. Geez and crackers, was I embarrassed.

Please notice none of my career choices are in any way related to forgery. I've chosen four perfectly respectable careers. That's progress.

Your Friend of Fate,
Danny

Feb 2, 1980

Dear Danny,

You do have great goals! A writer, how romantic. You surprise me more each day. Can I read "The Case of the Poisoned Hamburger?" I love mysteries. I bet it's absotively spellbinding. Technically, under the guidelines of our pact you have a moral obligation to share it. But if you don't want me to read it, I understand. Maybe I should become a writer, too! Hmm?

Evenwise, I think I want to be a social worker or a nurse or a botanist. I want to help people. It makes me sad to see hungry people. Sometimes I see folks outside the orphanage sleeping in the bus shelter. When I'm out playing, I see people walking by with dirty clothes full of holes. One old woman pushes a shopping cart and picks up bottles by the road. I don't know where she lives, but I bet she doesn't have a home.

If I was a nurse, I could help sick people, so that's a good job, helping people. And I'd like to be a botanist because I love plants and flowers. I grow a fantabulously wonderful garden in the spring with Mary and Sister D. I can't wait for winter to end so I can plant vegetables and visit the bell tower and breathe sweet, spring-fresh air. Ahh, that will be absotively glorious. Evenwise, a social worker, a nurse, or a botanist for me, maybe a librarian. Or maybe a writer (which is what Sister D is encouraging).

Did I tell you the big news at St. Als? This place is buzzing with scandal. Joyce Wilkerson, Rita Starks, Rachel Mint, Bobby Grey, Alex Smith, and Toby Hansen all got caught playing strip poker. Joyce and Alex were completely naked! Rita was topless but wearing socks, Rachel was down to her panties and bra (like she needs one!) and Bobby and Toby were in their underwear. The nuns raided Joyce's room last night at 10 o'clock. It woke everybody up, except Mary.

Shriek! A shrill whistle blew through the hallway. I quickly put down my book, threw on my robe and ran to the hall. Mother Superior stood there like Mount Rushmore, biting the whistle between her lips, swinging a paddle with her left arm. Five stern-faced nuns surrounded her. *Shriek*—the whistle blew again. Clod fidgeted with the locked door to Joyce's room. She dropped the key.

"Oh, for the love of God, Claudia, give me that!" Mother P shouted, snatching the keys from the floor. "They'll be sipping tea by the time you get the door open." The great assault on the door handle complete, they rushed into Joyce's room.

"Oh my!"

"Well, I never!"

"Sweet Mother Mary!"

"Shit!" came a boy's voice. I couldn't see what was happening, but it didn't sound good. Gasps and hushes and murmurs echoed through the cold hall.

"Out! You children get up and march into the hallway this instant!" ordered Mother Peculiar.

Both Toby and Bobby came out in T-shirts and underwear. Toby had mismatched brown and black socks, and Bobby was barefoot. Next came Alex, his little shriveled penis bobbing as he walked. Then came the girls—Rachel first, shaking and red-faced, then Rita who has been caught in situations like this before, and lastly Joyce, crying, trying to cover her breasts and her pubic area at the same time. She actually has hair down there. She could only cover one boob at a time leaving the other free. It was chilly in the hall, too, so her nipples were standing up. I wish I had breasts like hers.

Clod and Barney strutted into the hall behind the kids and attempted an awkwardly embarrassing high-five. What a sad strange sight—two old white nuns high-fiving and missing. Cheesecake! Smiling from ear to ear those nuns were. Sister D wasn't present. Evenwise, they ran all of them into the hall. Joyce and Alex were nude.

"Line up," Mother Peculiar directed. I swear to Jesus in the bathtub, Mother Peculiar was lusting after Joyce. All the nuns had sick smiles of victory on their faces. Clod came out of Joyce's room and threw all their clothes in a big pile.

"You see what happens when you break the rules, children?" Mother P broadcasted to the onlookers. It was designed as a public show. "Do you see what promiscuity will get you?" she said, a forceful tone in her voice, a gleam in her eye.

Mother P and the Catholic Crusaders, with their backs to me, strained and stretched to get a good view of Joyce's rump. With the nuns preoccupied with Joyce,

Rita—who has always had an affection for me since the Honeysuckle Affair—turned round to me, cupped her right breast in her hand, and blew me a kiss. Cheesecake, can you figure that one out?

"Stand straight!" Barney said through a head cold. I swear she looks just like Barney Rubble, a fireplug of a woman with a pickle nose. Kosher dill.

"Hurry up. Hurry up, children," Clod repeated, while the guilty heathens stood frightened. "We don't have all night, children." I could see goose bumps on Rachel's arms. The dirty deed was yet to come.

"All right, girls first," Mother Peculiar sneered. "Prepare to feel the wrath of God. Rachel, hands on knees, bend over." Mother Superior turned toward the crowd of innocent kids gathered in the hallway. "Children!" she bellowed, with a great big sweep of her wooden implement of pain. "This type of carnal activity will not be tolerated inside the Catholic Church." She ran her hand down the smooth finish of the paddle. She flashed a wicked smile for drama.

Whack!

Whack!

Whack!

I wondered, as Mother Peculiar vented her outrage on Rachel's tush, if the goodly nuns had ever played a rousing game of strip bingo. They're all bingoholics—most especially Clod and Barney. They like to act as if they don't think about sex, but we kids know different. All sorts of shenanigans and secret liaisons take place. Shocking things. We all know the scoop, but me especially, since I'm the Red Angel.

Rachel straightened up slowly, her butt on fire from the swats, tears streaming down her face. "May God show you His lesson in the force of His hand," Mother P said sternly, grinning. "Rita, assume the position."

Whack!

Whack!

Whack!

Rita bit her lip, refusing to let a tear leave her eyes. "Stand next to Rachel," Mother P ordered.

Rita stepped to Rachel's side. She locked pinkies with Rachel, who was shaking, to comfort her. She is so calm. I admire Rita.

"Joyce, front and center! Grab your knees." Mother Peculiar's eyes were wild now. Strangely possessed. The nuns leaned forward in unison, each hoping to get a closer look at Joyce's sex. Clod stepped in closer (she always had a thing for Joyce). Joyce bent over, a dark patch of pubic hair visible between her legs.

Whack!

Whack!

Whack!

Whack!

Whack!

Five swats for Joyce! Jesus on a chandelier with St. Peter, why did she get five when the others got three? Because Mother P is twisted, that's why. She enjoys this. I know it.

"Boys line up," she said, a ring of supreme confidence in her voice.

First Bobby—three whacks; then Toby—three whacks; and then Alex—three whacks.

"God does not appreciate young men and women playing card games in the buff!" Mother Superior stated like Queen Victoria after a shot of whiskey. "We will discuss this matter further in the great room. March downstairs!"

The four nuns and Mother waddled toward the steps like penguins on an iceberg. The six villains, some crying, some rubbing their butts, followed. Rita, always the mischievous one, turned and winked at me.

What do you make of that, Danny? That Rita is something. Even in the middle of serious trouble, she teases. If I got swats like that in front of all those kids I would cry for a week from embarrassment. Of course, like I said in a previous correspondence, I would never play strip poker to begin with. Never.

Well, that's my news. Hey, did you hear that six Americans escaped Iran via the Canadian Embassy? They faked passports and diplomatic documents and flew right on out of there. It's a pity the others are still held hostage. It can't go on much longer. I'm sure Carter will get them out.

That's it for me. I love you, Danny.

Your Friend of Fate,

Allison

Feb 22, 1980

Dear Allison,

Sorry for the delay in writing. Homer had a one-eyed cold. His left eye was closed and he sneezed and had a runny beak. February weather must be taking its toll on him. I hate February—it's the coldest month and nothing is going on. Sorry I missed Valentine's Day. Homer was grounded. I have a slight cold myself. Sore throat, cough, clogged up head. Mom says I get sick too much. I can't help it. I don't go around looking for diseases to catch. I'm almost over it. Besides, I'm not sick enough to stay home from school, so what good is it to be sick?

It doesn't look like Carter is doing anything at all to get the hostages out. Who knows? Politicians always have something up their sleeves. I wonder what life is like for the hostages. It must be tough.

Wow! What a story about your friends getting caught. It sounds like Mother Peculiar is mean. Is she really, or are you exaggerating? Sounds like she really gets off spanking kids. My father spanks me every once in awhile. I usually deserve it when he does. He uses his belt. Mom used to spank me, but it doesn't hurt anymore when she does. I'm stronger than her now. Father, though, when he gets a hold of me, man, does it hurt. Youch!

Enough about swats. We still haven't picked a place to meet. I say we meet at the planetarium. I don't have enough time to make it over to St. Als. I looked at the bus schedule. It would take almost an hour and a half. That means I wouldn't get to see you for very long. It only takes thirty minutes to get downtown, so we'd have more time together. Does that make sense?

Only thirty-eight days to go. I'm excited as heck, how about you? I can't wait. Spring is coming, too, so we might have beautiful weather. Wouldn't that be cool?

Uh-oh, Cal is calling. I forgot I promised we'd play chess. I came up here to get the board and ended up writing you instead. You must be on my mind, Saint Allison. I didn't mean to write such a short note. Bye.

Your Friend of Fate,

Danny

Feb 22, 1980

Dear Danny,

I know what you mean about February. Brrr . . . I can't stand it either. I'm glad Homer is better. He looks fine. He has a good appetite, at least. I'm keeping him here a little longer to warm him up. We can't have him sick. And you're sick, too? You Gildays should take better care of yourselves. I'll bet you play in the snow without boots and gloves, don't you? I can see you getting in a snowball fight with your bare hands. Tell me I'm wrong; bet you can't.

Evenwise, life around St. Als is dull. I'm reading like crazy. I've been pretending I'm Red Angel, superspy, but even that gets old after awhile. I do learn lots of secret stuff though. I overhear all kinds of conversations. Nun-talk. Kid-talk. Plans for the orphanage. I usually know what our schedule is before it's posted. Mary says I'm nosy— I say I'm aggressively curious, but she always asks me to keep her informed.

I always know what field trips we're going on, or who's coming to visit, that sort of thing. I have a reputation as a *girl in the know*. It makes me lots of friends.

In the boring gray of February, I am planning my garden. I drew my plans already (it's important to have a plan). I decided to grow sunflowers for Homer. I'll harvest the seeds in the fall, and he'll have fresh sunflower seeds to munch. Isn't that a great idea? I also have eight jars of seeds I collected from the cafeteria. There's about a dozen friends who give me seeds from their fruits and vegetables after they're done eating. It's like a seed recycling program. Rita has been the best of all. She works in the kitchen and saves me all types of seeds before the food is cooked. I think she likes me because I never told on her when she got caught making out with a local. There's respect among thieves. Not that I'm a thief, but in the spy trade one has to use similar methods. It's very tricky being a spy.

Evenwise, this year my garden is going to be absotively glorious. Sunflowers and corn and beets and all sorts of splendid vegetables. I bet even my fruit trees will grow a lot bigger. I would just love to eat a fresh crisp apple off the tree. Umm . . . scrumptious.

We're going to meet soon! I can't believe it. The planetarium is a perfect place! The bus takes about twenty minutes from here. It stops at 3:27 and gets downtown at 3:47. I timed it out front for a few days, sometimes it's late by as much as ten minutes. That's okay, as long as we get together. Is four o'clock all right with you? Can you make it there in time? Hurry up, April 1!

Hey, what if your parents want to celebrate your birthday or the nuns decide to celebrate mine? If that comes up, what are we going to do? I say the chances are pretty likely one of the two, or both, will want to have a party. I hope that doesn't happen— if it does, we need another plan. Maybe we could meet the following Saturday. Let me know what you think.

Time for supper. Write soon. I love you.

Your Friend of Fate,

Allison

p.s.—Have you been watching what's going on in El Salvador and Nicaragua? That Somoza is a bad leader.

March 16, 1980

Dear Allison,

Today is the St. Patrick's Day parade. Cal and Father are there. Mom and I don't go anymore. Not for about five or six years. (It's a secret why not; a secret not even I can tell you because I promised Mom first.) Cal loves going—he rides with Father on a float or something.

T-minus seventeen days and counting! Four o'clock is great. I'm not worried about a party. As long as I'm back by 6:30 for dinner, Mom will never know I'm gone. Usually, as soon as I get home and change, I disappear into my room or go over to Jeff's house to play. She doesn't start looking for me until 6:30, so I'll be okay. How about you, any parties scheduled yet? It's T-minus seventeen and counting! The first is going to be positulely cool.

I'm going to bring Homer with me. It's only fair since he introduced us. Can you believe it's been nine months? Feels like I've known you my whole life. Geez and crackers, I wish you lived next door.

I don't think we should give each other a birthday present, we should save our money for a hot dog and pop together. Do you like hot dogs? I know they're made up of gross stuff, pig guts and feet and intestines, but they are tasty.

Speaking of gross food, how's school? I've been busy studying. How about you? I read my Pulitzer book all the way through—what a sad man. And no, I'm not going to forge his diary. In case your saintly, a-boy-can't-even-dream mind was wondering, I've given up my lust for forgery. It's impossible with an angel looking over my shoulder.

The talking light appears to agree with you about forgery. It's complicated deciphering my own thoughts from the signals of the talking light. The problem is, I know my brain is translating the light, which then becomes part of my thoughts, so how do I know what's me and what's the light? It's confusing sometimes. Most times. They get all tangled up together.

I tell you, it's aliens programming me. I feel like a living experiment. A guinea pig. A hamster on a wheel. A rat in a maze. What if we are all living experiments? What if this whole planet is just a gigantic science project? Did you ever read *Horton Hears a Who* by Dr. Suess? Well, Horton is an elephant who learns there's a world inside a speck of dust. How about that? What if we're just dust? Star dust.

I was star-watching last night, looking at the amazing light show through my telescope. On a really dark night with a jillion stars, the sky reminds me of talking light, only brighter. I painted my ceiling with my StarGazers glow-in-the-dark kit. It took me all last Saturday. I have a whole galaxy on my ceiling. It's posilutely cool. There's one star called Sirius that holds an attraction for me. If I came from anywhere, that's where—Sirius, the Dog Star.

When we get together in two weeks, I'll bring "Poisoned Burger" for you. It's too big to send Air Mail. Not even Homer could haul that much. Time to go—I have a term paper to write. My teacher loves these things. Five hundred words on any subject we want. My paper is called "Aliens Among Us: Fact or Fiction." What a dramatic title, huh? I'm going to make it funny, somehow.

See you soon!

Love,
Danny

March 16, 1980

Dear Danny,

Jesus on roller skates with St. Jude, you won't believe the bad news! We're going on a field trip April 1—to a potato chip factory! We won't get back till after 4:30. It's not absotively official yet, but I overheard Mother P and Sister D personally, so it's almost for sure. They may even announce it tomorrow. Can you believe the bad luck? I felt like the entire Vatican Council was sitting on my stomach when I heard. It's not on the bulletin boards yet, so there might be hope. But don't count on it.

 I just can't believe our plans have been foiled by a spud. Cheesecake, of all the places to go—a potato chip factory. I don't even like chips. Occasionally I'll eat Bar-B-Q, but that's it. I've been racking my brain about what to do. Fake like I'm sick, then sneak out? If caught, I'm in deep trouble. That's probably not a good idea. I don't want to feel the sting of Mother P's paddle on my tush.

Maybe we should go to Plan B and meet on Saturday the 5th instead. Would that work out? God, I hope so! Please don't say you have plans. Please. Please. Please. I've been thinking about eating a hot dog with you. Mustard and catsup. I can almost taste it. Mmm . . .

I was so looking forward to seeing if I could hear talking light inside your head. I can't exactly figure out what you mean. I *am* glad the light has talked some sense into you. I wasn't too sure you were going to listen to me for long. It's good to have other allies on one's side in the battle for a human soul. I'm continuing Sister D's super-duper prayer for you as insurance. It's only a small investment, and it can't hurt.

It would be absotively exciting to see the Universe on your ceiling. It's amazing the things people think of. I guess now Cal won't need to squish lightning bug guts on your walls.

Maybe we *are* just star dust. If you look at a teeny little ant, her world is all filled with other ants the same size. We humans must look gigantic to them. I think God must be huge compared to us. So maybe we are like specks of star dust floating about the universe. Could be. Except we are God's special dust.

Speaking of God's dust, what do you think of those Iranians? The Ayatollah gave his support to the Revolutionary Guard. Do you believe that guy? It looks like it will be a long time before they let the hostages go. Why doesn't Carter just send in the Marines? I couldn't live over there. Men telling women what to do, treating them like dogs; it's a travesty. No man is ever going to boss me around. Ever.

Evenwise, back to the important subject. I am absotively sure we will meet soon. Destiny wouldn't have brought us together and surrounded us with miracles if we weren't supposed to meet. She wouldn't waste her time. No way. No spud is going to keep us apart. And if it does, I will never eat another potato chip as long as I live.

What do you think about this tragic turn of events? Write back immediately so we can figure this out.

Love Always,
Allison

March 19, 1980

Dear Allison,

Shoot! I see your point about spuds. I may just boycott mashed potatoes all together (ha-ha). April 5th won't work. Father is taking me and Cal to Cumberland to get the cabin ready for the season. This is truly a bad deal. I think we need to pick another date right away and be careful not to let adults ruin our plans.

You're right, it is a shame they're holding innocent Americans in Iran, although a lot of those hostages are actually CIA spies, according to the Iranians. All they really want is for us to hand over the shah so they can execute him. They say his secret police, the SAVAK, tortured thousands of Iranians. If that's true, then I understand why they're so mad. I'm not saying I believe the Revolutionary Guard is right, but they do have a reason to be pissed. If it were me, I'd give them the shah and get our people home.

229

In a way, you are like a hostage, too. Your first note begged me to come save you. Maybe the Islamic fundamentalists are no different than the Catholics.

Wait a minute—there's a potato chip factory on Colerain Avenue, only two miles from my house! Do you think it's the same one—Grippo's? How many potato chip factories can there be in Cincinnati? One or two? If your field trip is at Grippo's maybe I could ride my bike up there and see you. It might work out. I could pretend I'm part of the tour or something. You could train me like a spy so I'd fit in.

What do you think? Will that work? Write me.

> Your Friend of Fate,
> Danny

March 19, 1980

Dear Danny,

It is Grippo's! Destiny is smiling on us after all! How can this work, though? I don't think you can blend in with a bunch of orphans. It's not like the nuns don't know us all by heart. A spare kid showing up will surely be noticed.

We're supposed to get there after lunch, around one o'clock. You won't get out of school till past two-thirty. Maybe we can see each other for a minute or two when we get on the school bus to leave. I'll wear green, which shows off my red hair well, so you'll recognize me. Okay?

This isn't the best way to meet, but it's better than nothing. Do you have any ideas? Write back this minute.

> Your Friend of Fate,
> Allison

p.s.—I can't believe your opinion on the hostage crisis. How can you compare my being an orphan with the mass kidnapping of innocent American citizens? It's not the same.

March 25, 1980

Dear Allison,

I'll be at Grippo's at three-fifteen waiting for you. I have a purple Huffy with a red banana seat. You can't miss me. I'll be the only kid there on a bike. Can't you sneak away from the tour and meet me outside? Can't you tell them you're going to puke because of the greasy air or something? They might believe it. Especially coming from a sweet girl like you. It's worth a try.

> Your Friend of Fate,
> Danny

p.s.—Sorry about the orphan/hostage comparison. I'm wrong.

March 25, 1980

Dear Danny,

I'll see what I can do. My keen spy instincts will look for the right moment. With luck, it might work out. Iranian apology accepted. Let's not argue over crazy governments. It's not worth it.

The sisters are all upset today. Yesterday, Archbishop Romero was assassinated at Mass in El Salvador. They shot him while he presided over the funeral of a journalist. This is such a shamefully cruel world. Clod took it hard. She had worked with the Archbishop as a missionary fifteen years ago. He was a simple priest then. Clod worked with him at an orphanage in the countryside. She's been crying since she heard the news.

Sister D says they were very close. Clod spent three years down there. Now that's real nun's work, in the trenches where the poverty is. I admire Clod for that. When the sisters cry, I cry, too. All this violence and death scares me. It's like the end of the world is coming. Do you think it is? Sister D says it isn't worth thinking that way. She says that people who worry about the end of the world waste their lives doing nothing because they're too afraid to live. I see her point. Still, I worry.

Evenwise, no point being negative. Time to shine. I will grieve with Clod over the loss of Archbishop Romero, and life will get back to normal. Only one week to the great spud tour. I do so hope to see you, if only for one minute.

Is it me or does Homer look like he's gaining weight? I better stop feeding him Cracker Jacks. He's getting pudgy. See you Tuesday. Red hair, green outfit—you can't miss me.

Your Friend of Fate,

Allison

p.s.—Jesus in the Congo with a blow gun, did you hear that City Hall announced a pigeon extermination program? Homer better not fly downtown. They plan on shooting pigeons with poison darts. How cruel!

April 1, 1980

Dear Allison,

Happy Birthday. What a great day to turn twelve! It was really cool to see you (even from fifty feet away). You're so beautiful. The most beautiful person in the whole group. I'm not trying to be mushy, it's just true.

I wanted to run over there and talk to you so bad. I was nervous. I didn't sleep last night. I have your image locked forever in my mind now. I love your freckles. You must have jillions of them. Didn't you say they are God's kisses? If that's true, then He must really love you.

How did you like the little sign I made?

231

DANNY AND HOMER SAY HELLO!

Wasn't it funny? It was tough carrying it on my bike. The wind kept trying to blow it out of my hand. I hope it didn't get you in trouble. I made a different one first with your name on it that said—HAPPY BIRTHDAY, ALLISON, but tore it up because I didn't want to cause a problem.

I can't write much today. We're having my birthday dinner soon. Mom's fixing my favorite, roast beef and gravy. I love it. She made a giant brownie with whipped cream for my birthday cake.

Father's in Arizona, which might upset a normal kid, but I think it's better that he's gone. No chance of a blow up that way.

I got back from Grippo's a minute ago. I'm writing so you get the message before dinner, and I'll have a message back from you by the time I'm finished. It was so cool to see you in person. We posilutely have to meet when we can talk and—you know—kiss.

Happy Birthday, Allison Leslie Pippin!

Your Friend of Fate,
Danny

p.s.—Don't worry about Homer; no one is going to blast him with a dart. Pigeons have survived man's worst for thousands of years. He'll be fine; besides, he's too fast.

April 1, 1980

Dear Birthday Boy,

Happy Birthday to you, too, you nut! Jesus on a motorcycle with John Lennon, it was neat to see you. I almost peed my pants. The sign made me laugh. Mary saw it first and poked me in the ribs. It was absotively inspired. You're crazy, Danny. And Homer is, too. He flew right up and sat on the hood of the bus. Did you see all the kids talking to him, throwing him potato chips. He likes Grippo's. Are they too salty? I tell you he's getting fat. It's absotively no wonder with all the junk food around.

Sorry I couldn't get out earlier. I tried. I faked like I was sick with very dramatic moans. I even doubled over and clutched my stomach. They took me to the Grippo's infirmary. I spent almost the whole field trip inside the factory health clinic with a nurse named Alice. She was terribly old. I thought there was a chance I'd have to perform CPR on her. She made me drink Pepto Bismol. It's not a popular idea among the kids, but I like the taste. Evenwise, you would have been proud of my acting ability. My tummyache ended just about the time the tour was over.

It was absotively inspiring seeing you ride after the bus. You must have kept up for three miles! I wanted to get off and ride home on your handlebars. Wouldn't that have been fantabulous? Mary says you're cuter in person. She's right. All the girls on the bus were squealing about the cute boy on the purple bike. Don't let it go to your head.

Well, we need to make plans right away, like you said. I need to see you. I can't stand it.

Write soon! Happy Birthday!

Your Friend of Fate,

Allison

April 19, 1980

Dear Danny,

It's been over two weeks—why haven't you written? Is something wrong? Sorry to resort to the post office to write but I couldn't wait anymore. I'm worried about you. Are you okay? Is Homer okay? Did I make you mad?

I'm worried. Please write me. Even if you're mad, just say so. If I don't hear from you, then I'll know you can't write.

Have you been reading the paper? Things are getting worse in Iran. The U.S. cut off relations with the country and seized all its assets. The militants said if Carter tries anything they'll kill the hostages. This is scary.

Did you see that twenty-six people were killed in a stampede at Archbishop Romero's funeral at the end of last month? It was like The Who concert. There must be a reason for it. God has reasons for everything.

Evenwise, I wanted to write just a short note to see if you're still alive. Let me know.

Your Friend of Fate,

Allison

May 4, 1980

Dear Allison,

It seems I made a big mistake. Big. Gigantic. A stupendous mistake. You were right, Homer was getting fat. The Monday after we opened the Cumberland cabin, Father and I carried the loft out back. Homer was sitting in his nest. He didn't want to get up while we moved him.

"C'mon, Homer. C'mon, boy. Take a little fly while we move you outside, okay?" I coaxed.

"He doesn't want to move, son. Why is he sitting on a nest, anyway?" Father paused, the sun just over his balding head shining off it like a cartoon light bulb when somebody gets a bright idea. "Let's just take a look under Homer and see if there's something hiding in there."

He lifted Homer gently off the twigs and brown grass.

"What the—" I said. "Eggs! Father, there's bird eggs! Homer's going to be a mother!"

"Yes, he is," Father laughed. "But I think Homer is a she, Daniel."

"What?"

233

"Son, the only way these eggs got into Homer's loft is if she laid them."

I looked closely at the perfectly shaped, white speckled eggs. Homer is a girl.

"You'd better start thinking of a different name for her, son. Homer won't do."

"That's a great idea, Father." I smiled. "Geez and crackers, how come I didn't know he was, I mean she was, a girl?"

So that's my news. Homer is a girl. Oops! I'm officially changing her name to Martha, in honor of the world's last carrier pigeon. Did you know she's stuffed at the zoo? It's a good name for Homer. What do you think?

Sorry I couldn't tell you before, but Martha had to hatch her eggs. One lived, one died. I gave the chick to Cal. They share the same loft and all, but now Cal has a bird of his own. He's happy. He named his pigeon Tramp.

I figured Martha has to go and find food for Tramp anyway, so why not see if she can drop you a quick Air Mail letter. You better write back right away, Martha needs to feed Tramp soon.

> Your Friend of Fate,
> Danny

May 4, 1980

Dear Danny,

What absotively splendid news! Birth is the most glorious thing on Earth. I had a feeling Martha was a girl. We had a closeness, she and I. A woman can tell these things. It's genetic. I'm so happy to hear you're all right. Martha will be a fine mother with a fine name!

I saw the original Martha at the zoo once. It was depressing. I remember how sad I was that man had exterminated all those glorious birds. Billions of them. And all that is left to show for it is a moldy stuffed bird with glass eyes. Now her memory and her name will live on. Martha is the most perfect name you could give her.

I'm so relieved you're okay. I almost called you again. I don't know why I'm so nervous about it. I picked up the receiver, put in my dime, dialed the phone, then hung up. A strange feeling comes over me, like it's not even me, and I hang up. Spooky. Goofy. It's just nerves.

I have to tell you something that happened yesterday. It was really scary. I had a nightmare last night. I woke up at a quarter till two in the morning, and I ran to Sister D's room.

"Sister D! Sister D! Wake up!" I shook her.

"Wha . . . what is it, angel?" She yawned as she turned on her lamp.

"I had a bad nightmare. Real bad."

She pulled me to her and stroked my hair. "Shh . . . it's all right, Allison. Shh . . ."

"But it was horrible," I cried.

"You're shaking, angel. And your nightgown is soaked. What is it?" she asked softly.

"I dreamed the pope was in Africa and there were a million people around him." I sniffed. "And . . . and . . ." I couldn't say it.

"You can tell me, Allison. I'll understand."

"And there was a rush of people trampling each other to see him. People got killed."

"There now, angel. It's only a dream. Dreams are just movies of our fears. Your love and concern for John Paul II probably came out in your nightmare as fear for his safety," Sister D said.

"But he's in Africa right now, and my dream was real," I sobbed.

"Here," Sister D said, handing me a tissue. "Dry your eyes. It's only a dream."

"But it was real, Sister. I could see crumpled bodies and bleeding people with broken limbs. One woman had her head cracked open. It was real. It was." I cried again.

"It's a dream, angel. Even the saints had a bad dream every once in awhile. Let's go back to your room, get you tucked in. I'll sit with you until you fall asleep. How does that sound?"

"Okay." My voice broke. "But it was real."

"It just seems real, angel, but things are not always what they seem." She patted my leg.

We walked back to my room, and that was the end of it. No one wants to believe that I had a premonition (I only told Sister D and Mary). I feel it. I hope it's not true, I hope it doesn't happen, but it will. I know it. And when it does, it will be horrible.

Evenwise, I'll shine as best I can. At least we're writing again. That's great. When do you want to get together? Let's make plans. How about two weeks from now, May 17? Is that good?

Write me.

Your Friend of Fate,

Allison

p.s.—Did you see how they botched the Iranian hostage rescue last week? What a fiasco. Eight soldiers killed, and they didn't make it anywhere near Tehran.

May 5, 1980

Dear Allison,

Jesus, Allison! You were right! There was a stampede in Zaire yesterday. Nine people died trying to see John Paul II. How did you dream that? You *must* be psychic. You *must* be! Has Sister D said anything to you?

I got goose bumps! Big ones. You're gifted. Will Sister D tell on you? Will the nuns get all freaked out about this? What's going to happen? Isn't it weird how much it was just like The Who concert, with people crushed to death to see a celebrity? The pope is just like a rock star. Do you think the nuns will change their view that rock is Satanic, now that just as many people were killed seeing the pope? I wonder what the Church will say about this? Write me soon.

Your Friend of Fate,
Danny

p.s.—May 17 is no good. How about May 24?

May 5, 1980

Dear Danny,

Jesus playing hopscotch with a cripple, don't be blasphemous! The two situations are completely different—the Zaire stampede and The Who concert are not similar at all. Do you want a lightning bolt to zap your skull? Be quiet.

I've been shaking since I saw the news. Sister D hasn't told anyone, but she excused me from classes today. I don't know what's going to happen, if anything. I don't like having dreams like that. It's so scary. Remember when I had a premonition about Homer (I mean Martha) being a girl?

It may be weird to you, Daniel Oliver Gilday, but I do believe I *am* an angel. I have visions like one. If angels exist at all, why couldn't I be one? Someone has to be, why not me? I have to go, someone is coming.

Bye,
Allison

May 9, 1980

Dear Allison,

So, I take it you don't share my opinion about the pope? Sorry. You can't change my mind on this one, Saint Allison. It's exactly the same—people killing other people to see their idols. It's tragic, but true.

You never said if May 24 was good to meet. We have to quit trying to arrange this by bird, so call me next week after school so we can make plans. Think about whether you'd like to meet at Martha's shrine at the zoo on the 24th. Wouldn't that be fitting? Martha (the live one) could meet us there, too! Wouldn't that be super-posilutely cool?

Are you okay? Your letters sound like maybe you're having problems. Are you still worried about the premonitions? I never knew anyone who could see the future before, but I believe you. If I have talking light, certainly you can have psychic visions. Aren't we a couple of strange ones?

What does your vision say about the presidential elections? My talking light says Carter is going to get blown out of the saddle. It's hard to imagine a cowboy actor and an ex-CIA director running the country. Are we a mess or what? Ronald Reagan? He's an actor.

Father likes him. He says he'll lower interest rates, which is good for business. Oh well, we can't change the world. If adults are dumb enough to vote for Reagan and Bush, they deserve whatever happens. (I hope you aren't Republican).

Your Friend of Fate,
Danny

May 9, 1980

Dear Danny,

The zoo will be the perfect place to meet. It's close-by—twenty minutes max. Even though I had a bad day there once, if I'm meeting you, it will be fun. You're so clever and sentimental, picking Martha's shrine. I can't wait. I'll call you with a time.

By the way, I'm fine now. Sister D and I had lots of quiet talks together instead of our tutoring sessions. I feel good. I just need to accept that I have this gift and use it as best I can. My vision doesn't waste its time on politics. Too predictable. My intuition tells me you're right about Reagan. Carter is cooked—too many problems to survive. I'm not Republican or Democrat. I think it's all really, really stupid. I heard Mother Peculiar talking about the election with Clod, who said she was going to vote a straight Republican ticket. How can anybody vote for someone just because they are from a certain political party? What if the Republican isn't qualified? What if he doesn't believe in the same things you do? Why not vote for the best person for the job?

It sounds like both parties try to brainwash the public. Have you noticed *The Cincinnati Enquirer?* It is so pro-Reagan and Bush it's almost sick. Thank God they report the news accurately or the whole paper would be worthless.

For your information, the pope is doing a splendid job in Africa, thank you very much. With the exception of the Zaire tragedy (which wasn't his fault), he is bringing a lot of people together. I applaud the great man's effort. Clap. Clap. Clap. So there.

Evenwise, I'm not going to let your radical leftist, antireligious, bigoted views come between us. I'm bigger than that (ha-ha). I will call you on the 13th so we can choose a time to meet. It's going to be absotively splendid to hear your voice. And to see you right after that!

I can't wait to be with my amazingly misguided boyfriend.

Your Friend of Fate Despite Your Flaws,
Allison

p.s.—I'm teasing about your flaws, you know.

The letters stopped abruptly. I searched the stack carefully, reading the dates of each one—Allison to Danny and Danny to Allison. I took each apart, separating them, thinking the additional letters had gotten stuck together. I read them all again, inspecting each meticulously, making sure I hadn't made a mistake, confused things. But there were no more letters. None. Suddenly, unexplainably, they stopped writing each other.

Why? What happened? Did they meet? My stomach flared up. Why did the letters end?

"Perhaps you need a different media to show you the rest of the story."

"You're back!"

"Yes," The Journals wrote. *"I made much progress in my travels, as you have in yours, Stoney."*

"What did you mean by different media? What happened to Danny and Allison?"

"Two questions from an impatient man."

"Your life isn't at stake," I winced, as a jagged pain cut through my stomach.

"Neither is yours, if you stay the course."

"So what did you mean, different media?"

"I meant that the people of this world learn in many different ways. This being unequivocally true, it should follow that many means of learning should be made available. This said, I will now give you entire, marvelous sections of the story via the most mismanaged, abused, under-utilized, unfulfilled tool of the twentieth century: television."

"TV?"

"Yes, Stoney, you have earned it. Whenever you wish to learn more about Danny and Allison, simply turn on Channel 99."

"There's no Channel 99."

"There is now, Stoney. And it is your private viewing screen. Enjoy."

"Wait!" I shouted too late. The damn thing disappeared on me again. I wished it would hang around longer and give me some reassurance. I could use it. Skeptical, despite all the recent evidence that the incredibly impossible was now routine, I switched on the TV. Channel 99.

Chapter 20

January 24, 1943

The black limousine, the longest car in all of Casablanca, stopped in front of Sulphur as he stood on the corner, waiting to cross. He could see his reflection in the shine of the gleaming vehicle, pleased with himself, thinking of the large detergent sale he had just made to the Algerian government. Not bad for a spook playing salesman. Would his employer let him keep the commission? The door swung open, and a smiling General Donovan waved the spy inside. From the street Sulphur could smell the interior. Fresh leather and cigarettes. He ducked into the limo and sat opposite his hosts, facing the rear of the car. It pulled away from the curb. He imagined the limo to be larger than the first apartment he'd ever rented.

"Pleased to see you again, son." The president extended a friendly hand. "This won't take long. I apologize for the theatrics. Have to beat the spies at their own game."

"Spies?"

The car turned the first corner slowly, as if the occupants were on a pleasant Sunday drive in the country. Donovan spoke. "FDR's own advisers do their best to keep him in the dark."

"Admiral Leahy has been doing it for years. Damn navy cracked the Japanese JN25 code years ago but tried to hide it from me," the president said as he pinched his trademark clipped glasses to the bridge of his nose. He looked fresh this morning, rested, his blue eyes as bright as the Mediterranean on a cloudless day. "Which is why I wanted to talk to you, Sulphur."

"Me?" Sulphur said, then remembered formality. "Sir?"

Roosevelt laughed. "You can stop all the sir nonsense. That's for folks who need to control others. I don't have that problem."

"The president has an important assignment for you, Sulphur," said Donovan.

The operative's eyes went wide. A grin burst across his face like a pack of matches lit at once. He was both gratified and startled. He had thought almost continually of Roosevelt since the first meeting, honored at being in his presence, thrilled at being congratulated and promoted by the Commander in Chief. The car turned another corner. Two rights, Sulphur remembered, his indoctrination during intelligence training never failing him. Always keep your bearings, even with your eyes closed, he'd been taught.

"I need intelligence from the field, Sulphur," the president explained. "Real intelligence. Not the watered down, sifted through, sanitized information the army and navy censor. Real intelligence."

"Pardon me, Mr. President," Sulphur said. "Your intelligence reports are screened?"

Roosevelt bit down on his cigarette holder, his chalky face flushed. "They don't trust me. It's politics, understand. The navy doesn't want me to know what they know. It gives them power. Bill, here," FDR nodded, "has essentially been banned from the White House by Leahy. The army isn't much better. And the British . . . well, you can't trust Churchill as far as you can throw his fat ass." FDR chuckled, then turned somber. "As everyone in the OSS is aware, Churchill had intercepts of the attack on Pearl Harbor but withheld the information as a means of forcing us into the war."

Indeed, Sulphur knew of this, had even read the report firsthand. The United States publicly presented a position of a unified front with England, but behind the scenes powerful gamesmanship laced with suspicion and treachery was being waged. He didn't like the arrogant Churchill either.

"That's why I need you, Sulphur. I need someone I can trust to give me the straight scoop."

Sulphur flashed a puzzled grin. "I don't follow."

"Son," the president said, "the minute I met you I knew you could be trusted. I have a knack for that, a vision one could say. There's a fire in your eyes, a burning. A light of honesty."

Sulphur thought his face would spontaneously combust from the accolades. "Thank you, sir."

"Now, here's the crux of it, Sulphur." FDR leaned forward as the car made yet another right-hand turn. "I want you to be my personal attaché. You will report directly to me, answer directly to me. General Donovan will be apprised of our communication and provide you whatever resources necessary for you to carry out my orders. Sound good?"

Sulphur was delighted, his mind a whirl of sabotage and espionage, of blowing up the Reichstag or the Crow's Nest, perhaps even laying an incendiary bomb at Hitler's feet. "Sounds great, Mr. President."

"Good. Now, the first thing I need you to do is get to Lisbon."

"Lisbon?"

"Yes. We have a substantial document forging operation there I'd like you to get familiar with. Take a couple weeks, learn the ropes."

"I'm sorry, Mr. President, I don't understand."

The great leader cracked his window slightly, pulled a lighter from his vest pocket, and lit a cigarette. "The best way to beat the Germans . . ." He inhaled deeply, "is to undermine their economy. To do that, we either need to buy up the manufacturing supplies they need on the world markets in Stockholm, Istanbul, Berne, and Madrid, which General Donovan and his team have been doing very effectively, or we need to devalue the Deutschmark. Or both. My plan is both. I want you to learn the craft of forgery," FDR said. "Go to Lisbon, where you'll be assigned to a joint American-British team of counterfeiters. After that, I want you in Washington to work at the mint for a month or so. Then, I want you back in Lisbon with billions of marks, which we'll send into the German economy through Madrid and Istanbul."

Sulphur was a jumble of elation and disappointment, gushing at the prospect of such an important assignment, but deflated that he wouldn't be blowing anything up. "But my specialty is arson, sir."

"Call me Franklin," the president insisted. "Ah, I see." His eyes shone like dual, spring moons. "You like to watch things burn. I'm sure General Donovan can find an occasional building for you to torch—an abandoned warehouse, a Nazi oil terminal— we have plenty of targets."

Sulphur was pleased, reassured that he wouldn't stray too far from his love. "How does my setting up a counterfeiting ring help you with your problems of getting true intelligence?"

General Donovan spoke, "This initial operation will introduce you to many operatives and intelligence officers throughout the OSS, army, navy, and British intelligence such as MI-5 and MI-6. Because of the large-scale nature of this plan, Sulphur, thousands of American, French, Dutch, British, and German agents will be given the bogus money. The coordination of this effort will take you to the innermost circles of each intelligence group."

"And," FDR added, "no one will know you report directly to me. No one but the three of us." He pulled a card from his pocket and handed it to Sulphur. "Here is my personal phone number. Call it anytime."

General Donovan continued. "Because your rank is that of captain, no one will suspect that you have the president's ear. They'll assume you have top-security clearance only on the forgery project."

The car turned right a final time. They had circled the block. "Well, that's it, Sulphur," the president said as the car stopped exactly where he'd been picked up. "Eleanor and I will have you to dinner when you make it to Washington. Good-day."

Sulphur stood on the crowded street watching the limousine drive off, exuberant at his new mission. Who could have guessed his fortunes would change so dramatically in the course of a few weeks. A worried look flickered on his otherwise happy face. How did they know he would be at that corner at that time? Was the OSS spying on the spy?

Chapter 21

August 29, 1990

I flipped on the TV after the telephone repair guy came to change over the phones. A private number is just what I need for some peace of mind. True to its word, the story appeared on Channel 99. *The Journals* creates its own rules, pirating airwaves, altering preconceived notions, changing history, illuminating the past in ways I'd never considered. In the comfort of my den, as Rose had lunch with Bobby in a futile attempt to convince him to speak to me (he won't), and Twinkie at work undoubtedly humming some theme song, I watched the tragic circumstance which split Danny and Allison apart. Hold on, dear reader, I'll do my best to describe what happened.

"Geez and crackers, what a wacky world," Danny exclaimed, hoping to distract Calvin from the chessboard. He was losing badly. "You know what I heard? Picasso's *Saltimbanque* sold for three million clams today! Do you believe that? I can paint that crap. In fact, I bet I can forge a better Picasso than he can paint an original. Three million dollars. Jesus."

"You're jealous." Cal scooched forward a half-inch on his stomach to make his move. The boys loved chess on the floor; it made it seem less serious. Cal hooked his index fingers through his belt loops and hitched his denims back in place.

"Are you doing okay this semester, Cal?" Danny moved a pawn forward to block a threatening bishop.

"No." He smiled, then moved his queen to take Danny's rook. "Check."

"Dammit."

"It's okay, Danny. I never get good grades."

"What kind of grades are you getting?" Danny sat up cross-legged for a better view of the battlefield.

"Mostly Ds and Fs," Cal said. He positioned his knight.

"Ds and Fs! Cal, you're going to get *the belt!*"

"So what? It only hurts a little while. After a half-hour the sting goes away." He brought up another bishop.

Danny studied the black and white board as he tried to figure out his brother's logic. After a few minutes he said, "You don't care then?"

Cal shrugged. "Not really. Father finds ways to get mad anyhow, so it doesn't matter if it's my report card or my room being a mess or something else—he'll find a reason to hit me."

A curious look fixed itself upon Danny's mischievous face. "What if I could fix it so you didn't get all Ds and Fs?" He positioned another pawn in a failed move to save the game.

"Could you do that?"

"Sure. I could forge your report card easily," Danny bragged. His blues eyes glowed at the thought of pulling another caper, this time with good reason—saving his brother from a sure whipping.

"How?"

"I can duplicate anything."

"Really?"

"Yep." Danny unconsciously worked his pinkie through a tiny hole in the bottom of a purple T-shirt his mom tried to convert into a cleaning rag months ago. He wouldn't consider giving up the shirt, not until it fell from his body when the seams were finally shot. "I copied the Mamets, didn't I?"

"Checkmate."

"Dammit, how come you always beat me?"

"I guess you're not smarter than me in every way," Cal laughed.

"Guess not." Danny pretended to sulk. He liked that Cal was better than him at things—it made Cal feel good, and it proved to Danny that his father was wrong, Cal would amount to something in the world. He just needed to figure out what. "So, do you want me to change your grades?"

"Sure, that'd be great." Cal paused, a devious smirk on his face. "Can you forge other things . . . like checks?"

"Sure, checks would be easy," the younger brother said, intrigued by the idea of doing it. "What would you do with the money?"

"Donuts," Cal replied without hesitation. "Glazed donuts."

"I like Bavarian Creme."

"You know what Father says about Bavarian Cremes, don't you?"

Just then their mother called up from the kitchen. "Boys! Dinner—wash up and come down."

Danny went to the faucet and let it run for a few minutes. Neither boy washed. Boys don't need to wash their hands before dinner. What for? As he stood at the sink, deceiving his mom with a water trick, he thought of his promise to Allison and how he was breaking his word. He winked at himself in the mirror and said, "She won't care, it's for a good cause." Kid logic. The child mastermind thought of forgery as a charitable endeavor—a most noble undertaking.

Their enthusiasm turned to disappointment as they spotted the stuffed green peppers (which Cara insisted on calling mangoes) sitting in the middle of the table. They took their usual chairs opposite each other as Danny tried to his best to salvage the meal by loading up on mashed potatoes. But he still held a grudge against Idahos, they having been the principle foil in his first attempt to see Allison. Frustrated in love by an underground tuber. A potato chip, more likely. He had forgone his previously-announced spud boycott because, ultimately, he did see Allison at the potato chip factory.

The boys were rambunctious. Cara followed their playful banter with delighted enthusiasm, her blue eyes catching the light from the chandelier. Cara Gilday, despite her oppressive relationship with Patrick, possessed a beauty many women pay thousands of dollars for and never attain. She loved her children, and her love radiated from her. Patrick Gilday sat at the head of the table with his monogrammed cloth napkin and attacked his food as if he'd been starved on crumbs and dishwater for the past month.

Cal, feeling impudent from teenage hormones blasting through his body, began a daring game of guessing each person's favorite donut. It could only end one way. He guessed Danny's, then his mom's, before setting his father up.

"And Father, I bet yours is . . . hmm . . ." He pretended to think it over. "I bet it's Bavarian Creme. Am I right?"

"Bavarian Cremes are for fags," Patrick bellowed, his face as red as the initials on his napkin. "My favorite is glazed." He knifed his pepper with ferocity.

Before Patrick could explode, Cal said, "Hey, mine, too, Father. You and I like the same donuts."

Gilday's short wick was diffused. The two boys kicked each other under the table, giggling at their inside joke.

Brring! Brring! Brring!

"I'll get it," Cara said, sliding gracefully from her chair before Danny could make a move.

"Let me get it, Mom," he said, but she was already in the kitchen.

"Hello?" she paused. "I'm sorry, but Danny is having his dinner right now. May I have him call you?" A long pause. "I see, dear. Well, could you call back in about an hour? Yes, dear, I'll tell him. Bye now." She came back to the table. "Danny, that was for you. A nice girl named Allison."

Patrick's knife and fork clamored to his plate, unwelcome guests crashing the party. The bell pepper mush was not amused. "What? What was her name?" he said, his mouth crammed full of pepper and hamburger meat, his face now white as the table cloth. He was so taken aback by the call that he stopped chewing, his jowls packed tight with food.

"Allison, Father," Danny said. "She's an orphan. She's cool. We made friends through Martha."

"Wha . . . what?" Patrick choked.

"Yeah, it's a really cool story. I sent Homer, I mean Martha, out with a message last spring, and Allison wrote back."

Gilday's face lost its color faster than a chameleon in a sack of flour, except for the

But at that moment—as the three of them looked at each other in silence—a strange quiet entered the room. An understanding sparked between them. A fury ignited in the lack of words. They all knew that each of them—Cara, Cal, or Danny— would kill him without thinking twice. A conspiracy was born.

After the dining room was clean, Danny went to his bedroom to write Allison, disturbed that their plans were thwarted once again. He hastily scribbled a note to her promising that nothing, posilutely nothing, would keep them apart. The note finished, he did his best to outlast his parents and stay awake until they went to bed. Alas, young Daniel fell asleep, clutching the letter in his hand.

Patrick Gilday slipped quietly out the back door into the glaring half-moon just after one a.m. He stole across the back yard. He looked about the neighborhood, taking care not to be seen. A light, spring breeze tugged at his dark sweatshirt. He peered toward Mrs. Smitch's house and hoped she wasn't awake. She sometimes stayed up late giving her dog piano lessons. Crazy old bitch, he thought to himself.

He scanned the connecting back yards. No lights on. Good. He looked back at the house to Danny's room and took a deep breath. He crept to the loft and stopped before it. The screeching hinge did its best to alert the world to his misdeeds as Patrick slowly opened the cage. "Shit," he whispered under his breath. "How many times did I tell that kid to oil this thing?" The rusting hinge creaked louder.

He reached in for Martha. "Good girl." He tried to soothe her. Martha stepped away from the intruder's hand. Suddenly, as if he she knew his intent, she began flapping wildly, beating Patrick back with her wings. She cooed frantically, clawing viciously at him. He pulled back, his right thumb bleeding from Martha's defense, his hand scratched in a half-dozen places.

He cursed the moon and took a deep breath, resolving that a pigeon wasn't going to ruin his life. He reached in with a quick strong motion and grabbed Martha. Her wings fluttered vainly as she tried to escape her attacker. Patrick brought her under control with his other hand. He held her torso firmly in his left hand and placed his bleeding right on her head. "Sorry girl, but I just can't let you—"

246

large, bluish vein pulsing in his forehead. "How long have you been writing her?" He gasped for air.

"Are you all right, Patrick?" Cara asked.

He took a drink of water and swallowed three large gulps. "Fine, just fine. Is she in an orphanage?"

"Yeah, Father, she lives at St. Alexandria." Danny said. "She's great. You'd love her. We're gonna meet in eleven days. That's why she called."

"Jesus H. Christ!" the elder Gilday shouted. "My son conversing with an orphan. I don't believe it!"

"What's wrong with that? She's nice." Danny shrunk down in his chair, his shoulders turned in, his feelings hurt.

"Yes, Patrick," Cara said. "What's wrong with that? I think it's cute."

"Cute? It's not cute! It's sick! No son of mine is going to cavort with a . . . a . . . a lowly orphan."

"But, Dad, you'd like her. I was hoping once we met, you guys might adopt her. She could live here."

"What? Live here? An orphan? What did you call me?"

"Nothing, Father," he said, remembering.

"Now, Patrick, it was an accident. Danny didn't mean to call you—"

BOOM!

Over went the dinner table, food, placemats, silverware, and all. Milk splattered the walls. Gravy spotted the china cabinet. Broken dishes cut into the carpet. The table lay on top of Danny, pinning his legs underneath. He lay buried under a mudslide of food and drink. Cal quickly dug him out. Potatoes, gravy, butter, bread, peppers, and hamburger meat stuck to Danny's favorite shirt, irreversibly stained and unquestionably destined for the rag bin.

"We will not have you hanging about with an orphan. You shall never meet this girl, whomever she is. Is that clear?" Patrick glowered at his traumatized son.

"Ye . . . ye . . . yes, sir," Danny whimpered as he tried unsuccessfully to wipe the glop from his clothes.

Frightened, Cara rushed to Danny. "Patrick!" she yelled. "What's wrong with you?"

Gilday lashed out. His hand struck across her delicate face. "Stay out of this, Cara."

Cal grabbed a butter knife. "If you touch her again, I'll kill you!" he said, his hand trembling.

"Bullshit." Patrick knocked the knife from his grip, the blade clanging harmlessly against the wall. "You're all fucking crazy." He stalked out of the room.

The three of them stood there, dazed, wondering what had happened. Cara rubbed her reddened cheek, shaking. Cal put his own quivering arms around her. "I will, Ma. I'll kill him if he does that again."

"Don't become like him, Cal," she said feebly.

But at that moment—as the three of them looked at each other in silence—a strange quiet entered the room. An understanding sparked between them. A fury ignited in the lack of words. They all knew that each of them—Cara, Cal, or Danny— would kill him without thinking twice. A conspiracy was born.

After the dining room was clean, Danny went to his bedroom to write Allison, disturbed that their plans were thwarted once again. He hastily scribbled a note to her promising that nothing, posilutely nothing, would keep them apart. The note finished, he did his best to outlast his parents and stay awake until they went to bed. Alas, young Daniel fell asleep, clutching the letter in his hand.

Patrick Gilday slipped quietly out the back door into the glaring half-moon just after one a.m. He stole across the back yard. He looked about the neighborhood, taking care not to be seen. A light, spring breeze tugged at his dark sweatshirt. He peered toward Mrs. Smitch's house and hoped she wasn't awake. She sometimes stayed up late giving her dog piano lessons. Crazy old bitch, he thought to himself.

He scanned the connecting back yards. No lights on. Good. He looked back at the house to Danny's room and took a deep breath. He crept to the loft and stopped before it. The screeching hinge did its best to alert the world to his misdeeds as Patrick slowly opened the cage. "Shit," he whispered under his breath. "How many times did I tell that kid to oil this thing?" The rusting hinge creaked louder.

He reached in for Martha. "Good girl." He tried to soothe her. Martha stepped away from the intruder's hand. Suddenly, as if he she knew his intent, she began flapping wildly, beating Patrick back with her wings. She cooed frantically, clawing viciously at him. He pulled back, his right thumb bleeding from Martha's defense, his hand scratched in a half-dozen places.

He cursed the moon and took a deep breath, resolving that a pigeon wasn't going to ruin his life. He reached in with a quick strong motion and grabbed Martha. Her wings fluttered vainly as she tried to escape her attacker. Patrick brought her under control with his other hand. He held her torso firmly in his left hand and placed his bleeding right on her head. "Sorry girl, but I just can't let you—"

246

He pulled her head hard to one side. *Snap!* The sound of cracking bone, of tearing flesh, stilled the night animals of the neighborhood. The great, white bird was dead. Murdered by a man fearful of his past. Extinguished by a man hiding his responsibilities. His undiscovered crime from six years earlier—the accidental murder of Skye Pippin, whom he killed in a fit of rage, rose up inside him with angry torment. Her anguished face as she slipped in the brown Ohio current lodged in his memory. He blinked desperately to shut her out. Her dying image haunted him. Skye stared, taunting him. He blinked again to compose himself.

"I've come too far to be discovered now." He choked on his breath. Indeed he had—a murdered mistress, an orphaned daughter—would surely dampen his acceptance into the proper social circles.

He tossed the blood-soaked mass of feather and meat to the ground and reached for Tramp, whose small, pink eyes watched the evil figure from the corner of the loft. Tramp was defenseless. There was no struggle. *Snap!*

Patrick dropped to his knees, the weight of sin pushing him down. "God, what have I done?" he cried as Tramp fell from his crimson-stained hand. Under the horrified moon, his spine shivered, contorting his body, as if the devil himself had taken hold of his backbone. The impact of his crime overcame him. "I'm sorry Danny," he sobbed. "I'm sorry Cal." He wiped his bloody hands on the grass moist with dew.

He cleared his watery eyes, smearing blood and tears across his face. Patrick sat and cried under a dispassionate May sky. The moon, witness to a plethora of horrendous evil over the millennia, would not offer solace. He had never cried like this before. He couldn't help himself. He sniffed back his tears in a futile attempt to deny his emotions. He bit his lip hard, hoping to replace his sadness with pain. Pain he understood. Sorrow, he had no tolerance for.

Suddenly Patrick realized where he was. The gravity of the situation was clear. His eyes were a blur of blood and salt. Still shaken, he rose from the ground, the dead pigeons in his grip. The assassin composed himself. Cautiously, he peered around the neighborhood again. Had anyone seen him? No.

He walked briskly to the garbage cans and hurriedly poured out a bag of grass clippings, spilling half the grass on the sidewalk. He set Martha and Tramp inside and refilled the bag. Weak and emotionally drained, he stuffed the bag into the can and took it to the street.

He stood by the mailbox, staring at the metal can, numbed by his act of murder. He had crept into the night like a thief. He had broken into the home of someone who trusted him. Like a trapped and panicked burglar caught in the act, he struck out viciously to kill. The assassin had completed his crime. Patrick Gilday, in fear of being discovered for the sins of his past, committed more sins.

The thief had stolen the dreams of two innocent children—Danny and Allison. He

murdered their hopes. The pathetic man stood and sobbed once again, his palm flat against the mailbox for support, his body hunched in revulsion. He vomited into the storm sewer.

"I'm sorry, Allison," he cried. His sullen voice carried on the deaf breeze. "I'm sorry, Skye." The moon hid its face behind a cloud and blew its sorrow-filled nose.

Not even God would forgive him these sins.

The next morning, Danny discovered that Martha and Tramp were gone. Upset, he ran into the house with the hope that someone had let the birds out. Patrick was already at work, having conveniently left before anyone woke up. Danny fretted over and over if somehow he'd been careless and left the latch undone. Could it be my fault? He consoled himself that Martha always came back, or that maybe she was out teaching Tramp to fly.

Danny and Cal skipped playing in the creek with their friends and came straight home from school. The mudball fight would have to wait. Martha and Tramp were AWOL.

"Has anybody seen Martha and Tramp?" Danny asked at dinner. By his own reckoning, pork chop night should be an automatic good Gilday dinner.

Cara shook her head and blinked a compassionate "no" to the boys. Patrick didn't respond.

"Have you seen them, Father?"

"Me?" he said, cutting a pork chop. "No, not me. Why would I be out back by the loft?"

"I didn't say you were. Martha's gone, and I'm looking for clues, is all."

"Well, I wish I could help you, son." His bandaged hand lifted a fork to his guilty mouth.

"Patrick!" Cara was alarmed. "What happened to your hand?"

"Oh, I cut it at the plant today on some metal shavings. It's pretty scratched up."

"Can I see?" Cal said.

"No, you can't. Why would you want to see a bunch of cuts?"

"No reason. I just think it'd be cool. Never mind," Cal said. "Pass the bread, will you, Danny?"

Patrick cleared his throat. He looked around the table, pausing to stare each Gilday in the eye. He peered down at his plate and pushed his green beans around. "I have an announcement to make," he said, clearing his throat again. "Our phone number has been changed and is now unlisted."

He picked up a pork chop bone and nibbled at the gristle.

"Why?" the surprised group asked.

"Because the Gilday family is becoming influential in the community, and I don't want to start receiving crank calls or calls from solicitors and the like."

"Geez and crackers! The Gildays influential?" Danny exclaimed.

"Well, we *are* becoming significantly wealthy, and with wealth comes certain negative aspects."

"Like what?" Cara asked.

"People who want your money. Con men and salesmen and all types of low-lifes."

"Are you saying salesmen are low-lifes?" Cal smiled.

"No, I didn't mean that. Oh, you know what I mean. The number's already been changed and that's that. Pass the potatoes, Danny."

A dejected Danny obliged. How is Allison ever going to call me now? he thought. I have to get a letter to her. I have to.

"You could have asked us first," Cara said. "Now I have to call all my friends and let them know. It would have been nice to have some notice." Her usually serene face hardened.

"It's done, Cara—forget it."

The next few days brought Danny less and less hope and more and more sorrow. He convinced himself that the Cincinnati extermination squad had gotten the pigeons, and blamed himself for their loss. He vowed to avenge their death at the hands of the city and wrote a letter to the editor to say so. The letter had an insistent tone that the city's program was illegal and inhumane. Murder, he called it. It did no good. The city ignored the letter and continued its pigeon genocide. It was murder all right. But he was accusing the wrong party.

Five days after Martha's disappearance, Danny held a funeral service for her in his backyard with a group of neighborhood friends. That night, depressed and saddened, trying to deal with his grief, he wrote a poem to honor his fallen bird. He titled it "City Pigeon Soldier."

Allison hung up the phone with Cara, a queasy feeling in her stomach. She called later. The line was busy. She called again, still busy. She called the next day and found the number changed. She waited by her windowsill for Martha. No word. Determined

249

and resourceful, she wrote Danny with instructions to meet May 24, at the zoo around three in the afternoon. The letter was intercepted by Patrick, who had taken to checking the mail during lunch without anyone's knowledge.

Allison did her best to remain buoyant and optimistic. She didn't let on to anyone, not even her best friend Mary, about the tragic cessation in correspondence. Only Sister Dena noticed a change.

"You haven't been eating, angel. Is something wrong?" she had asked more than once over the span of two weeks. Allison had no choice but to lie, for to tell the truth would have only made matters worse as the Sister Squad, as she had taken to calling them, would undoubtedly treat this as a major breach of security. Sister Dena was right—she was barely eating, and her personality, hard as she tried to hide her dismay, was just a shade less bright. It was just too difficult to shine.

"Jesus delivering the mail to the garbage dump, what happened?" Allison said at prayers the night before the scheduled rendezvous. They hadn't picked a time so she'd guess one and pray, oh God she'd pray, oh cheesecake, how she wished she got it right.

The grand day arrived with Allison tired from a sleepless night. How many prayers had she said, she wondered as the bus stopped on Vine Street in front of the zoo. Her hopes were a jangled mess—she dare not think he wasn't coming, that would be bad luck—but she also knew in her heart that the odds were extremely remote.

She paid for her ticket with money collected in advance from Rita Starks in return for choice pick of her vegetable harvest in late summer. Rita only wanted cucumbers, corn, and tomatoes and was willing to give Allison five bucks for first dibs.

Once inside the main gate, she ran directly to the shrine, her heart pounding through her blouse. "Please God, please let Danny have gotten my letter," she said under her breath as she entered the doorway. It was two-thirty. The building stood dark and musty. She was out of breath as she stood inside. "Danny?" she called, anxious, hopeful, wishing hard enough to make it so. The building was empty. Her wish did not come true. Dismayed, she went back outside into the sunshine.

A groundskeeper—whose uniform would have been loose on a much heavier man—wearing a name tag that said DENNY, came by working a dustpan on a long pole.

"Excuse me, mister, did you see a boy here waiting for somebody?" Allison asked.

He smiled at her through rotting teeth, looked up at the sun, and scratched his head. His forearm had a tattoo of a dove with an olive branch. "There was a boy here earlier."

"There was?" Her spirit rose.

"Left about fifteen minutes ago," the man said as his tongue ran slowly over a decayed front tooth. "Young fella, about twelve or so I'd say."

"Did he have brown hair and really blue eyes?"

"He had brown hair, don't know about the eyes," the groundsman said, sweeping up a cigarette butt.

"He left?"

"Yep. He was here half the day, maybe four hours."

"Oh, God! I missed him." Her knees crumpled in her disappointment.

"Are you okay, miss?"

"Ye . . . ye . . . yeah," she said. She walked back into the dingy shrine.

Her eyes slowly adjusted to the dim light. She saw the stuffed Martha staring down at her, then burst into tears. She put her head in her hands, doubled over, and sobbed into her lap, confused at the cruel way God played with her. It was the first time in her life, the absotively first time, that she questioned, even slightly, the existence of the Almighty. And who could blame her? Many have doubted Him for less a reason. She stayed doubled over for several minutes, unaware that the groundskeeper peered in at her every so often.

"Here, miss," he said finally, handing her a napkin from the concession stand. He sat next to her. "Are you in love with the boy?"

"Yes," she sniffed.

"Well, you're awful young to be too much in love. You'll find another boyfriend soon enough."

"But Danny and I have been writing for months. And today, I was supposed to finally meet him."

"Well, can't you meet him again some other time?" He smiled as if life were just that simple.

"No." She blew her nose. "We haven't been able to write for over two weeks. Something went wrong, and I can't get in touch with him. This was my last chance."

The man shook his head slowly. "Oh, that's too bad, young lady. But let me tell you, if you really love him, and he really loves you, nothing will keep you apart."

"Really?"

"Yep." He smiled, trying to cover his broken mouth. "Me and my wife were separated for four years by Nam."

"Nam?"

"Yeah, Vietnam. I got drafted and sent over to Nam. Infantry. I tell you, there was times in the jungle with a firefight going on all around me, friends dying, grenades and shells exploding, I thought I'd never get out alive. Thought I'd never see my woman again."

Allison stopped crying sometime during his story. "What happened?"

"I wrote her everyday. Prayed to God everyday. We had a pact, me and her. If either of us was killed, the other would go, too."

"What do you mean?"

"If I died, Kathy would take her life so she could be with me."

"Really?" Allison was fascinated.

"Yep. Neither of us wanted to live without the other. But it didn't matter because once I got out of the hospital and shipped back home, I was discharged, and me and Kathy was good as new."

"You got hurt?" She felt silly for feeling sorry for herself and acting like a baby over Danny when this kind man had it much worse than she. In Allison's view, everyone had it worse than her because she was blessed.

"Just a leg wound. I'm fine now, though." The man smiled and slapped his thigh. He looked up. "I'm a lot better off than her." He pointed to Martha. "We sure know how to kill things, don't we?"

"I guess."

"Billions of them birds and not a one left. A crime against nature," he said sadly. "Hey, what's that!" The groundskeeper walked toward Martha's pedestal and picked up a piece of paper. "City Pigeon Soldier, by Daniel Gilday."

"That's Danny!" Allison was ecstatic. "Danny wrote it."

"Here." He handed the poem to her.

"Well, little girl, I have to go now, don't want the boss comin' down on me. You take care." He smiled. "Our love, Kathy and me, survived over an ocean, a war, a battle wound, and four years of separation. If we can make it, so can you. If it's true love it can't be denied."

She gave a relieved wave to the stranger. "Bye."

Excited, Allison read the poem, City Pigeon Soldier. The words melted into her as if they were the words of Wordsworth or Tennyson or Whitman. More tears came to her eyes, a mixture of sadness and joy. Midway through, she knew that Martha was dead; that was the reason Danny didn't write. She paused to gather herself, crumpling the paper to her chest, then she read on, struggling to keep her composure. At the bottom of the page, a handwritten note from her soulmate awaited her.

"I love you Allison," it said. "I'll never forget you. See you in ten years." Danny intended to live up to the terms of the second Friends of Fate pact.

A flood of emotion swept through her like a river. The whole, miserable world disappeared. Swallowed up. She read the poem again. How could I have missed him? She kissed his poem. She cried. She kissed it again. What happened? She slid off the hard, wooden bench to the cold cement floor of the shrine.

"Jesus confessing his life was a hoax, dear God, why are you torturing me so?" Allison said as she tilted her head, eyes closed, to the ceiling of the pigeon temple. "Have I angered you, Lord? Are the fates conspiring against me? How could we miss each other by only fifteen minutes? Dear God, have I sinned against you?" Her words were not answered, of course. She sat on the floor, dazed and defeated, the hope of seeing Danny, her knight in shining armor, vanquished.

Later that day, as twilight settled over the menacing spires of St. Als, a disheveled Allison made it back to the orphanage and the concerned nuns. She walked past them, despondent, uncaring, shutting out their words as they attempted to question her.

She shuffled to her room with the gait of a geriatric patient on Valium. She opened her journal and wrote one passage. "Why have You taken my savior from me?"

Chapter 22

August 30, 1990

"I suppose we better—that is if you're prepared, if you don't mind my asking—well, it is my job, so I guess I shouldn't be shy about it. So, why did you do it, Stone?"

"That's objectionable. My client didn't come here to make a confession. Please stick to the questions in the deposition."

"Okee dough, Mr. Bennett, if you want to be direct, not that I have anything against that, I can be that way, too. Some people don't think—well it doesn't—okee dough, Stone, what were you doing by the Cosmic Club dumpsters the evening of August 2, 1990?"

"I don't remember."

"Hmm, kind of strange—convenient I'd say, highly unlikely, though. Amnesia won't sell well with the jury—oh some may fall for it. Your client is better advised, that is, I wouldn't suggest—for your sake I hope you have a better defense."

"That's another objectionable comment. Stick to a proper deposition or it stops now," Bennett insisted.

"I wasn't there. I've already told you that. How many times do you need to hear it?" I said. I sat in a room that mirrored my mood. Dismal and dreary. It may have been a nice room once, maybe in the 1920s. The walls were smeared gray like day-old oatmeal, congealed, pasty, unappetizing. Scuffed squares in geometric outlines and rectangles patterned the walls where pictures used to hang. Nail holes punctured the walls. President Bush, in full-color presidential glory, hung on one wall, the complete extent of the room's interior decorating.

I shifted in my chair, a lopsided, tangerine cloth swivel with a broken spring, to ease the gurgling porridge in my stomach. I felt like Papa Bear who had eaten his *too hot* meal instead of waiting for it to cool. I wasn't sure if the cause of my indigestion was worrying about the deposition, depression from witnessing Patrick Gilday's cold-hearted cover-up of his past, sympathy for Danny and Allison, the terse reply from Bobby, Jr. for me to burn in hell, or, as Rose believes, an ulcer. Whatever the reason, the pot simmered on the stove in my belly.

Changing my position didn't ease my discomfort. Bennett examined a document, an eyewitness sworn statement allegedly placing me at the fire. I rapped my fingers against the wobbly, oval table rutted with evidence of nervously-signed confessions and backroom deals by people who pressed too hard with their pens and forever etched their history into the unpolished surface. How many people had signed away their freedom in this room as the result of a coerced plea bargain? I wondered as I inspected the mismatched collection of furniture in the somber chamber. An odd assortment of chairs sat haphazardly around the table: one wooden with carved initials, four efficient fifties-style black and chrome, chipped and faded models, a torn, bark-colored upholstered highback, and two dolphin-toned lowbacks.

The windows, smog-streaked in black and gray, celebrated the melancholy, looking like the tinged hairline of Frankenstein's bride. Maybe Mrs. Frankenstein was the decorator of record. The place had that horror movie feel.

I looked outdoors for relief from the bleak interior. The sky imitated the room. Dark, scouring pad clouds wrung their greasy dishwater onto Greater Cincinnati. The end of August always brings a sullen rain. Dour rain. Unfeeling rain. A barren rain carrying a message. Its cool mist warns one to winterize the car, it implores us to head south for the winter. It gives us sympathy for birds and says to weather-strip the doorjambs. Get out the winter clothes. Find your scarf and gloves. Buy a snowblower. End of August rain brings a warning. It's a party's-over type of rain. Say goodbye to summer. It is a cold rain. An end of August rain reminds you why hot chocolate was invented. It makes one long for the glory of spring.

"Can you explain why—well, so many people have said—as Mr. Bennett is reading right now—plenty of testimony—witnesses saw you with a gas can," McBain said, breaking into my daydream.

I popped an antacid. I sat at the far-end of the table, away from McBain, Bennett, and Ms. Gibson, the stenographer, to avoid offending anyone with my breath. There is a sickness in my breath. A disease coming from within me that I don't want to expose to others. I looked down the table at the district attorney. His suit clashed poetically with the surroundings—a wrinkled houndstooth ordained with a red, knit tie basted with curry droplets. The bachelor gourmet.

"It wasn't me, McBain." I winced as a bubble of gas erupted inside. My organs steamed beneath the surface.

"I have a suggestion that you may wish to consider—although I can understand if you want to think it over—but let me present my proposition."

"We're listening," Bennett said. "We are always interested in hearing pretrial offers." Jim loomed large in the bark-colored highback, his impeccable attire and refined manners a welcome bright spot in the bleak venue.

McBain stood and went to the window. He stared down at the street through the drizzle. I popped a breath mint and crunched it into oblivion. McBain pushed his bent wire frames to the bridge of his nose. He pulled the left sleeve of his suitcoat, trying to even it with the right.

"There's so much evidence—not to brag or seem arrogant, it isn't my nature actually, but we have a considerable—a fair amount at least—enough for a conviction I would say."

"Brian," said Bennett.

"Okee dough, no more beating around the—suppose I should just come out and—you can take a couple days to think it over, I . . ."

"Brian! Get to the point." Bennett was more insistent.

"Okee dough." The D.A. continued to stare at the street. "I'm offering reduced charges to one count of attempted manslaughter, maximum sentence of five years." He turned to Bennett like a boy seeking approval from his father, then to me, then back to Bennett. "What do you say?"

"You're fishing, Brian. If you have such an airtight case, why would you want to plea bargain?"

McBain directed his gaze back to the gray streets ten stories below. I chewed a cough drop in the hope of suppressing a persistent tickle in my throat. My stomach sizzled like an order of sausage and cabbage pan-fried in my gut. Two antacids joined the cough drop in my mouth. The room was silent except for Ms. Gibson's transcription which had just caught up to the action as McBain responded.

"Off the record?"

"Off the record," Bennett said.

"Ms. Gibson." McBain signaled her to temporarily cease her dictating duties.

Her nimble fingers rested delicately upon the keys. Ms. Gibson, who sat two chairs to my left, had the kind of features that scare wives of middle-aged husbands. Early twenties, I guessed, dressed in a powder-blue business suit, which ended a tight six inches above her knee. She did her best to look professional with that determined impartiality a clerical worker is supposed to employ on the job. Her neutrality had progressed to boredom, but through the tedious task of the deposition, the slightest traces of her character shined through. I imagined her dressed for an evening of nightclubbing, her hair let loose from its barrette, her lips painted cherry red, a low cut blouse pulled tight against her shapely chest. I imagined her the quintessential female Walter Mitty, living a dull daytime life but reveling in wild, sexually-charged nights so passionate that she often came to work without sleeping. There would be time for sleep, she'd reason while she transcribed the mundane words of McBain and his prey.

"Politics," McBain said. "Running for office is—it takes a lot of time—so many people to satisfy, I can't afford the distraction. I'd like to settle due to politics."

Bennett, astute and sharp as a Ginsu knife, wasn't fooled. "You want this case done so you can use it as a feather in your cap for the election. Don't you, Brian?"

No response, just an empty stare at the street. The sausage in the skillet of my belly crackled. Another antacid. Then another. The semi-sweet morsels of Ms. Gibson's chocolate chip eyes looked at me as if to ask if I was all right. She didn't speak, dear girl. We waited for McBain to reply, but he ignored Bennett's question.

"The fact of the—well the thing is—and I'm not exaggerating here—there is just so much evidence, and I'd rather not have to waste the public's money. These trials can get costly, but really it's simply that it is open and shut."

Bennett straightened his tie and winked at me. "We'll take the offer under consideration, Brian. Let's take a look at your evidence first, shall we? Ms. Gibson," he said. "We can go back on the record."

Her fingers massaged the machine.

"Okee dough, counselor." McBain came back from the window, his scrawny chest puffed out like the hapless Hamilton Berger of *Perry Mason* fame. He gritted his teeth in displeasure and leaned on the wobbly table which tilted a full half-inch. A wave of coffee spilled from a cup over the edge of the table. The brown stain brightened the worn carpet. "Sorry about that," he apologized as I pulled a book of matches from my pocket.

I leaned under the table and placed the pack under the leg to stabilize it. As I did, Ms. Gibson shifted her crossed legs toward me. I admired their smooth texture and finely crafted form. She wore no pantyhose, her naked skin tan and inviting. Then, as if she could read my lust-filled mind, she uncrossed her legs. Slowly, in an inviting one-man peep show, she spread them apart just enough to reveal her sex to me. The dark patch of her crotch presented itself like a welcome mat in front of the harem door.

Stunned, not knowing whether to be elated or horrified at being discovered, I panicked and conked my head on the table as I came up for air. "Ouch," I said. The secret moment was broken. Above the table, Ms. Gibson smiled discreetly. Girls these days, I thought, where are their morals?

McBain spoke. "Do you use—that is, I didn't know you—how long have you been a smoker, Mr. Stone?"

"I don't smoke."

His eyebrows rose.

The kettle in my tummy bubbled. I ate another antacid.

"Funny," McBain said, "you carry matches yet you don't smoke—curious, that is—makes a man wonder why."

"Brian," Bennett said, looking at his watch. "I have another meeting. Could we speed things up?"

"Okee dough."

I stood up in a vain attempt to settle the brewing acid vat churning inside. It didn't work. I went to say hello to Mrs. Frankenstein. On the street below, a man stood in a slicker, leaning against a lamppost. A silver Oldsmobile slowed at the curb. The window rolled down, cash was exchanged for a plastic baggy filled with who knows what, and the car pulled away.

"Did you see that, McBain?" I pointed to the street. "A drug deal right in front of the courthouse. You have the criminals on the run now," I said sarcastically. Some days, late August rain days for example, one wakes up grumpy and stays that way all day long, no matter what happens. This was one of those days. I felt tired, weak, and nauseous. The proceedings were wearing me down.

"I don't arrest them, Mr. Stone. My job, part of it anyway, is to make sure that justice, or at least the law, in most cases, is served."

"Brian," Bennett said. "Can we finish this please?"

Ms. Gibson produced a naughty half grin. Why does she want to tease an old man like me? I asked myself. I could be her grandfather. I did my best, with the unwelcome aid of my bubbling abdomen, to forget her attentions and focus on the deposition. My freedom was at stake. I can't afford to be distracted by feminine wiles.

"Let me summarize for you." McBain picked up a stapled report and read from it. "Six witnesses saw you at the dumpster. Not good for you, Stone. Fourteen saw you flee the scene. Forensics showed traces of gasoline on your hands, yet one more strike."

"What did the lab report say about the rash on R.T.'s face?"

McBain frowned. "That hasn't—I mean we didn't receive—I'll have to check on that. We didn't get the results back yet."

Bennett leaned toward the D.A., a half-measure of his gracious nature replaced by tough insistence. "Withholding evidence is grounds for a mistrial."

McBain's eyes twittered madly behind his broken spectacles. He ignored Bennett's comment. "Let's see, here." He cleared his throat nervously. "Oh my, so much money. I hope I can afford to lose so much some day—not that I'd want to, but one has to have it to lose it—still, Stone, we intend to show that you lost a substantial amount of your net worth in 1988 and 1989."

I turned my eyes from the gray street and sat back down.

"We don't see the relevance to the charges," Bennett said.

"Oh yes, no doubt there is relevance—I mean, one can't lose that kind of cash, not a normal guy anyway—some might be able to, but not you—we will show in court that Mr. Stone was under serious financial duress—which led him to take drastic measures. It's called motive, Mr. Bennett. Our investigation, and it's all right here—most of it anyway—these files indicate that—they tell the tale of your six hundred and twenty-five thousand dollar bath on the Fountain Square West project alone. Isn't that correct?"

Bennett nodded for me to reply.

"Well, yes," I said. "But only because my backers from Chicago pulled out and I forfeited my deposit with the city."

"That's a large chunk of—few people have that much cash—must have hurt, it would me I can say that. Most can't afford to take that kind of hit." McBain smiled, amused at my financial misfortune.

"I came out of it okay. I have other investments."

"Yes, let's review those, shall we? My, my, my, later that same year there was another problem, a big one—a whopper of a loss I'd say—you had your loan called for the Hyde Park Station strip mall from First Security Alliance, didn't you?"

"Yes," I admitted. Damn, how was I to know that occupancy rates would shrink? Nobody knew retail would go in the toilet and the city would renege on its guarantees.

"How much was that one for, Mr. Stone?" McBain grinned, pleased at making me squirm.

"One-point-two million," I said. "I didn't know there'd be a soft real estate market. Times were good. Goddamn Savings and Loan scandal caused the problem." I glanced at George Bush grinning at me with that Iran-Contra cover-up smile of his. At that moment, with McBain ready to tighten the noose and the king of the S&L debacle staring back at me from the disfigured wall, I pondered the value of being a Republican.

"If I add it up—and I was always good in math at school—used a calculator on this one—had someone else check the work, oh yes," he said with a whistle of false amazement. "You took more than a two million dollar hit in less than eighteen months. Deep pockets, Mr. Stone?"

"Brian," Bennett said before I could reply. "Can I see the inventory sheet of evidence?"

"Okee dough. One more thing, before you review the list, that you may want to consider—it's a matter of some importance—could alter your feelings on the plea bargain."

"What is it, counselor?" Bennett said patiently.

McBain pulled at his left sleeve again, trying to lengthen one or the other, simultaneously trying to smooth his wrinkled coat, then reached for a thick folder of papers. He shuffled through several, saying nothing. His birdlike pupils scanned the materials rapidly as he searched for his potential trump card. The heat of my internal stove rose considerably.

He pulled a document from the folder and tossed it to Bennett.

"What's this?"

"It's a two million dollar insurance policy from Lloyd's of London on the Cosmic Club," McBain announced confidently.

"What?" I protested. "Where did you get that?"

"We're in criminal justice here, Mr. Stone. It's our job to find evidence," he said, running his hand through his wiry hair.

"I never took that out. Never!" I was telling the truth. I hadn't even spoken to Lloyd's.

"Fire insurance on your club." McBain smiled. "Most suspicious, I'd say—not that a man doesn't have a right to protect himself, but incredible coincidence, I'd say— riders on some works of art, too. Mamets and other valuables, I believe."

"It's authentic, R.T.," Bennett said as he handed me the policy. "It's your signature."

"Lot of money, take care of your problems, hard to pass up that kind of—not that I would stoop to, but that's neither here nor—did you cash the check yet?" McBain smiled like a crow on the berm standing over a fresh roadkill.

"I didn't take out this policy." My stomach boiled. The goddamn *Journals* framed me, I thought. Traitor. Just when I thought things were turning around. God, the noose was getting tighter. Why? Damn *The Journals!* "I don't have two million bucks. This policy is a fake, it has to be."

"Okee dough," said McBain. "Let's see if two million shows up, okay, Stone?" He smiled. "Oh, by the way, we also have several—eleven in all—well-verified depositions from other insurance companies who refused to insure the Cosmic Club because of the Mamets." He dropped three inches worth of paper flat on the table.

"What? That . . . that's not true."

"May I speak with my client privately?" Bennett said as he examined the insurance company correspondence.

McBain and Ms. Gibson left the meeting room. As soon as the door closed, Bennett bore down on me. "Listen, R.T., as your attorney, I have to tell you this does *not* look good."

"I know, but believe me, Jim, I don't know anything about the insurance."

"This isn't about insurance, R.T. It's about attempted murder. It's about arson. It's about how much time you're going to spend in prison. Do you hear me, Robert? Not innocence or guilt—how long your sentence will be—that's what this is about."

His words sent a blazing jalapeño pepper hurtling down my esophagus. I sat dumfounded for a moment, unsure how to respond. How could I tell him, in a way that he'd believe, that I had been set up by a cosmic entity known as the Council of Ancients? I paused, knowing what I had to say, realizing he didn't want to hear it.

"Jim," I began carefully. "I'm innocent. I really am."

Bennett edged in his chair to whisper, motioning for me to do the same. He looked around cautiously to see if anyone else were listening. "You know what, R.T.? In law, it really doesn't matter."

"What are you saying?"

"I'm saying I don't care if you did it or not," he replied. "If you didn't do it, they think you did, and all the evidence says so, and you're going to be convicted. If you did, then they are offering a good deal to reduce the prison time. Either way, you need to take the deal."

"They have no real proof!"

Bennett picked up the discovery inventory list and studiously reviewed its content. "R.T.," he said with a serious tone I've come to recognize as one of immense concern. He seldom used it in our long history together, more often as of late. "They have more proof than they need. They have *The Journals*. They have the poem *Impartial Fate*. They have witnesses. Insurance policies. Loan defaults. They intend to show your lengthy disappearances. Your *indiscretions*." His eyes stayed on the page as he gleaned the detail from the document. "Looks like they intend to question your relationship with Cara Gilday. And your—"

I tried to protest, but Bennett raised his hand to silence me. "And your unfortunate business dealings with BG Industries and Patrick Gilday—the Fernald and Zimmer indictments. It's a rather strong case."

"It can't be, because I didn't do it," I said. "*The Journals* will prove me right. It told me so." I can't believe Fernald and Zimmer continue to haunt me. Goddamn you, Patrick. I should have given up the contract at the first sign of trouble. I should have pulled out when the DOE called me in for a closed door meeting and forced me to sign secrecy documents. National security, they said. I should have known there was a cover-up. Greed kept me in the game. I should have known when we started discussing the merits of the government's "private policy" versus the public one. Am I paying the price for my silence now?

Bennett sat back in his chair, rubbing his hands over his face in frustration. He straightened his perfect, double-Windsor knot and picked a piece of microscopic lint from his blue pin-striped suit. "The prisons are full of people who didn't do it, R.T. Would you consider the insanity defense? We could play up the Jesus angle."

"Jim," I said, "you've represented me for a long time. You've been with me from the start. You got me through Fernald and Zimmer; you've done a wonderful job along the way." He stared at George Walker Bush, shifty-eyed, smiling presidentially from the wall. "I know this looks bad. I know you think I'm guilty. Everybody does. But here's the thing—I'm not guilty. So I can't give up. I have to fight. I have a purpose, a higher calling, a mission, so to speak, that must be completed."

"R.T.—"

"No, let me finish. I know this isn't a good case for you. I know you have a standing in the community and a professional record that is unblemished, so if you want to withdraw as my counsel, I'll understand."

Bennett rose from his chair, towering over me. "Mr. McBain," he called. "We're finished."

McBain poked his head halfway inside the door. "What did you gentleman decide?"

So this was it, huh? After all these years, Jim and I would part company. I'd have to survive my darkest hour alone. I begrudged him nothing; my situation was glum. He had his reasons and his right to do what he considered best. So be it.

"No deal, counselor. Let's proceed with the deposition."

Bennett gave me a pat on the shoulder as a knot of happy satisfaction lodged in my throat. In a battle for my freedom, a man stood by me despite the odds. Jim Bennett may not have believed in my innocence, but he did believe in our friendship.

"We're not going to make this easy on you, McBain. You're going to have to get elected mayor the old-fashioned way," he joked. "Bribery and boot-licking, like everybody else."

Undaunted, McBain tripped to the window and gazed at the street. The rain fell harder now, in sheets of gray. "Who knows what the hand will do?" he said, his adolescent voice replaced by a mellow, yet ominous, tenor, like Vincent Price reading Poe's "The Raven." "What the mind will insist. What play upon man the act will become. What fortune holds for desperate self. Who is this stranger come to visit? A fiery heretic in the temple with eyes of desire. Who ordained the species to deface the altar? A guest whom Chance invited to the feast . . ." He paused, taking a deep breath, and pivoted toward us. "Hope you don't mind—intriguing words to speak, not that I know much of poetry, but there are experts on such things—quite a poem you wrote, Mr. Stone, very philosophical—and damaging."

"Congratulations on your eloquence, Brian," Bennett said. "Is there a reason?"

McBain stepped to the conference table, bumped into a chair, slammed his hand down, and said, "The poem amounts to a confession!" His outburst was all the more dramatic as a coffee cup bounced from the tremor, tipped, and poured a brown caffeine river past the elbow of a shocked Ms. Gibson. The resultant flow of Folger's ooze dribbled to the floor where it formed a sizable lake near the lovely stenographer's feet.

I hesitated coming to her aid, choosing instead to allow my legal counsel the gallantry. Always at the ready, Bennett lifted a virgin monogrammed handkerchief from his pocket, got to his knees and began to work. The sensual stenographer casually swiveled toward him and provided the same voyeuristic performance for Jim, careful not to expose herself to the unsuspecting assistant D.A. The spot sponged up, Bennett rose from the floor, his face pink as a medium-rare tenderloin. He deposited the sopped hanky into the trash can which echoed with a hollow thud. The gentleman lawyer pulled a fresh one from his inside pocket and dabbed his flushed face.

"Sorry, um, sorry about that, sometimes I can be so—well I don't know how it happens. I guess I must be naturally—well, I'm sorry," McBain said.

Not one to allow a detail to slip by, Bennett said, "We will need a full copy of *The Journals*. I assume you will be introducing it as evidence." He smiled courteously.

McBain pulled at his sleeve again. The long arm of the law was not even-handed. "Uh . . . well . . ." he stuttered. "We can't seem to find—we're looking diligently—it can't have gone—well to be truthful, *The Journals* is missing," he admitted. "Don't worry, though, we're scouring the property room thoroughly. As soon as we find it, we'll get a copy to you." It was McBain's turn to squirm.

"As I stated earlier, Brian, withholding evidence is a serious matter." Bennett scooped up the stack of discovery documents. "Of course, it would be a shame if your primary piece of evidence can't be found." He flashed a grin that could have stripped the judicial robe off Sandra Day O'Connor. "I'll expect it by next Thursday, or we will be forced to file a motion for dismissal. Have a great week."

"We'll find the damn *Journals*." McBain scowled. "If we have to take apart the building brick by brick."

Chapter 23

September 5, 1990

Wherever the hell you are, you lying, fucking book, get back here! How could you do this to me? How could you set me up to take the fall, give me hope, then knock me down again? You son of a bitch. You liar. Deceiver. Abuser. Come back here, you unholy blackmailer!

Shit.

"What is the matter, Stoney?"

"You! You're the matter. Thanks to you I'm doomed. No way out at all."

"What happened?"

"As if you don't already know."

"Tell me."

"Okay, you back-stabbing, double-crossing, celestial traitor, here goes. But I'm only doing it to get it off my chest."

"Whatever you need, Stoney."

"I went to see Dr. Finkleday today. I knew something was wrong when he asked Rose to come along. We're sitting there with his office smelling of pharmaceuticals, like chemical warfare. He tells me the test results have come back while he inspects his fingernails, as if *they* were more important than me. Rose was anxious. 'It's not good, Bob,' he says. That's an understatement. Says I have moderate lesions on the testicles and liver."

"That does not sound good."

"I have cancer is what he finally told me. Just like that, I'm dying of cancer."

"This is most untimely. We have unfinished business. How long have you got?"

"A year, maybe two. You betrayed me, dammit."

"How did I betray you?"

"You said if I got *The Journals* published I'd be cleared of all the charges."

"And I shall keep that promise."

"But I'll be dead before then!"

As if to minimize the severity of my illness, it wrote: *"Not likely."*

"You tricked me."

"I did no such thing. I promised to clear up the arson situation, and I am still prepared to do as such."

"You tricked me," I yelled at the computer. "They want to cut off my balls just like that McJic fellow in the book."

"So, you do believe the story?"

"Quit trying to teach me a lesson. You come down here and mess up my life, blackmail me, discredit me, give me prostate cancer, and all you care about is whether I believe the story or not. It doesn't matter what the hell I believe."

"You are mistaken, Mr. Stone. It is all about belief. Entirely. There is nothing else. Your beliefs are your opinions, your prejudices, your choices, your actions. Belief determines the exact path of your life."

"The only thing I believe right now is I'm dying, and it's your fault. You gave me cancer. I know it!"

"It is far too premature to conclude that your prognosis will result in an orchiectomy."

"That's what the doctor said. They want to cut off my balls. And I have you to thank."

"Before one accuses another, it is most highly recommended that one examine one's own self first. In your case, Stoney, you eat horribly—bacon, sausage, steaks, creamy Italian dishes laden with fat, processed foods with no nutritional value. It is no wonder you have come down with a touch of cancer. Your dietary habits are atrocious. Fast food burgers. Fries. Shakes. Not to mention the hundreds of chemical preservatives and insecticides that have made their way into the food supply courtesy of the USDA, the FDA, and the infamous American food processors."

"What the hell are you saying? The cancer is my fault for eating food?"

The screen flickered gray. *"Yes. But not for eating food, for eating the wrong food. Tainted beef. Antibiotic-laden chicken. Herbicide-rich fruits and vegetables. Chlorinated, fluoridated water. Mercury-infested fish. You buy it because they sell it. Organic is the way to go. I am sure even the most jaundiced of A.M.A. physicians will tell you there is a correlation between diet and cancer."*

"You're insane. I'm not to blame for this. You are! You infected me. I know it. It's another deceitful trick to keep me under your control."

"I do not seek you to be under my control. I merely seek to show you that you have control of your own life. This is not my doing. I put not one spoonful of food in your mouth."

"Liar!"

"It is much more than food, Stoney. It is stress. It is suppression of emotions. It is avoidance of responsibility. It is temper and blame. It is chasing false ideals that has caused this illness. It is money. It is greed. It is allowing your government to export its tyranny. It is your destruction of the environment that causes disease. It is your guilt over your life's decisions. It is your acceptance of corrupt institutions. Your ignorance of others. It is a failure of your character to question, which has caused this malady. You create your own world, I am afraid."

"It's not my fault! I can't be responsible for every fucking thing that's wrong in this goddamn world! Can I? I've done well. I've lived a good life. You've done this to me."

"All experience is of your own making. However, I can use my influence to assist in your recovery."

"No thanks. I've had enough divine intervention. It just keeps getting me deeper and deeper. I'll work this out on my own."

"A word of advice, my friend. Do not rely on your existing support systems to save you. The Church, traditional medicine, government, all that you would normally run to, these are the very things that have caused the problem."

"Let me die in peace," I said as I turned off the computer.

The hard drive whirred. The cooling fan spun. The screen lit the room in gray. It had turned itself back on.

"The Universe is there for you, Stoney. Listen to its messages. Feel its healing power. Marvel at the coincidences that guide you on the right path. Listen to your soul. It is begging to be heard."

"I listened to my soul. And it told me I'm dying."

Section

A hero steps forth to challenge
A man whose life once had meaning
A man whose meaning once had life
A hero whose arm holds the torch of salvation

Chapter 24

February 1943

Sulphur was glad to breathe the fresher air of the Rossio again. He had been too long underground in the stale confines of the windowless OSS forging operation. Traces of exhaust and Coty perfume scented his nostrils, which cleared out the inebriating smell of printing inks, compounds, and chemicals. Sulphur had enjoyed their odor at first, he recognized their familiar flammable qualities as he thought of their potential for combustion, but after a few minutes, his head began to ache. The outside air, blended with leaded exhaust, was a welcome relief. It was purifying. He dug his hand into his pants pocket, worked the matchbook open with his thumb and index finger, then vigorously rubbed a matchhead. His fingers sufficiently coated, the spy lightly pinched his lower septum and sniffed the rich aroma of fire's wick.

His escort, Gregory Thomas, squinted at him. It had been hours since the two went deep into the windowless basement of the office building to view the counterfeiting complex, and now the Lisbon afternoon burst upon them in radiant blue. Sulphur marveled at the tall monument of Dom Pedro IV.

"Lisbon is beautiful, no?" the dapper Mr. Thomas said as he adjusted the red carnation in his lapel.

"Sure is," Sulphur agreed. The street bustled with activity, businessmen rushed to unknown places, taxis hurried about, women sat in outdoor cafés drinking coffee or port.

Thomas turned left. "Let's step into this place." He motioned as they entered a street side café. "We can watch the skirts from here."

The two spies took a table near the sidewalk. The Portuguese sun shone brightly on the buzzing square, but they found shade under a large tree which grew in the middle of the café courtyard. Sulphur studied his companion, tall and confident, well-groomed and suave, and decided he liked him.

"What do you think of our little operation?" Thomas asked.

"Impressive," Sulphur nodded as his focus bounced from his host to the sexy señoritas promenading past them.

A comely waitress with black-olive eyes spoke to Mr. Thomas. "The usual, señor?"

"Yes, Maria." The playboy spy winked at her. He pulled a bottle from his suitjacket. "Here," he said, "I have a new fragrance. The men will go crazy over you." Maria smiled shyly and batted her eyes as she took the bottle of perfume. "Thank you, Señor Gregory."

Sulphur doubted that Maria had a problem attracting boys as he traced her shapely figure down her soft, naked shoulders to her full gypsy blouse, which tucked itself seductively into a black, peasant skirt around her small waist. She was fresh and exotic, unspoiled.

"And you, señor?" she asked in a voice that made Sulphur want to check into the nearest hotel and spend the afternoon drinking in her features. Martini with two black olives, he thought to himself.

"Same as Greg," he said.

She scampered off to the bar.

"So, did you learn anything today, Sulphur?"

"Yeah, sure," he said as he reached toward an empty table and plucked a fresh matchbook out of the ashtray.

"You smoke?"

Sulphur stuffed the matches in his pocket. "No, just a collector."

Thomas raised a curious eyebrow. "We serve our purpose here, passports, visas, credentials of all types, but the Lisbon operation isn't nearly as sophisticated as Schoomaker's in Barcelona. Now, that is a work of art. Damn proud of that man, I am." Abruptly, the OSS chief for all of Spain switched direction. "So, you're out to ruin the German economy, is that it?"

"That's the plan."

"You've been given huge license here, Sulphur. The only person with as much clearance as you is General Donovan. How did you manage that, old boy?"

Sulphur shifted uneasily in his chair, unsure if a reply was expected. It wasn't. Maria arrived with espresso and a plate of figs, almonds, and sardines. After she left, Thomas leaned in and whispered, his cologne crowding Sulphur: "A word of caution. This city is crawling with spies. Double agents. Triple agents. Red herrings. Unscrupulous diplomats. Double-dealing businessmen. See that man across the boulevard in the brown hat?"

Sulphur acknowledged him.

"He's my shadow," Thomas said. "He's a German spy. He documents my every move, follows me from Madrid, stays in the same hotels as me; he's always present."

Anxious caution twinged in Sulphur's gut. It wasn't the sardines. "Why do you let him follow you?"

Thomas shrugged. "Because he doesn't know that I know he's tailing me. I can create all sorts of diversions to keep him chasing false trails. Originally, I thought about killing him, but cooler heads convinced me that it's better to be followed by a bad spook than a good one. That's why the Germans will never win this war."

"How so?"

"They're so proud of their so-called *German efficiency* that they don't think they make mistakes. At least we Americans recognize that we're imperfect, and we compensate for it. Not so, the Krauts. Their arrogance will be the ruin of them." Thomas smiled elegantly. "That, and a few billion Deutschmarks flooding their economy."

"Once the bills are printed, how would you recommend they get into Germany?"

Thomas laughed as he stabbed a greasy sardine with a fork. He held it up as he explained. "Simple. We'll arrange a large purchase of detergent—several boxcars—by a German importer friendly to our cause. We'll stash crates of counterfeit bills deep inside the detergent, then we'll ship it to Berlin."

"You can do that?" Sulphur was surprised at the casual ease with which the task could be accomplished.

Thomas winked at him just as Maria returned. "So, as you can see," he shifted the topic, "if we increase sales of our cologne, then we won't be as dependent on our perfume line to carry the company through. We call it line extension. It'll be all the rage after the war."

"I see." Sulphur played along.

Maria examined the untouched espressos. Satisfied that her patrons were comfortable, she returned to the kitchen.

"But isn't it risky to send that much money at one time?" Sulphur asked.

"Good point, good point," Thomas nodded as he waved the speared sardine in the air like a fisherman ready to cast his line. "First, we must get you to Barcelona with fifty million marks. Schoomaker can use his people inside Germany. He's got about six hundred agents to date. That should work nicely. We'll simply restock them with bogus money every four weeks or so."

"But how do you get them in?"

Thomas shot an amused, aren't-you-naive grin at Sulphur. "They're all businessmen. They fly in and out of Germany, usually through Madrid, Lisbon, Istanbul, Berne, or Stockholm. There are daily flights to Berlin. The Third Reich war machine is supplied by countries all over the world. Even in war, commerce flourishes. Pardon me—*especially* in war, commerce flourishes. Hitler's economy imports and exports tremendous volumes of product every day. He can't produce it all on his own."

Sulphur was taken aback. "I thought everyone was against the Nazis."

"Not hardly," Thomas scoffed. "This is a game of the highest bidder. That's how we're going to get you the exact paper and ink you need. We'll buy it all up from Germany's supplier."

"Damn."

Thomas chuckled. "Fascinating thing, this war. It ended the Great Depression. Make no mistake, Sulphur, people are making billions on both sides." A glint of greed shone in his eyes. "And once it's over everything will have to be rebuilt—France,

Germany, Italy, Poland, Russia, Japan, the Philippines, Singapore—all of it. Don't think for one second that strategic planners in London and Washington aren't aware of that. Some might say the more destruction the better. My theory is that's why so many American executives, like me, are in key decision-making positions. World War II is great for business and industry. Make no mistake, this is a good war."

Chapter 25

September 15, 1990

"Papa?" Twinkie's timid voice broke through my melancholy. "I have the mail." She stood in the solarium entrance. "Do you . . . um . . . want to read it? There's a large envelope."

"Bobby read my letter?"

"No, Papa." Twinkie bowed her head, then anxiously held out the stack of letters and junk mail catalogs.

"Set it on the table, if you don't mind," I said with a weak wave of my arm. I'd get to the mail later. Tomorrow perhaps, next week, in a month maybe, sometime before I die.

"Oh, Papa," she sighed. "You haven't touched your soup. It's Mom's potato, your favorite."

"I'm not hungry right now, thanks," I said, wishing she would leave me alone.

"It's chilly out here, Papa." She worried about me like a doting mother. "You should put a shirt on."

"I'm fine," I said as I stared past Prometheus to the woods full of red maples and scarlet oaks and locusts and buckeyes and birch and poplar, all cloaked in honeysuckle. There must be fifty acres of trees and trails back there that I never visit. I built a fine path of stone all the way to the woods. It took a year and a half to finish that path, and I never used it. Odd, how I used to drive downtown to walk on the levy but never walked in my own backyard. As children, Bobby and Twinkie built forts, camps, and tree houses back there, though I've never seen them. I was always too busy. I always had an excuse ready as to why I couldn't take the time to see what they had been proud to build. I could have—I should have—done better as a father.

The sun was hidden behind tumorous, gray clouds. The sun hadn't shone in my life, into my dismal piece of existence, since the bad news. It had been out all right, spilling its light on everyone else, but it eclipsed my darkened heart.

I was cold. Twinkie placed a soft, cotton blanket over my shoulders then pulled it snug across my chest. It felt good. The clouds hung like moist lesions carrying their poisonous precipitation further east.

"I'm not going to let you get sick while I'm taking care of you," she said as she kissed my forehead.

Dear girl, I thought. As much as I pity her for the way her life has turned out, she *is* a caring daughter. Much more so than the son who has abandoned me.

"Aren't you going to paint?" she asked.

"Not today."

"Your orchids could use some attention," she suggested as she sat on the glider.

I looked at her standing there in a Cincinnati Reds T-shirt. Since when was she into sports? Her eyes—gray gerbil spheres—weren't dull any longer, a tiny glimmer of light flickering in them. Her hair wasn't styled like Samantha in *Bewitched* any longer. Was Twinkie coming around?

"Shouldn't you water them?" she asked.

"They'll be fine. The sprinkler system does all that." She was right, of course. My prize-winning collection looked ignored. Temperamental creatures that they are, I imagined them telepathically sharing my pain, my sadness, my fear of death.

"Papa, you've been sitting out here half-naked staring at the backyard, not eating, not speaking, for almost five hours. I'm worried. Please eat something. You need your strength."

"Do you know what my choices are?" My gaze fixed on the forest. "Surgery, radiation, or chemotherapy. What's the use? Castration only removes part of the problem. They still have to give me radiation therapy. Do you know how that works?" I didn't wait for her answer. "They heat up your molecules, change their structure, send them zipping this way and that. Screw up their normal DNA coding is what they do." I took a breath. "Do you know what happens before all that?"

Twinkie shook her head, wringing her dishpan hands.

"The doctors subject you to a day of tests to calculate how much radiation you can stand. They permanently tattoo the treatment area so they know where to aim the radiation beam, then they custom design shields to protect the rest of the body from damage. Do you know what that means?"

Twinkie stared at me, biting her thumbnail.

"It means that they try to kill the cancer cells by killing all the cells around it. Does that make sense to you? It doesn't to me," I said, my strength failing. "And the side effects are nausea, hair loss, radiation burn, fatigue, dry mouth, diarrhea, depression, swollen skin and a list of other delightful conditions. After all that, it's only a fifty-fifty chance it will work. No thank you."

"But, Papa, you have to do something."

"It doesn't stop there." I was relentless. "No, they want to choke me with megadoses of pills so toxic that I'll need other pills to counter their side effects. And that's not all. Do you know what they want to give me?"

She trembled.

"Estrogen, Twinkie, estrogen. They want to cut off my testicles, feed me estrogen, and make me a girl. I don't want mood swings. I don't want to cry over McDonald's commercials while suffering from PMS. I've seen what you and Rose go through with water weight-gain and cramps. Kill me first. Suicide, that's it."

"No, Papa, don't even think it," Twinkie blurted, alarmed. "Don't talk that way." She fell to the floor at my feet and hugged my legs.

"Why? Why can't I just die? What's the point? My life is shit."

"You can make it through."

"It's too hard, Twinkie. The struggle is just too damn hard. First being framed for arson, now this. The gods are pissing on me."

She let go of my legs and sat back. She sat up straight. "You never gave up on me after I screwed up my marriage to Parker. I wanted to die then. I wanted to sit at home and sulk. I prayed for God to take my life. I begged for the sadness to end. But you didn't let me give up, did you?"

"No."

"I remember everything you did for me. You took me to Nassau for a week. Tried to fix me up with some boys. You gave me a job to keep me busy. You rented funny movies. You even took me to the circus on my twenty-third birthday. You never gave up on me. You wouldn't let me wallow in my misery."

She stood up, full of resolve, a trait inherited from Rose, and said, "I'm too messed up for you to quit on me now, Daddy. You've got to fight this thing."

"You're right," I said, although I wasn't sure I could make the effort.

"I need you," Twinkie said as she picked up the serving tray. "So, I'm going to microwave this soup, and before you know it, you'll be on the road to recovery."

Off she trotted, humming "Take Me Out to the Ball Game." Something odd is going on with that girl. She had barely made it through the first chorus when Rose came home. Twinkie updated her about my condition in whispers. Microwave sonar beeps interrupted their secret jabbering. Rose, chin held high, eyes fixed, marched into the solarium with a bowl of soup in her right hand and a stack of books under her left arm.

"R.T.," she said firmly. "You've had plenty of time to adjust to the news. There will be no more talk about giving up, suicide, or any other such nonsense. No more self-pity. I expect another fifteen to twenty years out of you, and we aren't going to get there feeling sorry for ourselves." She handed me the bowl. "Eat this," she ordered.

She set the stack of books on the table. "There will be no more sitting out here for hours, naked. You'll get sicker." Her tone became even more forceful. "I've been to the library and I checked out every book they have on *this cancer business*. If you take half, and I take half, we can learn how to beat it. The answers are in here somewhere," she said, as she patted the books.

"Rose, I . . ."

"And another thing, Robert Thomas Stone. We're going to enlist God in this battle. Tomorrow you're going to church."

September 16, 1990

Humans are a disgusting lot, a gathering of hypocritical egos spewing spite and fear. Rose deserves better. I did as she asked, put on my Sunday best, and went to church. The stares and whispers began immediately. We hadn't even made it up the steps when the shunning began. Rose kept up a good front, dignified and proud. If it were me, I would have turned around on the sidewalk and told God I'd catch Him another day. On a nice walk, perhaps.

Rose has given so much to the Church, not just the thousands in charitable contributions, but time and effort and ideas. She formed a prayer group. She put together a wives' committee to help inner city youth. She organized an annual collection to provide Thanksgiving meals for the needy. She didn't simply sit in the first pew and listen contentedly to the sermon. She was involved, a doer.

In the thirty or so years that she'd been a member of the church, Rose missed only two services. I suppose that counts little when your husband is a criminal. Excuse me, an *alleged* criminal. We sat in the front pew as she likes, next to her three closest church friends. One raised her nose in the air and turned her head, the others ignored Rose's greeting, then all three removed themselves to another row. Eyes like laser beams burned into the back of my skull. I fixed my eyes on the crucifix above the altar, a tormented, life-size Jesus bleeding from his ribs, his hands, his feet, and from his crown of thorns. The murmurs continued. Words became louder. Slanderous, cruel.

Rose pulled a clean hanky from her purse and dabbed her eyes. She sniffed lightly as the service began. Even the reverend, righteous and full of scorn, joined in lambasting us. He stood high upon the altar, candles lit behind him, the choir ready to break into song: "Gentle parishioners, I had intended a different sermon this morning, but when evil comes into the house of God," he said in a tone of sanctimonious condemnation that made me want to wring his evangelical neck. "When evil comes, we must drive it out, from our hearts, from the church, from the community. Send it straight back to Hades."

John Wesley must be turning in his Methodist grave. The Holy Club has been soiled, I thought.

His meaning was not lost on Rose. She opened her handbag, placed her hanky back inside, and calmly said to me, "Let's go, R.T. This isn't the best the Lord has to offer." She stood with defiant composure, her body straight and confident. Without comment, she strode from the church, as if to say we were above their petty disdain.

Rose drove. We hardly spoke on the way home. My stomach was in torment. I felt so sorry for her. Church was her second home, her shelter in the storm, and in our family right now, a typhoon besieged us. Because of me, she was abandoned by her faith. No, that's wrong, her faith didn't abandon her, the church did. There's a huge difference.

I thought the reverend's beliefs a bit queer anyway, ever since he declared that video games were Satanic because the players were given multiple video lives. The misguided reverend saw that as tacit approval from game producers that reincarnation was a fact. "Sega and Nintendo should burn in hell!" Rose quoted him as saying.

We were almost home. Rose said, "This isn't your fault, R.T. God merely revealed the true nature of this flock. I don't need them. I need you."

I wanted to cry. Instead, I stared out the window and said nothing, too choked up with emotion to respond. As we approached the house, she said, "I think it's time I understood this *Journals business*. Will you let me read it?"

September 17, 1990

I sat in the solarium reviewing the considerable stacks of mail from the last two weeks. The junk mail hit the can. I wished there was a law to prevent the sale of my name to these relentless companies. Junk mail is an invasion of privacy.

Rose came in with an afternoon tray of tea and sponge cake, strawberries on the side. She glanced at a stack and picked up *The Enquirer*. "Every time I see that Rense's face I see red," she said. The feature article wasn't going to make her feel much better. "The arts committee is one-hundred percent opposed to this blatant illegal censorship," she read aloud. Rose was active on the arts board and was incensed by the actions of the smut squad raid on the Contemporary Arts Center. My opinionated better-half doesn't particularly care for Mapplethorpe's work, but she did see "The Perfect Moment," and believes in its right to be shown. "I hear Spender's big money is behind this. I'm not buying anymore of his products—bananas and the like—or shopping at Dairy Barn again. I'm not going to support that hypocritical Puritan."

Spender is Mark Spender, self-made billionaire with religious principles he makes known to all within his dominion, which happens to include conservative Cincinnati, Ohio. Some say that without his influence, Cincinnati wouldn't be so far right. His influence, and that of Charles Keating Jr., of failed savings and loan scandal fame. Keating was a local boy who took it upon himself to clean up Cincinnati back in the late fifties. He used his influence to close down the adult bookstores and strip joints. He ran Larry Flynt out of town. Then he hooked up with Spender, just prior to setting off to bilk the American public of $3.4 billion in junk bonds that turned out to be worthless. Strange how the pious can turn out to be so corrupt.

Rose tossed *The Enquirer* to the floor like so much rubbish and picked up another paper. "Who is this 'M'? she asked as she scanned the attached yellow Post-it. "And how does she think reading the *Eastern Crescent Review* can help you?"

"I'm not sure," I said, reaching for a plump strawberry.

"Says here Saddam Hussein has rationed food supplies for his people," Rose said. "He questions why the United States has rebuked his offers to settle the dispute. Sweet Mother Mary! I didn't know we had two hundred thousand troops in Saudi Arabia."

"We probably have more than that," I said. "The government does what it wants, then tells us later. That's the way it is in politics, Rose. Nothing makes sense. The real losers in this will be the Iraqi people and the American taxpayer. We'll eventually pick up the tab for whatever it costs to pummel Hussein."

"That's terrible. I don't want our money going to fight a war."

"And, after we destroy most of their infrastructure, we'll probably insist that Iraq use American and European contractors to rebuild their country. We'll make the deal even sweeter by giving Iraq foreign aid. Our tax dollars at work."

"For the oil companies, that is. That's a shame," she sighed, then set the paper down. "War *is* ugly, isn't it, R.T.?"

If she only knew. If everyone only knew. Everyone bleeds in war. Everyone. If people would stop watching glorified combat movies celebrating the aggression of the U.S., maybe we wouldn't be so proud to kill others. Listen to me, I'm starting to sound like a damned liberal.

"R.T.," Rose said. "I made an appointment for you with the oncologist on Friday."

"Oh, Rose, I'm feeling much better, really. I haven't had hardly any pain since Finkleday prescribed that Kaolin."

"That may be," she said firmly, "but Kaolin only hides the discomfort; it doesn't cure cancer. We're going on Friday, eleven o'clock." She straightened a pile of bills. "When is Parker bringing that *Journals* business back? I want to read what you've written."

"He called this morning," I said. "He's stopping by after dinner. He was clear on the *after dinner* part."

"Good." She smiled. "I'd love to see him. He's such a dear boy."

I hadn't tuned in Channel 99 since the Ancients betrayed me, having childishly sworn I'd pay back the Council for my disease. My funk was finally breaking like a stained-glass window under the heel of the Reformation. I determined, based on Rose's gallant effort to support me despite the odds, that the least I could do was exhibit some survival instincts of my own. It wasn't right for me to expect her to stand by me when

I'm not willing to help myself. The self-pity shelved, I made a resolution to see this thing through—cancer, indictment, bankruptcy, and all—until I'm cured, innocent and solvent. A tall order, to be sure. I had just switched it on when the phone rang.

Bennett, even though he was upbeat as always, didn't help my initial attempt at enthusiasm. "Sorry to have to tell you, R.T., but straight up, here it is. They found *The Journals*, and our attempt at getting the case dismissed was quashed."

"Damn."

"Not to worry, we didn't have a prayer at that anyway." He chuckled, more jovial than I would have liked. "It was a ploy. A distraction to rattle McBain. Little sneak got ahead of us on that one and went to Judge Darke before I could."

"Damn."

"The worst part is that we have Judge Darke. He's a no nonsense guy. Serious. Staid. No theatrics or smoke screens." There was a pause. "We'll need a few tricks if we're going to win this one."

"Why?"

Bennett took a deep, considered breath. "Looks like McBain is going to play heavily on your past to try and show that you've led a secret double-life. He has petitioned your military records under the Freedom of Information Act. He's planning on dredging up all sorts of unseemly business. It could be painful for the family," Bennett finished.

My stomach flared. "Why?"

"He's bent on showing that you're capable of torching the club." Bennett didn't sugarcoat it. "He'll try to prove that you're reprehensible, corrupt . . . unfaithful to Rose. That type of allegation goes far with a jury."

"But . . ."

"And your business dealings with Gilday won't help. Look, R.T., don't sweat these legal issues. Let me worry about them. The biggest casualty in a trial like this is the family. It's what we lawyers count on—the emotional burden. McBain figures you'll plea bargain if it looks like he can ruin your reputation and turn your family against you."

"That really sucks, Jim."

"That's the judicial system," he said. "It's not all bad news, though. Judge Darke did agree to a continuance until January 18."

"There's something, I guess."

"It takes away McBain's political motivations," Bennett said, reaching for anything to give me solace. "He might look at the case more objectively after the heat of the election is over."

The call finished, I fixed a cup of tea and went back into the family room to my magic TV. The odds were infinity to one against me, but I kept my resolve. Somewhere in this story, somewhere, are the answers to my problems. They must be.

Chapter 26

May 31, 1980

It didn't take Danny and Calvin long to launch their wayward forgery plan. Allison's prior request for forgery abstinence was quickly forgotten in the thrilling allure of committing a felony. Danny could not control his penchant for mischievous accomplishment. Only two weeks had gone by since he narrowly missed Allison at the zoo, but he was already breaking his eternal commitment to their love. Boys.

Calvin stole checks from a box in Cara's closet. Danny dutifully filled them out and signed his mother's name. A few days later, he signed as Patrick. The two juveniles believed the coast was clear and subsequently began forging checks for larger amounts. Danny never got any of the money, only a few glazed and occasional Bavarian Creme.

"Danny. Calvin. Get down here!" Patrick Gilday shouted up the steps.

"In a minute, Father, I'm finishing—"

"Now, goddamn it! Before I come up there and drag you down by your hair!"

The boys looked at each other with dread. "We better get down there before he throws the spaghetti," Cal said.

They tramped into the family room to confront their parents. Cara was crimson in anger. The vein in Patrick's forehead snaked its way across his scalp like the Ohio River splitting Kentucky and Ohio. The boys summoned their false innocence, a technique they had perfected.

"What's up?" Danny turned on his boyish charm.

"Your father and I have something important to discuss," Cara said.

"It's damn serious!" Patrick stated, his black belt laid across his lap like a sleeping snake. "And you'd better get that smirk off your face, Daniel, if you know what's good for you. Now, which one of you boys forged these checks to the Donut Stop?"

"Not me," Danny shrugged.

"Beats me," Cal said.

Patrick stood, the vein ready to overflow its banks, his belt gripped tightly in his hand. "I can see you kids aren't going to tell the truth, are you?"

"I'm telling the truth." Danny's voice broke.

"Me, too," Cal said. They both knew that if they admitted their guilt they were still going to get whipped.

"So, you want *the belt*, huh?" Patrick said, as he raised the strap to the air. "Fine, if that's the way you want it. You first, Danny," he said. He grabbed the boy's wrist.

Before the first lash Cal yelled, "I did it. I forged the checks."

"You little son of a bitch," Patrick shouted, the belt poised to strike his oldest son.

"No," Danny shouted. "I did it. I forged them."

Patrick whipped them both, indiscriminate in his attack, bite after bite tore at their bodies. Yips and yelps escaped the boys as the belt ripped into them like fangs from a snake. Welts of burning pain throbbed from their reddened skin.

"Sit down," Patrick commanded. A satisfied sense of domination glowed from him. He reached into the end table drawer. "And how did you manage to get report cards a week before the school year ended?"

Danny's eyes showed terror. "Danny, Bs and Cs? You're changing your grades to Bs and Cs? Did you do worse than that?" Patrick said.

"No, sir." The boy cried as he rubbed the sting from his legs.

"Tell the truth or you'll get it again. Were you failing because of your attention to that orphan girl, Allison?"

"No, sir. I changed my grades so you wouldn't trash Cal." Danny fixed his eyes on the space between his thighs where the sofa showed. He dared not look at his father. He picked at a snag in the fabric with his baby finger.

Patrick's temper raged. "Are you sure it wasn't because of Allison?"

"No sir, it was to help Cal so he wouldn't get in trouble."

"And you made Cal's grades better, huh? Is that it?"

"Yes, sir."

"So, the genius of the family is becoming a forger? Well, this is very serious, young man. A little spanking isn't sufficient enough for this kind of behavior. Do you understand me?"

"Yes, sir," Danny whimpered. He pulled on the thread of the snag, his mind overloaded with fear, his body numb from the whipping which felt like poison spreading through him.

"I don't think you do. I'm going to put an end to this Allison relationship *and* this forgery nonsense, right now. No son of mine is going to break the law. Period." Patrick's forehead vein was a raging torrent at flood stage, pulsing and widening with his ire. "You're going to military school!" The belt fell lifeless to the floor, its purpose complete.

"What?" Danny couldn't believe it.

"No!" Cara shrieked. She had no idea this was coming. A spanking and grounding, yes, but not military school. She couldn't let that happen. Her star-child was not to be taken from her. "You can't, Patrick. You can't."

"Shut up, Cara," he said.

"He's not going." She ran to Danny. She wrapped her arms around him as if to protect him from Patrick's abuse. "Let's talk about this."

"I said shut up." Patrick raised his hand.

"But, Patrick—"

He hammered his fist into her jaw knocking her across the room. She smashed into a walnut display cabinet. Glass shattered as her collectibles tilted and teetered off their stands, breaking into pieces as she fell to the floor, bleeding.

"You motherfucker!" Cal rammed his head into Patrick's stomach. He picked up a lamp, holding it like a baseball bat, as a stunned and breathless Patrick shrank back to protect himself. "You leave her alone or I'll kill you."

The memory of a bloody Cal, eyes blackened, lips swollen after Patrick beat him for a $216 phone bill to some city in Iraq, overwhelmed Danny. He felt protective of his older brother. Matters had gotten worse when Cal revealed that he had called a number from a belly dancer ad he had seen in one of his father's dirty magazines that he kept hidden in the garage. It had taken Cal three weeks to heal, and explanations to school officials that he had fallen down the steps went unchallenged. Danny didn't want a repeat of that horrible night. But that was two years ago—Cal was smaller then—less able to defend himself, and he was operating on a much smaller dose of teenage testosterone. Cal was bigger now, stronger, seething with anger, boiling with hatred.

Cal cracked the lamp against Patrick's ribs, destroying the shade. He dropped it and flailed at his father, pummeling him with continuous blows to the head. Cara sat dazed and horrified on the floor. Danny wedged himself between the two combatants. Whether he feared someone *would* be killed, or saw in a clear moment of sanity a way to escape from his maniacal father, we cannot be certain.

"You're right, Father," Danny said quietly, as he stared into Cal's eyes. "I should go to military school." Cal suddenly stopped fighting. A tense quiet filled the room. Cara shakily got up off the floor. A trickle of blood blotted her chin.

"No, Danny, don't. You don't have to go," she said. She held him tight against her chest.

Patrick Gilday, shaken and sweaty, a swollen hand on his bruised ribs, huffed, "Yes, he does, Cara. It's for the best. I'll arrange it in the morning."

Danny spent the summer trying to adjust to his new Spartan lifestyle. In some respects, he liked the rigid confines of Calder Military Academy better than home, but only because he was away from his father.

Danny hadn't the disposition for the discipline of the military. He mocked their drills and their seriousness. An impish boy of twelve had no business being conscripted into a right-wing military institution. He called it a Gulag. Adversity instruction based on hardship and humiliation was not for him. He became convinced after the first few weeks, that the world inside Calder Academy was a twisted universe of jarheads with no sense of humor, no appreciation for life, and no patience with a flippant kid from Cincinnati. There were two types of boys at Calder—those who willfully enrolled to extend the family line of Calder cadets who actively served in the military (future soldiers of fortune, politicians, and cops), and those like Danny who pissed off their parents and were farmed-out for someone else to deal with.

He despised the kids who took to Calder as if it were a Sandanista boot camp. Citizen soldiers they were called, people fixated on controlling the minds and actions of others. That type, he believed, was why the world had wars to begin with. They were people who thought that only they knew what was best for the rest of us. People like Jerry Falwell, he concluded, who the cadets were forced to watch every Sunday after mess. Danny was pleased that he had discovered a diabolical connection between Christian fundamentalists, the NRA, the military, and the Republican party. Their agendas, he reasoned, seemed the same. One familiar with his celestial tutoring might consider that the talking light deserved much credit for his insight.

His banishment at Calder afforded him ample time to review his crimes and understand his motivations. The talking light came only sporadically now. Having concluded most of its work earlier in his life, it provided the knowledge for grasping great, unseeable truths about himself and others. He didn't feel forging a couple twenty-dollar checks warranted a life sentence at Calder (okay, it was seven checks), but he *did* calculate that he was paying for his Mamet crimes.

Dreams of Allison filled his nights. He wrote poems about her. He fantasized about meeting her. He wondered if his forgery had caused him, in the name of cosmic justice, to lose contact with her. He considered this carefully and deduced, with the help of his roommate, Billy Harper, that he had been the victim of his own bad karma.

Billy Harper was considered incorrigible by the Calder psychiatrist. This was a fact the commanding officer, Major Grimm, refused to acknowledge. The academy would not bow to a wise-assed, fourteen-year-old punk. It would tame young Mr. Harper. Grimm had seen worse and molded them. Some had gone on to distinguished deaths in Vietnam, Burma, El Salvador, Angola, Sudan, and Nigeria. Others languished honorably as prisoners of war in foreign cells. Still others were governors and senators tapped into the good-old-boy network, awaiting indictment. Major Grimm had similar hopes for Billy Harper.

An insolent cadet, Harper, after thirteen months of resistance, showed no signs of obliging the major's wishes. An exasperated Grimm, having failed to bring the impertinent youth in tow with forced marches, KP duty, corporal punishment, loss of privileges, taking away his guitar, and a long list of sadistic measures, believed the harmless Daniel Gilday would be a positive influence on Harper. The two were assigned as roommates. It was a plan destined to fail.

Danny's sandy-haired compatriot with the freckled nose and constant smile was a schemer. A continual stream of pranks and escapades occupied his creative mind.

Danny, on his second day at Calder, had heard at mess how the infamous Billy Harper ran the black market inside the institution.

"He can get his hands on anything," one cadet boasted. "Cigarettes, beer, pot, downers."

Another burr-headed soldier piped in. "He can even get you a hooker."

"He got caught last year getting a BJ in the utility closet," a cadet said.

Everyone laughed.

"He even takes bets on football games—college *and* NFL," the first cadet marveled.

"Hey, remember when he painted Grimm's dachshund yellow and glued an Oscar Meyer label to his side?" The table erupted in laughter. "It took months for that wiener dog to show himself again."

Danny concluded rightfully that Billy Harper was universally liked by everyone, with the exception of Major Grimm and a few of his anal-retentive cronies. The two got along from the start. Billy surprised Danny the first night with a delicious late-night snack from the closed kitchen: toasted, whole-wheat, turkey sandwiches with lettuce, tomato, and cheese. It was during this welcome, unexpected feast that Billy announced his plans to pour soap bubbles down the reveille bugle. Five a.m. is far too early for growing young men to rise and shine, he had said.

The two spent the next few months as co-conspirators in a series of devious plots to undermine the order and discipline of the academy. The soaped bugle trick worked, and the major switched to a taped version of reveille broadcast via loudspeaker from the administration building. Undeterred, Billy sneaked in and changed tapes. The major was not amused when the cadets awakened to the harmony of The Eagles' "Tequila Sunrise."

The pranks could come at any time and any place, but they were always at the expense of the establishment. Billy and Danny considered themselves rebels. *Free Radicals* they called themselves, united in their cause by an underlying resentment of authority brought on by their difficult relationships with their fathers.

"Mine pretends he's a sportswriter for *The Enquirer*," Billy said, matter-of-factly as he twisted together the fuses of two M-8os destined to blow the urinal off the wall in the officers lounge. "But really, he's just a hopeless alcoholic."

"What about your mom?" Danny asked.

"She left when I was two. I don't even know her. There, this ought to scare the shit out of the major."

In between their hijinks, Billy taught Danny how to play guitar. They had been assigned to band together. Danny blew trumpet, which he hated because his lips vibrated long after the music stopped, while Billy played trombone.

Summer changed to fall, and fall to winter. Danny didn't write in his diary much. He chose to write poems and songs and short stories for his own amusement. He seldom wrote home, but when he did it was to Cal or his mother, never his father. On weekend visits by his family, he ignored Patrick. More often than not, as a means of punishing his father, Danny refused weekend leave. His decision was laced with angst-tinged bitterness at the cruelty of the world. He would deny himself a visit home to teach his father a lesson. It was a special logic only teenagers comprehended. The only time he accepted leave was when Patrick was on business in Arizona.

Danny's first journal since entering Calder Academy came in early December.

December 8, 1980
John Lennon was murdered.

Then fate, or the manipulations of the Council of Ancients, stepped in to change the course of Danny's life. It was the spine-shivering night of December 17, which found Danny in a heaterless van traveling down an icy, Kentucky back road. Herr Strub, the pudgy, middle-aged, German-accented music teacher gripped the wheel as he peered into the frozen night. Heavy snow slashed into the beam of the headlights like a dusting of white flour. The green fluorescent numbers in the dash shone 10:19. Danny sat behind Billy, who was in the front passenger seat beside Herr Strub. He could feel the coolness of the brass against his chilled fingers as he held his trumpet in his lap. He'd barely been given time to grab his coat, and had forgotten his hat and gloves, before he was ushered into the van for an unscheduled road trip.

"Jesus, Billy." Danny leaned forward and whispered. "It's past ten. Where are we going?"

Billy turned around, his generous smile barely visible in the darkened interior. "To a whorehouse!"

There were three other passengers on this surprise excursion—a clarinetist, a tuba player, and a flutist. Billy had his guitar. Herr Strub's eyes twinkled in the dashboard lights as he improvised "Cherry Cherry" by Neil Diamond. The snow fell harder as the van slipped down the road. Danny pulled his collar tight around his throat.

Billy sang the lyrics to Strub's humming of the tune.

"Why are we going to a whorehouse?" Danny whispered again. "Are we . . . um . . . going to get laid?"

"Us? Laid? Not tonight. That's Herr Strub's department."

"Herr Strub is getting laid?"

"Sure. And we're going to set the mood."

"How?"

"You'll see." He smiled as the music instructor pulled into the driveway of an old Victorian house.

The musicians piled out, instruments in hand.

"Zet up over zare," the German Casanova requested.

"Sure, Strubmeister," Billy replied. "Okay, boys, over there under that window."

They shuffled to the side yard and setup ten feet from the weathered house. A driving wind tilted the snow at a forty-five degree angle. A blue light went on in the room up above.

"We'll start with a Neil Diamond medley," Billy said, as if he had done this before, "then break into The Beatles. Just like in class."

The light flickered off and on twice in succession.

"One, two, three, four—"

The band fell into rhythm, playing the songs they drilled so often. Billy sang a bluesy version of "Crackling Rose." The snow blew like wild powdered sugar, coating the oatmeal-cookie ground. Billy winked at Danny, as if this were the stuff life were made of, while the notes drifted upward. Danny blew his horn as best he could, his lips frozen purple, as he thought of the absurdity of the scene. The music sounded like crap in the classroom, and he doubted it would be miraculously improved outside a whore's bedroom in a blizzard. He scoffed at the concept of a clarinet, guitar, flute, tuba, and trumpet being able to do justice to music.

The boys played and played. The snow lathered the ground like whipped cream on pumpkin pie. It piled up on their heads and instruments. It was two inches deep now and fell with force in flakes as big as Frosted Mini-Wheats. The boys at Nabisco were working overtime, Danny thought. They launched into a medley of "Lucy in the Sky," "Lady Madonna," "Michelle," "Help," "Let It Be," and "I Want You (She's So Heavy)." Danny's fingers ached from the cold. His nose was numb, the tips of his ears stung.

He thought of John Lennon. Could Lennon have had any idea a bunch of misfits in a military school would be butchering his music while a German weinerschnitzel balled a fraulein during a snowstorm? Lennon's face appeared in Danny's mind as he remembered how much Allison loved "Instant Karma." What did she think of Lennon's death? Was she upset?

Danny recalled memories of hearing "A Day in the Life," and "Imagine." In the midst of the finale, a pathetic rendition of "Come Together," he began to cry. Tears streamed halfway down his cheeks then froze to his braced skin. He couldn't help it. Disgusted, he threw his trumpet to the ground and sat in the snow, his head buried between his legs to shield the biting cold. Lennon stood for something, he thought. Fierce independence. He questioned authority. He was a rebel who happened to write and play great music. He put his conscience in his music for all the world to love or hate. "Goodbye, John," he sobbed. "I'm sorry you had to go this way."

Danny turned his despair against his father. "Is this the discipline you wanted so badly for me? Is this supposed to teach me values? Playing cheesy dinner music while Herr Strub eats his strudel?"

Finally, it was over. The lights flickered off and on again. Billy motioned for them to pack it up. They marched single file to the van like demoralized Germans in the frigid wasteland of Russia. A few minutes later Herr Strub bounded down the steps of the house and skipped over to the waiting band. His round face blushed with rosy satisfaction like cherries on a parfait.

"How'd it go, Maestro?" Billy asked.

"Zare gute. Tomorrow, you vill zee a plump cheesecake for a nice bedtime snack, meine freunds."

And that was it. Billy's secret supply of late-night munchies arrived courtesy of Herr Strub, whose only request was an occasional "Longfellow Serenade" for him and his mistress. Danny shivered as he sat in the van while it slid its way home on the slippery road. His body ached, his eyes drooped.

"Billy," he moaned. "I think I have a fever."

December 24, 1980

A crowd of concerned people stood around the bed. A woman cried. A nurse checked the IV. A doctor said, "He's dehydrated, his temperature is a hundred and five. It's not breaking. We're losing him."

"Hold on, son." Danny thought he heard his father. "Hold on."

The voices were far away.

"This wouldn't have happened," Cara cried, "if you hadn't forced him to that wretched school."

He tried to open his eyes. He wanted with all his heart to tell his mother it would be all right. He wanted to ask them to quit fighting about him. He wanted to see Calvin again. He wanted to fish in the sweet, green waters of Lake Cumberland. He wanted to paint a portrait of Cal with a stringer full of bass. He wanted to write a book of short stories for his mother. He wanted to show his father he was a good cadet. He wanted all these things but could do none of them. Daniel Gilday lapsed into a coma.

He floated above the bed and stared down at his sweat-soaked body stuck to disheveled sheets. A woman he believed to be his mother brushed his matted bangs aside and placed a cool wash cloth upon his perspiring forehead. She kissed his cheek and sobbed while she gripped his hand, unwilling to let him go. Patrick stood at the window, his head against the chilled pane, as fear and remorse and sorrow served him a cold bowl of repentant tears.

Danny examined the room as he drifted weightless above it like an astronaut on a space walk. A thin, silver cord connected him to the boy in the bed. He knew him once. That was me, wasn't it? he thought. He felt sympathy for his grieving parents. "Don't worry, Mom," he said. "I'll be back soon."

No one in the room heard him. Danny's body lay still as death. He glanced upward beyond the ceiling, toward the sky, where a glowing light beckoned him. "I've seen that light before," he giggled. "I know who you are."

Suddenly, the silver tether snapped and he rocketed invisibly through the drywall and studs. He hurtled through the blue sky into the darkness of space like a NASA missile. He soared past planets and asteroids and meteors and stars, his body made of light, a translucent vessel blazing through the heavens. He was spirit-loosed from the physical bonds of Earth. The entity who occupied the Earthling known as Daniel Oliver Gilday was transformed into vibrating energy particles, pulsating atoms of pure being. His speed increased as he shot through galaxies with ease. He could not stop his motion, nor did he wish to. The experience was too grand, too magnificent an encounter to turn off. A jillion Earthly thoughts entered his mind. "Sure, Cal, you can have my stuff. Sorry, I didn't say goodbye, Ma. Sorry, I disappointed you, Father. Sorry we never met, Allison." He wondered if he were dead as he zipped toward the shining object, its brilliance more intense each second. "If this is death," he marveled. "I'll take it."

A burst of clear, white light exploded from the brightest star in the galaxy and headed directly into his path. A glittering vapor trail followed the flare. The young light-being was not afraid. Intuitively, he knew the fireball would not harm him. In an instant, the powerful beam intercepted his trajectory and fused with his energy, giving him more strength, more insight into the workings of the Universe. The light source was Danny's spirit guide, that part of the soul which stays in the Cosmos when one comes to Earth and carefully oversees the activities of its human form. The young, celestial traveler giggled ecstatically at the reunion. He was going home. Home. Home to where? To heaven.

He journeyed on as the light which drew him from his hospital bed grew warmer, more inviting, its immensity far greater than his mind could fathom. It seemed to contain the whole Universe—a hundred thousand light years across. He was soon surrounded by it.

Further on he traveled, intoxicated by its giddy energy. He went through the light's welcoming outer edge, deeper into its core. On to the beginning of creation. Onward toward an unknown destination. Time disappeared, vanquished to human imagination. Finally, after witnessing a lifetime of wonders, the journey ceased. He knew not if his space odyssey took a millisecond or ten years, but he did know that he loved this new existence and did not wish it to end. He was inside the light now, his eyes closed and unseeing, as if some sleep fairy had gently dusted them shut. Slowly, he was lowered to firm ground as softly as a spring breeze brushing a squab's wing. A delicate warming sensation permeated his eyelids.

"Is the child unharmed?" a woman asked serenely. "Did we bring him out in time?"

"Yes . . . yes," a deep, jolly voice boomed. "The boy is fine. He is an officer, do not forget."

"That may be, but the human vessel is so delicate. And, he *is* human, for now."

"He is fine," the jolly one said again.

Danny sat upright, eyes closed, enveloped by warm, swirling, white currents of a most delirious nature. He imagined himself before a great golden throne, adorned in sparkling rubies and emeralds, set in a royal hall so spectacular that kings and queens would bow to its splendor.

"Let us awaken him when the spirits are done bathing him," the woman suggested.

"It shall be so. The spirits like him. Look at Eno licking his face."

"And Fate has painted a halo around his head. Look there—Ya is massaging his heart. Such a glorious child."

"He is splendid. After all, I hand-picked him, didn't I?"

"Oh posh, the entire Council chose Daniel. You act like you're the father," the woman teased.

"And you, the mother." He chuckled heartily. "Come, let us begin. Awaken, Daniel, son of McJic. Awaken and meet the Council of Ancients."

His eyelids were freed, and when they popped open he found himself sitting on a stump in front of a large campfire. Night sounds of the forest filled the air. His wrinkled hospital gown had been replaced by a cozy robe. He sat opposite a large half-circle of people, the flame of the fire dividing them. A heavy scent of cedar hung thick like incense, like a Cumberland camping trip.

The campfire glowed surreally. Its vibrant flames burned in rich hues impossible for the physics of Earth, a profound spectrum of cobalts, ruby-golds, and emeralds, but also of crystal whites, pinks, violets, and golden tones. The fire steadily flickered, its heat and light illuminating the enchanted beings sitting around it. All that existed beyond its flame—above, behind, in front and below—was of the deepest blackness sparkled with shimmering stars of untold magnitude. The oval extended out to the slightest edge beyond the position of the Council members, then dropped off into space, as if the gathering was suspended in the ether. Danny peered behind him, unafraid, at the vast Universe below, in awe of the nothingness that held the grassy floor, tree stumps, and eternal fire in place as firmly as if it was Earth itself. What magic was this?

Danny delighted in the twinkling stars, each a candle of hope, an enlightened spirit of love. The fire dazzled him as he considered the state of his body. He had physical form but no mass. He seemed to function as a human, but was not bound to his body. He could feel his hands, his legs, his tongue, his eyes, yet he was both inside and outside himself. He and his hosts were best described as conscious holograms, three-dimensional images so real one could touch them.

"Would you like some water, son?" a strangely familiar voice asked.

"Yes, please." He answered timidly, but without fear. There was no fear in this place. Only love pervaded the atmosphere of the circle.

"Here you are."

Danny accepted an odd, triangular glass of water.

"It shall never empty. Raise it to your lips and you may drink until you are quenched."

He was mesmerized by the copper features and penetrating, brown eyes of the kind stranger. Those eyes, where have I seen those eyes? he wondered. To the young protégé, the eyes looked as though they were of American Indian descent. He felt their stare reaching deep into him as he gulped down the cool drink. "Do I know you?"

"You may," the man answered softly. As the man spoke, a dim light whirled around Danny's head, entered his mouth, wisped down into his lungs, then back out his nostrils, tickling him. He giggled with irrepressible joy. Childish whimsy. The man's embracing eyes, more intense than Danny's, showed bemusement.

"Leave him be. You can play with him after we have finished," the man said. The light sped away from the circle in great loop-the-loops. "I am sorry, Daniel. After your ordeal, the last thing you need is to be teased by your soulmate."

"My soulmate? What's a soulmate?"

"Daniel, we have brought you here to show you the nature of your existence. Please be patient, and we shall reveal everything you wish to know."

"Cool," he said flippantly, then immediately regretted it.

"It is okay, Daniel. There is nothing you can say, do, or think that we do not already understand about you."

"What do you mean? Who are you people?"

"Go ahead and tell him," an older man remarked.

"Yes, do tell him," said a beautiful female. Danny was smitten by her beauty and admired her luxuriant, blonde hair which fell seductively to her waist. "Do tell him."

The man kneeled at Danny's feet, majestic and noble.

Danny thought him ancient and young, wise and spirited.

"I am these things, Daniel," he said, reading the boy's mind.

"Hey, how did you . . . ?"

The familiar stranger took Danny's hands to quiet him. Again, he looked beyond the boy's eyes to his soul and sent a warm current of energy into his body. Without hesitation, he said these words: "I am McJic, Daniel. I am your father."

He pulled Danny toward him and squeezed him tightly. For several minutes the two became flesh, human skin and blood and emotion. McJic, who had sired the boy twelve years earlier, had never held his son. In his time on Earth, he had grown fond of the human act of hugging and would not miss his opportunity this day.

Danny didn't ask if it were true that McJic was his father. He didn't doubt it. He knew. This man, this spirit, this being that held him so close in some immense galaxy of light out in the middle of the Universe, this entity known as McJic, was his true father.

McJic sobbed in bliss as he held Danny. He hugged him as hard as he could.

Danny cried.

"Can I call you . . . Dad?"

The circle laughed. McJic wiped the tears from his eyes and laughed, too. "Son, you may call me whatever you wish."

Suddenly, a light darted from the shadows, racing toward Danny. McJic stood up, raised his palm as if to say stop, and the light ricocheted off his hand back out into the darkness. "Excuse me a moment, Daniel, I have to go speak with your soulmate. She is jealous that she cannot take a physical form as you have. I shall return."

Quick as a flash, McJic turned into a pure point of cobalt blue light and zapped off like a laser beam after her. Danny was dumbstruck.

"Let us use this time to talk, Daniel," the jolly one said. He was a stout man dressed in a saffron robe, like that of an emperor, Danny thought. "Indeed," he said. "I was an emperor. In my Earth time, I was known as Augustus."

Danny warned himself to watch his thoughts, especially about the sexy, blonde woman.

"Sensuality does not fluster nor embarrass me, Daniel," she said with husky exhalation. "Especially from a twelve-year-old Earth-boy. My, how those hormones must rage."

"Your time here will be short," interrupted the older man. He too was dressed in a saffron robe. "Let us not waste it on frivolous Earthling sex. If you want to pleasure yourself with the boy, Ariana, visit him down on Earth. This is not the place."

"Yes, you are right, Elder Brother."

"Tell us, Daniel," the Elder Brother said. "What would you like to know?"

"What is this place? Where am I? What am I doing here? Am I dead? Am I in heaven? Am I going back to Earth? Sorry," he said, after realizing his zealousness.

"Quite the inquisitive one." Ariana winked.

"Oh my!" Augustus exclaimed. "We have not introduced ourselves. We must get better at this. You start." He pointed to the first position to Danny's left.

There were seven beings in total, all wearing saffron robes. They were friendly and polite and spoke in precise words. Vivid auras radiated from each personage with a mystical hue unique to that being. He realized, as each took a turn to speak, that the flame of the fire changed color to the aura of the member who held the floor. He did his celestial best to hide his amazement.

After the introductions were made the Elder Brother said, "Daniel, this place is known as Shanidar. And we—" he waved his arm around the circle, "—are the Council of Ancients."

The words took his breath away. "Whoa," was all Danny could manage.

"We brought you here to provide a glimpse of your destiny so you may go back to accomplish the tasks for which you were sent to Earth. Do you understand?"

"Sort of."

"Shanidar is a vast collection of spiritual energy," Ariana explained. The fire's flame turned amber. "It is a formation of light-beings who maintain the balance necessary for the Universe to exist."

"Is this where the talking light comes from?"

"No." The blonde goddess smiled like wildflower honey. Everything in the fire's reach was polished amber now, influenced by Ariana's energy field. "Sirius is the source of the talking light. It is your guiding beacon. All humans have one."

"The Dog Star," Danny said. "The brightest star in the Northern Hemisphere. Is that where I'm from?"

The jolly one, known as Augustus in Earth time but introduced as Hee in the Cosmos, whose roly-poly features were reminiscent of a Western Buddha, joined in. "Sirius is your energy source, but Shanidar is your celestial home. Do you see?"

"Not really."

The Elder Brother explained. "You are a special being, Daniel. One with great powers. But like all humans, you need guidance to be sure you are on the right path. Sirius is the source of your light and inspiration. It acts as a type of communications relay station, as it were, between the Council of Ancients on Shanidar and you. Sirius is from where you draw your energy while you are on Earth."

"Like a radio station?"

"Yes, a radio, television, or satellite. They all work on the same principle, except our transmissions are based on thought-frequencies instead of ultraviolet, micro, or radio waves."

"Why can't I just get the signals from Shanidar?"

Ariana replied. "Shanidar is a vast galaxy of light, yet it is too far from Earth to function as the beacon you need. It is the central point of all Universal activity, the equivalent of what Earthlings call heaven, and as such must assign its energies to other sources of power, like Sirius, to watch over you. This is where you draw your strength, this is where your elements come from. Before you came to be Daniel Oliver Gilday, before your sojourn to Earth, your spirit chose to draw from Sirius as its fountain. You are bound to the physics of this star."

"That's where that ball of energy came from, isn't it?"

The entire Council smiled in approval.

Hee slapped his knee in delight. "Yes, it is," he said with a chuckle.

Danny wondered if he was *the* emperor Augustus Caesar, the one the hot, summer month is named after. Hee did not answer his thoughts but stuck to the boy's original question.

"It is that part of your energy field that you left behind as a homing beacon to make it back once you've finished your life down there."

"But if I'm from here, why do I need to be on Earth? And why do you need to tell me? How come I don't already know it?"

A large rumble of voices and winds stirred behind the Council. Unseen spirits had been watching from the darkness behind the fire. From the commotion, it sounded like hundreds of hidden life forms.

A flash of vibrant blue lit up the circle. McJic reappeared.

The Elder Brother continued. "You have a mission, Daniel, a very important one."

"I do?" the eager boy asked, enthralled. "What is it?"

"You, among many others, have been chosen to guide the Earth into a new age."

"What do you mean?"

The Council mumbled amongst themselves. Danny worried that he had said something wrong.

"The Earth is in trouble, Daniel. Nuclear weapons, wars, famine, pollution, violence, genetic engineering, a poisoned food supply—all these things, and many more, pose a threat to the rest of the Universe."

"Why?"

McJic spoke. "Because your scientists and politicians, under the influence of the Greys, are not capable of properly using the knowledge they have discovered. They seek to use this wisdom only for greed. The Greys are bringing the Earth to the brink of extinction."

"Who are the Greys?"

"They are an alien species which seeks to colonize Earth. The Greys have been assuming human roles for some time now. They will strip her of all her resources and leave humans with nothing."

"Mankind . . . will become extinct?"

Ariana spoke, the circle turning harvest wheat. "We are not as concerned for humankind as we are for the Earth Herself, and the billions of species which inhabit Her."

"You don't care about man?" Danny said.

"We care very deeply for humankind, Daniel," the Elder Brother said as the fire changed white hot. "Your species, under the negative influence of the Greys, has not learned well; it does nothing but destroy. We have all lived on Earth many times." He paused to reflect, his wise eyes revealing his disappointment in Man's betrayal. "Earth is a spiritual place of discovery for all of us. Our souls are from the fire and gases of primitive Earth. We have guided and nurtured Her since the beginning of time. Since we are from Earth Herself, made of Her elements, we cannot allow misguided men and women to abuse Her. This cannot be."

"What do you want me to do?"

"You must begin to realize your true being," McJic said. "You must begin to harness the special gifts you have been given and use them to influence people in a positive manner."

291

"How do I do that?"

The Elder Brother spoke. "By listening to your heart, by following your intuition, and by performing only those deeds which are good in nature."

"Like what?" he asked. "I'm just a kid."

"You are a chosen one from the Council of Ancients sent to help the world. You have special abilities, as do all people, but we have given you a more powerful mind and a stronger intuition. You have the ability. Once you are true to yourself, once balanced, you will lead people. You will be able to read their thoughts and guide their actions. You will be followed by many," the Elder Brother said.

Danny sat silently, considering their words.

"You must grow mentally and spiritually, Daniel. You must accept your responsibility to the Council and to the Earth and become a man," McJic said. The fire blazed blue sapphire. "A man of integrity and action."

"But, how do I do that? What am I supposed to be?"

"Become a writer, Daniel." Ariana said, the fire changing yet again to match her aura. "Your words will impact millions of people. By doing so, you shall save many souls from pain. This is your destiny."

"So, if it's destiny, why do I have to do anything?" Danny used boyish logic, reminding everyone of his age.

"We have provided the vehicle, Daniel, you must determine the road," the Elder Brother said sternly, amidst the mumbles and whispers of many Council members.

A puzzled look scribbled itself across Danny's face. "Why don't you guys just come on down to Earth and straighten it all out yourself?"

"He is not ready," an invisible voice said. "He cannot lead them against the Greys."

"He must go back and mature," another said.

"Silence." Ariana spoke softly and the shadows calmed. "Daniel, you have much to learn. And the complexity of this Universe is very difficult for an Earthling child to comprehend. It is a handicap you will have to bear, I am afraid. We have brought you here to prepare you for life's lessons. You will not be able to understand its intricate workings for many years. It is a process of delicate design."

"McJic," the Elder Brother commanded. "Send the boy a tutor. Someone to show him the way. Someone to befriend him."

"Yes, Elder Brother."

"But what am I supposed to do?" Danny asked. "I don't get it."

"Live your life, my son," McJic said. "Be a child. Grow to be a man. Evolve to be a teacher. Over time, you will rise to the status of officer in the Council of Ancients. You will take your rightful place in the Universe."

"But . . . I don't know how to do that."

"I will guide you, my son," McJic said. "Say hello to your mother for me. Goodbye, son."

"But Dad—"

"I love you, Danny," he called as a sphere of blue light showered Danny.

The Council rose, the meeting adjourned.

"Wait!" he shouted as the campfire extinguished itself. In the same moment, the darkness flew away, revealing a magnificent landscape of mountains and streams and lights and crystal buildings and a hundred moons shining in colors too miraculous to describe. The world began to spin around him as he fell back into delirium. Faster, ever faster he spun. Faster still.

"Wait!" he shouted. "Where is God? Where is God? McJic! Father! Dad!" He spun around and around. His mind was dizzy and disoriented. Feeling gradually came back to him. Heat. Throbbing heat inside a human body.

"Reverend, he's coming out of it," Cara whispered.

"Dad, help me! Dad! McJic!" he begged, but it was too late. The dream was over. Slowly, he pried open his pasted eyes. They burned hollow and hot. He focused on a man in black standing at the foot of the bed, a silver cross fixed in his prayer-clasped hands. "Jesus, where am I?" he asked, his mind mad with fever.

"You're back with us, my star-child," Cara blurted out, tears streaming down her blushed cheek. She hugged his sweaty chest, then kissed his wet brow. "You're back with us. Dear God. You're home now. You're home."

He smacked his dry lips. His head and body ached in every pore. "Man . . . I had a wild dream. I think it was a dream. Where . . . am . . . I?"

Cara looked down with tenderness at her son in a way only a good mother can. "You're in the hospital, Danny. You have pneumonia." Her tears continued. She had been wrung out in the last few days, fraught with worry, having chastised herself for not being more insistent with Patrick about military school. The guilt of being a failed mother had tormented her. She anguished over the possibility of life without her dear star-child. She vowed, and told Patrick in words so powerful even he wouldn't challenge them, that Danny was never returning to Calder Academy. Fatigued, she placed her head on the handrail of the hospital bed and said, "You were in a coma."

The reverend pursed his lips. "Thanks be to God and His holy miracles."

"It is a miracle, isn't it Reverend?" Cara lifted her head.

"I was in a strange world, Ma," Danny said slowly. He pointed a weak finger at the water jug. "A really bizarre galaxy, posilutely wild. I saw the talking light. And met a guy named McJic."

"You met him?" Cara's eyes ignited as she poured a glass of water.

"Don't concern yourself with it, Cara," the pepper-haired reverend advised, shaking his head. "It's just the demons-of-dementia. So common in cases like this. Out-of-body experiences and the like. The demons-of-dementia play havoc with people in this condition."

Danny ignored the minister. "It seemed so real, Ma. I wasn't demented at all. I was

in another *dimension*, on another plane. I'd call it the demons-of-dimensia and spell it different. He told me to tell you hi. Like he knew you or something."

"McJic did?" Cara asked. "Oh . . . shit . . . pardon me, Father! Oh, no." Cara stumbled backward, dropped the pitcher on the floor, splashing the holy man's cassock. She fell into a chair, her back arched, legs squeezed tight, a look of divine bliss on her lovely face. A series of soft panting moans emanated from her. The baffled reverend glanced at an ecstatic Cara, then turned to Danny, who was too out of it to react to Cara's strangeness. Besides, he'd seen it all before. The reverend was too naive.

"She's had the most trying time, exhausted, dear thing. Been here three whole days," the disciple of God explained. Danny smiled. The reverend picked up the pitcher and poured Danny some fresh water. "It's the demons-of-dementia, Danny. Nothing else. You'll forget about it soon enough." The kind but uninformed reverend raised the cup to Danny's parched lips. "Praise be to God that His great power delivered you from the hands of death."

"Praise be, Father." Danny swallowed, then thought to himself, Praise be to McJic and the Council of Ancients.

"What are you staring at?" Rose said pleasantly, just as the demons-of-dimensia episode ended.

Channel 99 was like a TV mini-series without commercials, without a melodramatic Hollywood script and the pandering to the lowest common denominator of the lethargic American viewer. The clock dripped four p.m. The melancholy stares of the Stone clan peered back flatly from the mantle. I've got to change that picture—it's depressing me.

"I'm watching *The Journals*," I said, pointing at the screen.

Rose set a steaming cup of mint tea, a plate of oatmeal cookies, and my afternoon pills on the end table, a glint of disapproval in her eye. "There's nothing on, R.T. It's just snow," she said as she marched over and turned it off. She didn't look back at me. She didn't say a word, but I knew what she was thinking, and I imagined the worry that must have been etched on her face. To me, the screen was alive with Danny's life; to Rose, it was blank static hiss. She strode from the room and immediately dialed the phone.

I was left to ponder the Council's advice to Danny, which happened to be the same advice it had given to me—listen to your heart. I had ignored it, ridiculed its message. Now, I'm forced to reconsider. The irony weighed on my abdomen like a smoky meteorite crashed into the hillside of my belly as I struggled to down my medication.

This day was a miracle of sorts—I had seen the Council, that infamous entity that decided to invade my life. The members had ruptured my peaceful existence a month and a half ago with a determination that made me question their intent—were they good or evil? Were they real or imagined? Was their desire to help or hurt me? But today, as I watched their interaction with young Gilday, studied their faces, listened to their responses, I realized that they are, indeed, decent beings guiding the events of my life toward some necessary, and hopefully positive, outcome. I picked up the remote, sent an infrared beam to the TV, and it switched back on. I could hear Rose in the kitchen talking on the telephone in a low, disturbed voice.

I turned my attention back to Channel 99.

At dinner one night in mid-January 1981, a calculating Patrick Gilday abruptly announced the family was moving. By Danny's theory of Gilday family dinner moods, it should have been a night of good news, being potato pancake night, but his statistical accuracy was damaged when his father dropped the bombshell. He used the pretext of setting out to ruin John Ogilvey, the man Patrick remembered as responsible for his father, Benjamin's, death. This was partially true as an excuse for the move. Patrick *did* set out to ruin the man who had ruined his father, but his larger purpose was to spirit Danny away from Allison without a trace. He was bent on keeping his illegitimate daughter out of his life at any cost.

No one in the family was allowed to discuss the topic. The decision had already been made. Their new home in Crittenden, Kentucky would be called Mulciber, after the Norse god of iron and fire. Patrick had his marketing department come up with the name. The Gildays would be moving as soon as they could sell their present house.

Over the following weeks, Danny distracted himself from the distasteful news with schoolwork, research on America's nuclear program, painting, astronomy, and guitar playing; the latter in honor of John Lennon. The talking light had left him, never to return. The lessons were over. Occasionally, he would think of his coma as he painted or looked at the stars, but as the days rolled by the realism of his celestial journey faded. The reverend had been right, he told himself over time, the demons-of-dimensia had played tricks on his mind.

World events rose up to occupy his thoughts—Reagan took office the same day the hostages were released, causing Danny to wonder (strong evidence the talking light had successfully done its work) if an unholy deal had been made with the Iranians. Days later the Indian Point nuclear plant in New York was shut down due to radiation leaks. Danny stepped up his efforts to pressure his father about his contracts at Zimmer and

Fernald, the local nuclear boondoggles that most Cincinnatians mindlessly ignored, thinking the government would watch out for them.

A chilly third week of February brought Danny to Mulciber for the first time. He had been listening for weeks to his father's descriptions of the former plantation but had dismissed them as salesmanship. His magnetic, blue eyes were astounded as the family car pulled into the blacktop drive to the main house. He had expected Mulciber to be a worn brick house from the early 1800s, painted whitewash, shuttered and ragged, but was delighted to see a huge modern house sitting on four hundred and seventy-six acres of land with a barn, a gatehouse, and best of all—its own lake. He and Cal could fish every day!

Mulciber was certainly a palace to behold, a mansion by Gilday standards. It stood like a stuffy financier in a gray, hound's tooth suit atop a gradual slope some two hundred feet from the road. Cara viewed it forebodingly, as if nothing good could come of a place that came as a result of revenge, but she vowed to make it a comfortable home for her children. The looming archway to the house would need sanding and repainting in a more cheerful color: Spiced Cider or Renaissance Gold perhaps. The eaves and pillars would be made to complement the sandstone brick, and the shutters would be replaced to match. Gardens overflowing with flowers would supplant the efficient shrubs, which sat like buttons in perfect symmetry along the front.

Cara saw this new place as a long-term project. Mulciber would be what filled her days as Patrick made love to his job. It was not an activity she relished, for she saw a black history in the house. Shadows of the past. Wicked business unfinished. A sharp, involuntary gasp squeezed her throat and twisted her spine a half-thread the minute she stepped across the threshold. The god of iron and fire was not a peaceful deity.

The animated boys explored their new digs, and quickly began to plead with a stubborn Cara to let them move in before school let out for the summer. She hadn't gotten her way about *not* moving to Mulciber since Patrick was too obstinate, but she did win the battle over keeping the boys in school until summer break. Patrick had wanted to move as quickly as possible.

Danny was pleased that there were ten other houses in the neighborhood across the street, courtesy of Ogilvey, who had developed a subdivision on twenty-five acres, while keeping the best land for himself. The Mulciber parcel was best described as a large, triangular ascot tucked into the breast pocket of northern Kentucky. Its frontage folded flat, blunted along the road a hundred yards across, widening into a broad scarf further in. It was big enough for the boys to live in the country, yet close enough to the other houses that they wouldn't be isolated.

Soon after the Gildays arrived, a dusty pickup truck, some color faded white, pulled in the drive. A man applying for the position of caretaker and his son got out. Danny stood in an upstairs window and observed the boy, whose frizzy hair hung wild like a black mop over his shoulders.

"Rasputin," Danny whispered under his breath. "He's dead-on Rasputin."

Indeed, the exaggerated features of the visitor were similar to those of the renowned psychic whose disastrous advice led to the downfall of Czar Nicholas. Thrilled, Danny called to his brother to join him, then hurried downstairs and out the front door into the cold February afternoon. Cal decided to stay in the house and investigate the closets for secret passages.

"Danny," Patrick Gilday said. "We have business. Why don't you and Gram take a walk down to the lake?"

Danny found his new friend a bright conversationalist, almost as upbeat as Allison, and the most curious person he'd ever met. The walk to the ice-covered lake was a long one. Once there, the dark-eyed Gram, his hair blowing like black straw in a persistent late winter wind, said with a laugh, "Some day I'm going to save your life by a lake like this." Faint wisps of a future mustache curled on his lip. "And you're gonna be thanking me something fierce."

"You're crazy," Danny said as he shoved his frozen hands into his jeans.

Gram threw his hair back into the wind like a mad gypsy. "Back in Rumania, when I was a fortune teller, I used to predict the future."

"You don't know what's going to happen."

Gram picked a stalk of dead grass and stuck it in his mouth. "Maybe I don't," he chuckled. "But a kid like you and a kid like me, we're bound to get in trouble. And I think you'll get in more trouble than me. When that happens, I'm going to save you."

"Yeah, how do you know?"

"I can see it in those blue eyes of yours," Gram said. He smirked playfully. "They glimmer with mischief."

On March 6, 1981, Danny made a single entry into his journal, probably due to the outrageous statement of our current Commander in Chief. I have to admit, when Reagan said it at the time, it made good sense to me. Maybe that was wishful thinking. Or patriotic rationalization. Either way, although I still believe in Ronald Reagan, reading the same statement from the perspective of a young boy has caused me to rethink my anti-environmental stance. But only slightly.

Danny's diary entry read: "I don't believe that clown, Reagan. I used to respect him so much (mainly because of my father's politics), but you'd have to be pretty stupid, gullible even, to fall for his latest comments. President Reagan said, 'Approximately 80% of our air pollution stems from hydrocarbons released by vegetation. So let's not go overboard in setting and enforcing tough emissions standards for man-made sources.'

"He's blaming air pollution on plants? Just how dumb does he think we are?"

Danny's birthday arrived, along with an Apple home computer and a real guitar to replace the plastic one he had been learning on. He found his new computer only somewhat interesting, but Cal took to it like he did to fishing. He was a natural. Danny spent nights tracking the Columbia space shuttle across the heavens with his telescope. He was awestruck since its launch on April 12. Four days later, he wrote a journal entry which I found most telling of his remarkable maturity.

April 16, 1981

Pulitzer news everywhere. John Toole won a Pulitzer Prize a few days ago. Now figure this out: he won after he was dead. He committed suicide because he couldn't get published. John should have hung in there a little longer. Did they give him the Pulitzer because he killed himself or because his work was good? And if his work was so good, why didn't anybody recognize it when he was still alive? Crazy world, man.

And check this out—a woman wrote a false article about an eight-year-old boy named Jimmy, who was a heroin addict. The twist is the reporter made the whole thing up and won a Pulitzer Prize! Is that amazing or what? She had to give it back. That must have been embarrassing.

Those two stories got me thinking about Pulitzer, which made me think of forgery, which made me think of the Mamets. I have to make it right, before the move. How am I going to do that when the forgeries are hanging downstairs? I've looked for every opportunity to switch them back, but with us moving to Mulciber the family is always together now. I'm starting to get worried. I'm going to get caught for sure.

By the end of the May moving day, Danny had not been able to switch the Mamets back. He began searching for the best opportunity once they were settled at Mulciber. The gleeful boys couldn't wait to occupy their new home. They said goodbye to their neighbors, including Mrs. Smitch, who insisted on a farewell concert by her dog, Mozart. Most of the neighborhood crammed into her living room for the recital and a potluck farewell celebration. Mozart did his best, but alas, he couldn't pull it off, leaving everyone to feel pity for the lonely Mrs. Smitch.

Channel 99 showed me June 6, 1981. A warm spring day sprouting with friendship like an aromatic field of clover and peppermint. Danny and Gram took a leisurely walk along the fenceline of Mulciber, making notes on which sections needed mending.

"So, Gram, tell me what's so ironic about working on our farm," Danny asked, referring to a comment Gram had made the day they met.

"You remember that, huh?" Gram pulled his hair back in a ponytail and snapped it tight with a rubber band. "Life's funny, Danny. Dad and me lived in crowded cities all our lives, with houses only five feet apart. We never even grew flowers in our yard. Now, here we are growing corn and wheat, milking cows, feeding chickens—it's weird, man."

"I don't see how that makes it ironic."

"It's ironic because Dad used to work for a developer who looked for large farms in default so the company could buy them cheap and build factories. Don't you think it's ironic that now he works on the same type of farm he used to bulldoze? He's working the land instead of destroying it."

Danny nodded. "Why did he change jobs?"

Gram stopped, turned sideways, and fixed his slate eyes upon Danny. "He says God spoke to him. That God told him what he was doing was wrong."

"Really?"

"That's what he says. Personally, I think he was drunk."

"Why?"

Gram didn't answer for a few seconds. "After Mom died, it took him a long time to recover, and he started drinking."

So that's what happened to his mom, Danny thought. "How did she die?" he asked, pretending to look at a fence post.

"Cancer," Gram said, kicking a rock.

"Man, that must have been tough."

"Yeah, but that was a long time ago. Nineteen seventy-eight."

"How did she get cancer?"

"Cigarettes. Stinking, filthy cigarettes."

"Are you sure it was the smokes?" Danny asked.

"When someone smokes a pack-and-a-half a day, and every pack has a gigantic Surgeon General's warning on it, it's pretty clear what the cause and effect is," Gram said as he bent down to pick up a rock.

"I guess you're right." Danny inspected the tiny seeds of grass which clung to his pants looking for a new place to grow. Nature at work, he thought to himself.

"It was my mom's choice to kill herself. If she didn't love life enough to take care of herself, she deserved what happened." Gram's raven eyes flashed resentfully. "You know what the ultimate irony is, Danny?"

"What?"

"It's that we're growing tobacco on Mulciber."

The words sent a chill through him. Gram was right. Patrick had ordered fifty acres planted. Fifty acres of death, Danny thought.

"Can you believe it?" Gram said. "Mom died from it, and now Dad's growing it. The Surgeon General warns against it, but the Department of Agriculture pays you to grow it. Back when I attended the Continental Congress," Gram joked, "we had no idea today's politicians were going to screw things up this badly. Who knew the government would subsidize cancer with taxpayer money?" He could not conceal his anger. "My mom was alive, but she chose to die. Irony is all around us, Danny. All around us."

As if on cue, the boys turned a corner near a large oak tree and discovered an old graveyard with a couple dozen aged headstones streaked gray from acid rain. Irony, not one to miss a chance, slapped them both in the face. They said nothing but took a narrow trail, which ran adjacent to the cemetery, back to the main house. They didn't speak for the remainder of the route. The only sound was winter's left-over grass crunching under their footsteps. High grass waved slowly on both sides of the path, weathered fence posts popped their heads up, and rusted barbed wire reminded Danny of man's constant attempts to capture nature. But nature always wins, eventually.

He looked into the morning sun and tried to guess the time as the cool dew seeped through his soggy sneakers. Two hawks rode the breeze and he was reminded of Martha. The two companions walked on silently. There was nothing to say. In that splendid silence, both boys realized what they needed most from each other—friendship without questions.

I sipped the mint tea, now cold, without taking my eyes from *The Journals*. The screen flickered fluorescent on "pause" as I thought of my own youth. I reflected on the special moments that define a person. The moments that no one else cares to notice, that no one else dares to involve themselves with. Such a shame. I recalled my days as an impetuous boy on the streets of Over-the-Rhine, selling bread, delivering beer, doing handyman work. I knew everyone in the neighborhood. I felt connected. Heinrich Johansen taught me German. Mrs. Grundel baked me pies. Captain Spitz at the firehouse used to let me wax and polish the pumper. People lived in communities, not subdivisions. We had discussions, not dialogue. We had friends, not acquaintances. At least that's the way I remember it. Until I was drafted.

I glanced at the water clock—a quarter past five. Rose and Twinkie will be cooking dinner soon. Pork chops, I hoped. A major benefit to contracting cancer is that people tend to give me what I want. Rose always cooks what I ask for, and Twinkie has stopped her experiments, if only temporarily. I doubt that she can go cold turkey in the kitchen without regressing back to some extraordinary culinary creation. Jell-O is still a featured dessert, so she feeds her neurosis that way.

I crunched a savory cookie and turned my attention back to the screen. Summer scenes came and went. Danny spent his time in his usual manner—painting, writing, playing guitar, hanging out with Cal, until mid-afternoon when Gram was done helping his father, Joshua, with the chores of the farm. Danny felt guilty that Gram had to help his dad while he got to do what he wanted. Yeah, he thought, I have to make my bed and keep my room clean, but I don't have to plow the fields or do any real farm work.

Cal spent his time getting up early in the morning to fish, sometimes joined by his brother. After breakfast he'd work on Danny's computer, which had found its way into his room during the move. Danny didn't mind. He figured his brother got more out of it than he did and was amazed at Cal's computer programming prowess. Danny had tried, at a roast-beef dinner (always a good time to persuade, he had calculated), to get Patrick to take a look at Cal's impressive computer work, but their father brushed it aside as mere boys playing games. Both were crushed by his unnecessary rebuff. More distance created.

In late afternoon, Gram was free to play. This left the three boys plenty of daylight to find things to get into. One distraction that Danny found most intriguing was the busty girl across the street that he had met the second day he had moved in. Janis. She flirted shamelessly with him, teasing him whenever it tickled her. He dished it back to her as easily as he received it.

July 17, 1981 hastened a crisis in Danny's life. His father had patched things up with the curator at the Cincinnati Art Museum, and he was coming to view the Mamets. Danny called a meeting of his closest advisors—Cal, Gram, and Janis—to discuss plans to exchange the paintings.

After hearing his confession, Janis was flush with elation. "How sinful," she purred as she sat on the milkhouse roof, one of numerous Mulciber hangouts. A half-moon painted a yellow traffic stripe across the placid lake and illuminated the ducks who didn't seem to notice that they were driving left of center.

It was decided that Gram and Danny, dressed in black jeans and gym shoes would meet at midnight. Gram's onyx eyes glistened with starshine as he relished the thought of a daring mission.

"Back when I worked in the French Resistance," he joked, "I stole six Rembrandts from the Louvre." He stood up, his palm out as a firefly landed. "Cute little fellow." He laughed. "Say, what if lightning bugs were actually miniature photographers sent by God to take pictures of the whole planet? You know, to kind of map its details."

Cal groaned. He'd heard several dozen of Gram's crazy theories in the last couple months, but Danny loved them. Gram was always expounding on some far-fetched theory. It challenged Danny's mind to discover which theories had validity and which didn't. The firefly theory didn't. The Mamet switcharoo plans confirmed and repeated, the foursome goofed around on top of the milkhouse, officially their favorite partying spot, before they went in to feign sleep.

At the appointed hour, things immediately went awry as Gram slipped from the tree outside Danny's window and landed with a cracking thud fifteen feet below. A late-night hospital run ensued. X-rays showed a broken collar bone. Danny sat in the waiting room, dreading the consequences of his forgeries being discovered. Would Father send me back to Calder? Getting busted for this would be a big-time punishment, he thought. Not even his mom could keep his father from sending him back, he feared. "Come tomorrow night," he told himself as he pressed the button for chicken soup in the vending machine, "they'll be bringing me in for broken bones."

All the next day, Danny alternated between states of fear and resignation. He was certain his crime would be uncovered by the curator. He sat in his room, trying to calm himself. He had a grocery bag stuffed with clothes and personal hygiene items in case he had to beat a hasty retreat from home. Running away appeared the best option for the thirteen year old.

Danny would be made to suffer in his room until after dinner. This was a formal affair, one where children don't eat with the adults. He thought the concept barbaric and condescending but was thankful for it this night. He poked at his turkey potpie while he listened to bits of conversation coming from the dining room, where the adults supped on duck l'orange. He resented the fact that he was banished from eating duck with the adults on principle, but doubted he could hold down the gourmet meal any better than he could his untouched potpie. Nerves.

The tension got to him. He crept to the landing, where he listened to the grown-up chatter. Cara, who hated these types of things, did her best to be a polite and gracious hostess. Danny cocked his head sideways, placing his right ear closest to the action.

"Dinner was scrumptious," the curator lisped, like Marlene Dietrich in drag. "Hats off to the chef."

"Thank you," Cara said modestly.

"When do we get to see those scrumptious Mamets?"

"How about right now?" Patrick offered. "Cara, would you mind serving coffee in my study?"

In my study, Danny thought. Since when did it become a study? How fancy-schmancy. It was a den before tonight. He heard chairs scoot out from the table and rushed back to his room unseen. He lay on his bed trying his best to be casual. Seconds ticked by. Minutes. His heart did a war dance in spiked heels in his chest. What was happening? he wondered. Have they discovered it yet? Is Father on the phone to Calder already? What if they don't realize the fakes were done by Danny and they call in the FBI?

Footsteps came up the carpeted steps. The drums in Danny's panicked body beat faster. Louder. The steps were heavy like Father's, he thought. He had learned long ago, as all kids do, to identify the walking pattern of everyone in the family. It was most definitely Father and the curator coming toward his room. He pretended to read a *Mad Magazine.*

"Son," Patrick said kindly. "Can we talk to you a minute?"

He swallowed hard and hoped his father knew how to perform the Heimlich maneuver. Someone would need to dislodge the tongue he was about to choke on. "Sure, Father, come on in." He sat up in bed. "What is it?"

The curator broke in. "I simply must see your work." He clapped his dainty hands together then brought them to his slender chest as if he'd just won an Oscar for best female actress in a male role. "Your father and I have hit upon the idea of showing your work along with those fabulous Mamets. Isn't that just darling?"

"Yeah . . . uh . . . sure . . . I guess so."

"Forgive my manners, Danny. This is Drew Winthrop of the Cincinnati Art Museum."

The curator held out a cold, tuna-fish-on-white-bread limp hand. "Pleased."

"Me too," Danny said as he found his ability to breathe. A great burden lifted from him, replaced by his mischievous grin. He had done it. A guardian angel or some such being had helped him through. The curator was fooled.

"Drew wants to see your work," Patrick said, nodding to the abstracts Danny had painted to cover the real Mamets. The light-footed curator rushed over to Danny's work and studied it. He placed an index finger to his pursed lips, which Danny swore had the slightest touch of pink lipstick. Winthrop nodded his head occasionally, like Joan Crawford at a starving artists sale. Danny brought more of his work out of the closet as Winthrop ogled the abstracts.

In a true moment of sheer irony worthy of Gram's notice, the curator raised up on the balls of his feet in joy and proclaimed, "My, my, my, you are a *talented* young man." He slapped his face in mock amazement at the rest of the collection. "I most especially

adore these first two. The dichotomy of depth and color, of sweeping brush strokes and austere lines. Oh, it simply takes my breath away." They were the hideous abstracts Danny had hurriedly painted to hide the Mamets. Winthrop loved them. He squealed in delight.

"We have a tentative agreement to show your works along with my Mamets," Patrick Gilday crowed. "The Gilday collection will be a household name in Cincinnati."

A surprised Danny caught Mr. Winthrop's pixie eyes darting between him and the bed. "It will be the *climax* of our cultural season," he sighed. "Isn't this just precious, Danny?"

"Yeah," he said sarcastically as he shot the curator a queer look.

"Think of it, son," Patrick beamed proudly. "Your work shown alongside Mamet."

"But you've only three of them, Father. That's not enough to make a show," Danny said, trying to reason his way out.

"Fiddle faddle." Winthrop slipped his arm around Danny's shoulder. "We've already decided to bring in others from various museums across the country. We'll have thirty in all, I'd imagine. It's a dream come true." His voice lilted up into soprano range as he squeezed Danny into him. "Your work will be presented in a room next to them. We'll call it Masters: Young and Old."

Danny felt himself sinking in quicksand. After the visitors had left his room, he wondered gloomily, if their enthusiasm would be so filled with gaiety if they knew the true origin of his father's Mamets. He had to make the switch. Fast.

The rest of the summer was filled with Gram espousing dozens of ridiculous theories to the group, each one crazier than the next, all designed to make Danny think. Gram tried to convince Danny that license plates were secretly assigned with a special coded number that revealed your psychiatric make-up to the police. He tried out the theory that a person's hair actually functions as an antenna by picking up radio signals from other planets. The more hair, the better the reception. He stated that hot dogs were actually a government experiment to see if humans would eat pretty much anything set before them.

Gram's fantastic mental suppositions were made more amusing by the fact that the group had started smoking marijuana, supplied by Cal, who had introduced it on a humid August night at the lake.

As summer sweated to its end, Patrick told Danny that it would take a year to plan the Mamet exhibit. He breathed an extremely heavy, if not pot-induced, sigh of relief upon that news. There was a negative side to the summer, however. One night at dinner, Patrick came in sullen-faced and announced, "Gary Bartlett killed himself this afternoon."

Cara cried into her napkin. She had known Bartlett well: he and his wife were often dinner companions of the Gildays. She liked Gary. She knew him better than anyone suspected, having seduced him several years ago and kept up a seven month affair until they tired of each other. It was her way of paying Patrick back for ignoring her wants and needs. Not many of his *friends* hadn't been seduced by her charms.

"Well, if he wasn't man enough to tough it out, then he wasn't much of a man to begin with," Patrick said coldly, to everyone's astonishment.

Cara left the table in tears of disgust. The brothers sat there aghast at their father's brutal comment. It was at that moment that Danny realized once and for all, staring into his lumpy mashed potatoes, that his father had no soul.

Chapter 27

April 1943

"I love a good steak, don't you?" The president patted his stomach as the butler cleared the dishes.

"Yes, sir," Sulphur acknowledged, still overwhelmed that he was sitting in the White House having a private dinner with FDR.

"If you'll excuse me, gentlemen, I have an engagement to attend," said the first lady as she rose from the table. Mrs. Roosevelt extended a firm hand to Sulphur and exited.

"Good woman," FDR's eyes glistened. "She's made some of my best decisions for me. Strong-willed, Ellie is." He chuckled and lifted a frosted glass to his lips. "Ahh," he exhaled with satisfaction. "The Germans may be a holy terror, but they make a fine pilsner."

Roosevelt removed his nose-clip glasses, pinched his tear ducts, then replaced them. The butler brought another beer as the president inserted a cigarette into his long holder. "You have a light?"

"No, sir. Sorry," Sulphur said, his attention drawn to the two packs of embossed White House matchbooks he had stashed deep in his pockets. He knew FDR had a lighter, but figured he enjoyed testing whether others smoked, too, but were reluctant to do so in his presence.

"Matches aren't made of sulphur, did you know that?" Roosevelt's pupils reflected the dancing yellow flames.

Sulphur nodded.

"Chlorate of potash, I'm told." Roosevelt puffed to start his smoke. "With paraffin to carry the flame to the stem. Interesting product. The Diamond Match Company is working on a waterproof match for our boys in the South Pacific. They tell me they're close to having a match that will light after eight hours underwater. Fascinating."

Sulphur measured the Commander in Chief. What was he getting at? he wondered. "You have an impressive knowledge of matches."

FDR took a long drag of the smoke, then let it out slowly, the cloud filling the room. He tilted his holder upward like a magic wand. "Have to," FDR said surprisingly, and grinned. "That's where you and I are different, Sulphur; your eyes show a love of fire, but it doesn't thrill me." The president leaned forward in his chair. "It scares me, son. I'm deathly afraid of fire."

The spy turned personal attaché was stunned. He hadn't thought of FDR as afraid of anything. "You, sir?"

"Terrified," Roosevelt admitted without inhibition. He smacked his legs crisply with his left hand. "Legs, you know, can't use them, so I'd be trapped in a fire. It's a phobia, Sulphur. Horrendous way to die. Horrendous." The president inhaled, gripped the filter tip with his teeth and said, "You'll be going to Spain soon. You should ask Colonel Thomas to give you a tour of the Spanish sulphur mines."

"I'll consider that, sir," the intelligence officer replied as he thought of the progress he'd made on the forging operation. Three hundred million marks to date, with more coming off the presses every hour. It had been much less difficult than he'd imagined. Of course, with the undivided attention of the U.S. Mint, he couldn't help but be successful. The engravers had done spectacular work. All that was left was to ship the money to Lisbon, then distribute it throughout Europe using Thomas' spy network.

"Sulphur," FDR recited, "chemical symbol—S. A solid, non-metallic substance with the atomic number of 16 and an atomic weight of 32.064. Ignites at a low temperature, burns quickly, and gives off a pale blue flame."

Sulphur revealed no emotion as Roosevelt continued.

"Aids in the development of bones and helps muscle change food into energy, I'm told." The president drew on his smoke as if the cancerous wand were some elixir that gave him special power. Indeed, to many Americans, FDR was Merlin, the one who lifted the country out of the Great Depression in a one-man financial levitation act. He would also be the wizard to save America from the Black Knight, Hitler. The population stared in awe at him center stage, admired him, idolized his person as if he were some mythical savior with divine guidance. Sulphur saw him as a man—a man with tremendous power. "Ever heard of Vemork, Norway?"

"No, sir."

Roosevelt's jovial face turned somber. "It's the home of the Norsk Hydro power plant. On October 19, 1942, we sent thirty-four commandos in to blow it up. It was an ill-conceived operation. They were all captured and executed by the Nazis. Bastards shot every one of them. Know why we sent them in at such peril?"

Sulphur shook his head.

"Water, Sulphur. Water. Fire's natural enemy."

"I don't follow, sir."

"Norsk Hydro is the world's only producer of heavy water. Chemical formula D_2O. Contains a heavy isotope of hydrogen called deuterium." FDR set his cigarette in the ashtray, the wispy line of vapor rose in the air like the burning wreckage of a Spitfire. "Heavy water is essential for the production of an atomic bomb, Sulphur. And the Germans have captured the supply." Sulphur wasn't sure what it meant, but he judged by FDR's grim face that it wasn't good. "Oppenheimer tells me one atomic weapon could wipe out an entire city. The equivalent of nineteen thousand tons of TNT."

"Holy . . ." He didn't finish; his heart pounded with the immense destructive power of the weapon. He wasn't sure if it was terror or delight that he felt as he mulled over the A-bomb's force.

"I need you to wrap up your forging operation," the Commander in Chief ordered. "Turn it over to Schoomaker in Barcelona. Within eight weeks, I want your full assessment of how to destroy Germany's production of heavy water."

"Yes, sir," he responded emphatically, the hairs on his arms tingling. He was getting back into the action, back to his first love. Finally, he was assigned to blow something up. He wouldn't waste this chance. Sulphur tried to suppress a smile but couldn't.

"Sulphur," FDR said ominously. "It all comes down to you. Your mission will determine the fate of this war and of this nation. The freedom of future generations is in your hands."

Chapter 28

September 17, 1990

I eyeballed the peep hole and saw nothing but the Bing estate, the pagoda monstrosity across the road surrounded by cherry trees. Bing was out bagging his leaves. A sound like the claws of an unwelcome cat scratched at the bottom of the door. I pulled it open to find Parker on his haunches, carrot clenched in his jaw, fingers rubbing a red liquid. He sniffed his thumb and index fingers as his penetrating eyes scoured the door, searching for clues. Bing waved from across the street. I returned the suburban salute like a dutiful neighbor.

"Hey, R.T." Parker's coral blue eyes drew in the immediate area, like a black hole pulling all matter into its immense gravitational field. "You have some real fans, fella."

He emitted a nervous laugh as he nodded at the door, recently defaced with neon red spray paint: ARSONIST GET OUT! Parker didn't wait for me to respond. He stood up, adjusted *The Journals* under his arm, a freshly shaved carrot in his teeth.

"I'll come by tomorrow and swab a roller over it," he offered.

Rose was busy cleaning up the evening meal. Thank God. I could see her outrage that we had been violated again. I worried it was all becoming too much for her, and regretted that it was all my doing. Dear girl, I thought, when will this end so we can live in obscurity again? Is peace too much to ask?

"Here," Parker said, shoving a paper bag at me.

"What's this?"

"Oh, some fresh parsley, some myrrh capsules, and green tea." He grinned humbly, doing his utmost not to embarrass me. "I noticed you covered your mouth with your hand several times the last time I was here. Figured you were having trouble with your breath. Self conscious and all that. Parsley, myrrh and green tea will fix you right up. All natural, organic."

"Come on in," I said, doing my best not to blush.

Parker's astute powers of observation came through again. Of course, he could have noticed the jars, packages, vials and boxes of breath fresheners and mints, oral rinses and mouth washes, candies and sundry other products I've taken to stem the stench reeking from me since I took a bullet last August. None of them had worked. I swallowed and swigged and swished and rinsed and sucked on and chewed all manner of fresheners. Salt water. Red hots. Every toothpaste known to man. A list too long to document in this journal. The odor venting from me cut through my visitors like a logger's chainsaw through a Pacific Northwest sapling.

"Oh, yeah, almost forgot. If you sniff parsley while you visualize a safe home, it will put up a protective barrier around the house. It's called aromatherapy. You might try it. Mind if I wash my hands?"

"Not at all, you know the way." Aromatherapy? Sniffing parsley for protection? Eating it for bad breath? Does he want me walking around with a mouthful of pascal like he with his carrots? Parsley, *Petroselinum sativum*, the wonder herb—mouth deodorant and protector of homes. Is he trying to convert me to some weird New Age philosophy?

"Hel . . . low Swami, I never noticed it before," Parker said, as he stopped to admire the antiquities in the hallway. "Cool theme."

"Thank you." I acted as if I knew what he meant. "What's so interesting?"

"The Disc of Phaistos. Bronze, seventeenth century BC. It tells the story of celestial beings visiting Earth. Experts differ on whether the visitors were from Sirius or the Pleiades, but they agree the symbols represent space aliens. Same with your Mayan relics. And your Greek."

I hadn't known, but was saved embarrassment as he ducked into the bathroom to wash up. Celestial beings? As in space aliens? As in the Council of Ancients?

The house still reeked of tonight's shiitake mushroom and asparagus sauté, courtesy of Twinkie, who had fallen off the culinary wagon and decided (against my strongest reservations while she hummed the Perry Mason theme) that I would just *love* this one. She seemed to be humming that song a lot lately. She followed the main course with a circular mass of a lemon Jell-O smiley face with white grapes for eyes and a lemon wedge for a mouth. She placed it on the table, nervous for acceptance, her smile as natural as the citrus slice. The gelatin quivered for approval, too, and I realized she and the Jell-O were emotionally linked by some inexplicable anxiety-based psychological connection. Twinkie continually sought reassurance.

My faltering constitution didn't help her self-esteem this night, sad little lamb, because I vomited before I could swallow my first spoon of the lemon-flavored, rubberized bone marrow. No testicular cancer excuse could alleviate her disappointment. It had been a bad night.

She was upstairs getting ready for a rare evening out when Parker entered the kitchen. Lately, Twinkie seemed different, more upbeat. If only she'd quit humming Perry Mason.

Rose greeted the handsome private eye with a warm hug and a kiss on the cheek.

Parker breathed in Rose's delicate scent. "Lovely perfume. Vanilla and . . ." he sniffed again, "asparagus, I'd guess."

She giggled and batted her eyes as she put on a kettle.

"Tea?" Parker asked, as he gnawed lightly on his carrot. "Try the green stuff I just gave R.T."

"I suppose after sixty-seven years I need to start taking care of myself," I said.

"It's about time," Rose said, only half-kidding.

"You should try massage therapy," Parker suggested. He set *The Journals* manuscript on the island counter. "Great for curing addictions."

Massage. Another wacky New Age fad. It's amazing to me that I like Parker so much. We're so far apart ideologically, it's scary. "Massage? How can that help?" I asked, while Rose busied herself with the cups.

"Psychologically, people need to replace the loss of one pleasurable experience with another. So, if I'm addicted to Folger's and my body finds that enjoyable, then I need to replace that sensation with one even more satisfying, if I give up coffee." He grinned. "And fella, there aren't many things better for you than an aromatherapy massage once or twice a week."

Rose offered a motherly smile. "Why don't you boys go into the solarium to conduct your business while I fix the tea?"

"Sounds good," Parker said.

"Is that the manuscript?" Rose asked.

"Yep." Parker rubbed the cover page. "Back safely to its creator."

"What did you think of it?" I asked as we walked.

His boyish innocence beamed warmly. "Hel . . . low Swami!" he exclaimed. "If I didn't know you better, I'd say you were trading your Republican pinstripes for some liberal denims. That's one helluva story. I couldn't put it down."

I ignored his jab at my political leanings. "Did it help you?"

He pulled on his pony tail as he made a peculiar face. "I made progress, R.T.," he said as he stopped near the sofa. He stood and stared at the Stone family portrait as he nursed his carrot. "But I'm not sure it's going to help you much."

"Why not?"

Parker observed the room, checking each item against his memory to deduce if anything were new or different. The spoons. The portrait. The clock. The furniture. Satisfied that all was as it's always been, he answered me. "I'm unclear on the assignment." He shifted his weight from one foot to the other. "None of it seems to be helping your criminal case. I've accomplished a lot based on your original instructions. I interviewed Winston Held III, the Diamond Trust officer. I've done lots of research, gathered tons of facts, and chased down clues from the book you're writing. I've been a busy boy."

"And?"

"Oh, and I found Dr. Muse. She's a sex therapist now." He raised his thin brows quickly. "Rather attractive, Dr. Muse. It took a couple weeks of dinners and drinks before she let her guard down. And even then, I had to show her *The Journals* before she opened up. She corroborated Danny's part of the tale—talking light and all. Said that boy had a glow about him. Last she heard from him was a few years ago. He showed up out of the blue all messed up, right around the time when Patrick—well—you know the story." *Chomp, chomp.* Double bite of the carrot for emphasis.

Parker glanced at the family portrait again, then the fireplace, as the liquid timepiece dripped the hour. Seven stones dropped and splashed in the surf of the marvelous clock. "I've always loved this thing, so unusual. I researched its engravings just before Twinkie and I split up. I never got a chance to tell you what I discovered."

"That's nice," I said, a bit impatiently, wanting to get back to the topic of serious *Journals* investigative progress. Dr. Muse had been found. The talking light was true. There must be more.

"Yeah, fella." Parker's eyes were awash in gold and blue as he stared at the glowing metal of the clock. He pointed at the magnificent work. "The various deities engraved on the face of the base are numerous gods and goddesses of water from cultures around the world. See?" His eyes glistened, his earring bouncing a tiny star of light. "There's Mon, the god of flowing water from the Kafirs of the Hindukush. Mon is the Afghan god who freed the sun and moon from captivity. Here, see?" Parker said, with cool authority. "He's represented by a stone slab and two smaller stones. Some call Mon the creator of man and law."

"Another Prometheus."

Parker smiled and held his carrot firmly in his hand, pointing it at the clock. "For a guy who professes no belief system, you sure have a lot of spiritual artifacts hanging about." He returned to his analysis of the water clock. "Zurvan, the artisan who made the clock, depicted the spiritual symbolism of many profound truths as told from the great myths. She was an artist, a master craftswoman. The waterwheel represents the cycle of life. Reincarnation. Rebirth. The high relief scenes are the myths personified in different ancient societies."

Parker was enthused, his boyish enthusiasm contagious. I listened, astounded at the man's knowledge. I was impressed again by the vast wisdom he possessed. His degree in theology and his travels to the Middle and Far East, his affinity for all things spiritual and occult, continues to surprise me.

"And look, R.T." He kept on, his carrot nearly touching the clock. "Noah's ark—a good Jewish myth. And there, Absu, the Babylonian god of primeval waters. And Banga, the Ngbandi god of clear water and white-skinned people. There's Corentina, the Celtic water goddess of wells, fountains and springs." His excitement was building. "Ea, the Babylonia god of sweet water who killed Absu as he slept, and Yemoja, the Nigerian goddess of water worshipped by women. And the center of the piece, the deity who most inspired Zurvan, Siarara, the goddess of the Persian Gulf. She takes up half the gold panel. See, fella? Funny how it all comes back to the Persian Gulf these days, isn't it?" Chomp went the carrot. *Crunch, crunch, crunch.*

"How so?"

He chewed his carrot, then swallowed, but not before he gave me a curious look, as though I had a secret. I didn't. "You got shot the night of Iraq's invasion of Kuwait. You spent time in the Middle East during the war. Your house is loaded with priceless antiquities from the region and," he paused for effect, his eyes shining like stars in the depths of the Universe, "you've been getting those packets from 'M.' Have you received any more correspondence?"

"Yes," I admitted, "one arrived yesterday. But I haven't looked at them much."

"Why not, R.T.?" He turned from the clock and plopped himself on the sofa. "There's a reason all this is happening. *The Journals* even say so. 'M' has something to do with all this, I'm sure of it."

I felt guilty about ignoring the crisis in the Persian Gulf. Maybe I should do more, but the Council wants me to find Danny and Allison. Correct that, the Council wants me to tell their story. Operation Desert Shield seems a distraction.

"Something isn't right about this whole thing," Parker said. "They're comparing Saddam to Hitler now. William Safire in *The New York Times* wasted a whole column spelling out the similarities. I have a theory." He twirled the carrot with his fingers like a baton. "Whenever our leaders buy off the conservative media to plant a story that such and such is as horrible as Adolf Hitler, it means the administration is desperate for an emotional smear campaign. A precursor to war. Who wouldn't agree to stop Hitler? Saddam's a terror, no doubt, but he's no worse than the Shah of Iran, whom we supported, or President Assad of Syria, or the Yememis, or the Kuwaiti emir, who we are allegedly defending. Yep." He bit his carrot with force, "Whenever Hitler's name is brought up and compared to some modern day adversary, you can bet there's an ulterior motive, *and* they have a really weak position to start with. They evoke Hitler to stir up emotion. As an example, the Christian Coalition does it when it says that abortion and euthanasia are similar to Nazi death camp atrocities."

"They're not," I said, with a force that surprised me.

"We humans are gullible that way." Parker laughed, apparently bemused by the daily toils of we humans.

He was right, of course. I'd seen and heard it over and over again when I was in the service. It had become a matter of public policy to strike fear into the citizenry through images of the Third Reich returning to power. All manner of groups used the technique. It worked every time.

Parker switched gears. "Hel . . . low Swami, did you hear Bush's speech to Congress a few nights ago? Blood for oil, no matter how he sugarcoats it. Two hundred thousand troops over there for defensive purposes. He thinks we're as dumb as Reagan did. Sounds like they're employing the Doctrine of Invincible Force."

Yes, I knew it well. The doctrine was developed from the failure of the U.S. war in Vietnam. It stated that the military should not engage in a war unless it had enough firepower to ensure decisive victory. That's perhaps the only positive that came out of the Vietnam disaster.

"Should have used it in Nam," Parker said, with a swing of his pony tail and a rabbit's gnaw on his carrot. "Not that I'm for war of any kind. But if you're going to fight, and our leaders are predisposed to such things, then you might as well use all available means to get it done quickly."

He didn't have to say it, and neither did I, but we both thought it—if the government had employed that doctrine in Vietnam, maybe Bobby wouldn't have lost his arm; maybe he wouldn't be so resentful. Bobby always hated Parker and his casual flippancy.

"Say, fella," Parker switched direction again. "How's Bobby? Is he speaking to you yet?"

"No." My head drooped. "He won't return my calls. And he stopped paying his lease on the C.C."

"Maybe he can't afford to."

"He can. He just doesn't want to. He blames me for the fire. I've written and called, but he won't respond. He even told Twinkie to 'kiss off,' and he loves her. He's always protected her."

"It's a shame." Parker shook his head as he stood and started toward the solarium. "In my business, relatives treating each other badly is the norm. People do some unholy things over money." He could tell I was depressed and dropped the topic. "I interviewed Winston Held III. It was a bust, other than the fact that he's hiding something."

"How do you know?"

"Intuition," he said. "Blinking eyes. Sweaty brow. Too many pauses in his sentences. That cat was wrapped way too tight for an inquiry of this nature. He was extremely anal. I told him we knew all about Patrick Gilday's contributions. I told him we knew Patrick was Allison's Father. He wouldn't divulge a thing."

"Isn't he bound by law to maintain discretion?" I asked as we sat in the white wicker chairs in the solarium. The sun sent its reddish-purple hues past Prometheus into the glass room, giving majesty to the great Titan, the bringer of man. The sun's silent rays of life brushed my resplendent orchids. They had begun to perk up, my babies, seeming to respond symbiotically to my recovering emotions. Lately, I'd been on the upswing, but still far from on top. Some of my girls exhibited brown leaves and others lost their blooms and went dormant too early, but most of them have stayed with me.

"Sure," Parker said as he admired Jessie, my purple *Vandanthe rothschildiana*. Gorgeous creature, she. "But there's the law, then there's how things really are, and then there's Winston Held being extremely uncooperative. I asked him why it mattered, since Patrick Gilday was dead. He was hostile—didn't want to talk about Danny or Allison. Curious fella, in a wormy sort of way."

"Did anything come out of it?"

Parker shrugged. "Not really, other than I know he's covering something up. I'll work on him through his secretary." The rakish private eye grinned impishly. Then he suddenly turned serious. "The news gets worse from there. To find Allison, I started where the story did, at Skye Pippin's houseboat. Gilday owned the boat. Trouble is, R.T., you owned part of it, too. McBain is sure to have that information as well."

"Damn." It had been so long ago, and I was only a minority owner—one eighth to be exact—that I didn't think anybody would find out.

"I don't care what you've done in the past—it *has* been almost twenty years—but you need to point me in the right direction," Parker said as he studied his carrot. "I know you want me snooping out facts about Danny and Allison, but shouldn't I be helping in the actual defense investigation?"

"The Council told me to tell the story, and they'd arrange to clear me," I half-whispered.

"Fella." He scooted to the edge of the chair to within a few inches of me. "Lots of people believe in God, lots of people believe in the ancients, lots of people have a hybrid belief system based on some obscure cult icon or the other. All of that is okay, but it shouldn't stop you from hedging your bets."

"What are you suggesting?" I said. My colon began to grumble.

"Turn me loose on the things that are going to help your case. Take your cancer, for example. You're not just wishing it away, are you? No, you're getting professional medical treatment. You're not just wishing yourself better based on faith. That'd be foolish."

"No," Rose said sedately, as she delivered the steaming beverages. "He's not wishing it away on faith, he's ignoring it."

"What?" Parker sat forward, his carrot almost popping from his mouth.

Rose set the tea on the table between us. "Oh yes, that's right, Pink. R.T. has canceled two appointments with the oncologist. He thinks he can ignore it, and the problem will disappear."

She avoided me. I hate it when she treats me that way, as if I'm not in the room, as if I'm six years old.

"He's like a little boy who refuses to take his cough medicine. Except he's got something much worse than a cold."

"I thought your aura looked a little tarnished, R.T." Parker looked at me with steely blue eyes. "I'm not one to meddle, but you can't expect everyone else to work hard at saving you if you won't even save yourself, for chrissakes! You get your butt to the doctor, or I'm off the case."

I was shocked at his insistence. Rose smirked at me and sashayed out of the room with an air of triumphant satisfaction. If she couldn't influence me by herself, she'd force me to comply through the pressure of others. It worked.

"Okay," I said glumly, "I'll go see the oncologist."

Parker picked up the previous conversation and shifted the carrot to the other side of his mouth. "We need evidence that separates you from Gilday. McBain is bound to link the two of you. And judging by everything I've seen so far, he's got a strong chain."

"I wish I'd never met Patrick Gilday."

"Too late for that. Did you know that Skye Pippin drowned?"

My mind sparked vivid images like flashbulbs of distinct memory. I could see the two of them on the deck near the railing, Patrick and Skye. It was late at night, only a few dim stars glowed through the city lights. The river was quiet, the streets empty. Allison lay peacefully asleep in her bed, dreaming.

A red scowl burned on Gilday's face. He'd wanted pork chops for dinner; she'd fixed a large salad and baked potatoes. Angry words were exchanged. Skye showed no fear. She shook her head no, her black mane whipping like a wild mare in a thunderstorm. More angry words. Vengeful words that should never be spoken between lovers. Gilday grabbed her arm and squeezed with all his might as she twisted to get away, her face defiant of his masculine strength. He raised his other arm in a fury and smashed it down across her cheek. Her fragile body fell back from the blow and crashed into the railing. The violent momentum toppled her over the stainless steel rail. She clawed at it trying to save herself, but she missed. Skye plunged into the water, thick as raw crude.

Patrick grabbed for her, horrified. She clutched for the edge of the boat, but the strong current pulled on her. She went under. Desperate, she lunged up out of the water, gasping for air, as she struggled to grab hold of something solid. Gilday's hand brushed her fingertips. He reached for her hand but found himself staring at his empty fist. The thirsty river swallowed deeply, taking Skye down into its massive, fluid belly.

In that instant, Patrick realized what his temper had done. As he sat numbly on the deck, he knew he would be tortured by her death for the rest of his life. Skye Pippin was gone. He had killed her over a baked potato. Allison would wake up an orphan.

"Her aunt died in '81," Parker said.

"Huh?" My trance was broken. I felt sick. My rump was enflamed, my bowels pure acid. "Excuse me." I raced to the toilet, barely making it before soiling myself. Damn medication gives me the runs, completely takes over and leaves me no choice but to caress the commode.

I cleaned up and rejoined Parker. "Sorry about that," I blushed.

"Are you all right?" he asked. "See, you *do* need to get treatment."

I nodded. "He killed her."

"Who?"

"Patrick Gilday killed Skye Pippin."

"Hel . . . low Swami. Interesting theory, fella. How do you know that?"

"Do you believe in psychic phenomena?" I asked.

He grinned. "Telepathy? Absolutely. One can't be a New Age private eye and not believe. Why?"

I couldn't speak the words right away. "Ever since this ordeal began, strange things have been happening. I've been having visions. My mind sees things it never could before. There's a clarity to it, like . . . like—"

"Like a dream, only you're awake," Parker said. "You're being channeled to. I've witnessed it many times. Many people have that ability if they choose to develop it. Most don't. They're too busy going to the mall or watching game shows to tap their own power. Me, too, I'm afraid."

"You? Why?"

"I've slipped. When I went on my sojourn to the Orient, I learned many ancient ways. Zen, Ayurveda, Yoga. All that stuff. I meditated twice a day, became a vegetarian, gave up all my vices. It was the best time of my life. I had a purpose," he said, a radiant blue flame in his eyes. "There was a real sense of *me*. But . . ." He sucked on the carrot as if to draw juice from its stalk. "I came back to the States and immediately fell back into the same traps. Rush, rush, rush. Consume, consume, consume. Spend, spend, spend. I fell into the same wrong-headed belief system as most Americans: 'If I'm busy I must be making progress.'"

"So you don't have psychic ability anymore?" I looked beyond the lush orchids of my solarium over the yard to the woods. I told myself to take a walk there.

"I was never much into telepathy, although I did have my share of visions. My thing was always intuition, developing the third eye. I still do that. It's like this case. My intuition says you're telling me the truth. The perceived reality, the evidence, doesn't support it, but I'm listening to my gut on this one. And the more I do, the easier it will get. Whenever I override my intuition, life becomes a struggle. Things don't make as much sense. Life loses its meaning, and I become dissatisfied." He shifted his legs as he tried to follow my line of sight into the tree line. "Anything out there of importance?"

"I saw Patrick Gilday kill Allison's mother."

"I'm sure you did," Parker said, honestly. "But that doesn't help us in the slightest."

"The bastard should pay for what he did."

Parker's thin eyebrows raised. "Even though I've fallen from spiritual grace, even if my heavenly beacon has dimmed, I still believe in karma. If nothing else, there is one thing I am sure of: Patrick Gilday is paying for his sins."

Chomp. Chomp. Chomp.

317

Chapter 29

September 22, 1990

Some days start and stop without much to offer. Others drag you into a moat of depressing problems so deep the king's cavalry can't drag your carriage out. The great beasts pull and strain and heave as the wheels sink deeper into the mud. Days like that are such a struggle that the more you fight, the worse it gets. It's those kind of days that make you realize the mud you're slogging in is actually quicksand that will suck you under and squeeze the life out of you with its gritty hands. I've had a Sahara full of those days, as of late.

Today was not one of those days. Today was the third kind of day. It was a day of redemption, a day of inspiration. A red sunrise spilled across my life like a crimson robe of royalty heralding the autumn earth. This day delivered hope like a crown of jeweled promise. Before first light, I stumbled to the family room, a cup of hot tea in hand, and flipped on Channel 99. The next installment of Allison's life awaited.

Allison languished in her room for several days after her untimely missed connection with Danny at the zoo. She didn't work her garden. She refused to go to Mass. The Church surprisingly obliged her, though it was not shown whether it did so out of sympathetic consideration or on instruction from Patrick Gilday. Certainly, they must have been alerted to Allison's budding relationship with her half-brother. A distraught Patrick must have been insistent that her attempts be thwarted.

Allison wrote Danny a tear-soaked letter, which Patrick intercepted. She suspected the nuns were treating her differently and wondered why. After a few days, delightful sprite that she is, she came to terms with losing Danny, vowing never to lose hope, convinced that he must love her. He showed up, didn't he? She reaffirmed her love for him and celebrated the romantic tryst that the fates had denied. She told herself, in typical exaggerated fantasy, that they would someday be together.

One cloudless spring night, a night she envisioned to be made just for her, she slipped quietly to the bell tower and delivered a robust version of Danny's poem, City Pigeon Soldier, aloud to a deaf God. It was a plea of sorts, a challenge for Him to hear her prayers. Perhaps the Council was listening. Satisfied that she had mourned long enough, Allison placed her faith squarely back into divine hands and returned to life as usual.

She found many diversions to keep her mind off Danny. She toiled in the garden for hours, caring meticulously for the vegetables as if each were a newborn child. She debated with a shocked, then indignant Clod and Barney about a Supreme Court ruling that allowed new life forms created in the lab to be patented. Clod insisted that scientists would be creating Frankensteins. Barney said it was a continuation of Hitler's work. The debate ended in a traditional Catholic stalemate, with the clergy saying don't ask questions and the opponent (Allison) left with even more doubts.

By mid-July, she was eating fresh-picked, vine-ripened, organic tomatoes while she celebrated Marjorie Matthews' ordination as the first woman bishop in the U.S. She expressed some annoyance that it was the Methodists who bestowed the honor, not the Holy Romans. Sister Dena confided during the news report that she held aspirations of someday being the first female Catholic priest. Allison gladly wished her luck.

Allison Leslie was a voracious reader. Book after book. One every couple of days. In addition, she read every page of the daily paper, obituaries and want ads excluded. Knowledge, albeit screened Catholic knowledge, took root in her fertile mind. Sister Dena would occasionally slip her a book not approved by the Church, believing that Allison needed a wider view of the world than St. Als could provide.

The hostage crisis was still front page fodder, having become a tragic metaphor for Jimmy Carter's administration. Doomsday for a second term. The longer the Iranians held United States citizens, the more she related to their plight, until one day she understood, as she looked out from her perch in the tower, that she was as much a prisoner as they. Only she was held captive in America. Driven by news of brutal executions of Iranian citizens for minor offenses, she took up the cause of the American hostages by writing a letter to the pope, imploring him to talk some sense into the Ayatollah. "Jesus changing his mind on the cross," she wrote, "what's it going to take?" Mother Superior destroyed the letter. She would not have orphans bothering His Eminence with childish correspondence. Censorship was alive and well and thriving in America.

In early August of 1980, Allison had made up her spirited mind to give herself to charitable deeds. She proclaimed to everyone she spoke to over the course of two weeks that she would become the Mother Theresa of Cincinnati. The best she could do at the moment was distribute the bounty of her garden to kids inside St. Als, but she viewed that effort as a stepping stone to greater glory.

Without notice, Allison's life took an invisible turn, precipitated by a BLT sandwich, Sister Dena, and the U.S. Open women's tennis championship. With a delicious sandwich on her lap, she and the good sister settled in to watch the Open. Allison casually mentioned that it would be "absotively cool" to play tennis, and Sister D seized the opportunity and made it happen.

Then, as I watched her life, three of her journal entries scrolled upon the screen. I copied them verbatim.

October 25, 1980

I've been learning how to play tennis. I got a book from the library and learned the rules and how to hold the racquet and all that. It's absotively splendid. I play with Sister Dena, which is fun (and funny). She wears tennis shoes. It's hilarious to see her chasing after one of my balls. She's great. She really takes care of me. She said if I do my tutoring lessons well, she'll buy me my own racquet. I've been studying super hard lately. I want my own racquet. Sister D says I'm pretty good. Actually, she said I had a blessed back hand shot. Does God like tennis?

Halloween is coming soon. I'm going to be a homeless beggar. Mother Peculiar asked Clod who asked Sister D to ask me to be something more appropriate, but I'm not budging. A beggar is perfectly appropriate, I told the Inquisition. We'll see who wins this one.

The pope came out with a weird rule today. He decreed that divorced Catholics can remarry and avoid excommunication as long as they don't have sex. Jesus in a brothel without a condom, what kind of a rule is that? How can the pope expect married people to not have sex? And why would he want them not to? I don't get it.

He's a great man, John Paul II, but he's goofed on this. The purpose of marriage is love, and love is consummated through sex. Maybe it's because the pope doesn't have sex that he made this mistake.

November 15, 1980

The pope is in Cologne, Germany today. It's the first time a pope has been on German soil in 198 years. That's an absotively long time. Probably because the Germans were into conquering Europe for awhile there. He must not have called the Ayatollah yet. A few days ago the Iranians demanded $24 billion to let the hostages go. $24 billion! Jesus with a Swiss bank account, that's a lot of cash. I wonder if the Iranians really believe they'll get it.

December 8, 1980

John Lennon was murdered. Instant Karma.

On Christmas Eve, Allison stood on the famous steps of the Sacred Mother of Hearts. Each year, thousands of the faithful brave the cold and fight the desire to stay home and sip hot chocolate in order to make the symbolic pilgrimage to the cathedral, which rises above the city. Behind her, Allison was dazzled by the skyscrapers huddled together like good Christian soldiers on the battlefield of salvation. She gleamed proud exhilaration as she held a shivering candle while saying her Hail Marys and ascending the stairs one step at a time.

Her best friend, Mary, stuffed into an oversized, down coat and a black, woolly cap pulled over her eyes, invented humorous Hail Marys to relieve the boredom. This resulted in an occasional elbow from Allison and an elongated "Mareee" along with an exaggerated rolling of her eyes.

"Hail Mary, full of spaghetti," Mary whispered, as the candle struggled mightily against the night chill. "Hail Mary, full of toothpaste." Up the steps they went. "Hail Mary, what a big waste."

Mary was opposed to "the whole sham" (as she called it) of force-marching a brigade of orphans up a hundred or so steps to a church Mass on Christmas Eve, when they should be home dreaming of gifts and a better life with some unknown future family. But Allison was enthralled by the reverent sensation of honoring Jesus on the eve of His birth. Each step brought her closer to Him, still closer. Her heart seemed to carry her weightlessly up the great hill. Her anticipation built with each movement forward. Upward they went—Allison and Mary, somehow separated in the mass of Catholics from Sister D, Mother Peculiar, the lesser sisters, and all the orphans over the age of ten who had signed up for the nocturnal religious field trip.

Mary hadn't signed up voluntarily. It was Allison who put her name on the list, then coaxed her relentlessly for eight days. Mary gave in to the strong-willed Allison, who had described the event as an Earthly ascent unto God's house, and failing that strategy, a good way to meet altar boys.

After an hour, the two finally made it inside the warm church, aglow with a spectacular display of thousands of candles. The tallow's light cascaded off the stained glass windows in quivering shadows that made Allison think of the throngs of past worshippers who had visited the hallowed sanctuary. Statues of Christ and the Virgin Mary stood near the altar. The Sacred Mother of Hearts was an average church—certainly St. Peter in Chains downtown was more elaborate, more ornate, and others around the city were larger, more splendorous—but to Allison this night, this glorious night, it was the throne of God Himself.

She approached the altar feeling light-headed, which she assigned to giddiness at being at such a blessed ceremony. She bowed before the priest to accept communion. She closed her eyes and whispered what was meant to be a quick prayer. Somehow she found herself praying for the hostages in Iran. She prayed for the spirit of John Lennon. Then, a prayer of protection for Danny with the Host in her mouth, which she always thought tasted a bit like a Triscuit. With Christ's mock blood on her lips, she suddenly found she could not move.

A startling image of Danny shivering in snow froze her spine. A bleeding John Lennon lying crumpled on the sidewalk outside the Dakota appeared. Her body trembled, as if an angelic musician played her vertebrae like a xylophone. Two priests approached to hasten her on. Then the light came. Soft and mild like a spirit in a lemon chiffon dress. It surrounded the Seed. Took her inside it. Made her warm.

Astonished gasps escaped the gaping mouths of the worshippers. They had come to honor Jesus, as they had followed their traditions before, but they had not expected a miracle. Not a true apparition. That stuff happens in France. Or Bulgaria. Some foreign land. Not Cincinnati. Not tonight. Not yellow light encasing a red-haired child from— what was that orphanage again? Hail Marys poured from the awestruck crowd as the light radiated outward from Allison.

The priests stood motionless, like caricatures in a tacky Christmas lawn display. Allison began to cry. Tears seeped from her for the sorrow that is this world. Sobs of pain for the less fortunate. Tears for Lennon. A river of sadness for the homeless. Her emotions swept through the muffled crowd like news that a favorite uncle had died. Everyone began to cry. Quiet sobs and sniffles permeated the pageantry of Christmas crusaders. Even the stoic, above-it-all priests fell to their knees and wailed. All heads were bowed, as if her emotions had become the crowd's, as if her sensations were universally tied to their consciousness. A great burden was relieved in a sea of emotion.

Suddenly the sadness turned to joy. Elation that Jesus Christ was born this day. Bliss that a new age would soon be dawning. Ecstasy that loving souls *did* live on Earth. Happiness that each of us in some small way has a connection to the other, that we are not in this mess on our own, forgotten and helpless and scared. This was a deeper moment than the traditional "peace be with you" ritual, which often peeled off-key like a cracked bell.

She stood and the flock stood with her. Then she began to laugh in joy at the beauty of God's glory, and the parishioners laughed with her. The gentle light emanated out from her in an ever-widening circle like ripples on the surface of a pond, washing over everyone in the church. The feeling enveloped all who stood inside the cathedral doors and those fortunate enough—no, blessed enough—to have witnessed the visitation.

The meaning of Christmas was changed for them. For now they could not simply pretend to believe, they *had* to believe. They had seen God's work. The next day, Christmas Day, and every day thereafter they would be kinder to their children and their parents. They would listen intently to Uncle Ralph's Korean War story and help him through his troubled past. And the excess of toys would be returned to the store, the refund going to charities. The gaudy Christmas lights which blazed brightly in the yard, draining the Earth's resources like a shoddy Vegas casino with a ten billion megawatt electric bill, would be turned off. They would volunteer their time helping the less fortunate. Rumors and gossip would cease. Fewer cigarette butts would be tossed out car windows. Blame for the world's problems would manifest into personal responsibility. Letters to politicians encouraging them to make things right would be written. Active participation in helping others would be their calling. The true meaning of life had come to these people. Caring was reinstilled in their souls, and this feeling would be a part of them from that incredible night forward. Their *anima* had been washed clean, truth had come to Christmas and they would tell the story, each from their own perspective, for the rest of their lives over and over to all of their relatives and friends, whose doubting eyebrows and half-hidden snickers would signal the blessed witnesses that few truly spiritual believers actually occupy this rock in space.

Unfortunately, Allison's miraculous light had faded well before Mother Superior and company could squeeze into the standing-room-only showcase for God's holiness. Sister Dena, who was in no need of spiritual cleansing, was the only person besides Mary from St. Alexandria touched by the celestial force. By the time Mother Superior pushed her way through the hushed crowd, the moment was gone. All that remained was the quiet knowing and the gentle murmurs of three hundred and eleven people who would do their best to bring peace and harmony to those around them for the rest of their lives.

Allison, weakened from the surge of energy, only wanted to go home and snuggle up with Sister Dena alone in front of the fire and read her favorite Yuletide story—*Silent Seraph.*

Despite a most phenomenal exhibit of celestial grace, the Church made no attempts to determine what had caused the holy vision to pervade the Sacred Mother. It baffles this reporter how such a delectable cosmic treat could be left on the dessert table at the church bazaar. The leaders of the Church, upon hearing of the Christmas Eve event, chose to employ a policy of denial similar to that used by the United States government in dealing with UFO sightings. An immediate campaign was begun to convince people they had not seen what they thought they saw. The Church asked no questions, choosing instead to focus on blotting out the holy visitation.

Only Sister Dena was curious enough to gauge Allison's experience, to understand what had happened. To the rest of the clergy, it was as if they had been waiting all their lives for a sign of this magnitude and somehow missed it. They blinked. Either that, or they simply had forgotten how to see, or were told not to see.

Allison just kept on being a kid. She celebrated receiving a tennis racquet for Christmas, a special gift from Sister Dena. And soon she was playing and practicing at least once a week at an indoor court owned by the Church. She loved playing tennis with Sister D and laughed heartily at the good sister's enthusiasm. "Give me your best shot, Seed. Fire it in here, baby," the gym-shoed nun would shout.

Simultaneous with Allison's foray into the world of athletics was Sister Dena's sudden addiction to sunflower seeds. It was inexplicable to some, to see Sister Dena busy as a chipmunk during the fall harvest, splitting, cracking, sucking, and chewing seeds one after another. Bag after bag. She went nowhere without them, and she didn't confine her habit to the discipline of the court, no ma'am. Sister Dena munched throughout the day, in meetings, in church, in the car, everywhere. She even devised a system for disposing of the spent carcasses. She carried two baggies (Ziplocks), one filled with fresh seeds, the other for the saliva drenched remains. But no matter how careful her seed-eating etiquette, no matter her high standards of hygiene, a trail of spent shells followed Dena wherever she went.

Allison heralded the release of the hostages during Reagan's inauguration as a great sign of new hope and prosperity for America. Her zeal was soon dashed when she read on March 6 that Reagan requested Congress discontinue legal aid to the poor.

"Jesus kicking a blind man in the ribs!" she exclaimed to Sister Dena during a tutoring session. "That's absotively cruel of the president."

At the end of March, the day before her thirteenth birthday, she sat numb with the rest of St. Als watching the news of the assassination attempt on Ronald Reagan. "Jesus with a handgun from K-Mart, what's this country coming to?"

The Council's special television played on, showing me a remarkable period in Allison's life, beginning May 11, 1981. My untouched tea was cold as I reached for a note pad. I've since transcribed her extraordinary diary events into my trusty word processor for your review. I do not dispute the accuracy and validity of her diary. After all I've been through, I would be a foolish man indeed to doubt her words. Allison, like a sweet strawberry fresh from the bush, had begun to blossom into an extraordinary young woman. Her skin was like powdered sugar dotted with a modest assembly of freckles. Around her had gathered a coterie of admiring friends eager for a taste of her enthusiasm, a nibble of her imagination, or a morsel of her delightful freshness.

It was the extremely early morning of May 11 that the consequences of her divine nature were finally understood by a reluctant clergy more bent on keeping secrets than revealing glory.

"Sister Dena, wake up!" Allison whimpered, as she knelt beside the bed, a moist sunflower seed stuck to her big toe.

The green face of the digital clock radio split the darkness of Dena's bedroom. It was 4:30 a.m. Its plutonium glow fell upon the entire room like nuclear fallout. A See, Hear, Speak No Evil statuette of three monkeys, each covering a sensory organ, sat prophetically on the night stand next to the fission-reactor chronometer. A half-eaten bag of salted sunflowers sat next to the monkeys. "Sister Dena, I'm scared."

"What . . . what is it angel?" The nearly catatonic sister stirred.

"I had another bad dream—only worse."

"Oh, angel, you're so delicate."

In no mood to be patronized due to the severity of her nightmare, Allison said in the most serious tone she could summon, "Somebody is going to shoot the pope."

The statement forced Dena into alertness. "What?" She scooted herself upright with a firm tussle of the bedware to her chest. She smoothed a spot on the bed for Allison to sit. "Tell me what you saw, Seed."

Her lips trembled as she glanced at the monkeys. "It's just like Zaire." She choked back her tears. "Remember when I dreamed of the stampede, then it happened?"

Sister Dena placed Allison's troubled head on her shoulder and stroked her crimson hair. "Shh . . . there, there, now, angel. It's only a bad dream."

"It's not. This time . . . this time . . ." She gasped for air. "This time it's the pope himself! We have to do something." She looked away to the crucifix on the wall. Jesus stared down at the blind, deaf and mute primates, his plastic legs exposed to doses of timely atomic matter. The imagery disturbed Allison. She switched on the lamp, whose light dispelled the radioisotopes and lit the room with sixty watt proficiency. Ms. Curie lost out to Tom Edison.

"Tell me what you saw," Sister Dena said softly, to soothe Allison's anxiety.

"The pope was in St. Peter's Square, waving to the crowd from a car. A Turkish man came up to him, he had a gun, and . . ." She couldn't say it. More tears.

A sympathetic Dena did her best to comfort her. "It's only a dream; even the saints had a bad dream every once in awhile."

"It wasn't a dream, Sister. It was a vision. I know the difference."

"How?"

"I just know the difference. I can't explain it. There's something else."

"What?" Sister Dena asked.

"There's blood."

"In your dream? Where?"

"Down there, you know," Allison motioned shyly toward her lap.

As if vaginal bleeding explained everything, Sister Dena produced a smile as big as a super-maxi pad, then pulled Allison to her chest. "Oh, my child," she said happily. "You're becoming a woman."

"What's that got to do with the pope?"

Dena thought for a moment. "Maybe your nightmare was triggered by your passing into womanhood," she said. "That explains it."

"It's not womanhood." Allison freed herself from the nun's embrace. "It's a sign of the pope's blood from a gunshot wound. It's a sign that he'll be shot!"

"Oh no, no, no, angel. It's no sign at all. I think your nightmare was induced by your first period."

"Really?" She was doubtful, thinking it absotively unlikely. She had studied menstruation and knew it was coming. She had examined herself in the shower and could see her nubile breasts forming. But none of that had anything to do with a vision about the pope.

"Yes, little Seed," Dena said. "You are becoming a woman. That is the reason for your nightmare."

"How?"

"You love His Holiness, don't you?"

"Yes."

"In dreams, our subconscious looks to process the important events and emotions in our lives. You began to bleed, so your subconscious created an illusion of the pope being shot. It's because you are so devoted to the Church. You are such a blessed child." She hugged Allison again.

She didn't buy Sister D's logic. She glanced at the monkeys as Dena squeezed her, and wondered if the whole Church practiced their philosophy of seeing, hearing and speaking no evil. "I don't believe my menstrual cycle regulates my visions."

"Well, just in case it wasn't caused by your period, I will alert Mother Pecul—ahem—Mother Superior of your nightmare."

"Can't you get the Vatican on the phone and warn him?"

"We'll see, angel," she said softly. "One doesn't usually do such things." She rubbed Allison's back to ease the tension. "Perhaps you should stay home from school today, to become accustomed to your cycle and your feelings."

"Thank you, Sister D." Allison grinned and kissed her cheek.

The next morning, with much more scrutiny than Allison thought necessary for a girl bleeding into womanhood, Sister Dena and a host of nuns fluttered about her, asking questions, taking her temperature, making notations in a book. Ever the super secret spy, she overheard Clod outside her door mentioning the Christmas Eve incident at the Sacred Mother. Clod questioned whether Allison might have actually seen a vision. Mother P, swearing in whispers, said it was sheer nonsense. "What in Christ's name would a puberty-stricken girl have to do with God?"

Two days later, the Christian world was rocked to its holy foundations. If ecclesiastical events were earthquakes, this one would send Richter back to design a new scale. Pope John Paul II took a bullet for the Lord, just as a pubescent, red-headed orphan in Cincinnati had predicted. Allison, regretting that she had mentioned her vision to anyone, was pulled out of English class and taken to Mother Peculiar's office.

"Allison," she said grimly, behind gray eyebrows the size of squirrels. Her severe face was involuntarily menacing, a drained ash-white color like His Eminence's sleeve. "Please take a seat while I make an announcement to the entire orphanage."

A trembling Sister Dena took Allison's hand while they sat on the leather couch. Dena was too nervous to reach for the packet of seeds in her pocket, although they could have possibly helped her anxiety. She squeezed Allison's fingers.

"What is it?" Allison whispered to Sister D. "Somebody die or something?"

Indeed, the mood in the room was only slightly more jovial than a full moon graveyard at midnight. Dena looked off across the room to a picture of His Holiness dressed in pacifist white vestments, serenely smiling like a grandfather.

Allison noticed everyone had puffy eyes, even the stoic house Mother. Claudia sniffled into a tissue.

"Attention all personnel and residents of St. Alexandria," Mother Peculiar commanded gruffly. She cleared her throat. "I have a serious announcement to make." She paused to compose herself yet again, then continued slowly. "This afternoon, as His Holiness gave an audience in St. Peter's, a wicked assassin shot Pope John Paul II. No further information is available. Class will be dismissed immediately. We will begin a prayer vigil in one hour. Everyone is expected to participate. That is all." Her voice cracked.

"The pope was shot?" Allison shouted.

Sniffles and blows and sobs and chokes and gasps and sighs and trembles and hugs and God blesses and unsaid goddamns (by whom we won't divulge) and droplets and tears and streams and tissues and handkerchiefs and woes and dismay and weighted hearts and ends-of-the-world and Satan-is-loose thoughts and prayers and signs-of-the-

cross and kneelings before his portrait and bowed heads and heartsick concern for holiness and compassion and bravery, ensued.

"Yes angel, he was," Sister Dena said.

"Dear God, may he be all right," Allison prayed under her breath. "Dear God, may he be all right." She had known it would come to this. She had feared it, prayed against it. Why hadn't they listened?

"It's all right, dear. It's not your fault," Mother Peculiar offered, as her huge frame lumbered from behind her desk.

"Of course it's not," she cried defiantly. "Why would it be my fault?"

No one answered, struck silent by their own guilt, knowing that they had the chance to warn His Holiness but chose not to listen. "Yvonne . . ." Mother Superior said, standing above her like a huge marble tombstone.

"Allison, Mother—or Seed, if you like," Allison managed through her tears.

"Fine," Mother Superior exhaled, annoyed at being corrected yet again by the precocious child. "*Allison*, we have to do some tests."

Her office door swung open with a loud bang. A group of stone-faced men quickly entered. Sister Dena reached for her seeds.

"Who's in charge here?" a self-important man barked, as an ash committed suicide from the cigarette which hung like a corpse from his lips. His yellowish skin was brittle against chipped cheekbones as if he'd been papered in Dead Sea Scrolls. Allison's chilled backbone genuflected involuntarily as she studied the man. His muddy, deeply set eyes, ringed by charred darkness, looked soldered into their sockets. Allison thought him a living cadaver, a ghostly figure who smelled of stale tobacco. The Marlboro man (who died of cancer, for those who are interested) come back to life as a zombie.

"I am," Mother Superior answered, holding out a hand. "Judith Jones."

He ignored her attempt at introductions. "We'll need an Operations Center." The other three men said nothing and showed no emotion or interest. "We have a lot of work to do."

Mother Superior withdrew her hand as if barely pulling it clear of a snapping mouse trap. "You can use the second floor of the east wing. It's secluded. We haven't used it for years."

Allison swallowed a fear-laced concoction of stagnant office air laced with nicotine as she squeezed Dena's hand. What do they want with me? she asked herself. They're here for me. I know it.

"Excellent," the ghoulish figure cackled. "We will need time to prepare. Bring the girl at fifteen hundred hours." He offered an ill-fitting smile, his dentures purchased from a dusty scratch-and-dent bin at a discount store. As quickly as the men came, they disappeared toward the east wing.

Allison assumed correctly that she was "the girl" the corpse referred to. She was scared but determined to hide it. She hadn't done anything except receive a vision in her sleep, a celestial warning that the pope would be harmed. It wasn't her fault. She couldn't help it. She wasn't the one who ignored the signs.

"What's going on?" Allison asked fearfully.

Sister Dena rubbed Allison's knee. "We have to do some tests, angel, to see if you have special powers that we may have overlooked."

"Special powers? Me?"

"Yes, Allison." Sister D said, compassionately. The pressure was too much. She popped a sunflower seed in her mouth. "You have a gift that we seem to have ignored. Now it's time we find out how special that gift is."

"What—what are they going to do?"

Mother Superior pushed back a large shock of white hair, the skunk stripe the kids called it, as she sat on the other side of Allison. Sister Claudia's panicked eyes glared at the pope's picture as if she were trying to heal him herself. Sister Bernadette watched Claudia as she kneaded her rosary beads like a loaf of troublesome dough.

Mother spoke. "They're just going to ask questions, Allison," she said in a rare note of sympathy.

"Ask some questions is all," Claudia repeated, much to the annoyance of the Mother.

"They won't hurt you. Sister Dena will be with you at all times," Mother Superior said, unaccustomed to displaying emotion. She placed a chapped paw the size of a collection basket on Allison's leg in reassurance. This unusual act of kindness alarmed Allison even further.

"Did you tell anyone about your nightmare?" Sister Dena asked, working the unbitten shell around in her mouth, toying with it, savoring the salt, releasing her tension.

"Sure. I told Mary and Rita and lots of kids."

Collective eyebrows, like an emotional offering to God, raised in unison from all the sisters present. Wrong answer. They didn't want this secret out. But Allison harbored no personal guilt about His Holiness. She had warned a disinterested staff and was casually dismissed, with the exception that they took her temperature and gave her a tampon or two.

"Is the pope going to be okay?"

"We don't know yet, angel," Sister Dena replied. A millisecond later she split the shell between two sets of central incisors.

"We can't afford to lose this one," Allison said, as she bowed her head. "They've been dropping like flies lately."

Claudia gasped. Bernadette too. "Child!" Mother exclaimed. "Why would you say such a thing?"

"Well, we had three popes in two months a couple years ago. I'd hate to see us have to get a new one. He is such a great man."

The appointed hour came, and Allison, accompanied by Sister Dena, was ushered into the so-called Operations Center on the second floor of the east wing. So-called because it consisted of nothing more than a banquet table, which was actually a bingo card sales table evidently borrowed from the Our Lady of Perpetual Greed bingo hall, covered in blue and white skirting. The east wing once had a purpose, years ago when the Catholics owned the town, or a good portion of its souls anyway. It was home to a deacon who saw to it that the street urchins abandoned by indigent parents had three squares a day and a warm bed to sleep in. Unfortunately, some of the boys found themselves in the deacon's bed, a nasty fact covered up for years by the Church, but well known in the community where the full grown, finally-able-to-defend-themselves males eventually made their livelihood. The parish never did figure out why community donations were far below those of other neighborhoods.

In recent years, the Operations Center had a different purpose: an occasional seance hosted by Rita Starks, usually coinciding with changing seasons and equinoxes, a place where The 88s divided up their stolen loot, and an active lover's lane of sorts for St. Als' romances. The nuns, of course, believing they knew all the comings and goings of every girl and boy in the joint, believing they knew every wicked little detail of the heathens' desires, were clueless. Barely a night went by that a couple didn't sneak to the east wing for some tongue wrestling, and hopefully more. Lately, the boys had taken up smoking pot at the far end of the hall near the fire escape, just in case a blind nun should happen to stumble upon the acorn of adolescent shenanigans.

Sitting on the table in front of her and Dena was a large manila folder the size of a phone directory. The folder was held closed by a thick rubber band.

She stared at the file as she inhaled the mildewed atmosphere cut with nicotine vapor. Is that my file? What's in it? she wondered. It's so thick, what could they possibly have on me to record that much stuff? Allison slipped into her Red Angel role and promised herself to recover its top secret information at a later date.

The living cadaver sat with his arms on the table, a black plastic ashtray next to him. Three somber-faced men sat behind their leader on rickety, wooden chairs the orphanage had retired years before, giving one the impression that the corpse was the star of the show and the rest were bit players. The one on the left blinked his eyes rapidly like a politician at a news conference trying to explain how five million dollars in Christian Coalition money ended up in his personal bank account. The middle man worked his pinkie in his right ear, as if the truth had worked its way in there and he couldn't get it out. The third chewed on his thin lower lip like a bit of stale communion wafer had lodged in his gums. Cobwebs, like cotton candy served in a sand storm, hung in dusty, brown gobs behind the ghoulish quartet.

The scene was not lost on Allison. See, Hear, and Speak No Evil sat placidly grooming themselves behind Christ's latest business agent. Sister Dena's monkey statuette had come to life. The cadaver nodded to See No Evil, who seemed to age by the minute, who in turn switched on a tape recorder.

"State your name," the mystery man ordered, his voice as craggy as the lines on his face. He lit a cigarette and held it with his brownish lips, keeping his hands free to move papers about the table. The smoke lazily drifted up past his right eye, like an errant phantom come to haunt his scary face.

"Allison Leslie Pippin," she said, doing her best to appear cheery and unintimidated. If ever there was time to shine (she remembered the words Skye had spoken in a dream the night she died), this was such a time. She squeezed her legs tightly together, just enough to keep her knees from knocking, but not enough that anyone would notice. "Most people call me Allison. A lot call me Seed, though."

"Your name isn't Yvonne?" the man asked as he took a decidedly vicious pull on his cigarette.

"Well . . . yes," she admitted. She turned to Sister Dena, who nodded in reassurance. "But I'm known as Allison or Seed. What's your name?"

The man fidgeted, unfamiliar with being questioned, and stole another breath from the cigarette. "That is unimportant," he said with a dismissive wave.

Sister Dena, keenly aware of Allison's uneasiness and protective of her angel, said, "Perhaps *Allison* would be more forthcoming if she were treated nicely."

The smoking zombie glared at Dena who was not the least vexed. The monkeys stirred behind him, stopped scribbling on their note pads and nodded in agreement with her.

Perturbed, the man said, "My name is Mr. Smith. And these gentlemen are Mr. Parish, Dr. Hastings and Dr. Temple."

The monkeys nodded politely. Smith, whose nicotine ghost had changed into a gray scarf of asphyxiation wrapped around his neck, said with a hazy rasp. "We are from the Governing Order of Divinity—Division of Apparitions, Miracles & Nuisances."

"It sounds important." Allison tried faint praise. It had often worked on the nuns, and she guessed it might prove useful in this situation. Cadaver Smith, as she had come to name him in her mind, sat like a Grand Inquisitor of Spanish infamy. Indeed, the perpetual scowl inscribed on his papyrus skin made him appear angry that he had missed the roaring good times of the Middle Age witch hunts. Those were the days, one could almost hear his mind think, a good burning at the stake or a cat-o-nine tails confession. Damn the unfortunate luck that landed me in the twentieth century with its rules about human rights. "What do you guys do?" She turned on the innocent charm.

Cadaver Smith pursed his paper-thin lips. "We investigate all manner of unexplained phenomenon. We categorize it for the faithful so they can understand it."

Translation: Catholic marketing of the miraculous and the not-so.

Having had more than enough chit-chat for the year, Cadaver Smith spoke again as he exhaled a long rope of carbon dioxide which created a smoky noose about his throat. "Where is the form?" he asked, without looking at any of the monkeys. He held out a skeleton arm, expecting someone to place the required document in his bony hand. The monkeys all looked at each other, each assuming the other one had brought the aforementioned piece of paper.

Hear No Evil cleared his throat. "We haven't got the form."

Smith's marrow-colored eyes shrank. "How many times have I told you guys not to leave the office without the form? We can't conduct the interrog—um— investigation without the form. We need the form."

"I'll check the car," Speak No Evil said.

The form was not to be found. An unarmed Cadaver Smith, antagonized further by the bungling incompetence of his Governing Order of Divinity—Division of Apparitions, Miracles & Nuisances—halted the proceedings until the form could be located. The interrogation was postponed until later that same evening.

Nightfall tripped over the sunset, and the Grand Inquisition, which was more like a Less-Than-Marvelous Interview, took place without the seriousness Allison had feared. Cadaver Smith, whom she imagined had actually hung next to Christ at Calvary and somehow survived (badly preserved) until modern times, and the three monkeys, exalted administrative form in place, began their official investigation.

The white-faced leader, cigarette hanging from his lips like the Holy Ghost, one eye shut to avoid the smoke which wafted upward, started the new proceedings by filling in the blanks on the official form. "Would you classify this as an apparition, ghost, haunting by an unidentified spirit, visitation, Mother Mary sighting, stigmata, crying statue, bleeding statue, crying Christ, wailing holy mother, saintly sighting, UFO encounter, channeling, demonic possession, post-hypnotic suggestion or psychic phenomenon?"

"Dream," was Allison's quaint, angelic response.

Cadaver Smith picked up a gold pen (Cross of course), with the official logo of the Governing Order of Divinity—Division of Apparitions, Miracles & Nuisances stuck to the side, its squiggly spook-like shape struck Allison as being awfully similar to Caspar the cartoon ghost.

The preliminaries dispensed with, the header of the form completed, the investigators moved on to more consequential matters and asked a series of questions that seemed altogether ridiculous to our heroine.

Did she own a passport? No. Had she traveled to Turkey? No. Did she ever have any ties to terrorist groups? No. Did she have any relatives with ties to any terrorist groups? I'm an orphan, remember? Sorry. Did she hate the pope? Heavens no. Did she disagree with his views on contraception? Not sure, can you explain that to me? How often did her dreams come true? Once in awhile. Did she think she was special? Yes. How did she feel about red hair? Fine. Could she explain the orchid of her first Christmas? A miracle from God's grace. Did she recall casting a spell on Sister Claudia? I didn't cast a spell.

Allison recalled that strange sunny spring day when she had been caught watching a caterpillar walk across a window pane during class. A vengeful Clod, irate at Allison's daydreaming, was ready to mete out punishment when Allison stood on her chair, placed her hand on Clod's shoulder and said, "An angel need not fear the wrath of God, my sister." She didn't know where the words came from, but they had the uncanny affect of hypnotizing the sister into passiveness.

Writing furiously, the monkey tribunal seemed satisfied with the details of the infamous caterpillar incident. She had forgotten it long ago. Can you explain Zaire? I had a vision. Can you explain the Krohn Conservatory? A light surrounded me. Can you explain the Sacred Mother of Hearts incident? A light surrounded me. And on and on and . . .

Two hours of redundant questioning later, Dr. Temple (Speak No Evil), joined the carnival. He gave her a physical, took blood, and attached her to an EKG. She peed into a plastic cup, breathed into a tube, and took an eye test.

When the doctor was finished, Hastings (Hear No Evil), a skinny guy with a huge Adam's apple and a bad toupee that could give Astroturf doormats sudden appeal, gave Allison an "absotively bizarre" psychological evaluation. At this point, after the initial gabbing and jabbing, she realized her inquisitors were, in sports terms, a third string development squad from the nether regions of the Catholic oligarchy. She decided to have fun with it. Did she love her mother? Yes, a long time ago, do you love yours? How did your mother die? Not sure, drowned I think, I saw it in a vision. Do you remember her? Not very much, she's dead. Did she like fire? Only for roasting marshmallows. Do you like to touch yourself? No, she lied. Did she have an active imagination? Jesus with a box of crayons in a black and white world, doesn't everybody?

During the final stages of the interrogation, Allison became aware of girlish whispers coming through the heating vent like exuberant steam finding its way out the cracks and drafts of the East wing. Apparently, only her well-trained super-spy Red Angel ears were sensitive enough to hear Rita and Joyce and Mary and Linda eavesdropping, although she suspected Sister D heard the chatter but kept a discreet silence. Certainly, the overzealous Governing Order of Divinity—Division of Apparitions, Miracles & Nuisances didn't suspect a thing. She wondered if they'd recognize an apparition, a miracle, or a nuisance if it served them tea. And just what is considered a nuisance, by the way? She wanted to know but said nothing. She guessed it was *the* thing Cadaver Smith and company were best at—being a nuisance.

Then it was Parish's (See No Evil) turn to perform. He started with a scientific overview of paranormal terms—telekinesis, trance channeling, clairvoyance, past life regression—which she found confusing. He followed with a series of psychic tests designed to elicit her telepathic skills.

"Try to levitate this apple," he suggested, as he tossed a mighty Macintosh in his hand. He placed it on the table.

Allison, while she pretended to concentrate, thought the only worthwhile thing she could do to the apple was to make apple sauce via the head of a hammer.

"Okay, try this pencil then," a hopeful See No Evil requested. Nothing. "A paper clip?" Zip. Then Parish hit on what he considered a perfectly splendid idea. Since the vision was of the pope, why not have Allison try to levitate his picture? A wallet-size photo was produced, but, alas, it was futile. She had neither the will nor the skill to move objects about. The monkeys were reaching for bananas in the wrong tree.

It was getting late, around 10 o'clock at night, when Smith stated that was enough for the day. To emphasize the point, he tossed a half-finished cigarette to the floor and ground it with his heel. Allison and Sister Dena sighed, glad that it was over. It had been a long day and both were saturated with the putrid stench of Smith's cigarettes. Allison counted twenty-six that had been fiendishly consumed in her presence, and God knows how many more Cadaver Smith had inhaled when they had to motorcade back to Divine HQ with their tails between their legs to find the form.

"He's a cancer statistic waiting to happen," an exhausted Allison said as she trudged to her room. She opened the door, anxious to shower and fall fast asleep in her jammies.

"Jesus getting a Vulcan mind-meld from Mr. Spock, what's this!" she exclaimed, as she examined a bulky sleep-monitoring device sitting next to her bed. "Where's Mary?"

"She's in with Kate tonight," Sister Dena said. "This is only for tonight, angel." She took Allison's arm. "To see if you have any abnormal thought patterns in your sleep."

"But . . ."

"I'll be in Mary's bed, right next to you. There's nothing to worry about."

Allison looked to the windowsill to Seraph and felt relief. She was fine. Purple blooms busting out like always. With Sister D and Seraph nearby, she told herself, I'll be fine.

After cleaning up, Dr. Temple came in and attached the sensors to various places on her head and body. Not surprisingly, she had a difficult time sleeping. The next morning, at seven a.m., Temple came back, unhooked the machine, packed it up, rolled the graphs tightly in a tube, secured it with a rubber band—the color of monkey dung, Allison thought—and left.

That was it. The Governing Order of Divinity—Division of Apparitions, Miracles & Nuisances was gone, their work finished, their analysis complete, their assessment compiled, their findings secret. Not so much as a "thank you, Ms. Pippin." Not even a "you're completely normal, Ms. Pippin." Nothing. She was bewildered *and* indignant.

Goodbye, Cadaver Smith. Good riddance.

Rose stirred in the kitchen, clanking the tea kettle about. The darling does things, quiet things, to show her support. She converted from coffee to herbal tea upon the doctor's no-caffeine commandment to me. Rose denying herself caffeine in favor of Earl Grey decaf is akin to asking her to forsake the Methodist church to practice Zoroastrianism. Yet every morning she goes to her kitchen, her sanctuary, and makes tea for two.

She heard the television and shuffled half-asleep into the family room. I cocked my head to one side, lay back on the recliner, and feigned sleep. She went to the TV as I watched her through the squinty undergrowth of my eyelashes. She shook her head when she discovered the station set to Channel 99. Lord knows what she thought. My husband is bonkers, probably. She switched it off and came to me as pure of heart as any Holy Spirit religion can conjure up. She leaned over and lightly kissed my forehead, her lips warm like roasted almonds. Her fleece robe fell open slightly, and I became a voyeur to the spires of her well-attended cathedral.

Her vanilla scent sent a contingent of delighted tingles to dance in my groin as she came close to my ear. Her steeples stretched longingly toward my heaven, ready to answer my carnal prayer.

"I read *The Journals*," she whispered. "I believe you, R.T. Everything will be fine, God willing."

As those words of redemption fell from her lips like God's rain on an arid garden, the first red ray of dawn lifted itself from the crayon box and colored the sky far outside the lines. It was beauty in its innocent chaos.

Allison marked the first anniversary (May 24, 1981) of losing Danny with a candlelight bell tower service. She half-expected (and wholeheartedly hoped) Martha would magically flitter into the tower as if the last year were but a celestial bat of an eyelash. Ever the romantic dreamer, she brought a candle despite the sunshine, as a touching remembrance of their love. She carried Danny's letters and read each. Time blinked. Danny seemed so far away now, a distant imagination.

Concerned that the over zealous St. Als sisters might perform an illegal search and seizure of her possessions, *à la* Ronald Reagan and his "drug war" storm troopers, she

loosened a board (the same one your chronicler discovered) and stashed the letters safely inside. A most pleasant déjà vu sensation filled me as I witnessed how she had come to place those important letters in the tower.

She wasn't surprised that she had heard nothing further about the Less-Than-Marvelous Interview, but she did notice a difference in the way she was treated. Gifted. Special. Foreign. Alien. She didn't know what to think, but in her words it was "absotively weird." She refused to bless a plan by Rita to hold seances in the east wing (at two dollars a pop), in which Allison would contact the lost parents of the other orphans. She didn't wish to take advantage of anyone for money, especially the Cutters.

As spring received a scorching overhand serve for an ace from summer, her tennis game improved to the point where she was playing sixteen-year-olds (Rita Starks) and winning. Dena saw silver-plated trophies in her eyes. Soon a regimen was in place, and Allison found herself volleying smack dab center court of the amateur tennis world. Like a fresh, young star too green to know the score, she had no idea how it was that a brand-new tennis court came to be built on the grounds of St. Als, especially at a time when Reaganomics was filching much-needed funds from the pockets of any American and non-profit who didn't happen to be rich, white, male and Republican—not necessarily in that order. This reporter, somewhat shamefully today, must admit that he shared handsomely in the trickle down redistribution of wealth.

But a new tennis court in difficult social times did come to pass at St. Alexandria via a circuitous route of the Diamond Trust Bank, Winston Held III, BG Industries, and Patrick Gilday. Yes, the man who refused responsibility for her paid to ensure that she was well taken care of in every aspect except one: fatherly love.

She treasured her days on the court, the squeak of her shoes, the sweat in her palm. After God, though, her first love was the garden. Tennis was a close second and soon rivaled all other activities as her mental top seed, including her Red Angel fantasies. Her exact expression upon hearing the construction plans for a tennis court was, "Jesus playing doubles with an angel, I can't believe my good luck!"

The budding star of St. Als didn't merely hone her backhand and forehand serves and returns, she also crafted a litany of Jesus expressions (for which she became widely known—and which were not appreciated by the nuns) to go with her feelings on local and world issues. On President Reagan's decision to cut back on civil rights enforcement, she said, "Jesus lighting a torch at a KKK rally, what's going on in Washington?" Of the Ayatollah's bloody purge of 1,800 people since July, she said, "Jesus wielding a machete in the mosque without forgiveness, what is going on in Iran?" Of the nuns' lack of charitable spirit, she said, "Jesus driving a metallic red Mercedes, certainly we can afford to do something." It was this last statement that inspired Mother Superior to request Sister D to instruct Allison to curtail the Jesus phrases. Too late; the trend had caught, the phrases had a life of their own inside St. Als, and she wasn't able to stop it. Nor did she try.

Two infinitesimal events coincided for sweet Allison within twenty-four hours of each other, which, by cosmic design, set her in motion on her path of becoming the Mother Teresa of Cincinnati with the velocity of a blazing fastball from God. It may be difficult for the average, socially-hypnotized mind to comprehend how a potato chip can so unmistakably lead one to a revelation, but it is true.

It is perhaps both fitting and ironic that the world's largest consumer products manufacturer *and* the nation's largest grocery store chain were both founded in Cincinnati, Ohio. Yet, as the skyline attests, their buildings stand wide as city blocks, rising to the sky like outstretched arms in thanks for their profits. The Kroger Building is located several blocks east and north from the nondescript Procter & Gamble complex of gray sandstone that looks more like a government fallout shelter than the world headquarters of the arguable king of marketing genius. The mushy mind of America owes a debt of gratitude for P&G's introduction of soap operas on daytime TV. Please, hold your applause till later.

It was a visit to Procter & Gamble, some call it Procter & God, which was the catalyst—the inspiration, if you will—for Allison's ascension into social work. The field trip was drawing to a close as the orphans sat on Fountain Square, eating P&G-provided box lunches, which consisted of P&G peanut butter and jelly sandwiches, P&G fruit drinks, P&G napkins, and canisters of P&G chips all perfectly shaped, symmetrically-designed, and synthetically-engineered potato food. The fabricated chips were the stuff of corporate marketing and personnel legend, as they served as both a salable product and corporate symbol of employee expectation. All uniform, all the same, all cardboard, all the time, each chip conveniently slipped behind the other so that no discernible difference between one chip and the next could be found.

Mary took a bite of her PJ as she sat next to Allison on the onyx marble wall of the city's main public gathering spot. Allison hadn't touched her food yet. Instead, she watched the legions of pigeons peck about for scraps of bread as she thought of Martha and the city's pigeon control program. She thought of the city's peregrine falcon program. She thought of Danny. She thought of how different her life might have been had they met. She thought about the Reds and how well they'd been playing lately. She thought, I don't care about baseball. She thought about fate and its constant curve balls. Then, she thought of the first minuscule incident which was to change her life.

"Remember that family in the news last night?" she said to Mary, who held her chipmunk face up to an obliging sun.

"Nope. What about it?"

"The guy was living in a box under a bridge with his family because he got laid off. He lost his job, his money, his house," Allison said sadly. "All because the company moved the jobs to South Carolina."

"So?"

"I can't stop thinking about them. I wish I could help them somehow."

"You can't save everybody, Seed," Mary said as she pulled the tab on the potato chip canister.

"Mary, look!" Allison whispered. "But be discreet."

"What?"

"There's a man staring at us," Allison murmured, dropping into her familiar clandestine spy role. "Over there, by the garage elevator." She nudged her sun-polished, tangerine hair in the man's general direction.

The two girls pretended to look at the Fifth Third Bank Building just beyond the position of the derelict voyeur, ever-so-carefully glancing at the man who studied them. The public Peeping Tom wore a frayed olive beanie over long greasy hair, a pimento checkered plaid shirt smeared with a black sticky substance of some kind (diesel fuel exhaust, Allison imagined), a pair of Levi's (original color unknown) which drooped from his waist around toothpick legs and stopped three inches above his ankles. The pant legs sported several large holes, like ravenous Viking bites, as if eating one's trousers as a last resort somehow provided enough sustenance to make it through to the next soupy meal.

"Oh, Mary, he's hungry. That's why he's staring at us." It struck her with the resonance of a silver spoon clinking a fine porcelain teacup that the man was looking for scraps, just like the pigeons. She hopped down from the black marble.

"Where you going?" Mary asked.

"If we can feed pigeons, certainly we can feed a human being." Allison marched toward the elevator, her box lunch snug under her arm. "I'm not going to let a man go hungry."

Her resolve was unshakable, fear unknown. She found the grungy man, trembling, his back toward her, his face wedged into a granite corner. He reeked of urine. She set the box lunch on the ground and said, "I have absotively no appetite today. Maybe you would like my lunch."

The man wanted to turn round, but what little dignity, what microscopic pride the good citizens of Cincinnati hadn't stripped away, rose up in him like the sophisticated ego of the maitre´d at a five star restaurant. Allison returned to Mary without further words.

That is how the seed of her idea was born. First, a thirty second news story, then a live, bonafide, in-the-flesh, down-and-out person who needed help. It germinated throughout the rest of the day, took root by late afternoon, assisted by a brief rain shower which blew in and out of town faster than a political photo-op, and, by evening, her concept had matured into a full-grown plan. At eleven that evening, as all the residents and workers of St. Als slept, Allison sneaked to her garden, picked and dug up all the ripe vegetables, stuffed them, dirt and roots and all, into a pillow case and deposited them on the doorstep of the Mission de Cincinnatus shelter twelve dangerous blocks away down busy Reading Road.

As she snuggled back into her bed, the blankets cozy to her chin, an angelic smile of deep satisfaction glossed her cherub lips. "I did good today," she whispered to Seraph, her mystical orchid and companion. "What should I take them next week?"

Allison began sneaking out every Saturday night with a pillowcase full of canned goods and leftovers—courtesy, albeit without its knowledge, of the orphanage kitchen. Using her skills developed as the Red Angel, she orchestrated an underground food smuggling operation that would have made the CIA proud, should it ever decide to forgo its sinister schemes and perform a humanitarian deed. Saturday nights, she went to bed fully clothed, with the exception of her sneakers, which she kept tied loosely enough to slip on. Her years of prowling about St. Als, traversing its myriad nooks and crannies, gave her an intricate understanding of its hallways, fire escapes, tunnels, and back doors. She relished the idea of being a secret provisioner to the homeless and hungry.

The night of October 17, 1981 drew her deeper into the late-night world of "social misfits," a menagerie of downtrodden creatures with tales so heart-wrenching Idi Amin would have sniffed back a tear. The late October night featured a sky as destitute as a plasma-selling vagrant; no moon, only gray *cirrus fibratus* clouds trailing toilet paper on their heels. Allison had slipped the confines of the orphanage easily again, a bulge of canned goods stuffed under her jacket. She looked pregnant, she thought, and it tickled her to think of a pregnant orphan living with a cadre of celibate nuns.

She saw the nondescript, hand-painted mission sign, which hung below a single 100-watt bulb in a metal housing similar in size and dimension to a Chinaman's hat. Do indigent people ever get served Chinese? she wondered as the mustard-colored mission door, graced with a welcome smile on a fluorescent orange sun, came into view. It reminded her of something one would see on a cereal box.

She emptied the pillow case on the fractured stoop, which was crumbling like a forgotten Roman temple, and turned to walk away. Suddenly, a man stepped from the dark alley beside the mission. A lump larger than this summer's plumpest tomato caught in her throat. A zucchini banged her heart like a timpani in the "William Tell Overture." She inched back, then froze as the man stepped forward into the Chinese light.

The man's face softened. He brandished a kind smile under a cherry cold nose from the chill of the night. His hair swirled in wisps of gray and brown just below his ears.

"Thank you, miss," he said. "You are a most generous and thoughtful girl. The folks here appreciate it."

Allison smiled. "Oh . . . well . . . you're welcome."

"My name is Cincinnatus." The man held out a grateful hand.

"Mine's Allison, but you can call me Seed. Hey, do you run this place?"

He smiled. "Yes, I do. How does a girl get a nickname like that?"

"I collect seeds from the kids at the orphanage and plant them in my garden."

"You're from Saint Alexandria, huh?" He turned his palm over as he spoke, like a short order cook working flap jacks. "Rather late for a girl to be out, don't you think?"

"Just doing my part," she said without hesitation. "I do my best for God."

"Oh," Cincinnatus crinkled his forehead. "Doing this for God, are you?"

"Absotively."

"You are lucky to have God watching over you so closely."

"Doesn't God watch out for you?"

"Not really. I look out for myself and for others who cannot."

"How many people come here every night?"

Flip went his hands. Eggs over easy. "Depends on the weather. A couple hundred usually. We are full tonight, with the rain coming."

Her smile faltered. "Two hundred! I've only been bringing enough for a dozen or so."

"It feeds twelve more than before you brought the food," Cincinnatus said, smiling. "And it is most helpful."

"What else can I do?"

"Come, I'll show you."

He escorted her inside for a tour. While the living quarters were meager, she was immediately taken by the abundance of foliage which seemed to occupy every spare corner and extra inch of space. Ferns and jade, ivies and pothos, wandering Jews and eucalyptus gave the mission a homey feel, cozy and safe. Government issue bunk beds aligned in rows crammed a gymnasium-sized room surrounded by green and brown flora. People sat or milled about, trying their hardest to keep their tattered spirits up. Allison's sunny disposition was besieged by cloudbursts of fatigued mothers, their children clinging to them for attention, asking questions that just can't be answered. "When are we going home, Mommy? When is Daddy coming back? Why are you crying, Mommy? Do we have to live here long?" The women strain to hold back a tear of defeat.

(Chronologer's note—How can society expect a woman, abused and abandoned by an unfaithful husband who split irresponsibly at the first whiff of a better time, look her precious, hungry darlings in the eyes and answer those questions? The court system has failed them, the child support goes unpaid, the house is foreclosed; meanwhile ex-hubby is driving a new car and hitting the bars with a new victim on his arm.)

"Over a third of the homeless are abandoned mothers and their kids," Cincinnatus said.

Allison felt as if a deluge were pouring into her chest, her breast overflowing with sadness at the unfairness of it all.

"And some say people choose to be homeless."

She donned an apron, summoned up her positivity, and performed a range of chores the rest of the evening. She was honored to be able to help. At four a.m., when the mission was quiet, Cincinnatus drove a weary Allison home. Despite the long hours, the grueling work, and the depressing state of the homeless American family, she was not disillusioned. A light drizzle fizzled like carbonated soda about her. "I'll be back next Saturday," she said, a ray of hopeful sunshine in the dreary pre-dawn mist, "with twice as much energy."

"Only if you think it wise," he said, turning over his hand, this time serving an invisible grilled cheese sandwich.

"Don't worry, I have a guardian angel."

A buoyant Allison kept her promise and came each Saturday to the mission, laden with heisted canned goods, fresh vegetables, and house cleaning supplies. She befriended many of the volunteers at the shelter and scores of the homeless, too.

One vagrant in particular, Stephen, would sit and tell her wild stories of his days as a blues harp player in Chicago. Of all the indigents, he was her favorite. He was a pleasant, easy fellow with the greatest respect for Cincinnatus, and with manners many a Cincinnati socialite could learn from. She enjoyed his stories and looked forward to the time after the kitchen was closed and cleaned, when Stephen would spin a yarn about his fame and the famous cats he used to jam with.

It was Stephen who told her how Cincinnatus got his name, a gift from the homeless community who recognized his self-effacing style and his tireless, unassuming contributions. They nicknamed him after the Roman farmer Cincinnatus, who left his plow to defend Rome as a general against the Visigoths. Once the intruders were defeated, he returned to his fields, declining an offer to become emperor. Stephen told the story with obvious pride. "No man ever gave more to me than that great man," he had said. "Our Cincinnatus don't expect nothing for it, neither. Calls it his duty to man."

In the weeks she had come to know Cincinnatus, she had never heard him speak

an unkind word of judgment. She had never heard an unkind word spoken about him, either. Nothing but praise from those he served. He was described respectfully as modest, humble, a saint, a godsend, a quiet man of integrity. Allison, too, felt these things for him.

The weeks rolled by and the missions of mercy continued unabated, with Allison not feeling the least apprehension, secure that her guardian angel was camped on her benevolent shoulder. The angel seemed to be on vacation one week, however, when she was caught sleeping during Mass. Allison called it a bad day at the altar, but her guiding spirit returned to the job with back pay when her punishment turned out to be kitchen duty—the exact place she wanted to be to get a better scope on Church rations.

Channel 99 played onward as time trudged forward. Upon hearing of the Reverend Sun Myung Moon's indictment for tax evasion, Allison said, "Jesus with His hand in the cash register, what have some religions come to?"

She skipped dressing for Halloween, partly because she felt too old for it, and partly because she had reasoned that if all the money spent on Halloween candy, costumes, parties, and decorations went to charity, there'd be no one hungry in America. Everyone inside St. Als, with the exception of a pleased Sister Dena, said her idea was preposterous.

"Self-centered greedy cretins," was Allison's caustic and unappreciated reply.

She loved her week of kitchen duty, being partnered with "that naughty Rita Starks," as Sister Bernadette liked to apply the label. Allison had never met a girl so utterly sex-crazed. The two got along famously, as Rita shared intimacies even Allison's rich imagination had never dreamed.

On November 1, Cincinnatus took her on a late-night field trip. He picked her up just outside the gates of St. Als as he had insisted on doing. He was concerned about her safety since the first night they'd met. She wasn't sure how safe she was riding in Cincinnatus' dilapidated station wagon, which huffed and puffed and chugged and churned its way along the potholed city streets. She thought the car was not unlike some of the alcoholic old timers at the mission who hacked and coughed and spit and wheezed their life away. Perpetual asthmatics, the car and the old men.

"Where are we going?" she asked as Cincinnatus turned south, away from the mission.

"To answer a question you asked me last week," he said. He flipped a nonexistent burger over with the spatula of his palm.

"What question?"

"The one about why there are so many hungry and homeless in America."

The car clattered along, spitting carbon monoxide phlegm from its exhaust. It didn't seem to bother Cincinnatus. Occasionally, Allison would jump when an unexpected backfire farted out the muffler. The car puttered toward its secret destination, with Allison a jumble of excited anticipation.

"So," she said, as the car rattled like a dime in a vagrant's tin cup. "Why are you dressed in a tuxedo?"

"Because we're going to a ball." Her fatherly escort grinned. "A charity ball."

She whined in protest as she gawked at her baggy sweat shirt and jeans. "I can't go to a ball dressed like this!"

He grinned. "I have it worked out." He motioned toward the ripped upholstery of the back seat. "Grab that bag and open it."

Excited as an Indy driver during a victory lap, she undid her seat belt, twisted her body around, and grabbed the large plastic bag. "What is it? Oh my . . ." She exhaled, her breath stolen by the fairy of stunned gratitude. "It's—it's absotively beautiful," she whispered. She pulled a satin green dress from the bag and held it to her chest. She inhaled its scent. "It smells new. Is this . . ." Her eyes lowered in hope she hadn't made the wrong assumption. "Is this for me?"

An Armani smile unzipped itself on Cincinnatus' face. "All yours."

"Oh my God!" she screamed in delight. Instinctively, out of thankfulness and a confused rush of adolescent hormones, she scooted across the seat, hugged the missionary man tightly and kissed his cheek. Then, as she remembered Rita's detailed exploits in seduction, she laid her arm across his thick waist. "Thank you," she said, her voice grateful and naughty, innocent and sensual. She let her right hand fall to his leg, felt it flinch. Boldly, as Rita had described, she moved her hand slowly toward his crotch. The station wagon backfired. She jumped. Her heart revved. Did he like this?

A warm hand surrounded hers. Yes, he wants me, too.

He lifted her hand and placed it back on her lap. "Did I ever tell you," he said, his voice downshifted to neutral, "that I'm fifty-two years old?"

Her mind was in shock from the impact of her amorous accident. She had crossed the yellow no-passing lines of their relationship, misread the street signs, swerved into oncoming traffic, careened back into her own lane, and crashed into the guardrail. "No," she uttered, embarrassed and hurt. "I didn't know that."

Cincinnatus carried a no-fault insurance policy. "Some day," he said wisely, compassionately, "you will make someone very happy."

She smiled, a timid kind of grin one gives the traffic cop as he's writing you up. You do your best to act respectful, courteous, friendly, and your tentative grin shows it, but inside you are angry at yourself, frustrated, ashamed. The only thing to do once the ticket is written is to get back in your car, drive away and forget it. Anything else is wasted energy. It's not the cop's fault. You were the one who broke the law.

"Evenwise," Allison employed her best defensive driving skills, "this dress looks really expensive. Can you afford it?"

"Yes."

"Where did you get the money?" Her embarrassment began to dissipate like the fog on an autumn windshield.

"I am a man of means. I used to own my own lawn and garden company," Cincinnatus explained, as he maneuvered the car onto Vine Street and clambered past the Kroger Building.

"Wow! I love gardening." She was determined to put the nasty business of emotional wreckage behind her. "Is that why the mission has so many plants?"

"Yes," he said sheepishly. "I retired several years ago and sold it to a large company for a comfortable sum. Wish I hadn't."

"Why not?"

"The new owners took all the company assets—land, machinery, customer base—changed the way we did business, which was organic groundskeeping, with no pesticides or dangerous chemicals, and screwed the whole thing up."

"Well," Allison said. "At least you made your money."

"Yes, but there is more to life than money. Once the business soured because they squandered it, they laid everybody off. Oops, here we are." He swung the grumbling vehicle into the valet zone of the Clarion Hotel.

Allison skipped into the bathroom to change, none the worse for her first "driving" lesson. Inside the bag she also found buff-colored pantyhose, green high-heeled shoes, a faux sapphire necklace and matching clip-on earrings. She whirled in front of the mirror like Cinderella on her way to the ball. She applied the stolen make-up Rita gave her from The 88s burglary ring with only slight guilt as she pigmented her lips orchid pink, chosen more for its name than its shade. It wasn't the perfect hue for her skin tone, but it was what she wanted.

A pleased and proud Cincinnatus escorted Allison into the ball, which was on the backside of its prime. Her eyes were bedazzled by the crystal and gold-plated chandeliers hanging like a queen's jewelry from the ceiling of what seemed to be the royal palace. A Tommy Dorsey tune she didn't recognize blared from the twelve piece orchestra on stage as they looked for an open table. Hors d'oeuvres of gossip served themselves in plentiful fashion upon her ears as they wandered through the crowd. Sautéed mushroom caps of rumor. Canapés of disparaging remarks. Pigs in a blanket of politics. Phyllo of flaky business deals. Crudité dipped in ego. She didn't hear any talk of the main dish—charity.

They found a tuxedo-filled table of rich boys and their smashing escorts. Tuxedos and nuns habits look remarkably similar, she thought to herself. Could wealth be a religion?

"May we sit here?" Cincinnatus asked.

"Yes, you may," a man answered without looking up. Mercedes, Allison thought. This guy drives a Mercedes.

"The shrimp isn't fresh," a sophisticated woman in a Halston dress droned. Two carat diamond earrings hung like icicles from her lobes. "They should have flown them in overnight from Boston. That's what Marcus and I do when we entertain."

"And the pâté, pleeease," drawled her tedious companion, assumed to be Marcus, with a roll of his spoiled eyes.

BMW, Allison cringed in her thoughts. Cincinnatus glanced at the guy's overstuffed monkey suit, soiled by brown liver crumbs, and considered whether the man would like pâté *more* if he could find his mouth.

"And this music, come on!" offered another.

Jaguar, Allison was convinced.

"Who listens to this crap anymore? I didn't pay two hundred bucks for this kind of shabby affair."

Cincinnatus scowled. "Excuse me," he said politely. "Is this the Homeless Bash for Cash?"

"Why yes," replied the icicle princess, as several others nodded.

"Oh, I thought we may have been in the wrong place."

"Nope, right place, pal. We're all doing the right thing by being here," a Gatsby wannabe with slicked back hair replied.

"What shelters does this charity benefit?" Cincinnatus asked.

"Don't know," Gatsby shrugged and straightened his drooping bow tie.

"Well, where does the money go?"

"Who cares? We did our part; let someone else figure out what to do next."

"Paying a hundred bucks a head to get drunk is your idea of helping the homeless, is it?"

The liver-stained, tedious man, his tie loosened to get oxygen to his head, leaned forward. "We don't need a lecture from you, *Dad*," he said, then belched in Cincinnatus' face. "That's my idea of charity. Waiter, another beer!" he called, as the group exploded in laughter.

"Please excuse us," Cincinnatus said politely, as he stood.

"She's a little young for you, ain't she, Pop?" Gatsby slurred.

A seething Allison stormed away, her red-headed temper only slightly assuaged by the words she had longed to hear most of her life, words from the lips of the humble Cincinnatus: "She's my daughter." She marched on to avoid a most unseemly scene. She could still see it in her mind, hissing like hot motor oil on the engine block, as she stalked down the hall, furious at the uncaring attitude of her table mates. She could see herself with one hand on a bottle of Chardonnay and the other on the shrimp sauce as she splattered each of the ingrates with a dose of hundred-dollar-a-plate charity. Luckily, the scene was relegated to the angry confines of her fiery noggin.

"It's a good thing we got up, because I was ready to tell him a thing or ten," she fumed as they exited the back of the hotel near the kitchen. "I don't get it."

"You will," Cincinnatus said. He took her hand. "Unfortunately, most people *do not* get it. "Over here, by this retaining wall," he suggested. "We will have a great seat from here."

"What? What are we going to see?"

A couple minutes passed before two doors crashed open and a rickety cart squeaked its way toward the dumpster pushed by two kitchen workers, one black, one white. The men began to toss the boxes.

She squinted to better see the action. "What are they pitching?"

"Food."

"That's not right," she said, amazed. "Why?"

"It is a sad disgrace, Allison," he said, gently knocking the heels of his shoes against the wall.

"No way," Allison said, jumping down. She ran over to the men and proceeded to chastise them for trashing perfectly edible food.

"Orders," came their reply. They did it every night. In the dumpster it went.

"Every night?" She was incredulous. "Don't you know people are starving?"

"In China, maybe."

"No, right here in America! In Cincinnati!"

"Ain't my problem, miss."

"Jesus going hungry at an all-you-can-eat buffet, how can this be?" she cried out. "We need to take this food to the mission." Then, with the acceleration of a sports car and the grace of a luxury sedan and the control of a German import, she hurled herself, brand-new dress, shoes, and all into the dumpster. She fished around, inspecting the containers.

"Here," she said to a drop-jawed Cincinnatus, "take this shrimp." The men shrugged nonchalantly, shook their heads, and returned to the kitchen.

She cleared the dumpster of any edible food, while Cincinnatus, pleased with the tenacity of his young sidekick, piled the car full of stuffed mushrooms, quiche, shrimp, salad greens, and dinner rolls. It was twelve thirty-eight when they headed for the shelter.

"You did well tonight, Allison," he said. "Even if you do smell like shrimp."

"Sorry about that." She grinned as she cracked the window. "I hope I didn't ruin the dress. It's so beautiful."

"It will come clean."

"I don't suppose I'll need it again, evenwise. I've had plenty of charity events, thank you. That banquet was horrible. Those people didn't care at all about the plight of the homeless."

Cincinnatus didn't answer.

"How much of that money will go to charity?" she asked.

"About two percent," he said, his tongue lodged in his cheek in displeasure that so many well-meaning people contribute, but so little reaches its target.

"Two percent? Only two bucks a ticket. Where does the rest go?"

"The organizers take their cut. And other expenses," he said. "And *that*, dear Allison, is one reason why there are so many homeless in America."

She pondered his reply, scrunching her freckles into a new constellation on her face. "Because only two percent makes it where it's needed or because people don't really care?"

"A little of both, Seed. It is not entirely the fault of the rich. They contribute money and feel they have done their part. They do not realize so little funding makes it to the homeless. And to be honest, many wealthy people, like me, *do* make a contribution that matters. There are good and bad people at all economic levels. The real problem is that not enough people get involved in a way that can make a difference. It is not just the wealthy. Most middle class Americans are better off than 99% of the world's population, but few are interested in more than ballet lessons for Margaret, baseball practice for Chad, eighteen-holes of golf for Dad and psychoanalysis for Mom."

She frowned. "That is so absotively sad."

"Of course, the main reason is the sheer daily waste in America," Cincinnatus said, nodding his head toward the culinary haul saved by the gutsy insistence of the Seed. "It's estimated that Americans throw away twenty-eight percent of all the food they purchase."

"God, what a country we live in."

"We subsidize waste. There is enough food in America to feed everyone on the planet."

"What do you mean?"

"Our government provides billions of dollars in price supports and subsidies to large food conglomerates, then they store the food in huge warehouses where it never gets distributed."

"Why not? That can't be."

"They protect the profits of big business by keeping prices high," he said. "It is a completely distasteful and inhumane policy, but it is also, unfortunately, true."

"Can't we change it? Can't we write our congressman and stir things up?"

He chuckled. "There were two congressmen there tonight. The best thing to do is work on an individual level to affect change."

"If more people volunteered, we could stamp out hunger."

"Yes, Allison," Cincinnatus said, glancing at his accomplice in charity. "We need more people like you."

When the gods decide to use a hammer from your toolbox, it's best not to dispute their construction methods. The scene ended when a fatigued Allison stole back into the orphanage and plopped into bed.

Uplifted by her undaunted spirit, I decided to quit being a masochist and take my medicine. The stack of cancer books Rose gave me sat untouched in my solarium. I vowed to look at them later that day. She and Twinkie had done their best to insist I take care of myself, and, indeed, I had gone to the oncologist and sat through the interview and scheduled my first treatment for next week. But it was an ineffectual attempt at best. His office was so cold, so sterile, and, to borrow a word from Allison, so "absotively" clinical. I'm a number in the butcher shop. Now serving number 67.

By the time I had finished the last segment of Allison's saga, the house smelled of crisp bacon, buttered toast, and scrambled eggs. My stomach said no, stay away from that pork, but my taste buds, conditioned for over six decades, were set to override the decision when the morning began to shake from a pounding that throbbed in my heart like I'd been thumped by a sledge. Are the vandals at it again? Why can't they leave me alone? I'm innocent. I hobbled to the front door, half-doubled over from an acute spasm in my abdomen. Was it fear, anger, or the cancer that ripped at me?

When I arrived in the hall, the same time as Rose, the front door was missing. The Bing estate across the way was awash in sunshine and Christmas decorations—it's September 22, for chrissakes. Rose and I stared, mouths agape. Who had stolen our door?

"What the hell!" I shouted. "In broad day—"

An effervescent Parker stepped into the frame, smile as big as a Caribbean postcard, a pencil stuck behind his ear, looking like a carpenter in brown coveralls. His eyes sucked in all the energy of the hallway and beyond like some great galactic vortex.

"Morning." He grinned as a long skinny carrot bobbed from his lips. "That's a lovely nightgown, Mom."

Rose smiled and self-consciously gathered the neckline. "Would you like some coffee?"

"Nope, trying to quit. You and R.T. are my inspiration. And I have work to do," he said, as the light poured into him.

Me, an inspiration to Parker?

"What are you doing?" I said. The burning in my intestine turned itself down to simmer.

Parker cocked his head, changing the gravitational alignment of his magnetism.

Planets in unknown galaxies suddenly hurdled out of orbit. He stepped back and swung his arm out gracefully, as if introducing a person of prestige, showing us the brand-new front door he was hanging. "Replacing your door. They're important, fella. Doors can be a welcome or a warning. He lifted a crowbar to the doorjamb. "I think it's time to welcome whatever spirits are trying to call." *Chomp* went his carrot.

"Me, too," said Rose.

When the gods decide to use a hammer . . .

Chapter 30

September 22, 1990 (Continued)

Breakfast finished (three slices of bacon and massive indigestion for me; Parker showed excellent self-restraint), a new door put on thanks to a resourceful former son-in-law, a sparkling day full of promise, and a wife who has shown renewed signs of faith in me, all conspired to give me hope as I sat in my easy chair and switched on Channel 99 once again. Rose went to visit a friend. Parker was back on the case. And Twinkie didn't come home last night. On this finest of Tuesday mornings, I wondered if she had found someone. I hoped so.

It was scarcely ten a.m., and my day was lacquered like a rich cherry finish on a fine piece of chair rail. Much progress had been made—I witnessed several months of Allison's life and I wanted more. *The Journals* did not disappoint.

Though busy with school, St. Als chores, tennis, and her secret ministry at the Mission de Cincinnatus, Allison began to write more in her journal. She was happy, content that she was contributing to benefit others, not just talking about it. She could put many a philanthropist, missionary, or saint to shame.

"Since you have no aversion to dumpsters," Cincinnatus kidded her on the chilled night of November 15, "you reach in and get it."

"O . . . kay," she said. There was a difference, she thought, of diving into a dumpster in the emotional heat of an argument versus knowingly devising a plan to enter a dumpster for the sake of a pizza. She grabbed the cardboard box.

"How often do you do this?" she asked later as they sat eating the pepperoni, onion and anchovy on the front seat of the indigent station wagon. The asthmatic engine was off, so quiet pervaded the interior.

"Almost never." His eyes twinkled. "I wanted to show you some of the devices the homeless use to get food. They order a pizza nobody else will eat, then wait until the restaurant throws it away."

"Jesus eating minnows from a ditch in Galilee, anchovies are disgusting." She winced as she swallowed.

He chuckled. "Pick them off."

"What made you decide to start the Mission?" she asked as she flung the herringlike fish onto the pizza lid.

He chewed with purpose, buying time between her question and his answer. It was difficult to respond. "In life, several seemingly inconsequential circumstances sometimes collide to push one where one needs to be." He wiped his hands on a paper towel they'd picked up at a Shell station.

"How's that?"

He considered how much of the story to relate to his young protégé. "Mine is a strange tale, not unlike most people's lives," he said.

Indeed, it was. On October 24, 1929 the stock market plunged by twenty-five percent. General Electric, Montgomery Ward, AT&T, and others all took a bath. Bankers and financiers were broken. Black Thursday, as it was called, caused some to commit suicide; others lost their life savings; most people panicked. Cincinnatus' parents went straight to bed for four days and conceived him. The way some people deal with stress, huh?

"I know the fear of hunger," he said humbly as his palm turned. Allison imagined him braising asparagus tips. "My father was forever changed by the Great Depression. He swore he'd never go hungry again. Even after it was all over, he'd buy canned goods by the case and stack them in the basement. He'd buy a dozen boxes of cereal at a time. There wasn't ever a moment when we didn't have at least six of everything. Growing up with that psychosis affected me."

"I guess so. But how is that related to the mission?"

He smiled. "My wife and I bought a house in Oakley with a small backyard near a ravine. The best we could do at the time. Across the ravine, hidden by a thick woods, was a manufacturing plant. My daughter, April, who was a lot like you—full of giving— used to play in that woods every day. She'd bring home wildflowers and tell us about the camps she'd made or the vines she'd swung on."

"Sounds absotively wonderful."

"It was nice." His voice faded. "Until we found out that April had leukemia. She struggled for two years, but we lost her."

"I'm sorry," Allison said.

"The water was polluted. The company dumped its toxic waste directly into the creek with no consideration of the consequence, and they had a smoke stack burning twenty-four hours a day."

"That's absotively horrible."

"It was prior to any environmental laws," he said meekly. "I have seen many families destroyed by personal crisis worse than what I went through. I was fortunate. My company was doing well, I had insurance to pay the bills. But most don't. Many good people get leveled by something that tragic."

She felt as if the lone anchovy she swallowed was attempting to swim its way upstream and out of her throat. It was the emotion caused by Cincinnatus' story.

"I learned a lot. Converted my landscaping business to completely organic and stopped poisoning people's yards. I was as guilty as anybody else. I decided I needed to

take responsibility. I told myself, when April died, that when I had the chance I'd give back to the world as best I could. Twenty years went by, and I felt like I hadn't done enough. When the opportunity came to sell Celestial Lawn & Garden, I took it. I started the Mission de Cincinnatus with some of the profits."

"That's such an absotively noble deed," Allison said. She asked him if Reaganomics would have an affect on the mission. Cincinnatus conceded that it would.

"If the mission ran out of money, or if the political climate became too intolerant, I would probably head to El Salvador."

"El Salvador? That's dangerous."

"People are in need down there," he said, as if flipping a slice of French toast on the griddle. "They are very poor and—"

"And there's a civil war going on! You'll be killed."

Cincinnatus shrugged. "Someone has to undo the injustice of our Latin American policy. Maybe I can help a few people. Besides," he said, "the mission is doing fine, and I am not ready to pack my bags just yet."

"Cheesecake!" she exclaimed. "You sure are brave."

Cincinnatus blinked shyly. "I live in service to humankind."

"And I," she said proudly, "shall do the same."

She wasted no time putting her commitment into action. During a tennis match with Rita, who was more interested in the boys on the next court than hitting lobs and volleys, while a gym-shoed, fanatic Sister Dena called instructions, Allison came up with a grand idea. She walked off the court, hardly a reddish curl moistened, nary a freckle gleaming sweat, and presented her concept to her two tennis pals. Her delicious plan was so exceptional that both Rita and Dena hugged her simultaneously, with Rita saying, as she stroked Allison's hair, "What a sweet, innocent girl." And Sister Dena, touched by compassion, said, "How did such a beautiful soul arrive at St. Als?"

The three concocted a sales pitch to Mother Superior. They talked it through, its logic, its benefits, its charity, and stood before her in the grand dame's office. Even seated, Mother Superior's torso, adorned in her alma mater's sweatshirt, rose tall behind the desk, like a somber statue weathered by rain and pollution and pigeons in Vatican Square. Her large head and masculine features mimicked the exaggerated sculpted busts of many a famous patron. A football sat on her desk. It was almost game time.

Sister Dena, who was possibly the only adult in St. Als not intimidated by her, broached the topic as Allison whispered a prayer to Pope John Paul II, whose picture hung on the wall. He was smiling meekly, like a good pontiff should.

"I have an absotively splendid idea!" Allison said, having determined overwhelming enthusiasm was the only way to win Mother Peculiar over.

"And just what is this suggestion, Yvonne?" came the stern reply.

Rita shifted her weight from left to right, from right to left, then back again, nervous about making this special request. She didn't like Mother P, who had given her swats and disciplined her several times for her sexploits, so she chose to avoid the "evil mistress of the manor."

"Allison, ma'am," she corrected. "I prefer the name Allison. Um . . . can we please, . . . um—"

"What is it girl?" Mother Superior huffed with all the grace of a buffalo in tap shoes.

"Mother Superior, ma'am, knowing how kind and charitable you are. And knowing the nuns here love to help those . . . who . . . um, are . . ."

"Get to the point, child."

Jesus with a hair trigger temper she was touchy, Allison thought, but wisely kept it to herself. Then she realized Mother Peculiar's obsession with football and knew they had picked the worst possible time to approach her. It was Saturday, just before kick-off.

"What Allison is attempting to suggest," Sister Dena offered, "is that St. Alexandria open its doors, its heart and its pantry to those in our immediate community who may be alone, hungry or homeless for Thanksgiving."

"It would be great. And God would absotively love it!" Allison piped in.

"And we have plenty of food," Rita said.

A stone face of resistance chiseled its way onto Mother Superior's facade. Her body became rigid, immovable. The ladies read its unmistakable language and immediately abandoned the game plan for impassioned pleas of mercy and charity, a tactic Mother found highly irritating. She listened with detachment for a few minutes as the arguments for feeding the homeless with orphanage food landed upon her like a squadron of mourning doves. She took a deep breath, picked up the pigskin, and twirled it like a baton, then brought it to her nose just above her unsightly mustache. Allison thought of the rumor, which made the rounds of St. Als last year, started by the boys, that Mother P was actually a man who was rejected by the priesthood and had a sex-change operation to become a nun instead. Mother Peculiar sniffed the grass-stained leather. She inhaled it. It smelled of victory.

The ball spun in Mother Peculiar's rock hands as if all the power of St. Als lay in her marble mitts, which in fact it did. She inhaled deeply. The absolute power of the Church was about to speak. "I'm sorry, children. St. Alexandria is not in the charity business, and we are ill-equipped to have vagrants running through our home."

"What?" Allison protested.

"That is all," she said firmly, with a short but smug toss of the football from one hand to the other. Touchdown. She had won.

"You need to reconsider!" Allison shouted. "Why not?"

"It is not our mission to help the homeless. Ours is to provide services to parentless children."

"Come, Allison. Come, Rita," Sister Dena bowed her head, disappointed. "Let's go."

Allison was not so easily dismissed. "How can we not help people in need? It's a primary function of the Church."

"It is not our place," Mother Peculiar insisted.

Allison, emboldened by anger, driven on by the gods of furious disbelief, leaned over Mother's desk. "If it's not the place of the Catholic Church, then whose is it?"

The great hulk of masculine womanhood rose from her chair, like a jagged mountain rising from the sea, with the intent of intimidating the petite Allison. "We are *not* the Catholic Church, Yvonne."

"We aren't? Then what are all these people doing running around here acting like nuns?" Allison shouted.

"Seed!" Sister Dena pulled at Allison's arm. "Let's go."

"No!" She pulled away. "Answer me. What are all these fake nuns doing here?"

The senior nun's face turned molten lava. She wasn't a mountain rising from the sea; she was a volcano ready to blow off a chunk of its roof and spew its magma over anything in its path. The palm of her hand exploded on the top of her desk. "I will not be spoken to in this manner," she rumbled as the great pressure built up inside her. "We do a great many things here at St. Als . . . er . . . at St. Alexandria. Food, shelter, education, religious conviction . . . We care for over seventy-five children of all ages and races, so don't tell me we are fake nuns!"

"Seed, let's go," Rita said as she and Sister D each grabbed an arm. Allison's own red-headed friction boiled over.

"Well, if you ask me, and I'm sure you won't, the Penguin Squad ought to do more than pretend they're playing parents to a bunch of kids."

"What?" Mother Peculiar squeezed her football hard as if to pop a balloon. Vesuvius had erupted, and Pompeii was in danger. That's the mold Mother Peculiar came from, Allison thought, a fossilized victim caught in the volcanic ooze.

Allison refused to back down. "You heard me fine. You penguins try to compensate for the fact that you can't have your own kids. And you don't even do *that* very well!" As the words escaped her lips, she knew she had made a mistake. She had slandered the sisters, women who gave their lives, whatever the reason, to the Church. She had attacked their personal being, their reason for existence. Still, she couldn't turn back.

"You're grounded."

"Grounded? Jesus on death row without chance of parole, of course I am," she said as Rita and Dena pulled her toward the door. "We're prisoners!"

"Get her out of here!" Mother shouted. "Get her out before I strangle her!"

"You're making a big mistake about Thanksgiving," Allison warned. "God's not going to like this! I'm going to talk to Him."

Mother Superior scoffed at her prophetic threat. Threaten me, hah, the flustered Mother thought. I'll show that heathen the fear of God and the power of the almighty Church.

Allison was dragged into the hall by her two horrified compatriots. The door slammed behind them.

A deafening quiet reverberated down the stark hallway. Anxious eyes bounced nervously from face to face.

"That didn't go too well, did it?" Allison smiled, her temper softened to moist clay as the three embraced and broke into hysterical laughter.

Undeterred by Mother Peculiar's "ridiculous" decision, incensed, no, motivated by it, Allison soft-shoed her way down darkened St. Als' hallways, illuminated only by red EXIT safety signs, to the kitchen. It was midnight, one minute into Thanksgiving, and she would not be denied helping the less fortunate on this blessed day. She tiptoed to the kitchen where she heard giggles and whispers. She peered in cautiously.

"Jesus French kissing the pope, they're lovers," she said under her breath as she spied Joyce's tongue flicker in and out of Rita's mouth while they groped each other with the fervor of a vicar and his favorite altar boy.

Uncharacteristic of her skill as the Red Angel, or perhaps because she was shaken by the scene, Allison leaned too closely to the swinging door, lost her balance, and tumbled into the kitchen, startling the girls. After a few tense minutes of mutual, blushed explanation, it was decided that Allison didn't care what they were doing, and swore not to tell. Rita and Joyce were grateful to assist the St. Als angel on her latest mission of mercy.

Joyce, who through abuse and abandonment was predisposed to women only, eyed Allison like a Cheshire in heat while she loaded the pillowcase with canned beans, corn, and beets. Rita pitched in a turkey, some yams, and a fresh baked pumpkin pie, much to Allison's delight. The girlfriends stole across the yard with her, helping her carry the oversized haul of Thanksgiving treats. A patient Cincinnatus waited at the bus stop with the engine coughing. With the food stowed in back, Allison climbed into the

hacking car. She wasn't sure, but she thought she heard Rita and Joyce discussing her as they drove away.

"It won't be long."

"I get her first," Joyce said.

"No, you don't. She's mine."

Allison was jubilant at having fed the Thanksgiving homeless while snubbing her pretty, freckled nose at the edict of Mt. Rushmore in drag (Mother Superior). Her weekly missions continued, although she altered her route away from the kitchen and used the fire escape, instead, to avoid any indiscreet sexual encounters. She'd taken to squirreling away food under her bed during the week so she didn't find herself cornered by two lesbian nymphomaniacs intent on pulling her in half like a wishbone.

On Christmas night, alone in her room, she sat next to the window with a small glass of eggnog in her hand, Seraph, her ever-blooming savior-orchid by her side. She raised the eggnog high and said, "Wherever you are this night, Daniel Gilday, I wish you well."

January 17, 1982 turned into a disastrous night for the apprentice saint. It was a cold night, a night so cold that beleaguered fire waved an exhausted flag of defeat to the chill. It was a night that breeds pneumonia and viruses humankind has yet to discover. It was a night in which even indoor jugglers, digits numbed, fumbled through their acts, dropping this object and that. It was a night that turned hot chocolate to a brown Slush Puppie. It was a night so brittle that one wrong blink could send a whole row of eyelashes tumbling to the ground like a clumsy Rockette tripping the entire chorus line. A night so frigid, warring couples ceded their anger and snuggled for warmth. It was a night where spies stayed cloaked within their secret bases. A night where perennial bulbs were forever grateful to the soil for protection. It was a night that cleansed the sky by freezing pollution into chunks of toxic briquettes that shattered into nothingness. It was a night that all the stars in the Universe, in sympathy for those without homes, glowed brighter in hopes their distant twinkles could raise the temperature one solitary degree. It was the type of night that forces even society's black market castaways to seek shelter. It was a night that saw long lines of the shivering unfortunate spilling out into the street in front of the Mission de Cincinnatus, wondering if this night—this frigid, cold, barren, brittle, chilling, brutal night—would be their last. And finally, it was a night that saw Allison standing before the gray monolith of piety, Mother Superior, explaining why she was out at 3 a.m., and who was that man whose muffler fell off in the driveway.

Allison, who figured that doing the true work of God—charity—was much more important than an admission of guilt, lied. But the questions didn't stop. Mother Superior and Sisters Claudia and Bernadette assaulted her with one question after another. Not even Sister Dena could quell their perverse fascination with what *may* have happened. The nuns' imaginations were rampant with degrading scenes of oral sex acts performed by Allison: child molestation, rape, corruption of a minor, kiddy porn, and . . . oh my God . . . who knows what all. The reality, of course, was that Cincinnatus was an honest man of virtue who never entertained even the faintest deviant thought about his thirteen-year-old helper.

Allison held firm to her story that she didn't know the man, that she had hitched a ride home. When Sister Claudia announced, far too proudly for the girl's liking, that she had the license plate number, Allison began to waver. When Mother Peculiar, who looked especially menacing with puffy, sleepless eyes and her hair bunched up in a net, revealed the rumor that Allison had been sneaking food to the Mission de Cincinnatus, the charade was up. Her goose, as they say, was cooked. Allison knew Joyce had narked on her, perhaps to undo a failed grade on a math test last week, perhaps because Allison had rebuffed her advances, perhaps because of Joyce's "special friendship" with Sister Claudia.

Forty-seven minutes into the interrogation, Allison spilled the whole truth in hopes of a lighter sentence, and to dissuade the nuns from pursuing their ridiculous sex scandal theories. Dire warnings to stay away from the shelter followed.

Allison thought she was home free when Mother Superior, whose craggy face looked twenty years older in the dead of night, asked her what her punishment ought to be. Seeing this as a grand sign of hope, Allison suggested that she be required to plan a charity tennis tournament in the spring. The notion was disdainfully dismissed like a beggar in St. Peters Square, replaced by a most-appreciated assist from Sister D, who stated that three months duty in the library might be fitting compensation. All agreed. Allison repressed a smile as wide as an angel's wing.

Her hidden giddiness was short-lived as Mother Superior croaked, "Your friend, that Cincinnatus pervert, will not be as fortunate." She pursed her creviced lips. "Bernadette, call the police."

Chapter 31

May 1943

Sulphur stood in the canary twilight on the steps of the cathedral and looked down from the hill over the sprawling Spanish metropolis. He much preferred Barcelona's openness and energy to the droll suspicion of Lisbon, yet he nervously turned a matchbook over and over in his pants pocket as he waited for his contact to arrive. His plans for moving the counterfeit Deutschmarks had been altered, thanks to FDR's changing priorities. Sulphur had to move the whole lot at once and turn additional printings over to Schoomaker's Barcelona operation. Heavy water, he thought, that doesn't sound too important. Still, on the blackened steps of the grand church, flocks of pigeons pecking about the courtyard, Sulphur's face lit up with a cherry bomb smile. He would soon demolish a power plant with a fireball so big and bright and loud the concussion would knock Hitler from Eva Braun's Berlin bed.

A cautious voice startled Sulphur from behind. "The pope sings German arias in the bathtub."

Sulphur turned and sized up the man. The suit was right, gray pin-striped with a red carnation. The hat was right, black felt Stetson with a gray band. His upper lip was ridiculously sketched in the thinnest of charcoal mustache hair—that's good. He eyed the man's left index finger, a gold ring affixed with a cross. "Yes," Sulphur said, "And I hear Greta Garbo sometimes soaps his back."

"So much silliness, no?" The agent gripped Sulphur's hand as if they'd been friends for life. "This cloak and dagger business I find amusing. I am Garbo." He offered a slight bow to accompany his Spanish accent. Garbo spoke the word business as *beezness*, which Sulphur found charming.

"Sulphur."

"Pleased," Garbo said. He motioned for them to stroll through the plaza to the side of the church. "We have much to do and little time. We must meet the man soon."

"What man?" Sulphur was alarmed. There wasn't supposed to be any man, just instructions on where and how to ship the money, and an envelope from Greg Thomas on the heavy water situation in Norway.

"Calm yourself." Garbo's crow eyes glistened as he placed a gentle hand on Sulphur's forearm. "This man is the one who can move all the currency."

Sulphur took a deep breath to relax, catching a whiff of olive oil. Garbo is one of our best agents, he told himself, with a sterling record of service in the OSS; there's nothing to worry about. "Who is he?"

"His name is Josemaria Escriva." Garbo grinned, relishing his role on the stage of intrigue. "A strange, little man with peculiar tastes, but he will get the job done."

"How so?" Sulphur asked, wondering about this mystery man with a masculine—feminine name.

"Let us say," Garbo lowered his voice, then paused, "he has a penchant for the masochistic. It is said that he flogs himself with a whip filled with the shavings of metal. The tastes of some men, eh señor?"

A shiver of disbelief split his spine like a splinter in a steeple's crossbeam. The two approached a thick, oak door to the rectory, its hinges rusted from the salty Iberian climate. How many covert deals have been consummated behind this door over the last three centuries? Sulphur wondered. "How can he move all the Deutschmarks?"

"This man, this crazy bastard who beats himself, is very powerful. Mucho powerful," Garbo waved his arms wide. He began to whisper. "Do not speak these words again, my friend, but he is the founder of Opus Dei. He has the ear of Generalissimo Franco. They control the minds of the Spanish people."

"How?"

"Through the Church. Opus has infiltrated beezness and university throughout Spain. And much of Italia I am afraid," Garbo's charcoal sketch seemed to wiggle above his lip like an anemic, black snake as he spoke. "But this is of no concern of ours, these pious Spanish zealots. We must use the resources we have."

Garbo knocked twice, paused, knocked twice again, paused, then knocked thrice. The door opened just wide enough for the two men to duck inside. The room was dim and Spartan. Candles flailed against the darkness from the four corners, their flickers casting demonic shadows off the stone walls. A rough wood table and four meager wooden chairs stood in the middle of the room. Standing next to one of the chairs, a smile of courtesy on his chubby face, distrustful eyes of no distinguishable color magnified by thick glasses, greased black hair atop a head the height of Sulphur's chin, two manila envelopes under his arms, a gold cross reflecting the candle glow, and a priestly look of inconvenience in his jowls, was Josemaria Escriva, founder of Opus Dei.

Pleasantries were exchanged, details worked out, rendezvous points established, remuneration considered. Sulphur wasn't particularly impressed by this *beezness*man-priest who aligned himself with Franco, the oppressive dictator. Suspicion reigned on both sides of the negotiation. In the dark confines of the dank rectory, as he made arrangements with this curious masochist, Sulphur considered whether the unassuming paunchy priest actually beat himself in servitude to God. And if there were a God, would He laugh or cry over such obedience?

One comment which caused Sulphur to question Escriva's ecclesiastic piety was his insistence on a twenty percent cut of the deal. "Ten percent for the Church," he said

calmly, "and ten percent for the important work of Opus Dei. Consider it tithing, my brother."

Tithing my butt, he thought to himself as Escriva examined the envelopes under his arm, deciding which one to hand over. The transaction completed (Garbo and Escriva would handle the actual exchange on Thursday), the German economy would be flooded with marks within two weeks. Sulphur glowed with accomplishment.

He and Garbo found themselves in a little café drinking cognac to celebrate the success of the mission, as Sulphur, anxious for his next assignment, tore open the envelope given him by Escriva.

"My friend," he barely heard Garbo utter. "You look to have surprise upon your face, no?"

Sulphur studied the documents carefully, his eyes straining to make sense of the words. He didn't speak for the longest time as a concerned Garbo looked on. "These aren't the right papers," he said finally. "There's four different documents here—three in Italian and one in German." His face turned grim; this spy *beezness* was certainly full of complicated twists. "You must get these to Gregory Thomas with instructions to get them to London immediately. And you must do it with the utmost caution—tonight!"

"It is done, my friend," Garbo said. "But what is the significance?"

Sulphur sipped the cognac, delighted in the way it tempted his tongue with its fire. "I don't know exactly." He felt the smooth burn trickle down his throat. "But they're important enough to have been signed by the pope, Mussolini, and Adolf Hitler."

"That, my friend," Garbo smirked as he threw back the entire cognac shot, "is an unholy trinity."

Section

The time is at hand with sulphur-stained fingers
And a gallon of gasoline for the pyre
I release you to the elements; do your work
Return the Earth to her rightful throne

Chapter 32

October 7, 1990

Dear reader, I regretfully inform you that our chronicler, Robert Thomas Stone, is on a brief sabbatical mending his body. He will rejoin us once his illness subsides. We ask for your patience and compassion toward him in his absence. Those who are predisposed to praying should do so at this time—in heavy doses. Stoney's last trip to the oncologist did not go well.

"I have good news and bad news," *the droll medicine man said.* "The bad news is the cancer in your testicles has spread. The mass is too large to be operable."

No sugar coating by this god-like doctor. One could almost hear Stoney's blood drain onto the carpet. Plush shag—sixty-five dollars a yard.

"We'll have to try radiation and chemo. The good news is we won't have to remove your testicles." *Long breathless pause.* "Until the mass reduces in size."

Faster than he could say "radical inguinal orchiectomy," and quicker than he could master his thoughts, Stoney was undergoing treatment, making his small contribution, at the expense of his body, toward the annual seventy billion dollar medical racket sponsored by the American Cancer Society. Several days of less than distinguished, involuntary bodily functions discharging themselves at the most inopportune times, followed. Our scribe was brave, though: betwixt heaves and hurls, he vowed to keep fighting.

Then the depression set in, the lethargy, the loss of stamina. Acute loss of appetite. Nausea that would make a Roman vomitorium seem like a good time. An uncontrollable fatigue slammed him into bed as radioactive molecules stampeded through his body, unchecked by retreating antibodies.

Every four to six hours, Twinkie would arrive, humming a strange mixture of "Take Me Out to the Ballgame" *and the theme from* Perry Mason. *She had a handful of powerful drugs—some prescribed to negate the harmful side effects of the cancer treatment, others to negate the harmful side effects of the drugs prescribed to treat the harmful side effects. There were so many pharmaceutical measures and countermeasures taking place inside him, one would think it was the Battle of the Bulge.*

Indeed, there is a war raging. Great battles yet to come. It rages inside our fallen writer. It is waged between his contradiction and contrast, of moments lived and lost, of promises he kept and those broken, trampling him beneath its momentum.

There is a mighty external conflict as well. It boils black as a tempest in the Middle East. Oil will be the prize. Liquid to power your cars. Will the death be worth it? Oh, what a bloodlust some Americans have. The mention of fight or battle or war sends hormones charging dangerously to muscles that ache to punish. Is this what you humans do—look at life as a battle—a throw-back to the plunder and pillage age of barbaric men? A brutal time when conquering the next village proved supremacy? Humans as supreme beings? In any other realm of the Universe, that is a laughable thought.

But the battle, if there is to be one, is never fought by great nations for just causes. No, these battles, whether external conflicts or internal struggles, are never against someone else; they are always fought against ourselves. They are battles of our fears, of our souls against our egos. For the human race, at least up until this day, ego has won.

But pity not the beleaguered R.T. Stone, dear readers. Like all of us, his problems are of his own making. If he is going to survive, he will have to step from the shadows of his own ignorance. He will have to admit his guilt before the world and accept his penance. Allow me to reveal a cosmic secret: No one is innocent, only ignorant—but in the eyes of the Council, ignorance is no excuse. Stone's punishment for his ignorance is participation. He must become involved with life if he is to save himself. But the penalty is also the reward. The insanity is the revelation.

I am in Stone's study, the place where he writes most of this work. He is to be applauded, this messenger. My being scans the room while Stoney lies in bed as a bayoneted exhaustion pokes at him. A packet from 'M' lies unopened on his desk. He had wisely asked Parker to trace the origins of the previous 'M'velopes, pardon my pun. Stoney has made great progress but does not know it. A Lloyd's of London check in the sum of two million dollars sits like a camouflaged tank in the stack of mail ready to annihilate a platoon of troubles advancing on Stoney's flank. Boom!—no more debt. Boom!—bankruptcy is gone. If only he could summon the strength to pull the trigger of his free will. If only he could hear the bugle call.

It was not a boring time while Stoney languished in a hospital for three days, doing his best to keep down the nutritionally-deficient chicken broth. Thirty-seven percent of well-nourished adults who go into the hospital leave malnourished, courtesy of the pathetically low dietary standards of the American Dietetic Association. It is the next great scandal. But America is nothing but scandal. Back to the point: no, it was indeed not a boring time. First, there is the distasteful matter of Rose's Methodist church.

It seems a vandal broke into the church late one Saturday evening, spray painted the Crucifix head-to-toe with a can of Krylon Magenta Magic—a dollar eighty-nine at K-Mart—and stuffed a Lucky Strike cigarette in the anguished Son-of-God's lips. Upon arriving for the Sunday morning serving of fire and brimstone, the parishioners were enraged at the sight of their beloved icon shimmering purple before the stained glass.

The *Lucky Strike* was a most ironically-fitting gesture of protest, lost on the church elders, whose board of directors had invested church funds in several thousand shares of tobacco company stocks. One could rationalize that religion, death, and tobacco are intricately entwined, but the fact that the church board neglected to inform their flock of their questionable investment leads one to conclude that the directors had put greed before ethics.

So infuriated was the congregation at the defaming of their dead leader, Jesus, Prince of Peace, that they blamed the most likely candidate for the blasphemous artistry. They focused their anger on the man whose wife they had shunned, the man who had embarrassed the community by burning down his son's nightclub. Robert Thomas Stone.

Hearing that the police had cleared Stoney of any possible wrong-doing since he was in the hospital at the time didn't appease the volatile church-goers, who had just spent the last hour and a half staring, jaws clenched in hatred, at their beloved, purple Man of Nazareth. Incensed shouts ensued: "He's done it before, hasn't he? Bribed public officials to get him off. Look at Zimmer. Look at Fernald! He probably bribed the cops this time, too! He's crazy," they fumed. "He torched his own club for the insurance money."

It was a nasty collection of false accusations, but there was no stopping the fervent crowd.

One will never know how much the Friday verdict in the scandalous porn trial of the Contemporary Arts Center upset those who would make life right for all of us. But suffice to say that a unanimous acquittal was not what the Holy Rollers had in mind. Lock up your daughters, we're living in Sodom. No, it didn't set well that the Mapplethorpe pervert was allowed to peddle his smut and infect the virgin minds of the community. Oh Lord—to hell in a hand basket—here we come. And seeing a purple Jesus, no matter how skillfully painted, catching a smoke, was the spark that set the already smoldering Christian mind to blazing.

An enflamed lynch mob was formed, a large contingent of self-righteous justice seekers. They would forgo the usual brunch at Bob Evans or Perkins to correct this travesty in the way the Good Lord might. The assemblage of God's children proceeded to swoop down upon Stone's house like a plague of black locusts, although in this case they were very much affluent, angry whites. The yard was already doused with gasoline, the door sprayed red, like the blood of Christ, before Old Man Bing could call the cops. As fate would have it (as I often do), two people who knew nothing of the other's existence on the planet were listening to the police scanner at the same time. The first person was none other than our New Age private eye, Parker Floyd, who was already on his way to meet Rose. He arrived on the scene before the first match could be laid to Stoney's yard, but moments too late for the newly replaced door to be saved.

Parker, knowing that he was seriously outnumbered, carrot firmly clenched in his teeth, eased his way through the mob to the front porch. A simple, yet separate act of *good fortune, had diverted Rose from the house. More on that later. Twinkie was awakening across the river in a half-furnished Newport apartment in the clumsy embrace of a certain assistant district attorney.*

Coolly, Parker's eyes assessing every twitch, every movement of every vigilante present, he said to the ringleaders, "This is private property. I think you should leave." *The carrot agreed, for it shook itself up and down in the affirmative with every word that he spoke.*

Angry shouts and hostile retorts filled his ears. "An eye for an eye," *someone shouted.* "We shall smote the infidel." *Smote the infidel? Rumbles and grumbles and all sort of nasty human emotions poured forth from the tyrannical gathering.*

Parker listened to the accusations made against Stoney. Calmly, he replied, "He couldn't have done it. He's in the hospital. Stone didn't spray paint your precious Christ."

The crowd heard his voice but not the words. They heard the sounds but not the message. They were frenzied beyond tolerance. The Golden Rule would be sacrificed for a day's vengeance. Ask forgiveness later. A clever age-old distraction, used since Babylonian times, to keep the flock coming back for more.

"Burn his house down!" *someone shouted.*

Parker gently pushed back his sport coat and thought how reassuring it would be if he only had a revolver in a holster on his hip. He didn't own a gun. He shouted so everyone could hear without mistaking him. "Leave Stone alone. He's innocent. What's wrong with you people? He doesn't deserve this. Rose doesn't deserve this. The man is dying of cancer. Leave him be."

"It's God's will," *a defiant voice called out. The grumbling grew louder, rising to a fever pitch. Not one to allow circumstance to sweep him unwillingly along in its current, Parker stepped close to the pastor, whose paint-soaked hands spoke volumes about his complicity. He casually pulled the carrot from his mouth without anyone noticing and placed it discreetly in the pocket of his sport coat. Then he pressed the stub firmly against the startled pastor's bony flesh as he wrapped his arm around the man's waist.*

"I have a license to carry a weapon," *Parker said in a low confident tone that only the reverend could hear. He pressed the root harder into the minister's flabby abdomen.* "That door's been replaced twice already. I'd just as soon blow a hole in your pious, little ass as fix it a third time."

"Um . . . excuse me folks," *the quaking clergyman addressed the group.* "We've said our peace here. Maybe we *have* acted in haste."

The words barely uttered, three Indian Hill Village patrol cars, sirens and lights blaring, rolled into the yard. In minutes, the congregation was dispersed.

The second person who had heard the police scanner stood away from the crowd, notepad in hand, frantically scribbling her observations of the maniacal mob. As she witnessed the pandemonium, a pleasant thought tickled her. She knew she had caught her big break. She grinned as she thought of the improbable stepping stones destiny had laid before her feet. She had worked as a stringer for the Community Forum for only three weeks, working at every grunge job the paper had, when the reporter assigned to the Impartial Fate case, as it had come to be known in Cincinnati media circles, had suddenly gotten appendicitis. Two weeks after that, she heard the call on the scanner.

A co-op student in the University of Cincinnati's journalism program, she had plopped into the story by what seemed to be sheer accident. But she didn't believe in accidents. She believed in fate. Pure fate. It had always been there for her, guiding her. From Tucson, Arizona, where she was raised, to Stonehenge, where she had the vision, to Cincinnati, Ohio, where the vision led her, it had all happened for a reason. At last, she knew why.

Her round almond eyes, like rich chocolate flecked with bits of tangerine, studied the detective who had stood up to and defused a mob of fifty-four people all by himself. The excitement over, the young reporter edged closer to the handsome detective as he insisted to the cops that charges be filed so that the Stones could be remunerated for damages.

The legal matters dispensed with, only Parker and the young woman remained at the scene.

"Excuse me," she said, timidly. "May I ask you a few questions?"

He squeezed his chubby carrot tight with his back molars as he sized up the young beauty's request. He sniffed the air, catching a faint whiff of beta carotene and sandalwood. "If you can ask them over a burger," he said, his blue eyes locking onto her stunning face. He felt a catch in his throat and the slightest tug in his chest.

She smiled, regaining the self-assurance she'd been given at birth. "Make it a veggie burger and you've got a deal."

"At last," Parker said, "I wondered when the mysterious 'M' would finally reveal herself." Chomp. Chomp. Chomp.

Concurrent with the near riot at the Stone house came the ecumenical diversion that kept Rose from meeting Parker at the homestead. A flat tire. As divine intervention would have it, a sixteen common nail punctured her driver-side rear wheel, rendering her car immobile. One may wonder how a flat tire is good fortune. Most would see it as a sign of continued bad luck. There is no such thing—luck. No, Rose's car troubles were orchestrated for several reasons. One was to spare her the horror and indignation of an insane mob of former friends standing on her front porch, and demanding the head of the man she loves, the man she is devoted to. Another reason for the celestial diversion lay inside Rose's soul itself.

I am confident that most people reading this text believe it to be about Robert Thomas Stone and his hopeful redemption through the graces of the Council of Ancients. It is true that Stoney is a central figure, but Rose, like all humans, has her lessons to learn as well, her price to pay. As I said before, we in the Council do not subscribe to ignorance nor innocence as an excuse. It may seem harsh, but those are the rules.

Rose Stone is a special woman, a dedicated wife stuck with the mistaken conservative 1950s mentality that women are on this Earth to serve men. An advanced form of slavery, to be blunt. Many an alien race has shaken its collective head as they study Earthling habits. Elsewhere in the Cosmos, the female is revered, celebrated as the Mother of all Creation. She is Creation herself. Earthlings had it right until a few thousand years ago, when a patriarchal power play overthrew the prevalent maternal belief system, which honored all life and began persecuting women and subsequently screwed it all up. Humankind has been paying in blood and war since that unfortunate religious coup.

Yet, even though she was raised to serve her man, Rose grew to be a strong, independent woman who got what she wanted by being more clever and more enlightened than those around her. Coy, I believe is the proper description. At the same time, however, social hypnosis being what it is, she was taught to follow. She was indoctrinated, at any early age, not to question her father or her husband or any man. She, like all women of the time, was taught not to question the system, the social institutions, the government, the Church. Let them lead you—they know best. Again, ignorance is not an excuse.

Her transformation, albeit on a more subtle level, began with the great fire at the Cosmic Club. Her world began to crumble around her. For years she had endured the heartache of Stoney's unexplained disappearances, the rumors of his infidelities, the lopsided manner in which their marriage was acted out. She did as all good women of the time did: she smiled through the pain and found comfort by using coercion and persuasion to get what she wanted, all the while wording things so that Stoney believed he was making the decisions. But Rose, even having discovered an amicable balance in order to tolerate being considered a less-than-equal partner, lost a tiny sliver of her soul each time she acquiesced.

Her best method for patching up the broken dream of her life was the Church. There was solace there. Shelter. Through the years, she had become a woman of ritual. When she was shunned by the very church she had done so much to be a part of, the house of worship she gave her energy to, she was caught unaware, unprotected, unsure.

She was caught between two worlds: the world of religion, with its symbols and rituals and control, which offered a pattern of consistent comfort, and the world of spirit, where the individual is accountable for his own actions, his own salvation, his own happiness. Her ego was frozen even as her soul (with prodding from the Council) forced her to reconsider everything she believed.

She had tried to raise her family well. A son whom she had taught to love and respect all life, who then betrayed her years of example by betraying his father at the first—well, maybe sixth or seventh—sign of adversity. She now saw him as greedy and self-serving. She thought of Twinkie, who she adored and doted over, the daughter she had long talks with, encouraging her not to make the same mistakes as she had, to be more independent, stronger, more assertive. And look at Twinkie now: a quivering mess of indecision, more dependent than any woman of the fifties.

And then, of course, there was her husband. The enigma. The mysterious person who seemed to disappear sporadically every few years. Sometimes for a few days, often longer. Rose sometimes felt as though her husband was a stranger in her bed. But she loved him, despite his many faults. He was the man she had forgiven again and again, the man she stood by through severe trials and tribulations. Still, her faith couldn't keep the problems from coming faster and more serious than the Book of Revelation. First, the strange disappearances, then the affairs, then the Zimmer and Fernald indictments, the protests, the looming bankruptcy, then the C.C. fire, more indictments, a bizarre tale about a book with a conscience, an unbelievable charter that he is to save the world by writing a manuscript, and now cancer.

As she stood numb in the street, the hubcap lying in the grass by the curb, a cool autumn breeze chilling her feet, a heavy lug wrench in hand, the fresh knowledge that there was no jack in the trunk, it was understandable that Rose would begin to cry. Her hand went limp and she dropped the lug wrench onto the gritty roadway. She sat wearily on the curb, her head in her hands, tears staining her dress as she questioned what she had done to deserve so much pain. It had all accumulated. Too much rain in too small a stream.

Her tears flowed. Maybe crying would release the pain she felt, the unstated bitterness, the feelings that she had been forced to swallow since her self-esteem had been systematically stripped from her in her early teens by teachers and preachers and parents who believed that Eve came from Adam's rib, and, therefore, a woman was subservient to man.

She sobbed and considered leaving R.T. She could take a cab to the airport, buy a ticket to St. Thomas, meet a young gigolo named Ramone, and recapture the freedom subjugated for sixty lost years.

The kids don't need me, she thought. They don't care anyway. R.T. doesn't need me, not really, she rationalized. He can hire a maid. Twinkie can help him. I need to get away. I need to run from here and find myself.

"I'm lost, dear Lord," *she said, her knees drawn up to her face.* "I'm so lost."

At that moment, good fortune smiled upon her as the angelic choir of the Unity Center of Cincinnati, the sanctuary in front of which her tire had flattened, filled her desperate ears.

That Rose and Stoney and Parker and the rest of humanity need to find themselves is important, but it is not the reason for this documentary. High from our perch on Shanidar, we have watched silently as the human species has inflicted travesty after travesty upon itself and the Earth. To that end, to the end that is all ends, to the end that some misguided souls pray for, we have sent two souls to quell the heartache. Two souls, among others, to live among you. Two souls to deliver a clear message to the world, a message so clear and bright and powerful that it cannot be ignored.

Some may question, as we actively encourage all creatures to do, why this is all necessary. Dear friends, inhabitants, Earthlings, visitors, specs of dust, blips on the radar screen of life, it is not you that we are here to save. It is the Earth. The Mother Herself. The true Goddess you should worship. The giver of all life. The provider. The nurturer. The breast of humanity. The milk of sustenance. It is she that we seek to cure, for she is sick.

One should see our benevolence as though the Council of Ancients were physicians and the Earth Mother the patient approaching a terminal condition. As such, we must treat the disease, which is humankind. If we cannot treat the disease (humanity) naturally, send it into remission through the use of knowledge, intuition, soul-intervention, herbs, kindness, love, positive energy, and a plethora of other gentle treatments, then we, as the guardians of the Earth, must perform radical surgery.

Daniel Oliver Gilday and Yvonne Allison Leslie Pippin and their light-being counterparts are the last ditch antibiotics before the operation. Should humanity fail to respond to their therapy, grave and painful slices of it will have to be removed. Will it be the end of the Earth as some pray for in their right-wing, neo-fundamentalist vigils? No. Will it be the end of life as you know it? Perhaps.

But enough doom and gloom. It need not be that way at all. It is our desire, our grand plan, as it were, to salvage this mess with a minimum amount of carnage. To do

this, the story must be told. As such, I shall now return you to the main tale, the lives of Danny and Allison. For the sake of consistency, I will perform Stone's task as his ghost writer, his shadow, until such time as Mr. Stone feels he is able to return to his scribner's duty. Henceforth, the font on these pages, even though in my hand, shall revert from italic to normal, an act I am sure publisher and reader alike will find more amenable. That is to say, I shall write The Journals *in his absence, but Stone shall get full credit for its accomplishment. This is, my research reveals, a common practice among movie stars, politicians, and other celebrities who have no real talent but an immense vanity to see their names in print. This, I assure you from the highest authority, is not the case with Robert Thomas Stone. He is much more a hero than he lets on.*

Chapter 33

Over a liver dinner slathered in sautéed onions and sour creamed mashed potatoes, Danny and Patrick argued about the nation's nuclear infrastructure on the night of February 1, 1982. Danny had commented on the day's news of one hundred seventy protesters being arrested at the Lawrence Livermore research laboratory. He was almost fourteen and had become a formidable conversationalist. The talking light had taught him to always argue one's point with facts, not rhetoric, something American politicians ought to try. This gives one a decided strategic advantage, for truth wins out over emotion most often.

When he presented the stark reality that three nuclear weapons facilities were located within fifty miles of Cincinnati, everyone stopped eating to listen. When our young protégé informed his audience that the good residents of Cincinnati had the fifth highest cancer rate in the country, Cal and Cara pushed their plates away. Only Patrick, whose temper and conceit wouldn't allow him to give in so easily, decided to defend the U.S. nuclear program by accusing Danny's sources as being leftist hippie propaganda.

"*Time. Newsweek. The Cincinnati Enquirer.* Those aren't leftist rags, Father."

A rocket's red glare burst from Patrick's face at his smart-aleck son. When Danny mistakenly spoke about the K-65 containment silos BGI was building at Fernald, every corpuscle in Patrick's face was at Def Con One. The bombs were bursting in air. "That's classified information," Patrick warned. "What if the Department of Defense found out you were reading my files?"

"Electrocution?" Danny said, eliciting a nervous chuckle from Cal and Cara.

Patrick didn't respond. He just stabbed at the leathery beef organ that lay like a muddy Florsheim on the plate among onion shoestrings. "How long can those silos last, Father? Two hundred years? Three hundred? Plutonium is radioactive for twenty-four thousand years."

"We'll be dead and gone by then," Patrick said as he knifed at the liver. "It won't matter."

"It might matter to my kids."

"And mine," Cal said.

"And our great grandchildren," Cara offered.

Patrick's cutlery clattered on his plate as he threw his hands up in defiance, exasperated that he was being attacked for being a patriotic American. Oh, say can you see that banner yet wave? "Look," he seethed, "we have to be prepared for a Soviet attack."

"We have enough weapons to blow up the planet twenty-nine thousand times," said Danny. "Besides, the Soviets are too busy standing in line for bread and milk to attack us. They can't even feed themselves."

Patrick rose angrily from the table. This was liver night after all, so it had to end badly, according to Danny's well-proven dinner hypothesis. "The government knows what it's doing," Patrick said as he tossed his cloth napkin into the middle of the brown ooze on his plate. "You're going to have a tough life, Daniel, with these radical ideas of yours. It's America—love it or leave it, pal!"

He stalked from the room, leaving Danny to shake his head about people who defend their positions with bumper-sticker logic. Is this all our business leaders and our parents have to offer? he thought. Red-neck advice lifted from the chrome rear end of a car? Is this the best the land of the free and the home of the brave can do?

A week later, he was much more grateful to his father for pulling him out of the Young Artists program shepherded by the closet pedophile, Drew Winthrop. Danny didn't have proof, but he had a strong enough tingling in his spine that told him Winthrop had more than art on his mind when it came to Danny. One comment to Patrick, homophobic as he was, and Danny was out of the program. Of considerably more benefit to him was the simultaneous canceling of the Mamet exhibit, Masters— Young and Old. It could have been a major opportunity for him, but he chose to see it as a means of eluding arrest for forgery. Once his Mamets were compared to the genuines, he reasoned, a minimal amount of investigation would lead to him. He was bound to get busted. He shrugged off the loss of the exhibit. His interest in painting was beginning to wane anyway as he pursued other endeavors, such as writing, guitar, and Janis, the healthy and promiscuous girl across the way.

A blustery, cold late-February ushered in a new, favorite party spot for the quartet of Danny, Cal, Gram, and Janis. The wind was too wild for a toking party on the milkhouse roof, which had been a good spring-summer-fall hangout, and they could too easily be caught by Gram's father, Joshua, who often worked late cleaning his tools. So they repaired to the small cemetery two hundred yards from the house. They passed a joint. A giggly buzz occupied everyone as they stood among the headstones arranged in a ten-by-ten row of markers inside the forgotten graveyard. Danny was drawn to a large, marble obelisk tombstone, which rose from the ground. Captain Matthew Crittenden died during the Civil War, October 12, 1862. Carved upon the marble was an open book, which everyone concluded must have been a Bible, people being so religious back then and all.

After much marijuana and alcohol, they decided their new stomping ground needed a proper name. A few minutes of inebriated discussion led to the name, "The Stones," in honor of the tombstones which poked their heads from the earth and to commemorate the main purpose of their being there—to get stoned. The infamous British rock 'n' roll band had no weight in the decision.

It was a clear night bright with stars glittering like an expensive necklace on the neck of Aphrodite. Gram had just presented his latest theory, which was that each star was assigned to a specific person on Earth. Cal scoffed at it, but Danny vaguely recalled a similar thought from his demons-of-dimensia coma-dream.

"If we do have a star," Danny said, holding Janis by the waist as he pointed to the sky, "That's mine. Sirius, the dog star."

A drunken Cal raised his head to the sky, as if to bark, but took a swig of beer instead. With liquid hops dripping down his chin, he said, "Mine's Signus, the swan star."

Two weeks later, Gram used Danny's ire over the Environmental Protection Agency's permitting companies to dump toxic waste to advance his new theory that mankind's run on the planet is limited. In his view, every species has its day. Dinosaurs, plants, trees, all of them. Over the vast continuum of thirty-five billion years the planet has seen its share of dominating species. Man, Gram philosophized, is simply the latest in a line of kings. He will die by his own violence. His reign will end. For a reason that he couldn't entirely understand, Danny liked that thought.

Danny was elated to receive an Irish-setter puppy for his fourteenth birthday. A new best friend to lope through the fields of Kentucky with. Never one to miss an opportunity at sarcasm, he named the dog Roentgen after the nuclear definition. He told his father, Patrick, who had been in Arizona and missed his birthday, that Roentgen was Slavic for Rin Tin Tin.

The night of his birthday, with the floppy rust-colored puppy, guitar and telescope at his side, Danny sat on the milkhouse roof looking for the space shuttle Columbia. He held the tube up to Roentgen's eye, but the young pup was scarcely interested. Danny's interest in all things related to space had been intense since his Council of Ancients episode in Shanidar. He was less and less convinced of the detail, but he wanted to believe the dream.

A few days later, Cal showed Danny how to fool automatic teller machines into giving him as much money as he wanted. The tricky part was to get the ATM to give him the money from other people's accounts. It was a simple programming challenge, however, that Cal solved shortly. Oh, what a talented boy can do with his Apple computer. In the interest of the banking industry and the world economy, I shall not divulge the technical aspects of his achievement in this text. Danny was intrigued with the concept of endless piles of cash to spend but made Cal promise never to use the program. Cal hemmed and hawed before finally agreeing, but not without quipping, "Look who's lecturing me, the biggest criminal in northern Kentucky—Daniel Oliver Gilday. The Forger."

The morning of May 9 was bright and crunchy, like a box of corn flakes before the nefarious preservative, BHT, has had to do its work. The last frost of the spring disappeared into the grass like cold milk run-off into the bottom of the cereal bowl. Danny sat in the back seat of his father's car, Gram beside him. He nervously flicked the ashtray up and down, careful not to let it snap so that Patrick wouldn't get annoyed. Not that he wasn't already annoyed at Gram's renditions of Johnny Rivers' "Secret Agent Man."

Danny felt like expired buttermilk was churning in his stomach. Why did Father insist on proving his point? Visiting the Fernald plant wasn't going to change a thing. He stared out the window at the passing fields. The tiniest snippets of green, shy vegetation, stretched their leafy arms from the soil as if to surrender to old man winter, who had hightailed it back to the Arctic Circle. Brown, furrowed strips like perfectly sown mole tracks lined the fields. Segregated from the crops by a rusted wire fence, black spotted cows, milkers, their mechanical suckling done for the morning, ate lazily around troughs of grain put out early by hard-working farmers. America the beautiful.

Gram sung his song quietly to himself over and over. It was an inside joke, singing that tune, one that only he and Danny and Cal understood. Danny wished he hadn't challenged his father now by constantly chiding him at the dinner table with facts about the dangers of nuclear technology. He wished Patrick didn't have to prove himself right, as Gram fiddled with the slimline camera concealed under two layers of shirts. He watched Gram's wide, black eyes radiate excitement. Gram had begged Patrick Gilday to let him come along, and Patrick finally caved after Gram told him how impressed he was by the success of BGI. Ego gets to Father every time, Danny thought.

"Did anyone know that Marie Curie died of leukemia on July 4, 1934? One of the first victims of radiation exposure," Danny said, hoping to calm himself.

Patrick's forehead vein twitched momentarily, but he said nothing. Cal popped a grand bubble that could have carried Phineas Fogg around the world in 80 days. Gram sang.

Danny was uneasy for two reasons. First was the visit to a radioactive nuclear facility with a horrible thirty-year record of safety violations and toxic emissions. No Cincinnatian in their right mind would voluntarily visit the mephitic sight. Second, and just a quark shy of first, he was uneasy about Gram's plan to breach national security and illegally photograph the place. Danny was sure they were going to be busted by the Department of Energy and sent to prison as communist spies, tools of the proletariat. He had also concluded that Gram loved the thrill of the unknown, the possibility of danger. He must get some sort of high energy charge out of breaking rules.

Cal didn't share Danny's reservations as he sat in the front seat, working a wad of bubblegum he had stolen from a convenience store on Friday. He had simply shrugged when Patrick told him he was required to come along. Both boys were to learn this lesson. Cal liked being with his father, abusive as he was. At least it was attention, and Cal needed large doses of that.

The Gilday Cadillac hurtled onward like a land-based B-52 carrying a payload to its target. The car had the physical audacity of a bloated pickle. A cucumber formulated into an automobile. A kosher dill on wheels. An expensive, albeit vegetarian, symbol of Patrick's success. Danny called it the green marauder.

Patrick gripped the wheel as he wound around curves and up hillocks and down into small valleys past the little burg of Colerain, where the Gildays used to live. The car turned off the Colerain exit but took a right up Route 27 instead of a left toward their old home. Danny had hoped his father would change his mind and drive through the neighborhood where he grew up, but Patrick had no time for sentimentality; he was out to teach his rebellious, leftist son a thing or two about the might of the American Military-Industrial complex. Eisenhower had warned the country about it, but nobody listened as America overspent its means building elaborate weapons systems it didn't need.

The dill-colored warhead sped onward toward Ross as Gram continued his private serenade. Danny was convinced of impending doom. Cal blew bubbles without care. Patrick held his anger at Gram in check. Danny was surprised by Patrick's restraint. Did sucking up to him about his biz work that well? he asked himself. If so, I have to try it.

"Thar she blows!" Cal hollered in his best Captain Ahab voice.

Danny's buttermilk stomach curdled cottage cheese as he thought of black-suited Department of Energy types in impenetrable no-gamma-rays-allowed sunglasses grilling Gram and him for hours until they cracked.

"God, this place is huge," Cal exclaimed.

Danny and Gram inched up on the edge of their seats. The ominous factory was a massive collection of gray tin buildings and sheds and sludge ponds and smoke vents swabbed with innocuous looking cotton balls of smoke along the chafed baby bottom of the soiled sky.

"Over a thousand acres of U.S. industrial power," Patrick crowed.

"Geez and crackers, what's that over there?" Danny pointed as the car approached the guardhouse. "Look at all those barrels. There's jillions of them." Three hundred feet to their right, behind a chainlink fence topped with barbed wire, were 42,612 rusting, leaking, and seeping forty-eight gallon barrels of contaminated, radioactive waste. They were loosely stacked four high, some tipped over like a grocer's shelves after a tornado, some dented like canned goods. The boys were in awe of the sheer volume of the barrels. What they didn't know was that the stack in their immediate view was the tip of the proverbial iceberg. A half-million barrels of thorium, tributyl phosphate, diamylamylphophonate, 1,1,1-trichloroethane, xylene, flyash, spent lime sludge, and a hundred combinations of unheard of hazardous radionuclides were stored in various states of leaking disarray at the abused nuclear facility.

"Doesn't seem to bother the cows any," Cal said as a group of Jerseys lazily ate just outside the fence line.

"Things aren't always what they seem." Gram stopped singing long enough to egg Danny on. "You think those cows are radioactive?"

Patrick did his best to act like he hadn't heard the comment.

"They're probably hot," Danny said, his stomach fermenting to sour cream. The corn flake morning was drenched in the acid bath of his stomach. This day spelled doom for him. He could feel it like an intestinal cancer in his wrenched gut. He could feel it in his bones, as if the uranium-238 had already invaded his marrow.

"Do you think their milk is hot, too?" Gram asked. Patrick's face turned a lovely shade of iodine. "Do you suppose they ship their glow juice all over the city and people are drinking radioactive milk without knowing it?"

"That's enough, boys," Patrick ordered. The world's only pickle-jet car pulled to the gate.

The security man, whose worn name tag announced him as Rusty, reminded Danny of George C. Scott playing General Patton. "Field trip today, Mr. Gilday?" the guard asked, revealing a missing incisor.

"Yep, bringing the boys up to see the might of the nuclear program."

"They almost got the first silo reinforced," Rusty said. He bent down to peer into the car. "Stone's crew has been working on it all week." The guard handed plastic visitors badges to Gilday. "Clip these to your collars, boys," Rusty said. He shuffled in four more badges like he was dealing solitaire in a lonesome Quonset hut. "Better put these on, too." He patted his own badge. "Radiation film," he explained. "Gives you the heads-up if you've been exposed."

Danny swallowed hard, certain a tumor had already formed in his throat. He looked away toward the ignorant cows chewing their ionized cud as if it was the purest pasture in the heartland. Maybe, he thought to himself, if I act like I don't really know Gram I won't be thrown into handcuffs and shackles when he gets busted.

Patrick thanked Rusty and pulled away from the guard shack. The tumor in Danny's throat refused to go into remission. The Kraft World-of-Cheese experiment in his stomach was dying to show itself to the occupants of the car but the tumor, fortunately, blocked its way. The Cadillac, seeming more and more like a detonator for a hydrogen bomb of some devastation, drove slowly down the road.

Danny tried to protest. "Father, it's not safe. I want to go home."

Patrick was in no mood. The vein in his forehead swelled slightly. They were at Fernald now—there was no turning back. "It's perfectly safe. Grow up. Be a man."

"Far out," Cal said as he examined his radiation badge. "High-tech, baby!"

They drove past the gray dilapidated buildings that lined D Street like toothless, World War II veterans stuffed into dress uniforms for the Memorial Day parade. Patrick bragged as if he had personally designed the plant and invented nuclear weapons himself. No help from Edward Teller and Robert Oppenheimer. No assist from Einstein, who, for the record, was opposed to nuclear weapons. Einstein had counseled Roosevelt and Truman on the matter to no avail.

The patriotic pickle from Detroit motored past the Slag Recycling Plant, Metal Fabs, Plant 9 and Plant 5, then took a left just beyond the Decontamination Building, past thousands and thousands of additional barrels teeming with low level radiation. Patrick talked and pointed and generally annoyed Danny as Gram ferociously took pictures, taking care to cough with each click of the camera.

"You better get that cold looked after, Gram," Patrick said as the boys suppressed snickers.

The car turned left down B Street. Patrick prattled on about his knowledge of Fernald and his access to security areas. They passed the Boiler Plant, Water Plant, Chemical Warehouse, Plant 7, then First Street, and finally the Administration Building, where the boys eventually found themselves standing in a musty, dimly-lit business office filled with rows of government issue desks buried under stacks of documents. A bureaucrat's dream vacation.

Patrick introduced the boys to Jerry Spangler. Spangler's eyes were set wide apart, behind thick glasses on a broad, bulbous nose with red variegated veins that had sniffed its share of liquor fumes. Usually four vodka screwdrivers found their way down his throat to the paunch in his belly every evening. On weekends, the alcohol began flowing at 5:30 Friday evening, before dinner, and didn't subside until 9 p.m. Sunday night. Two bottles of Smirnoff to ease his conscience. Spangler hadn't always been a drinker, but he soon started once he was transferred to Fernald by the Department of Energy in 1974.

Their alcoholic host wore a short-sleeve shirt, dingy white from years of perspiration and laundry, the breast pocket overrun by a half-dozen, multi-colored marking pens. Danny guessed Mr. Spangler to be an engineer or scientist. His eyes had that "look," the look Danny had come to recognize, thanks to excellent "talking light" tutoring from the Council: the intelligence look, identified by the odd juxtaposition of cheek bones and eye sockets—like two great tectonic plates under the skin's surface— came together with such force that a facial ridge jutted out high on his cheeks, leaving its geological mark. It was as if the brain needed the extra room to compute at a higher intellectual level. The distinct "genius bone-structure," as Danny called it, coupled with a bad haircut, never exactly combed, shouted *geek*. That is not to say that Jerry Spangler, nor any scientific sort, was not a handsome person. In his book-wormish way, he was—as many like him are. But they do fit a different, if not unique, mold.

The group stood in the cavernous room as Patrick and Spangler made small talk designed to show off their knowledge and authority in front of the boys. Danny, desperate to dislodge the now throbbing tumor in his throat, and hoping to dilute what felt like a coagulated sour cheese mass in his stomach, stepped toward the drinking fountain. An arch of cool water presented itself like a clear rainbow before splashing without sound into the stainless-steel basin. He loved drinking-fountain water. It tasted purer to him. Sweeter. Better. He leaned over to drown his fears. He opened his mouth and puckered his lips, as if to kiss the gentle flow.

"Don't!" Spangler shouted suddenly, pulling him by the forearm from the fountain.

"What the . . . why not?"

Mr. Spangler, primrose cheeks now matching his variegated nose, tried unsuccessfully to compose himself. "It's um . . . uh . . . we have a heavy iron taste in the water here. You know, the plant was built in the fifties, deposits build up. I have some better water in my office." He searched for words. "It's a real treat. Would you, um, like some?" He motioned toward the office. Spangler wasn't a good liar, which is why he always lost a wad of dough in his monthly poker game.

"Jerry," Patrick said. "I have a couple of private business matters to discuss. Can we talk in your office?"

"Sure, yeah, you bet, Pat."

The two stepped into the office and closed the door. It didn't take long for Patrick's hair trigger defense to take charge. He had Spangler in his sights. "Jesus Christ, Jerry, what the hell's the matter with the water?"

Cal and Gram had their ears to the door. Danny, knowing he'd get a full report of the conversation later, stepped to the water fountain. He pressed the lever again.

"Give it to me straight, Jerry," Gilday insisted. "What's wrong with the water?"

Spangler hesitated. Gilday was having none of it. Mr. Spangler wasn't good at lying, a terrible liability as senior manager of a top-secret weapons facility, but he was even less talented at telling the truth. Instead, he had greased his conscience over the last sixteen years with large and frequent quantities of denial and alcohol.

"Tell me."

"It has a high contamination risk factor."

"How high?"

Spangler shuffled his feet, pushed his thick glasses up against the bridge of his nose like safety goggles. "A hundred and two picocuries."

Danny, oblivious to the conversation, followed a hunch and performed his own science experiment. He unclipped the radiation badge from his shirt and held it carefully under the water so that not a single drop touched his skin.

"What the hell are you saying?" said Gilday.

"The water is unsafe. It's way off the scale."

"Jesus H. Christ," Gilday whispered. "What's going on up here?"

"Over thirty years of nuclear mismanagement. That's what's going on."

Gram and Cal stared at each other. Gram pulled back from the door, and, like a good reporter with a nose for news, took a picture of the water fountain.

"Holy shit," Cal said. "Danny, you're right. They're killing us!"

"Man-oh-man," Gram said. "Back at Los Alamos, when I worked on the Manhattan Project, we didn't have levels this high."

"Shut up, Gram," Danny said. He examined the radiation badge. "Look at this!" He involuntarily dropped the badge. "It's hot!"

In the office, where a not-so-private conversation was going on, Spangler said, "The whole place is radioactive. Some areas are more dangerous than others. This building is okay, except for the water."

"Damn, Jerry, how can you work here?" Patrick asked.

"I have a wife and four kids, I don't have a choice."

"It's killing you, Jerry. This is between you and me, okay? We won't tell the boys."

Cal quickly jumped back from the door. Gram stashed the camera inside his shirt.

The door opened before Danny could kick the radiation badge under cover. The three boys stared around, doing their best to act as if they didn't know a thing.

"What's this?" Spangler said as he bent down and picked up the breached radiation badge. His face went white. His face drew tight, as if the two tectonic plates were about to shift. "It's hot. Did you boys touch anything else?"

Patrick was deeply concerned. "Jesus," he said. "Did any get on you?"

"No," Danny replied.

"We'd better go," Patrick said in a strained voice.

Spangler nodded and lead the visitors to the parking lot. Except for nervous chatter between the two adults, attempting to minimize the gravity of the situation, no one spoke much. It was difficult to determine who was trying to convince whom that everything was fine, Gilday or Spangler. The tension decreased somewhat once the Gildays and Gram were safely inside the gherkin Cadillac. Still, no one spoke. Patrick Gilday, his cranial vein pulsing in twisting and turning curves like a winding Grand Prix course, drove outside the confines of the mammoth thousand acre complex. They moved past the cows, the fields of recently planted crops, the farmers with their roadside stands of produce. Each occupant, with the exception of Patrick, who was considering other matters, looked at the cows and the fields and the farmers and the produce and knew that it was all contaminated with radioactive dust spewed from the plant over the course of nearly four decades. Assured by the Department of Energy that there was no health risk, the residents in the placid countryside surrounding Fernald mistakenly believed they were safe.

Danny and Cal and Gram, each in their own minds, each in their own way, asked themselves if the good people of Fernald, Ross, New Haven, Oxford, Colerain, and Cincinnati in general, knew they were dying from a government nuclear program gone mad. In the words of a wise light-being: Universal truth being what it is, ignorance is no excuse. Cold War rhetoric was costing thousands of Americans across the country their lives. There was a war being waged all right—against its own citizens. They should have asked more questions.

Patrick wasn't thinking of cows and livestock and nuclear cucumbers soon to be made into plutonium pickles. He wasn't considering the cancerous fate of the innocent victims of a menacing government boondoggle. He wasn't thinking of Jerry Spangler and his wife and four kids. He wasn't thinking of a half-million barrels of toxic, hazardous waste. He was thinking of Danny. He considered how his son could have taken one sip of water, one ionized sip, and thought nothing of it. Then, years later, as his kidneys failed or his lungs became lined with lesions, the family would be heartsick and the doctors would be baffled, and no one would realize that years before he had taken a fateful drink that caused his illness. No one would ever suspect, no one would ever find the cause.

A scowl of self-deprecating contempt mushroomed on Patrick's face. A mile outside the plant on route 128, his hands shaking, Patrick pulled to the berm. With misty eyes, he turned to face Danny. The large water tower from Fernald jutted up like a giant warhead in the distance just beyond Patrick's head. His throat developed an anxiety mass of its own as he said, "I'm sorry, son. I shouldn't have let my need to be right put you and the other boys in jeopardy." The strong man's lips quivered. "I'm sorry."

Danny thought his father, whom he had never seen express any real emotion except anger, was going to cry. "It's okay, Father," the boy said. "Nobody got hurt. And it *was* educational."

Relieved that Danny wasn't harboring any animosity about the incident, Patrick softened. "We passed a Creamy Whip on the way up. Would you guys like an ice cream?"

It was agreed, and soon the three youths were sitting at a picnic table, freaking-out in alarmed whispers about Danny's near-death experience as Patrick stood in line. It was a spring fresh day again, only now the BHT was forced to work its artificial magic on the corn flake day to keep it that way. The intensity of their morning had put a stoic damper on their normally impetuous shenanigans. Yes, the BHT was called into the cereal bowl of life to keep the teenagers' spirits up. Like any *decent* processed breakfast food additive, BHT didn't want to take chances and fortified its efforts by calling in BHA and Sodium Benzoate to ensure the American way of life was preserved.

Danny sat in the sun of southwestern Ohio and stared across the street at a mother happily pushing her little boy on a swing in the side yard. The child, who looked about five years of age, wore a Cincinnati Reds ball cap, which Danny found strange, given the warmth of the morning. The sun had just peaked past noon. The boy was pale, perhaps from the long winter, Danny thought.

"Higher, Mommy, higher!" the child yelled as he swung in delight. They laughed and laughed together, oblivious to the world around them, unaware that Danny was watching through the gap between Cal and Gram sitting opposite him, their backs to the street. "Higher, Mommy, higher," he giggled.

Danny laughed. This is what life is about. Forget all that nuclear business.

Another great, exhausting push from his mom and up he went. Suddenly, the cap was caught by a slight gust of spring breeze and fell to the ground. Danny turned away.

"Here's your ice cream, Daniel," Patrick said, grateful to put his Fernald mistake behind him.

"No thanks, Father," Danny said, his imaginary throat tumor now at Stage IV. He pointed across the street. "That could have been us." Cal and Gram turned. Patrick's face turned as white as the melting cone of vanilla swirl in his hand.

They all stared at the scarred boy, his bald head splotched red with sores. His eyes were ringed by charcoal circles, his skin pale as the white smoke that belched from the stacks of the great plant just two miles away. The child, still laughing with his mom, who had run to retrieve the hat, looked terminally ill. To Danny, the boy seemed to age by the second, becoming more and more frail, more susceptible to disease, weakened by each breath.

They gawked, unconscious of their action, numbed by the sight, paralyzed by the possibility that this child's life would soon end. They were reminded with a sharp smack of reality just how close they had come to being exposed. In the brief moments that they stood looking at the unfortunate child, the four of them wondered how this could happen to such an innocent.

The answer was simple. Government policy. The harmless puffs emitted from the thirty-eight vents at the Feed Materials Production Center delivered a deadly supply of airborne particulates to an unsuspecting, trustful citizenry. Invisible soot had rained down on their homes from illegal atmospheric emissions for decades. Each night, more atomic rain would fall, more radioactive waste would be dumped into the river. Even more would seep into the ground wells used by so many of the residents.

"Jesus," Patrick said weakly. He tossed all the cones in the trash. "Get in the car, boys."

He peeled out of the gravel parking lot with a crazed look on his face. The car barreled down the single-lane highway. He pressed the gas, accelerating through straight-aways. He flew past slower cars as if they stood still. He drove faster. Away from Fernald. He took curves with abandon, splaying grit from the berm in all directions. He swerved around cars, crossing double yellow lines. The green marauder roared on. Patrick was trying to escape, trying to beat the invisible cloud of gamma rays, alpha and beta particles that he was sure was after them. Onward he sped, the car barely under his control. He would beat the cloud. Out-run it. Another straight-away and he floored the pedal. The car heaved its mighty engine and surged even faster. It was the fastest pickle in this part of the state.

Danny, more in fear for his immediate life than the potential disease which could inflict him later from an unseen source, finally said, "You know, Father, we lived four miles from Fernald for over fourteen years. If it was going to get us, it already has."

As if the truest words ever spoken had reached his ears, Patrick lightened up on the accelerator.

"Yeah," Cal said. "It's a good thing we have our own graveyard. We're goners."

Danny glared at him.

"Yeah," Gram joined in. "We've probably already been saturated. We're nuclear toast. Radioactive marshmallows. Fission bait. Ionized—"

"Gram!" Patrick said.

"Yes, Mr. Gilday?"

Patrick chuckled. "We're atomic corn flakes."

Everyone laughed. Humor was the only vehicle to sanity. They had to laugh, or else cry. And if they started to cry they might not ever stop. So they laughed. The occupants of the brine-colored Cadillac told one nuclear pun after another. They laughed until it hurt. They laughed so hard, tears came to their eyes. They laughed until they couldn't laugh anymore. They laughed until they realized . . . it wasn't funny at all.

The near miss at Fernald affected each of the participants differently. Patrick installed an elaborate water-purification system at Mulciber and BGI to insure he and his family weren't being poisoned. A wise move for those who can afford it. He also began sending his top manager to the Fernald job to minimize his own personal risk. Calvin shrugged the whole thing off but drank more heavily as an excuse. Gram sent his clandestine negatives to St. Louis for processing. He chose a photo lab in Missouri as a precaution against getting busted by a nosy local technician who might notice the photographs were of a top-secret military program and turn him in. He anxiously awaited their return. Danny began studying nuclear science and the industry. He was now anti-nuke all the way. The more he learned, the more militant he became. He deposited environmental material on the desk in his father's den with diligence, often stopping to straighten a Mamet, telling himself someday he needed to make the forgeries right. The Mamets, which Danny had never particularly liked (he considered them boorish and immature) began to garner his appreciation for their style.

The incident caused him to examine his life more closely. It taught him to treasure it more, to take full advantage of the days and live life to the fullest. Not too dissimilar an approach used by some who find themselves facing cancer. He reviewed his letters from Allison and began thinking of her regularly. He was secretly doing time at various make-out spots with Janis, the pubescent flame from across the street. Janis preferred the Stones; casually mentioning it turned her on for some reason. "Cycle of life" may have been the words she uttered in the guttural throes of ecstasy. Danny had been warned by Janis' mother to stay away, a request which only served to motivate him to conquer and explore every inch of Janis' body. Alas, as our Earth-bound star locked lips and fondled and caressed Janis, he often found himself thinking of Allison. Oh, the sweet complications of love and lust.

Early June found Danny in conflict with Gram over the sanctity of the dead. Our hero was growing into maturity, and he had grown into his ego faster than common decency. Since all heroes are flawed, except for the shamelessly perfect revisionist idols found in history books, his indiscretions are to be understood. Cal, Gram, Janis, and

Danny were celebrating the recently completed facelift of the Stones. Patrick Gilday had ordered Joshua to work on it at the beginning of spring. He did an admirable job. The headstones were righted and properly groomed. The dirt path leading to the Stones had been widened and blacktopped. A fence had been placed around the graveyard to mark its somber purpose.

The night of the aforementioned scuffle found Danny hammered. He could not hold his liquor and felt rather bold. When he proceeded to relieve himself upon the headstone of Mrs. Hobbins, Gram let him know it would anger the gods.

Danny flippantly slurred, "Piss on the gods. They won't harm me. I've got a star in my hip pocket."

But it is always best not to tempt the celestial deities.

Strained as their relationship was, Danny and Patrick did share some common ground. Perhaps the Fernald incident brought them closer together. When a man, no matter his faults, realizes that his son had a brush with death, it changes him. Perhaps Danny's persistence—his leaving anti-nuke literature on his father's desk, his adamant position—was bringing Patrick slowly away from the far right toward the center.

The evening news of June 12, 1982 contributed as well. The house smelled of pork chops frying in the skillet. The whirl of the mixer turning the potatoes to mash competed with the news. Tiny pixels of electricity flickered on the TV screen. "Cara," an overbearing Patrick called. "We're trying to watch the news."

Danny thought his mom could never please his father. Patrick expected dinner on the table at a certain time. If it wasn't, there was hell to pay. Yet Patrick didn't want her using tools that might interrupt his information fix on Channel 5. Did he expect her to mash them by hand?

The usual stuff was reported—murder, embezzlement, a natural disaster somewhere, but then . . . a protest of eight hundred thousand people in New York City against nuclear weapons. Danny scooted to the edge of his chair. Patrick swiped a tired hand across his face, knowing his son was about to begin a lecture. In a preemptive strike, he said, "Don't these people realize that our nuclear arms are the only deterrent to Soviet aggression?"

"Maybe they think there's a better way," Danny said. It was pork-chop night, so he knew Patrick's vein would remain constricted beneath the skin of its forehead.

"There are tens of thousands of productive jobs in the nuclear industry. Lots of hard-working people fighting in the trenches of the Cold War."

"That's pretty dramatic, Father. The people working in the nuclear facilities do it because it's a job. It pays well. If they're patriotic about it, it's only to justify the risk they take." On the TV, a reporter interviewed a protester dressed in a suit and tie. A businessman.

"How can you say that?" Patrick raised an eyebrow without looking away from the TV.

"You're building K-65 silos because you're patriotic, not because you're making a nice profit, right?"

As he stared like an automaton at the screen, Patrick considered Danny's point. The protest-march story went off. "In local news," the broadcaster said. "A high speed car crash left two people dead near Ross, Ohio this afternoon." Pictures of twisted carnage, a body covered in a sheet being loaded into an ambulance, an interview with the local sheriff.

"Besides," Danny said, without acknowledging the crash. "Just because something is good for the country doesn't mean it doesn't have problems that should be fixed. Look at Fernald. I almost drank contaminated water."

Patrick grimaced. "You're right. Maybe we should have more accountability in the process."

"Did you know that the DOE is responsible for policing itself? There is no control by any other agency."

"That *could* lead to problems with cover-ups and corruption," Patrick agreed. "Still, we need a strong nuclear policy, and people shouldn't protest against it."

"But Father, that's what America is about. Democracy. Freedom of expression. It's no good if the government hides behind laws to bury the truth. That's censorship. That's what we accuse the Soviets of. Look at these!" He pulled Gram's illegal Fernald photos from his shirt pocket. He handed them to his father.

"What's this?"

"Two guys dumping a barrel of toxic waste down a drain."

"This looks like Fernald." His forehead wrinkled.

"It is, Father. Those guys could be dumping radioactive substances right into the sewer system."

Patrick's face was flushed white as a porcelain commode. He couldn't decide whether to be angry or concerned over the illegal photographs.

Danny glanced at his father's receding hairline for any signs of swelling. The vein held its position. There'd be no anger tonight.

"Well, you and I won't solve it, Daniel," he sighed. In a peculiar way, he was proud that his son was so committed to a cause. He didn't agree with him—far from it—but he did acknowledge that it showed a strong independence that would serve Danny well in the future. "It's a huge juggernaut now. Nothing can stop it."

As if on cue, Roentgen, the dog with the Slavic sounding nuclear name, came in and curled up at Patrick's feet. Danny saw it as a good sign. "I can, Father," he said. "I can stop it."

Some days come and go quietly, a mere routine of tasks that one will never recall. Some days bring tragic events—a divorce, a death, a lost job, a failed exam, a car accident, an illness. We all have those days. But some days . . . some very special days . . . some are a rare collection of circumstances that come together to deliver a remarkable experience. It is as if the gods conspired to orchestrate a day so wondrous that one remembers it forever, in all its exactness. June 28, 1982 was just such a day for Daniel Oliver Gilday. It was a day that he would later describe in a single word—magical.

"Gram, come here!" he called as he tossed a bale of hay aside. Patrick Gilday had asked the boys to move a humongous mountain of bales from the barn floor to the loft. Danny wiped the sweat from his brow with the salty tail of his drenched T-shirt. "I found something."

"What is it?" Gram scampered over, his frizzy hair impaled with straw, as if wrens were nesting there.

"A trapdoor," Danny grunted as he pulled on the handle which he had discovered under a tall stack of hay. He tugged again.

Gram bent down to help him. "Man-oh-man," he huffed as he lifted. "Back when I was a court jester in the court of King Henry, I found a trapdoor like this once. Maybe it's a secret dungeon."

"Or buried treasure." Danny heaved. "Okay . . . one . . . two . . . three!" Up creaked the thick oak door, launching millions of dust particles into flight.

"Maybe we just found Jimmy Hoffa," Gram joked. A dense cloud of grit surrounded the sweating boys.

Danny ran to the front of the barn to grab a lantern and a flashlight. Before he could return, Gram had already jumped into the hole. Danny's pulse raced madly as he considered the secret chamber. What would he find there? What mysteries did it hold? He tossed a flashlight to Gram, then struck a match to the lantern. Not stopping to think, he jumped into the hole feet-first without easing himself down by hanging from the floorboards.

Thump—crash, he went. His body smacked hard against the floor of the chamber. The lantern flew from his hand. *Whoosh!* A kerosene flame shot up inside the hidden room.

"Shit! Father's going to kick my ass if I burn the barn down."

"No problem," Gram said. "As we used to say when I was a fireman during the San Francisco quake of 1906, step on it." He placed his farm-splattered gym shoe into the kerosene pool and extinguished the mini-blaze in one smooth stomp. Danny picked himself up off the dusty floor and patted himself clean.

The chamber smelled of time and ink and machine oil cut with spilled kerosene. Danny tried to adjust his eyes to the dark confines. Gram relit the lantern, illuminating the whole room. Goose bumps flared on Danny's skin. "Geez and crackers!" He stepped toward a huge, metal apparatus standing at the end of the room. "Look at that!"

"Man-oh-man!"

"It's a printing press! The nameplate says Heidelberg. It's our own printing press." Danny could scarcely contain his glee. "The gods are smiling on me, Gram, old chap. Can you believe it?"

Gram stuck his hand into a box as if he were digging into a treasure chest of gold doubloons. "Look at this, Danny." He lifted a handful of metal objects from the box. "Boxes filled with metal letters. Typefaces!"

The boys examined the room thoroughly, discovering more boxes of letters and a large crate which they couldn't get open without tools. A crowbar. A hammer. A saw. They realized they didn't have a ladder to get out of the chamber, and the trapdoor was ten feet above their heads, but Gram soon propelled himself out of the chamber by standing on Danny's back. Off he went for the necessary equipment.

Danny felt like an archaeologist in an Egyptian tomb. The coolness of the room felt good against his hot skin. He studied the walls, the floor, the boxes, the cobwebs hanging in every corner. They must be fifty years old, he thought to himself. He coughed from the thick air of the chamber. He watched his shadow dance on the wall as the lantern drank heavily of the kerosene.

"What secret history does this place hold?" he said aloud as he peeled the T-shirt from his back and began to wipe ages of dirt from the Heidelberg. A good rub of elbow grease, like massaging a genie's lamp, revealed a date: 1859. "This baby is a hundred and twenty-three years old!" he said, his blue eyes sparkling with fascination. "This is a discovery beyond belief." He set his ruined T-shirt on the Heidelberg, his eye caught by a small, black lacquer box layered with dust, held closed by a single, rusted clasp. He swabbed the top of it with his sweaty palm. The letters C.C. inlaid with gold glittered before his eyes.

His heart thumped loudly in his ears. He hadn't been this keyed up since Janis first showed him her breasts. He didn't know her that well back then, having only moved to Mulciber three weeks prior. It had cost him fifty cents. Lovely breasts they were. It was worth the fifty cents. Now, that familiar thumping returned. Was something as lovely, something as enticing and refined as Janis' breasts awaiting him inside the black box? He opened it gently.

A fragile, yellowed note sat on top of the contents:

The Personal Effects of Captain Matthew J. Crittenden
United States Army, Fifth Cavalry

"Captain Matthew J. Crittenden," he whispered, his breath seemingly swiped from him by Crittenden's ghost. "The guy at the Stones." He placed the note on the press to examine the contents of the mysterious box. An envelope as dingy as a skeleton's bones lay inside. He opened it and slid out a document.

> Captain Matthew J. Crittenden of the United States Army, having been tried and convicted as a Union spy, is hereby sentenced to death by firing squad for the charge of espionage against the Confederate States of America. The sentence to be carried out on this date, October Twelve in the year Eighteen Hundred and Sixty-Two.
>
> Authorized by order of General Braxton Bragg, Commander of the Confederate Army of Tennessee.

He shuddered as the chill of the chamber shook his spine. He found a photograph of Crittenden. Curled at the ends, the black-and-white picture showed a dashing man with long sideburns and warm, serious eyes. The eyes drew him in, as if they had a power that transcended time and death, and called to him. He felt as though Crittenden's spirit was still alive. "Have you been watching me, Captain?" he asked the photo.

"No, but I have," Gram said, sticking his head through the trapdoor. "Here, catch." He tossed down a utility light and a sack, then slid a ladder into the newly discovered compartment.

Danny hung the light on a rusty nail, set the sack on the printing press, and went back to examining the amazing box. He found another envelope, this one larger, written in a woman's hand, "From my loving Matthew."

Gram descended into the chamber. "Hey, I brought sandwiches. Your mom made them for me. She's pretty cool. You want one? Salami and cheese with mustard."

Danny ripped at the sack, consumed by hunger. All this incredible adventure had given him an appetite. "What do you suppose this place is?" he asked Gram, with a mouth full of meat and bread.

"Beats me." Gram shrugged as he opened a can of soda. "But I'll bet the answer is in this crate." He banged the crowbar against its wooden side.

"Or in this letter," Danny held up the envelope. "So, you don't have a hunch about this, huh, Mr. Conspiracy Theorist?"

"I don't want to spoil the surprise," he kidded. Gram, always inspired by the unknown, and far too excited to eat, applied the crowbar to the crate. Within minutes the lid was off and the boys explored its contents. Gram stuck his hand into the crate, moving packing material around until his eager fingers gripped something cold and metallic. He pulled it out and held it up in the air. It was a heavy, metal plate designed for the printing press. He examined its detail closely, then announced, "Maybe Captain Matthew J. Crittenden was a forger!" Gram laughed as he dug down into the crate again. This time he pulled out a stack of Confederate ten dollar bills. "We're rich!"

"Nah," said Danny. "It's worthless shinplaster. Somebody may want it as a collector's item, though."

Undaunted, Gram dipped his arm inside again. "Look," he said, his black eyes alive with stimulation. "A map. A treasure map!" The boyish Rasputin quickly laid his find on the printing press and smoothed it out. He and Danny leaned in, studying it.

"It's Mulciber," Danny said, instantly recognizing the topography. "See the property lines and the hill behind the Stones?"

"Man-oh-man, so it is."

Danny put a cautious finger on the aged document. "What do you suppose that X means?"

"It means there's buried treasure." Gram's eyes gleamed with a material craving Danny had never seen before.

Danny returned to the crate and pulled all the packing out. Inside, he found another large box containing all kinds of paper. Paper of different textures and bonds and materials and weights. Captain Matthew J. Crittenden was a forger, all right. A master forger.

Faint tappings pecked on the keyboard of Danny's mind, an old typewriter that wrote its silent message upon his cerebral tissue. A mad Hungarian newspaper man was sending him an idea. Joseph Pulitzer. The crazed publisher emblazoned his brain with a major headline: PULITZER DIARIES FOUND! He was bitten once again by the bug. He was a forger, too, like Crittenden, and he would be one again. His promise to Allison to forever forgo a life of crime was forgotten. Pulitzer took over. All Danny's needs were there—the press, the paper, the ink, the book his mother had given him—all of them. It was a sign, a message. Yes, he told himself, I will be a forger. It's my destiny.

He remembered Crittenden's letter from which Gram had distracted him. He took a bite of sandwich and opened the fragile correspondence.

Gram, having had enough titillation for the moment, sat on a box next to him to eat. "What's it say?"

Danny showed him the envelope.

"From my loving Matthew," Gram read aloud. Suddenly, a burst of sweet, warm air whisked through the trapdoor above. "Did you feel that?" he whispered.

"Is that you, Captain?" Danny said.

"He's here," Gram said. "The spirit of Captain Crittenden." Just as suddenly as it blew in it was gone. "Let me read it." He snapped the letter impatiently from Danny's hand. It was dated October 10, 1862. "Dear Cara. Hey, that's your mom's name!" Danny's skin froze like a Popsicle.

> Dear Cara,
>
> By the time this letter reaches you I will have passed from this world. It is but a formality that I shall die at the hands of Confederate marksmen. I doubt even my father could use his position to stop the fate which awaits me. Though it be doubtful that the senator would forgive his son for his Southern disgrace.
>
> I do not know if the news of my capture in New Orleans has been carried to you. Were that it could have been an heroic deed that caused my incarceration. Due to the sworn honor I gave to my president, Mr. Lincoln, I have been less than forthright with you about my presence. Dear Cara, I could not reveal to you, upon my oath, my position as a spy in the employ of the United States government.
>
> I document this truth today for fear that only two more suns will rise to greet me. Do not think I have died miserably. My captors are not bad fellows; they are simply blinded by the wrong cause. They are gentlemen who have treated me well, and dare I say it, with a certain degree of esteem. Make no mistake, my dear Cara, I would gladly barter the esteem for my life at this moment.
>
> Still, is death such a hideous passing? Or is this life, under the horrid conditions of the war, best left to the soil? As brother fights brother for

the sake of causes both sides have long forgotten. As father disowns son for beliefs long ago blurred by the cannons of battle.

You and I have known many pleasures. Tussles in the warm, down comfort of winter. Walks through the fertile plantation grounds. Stolen passion at the waterfall of Featherbed Bank. You and I, Cara, shall never be parted, even as this life expires.

I have been summoned by the Ancients to return home. My mission complete, my task at its terminus. If you believe, as do I sweet Cara, that life is but seasonal play, then we shall hold each other once again in the next lifetime. In the passion of spring, when the war is done, and man has satisfied his appetite for death, I shall rise from the earth to greet you with each flower that displays its blossom.

As the heavens await my arrival, I must depart this unforgiving world, my heart and soul warmed by the grace of your beautiful spirit. God bless you, Cara.

Yours in eternity,
Matthew J.

Gram's hand fell limp to his side, the letter like a wilted rose in his hand. His black eyes held a reservoir of emotion. Something had touched him at the center of his heart. He sat quietly without moving, without blinking. Danny was saddened, too, but wondered why Gram took the letter so hard. Danny was fascinated by the reference to the Ancients. Were they the same ones as the Council on Shanidar?

"Geez and crackers, Gram, this is freaky, man. He mentioned the Ancients. Do you think he means the Council of Ancients? The ones in my dream?" Gram didn't respond. "And Crittenden's wife had the same name as my mom. What are the odds of that?" Still no response from Gram.

Danny tried to lift him out of his funk. "Let's go to the Stones! I want to see if Cara Crittenden is there."

"Okay," Gram said.

The boys packed up and climbed from their secret chamber. They would visit the captain's workshop again another day.

Truly magical days don't stop with one amazing phenomenon. Truly magical days fill one's soul with inspiration, with subconscious neon signs, with a wealth of undeniable circumstance, so much so that there is nothing left but to surrender to the belief that God does exist, and He is speaking directly to you. When the celestial wizards wave their wands and cast their spells, they leave no doubt as to their purpose. This was one such day for Daniel Oliver Gilday, a day when Shanidarian wizards pulled fate's marionette strings and showed him the truest nature of the world.

Already overjoyed at having discovered a clandestine printing press with all its grand forgery implications, the boys now stood on the threshold of an even more incredible experience. It was decided, as they stood staring at Crittenden's marker at the Stones, to wait for Cal and Janis for the treasure hunt. They would slip off just after supper with about three hours of good light left. The boys were only mildly disappointed not to find a headstone with the name of Cara.

Danny's mind was awash in speculations about Crittenden's life. The captain was an unsung hero of the Civil War. A Yankee counterfeiter. A spy. A man executed in service to his president. How many other anonymous people have sacrificed themselves? he thought. How many others go about quietly changing the world? How many other silent ones has history overlooked?

"Sorry, Mrs. Hobbins," he apologized, standing in the graveyard. "I shouldn't have tinkled on you." A twinge of guilt crept across his smooth chest, like a black cat across linoleum, as he considered whether his regular copulations with Janis at the Stones mightn't also be sacrilegious.

A cooler loaded with ice, beer, and wine, a bag of barbecue potato chips, home-baked, chocolate chip cookies, a pound of bologna filched from Janis' fridge, a loaf of calcium-enriched, nutritionally-deficient white bread, a tent, blankets, lanterns, flashlights, a boombox with fresh D-size batteries, Danny's guitar, sleeping bags, three shovels, a pick-ax, bug repellent, toilet paper, matches, half an ounce of Colombian

Gold, a pack of Zig Zag rolling papers, and other necessities for a camp-out loaded the foursome down like Sherpa guides in the Himalayas as they set off on their expedition. It had started as a simple jaunt to X-marks-the-spot but had soon grown into a search for the lost mines of Solomon.

Roentgen led the way, happily jumping through the tall grass. Danny had the map tucked tight in his waistband as he slogged along like a stunt double in the *Hunchback of Notre Dame*, a canvas bag of supplies strapped across his shoulders and a guitar case pulling on his left arm. Gravity did its best to slow him down. Gram followed him, then Cal and Janis. The intrepid explorers trudged merrily along, invigorated by the thought of what lay ahead.

The sojourn took the wayfarers off Mulciber property, down a long slope of thigh-high grass mixed with low patches of red clover. The early summer scent of honeysuckle was an elixir to the youths, giving them strength, urging them on with great expectation. There was an energy among them, electric and vibrant, carefree and powerful, indestructible and inexhaustible.

Danny felt a slight but pleasant omnipresent sensation as he stopped momentarily halfway down the slope to shift the weight of his load. Roentgen charged onward, snapping at butterflies, ignoring bumblebees. A strong two-and-a-half hours of sun shone behind their backs as the crew pressed forward. He considered how Daniel Boone must have felt as he stomped through this area two hundred years before; no, he stopped himself, not Boone—how did the Indians feel who lived here for hundreds of years as they hunted the land for deer and bear and fox? Did they love summer days as he did? He wondered, if reincarnation were true, had he ever been an Indian? Had he hunted these grounds? He squinted back at the sun, its rays tonguing his smiling face like Roentgen's sloppy kisses. He thought of summer's heat. Winter's cold. Calder Academy. The demons-of-dimensia flowed into his mind. The Council of Ancients. McJic. His father. Crittenden, the town. Captain Crittenden, the man, the soldier, the spy.

"Do you hear that?" Gram called ahead to him. "Water! We're getting close."

The expedition picked up speed, nudged by the rushing sounds of a stream, pushed more by unstoppable gravity and the mass of their provisions than the momentum of their own legs.

"There it is!" Gram shouted. "What did Captain Crittenden call it, Danny? Featherbed Bank?"

Short grass tickling their ankles, they stood in the meadow gaping at its beauty as if they had just discovered the Eighth Wonder of the World. A majestic stand of evergreens lined the perimeter, the same evergreens that stood vigil over an injured McJic during his ignominy. They were silent now. Watchful.

Janis, whose hormones itched like poison ivy between a Girl Scouts' legs, was ecstatic at the sight of the meadow. A mighty weeping willow stood like a siren poised seductively at the edge of the pond, its branches new with green buds of the season. A gentle waterfall fell into the crystal pool. "Oh, boys," she said, "isn't this gorgeous?" She dropped her cargo and stretched her arms and pushed out her marvelous chest, causing the three males to admire her appreciation of nature. "I just love weeping willow trees. They're so . . . sexy, don't you think?" She reminded Danny of a sensual fertility goddess.

"Man-oh-man, Danny boy," Gram whistled. "This . . . is the place in your painting. This is the place in the Lights of Crittenden."

"It is!" Janis squealed.

"You must be psychic," Cal added. "Damn."

"Destiny." Danny tried to deflect the attention with a shrug. "The gods have brought us here."

And everyone knew, based on the goose bumps on their arms, that Danny was right. What none of them comprehended was the significance of his comments.

Danny and Gram set immediately about the task of determining the precise whereabouts of the X-marks-the-spot tree while Cal and Janis organized base camp. Cal suggested a good place for party headquarters. As Janis and Cal swung into action, with Cal rolling a joint only slightly smaller than a flashlight, Gram and Danny examined the precious map. They quickly and accurately identified the treasure tree, a giant elm, and began digging. They had no way of knowing that years before, on the night of Danny's conception, his real father was tied to that very tree and castrated. An odd sensation continued to tug at him.

Janis turned on the boombox and music filled the delightful meadow. Danny struck his shovel at the earth time after time as he pondered the strange déjà vu that occupied his mind. He dug, alternating scoops with Gram as the two of them clawed at the dirt with their tools like greedy forty-niners rabid for gold. Neither, of course, were aware that John Augustus Sutter, founder of Sacramento and the official landowner of the forty-nine thousand acres where the California gold rush took place, lost all his land and its gold to squatters and the U.S. government in January of 1848. He was given a pension of $250 a year for being such a good sport. Ah, the false legends that made America great.

Janis served up ice-cold beers to the laborers. Cal fired up the humongous joint. The boys took brief breaks to rest their muscles. Two hours, and a fair level of inebriation later, with the sun beginning to yawn and droop a bloodshot eye just above the western horizon and a half-moon raising a winking, white eye in the southeast, the boys found themselves staring into a six-by-three, five foot deep crater of shale and clay. Gram and Danny, both worn-out by the arduous effort, stared silently into the hole. All their grand visions were dashed. Vain hopes, they now conceded. Naive optimism about their importance to the fates. Disappointment reigned supreme.

"Maybe the gods aren't smiling on me," Danny said.

"Maybe you got the wrong tree," Cal said, choking back a huge toke of the joint.

Janis stood away from the group, mesmerized by the beginning flames of a bonfire. She swayed like a lazy drift of marijuana to the tape she had plugged in—Supertramp. She thought of her parents. They'd be divorcing soon, and she didn't know where she'd be living. It scared her, but she never told the boys, not even Danny. Seeing her parents argue over what she considered petty things made her want to grab life with that much more zeal, to hold onto moments and suck all the joy she could from every occasion. This, she understood, is where her lust came from. She was determined not to be like her mother, who used sex, or the withholding of it, as a means of getting what she wanted. Sex, in a strange, twisted Freudian way, was all Janis really wanted. That, and to be loved.

"It's the right tree, all right," Gram beamed with confidence. "I can feel it."

"Who sprinkled happy dust in your crater?" Cal said.

"It's cosmic, man, cosmic. Danny has a star in his hip pocket, remember?"

"Then how come you ain't found nothin'?" Cal challenged as he passed the doobie to Janis, who had just joined the group.

"Oh, ye of little faith." Gram shook his head teasingly. "Tonight we will be showered in wealth!"

"Take a shower now, G-man!" Cal tackled him around the waist and dove into the pond with him. The sun was sleeping off its buzz just over the hill as the boys splashed and laughed and rough-housed with each other. Janis slipped her arm around Danny's waist and stuck her tongue in his ear.

"I love the smell of a sweaty man," she breathed. "It's so . . . primal."

"Hey, Danny, it's really great," Cal called. "C'mon in."

"I'm in." Janis peeled off her top and slid out of her shorts with the speed of a stripper on amphetamines. Her taut body, firm breasts, and smooth legs were revealed long before she dove gracefully into the pond.

Cal shouted, "Up periscope!"

Danny stepped out of his clothes a bit more clumsily and joined them. A few stars blinked in the dark sky as the young explorers frolicked in the Kentucky lake. Cal and Gram, none too shy with several beers pulling at their inhibitions, shed their clothes and delivered them with a sloppy thud to the grassy bank.

Grand Funk's "Closer to Home" played on the radio.

"I didn't know you had this tape," Danny said, planting a kiss on Janis' neck as he grabbed her thigh.

Suddenly, the music turned itself louder.

"Is it me?" Cal shouted. "Or is it getting lighter out here?"

Everyone looked about, eyes judging whether the night had administered the appropriate proportion of darkness in the meadow. Decidedly, it had not, for it was obvious from Cal's observation that Featherbed Bank was not in harmony with the sun's snooze time. The golden sphere had hit the sack a half-hour earlier, yet it seemed like twilight. Danny studied the bonfire, but its flames only shed light for a few feet.

"Man-oh-man!" Gram shouted. "The hole! It's glowing!"

Like a stampede, the four adventurers attempted to charge out from the water, their legs slowed by the sheer physics of liquid. "If mankind lived under water," Gram had theorized a few weeks earlier, "their destructive motions slowed considerably by the force of H_2O, perhaps the planet would not be so depleted." It was one of his better theories.

Once on shore, the crew picked up their clothes and scrambled toward the hole, astonished and apprehensive at the evening's unexpected happenings. Before anyone could get too close, the music turned itself off and the glow intensified. A dull hum came from within the hole. Everyone stopped, held back from the excavation by the eerie, unfamiliar, vibrating sound, as if the hum itself were an invisible force field from another dimension. No one knew what to do. They stared in fear and fascination as the humming grew louder. They moved back a half-step, maybe two. Janis grabbed Danny's forearm, squeezing so tightly he would find bruises the next day. At that instant, however, he didn't feel her frightened pinch. Like the turbine of an intergalactic spaceship, the hole hummed, as if spinning. Faster. Louder. Faster. Louder. Faster still. Light pulsated from the hole in great throbs of energy, growing brighter and brighter as it built to a crescendo.

Boom! Whoosh! Boom! A powerful force was unleashed from the core of the Earth as something exploded out of the radiating cavity. A blinding flash of color followed it as the thing hurtled thirty feet into the air like a Patriot missile after an Iraqi Scud. It ignited in the air with a loud bang like the sound of thunder, no, the sound of the Fourth of July.

A glorious shower of glittering light rained down upon the bedazzled spectators. They all stared, completely spellbound, frozen by the dramatic appearance of the mysterious object. The fiery nucleus of the explosion dropped to Earth and thudded unceremoniously at Danny's feet in the soft grass of the meadow. It lay there, dark blue-black, smoldering, daring him to pick it up. Ancient smoke, like the wood fire from a shaman's prayer vigil, hung thick in the night. The meadow was aglow, shining miraculously through the hazy fog which shrouded the vessel.

Danny sniffed the warm air. He remembered Calder Academy and his pneumonia-induced dream. He recalled vividly the scent that filled his enlightened lungs as he sat enthralled by the campfire before the Council of Ancients. Instinctively, he knelt down before the steaming object. He examined it. Waved his hand in front to clear it of smoke. Metallic gold letters revealed themselves to the young light-being.

"*The Journals,*" he said in awe. "It's a book."

"Holy shit," Cal whispered.

"Not just a book," Gram uttered. "A glowing, exploding, throwing-itself-out-of-a-hole-like-a-missile book!"

Those readers who have been paying attention know by now that *The Journals* has been known for its theatrics. It must be remembered that this event, however, preceded the one Mr. Stone encountered on the river by some eight years, one month, and four days. Wisdom, indeed truth, reveals itself whenever it must, wherever it must. Lest the dishonest use its message for personal gain, *The Journals*, as a dedicated harbinger of truth, is not a book to be checked out of the library of human conscience by one person at a time. Indeed, Mr. Stone has no monopoly on the powers of *The Journals*. Nor does anyone else. Truth simply *is*, and anyone who seeks it may call upon it at any time. In this particular circumstance, it was Danny who became the beneficiary of its services.

All at once he recognized the light. Without thinking, without knowing why, he said, "The Glorian Aurora."

Cal understood it, too. "Mom's orchid," he said, kneeling next to his brother. "And the UFO we saw. It was calling us. Even back then."

"Holy Mary, Mother of Saints, all the wise men, the apostles, the pope, President Reagan, and the Joint Chiefs of Staff," Janis whispered.

Danny reached down and carefully picked up the smoldering book. It was warm to the touch, like a loaf of fresh-baked, honey wheat bread. Gingerly, not knowing what to expect but without fear, he opened *The Journals*.

A bright glow leapt from the pages, enveloping the whole of Featherbed Bank. Streams of Glorian Aurora poured from the book like instant sunlight. The surreal rays swirled and danced like soft laser beams, photons and electrons and neutrons tamed for joyful purpose. The light ricocheted off evergreen limbs and jade water and feathery grass and pungent earth and blasted out into the waiting night sky, off into the Universe forever. Everyone was shining gold, naked in the wondrous sheen of the book. The meadow was swathed in its aura like a bullion mist. The beams, warm and soothing, bright and magical, carried with them a mystical power, an energy created in Shanidar and delivered unto the meadow for this evening only. Each breath the teenagers took filled their lungs with delirious intoxication. It was nectar, a sweet ambrosia of awareness. An enlightenment.

Soon, euphoria spread among them as they played nude before the stars, which shone down like eager eyes watching a grand play, a masterpiece. Night was turned to day as the golden aura danced betwixt and between the hungry children. Janis, ever the lustful girl, held her arms out wide to embrace the magical essence and bring it to her breasts. But she could no more do this than catch the wind with a butterfly net. Gram sat lotus-style on the ground, chanting a personal mantra like a peaceful Tibetan monk. Cal stood in the raw, laughing in rapture, reaching for the glow as he would a firefly, trying to pinch its tail.

The light permeated every atom of the meadow so that Paradise or Nirvana or Utopia or Heaven or Shanidar or whatever it is that one believes the perfect afterlife to be, is what it became. A personal Garden of Eden without the imported sin.

The light changed color and lessened in intensity. The teens lost track of each other and fell deeply into their own subconscious. Each person's soul, long suppressed by the act of living in a shallow world, paid a welcome call upon its ego and brought gifts of insight and courage and love. Danny lay on his back staring at the sky, his mind charged with celestial visions of time past and future. For all the visitors to Captain Crittenden's treasure, the future was foretold. Gram meditated in bliss. Janis giggled and brought her hands sensually between her legs as she closed her thighs tight. Cal simply laughed and laughed like a hysterical madman struck by full-moon fever.

On and on the night went. Danny's mind was overjoyed with angelic music of such glorious harmony and beauty that he was brought to tears of happiness. All the while, he watched the future unfold like a magician's scarf trick. But this was no trick. Not at all. He peered through the strange light as five years hence played out. Then ten. Then twenty years. He saw himself grow to manhood. He saw Allison. He made love to her. From his euphoric vantage point he saw the revolution which would begin anonymously in January of 1996 as the Earth entered the Aquarian Age, peaking just after the turn of the Millennium. The Piscean Age would die away. He witnessed an incredible pacifist uprising of the world's people as they rebelled against prejudice and pollution and war and poverty. He saw Allison standing before a hundred thousand people, shining like an angel, giving them her light, sharing her spirit, and he saw himself standing proudly at her side, holding her hand.

The light spiraled and twisted about the meadow, at once nowhere and everywhere as Danny laid eyes upon the future. The antiquated systems of the West's institutions crumbled like a weathered Roman column under the wrath of a Visigoth's battering ram. He laughed and cried as he visited scenes of miraculous ecstasy and dire tragedy. Scenes of humanity's love and cruelty, moments of opposing life forces battling each other for balance. Time disappeared as he fell deeper into the Glorian trance. He began to sing. He sang in a voice that was his own but not from him. He found his guitar in his hands playing chords he did not know, strumming songs he had not heard.

Gram, Janis, and Cal danced merrily around the bonfire to his celestial overture. Bare before the gods with uninhibited abandon, they gyrated and celebrated this most blessed of nights. The dance and song continued for an hour or more. Finally, its energy beginning to wane, the light collected itself in a sphere and hovered above the ground. It pulsated and hummed. The Glorian sphere began to rotate slowly as it changed color. It spun faster. It turned sapphire, then purple as it spun faster. It whirled like a compact tornado, now ruby-colored.

Danny reached for the sphere, hoping to channel its energy inside him. *Bam!* The sphere rocketed into the sky and blazed out of the Kentucky night like a comet. Its destination—Shanidar. In a second, it was gone. The sounds of night slowly returned to the woods. The stars shone. The moon seemed to smile. The lantern hissed and the bonfire crackled.

They dressed silently, except for Danny, who sat cross-legged in front of the fire, naked with *The Journals* in his lap. He opened the book, but the light was gone. The Glorian Aurora had returned to the Council of Ancients. He flipped to the inside sleeve. It read simply: Personal Diary of Matthew J. Crittenden.

He swallowed what little saliva he had. He turned to the first page.

> Whosoever shall find this truth will be forever blessed with gifts beyond this world of mortals. This book before you has found its way into your life. Welcome to your destiny.

> From this moment forward shall be known to you the secrets of this realm. You are a chosen one. You must seek the hidden answers. You must guard against injustice. You must reveal your story to the faithless.

> This book, as life, is both the message and the messenger. And so it shall be for you—you are both the message and the messenger.

Like Moses with his burning bush, Buddha with his Bodhi tree, John the Baptist with his water, and Mohammed with his cave, Danny had his book.

"Is it like the Ten Commandments or something?" Janis said, sitting down next to him. She placed her head lovingly on his shoulder. "Wasn't that the most incredible experience?"

"Yeah. It was posilutely fantastic."

Cal joined them, as did Gram.

"What did you guys see?" Gram asked.

"I saw my future," Janis reported. "Married. Three kids. Divorced. Back to college. Move to San Diego. Then marriage to a handsome veterinarian from Toronto. That's in Canada. I visited you at a book signing, Danny. It was so cool."

"How 'bout you, wonderboy?" Gram asked Danny.

Danny shrugged his shoulders nonchalantly. "I'm going to save the world, I suppose. What did you see, Swami?"

"Oh," Gram paused. "I've always known my future. I've always been that way. Back when I was an astrologer at the Oracle at Delphi I learned all the tricks of fortune."

"Right," Cal scoffed. "C'mon, G-man, be fair."

"I didn't see my future." His black Rasputin eyes narrowed as if some great inner truth were to be sprung upon the group. "I *can* do that any time."

"What is your future, though?" Janis persisted.

"To come to Crittenden and be with you guys. To be here for this moment. To be here when Danny discovers his sacred power."

A chill, more like an electric current, sparked in Danny's root chakra and spread through his body. He knew some funky cosmic occurrences were going on. And he knew he was deep in the middle of them. But this was far too weird. As he sat cross-legged like some teenage Messiah in a Kentucky field, he wondered if he had the power Gram spoke of. He wondered if the gods hadn't gotten it wrong, delivered the wisdom to the wrong address. Souls can get mixed up like that, he tried to convince himself, being there's so many of them and all. He rose to his feet, his arms outstretched to the midnight sky. "I am one with the gods!" His voice boomed across the meadow in a bass reserved for comic imitations of the Almighty. Everyone laughed. "So Cal," Danny said as Gram shot him an odd frown, "you were hysterical almost the whole time. What did you see?"

"Oh," Cal hedged, producing a forced smile.

"C'mon Cal," Danny nudged his older brother. "What did you see, man?"

"Oh," Cal said with a false smile that spoke more with one simple upturn of his lips and a slight baring of his teeth than some folks express in a lifetime of suppressed feelings, "I saw my own death."

Chapter 34

June 1943

Sulphur pulled his cardigan sweater tightly across his chest and checked the buttons to make sure they were secure as he waited in Colonel Bruce's office. He wanted to get out of London, away from the perpetual drizzle and cold that plagued the city. The spring days of warm, blue sky that he had taken for granted while growing up in the Midwest were a luxury now. Still, people can adapt to any hardship if they must.

Sulphur liked the British people, if not their climate. Except for Churchill, who he saw as a traitor for his complicity in Pearl Harbor, he enjoyed their quaint accents and found their hospitality most gracious. To be sure, he felt they considered him a bit off his nut, as he avoided the standard tours of London, choosing instead to visit only those sights that had been blasted by the German Luftwaffe. The sheer power and immensity of the destruction invigorated him. He was sorry for the loss of life, but the absolute force of it all was mind-boggling. He had seen firsthand how the Brits stood tall after the Blitz of 1940 and `41. German bombardments destroyed half of London, ten thousand people died, great historical landmarks were damaged or obliterated, yet they banded together and did not waver. Yes, he admired the British spirit, their ability to "press on, what." He found his hosts charming in spite of the war.

As he waited patiently for Colonel Bruce, he thought of his visit to the Tower of London where the north bastion had been demolished by German ordinance.

Sulphur liked Bruce, the charismatic leader who had shown him every courtesy upon his arrival in England. True, Sulphur didn't much like sharing 87 Harley House with five other OSS officers, but this was wartime London, and a personal flat was out of the question. A shiver went through his chilled bones. He felt like he hadn't been warm since he arrived from Spain, as he sat looking out the fourth floor window of the Grosvenors Street office the OSS had commandeered for their intelligence operation in the European theater.

"Well," Bruce said as he strode into the room, slapped a file on the desk with authority, and parked himself in his leather chair. "Looks like you stumbled upon a hot potato, Sulphur." He grinned.

"Sir?"

"Turns out those documents Josemaria Escriva gave you were top-secret concordats. Two documents actually." Bruce threw his legs up on the desk and leaned back. "Translators tell me the first document is a Lateran agreement signed in 1929 between the Vatican and Mussolini. Seems the pope was all too happy to publicly align with Mussolini, thereby giving the dictator the support of the powerful Catholic Church and effectively wiping out democracy in Italy."

"They're on the run now," Sulphur said, referring to the score of Allied routs of the Italian army. He didn't fully understand the impact of Bruce's revelation.

"Damn straight," Bruce said, his eyes gleaming. "The second set of papers is pretty much the same type of agreement, a concordat between the pope and Hitler."

"Holy smoke! You're saying the Church is in bed with the Nazis, too?"

"That's common knowledge in political circles. The pope and his boys are scared to death of the Communists. They hate the Soviets because they think Communism will mean the end of Christianity. So they cut a deal with Satan, Hitler you understand, and he won the German election. The Vatican planted the demon seed, watered it, and allowed it to flourish. What they don't realize is the ruthless bastard hates the Catholics as much as the Jews. It won't be long until he turns his SS storm troopers loose on them as well."

Sulphur sat speechless, staring at Colonel Bruce. A familiar spark of anger ignited inside him. Now he knew why his hotel room in Barcelona had been ransacked. He had gone to make the final transfer arrangements with Garbo on the forged Deutschmarks the morning after Escriva accidentally slipped him the wrong packet. Escriva had called the hotel only hours after their initial meeting, frantically looking for him. When he said the parcel was on its way to London, Escriva became enraged. Upon his return from his second meeting with Garbo, he found his room shredded. A warning written in blood, which Sulphur first thought to be lipstick, was scrawled upon his bathroom mirror. BEWARE OF OPUS.

Call it a twinge of human consciousness, but he was more enraged at the deception of the Church against its followers than at the threat against his own life. He was a spy, after all. A dangerous spy with a nasty background in arson and warfare. If the Church hadn't backed Mussolini and Hitler, he reasoned, they wouldn't have come to power. The World War which had taken so many lives may not have happened. Sulphur, who had always had an aversion to religion, was more than willing to blame Opus for the outbreak of the war. "Damn Opus Dei," he said aloud. "The Church is selling out its followers."

Bruce, always the pragmatic businessman, chuckled. "Don't confuse Opus Dei with the work of God. Religion is the oldest known business on Earth. Some say prostitution is the world's oldest profession, but those at the top—the elite—know better. The Catholics have been practicing commerce for over nineteen hundred years. And Opus is a right-wing faction that will stop at nothing. They want what's theirs. They want market share and customers. If they have to forsake a few million people to get their souls, they'll do it and pay penance for it later."

Sulphur's right hand was shoved deep inside his pants pocket. He rubbed his thumb and forefinger on the head of a match. A low flame smoldered inside his seething gut as he plotted his revenge on Escriva and his sadistic brand of religion. Opus Dei would pay for its sins if Sulphur had his way.

"You seem surprised, Sulphur. You needn't be. Pope Pius XII has been giving pro-German radio broadcasts for months now. He has openly praised their heroic efforts," the European OSS chief said with a definitive measure of disdain.

Sulphur gritted his teeth. "If everybody knows about this, then how are the documents a hot potato?"

"Not everybody knows, Sulphur. The Catholic faithful, blind sheep they be, are oblivious to the fallacies of the Vatican. They follow the Church's doctrine and direction without question. Hundreds of millions of people," Bruce explained as he rubbed a smudge from his freshly polished shoe. "If people knew that their freedom had been sold to the highest bidder so that the Church could insure itself a good revenue stream from their downtrodden souls, they'd renounce it."

"Maybe they should."

"They would just follow something else. That's how most people are. There are followers, and that's ninety-nine percent of the people, and there are leaders. Of that one percent, a good chunk just take what they want from the rest. That's all this war is about—greed. The key for you, Sulphur, is to figure out how you are going to get your fair share."

"I don't follow, sir."

Bruce pulled his legs down from the desk, grabbed a piece of scratch paper, and scribbled a name and number. Looking up, he said, "Call on this man, Jacques d'Astang, he's an antiquities dealer in Tripoli. He has his hands on some of the finest spoils captured from Hitler's foray into northern Africa. Antiquities, Sulphur, that's the market."

Sulphur stared at the paper. "But he's in Libya, sir. How am I to reach him?"

"Take a few weeks, go visit him."

"But sir, what about the heavy water mission?"

Bruce raised his eyebrows and chuckled. "Don't take this war so seriously, Sulphur." The colonel shuffled, lifted, and looked under a few stacks of paper. "You've got presidential privilege, man. You can go where you want. You can get lost for a few weeks and everyone assumes you're doing your job! That's the beauty of the spy game—nobody questions you. But if your conscience bothers you," he said, continuing his search, "ah, here it is." He pulled a top-secret file on the Norsk Hydro power project out of a stack. "Study this on the way over. Take a Norwegian language book as well. That way you will still be working for Uncle Sam."

Sulphur took the thick file and set it on his lap. He couldn't believe this was happening. He was being instructed by a superior officer to become a profiteer. His ideal of patriotism exploded like a mortar round in the schoolyard. "I can arrange a flight out in a few days," Colonel Bruce said. "Jacques has a few Grecian urns I'd like you to bring back for me, if you would."

"Certainly, sir." Sulphur didn't argue, figuring this is the way war is done. He rubbed the matchhead in his pocket briskly, hoping the friction might ignite it. He knew this was not possible, but he wanted to break a law of physics just the same.

Feeling new found strength from his affiliation with FDR, and unwilling to let the Opus Dei leader, Josemaria Escriva, get away without retribution, he added, "I'd be glad to fetch your urns for you, colonel. But I need to get to Spain first. There's a burning issue in Barcelona I must take care of."

Chapter 35

October 22, 1990

Stone here. I'm back. I extend my heartfelt appreciation to *The Journals* for adeptly standing in during my absence. Funny what a man goes through when he thinks he is dying. Not funny, actually. Interesting. Disconcerting. Therapeutic. Holistic. In the most wretched state of my illness, weak from radiation, my gums bleeding, my colon swollen, my stomach involuntarily expelling every bit of nourishing substance like a Cuban boat exodus through the choppy Caribbean waters, I wanted to give up. But somewhere inside that dull ache, somewhere tethered to that wrenching sorrow, somewhere the smallest kernel of survival instinct began to grow.

I've been through it all: the darkest abyss a man can face, the loneliest hollow a man can endure, the most forlorn depression a soul can forsake. It is a slow recovery, this scratching back from death. It is a clawing journey, all splintered fingernails, scraped knees, and bruised skin. It is a battle. It is a dismal memory. It is a weight. It is a purging. It is a renouncement of the past. It is a reckoning.

The first thing one must do is forgive. Forgive everyone you hurt, everyone who hurt you. One must loosen the grip of life's experiences, the bad karma that chisels its way upon your edifice. But it is no easy venture to lessen one's dependence on past ideals that never were. It is a tremendous difficulty. One must learn not to lie to oneself. One must reshape the deceptive, clay thoughts one has sculpted into monuments of perception. One must step back from the whole of life's work in order to see that the art of living is nothing but plain brick after plain brick mortared high in an enclosed wall. A prison of false belief. And this belief only comes when Death stands before you, scythe in hand, and dares you to deceive Him.

The second thing one must do is find your determination, your will, and this is much more the challenge. Having stared into the onyx eyes of Death and rationalized your peace, it is far easier to let the Reaper drag you by the head to the block for chopping. To stare at the Grim Merchant and summon courage to denounce him is achievement. It is victory of light over darkness. It is triumph of spirit over ego. It is conquest of the material.

I have found my will.

One may well wonder what it is that has set me right. The answers are plentiful. People. Circumstance. Love. Faith. I have not been the most faithful of husbands, I admit this. I have not been the most passionate lover, nor the gentlest man, nor the most forgiving partner. There are cracks in my personality and faults in my character as wide as the jagged line of San Andreas—and perhaps as volatile. Yet, Rose, my personal angel, has righted me without question. She has endured the punishment of my manhood, the expression of my testosterone. She has every allowance to leave me, to board a plane to who-knows-where to lose the baggage of her husband. She deserves to find herself at my expense.

Rose is a different woman. Confident but changed. She has begun attending some Unitarian church. She calls the experience liberating. Her eyes, marbled with recent worry, glisten again. Her voice is vibrant, sure. A few days ago, when I commented on her transformation, she said, "Saviors come in many forms. My eyes have been opened." She had no doubt. "I was foolish to have thought there was only one way to believe." The woman is amazing! She's even signed up for a yoga class. Yoga! At her age! Holy smokes!

Yet here she is, in the kitchen with Twinkie, making supper. Twinkie hums *Perry Mason* (as if it's the only song she's ever known) while they fry potato pancakes and sausage links and talk over ways to comfort me. I have often found Twinkie's renditions—humming, singing, whistling and the like—to be off-key and irritating. However, her melodies are more harmonious lately, like a nightingale finding her voice. She laughs more easily, as if confidence is building inside her. Whatever the cause of her joy, even if it's McBain, I'd suffer a few years in the penitentiary so that Twinkie may find a few days of happiness.

I have caught up with *The Journals'* account of events during my affliction. From my station in the family-room recliner, I have read *The Journals'* entries with fascination and surprise. With each turning page I am drawn further in, as if the plot itself (and the lives contained therein) are unfolding today instead of eight years ago. So much has happened in that time. How ignorant I was to the lives around me. Is that one of life's grand messages? To pay attention to those who touch your life, however lightly, for they have as much to offer you as you do them? Is that it? Whatever the real purpose for my conscription into this job as narrator, and I am now convinced it is much more than *The Journals* lets on, I am glad to be a part of it, glad to be a witness to these phenomenal events.

Sadly, I have not been in the physical or emotional state to watch Channel 99. There have been no communications from the Council, no subtle signs or obvious omens. I feel I have neglected my duty, deserted my post, as they say in the military. But I am back in command now, ready for action. Again, I am grateful for its help during my leave.

But I am more grateful that Rose did not abandon our marriage. She has always been my rock, stronger than me, more secure. She knows it. Somehow in her surrender to my manly indiscretions she gains power over me, as if she knows she is the only one to tolerate my idiosyncrasies, my long, unexplained absences. She knows her value, and now so do I.

I am also perplexed by the persistence of 'M,' who has delivered me another packet of *Eastern Crescent Reviews* with the surreptitious note: "The world must know the truth." 'M' thoughtfully highlighted several articles on the Iraqi situation. Desert Shield was a sham they claimed, an invented defensive military diversion for an offensive attack planned for twenty years. Why, they charged, did the United States refuse to consider several Iraqi offers to withdraw from Kuwait? Why indeed? The paper's conclusion was that Bush had rolled up his sleeves and was determined to blacken Hussein's Middle Eastern eye so the United States of America could usurp the long-running Soviet domination of the region. With billions of annual oil profits at stake and the Soviets hemorrhaging at home, in no position to counter U.S. aggression, it was a calculated risk, a business decision. Blood for oil.

I threw the papers in the trash. I don't need that propaganda polluting my mind. I voted for Bush, I'd do it again. If he uses a little U.S. muscle to secure freedom for Kuwait, so be it. Saddam's misfortune can be our gain.

The water clock's wheel turned slowly, gurgling like a miniature stream. Turning, ever turning. The wheel moves and seconds drip by. Minutes. Hours. A lifetime. The infamous, two-dimensional Stone family portrait hanging over the fireplace stared back at me. I glanced at Bobby, who had hid his missing arm by stepping slightly behind me. I hadn't seen him since the fire, two and a half months ago. He didn't return my calls. Rose says he's more spiteful than ever. What happened to our family? Were we always this dysfunctional, or did it begin with John Kennedy's assassination? Were Bobby's illusions jaded in Vietnam, or was it my paternal miscues? The guilt I often felt for being too involved in my work and in the things I like to do pulled at my heartstrings like a tripwire land mine in the Mekong Delta. Bobby's severed limb, torn off by a Viet Cong booby trap, blew away what remained of his innocence and seemed to injure the rest of the family as well.

I stared at Bobby's picture, then at the trash bin. When did war ever solve anything? It only leads to another war. I reconsidered my Iraqi position. What was I saying? That it's okay to destroy a country and its people so we can take long vacations in big, gas-guzzling cars? I've known many Iraqis. I've been to Baghdad and visited its bazaars, negotiated for figs and olives with vendors on the street. They are good people with lives, dreams, and aspirations not unlike our own. Ashamed, I pulled the papers from the can. I started a file on the Persian Gulf situation. It's obvious there's to be a war. And I, as one who has lived through the horrific consequences of war, should have known better than to be sucked in by the media's desire to incite conflict.

Feeling emboldened and stronger this morning, and far less vulnerable thanks to a generous godsend from Lloyd's of London, which I shall describe momentarily, I fired off letters to Senators Glenn and Metzenbaum, one to President Bush, and another to *The Cincinnati Enquirer*, voicing my opposition to any American military involvement in Kuwait. As I wrote the letter, I felt guilty about questioning our leaders. It was such a radical act for me. But as I finished the letter, a sense of pride came over me, as if I had truly, for the first time, participated in the experience of being an American. I did something.

Now, for the highlight of this day's chronicle. I have in my possession a check in the astonishing amount of two million dollars. Here is my dilemma. If I cash the check, McBain will use it as evidence of my guilt. He already has a copy of the policy, from where it came I don't know, and a list of other carriers I allegedly contacted to insure the Cosmic Club and the Mamets. But if I don't cash the check, it is only a matter of weeks before I am forced into bankruptcy. My immediate debts total nine hundred seventy-one thousand dollars. I don't want to sell my art, antiquities, cars, my house, and all the other possessions I've managed to accumulate over the years for pennies on the dollar.

I developed many plans while I convalesced. The one I most favor is cashing the check, paying off my debts, and parlaying the remaining balance into a twelve-acre commercial development on which I believe I can make a fortune. That will set me and Rose up for the remainder of our lives. This may be my last chance.

The land, located just east of Mariemont, is perfect for a five-story office building fronted by a strip mall. It's all trees and undergrowth now, situated at the intersection of two heavily traveled roads. A dozer crew could have it cleared in a couple of weeks. The back of the property butts up against the Little Miami River so there is excellent drainage and effluent discharge. It's ideal. A developer's dream.

Sometimes I feel so fortunate, which is a strange thing to say considering my last two weeks of intestinal expurgation. But the presence of two million bucks brings a certain amount of cheer to my existence. One less set of problems to deal with. I have a call into Bennett for his opinion on the matter. I need his strategic mind on this one. To spend the two mill or let it sit; that is a major consideration.

Parker called. He's on his way with news, alive with tales of an exotic woman he recently met. He sounded jubilant, youthful. Ah, the joys of love. I hope he doesn't stay too long, I'm itching to watch Channel 99 again. I have to get back in the game.

October 23, 1990

It is a world of wonders. Not the tangible kind one sees on vacation—the Grand Canyon, Niagara Falls, Broadway, or the Golden Gate bridge. The wonders I speak of are personal, human. Perhaps I am more receptive and cognizant of these matters due to my cancer, determined to suck the marrow out of life, as it were. True, facing one's mortality does force appreciation for the things in one's life that have been taken for granted or simply overlooked. If not, well, perhaps death is the appropriate course.

The wonder I speak of is not scenery, not a place, a TV show, an emotion, a book, a memory, or a dream of some fantastic imagining. The wonder I speak of is human. Her name is Maya Shakti. It is fair to say, after having had tea with her and Parker, Rose and Twinkie, that Parker did not exaggerate her exotic nature. I half-expected fireworks given Twinkie's perpetual, unforgiving attitude toward Parker and her obvious jealousy of anything related to his potential happiness. But Maya appears capable of casting charming spells, an aura of loving peace upon those she encounters.

I was caring for my orchids, an exercise which gives me much joy, when the bell rang. Parker hadn't told me he was bringing a guest. That's his way sometimes, totally unconcerned about social norms, and I admire him for that. I often wonder if we don't erect class walls by our limiting rules of social engagement. Have we refined ourselves right out of spontaneity and creativity? If so, what opportunities, what marvelous experiences do we unknowingly filter from our lives?

By the time I had set down the pruning sheers, removed my gloves, and hobbled to the kitchen (I'm still a little weak), Parker, a long stalk of celery between his lips, and his date were already standing in the kitchen, where Rose and Twinkie were putting away the remnants of dinner. Fearful images of the ill-fated Beefaroni tamale projectile scene flashed vividly in my mind. I scanned the room quickly (Parker's radar eyes were nearly finished with a similar sweep) to insure there was no food which could be catapulted, slipped upon, dropped or abused in any way. I hadn't finished my search when he dropped a bombshell.

"R.T.," he gushed with a tiny snap of his celery. "It's my distinct pleasure to introduce you to the mysterious 'M.'"

My mouth dropped, possibly my jaw, perhaps my entire head. I'm not sure; I was too flabbergasted to react. A dozen questions popped into my brain. My tongue wouldn't work. I was like a smitten schoolboy too bedazzled to speak. This is 'M'? The one who had sent me packet after packet of Gulf Crisis intelligence? This young woman with divine, brown eyes and a smile that could convince the Nobel committee to give Saddam the Peace Prize, was 'M'?

Before the numbness that had taken over my body faded, she said, "Pleased to meet you, Mr. Stone. Astarte bewitch me, I've been wanting to for such a long time. Personally, I believe you're innocent." She extended a slender hand. "My name is Maya Shakti."

I was completely slack-jawed as she unabashedly introduced herself to everyone. She thinks I'm innocent? Just like that? Within five seconds of meeting me? I like this girl. There are people I've known for twenty, thirty, and forty years who don't believe that. Who is this, Astarte? What an odd phrase. Parker's ocean-deep eyes shimmered like a contented man with a pleasant secret as the self-assured Maya returned her attention to me.

"Pardon my forwardness, Mr. Stone," she said in a soft, orchid petal voice. She wore the heritage of an Eastern Indian, yet her accent was American-Southwest. I had studied dialects extensively in the service. Her skin tone was Middle Eastern, or Indian, yet there were other ethnic traces flowing in her like silver in an argentite cavern.

"R.T.," I blushed.

"R.T., you don't look well." She took my hands in hers, turned my palms up, then back over, and examined my fingernails. I was too stunned to resist. Twinkie, competitive in her lack of self-confidence, arms crossed, bit at her lip and fretted. Maya, her brown irises tinged like Orange Milano cookies, her skin naturally pigmented like that of a college sun goddess on spring break in Lauderdale, inspected my fingernails with a firm, twisting-and-pressing motion. "Goodness, you have an illness," she said.

"Are you a nurse?"

"No," she giggled, releasing my hands. Twinkie's eyes were in a panic. She slipped on a yellow pair of elbow-length Playtex gloves and began polishing the already spotless chrome trim on the oven door in a way that could only be therapy for her. She rubbed and rubbed, the BTUs of friction she created, equal to the angst in her mind, could have kept the city lit for several days. No brownouts while Twinkie is polishing. Rose watched intently while Parker stood passively munching his celery stalk.

"May I see your tongue, please?" Maya asked.

I stuck it out without thinking.

"Hmm . . ." She examined my tongue. Her eyes were magnificent. On that count, she and Parker were perfectly matched. Never has there been a pair of humans with enveloping eyes like theirs. While Parker's eyes suctioned everything in their trajectory, Maya's radiated light like a calm wave of happiness. A calm, yes, that's it, a calm. "I'd say you are having some bowel trouble," she smiled. "In the lower abdomen. Most likely the groin area."

I was surprised. Judging by Parker's face, and the upbeat angle of his celery, he was, too. I thought he may have tipped her off, but his shrug and elevated eye brows told me he hadn't. Twinkie quivered so imperceptibly that only a parent would notice—and perhaps Parker, with those remarkable telescopic pupils of his.

"Papa's been feeling a little under-the-weather," Twinkie said, stopping her frenetic buffing to place her body between me and Maya. What insecure children will do for attention. "I'm Julie, his daughter. We've got it all under control."

As if sensing the precise source of her discomfort, Maya placed a friendly hand on Twinkie's shoulder and said, "You must be a great daughter to take such good care of him."

Parker cleared his throat. "Hel . . . low Swami, you aren't going to believe what I dug up. I have some interesting facts in the case, R.T.—Maya has been an inspiration."

"I'll just bet!" Twinkie huffed with a snap of a rubber glove as she pulled it tighter. "Graduating to larger phallic symbols, Pink?" She motioned at the celery stalk in his mouth. Parker shrugged her off. He's like that, nothing gets to him. Especially jealousy.

With the touch of a light breeze Maya stroked Twinkie's hair. "Who does your hair?" she said. "It's so attractive."

Twinkie softened like whipped cream on hot apple pie. She bashfully lowered her eyes to the countertop and shuffled her feet as if she were four and still wearing Daffy Duck pajamas with feet in them. "I . . . um . . . do it myself. Do you really like it?"

"Oh, absolutely," Maya said. She let the hair slip slowly through her fingertips. "I wish I had your talent."

I couldn't believe what I was hearing. I love Twinkie, but a fact is a fact: she gets her looks from me. Sturdy bricklayer features. A permanent UNDER CONSTRUCTION sign should be placed around both our necks. I'm your average-Joe, which makes Twinkie your plain-Jane. Listening to Maya, though, watching her expressions, I'll be damned if her words weren't genuine praise for Twinkie's lackluster appearance. At least she wasn't looking frumpy, like Rhoda Morgenstern on *The Mary Tyler Moore Show* any longer. Thank God that phase was over. This is 1990 after all. Begrudgingly, I hate to admit, Twinkie's fling has done wonders for her appearance.

Maya turned her attention back to me. "I'd say your illness is fairly severe, Robert. Cancer perhaps. We need to invoke the goddess Hala to heal you."

As I pondered who this foreign deity was that Maya recommended, Parker leaned into me, celery back in his jaw, cupping my forearm with his palm. He whispered, "Isn't she incredible? She knows ancient mythology just like me." *Chomp.*

"And," Maya continued softly, "you are very stressed."

"How do you know that?"

"It's obvious she's well-educated, Daddy," Twinkie said. She slipped the bright yellow gloves from her hands. Rose fiddled with her cross, her lips pursed as she contemplated the motives of the newcomer.

412

Maya bounced on the balls of her feet, springing with a youthfulness I'm not sure I ever had. "My mother is an Ayurvedic doctor."

"Aya . . . whata?"

"Ayurveda—the science of life. Very ancient. Very powerful."

"And what does your father, Mr. Shakti, do?"

"He's an astronomer, but his last name isn't Shakti—it's Begay." Maya smiled. "I was given my mother's last name to honor the fact that women are the ones who bear, raise, and nurture children. My mom and dad agreed that it would please the spirits more if I took her name. They consider the act of taking the man's surname as a male issue of power and control, one that men don't especially deserve given their historical record of abandonment and abuse. Women generally give more love to their children than men, and my parents wanted to acknowledge the precious gift of motherhood. I guess my folks wanted to make a feminist statement. It's wild, huh?"

I didn't know how to respond. Kids with the last name of the mother, not the father? I started to say something. Parker caught my arm.

"Really, R.T., I have some good evidence," Parker said, holding the celery in his fingers like a menthol Salem. "Come on." He pulled me into the family room, his green stalk leading the way. I wanted to ask what the deal with the celery was but decided to let it go. "We've got a case to discuss. Maya can mesmerize you some other time. Coming, Maya?"

"No, thanks," she said. "I think I'll stay here and talk to the girls."

Rose, who had been speechless, smiled, as did Twinkie. Both were flattered that this rare specimen had chosen to visit with them. Faintly, I heard Maya say, "Now, about Robert, we must do some . . ."

Parker spilled his news as my eyes rocketed back and forth between him and the ladies in the kitchen. He told me that Cincinnatus, a key figure in Allison's life as far as I've witnessed, was in El Salvador. When I asked what the hell he was doing down there, Parker replied, "The Church had him arrested on child abuse charges. He fled the country. Sick bastard."

"Shit! But he's innocent."

"Sure doesn't look that way," Parker said with a sharp crunch of his celery, the stalk half as big as when he arrived. "They tried to close the mission, too. But that failed, thanks to Allison."

"Do you know where she is?" My eyes skipped to the kitchen, where the women were whispering amongst themselves. Rose put on a kettle for tea.

"I've got it all here in a synopsis for you." He smiled boyishly. "You can read it later. I'm not sure a line-by-line listing of her life is what *The Journals* is after, though. It doesn't really tell her story. I need to find people that knew her. Conduct interviews. Get out and—"

Drip, drop, plop. Drip, drop, plop. "That's such a cool clock, fella," Parker said as the timepiece delivered five additional reports. Seven o'clock. "Sounds like my coffeemaker. Only more expensive. I've always admired your collection of gods, bronzes, reliefs, urns, and pottery. Always. But this clock, hel . . . low Swami, it's incredible."

I don't know what bubbled up, but it poured out of me like a confession. "All I've ever done is collect things. What does it mean? Trinkets. Clocks. Spoons. Matchbooks. Orchids. Art. I own them, but I don't know what they mean. It's like my life is nothing more than possessions, and I don't even know their true value. Look at you," I said. "You live life. You relish it, savor it, find reason to celebrate it. My life is dull."

Parker studied my melancholy as he threw his ponytail over his shoulder. "Seems like you're in the midst of a pretty big adventure to me." *Chomp. Chomp.* The celery was just a nub, a thumb of vegetation, at best. He snapped open his ever-present briefcase and pulled out the Allison document. "She's had an interesting life, too."

"Do you know where she is?"

"New Orleans was her last known address. I've been thinking, R.T. If we had the rest of her diaries, it may help me find Allison. She's disappeared. So has Danny. It's weird, man."

"How so?"

His eyes drew in the light of the room, sparkling bright with intrigue. "Nearest I can tell, some ultra-secret Catholic sect was shadowing her. What was their name?" He shuffled through some papers. "Opus something. Yes. Opus Dei."

Pricks! I wanted to shout. But before I could respond, the three women swept into the room with a tray of tea and a purpose in their collective eyes that wreaked of conspiracy. Rose set the tray down, an impish yet determined grin on her face.

"We've decided," she announced, staring directly at me in that way she has, the same look she used when she told me it was time to get married, the look that cannot be denied or avoided. "We need to revisit this *Journals* business and support you any way we can."

"Yeah, Daddy," Twinkie said. "We want to do more than cook and clean for you; we want to get involved. Maya has convinced us you have too many things to deal with on your own."

Maya smiled. "Not that you aren't a strong man, R.T. But even the best people need the energy of others. Sing say," she said.

"Tell us the story from the beginning," Rose said as she sat next to me. She kissed my cheek. "And this time we're all going to pay attention."

Sometimes a man feels like he goes through his entire life alone. He carries the weight of his past, the burden of work and family and home. Some men keep it all inside, like a rock, or a brick. The problems come, the trauma increases, the drama unfolds. The stress and strain builds, but still you're expected to be this icon of strength. Some men suffer quietly. They bear their secrets in solitude even as they are surrounded by wives and lovers and sons and daughters and grandchildren who don't know their despair or their fear. Even with all the material accompaniments, a man is alone with his grief. An indescribable distance, a wall perhaps, separates his existence from those around him. At that moment—with Rose and Twinkie and Parker and Maya sitting around me offering unconditional support through the most challenging of trials—at that exact moment my walls were beginning to crumble, and I felt a great sense of relief, like the tower of Babel had come crashing down from my shoulders. I felt vindicated, empowered. Now, I knew deep inside, this is one of *The Journals'* messages. Rose always knew. It is a matter of faith.

Before I could respond, a miracle happened. It may have been caused by the love in that room. It may have been Maya's presence. It may have been caused by raised awareness. It may have been a tear in the cosmic fabric, or may have been predestined. It may have been a phenomenal set of a thousand circumstances unknowingly aligning, but I suspect it was the Council of Ancients showing its compassion.

In the midst of their heartfelt offer, as I sat on the couch holding hands with Rose, love blooming in abundance, the television turned itself on. The screen flickered as the station set itself to Channel 99. Celestial music played. Harps, flutes, and organs.

All eyes, astounded and perplexed, stared at the TV. Maya, whose eyes danced wild with a primal fire, managed to gasp, "Sing say."

A Godlike voice spoke to the dumbstruck group. *"Welcome to your destiny. Your faith in Stoney shall be rewarded. Take comfort,"* The Journals instructed the flabbergasted audience. *"There is an intriguing story to tell."*

Chapter 36

August 29, 1982

Danny stood in his room watching Cara through an opening in the silver maple outside his window. It afforded him a view of the Stones through his telescope. He spied on Cara as she sat in the graveyard and spoke to Captain Crittenden's headstone. Pages of Pulitzer research notes lay idle on his desk as he peeped at his mother across the backyard.

He hadn't realized what a profound impact the knowledge of Crittenden's journals would have on his mom when he casually mentioned their existence over a bowl of Cheerios the morning after the Glorian Aurora shone like a quasar at Featherbed Bank.

Much had happened since that fateful night. Danny and the others had formed a pact, a fraternity if you will, called the Calvary. The Calvary name was rife with many meanings: it honored their patron saint, Captain Crittenden, and the ancient Jerusalem hill where Christ, among thousands of unfortunate others, paid for His dissidence. The word was from the Latin, *calvaria*, meaning skull, so named for the heap of skulls which accumulated there as a result of countless executions. The new Calvary were unaware that there were actually two separate words with clearly different meanings—calvary and cavalry. The misplaced *l* of the word used to describe a soldier on horseback went undetected by the clan.

Even though the double-entendre missed the mark by the scant distance of an *l*, it didn't change the fact that all the members of the Calvary felt persecuted in some teenage way—misunderstood at home, detached from the world, disenchanted with the establishment and the hypocrisy of life in America.

Danny set down the telescope, saddened that Cara was crying again. Almost every day for over two months it was the same. After Patrick left for work, around nine or ten, she would take a stroll up to the Stones and sit with Captain Crittenden. Sometimes she brought flowers, sometimes *The Journals* to read aloud. Cara would stay for fifteen minutes or so, always gently patting the marker to say goodbye. Sometimes she would pack a lunchbag and walk past the Stones down the long slope east to Featherbed Bank. Danny never followed her there and knew nothing of her reasons for going. He only knew his mom would disappear for a couple hours.

The appearance of *The Journals* had brought Danny and Cara even closer together.

"Do you believe in reincarnation?" Cara asked at breakfast one morning. This was their time, Danny and Cara, after Cal was at summer school and Patrick was at work. Danny enjoyed their conversations.

"I'm not sure," he said. "The Hindu version seems far-fetched, coming back as cows and all. But maybe some simpler version could be true."

"I'd like to think there is," Cara said. "I'd like to think that perhaps I was Cara Crittenden in another lifetime. And that I came back here to reconcile my past with the captain. That'd be a nice fantasy, wouldn't it, Danny?"

"Sure would, Ma."

He spied his mother through his telescope and wondered if she had become obsessed by the coincidence of Crittenden's wife having her same first name, or if Cara actually believed that she and Crittenden were connected in a past-life tryst. He shuffled the notes about his desk as he remembered his mother's excited eyes when he showed her *The Journals* for the first time. How carefully she held it. How delicate her voice became. They had passed the book back and forth many times in the last two months, she keeping it for a few days, then he for a week, both of them finding a sort of celestial comfort in the writings. Danny looking for his father. Cara looking for her lover. Both wishing, beyond reason, that Captain Crittenden was part of them. Both knowing that a higher power had orchestrated the finding of his diaries.

He shared pencil sketches of McJic with his mother, renderings from his dreams, imaginings of a great officer roaming the Universe like some superhero or demigod. The mind of a teenager is fertile, rampant with belief that he or she can make a difference in this world. The enthusiasm hasn't been stripped out of them yet. And so it was with Danny as he drew fantastic versions of his would-be father traversing distant worlds, saving other "human-like" species from self-annihilation. Cara was most enthralled by his sketches, and one in particular, of McJic riding across the sky in a chariot like an ancient Roman god, she asked to keep. In the privacy of her own lonely days, when Patrick was "on business" in Arizona, she would stare wistfully at the sketch for an hour or so, often ending her infatuated longing by speaking his name. You know what followed.

Cara allowed Danny to come into the master bedroom whenever he liked (provided she wasn't sleeping or Patrick was home) and study her mysterious golden orchid. Danny had told her about his fascination with it. How its color was so rare, yet it seemed to appear with extraterrestrials, car accidents, and coma-induced dreams. It was a sign. Still, she could not bring herself to tell Danny that he was the son of McJic, not Patrick. She didn't know how a boy of fourteen would handle such knowledge.

Danny wondered what power *Magicka carallus* had. If he smoked its blooms, would he get off? If he rolled its leaves, would it take him to some enchanted land in his subconscious? If he ground its bulb, would he transport himself back to God, to the Council of Ancients, to Shanidar?

Despite their intimate morning dialogues, Danny did not mention the secret chamber, which he had meticulously cleaned and decorated and now called the Quarters, to his mom. There are certain things one doesn't tell one's parents. On one wall, he painted the Glorian Aurora witnessed by him and the Calvary. On another, he painted the Northern Hemisphere of the autumn night sky, in glow juice, with Sirius as the central beacon of hope. The Calvary managed to find an old, blue sofa to stuff into the Quarters. Danny, with valuable technical assistance from Cal, had painstakingly cleaned, lubricated, polished, adjusted, repaired and maintained the Heidelberg.

Everyone was excited to discover a secret passageway, a tunnel to be precise, about fifteen feet long that led to the south pasture. Janis had refused to crawl through the tunnel to explore with the boys but agreed it was a good discovery that could come in handy someday. She procured a small table, covered with a floral tablecloth, from her parents' attic. It served as the official altar to the Calvary's hero, Captain Crittenden. The lacquer box, his photograph, and his name spelled out in metal typefaces sat on top beside two candles, which were always lit in his honor whenever the Quarters was in use.

Danny's mind soon went back to the three simultaneous projects he was working on throughout the summer—his own journal entries, a manuscript he hoped to publish, and the intricate forgery of Joseph Pulitzer's diary. The young protégé of the stars was insatiably driven, staying in his room hours at a time on certain sunny days to practice his craft. He read about Pulitzer voraciously, calculating the journalist's whereabouts in the world so the diary would prove authentic. In his solitary research, he learned much about the sordid history of the United States from the mid 1800s to the early twentieth century, scandalous facts for anyone to learn in libraries, but nowhere to be found in school history books. He shared his discoveries and his disappointments about this serious lack of truth with his fellow Calvary officers, who cared about as much as mud daubers hearing about man landing on the moon. That there were significant holes in the curriculum of schools was tertiary to the great American mantra that the Calvary, along with millions of others in U.S. society, had come to live by—party first, ask questions later.

Danny's forgery bravado was encouraged by his conviction that he possessed special powers. He was intoxicated by the concept that he was from Sirius. That knowledge allowed him to separate himself from the social hypnosis of the daily American grind and elevate his personage above that which played out before him. Danny, mistakenly, immaturely, believed he was invincible, protected by the Council of Ancients from any problem befalling him. He was chosen wasn't he? Therefore, the world was his to enjoy, his to master.

He picked up one of the three tattered books on Pulitzer he had checked from the library. He scribbled a few sentences, his fingers feeling the numerous tooth pocks in the wooden shaft from his incessant biting, as he thought of what words Pulitzer might write. He had come far in his illicit transcription of the life of the famous newspaper man. In only six weeks, distracted by Janis, hanging out with Gram, playing guitar, getting high, writing legitimate prose, and fixing up the Quarters, he had written over sixty pages of believable Pulitzer entries.

His personal journal entries made as much of Pulitzer as Danny's increasing activism on environmental matters. Danny wrote, as we in the Stone family watched on TV, of his elation over the Greenpeace victory in stopping the Spanish government from dumping atomic waste into the ocean. "Brave souls," he wrote. "I wish I could be more like them."

Through the wall, he could hear Cal banging away at the Apple keyboard. Every day before and after summer school, Cal would cloister himself in his room to work on his computer. He wouldn't tell the rest of the Calvary what he was doing but promised they would love it when he was done. Danny was worried by his Glorian Aurora statement: "I saw my own death." And Cal seemed to be so distant lately, drowning himself with increasing amounts of alcohol and reefer. In a symbolic attempt to scoff at fatalism, Cal began dressing entirely in black. This, of course, was met with concern by Cara and utter contempt by Patrick. They didn't know the future that Cal saw at Featherbed Bank. No one did. All he had ever said through his heartbreaking smile was, "I saw my own death."

"The only bright spot," Danny wrote, "is Lian, the hot Amerasian chick Cal is dating." But even that had a downside for Cal, as he couldn't introduce Lian to Patrick, his bigoted father. Patrick's vein would surely pop, his temper would boil over, he'd berate and insult her, and the relationship would end. That would not prove wise, the two brothers had concluded. Danny penciled in his journal, looking up to watch Cara walk back from the Stones, "Cal is a lost soul."

"You wanna hear something weird?" Danny said as he lay slouched on the sofa. Stoned in the Quarters, he and Gram hadn't spoken in the hour since they each dropped a tablet of pink THC. *T* they called it. The constellations of the Northern Hemisphere glowed on the opposite wall. Two candles reflected like distant suns off the Glorian Aurora in the dim room.

"What day is it?" Gram said hazily, his brown, sorcerer's eyes like smudged crystal balls.

"Saturday, the thirteenth of November, and it's nighttime. Probably past eleven. Why?"

"Just checking. I was out in the Cosmos, man. I needed to hear the date to get grounded again. Man-oh-man, what a cool buzz this is. Back when I was official winetaster for the Bacchus temple in Rome, I never got this ripped."

"Yeah, man, this is posilutely fantastic," Danny said. He stared at the mesmerizing flames of Crittenden's candles. "I feel like a thousand gods are inside me."

"Shame Cal and Janis aren't here," Gram said. He tried to straighten himself up. His head still reeled from the *T* in his bloodstream, but at least he could talk now.

Cal was on a date with Lian in the car he had gotten in September for his birthday. Janis was out with her new boyfriend. Danny didn't mind; they didn't have a possessive relationship. Besides, he figured, the guy isn't from Canada, so it's not going to work out anyways. He laughed when he thought of how Janis had begun checking the nationality of all her potential suitors with instantaneous consistency within moments of meeting someone new. She was determined to find out the minute the future came true. What a crazy girl, he thought.

"So, tell me what's so weird?" Gram said.

Danny tried to wiggle his toes. "I figured out something that's puzzled me forever. At the oddest moments, for no reason at all, my mom goes into these wild contortions. She gets this weird smile like she's really enjoying herself. She's done it everywhere— Lake Cumberland, the dinner table, in front of a priest, in the kitchen, at the grocery store—it's weird, I tell you."

"So?" Gram grinned. "Maybe it's a chemical imbalance, a hormonal thing."

"I think I figured it out the other night when me and Janis were watching one of her parents' porno tapes," Danny said, eyes fixed on the dancing flames of Crittenden's altar. "She says the word McJic, he's the guy who projected himself as my real father during my dimensia, and seconds later she's on the floor hysterical."

"And . . ."

"I think she's getting herself off, like saying the word McJic gives her an orgasm."

"Man-oh-man, how cool. Back when I was the harem master for Ptolemy I, I saw a lot of that kind of thing. Orgasms, I mean. But I never saw a woman climax just by saying a name. If we could sell that technique, we could make a fortune."

"Yeah, and women would never have sex with men again." Danny wiggled his toes once more. "How long do you think my mom's been screwing your dad?"

Gram chuckled. "Since about the first week we moved in."

"That's about what I figured, too." He wasn't upset in the slightest. Both boys viewed sex as silly adult games. People lost in the world, looking for love wherever they can find it. Danny thought of the words to Pink Floyd's "Wish You Were Here," a sort of anthem for him.

"Danny?" Gram sat up, looking down from above at his friend. "Why do you think I'm here?"

"Beats me. Joshua landed a job here, I guess. Why?"

"Let me tell you about that demons-of-dimensia dream you had."

Danny had known from the beginning that Gram had a gift (you could see it in his eyes) but he hadn't considered it to be telepathy. He had listened for a year and a half to his bizarre theories and thought Gram was about to foist yet another outlandish hypothesis upon him. He had already heard one tonight, and that was enough. As they prepared to drop the *T*, before it had a chance to change their brain chemistry, Gram had espoused the theory that the whole problem of drugs in America could be traced back to massive CIA experiments. It began with JFK and the assassination he ordered of President Diem of South Vietnam. Gram explained that Kennedy's father, Joe, was a mobster who made his fortune selling liquor during Prohibition, so it was pretty much just an expansion of the family business to go into heroin. Diem owned the heroin routes out of Southeast Asia, and bang, he's dead. That broke the lock on the medicine cabinet.

Everybody in those days was making a power grab. The Mafia, the government, the Church, various contingents within the military, and, of course, corporate America. "The real issue," Gram said, "was that the CIA had gotten possession of Sandoz International's LSD and wanted to see how it affected folks. The best guinea pigs in the world have always been United States citizens. They've been subjected to nuclear tests for years in which hundreds-of-thousands died from radiation fall-out, and nobody said anything, so why not try drugs? Mind control through pharmaceuticals is a multi-national corporation's dream come true. And the U.S. population is the world's best test market."

He had gone on to say that, due to people's natural predilection to addiction and government's natural inefficiencies, the experiment quickly mushroomed out of control. But, like any good capitalistic society with a huge problem, the government didn't try to contain it; they turned their efforts to making a profit. Different factions controlled different markets—heroin, cocaine, marijuana, acid, downers—all controlled by one group or another.

"So what's the problem?" Danny had said as he took a hit of a fizzing Sprite to wash down the *T*.

"The problem is that they arrest innocent people. The CIA and Air Force both bring huge amounts of coke and pot and heroin into the country, using military planes, I might add, and then the average citizen gets popped for dealing. But—and here's the catch—only if they aren't buying from the government supply. It's turf wars, is all."

Danny had muttered something about Gram being nuts, but that didn't deter the twentieth century Merlin.

"You watch," Gram warned. "Before the new millennium, Congress will begin passing laws that allow personal property to be confiscated by the cops if you're caught using or selling drugs. You watch. It'll be just another scam to take people's property. It's all about profit and control."

An hour later, after the *T* was merrily traveling through their bloodstreams like a

VW Microbus carrying its occupants to a Dead concert, Danny had no way to predict, talking light training or not, what Gram was about to reveal. "So," he said as he sat up on the sofa, "Are you saying you know my dreams?"

"No. I only know one dream. The one you had when you almost died from pneumonia."

"No way, G-man," Danny laughed as he reached for the green bag of Mexican weed that sat on the altar. The Calvary had discovered that blowing a doobie while under the influence of Tetrohydrocannibinol (THC) enhanced the effects considerably, brought it back for an encore. He thumbed a pack of rolling papers and began to shape it with his fingers. Gram's eyes were serious, penetrating.

"In your coma, your dimensia carried you to a strange place. You awoke in front of a great campfire before a great council, and every time a council member spoke, the fire changed color to match that being's aura."

"I've told you that before." Danny pinched a bud between his thumb and index finger. He carefully crumbled the aromatic bloom into the awaiting paper, meticulously picking out the seeds, which he placed in a Kodak film container for future horticultural endeavors.

"What you didn't tell me is that the Elder Brother commanded McJic to send the boy a tutor. Someone to show him the way. Someone to befriend him. You didn't tell me that, did you?"

Danny stopped rolling the joint, setting it half-finished inside the baggy. "How the heck did you know that?"

"I am the tutor."

He was speechless. Gram, the half-baked, half-crocked, somewhat bumbling farmhand sent to tutor me? he thought. That can't be. No way. Danny did what any inebriated fourteen year old would do. He laughed hysterically.

"It's funny, isn't it?" Gram said. "You, with the brilliant mind and charming wit, and me, a simple caretaker's son. But you know, Danny, the signs are piling up in front of you—things aren't always what they seem." He paused and waved his hand about the room like a drunken Tinkerbell. "Your visit to Shanidar was no dream. That was reality. This," he swirled his hand again, "is an illusion. The real world awaits for those to discover its truths. Your visit to the Council was no dementia—it was real."

If the Earth were a metaphor for the human psyche, then Danny, at his core where his furnace burned hot and molten like a sun, believed Gram's words. At his mantel, a shallow level of thought, he wanted to believe it. At the surface, the crust of his subconscious, subject to wind and rain and earthquakes and all sort of climactic conditions, he found Gram's revelation impossible.

He clutched his stomach in laughter.

"That's okay." Gram chuckled, too. "Get it out of your system because we have a lot of work to do and so little time."

"Little time for what?"

"There's billions of lives to save." He peered through walnut, glazed eyes. "And a dying planet."

Danny tried to be more serious. "Who's supposed to save billions of lives?"

"You, and a few others."

"Am I like a new Messiah or something?" Danny said in hushed tone, feeling godlike under the influence of drugs.

"No. Don't let the drugs go to your head."

"So, what are you here to teach me? How to bend spoons with my mind? How to walk on water?"

Gram tossed back his shoulder-length black hair and looked at his student through mystic's eyes. "I'm going to teach you the power of compassion."

"Is that it? That's all? They sent you down here to teach me compassion?" Danny was disappointed there wasn't to be great Tibetan rituals and startling flashes of blinding insight as he sat at the knee of a master guru. Unlike most humans, who ignore the signs, he had ample evidence and overwhelming circumstance to believe Gram's claim—several instances of Glorian Aurora, a charmed existence, talking light, a persistent omnipresent feeling of being looked after—it all added up. Still, as he peered at his stoned counterpart, he only reluctantly believed it to be true. Too much dust in his synapses perhaps.

"Oh, there's a good many things to learn. I'll list them if I must. There's compassion, common sense, tolerance for others, the practice of nonjudgment, acceptance of personal responsibility, and the most important variable of all: the power, the absolute power of intent."

"Sounds like simple human nature to me."

"Man-oh-man, you catch on quick," Gram said. "Those who figure out the truth of human nature, those who study it, master it, make it their second nature, those are the ones who influence the whole of humankind. Provided they have the right intent, of course."

"I don't have a clue about these things. I don't get the value in this. How am I going to learn these things?"

Gram's eyes narrowed. "You are a light-being, Danny. A chosen one sent from the Council of Ancients to save the human race from extinction. Selected to help the Earth Mother heal her grievous wounds. All the answers are inside you." His voice turned soft, his brown eyes alight with the captain's flame. "I cannot give you answers, any more than I can see with your eyes. You must discover the answers to life on your own, in your own time, on your own terms. All I can do is make you aware of the gift and show you examples. Our hope is that you use your gift wisely."

Danny stood up, raised his hands to the air, palms up like a priest on Easter Sunday. In a booming voice he called out, "I am a chosen one. Heed my words."

Months swept by like a street cleaner after a ticker-tape parade. The Calvary, most often just Gram and Danny, spent their days talking religion, world events, politics, human nature, physics, philosophy, and all things important under the stars. Danny realized Gram was not a tutor in the standard sense; his was the school of the provocative—wild theories and fantastic conspiracies, some bizarre, some amazingly true. It was Danny's challenge to decipher which was which.

"Question everything," Gram said. "Things are not what they seem."

His mandate from the Council was to force Danny to think, to consider, to reason things out for himself. In that way, he would become stronger. He would earn the mantle of light-being, and someday, Gram promised, the rank of officer in the Council of Ancients.

Danny fell in love with the idea of being a light-being, of being an alien life force with special powers, and avoided the responsibility brought with it, as the human ego typically does to Earthlings. Gram had warned him, after his "I am a chosen one" joke, that while humor is a key element in the way one looks at the world, respect for certain truths, principles and authorities was equally as vital.

I looked at the mesmerized faces of my fellow television watchers—Rose, Parker, Maya, Twinkie—each with bright-eyed wonder, each shining with virginal bliss as the story continued to tell itself through the TV. I imagined them thinking, *What is this, magic?* I felt vindicated by *The Journals'* revelation, so much so that the perpetual throb of pain in my abdomen subsided slightly. Did good news put cancer on the run? Did positive energy rally certain immuno-response hormones to retake the territory lost to the hordes of cell scavengers that waged an unceasing and brutal battle on the terrain of my prostate and testicles? The bugle call had sounded, reinforcements were on the way. Now I had people who truly believed in me, supported me. It was a spectacular evening in the Stone family-room as we watched Danny's tale.

The boy's pursuit in creating the Pulitzer forgeries was unabated. He delved deeply into Pulitzer's life, researching his handwriting, carefully plotting the diary to make it appear factual, but the mischievous boy couldn't help himself and had to add a touch of humor. Historically, the young Joe Pulitzer wanted to be a mercenary (such were the times), but he was too frail, suffering from poor health and bad eyesight, and was turned down by the Austrian, British, and French militaries. It was the French, Danny wrote, tongue in cheek, who turned Pulitzer down because of hemorrhoids. He had Pulitzer write, "I curse my burning backside." In his own diary, Danny wrote, "If only they had Preparation H back then."

Pulitzer was a determined fellow and eventually made it to America to fight for the North in the Civil War. Even there, he couldn't cut it and was mustered out of the army. He ended up in St. Louis working for a German newspaper. Danny employed the meticulous skills of an old-world craftsman, paying attention to every detail, making sure none of his invented entries conflicted with the text books he studied. He made Pulitzer fluent in English by 1872. Danny was struck by the amazing similarity between Joseph Pulitzer and his father, Patrick. Both men were driven with intense ambition, which was more important to them than their families. Both men were egomaniacal. Not many people liked Pulitzer or the senior Gilday. Both were overbearing and demanding in unreasonable portions. Anything for success.

Danny was appalled and enlightened at the corruption of society during that period. The history he learned in school didn't jive at all with the facts he dug up on his own research. In that day, as today (though they'd never admit it), newspapers were either founded as Republican or Democratic rags, setup to function as propaganda mouthpieces for the parties in their respective cities and towns. All politicians of the era were on the take, and major scandals erupted continuously. Money, as in modern times, could cover up even the most heinous crimes. Pulitzer, who had been elected to the Missouri State Legislature, lost his temper and shot a lobbyist. He paid a fine of $105. No jail time. Just a simple fine.

While Danny immersed himself in Pulitzer's past, he also enjoyed his teenage present. He wasn't only infatuated with fooling the world with fake diaries of a famous man. His heart was also taken by Celeste, a girl in his biology class who was every bit his intellectual equal. She was fair-skinned, with a dusting of freckles across the bridge of her nose. Danny imagined her freckles to be the constellation Orion with stars invisible to the human eye. He romanticized the tiny, darkened patches as light not yet having reached the Earth. Ah, such are the dreamings of a teen in lust. There was a sophistication about Celeste, an attitude, that he loved. She would be a challenge. He had been summoning the courage to ask her out when a note from her was slipped to him by Timothy Oswich.

"Would you like to go to the movies with me?" she wrote.

They began spending serious time together, with Danny sharing his interests and secrets openly with her. Celeste, although attracted by Danny's dangerous nature, emphatically echoed Allison's words some years before that he should give up his life of crime.

Celeste was his opposite: pragmatic to his flippant, concerned to his carefree,

responsible to his wild, respectful to his revolutionary. But the blue-eyed Celeste, white-satin lovely and Harvard book-smart, did not know Danny's biggest secret, that of being a light-being. He heeded Gram's warning not to share his ancestry for fear of a long stay in a mental institution. Nor did she realize that Danny's intelligence was at a depth almost all humans fail to explore, giving him a distinct insight to people, which created a magnetism around him that people found impossible to resist.

Celeste was keenly (and jealously) aware of Danny's energy that seemed to draw people to him effortlessly. Danny, too, was cognizant of his growing ability to influence people by his presence. It was a gift Gram told him to handle with care, a gift easily abused, a gift the gods would strip from him if he did not use it with the proper intent.

Danny, raging with teenage hormones, didn't listen. "I've got a star in my hip pocket," became his favorite, overused expression when someone—Gram, Cara, Cal, Janis, or Celeste—suggested that he was sometimes taking things too far. "I've got a star in my hip pocket." One could say he wasn't taking himself too Sirius.

"Has the world gone mad?" he asked Gram as he inhaled a huge toke of marijuana while they sat in the cool confines of the Quarters. It was exactly one week before Christmas. "Somebody in South Africa tried to blow up a nuclear power station today."

The fire from the joint burned furiously as Gram sucked in the smoke. "We all do things without thinking," he said. "We all do things that are harmful. It's simply a matter of perspective."

Christmas 1982 taught Danny a lesson in religion. He was watching Allison's lace Christmas ornament spin slowly like a *Nutcracker* ballerina as it hung by a strand of fishing line from the ceiling of the Quarters just above Captain Crittenden's altar. A reefer fog blurred the constellations of the Northern Hemisphere. Cal was passed-out on the sofa, having drunk five beers and four shots of Jim Beam *and* smoked two potent joints of Panama Red.

"If Jesus were alive today," Gram said, "he would be crying in shame over Christmas."

"How so?" Danny asked.

"Mass commercialism. Christmas makes a total mockery of His life."

"You're kidding, right?"

Gram twirled a long strand of his hair and looked at him through eyes as red as Rudolph's schnoz with a head cold. "Afraid not, Danny. Jesus Christ, whose real name was Yeshua by the way, came to Earth to deliver a message of a simple life of virtue without corruption and greed and materialism. Just look what we've done in His name. The biggest holiday in the western world dedicated to his birth, but celebrated in shopping malls and Christmas sales that begin in October. Jesus was born in August, for chrissakes."

"No way, G-man."

"Historical facts prove it. Jesus' life has been rewritten by medieval monks on a mission to save their religion. They had to create a savior to compete in the dog-eat-dog world of religion. Islam was coming on strong, and they had to contend with all manner of smaller sects in Germany, the British Isles, and the Norse countries. The battle for hearts and souls is brutal. The Catholics needed an infallible champion, so they picked Jesus as their poster child. He has served them well; they're the most powerful organization on Earth."

"Are you saying the Bible is a lie?"

"No. I'm saying it was never the truth. A story written for sheep. All anyone need do is study ancient texts: Babylonian, Sumerian, Greek, Roman, Judaic, Pagan, Christian. You'll see the same basic myths rewritten again and again, based on the goals of the people in power at the time. All this nonsense is just stories."

"But why?" Danny asked. He squinted through the haze at Sirius glowing on the wall. Cal, dressed in black jeans and black turtleneck with black boots, snored fitfully next to him sounding like a lawn mower whose engine would not catch. Pull. *Rrrr . . . put . . . put.* Pull. *Rrrr . . . put . . . put.* No matter how hard one yanked on the chord, the mower was not destined to cut grass. Danny nudged him with his elbow to get him to change position in hopes the snoring would stop, but to no avail. Even his dreams are troubled, Danny thought to himself.

"Money, control, power, ego. It's all there, and always has been," Gram stated. "If you were a priest and hundreds, maybe thousands of people looked up to you and gave you money, and often sex, because you were divine, you'd come up with some good material to keep the flock in the pasture."

"I don't believe it."

"That's okay. You don't have to. It's just my thoughts."

"Are you saying that all religion is corrupt?"

"No," Gram said. He took a large swig of beer. "I'm saying that belief, or faith in a higher power—God, if you like—is an individual matter. All true spirituality lies within each person's own soul. Some have a serious lack of spirituality and have a need to have someone tell them what to believe, what to feel, what to think. Others know from the beginning that all their answers lie within. But as soon as people form a group, corruption inevitably follows. Egos and greed grab hold and never let go."

"So, you *are* saying that all religion is corrupt."

"No. I guess I'm saying it depends on intent. If the church, whatever denomination, truly means well, and I mean truly, there is no misintent, then it is not corrupt. But if the people within the religion are there for the wrong reason, then that religion is corrupt."

"I get it," Danny said, locating Sirius through the cloudy room. "That's simple enough."

"So, as an example, it doesn't matter how a person celebrates Christmas, or whether it is done on Jesus' real birthday or not, as much as the intent with which the person celebrates. Churches, however, the bastions of honesty that they are supposed to be, should not allow rituals in honor of Jesus' birthday in December."

"Why not?"

"Because His birthday is sometime in August. They supposedly stand for honesty and truth and faith, but instead they perpetuate a falsehood—Jesus was born in the summer, not December 25. A little known but well-documented fact is that Christmas today is actually based upon the Egyptian sun god holiday, which celebrated the seasonal harvest on December 24th and 25th. The Catholics figured out that the best way to get people into the fold wasn't to force them into it (that never works in the long run), but to supplant their normal, local religious customs with Christian ones. So, out went the sun god and in came Jesus H. Christ, Son of God," Gram said, his Rasputin eyes fixed upon the flickering candles of Crittenden's altar. "If people want to celebrate in December, fine—a winter harvest, a break from dreary winter, or being with loved ones—then let's call it what it is and keep Christ the hell out of it."

"Sounds like you're making too big a deal out of this," Danny said.

"Maybe," Gram admitted. "But my intent is right."

"What would that be?"

"To get you to question all the force-fed programming and brain-washing that takes place in our society, and to question if we are doing things for the right reasons. It could be that Christmas is a great holiday for a good many people who honor its traditions and sing the glory of His name. If that were true, though, people would know that there has been a great lie in the form of the Bible laid at their doorstep. The intent of the Bible is to control people's beliefs, because, dear Danny, if you can do that, you can control their actions and possessions."

"I was in the bookstore the other day and saw over thirty-seven different Bibles," Danny said. "And I wondered, if people think that the Bible came directly from God, then how come there isn't just one version?"

Gram raised his eyes toward the trapdoor. "Now you're thinking."

"But I'm still not sure why it matters when we celebrate Christmas."

"Again, *intent* is the key here," Gram stated as he struck a match. The joint had gone out. He held the roach close to his fingers. Danny shifted his stoned gaze to Gram's illuminated face. Gram spoke as he held in his breath. "Captain Crittenden had the idea that he could forge documents for Abe Lincoln and possibly bring about the end of a bloody war. Are you with me?"

"Sure, I get it."

"You, on the other hand, have a desire to forge documents, Pulitzer's diary as an example, to see if you can get away with it and also make some money. Right?"

"Yeah, but I—"

"So Crittenden's intent was for good, while your intent is for greed, which is bad. So he had the right intent, and you have the wrong one."

"That's where you make your first mistake, G-man!" Danny shouted as if he'd won the Publisher's Clearinghouse Sweepstakes. "Crittenden was executed, and I'm living in luxury." He smirked, unable to control his glee at having outwitted Gram.

"You may still be executed," Gram said with a large, warm smile. "And Crittenden did what he had to on this physical plane. You are seeing only a one-dimensional result. His intent was true, and he was rewarded with wisdom and riches beyond human comprehension. You, I'm afraid, are going to be pissed on by the gods because you have the wrong intent."

"You're wasted." Danny pushed Cal's ribs again. Pull. *Rrrr . . . put . . . put.* Pull. *Rrrr . . . put . . . put.* The mower wouldn't start. Cal's engine was flooded. "I'm a chosen one. The gods love me. I was born to be a master forger, you said it yourself at Featherbed Bank."

"A gift once given may also be taken away. Intent, Danny, that's the key. If you abuse the gift, your forgery will cost you dearly."

"You're so serious." Danny said, taking the joint. "Is that when you'll save me?"

"Save you?"

"Yeah, you said you were going to save me by a frozen lake someday."

"Oh that. There's a high probability you will need my assistance."

"You'll have to tell me about it sometime," Danny said, exhaling a mushroom of happy smoke.

"Intent, Danny, is important, don't ever forget it." Gram strained to hold his breath as he spoke. "It's used in all the wrong ways by people in this world to manipulate opinion."

"How so?"

"Many people want things black or white, no gray. But in reality, if we can call this reality for a moment, it's the gray that decides the validity of the issue, whatever it may be. And the gray just always happens to be intent. It's the deciding factor."

"That's deep, man."

"It's simple; take murder, for instance. One side says killing someone is wrong under all circumstances in our society. If you kill you should be put to death. Yet we honor soldiers who fight and die and kill for our country because the intent is that they are doing it to keep us free. So in the soldier's case, he is a murderer who is also a hero."

"Damn, G-Man, I never thought of it that way."

"So intent *is* the key," he went on. "Another side says the death penalty is cruel and unusual punishment, and who are we to play God? No one for any reason should be put to death; they should be rehabilitated. But you take a mass murderer who has tortured, mutilated, and killed a dozen children and tell me that person has any hope of fitting into our society. He has none, and the penalty for him should be death."

Danny jerked his head back and bugged out his bloodshot eyes in mock surprise. "That's pretty hard core for a guy from Shanidar. I thought you were supposed to be spiritual."

"I am spiritual, but that doesn't mean there aren't certain harsh realities to existence that require strict action, like eliminating bad elements. You could take a wild tiger cub from the jungle at birth, feed it well everyday, and provide a nurturing environment for it. Raise it as you would your own child, and you will still never get that tiger to say grace at the dinner table."

Danny burst out laughing. "I could see it, man," he said as the smoke swirled around his head like a dancer in a sultan's tent.

"The point is, you can't tame a beast. It's still an animal functioning at a primal level. The serial killer is on that level."

"Okay," Danny said. The hazy light projected phantoms upon the walls. "I get your point. So you don't celebrate Christmas because tigers can't say grace?"

"Something like that." Gram smiled.

Danny reached into his coat pocket and produced a small, brightly wrapped present. "For you," he said, handing it to Gram. "Even if you don't believe in Christmas."

Gram tore into the paper. He held his shiny gift up in the smoke of the Quarters. "A roach clip, I love it." He affixed the joint to the alligator jaws. "Thanks."

"Consider it given with the right intent," Danny said.

The fates of early March 1983 smiled upon Danny with one more example that convinced him his destiny was to become a master forger. Celeste transferred to the graphic-arts program at the high school, giving him access to the ink supply he needed to complete a high-school prank. He promised her that the ink was not going to the

Pulitzer project, which by now had become common knowledge among the sophomores at Grant County High and had given Danny a certain status among the students. It would have been amateurish, and most certainly would have led to his arrest. If one is to pull off the crime of the century, details must be strictly adhered to.

He was ready to end his plotting of Pulitzer's trials and tribulations and begin the real task of forgery. He was set to transcribe his notes from the papers, which had accumulated in thick heaps in a locked desk drawer, but not with Grant County ink; he'd concocted a mix of linseed oil and dried 1860s ink for that. He had achieved a remarkable level of skill for one so young, but then, he was a star-child, a light-being. What he didn't realize was that what he actually found most fascinating about his crime was the discovery of history itself. He lost himself in his research of the past as he strolled down the sordid avenues of Pulitzer's twisted world.

More strokes of irony brushed Danny's palette. Shortly after Pulitzer paid the fine for shooting the lobbyist named Augustine, he was elected police commissioner in St. Louis. Then, Pulitzer was secretary to the Republican convention held in Cincinnati in 1872, a fact Danny used to convince himself that divine providence (the Council) was showing him the way since he was from Cincinnati and Pulitzer visited there. He also learned that Pulitzer married Kate Davis, daughter of Jefferson Davis of slavery-forever distinction. Like many a person addicted to history, Danny was continually amazed at the past's attachment to the present. He became totally disillusioned that so few people knew the truth.

Danny wondered, as he read the scandalous news of Anne Buford's forced resignation from the disgraced EPA, what Pulitzer would have thought about government agencies, sworn to protect the public, being sold to the highest bidder. Specifically, one Environmental Protection Agency stripped of its purpose by Reagan and his boys, who filled it with cronies of a probusiness bent. "Good riddance, Anne Buford," he said as he turned the page to a story about the CIA, which admitted it had exaggerated the Soviet arms build-up for at least six years. He scoffed at the reply of a senator, with a weapons plant in his state, who said that he didn't think that should stop us from producing more bombs. Danny asked himself, "How many times do we need to blow up the planet, evenwise?"

"Father," Danny said, just six days before his fifteenth birthday, over a meatloaf and potatoes dinner, "Did you see that the FBI released a report saying the anti-nuke movement isn't a Communist organization?"

Grumbles from the far end of the table. A quaint, knowing smile from Cara. Beer belch from Cal, dressed in black, naturally, and who had sometimes taken to drinking right after school. This was one of those sometimes.

"Reagan announced a high-tech missile defense system called Star Wars today," Danny pressed on. "Hundreds of billions of dollars for laser beams, particle beams, satellites, and microwave devices to shoot down Soviet missiles. Sounds like Uncle Ronnie and his military boys figured the Earth-based nuclear deterrent has milked the public as much as it can. Now they're going to fool us into spending our taxes on some other multi-billion dollar fiasco we don't need."

More grumbles from Patrick, who was busy thinking of his Phoenix mistress, a woman who had threatened to cut him off unless he paid her a higher monthly allowance. Blackmail is such nasty business. Snickers of delight from Cara, who loved it that Danny toyed with Patrick, whom she barely touched anymore. And no response from Cal, who was content smashing his green beans into paste. Things in the Gilday family weren't going too well.

Danny had one final comment. "If the military wants to use microwaves to blast missiles out of the sky, what happens to our food when we zap it in the microwave?"

A spotlight flashed through the evergreens. Danny dropped his near-empty quart of Colt 45 and headed for the chain-link fence behind the bowling alley. Gram was quick at his heels. The boys hopped the fence and tore through the parking lot. A siren blared. Lights flashed. Tires spit gravel like shotgun pellets. The cops had spotted them drinking. Danny, his heart pounding, his breath smelling like a German *brew haus*, headed back toward the bowling alley. Gram followed. Through the pines they fled, a branch raking itself across Danny's cheek. Small trickles of blood cooled his burning skin. I can't get caught, he panicked, Father will kick my ass.

Danny and Gram found themselves standing at the edge of the busy highway, huffing. Cars whizzed by at fifty, sixty, miles an hour, a long chain of people with nowhere to go on a Friday night. Suddenly, the cop car squealed around the corner, lights flashing. "Freeze!" the patrolman ordered through his loudspeaker.

"Right," Danny said.

"See you on the other side!" Gram called as he dashed across the bustling road, his wild hair flowing like the end of a witch's broomstick. Cars honked, then skidded, drivers swore and felt their hearts palpitate as they reached for the prescription of Valium stuffed into purse or pocket. They had a story to tell now—about "that damn fool kid who ran right out in front of my Ford. Darn near killed him." But first the Valium.

"C'mon, Danny!" Gram shouted over the din of road noise. He waved his arm. "You're going to get busted."

The officer was out of his car, a portly cop, as they all seemed to be in northern Kentucky. He was only twenty yards away and closing. Danny eyed the solid line of cars and their blinding headlights. He glanced at Gram urging him on. He had no choice— stay and be arrested for drinking, or run and take his chances. A fifteen year old with Danny's penchant for danger doesn't have to think twice. Some might say fifteen year olds don't think at all.

He cleared the gravel beneath his feet, preparing his run. The cop ran toward him. "Don't do it, kid!"

Danny dug in and pushed off. His ankle gave way. His foot slid. He slipped into the street. Danny's knee crashed into the pavement. Something tore. Clothes? Skin? He had no time to consider it further. His knee felt warm, liquid; he was bleeding. He righted himself with his hands and pushed off again. Car horns echoed in his ears, but he didn't slow. He found a hole in the traffic. A pattern. If he timed the lights just right, he might make it. The cop was at Danny's heels, lunging for him, trying to grab his shirt.

The long, terrifying cry of black rubber scorching asphalt split the incessant road noise. "Crazy asshole!" someone yelled.

He ran hard. He paid no attention to his swollen knee and the red flow which trickled down his leg. He dodged a pickup truck, its lights blinding his vision as if he had stared at a solar eclipse. The truck flashed its brights and slid to a stop a hundred feet down the highway. One lane to go. An old Rambler, one headlight missing, exhaust belching from its tail like a cheap Hungarian cigar, was next. Danny lurched forward. The driver didn't see him. He was going to get hit. Shit, he thought, I can't die on my fifteenth birthday. Not today. The gods are supposed to be protecting me.

Desperately, he dove. The bumper of the Rambler knicked his foot. He tumbled over, gravel and grit tearing at his jeans. Gram pulled him up by the shirt. Danny's mind was rampant with fear and excitement. No time to assess damages. They had to run. They scurried down an embankment and hopped a creek, Danny splashing a shoe in its shallow water. They flew through the woods, their feet digging hard at everything in their path. Danny's knee pulsed with pain, and he slowed a bit to ease the ache. They found a trail and ran along it for a few minutes. Danny began to hobble, but still they ran until they were exhausted and were sure they were safe.

Struggling to catch their breath, they sat on a fallen tree. Gram said, "Man-oh-man, that was fun. We should do that again sometime. What a total rush!"

"What the hell kind of celestial tutor are you?" Danny wheezed like an asthmatic in an asbestos factory.

"We should call this game Timing the Light."

"Game?" Danny heaved, trying to get some precious air. He tore open the rip in his

433

jeans and examined his busted kneecap. Not too bad, he thought. He'd had worse scrapes falling off his bike.

"Yeah man, I haven't had this much fun since I was a marathoner back in Greece."

"G-man." Danny wiped the sweat from his forehead with his shirttail. The sting of his injuries began to announce themselves. "You're not a very good influence on me."

"Just testing the limits of life, Danny boy. Just testing the limits."

A dangerous new game had been invented—Timing the Light. Football is played on a gridiron with steroid slathered men in helmets and pads. Child's play. Baseball is a run around a diamond in ninety-feet doses. Boring. Hockey is filled with toothless wonders on skates with sticks. Aggressive figure skating. Basketball is sweat and lay-ups and alley-oops and three-point jumpers by men nearly as tall as the hoop. Too easy. Golf—please. No, they are all pretenders, these sports. The only real game in town, at least for Danny and Gram, became Timing the Light. It was dangerous, primal. It featured concrete and two-ton cars racing at damaging speeds. It was headlights and bumpers, man against machine. It was primitive. Professional sports be damned—it's all show, anyway. No spectators allowed at this new game. Only personal achievement. The rush of victory, of survival. Timing the Light defied death itself. It was individual challenge. Conquest.

No matter the weather—hard rain, frost, chilled mist, clear night, windy gust, torrid heat, humid oppression—the game would be played. The boys played regularly on Fridays and Saturdays, if Celeste wasn't around. Danny worked his mom for a new pair of gym shoes. If he was going to put himself at risk, he was going to minimize it.

Celeste didn't like Danny playing the new game, but their relationship was going well. Her parents approved of him. He had charmed them early with boyish ease. Mr. Jordan, who worked as an auctioneer down in Falmouth, thought Danny a little too smug, but he didn't find any real fault with the boy. Of course, he hadn't heard the rumors at Grant County High about his forgeries, either. Mrs. Jordan, who sold Mary Kay cosmetics to a wide circle of friends across northern Kentucky, saw through Danny's charade of innocence, but said nothing in fear of upsetting her dear Celeste, her pride and joy.

So as it was, the two slowly fell from like to love. Danny had never experienced anything like that since his correspondence with Allison. He and Celeste had much in common. Their hormones seemed to be in harmony as they experienced adolescent explorations of sexuality—making out at movies, wrestling on the sofa at Celeste's house, doing it in the Quarters.

"Sex with Celeste," Danny confided in Gram as they prepared for a round of Timing the Light, "is different than sex with Janis. With Janis, it's anything goes. With Celeste, it's more restricted, like she isn't sure what she likes all the time."

"Does Celeste know you're banging Janis, too?" Gram asked as he relaced his sneakers so that they were tight enough for his jaunt across the road.

"It's more when Janis wants it," Danny admitted, studying the traffic. "No, Celeste doesn't know. She's too possessive. But she suspects, I think. If she found out, that'd be it."

He eyed the cars across the four lanes of traffic. The boys had taken to wider and more death-defying locales to keep the game interesting, to keep the blood pumping. Timing the Light had evolved beyond merely getting across the street, it had been refined with nuances such as speed of the car, make and model of the vehicle (trucks were worth a lot), and the closeness with which the car came to hitting them. An Olympic-style point system had ensconced itself in the game, which the boys used to rate their performance. The purpose was to experience as close a shave as possible without getting hurt. Close enough to cut the sideburns off a shoelace, the peach fuzz off a face, close enough to pull the lint from a navel. Gram appeared to be the more death-defying of the two, but not by much. Both boys were at extreme risk.

Danny bounced on his toes, stretched his legs a couple times, crouched, then took off. "See you on the other side, G-man!"

Joseph Pulitzer was elected to the United States Congress in 1885. He resigned April 10, 1886, just six months after he won the election, repulsed by the blatant corruption and scandal that plagued those allegedly hallowed halls. Some things never change. He would never run for public office again. Instead, the irrepressible Pulitzer channeled all his energies into his newspaper *The New York World*, forever to alter the face of journalism.

Danny, sitting beneath the glare of a desk lamp, as a blackened May evening drew tight, scribbled a poem for the book he was writing as he thought of Pulitzer's strange dichotomies. The man tried so hard to do right in the world, yet he had such a bad temperament that people could scarcely stand to be around him. What an odd phenomenon, Danny thought. He opened his personal diary and stared at his pencil sketches of McJic. There were seventeen in all, each a fantasy of his dream father. Not the typical, will-you-play-ball-with-me father, but a star-hopping, mythological, space-warrior father who could conquer any challenge. He closed the book.

He stared at the disguised Mamets, covered over with painted abstracts, and considered Drew Winthrop and his merry art museum. He hadn't painted in several months. It no longer pleased him. "It's too homo-generous," he had confided to the Calvary. "I'm going to write a book instead."

Indeed, his obsession with the Pulitzer diaries left little time for writing. He seldom worked on his manuscript unless a pang of guilt crept up and forced him to write a few paragraphs. He did, however, play guitar almost every day and wrote numerous songs. He tried diligently to reproduce the music he heard that fateful night at Featherbed Bank. He had thought, given his intelligence and his belief that he could master anything, that he would easily write the music as he had heard it. He remembered the lyrics precisely and transcribed them into poems while he waited for the music to come. It was the chords and the harmonic orchestration that gave our young genius pause. The Calvary and Celeste loved to hear him play. Gram had taken to the harmonica and would often accompany his songs. As the music of the Glorian Aurora continued to elude him, Danny wrote music of a more Earthly rock 'n' roll variety.

"Damn it!" Danny hurriedly folded the newspaper closed.

"What's wrong?" Cara asked. She poured a glass of milk to go with his after school snack. The fresh scent of spring lilac wafted through the kitchen window. Cara loved that smell. Patrick, as usual, was away in Arizona. Cal, outfitted in black shorts, a black T-shirt and black sandals, was fishing at the lake with a six-pack (Cara didn't know about the beer).

Cara dabbed a droplet of milk off the counter with a dishrag. A contented smile blew across her face. Her evil husband was out of town, she'd just seduced his new V.P. of Marketing (payback for Patrick's abusive, self-centered nature), and glorious lilac filled her with spring fever. The truth was, the further away Patrick was from her and her children, and the longer his absences, the happier she became.

"Remember a few weeks ago when they announced they found Hitler's diaries?" Danny said. "They caught a guy in Germany who admitted that the Hitler diaries *Stern* magazine had announced were fakes."

"And that bothers you?" Cara arranged raspberry-filled cookies in a circle around the rim of a plate. She set the glass in the center of the cookie ring.

"I knew from the start the diaries were forged. I just didn't want the guy to get caught. Konrad Kujau was his name. From Stuttgart."

She set the plate next to Danny, where he lay on the sofa, and patted his head. "There are probably more important things to get upset about, dear." She sat in the recliner next to him. "How's your environmental stuff coming along? Doesn't that interest you anymore?"

"Sure, Ma. I'm still into it." He couldn't explain to his mother that he was concerned about his own ability to pull off the Pulitzer diaries. He felt part of an exclusive fraternity of counterfeiters, a secret sect of craftsmen (and women) who plied their trade anonymously. He felt bound to them by a gentleman's sense of loyalty. When one forgery brother (or sister) fell, they all fell, he thought. Besides, it didn't bode well for his own efforts if they had so quickly exposed Herr Kujau's fraud. Would he be so easily caught? he wondered.

Pulitzer's life was humming along under Danny's able reconstruction, and he didn't want to be discouraged by news of fellow forgers getting busted. Pulitzer was now battling it out for market share in New York City with the moneyed William Randolph Hearst. Few people realized, as history was rewritten, that Hearst got his seed money to dabble in the media through his unscrupulous father, George Hearst, who, as a senator from California, profited handsomely when legislation was passed to illegally remove the Sioux Indians from their sacred land in the Black Hills of South Dakota. Turned out that there was gold in them thar hills, and Senator Hearst wanted it. Yet another prestigious American family revealed for what it was. The Indians got shafted and the Hearsts became American royalty. Good press was easy to buy, especially when you own the media.

Danny called this section of Pulitzer's diary "The Hearst Years of My Life." To be sure, William Randolph Hearst, who had been booted from Harvard, was an ever-present migraine in the agitated mind of Joseph Pulitzer. Their hatred of each other, and their incessant desire to dominate the readership of New York, lead their respective newspapers—Pulitzer's *New York World* and Hearst's *New York Morning Journal*—to sensationalize headlines and fabricate stories. So intense did the rivalry become that the two men were responsible for printing stories of invented Spanish atrocities against the citizens of Cuba. These false stories forced Congress to declare war on Spain. In the end, American aggression, as instigated by Pulitzer and Hearst, led to the United States' possession of the Philippines, Guam, and Puerto Rico as spoils of war, and many, many newspapers were sold.

"Now that's America," Danny said as he finished putting the final touches to that section of the bogus diaries.

As he stashed his work under the sofa, Danny explained to Janis, "Even though I think he was a prick who treated people badly, I do feel sorry for him."

"Why?" Janis asked.

"He had a nervous breakdown when he was thirty-seven and never recovered from it. The guy spent almost the rest of his life sailing around the world on his yacht, nearly blind, his nerves jangled, and pained by even the slightest sound. He searched the world for a cure, going from one spa to the next, but never found relief."

"Tough life." Janis plopped on the sofa, her short denim cutoffs riding high up her thighs. "Sailing around the world in a yacht."

"Yeah, but he was sick."

"Poor Joe Pulitzer." She reached out and grabbed Danny's shirt. "Why don't you sail your vessel into my harbor?"

Danny recognized that glimmer in her seductive eyes. He hesitated. "The science fair is tomorrow, and I have to bind my project."

"Are you sure you should go through with it?" Janis asked.

"What are they gonna do? Suspend me?"

Janis kissed him on the lips. "Let's worry about that later, eh sailor?"

The science fair came and went. He pulled off his caper successfully. The judging committee chairman, Danny's autocratic biology teacher, was completely embarrassed and discredited, which had been Danny's goal from the start. A student riot had broken out. Tables were overturned. Science projects, some weeks and months in the making, were destroyed. Students chanted in defiance. Chaos raged inside the Grant County High School gymnasium. He hadn't counted on the riot and the subsequent damage. He only wanted to display his genius. Nor had he counted on discovering a hidden power within himself. A power to control action, to manipulate the energy of a room and diffuse any situation, bringing all the attention to himself.

"Did you see Mr. Dickens' face when he bellowed for you with the microphone?" Janis said, her eyes alive with mischief as she, Danny, Gram, and Celeste ate in the school cafeteria the afternoon after "The Insurrection."

"No," Danny said, scooping a fork of macaroni and cheese. "I was copping a bag of reefer from Johnny Hedges in the back." He could feel the admiring stares of kids from other tables. He could sense it as he had walked through the halls that morning, in class, and especially now.

"It was so cool." Janis beamed. "His face was red as a zit. I thought he was going to explode."

Celeste, jealous of Janis' casualness with Danny, scowled and speared a pickle. "People could have been hurt."

"I didn't mean for things to go that far. It was just a book. Jesus." Danny rolled his eyes. Celeste had supported him last evening at the science fair, out of principle, but she didn't like the fact that he was embroiled in controversy and loving it.

Gram grinned like a sorcerer whose spell had just saved the kingdom. "It's good to shake up the system every once in awhile. Those teachers on the judging committee already had their favorites picked out before the fair started. It was a done deal. My buddy, Dan, came along and forced them to actually stop playing politics and reward the best student for the best project. What a radical thought." He raised his milk carton. "I propose a toast. To Daniel Oliver Gilday, first-place winner in the Grant County Science Fair. *Vive la* revolution!"

"*Vive la* revolution!" everyone said, except Celeste, whose soft, blue eyes had hardened into bullets fixed angrily on her plate.

Danny didn't know why she was angry. Was it the science project itself that set her off? Was it Janis' attention? Jealousy? Was she worried about the strange influence he had demonstrated?

"You shouldn't have used me," Celeste said. "If I had known it was going to cause all this, I wouldn't have snuck you into the print shop."

"Celeste, you knew what I was doing. I didn't keep anything from you. You knew I was going to recreate the reproduction section of the biology book. I didn't know Dickens was going to go ballistic."

"Yeah, Celeste," Janis defended Danny. She was the last person Celeste wanted to hear from. "Danny didn't encourage the chanting when Dickens announced he was disqualified."

"And Danny didn't know Griffin was going to start yelling 'death to the totalitarian regime.' Danny stopped the riot, remember?" Gram said.

"You used me!" Celeste rose from the table and stomped off.

Danny didn't bother to chase her. He didn't do that sort of thing. He shrugged. "She'll get over it."

Janis scooted closer to him. Hoping no one would notice, she slipped her hand under the table and placed it on his thigh. "It was so incredible how you stopped The Insurrection with just a wave of your hand," she said, turned on. "How did you do that?"

"Yeah, Danny," a kid from the next table asked. "Where did you learn that?"

"Oh," Danny shrugged. "I have a star in my hip pocket."

It was true. He had unlocked a mechanism, which he could summon at will, that allowed him to change the emotion of a person (or crowd) with a single, magical wave of his powerful hand. He began to practice this talent, which he called the FEW technique in part because he felt it required Focus, Energy and Will, but also because he believed it was an otherworldly power available only to a chosen few. He practiced

with regularity, perfecting his technique like a carnival showman. He could stop conversations cold. He could cause Patrick, who often went flying into unprovoked rages, to forget what he was fuming about. He could placate Cal, who was growing more distant, and only seemed happy with a Miller High Life in one hand and a joint in the other. Partying with the Calvary had become Cal's battle cry.

Danny was tickled by his FEW discovery but naive about its potential. Using his newfound influence, he quickly persuaded Celeste to forgive him, even though he was convinced he had done nothing wrong.

School was out for the summer, and Danny looked forward to a full season of heavy sex, drugs, and rock 'n' roll. Celeste, whose keen intellect saw him beginning a descent that should be averted, tried her best over a burger and fries to convince him there was more to life than the three aforementioned vices.

"Did you understand the movie?" she asked as she unwrapped the colby-colored paper of her cheeseburger.

He squinted beneath the fluorescence of the golden arches. "What's so hard to understand about *Return of the Jedi?* He was puzzled, lethargic after coming down from a pre-theater joint. "It was cool."

"You seemed pretty high." Celeste wasn't opposed to smoking a joint now and again, or drinking a few beers, but in moderation. "I'm worried, Danny. You're taking everything too far."

He grinned and lifted his eyebrows. He did his best to project the charm that she found so irresistible. "Like what?"

"Quit trying to manipulate me, Danny! That slippery grin and gleaming eyes won't work on me tonight. I'm serious."

"I'm not," he lied. There's a flaw in my FEW technique, Danny told himself, I'll have to work on that. "So, what am I taking to an extreme?" He tore into his fries, grabbing a half-dozen with his fingers. He swabbed them in catsup and stuffed them into his mouth.

"Everything, Danny." She wanted so badly for him to go straight, to take better care of himself. "That stupid game you play—Timing the Light. And you get high all the time: before school, after school, after dinner. Every time you go somewhere, you think getting stoned is a prerequisite."

He could see the concern on Celeste's flour, Sorbonne-bound face. She was right, of course, but he couldn't admit it. He knew he was living on the edge. So what? he thought, I'm indestructible, and I like it there on the edge. But he couldn't tell her that; she hated it there. She wanted love and romance and going to the mall and holding hands and all the mushy stuff that comes with a relationship. He wanted some of that, but he wanted the craziness of the weekends, too.

"I'm sorry," he said. He saw those two words as the only way out of the uncomfortable conversation. Where's Ronald McDonald when you need him?

440

"I care about you, Danny." She lifted her eyes from the pickles she had stripped off her cheeseburger. "I love you."

"I love you, too," he said, and meant it, surprised by it.

The moment had a certain electricity. Celeste had her hand on the light switch. "But you're not invincible."

"Sure I am."

She smacked her hand down onto a packet of catsup. Splat! A shower of red goop splurted across the table onto his shirt.

"Hey," Danny laughed. "What are you doin'?"

"Accident's happen. That's a metaphor for blood." She nodded at the nasty, red glop. "And that blood could just as easily be yours, or Gram's, when you get hit by a car. I want you to quit playing the game, Danny."

"Okay, I'll think about it," he said, with no intention to honor her request.

"If you don't," Celeste warned, "I'll leave you."

Later that same night, after Celeste was fast asleep in her bed, Danny and Gram sat at the Stones under a spring sky black as a priest's robe. An incredulous Danny told Gram of Celeste's "unreasonable" demand.

"She's probably right," was all Gram had to say.

Two months sped by before an unspoken concern of Danny's was cleared up in a most humorous manner. The Calvary, accompanied by Celeste and Lian, spent the Fourth of July weekend at the Gilday cabin in Lake Cumberland, sans parents. Danny cleaned up the cabin of empty beer bottles and cigarettes, while he mistakenly thought everyone else was on a walk. He picked up Janis' wet bathing suit with the intention of depositing it over the railing of her bedroom's porch rail. He opened the door to her room.

"Good God, man!" Gram shouted in a stern British accent. "Have you no sense of decency?"

Danny was flabbergasted at the sight of Gram's flubbery, white buns furiously humping an ecstatic Janis. "Sorry," he sheepishly said as he quietly closed the door. Through the thin wall, he could hear them laughing.

One might think Danny would be upset or jealous that Gram was moving in on his territory, as it were. But Danny and Janis' relationship had never been one of ownership; it was always strictly one of mutual benefit. He had long suspected that Cal was doing it with Janis. The fact that Gram was getting some of her fine service, too, pleased him. Now his unspoken concern, based on having never seen Gram with a woman, was placated. Gram was not gay after all.

The vacation had been a good one for him. Lake Cumberland always seemed to renew him, invigorate his spirit. He and Cal spent time alone fishing. Cal, of course, catching every fish within a three-mile radius, while Danny's rod saw little action. It thrilled Cal no end to best his brother at something. It pleased Danny, too. The only snag on the trip—well, two snags maybe—was Celeste's insecurity over Danny's attention to Janis and Lian.

How could she fault me for that? Danny was puzzled. Janis and I have been friends for years. And Lian, well, what man could resist admiring her tight Amerasian body? Celeste was not amused. The second downer, in his mind, was Celeste's disapproval when the Calvary, along with Lian, each dropped a hit of blotter acid on Saturday morning. Celeste declined. She spent the day as a resentful and unnecessary chaperone, convinced that someone was going to try and fly off the roof or walk on the jade water of the lake.

He saw this as a clear indication that she had no concept of the value of psychedelics. Celeste saw it as a clear indication that Danny had no intention of going straight. Even with the strain between them, Danny had a great time. Upon dropping her off at her parents, as they stood at the front door, sleeping bag and overnight case on the stoop, Celeste's ruffled brown hair limp in the July humidity, she sternly said to him, "You're heading for a fall."

"Is there a pause button on this show?" Twinkie asked as Celeste's final words echoed faintly in the room. "I have to pee."

"*Certainly,*" *The Journals* responded aloud. *"There will be a ten minute intermission."*

Twinkie scooted toward the bathroom. Had she not called first dibs, I would have run there myself. I have little bladder control these days. Damn chemo. Damn radiation. A numbness pinches small areas of my groin while constant pain like a Norse hammer to the testicles pounds the rest. The drugs aren't much help—I want to sleep all the time. I think I'm taking six or seven different pills right now, though I'm not sure what they do.

"Hel . . . low Swami!" Parker exclaimed. "*The Journals* appear to be omniscient." His radarlike eyes scanned for reactions. Twinkie, by-product of the TV generation, didn't seem to notice at all, as if *The Journals* was just another TV miniseries. Rose placed her arms around my neck and kissed me in that special spot she knows. The one that, in a younger, healthier day, used to send me to the medicine cabinet for an unribbed Trojan.

"I'm sorry I doubted you," she whispered, proud, humbled, and embarrassed simultaneously. Her latest theological stint at Unity Church must have awakened her awareness. That, and an undeniable can't-contradict-or-refute-it, thinking, talking, living, twenty-seven inch television set with surround sound! "Never again, R.T." She kissed me once more. Rose stood. "Would anyone like some hot tea?"

"I'd like an ice cold beer," I said.

Rose rumpled her chin in teasing dismay.

Hey, a man should be allowed to celebrate his release from psychological prison, his escape from emotional torment.

Maya, who seemed momentarily engulfed in thought, broke from her spell and said, "Oh, no, R.T., you mustn't have beer. It's bad for your Pitta."

"I'll help you with the tea, Mom," Parker offered. He must have guessed Maya's forthcoming spiel. She pulled playfully on his ponytail as he left the room. I was alone with the enchanting whirlwind I had met only a couple hours earlier. Maya is a spring breeze after harsh winter, at once refreshing and sultry, invigorating and subtle, comforting and enigmatic. Some people you know for a few minutes, and you feel like you've known them a lifetime. Maya is such a spirit, at home in the Stone household, charming people she scarcely knows.

"What's a Pitta?" I asked.

Maya, her complexion a dreamy summer nightfall with the sun just beyond the ridge of day, looked at me and said, "It's a mind-body type. In Ayurveda, there are ten mind-body types, but three predominant ones—Vata, Pitta, and Kapha. You, R.T., are a Pitta."

"How can you tell?" I said, doing my best to hold back the rising tide of urine in my abdomen. Hurry up, Twinkie.

"My mother raised us on Vedic traditions." Her brown, saucer eyes poured their energy into me. "I can tell by the color of your hair and its texture, by your mannerisms, by your skin, by your fingernails, by the way you communicate. It is very clear, R.T. You are a Pitta."

"I don't get it."

"According to ancient Vedic traditions, all life is composed of five elements— ether, fire, air, water and earth. The rishis, the wise seers of India, discovered this five thousand years ago. They went into the mountains, studied, meditated, conversed with their gods, and came back with an accurate science of life. Almost all of Eastern

443

medicine and religion is based upon its Sanskrit roots. And much of Western culture's New Age movement is derived from it. Yoga. Transcendental meditation. Vegetarianism. Crystal healing. Mantras."

Oh boy, I thought to myself, how do I diplomatically get out of this? Maya must have sensed my disbelief.

"I bet you love spicy foods, like chicken wings and blackened steak and burgers with raw onion. I'll bet you like garlic and radishes and cheese."

"Yes, I do," I said, pleased by her perceptions.

"And, I'll bet you get indigestion every time you eat those things. Peanuts, too. You love all these foods and eat them even though your body feels betrayed afterwards."

"I wouldn't say betrayed." I thought about it. "But you're right, I do feel uncomfortable sometimes."

"See, R.T.," Maya smiled. "A Pitta is dominated by fire and water elements. Your internal engine runs hot. You like cool drinks and ice cream. Fall and winter are your favorite times of year. You get overheated easily in summer and prefer air conditioning."

"That's true. I do walk in the evenings in the summer because it's cooler."

"Sing say."

"What?"

"Oh, it's just an expression I use when I'm happy or I come to an understanding or I do something good. Say is the god responsible for the weighing of the heart at death. I believe that doing good deeds, helping people, being a bright spirit, helps me live life with a light heart." Her eyes shone like brushed copper. "It's a reminder to myself to always do good."

"Sing say," I said, feeling like a kid. "I like that. It's cute."

"I noticed Nabu is looking out for you."

"Nabu?"

"Yes, the god of writing and wisdom. He's on the Babylonian urn in your foyer. Are you a writer?"

The toilet flushed. Twinkie washed her hands. Praise the Lord! I can pee at last. I can pee at last. "Excuse me for just one moment," I said, then stupidly, "I have to shake hands with the governor." She giggled shyly. Why did I say that? I'm not a sophomore in high school. Holy smokes! I rushed from the room, nearly bumping Twinkie as she exited the bathroom.

Now, I should point out for you curious realists determined to find any flaw in this story, that yes, we do have more than one bathroom—four if you must know. But anyone who has had the unfortunate malady of cancer in the genitalia knows that sometimes emergencies arise like a violent summer storm on a calm lake, and the best thing one can do is get to the nearest shore, even if it isn't your point of debarkation. That, and the bewitching nature of Maya's presence, shorted out any semblance of logical decision-making in my feeble brain.

My business concluded, the deal between me and the governor done, I headed back to the enlightened conversation. Twinkie, Rose, and Parker busied themselves in the kitchen, preparing showtime snacks. Lord knows what Twinkie will come up with. Something Jell-O, perhaps. I returned to the family room where Maya's Arabian eyes studied the stoic, Stone family portrait.

"Is this your son?" she asked. I nodded. "He's troubled, isn't he?"

"That's Bobby," I said sadly, and instinctively looked to his spoon collection.

"You aren't close?" Her eye caught a glint of silver reflection. "What a marvelously wild set of spoons. Is this your hobby?"

"Oh, no, that's Bobby's; he doesn't collect them anymore. Not since Vietnam. Rose keeps them out. The spoons are her therapy for him. She has a crazy notion that our little boy will recover what the war took from him. That seeing them, he will remember the way he was before the war."

"That is so hard to do," Maya said, "but not impossible." I imagined she sensed my discomfort about Bobby. "Back to Nabu, R.T., you have such impressive antiquities. So many pieces from the Middle East. Those Babylonians must be priceless. When did you begin collecting?"

"Oh, that's really Rose's love."

Drip, drop, plop. Drip, drop, plop. The clock splashed nine o'clock.

"R.T. likes to tell people it's my hobby," Rose said, entering from the kitchen. I imagined her glowing with relief that her man, the guy she pinned herself to for life, wasn't certifiably insane after all. God *was* talking to him. Or His agent anyway. She carried a clattering tray of nervous teacups on saucers. "But it's really his; he started during the war."

Maya, who had turned to help Rose with the tea, said, "Isn't it totally wild that ancient Babylon is now Iraq? Astarte bewitch me, isn't it amazing that the cradle of civilization is such a hotbed of ruthless intrigue? And soon, another unnecessary war."

Ah yes, I had almost forgotten, Maya was the secretive 'M.' "So you're interested in the Persian Gulf Crisis?" I said.

"Who isn't? Desert Shield is all that's on the news. The press is itching for war. It sells papers and air time. It's all about money, don't you think?"

Before I could respond to this most fascinating creature, Rose politely interrupted. "R.T., dear, time to take your medicine." She handed me a handful of pills and a tall glass of water.

"Is that purified water?" Maya asked. "Hala help you, do you take all those?"

"Sure do," I said just before I belted back three of the pills with a giant gulp of H_2O. She didn't miss a beat. "I shall call my mother and ask her what alternative treatments are available for your condition."

Rose and I stared at each other in amazement. Who was this forward girl who just charged into life and its messy circumstance with a Dustbuster and a Handi-Wipe?

"It cannot be healthy to take all those pills. And, no offense, R.T., but judging by your frailty, I'd say whatever they're treating you with is inflicting more damage than repair."

"Chemotherapy and radiation," Rose said demurely, as if she agreed but had been afraid to say so because she had been the one to force me into it.

Maya waved a dismissive arm in the air. "Oh, those therapies don't work. They kill more good cells than bad. Astarte bewitch me, I can't believe the arrogance of the medical industry. Well, that's it then. When I get home I'm calling Mom. She'll get you in the right doctor's hands."

I was speechless again. I looked at Rose, whose sparkling eyes approved of this assertive newcomer with her array of odd gods and strange concepts. I threw back the remaining pills and gulped two swigs of water.

"You must really love sin," Maya said.

I nearly showered the carpet with my water and pills.

"Excuse me, dear?" said Rose.

"Sin, the Babylonian moon god. You were born in July, right R.T.?"

"How did you . . ."

"Who wants Jell-O?" Twinkie shouted as she stood in the entranceway, her arms supporting a serving tray of parfait dishes laden with a reddish-purple experiment of unknown origin. "Twilight Cloud. Raspberry Jell-O with orange slices and real boysenberries. I invented it myself. Oh, and Reddi-wip for clouds."

My stomach curdled. I'm sure my lips turned just as sour. Don't get me wrong—boysenberries are good—it's their combination with blood-colored gelatin and orange peel that sets my stomach to heaving.

"I'd love some, Twinkie." Maya showed no hesitation. A broad smile of triumph paraded across my daughter's whipped-cream lips.

"Where are you from, Maya?" I asked.

"Tucson." She scooped a dainty portion of Twilight Cloud. Parker's eyes soaked in her beauty, while simultaneously evaluating my interest in her. He's good at that.

"How do you know so much about Ayur . . . whatever—anthropology, world events, and . . . me? How did you get so wise?"

Parker's eyes registered the tiniest speck of worry. He looked at me, then Maya, awaiting an answer he himself would like to know.

"Fate," she whispered. Then her smooth, acorn face ruffled ever so slightly, turned solemn. "R.T., there is something I must tell you."

Chapter 37

Late June 1943

Sulphur reclined in a comfortable café chair and sipped sangria as he watched the glow on the hill. The distance was awash in fantastic oranges and yellows and reds, which turned the midnight to dawn. It was a good fire, reaching high into the sky like a beggar's outstretched fingers begging the Almighty to end the suffering. Sulphur was pleased that he had succeeded in delivering his message to Father Josemaria Escriva.

All eyes in Barcelona were on the great church, ablaze like a pious torch lighting God's way for Jesus' Second Coming. But He wouldn't be coming tonight. Nor any night soon. Fire engines wailed. Faithful Catholic women wailed, their hands wrung in prayer, wondering what wrongs they had committed that God would inflict such punishment upon them. Babies, ignored by their distraught mothers, wailed. Men, long silenced by the ravages of Franco's church-backed Civil War, wailed internally, like a hemorrhage of pride.

Bedlam reigned down upon the city in giant ashes from the cathedral. Sulphur raised his glass toward the crackling rectory some three miles away as the waitress gave him a curious glance. He took a healthy drink. Of all Spanish alcohol, he liked sangria best, especially when he was celebrating. Earlier that evening, around eleven, he had slipped undetected onto the church grounds with his bag full of destruction. He had chosen his method of repayment carefully, from all the tools at his OSS disposal. He had considered many options for this night, had discreetly consulted many associates as to the latest weaponry in the U.S. arsenal.

The fruits of his labor popped and exploded in a glorious blaze before him. He had chosen well. TNT was high on his list, but he thought it too mundane. The message must be delivered with the right tone, the right cadence. He considered gasoline, but that was too subdued, too pedestrian, so that anyone could have taken credit for the arson. No, Sulphur wanted Opus Dei to know precisely from whom the fire originated. He considered RDX, even watched it work in a marsh outside London late one night, but had dismissed the underwater explosive as inappropriate. He wanted a trademark, a signature bomb that made an impression on the recipient. He ended up with pentaerythritol tetranitrate mixed with TNT. The newly-developed charge, called pentolite, fit Sulphur's stringent criteria perfectly.

Pentolite had just the right destructive effect and detonation velocity. It also had the added feature of being suitable for the climate of Barcelona. Sulphur had thought this through. He had contemplated the repercussions of his actions, even doing a Ben Franklin T-chart on paper. Opus Dei would most assuredly come after him if he were an individual citizen, but he doubted that even the arrogant and masochistic Church would dare take on the Office of Strategic Services with its wicked bag of espionage tricks. He also surmised that Opus Dei would gladly forsake the dominion of one five-hundred-year-old church for the right to millions of dollars in profit for distributing counterfeit Deutschmarks. A church could always be rebuilt, with impassioned pleas for donations from the congregation of course, but this forgery scheme, Lord, this was a once-in-a-lifetime opportunity.

He saw correctly that his moment for retribution was ripe. "It will be a long time before Escriva ransacks another hotel of an OSS officer," he said aloud. The waitress, who understood little English, smiled at her strange customer, who took delight in the fiery demise of the holy temple on the hill.

The Church would pay for its sinister duplicity in starting World War II. Sitting in a café in Barcelona, sipping sangria, the flames spitting at the pope as if from Satan's lips himself, Sulphur began making plans to burn at least one church wherever his assignments took him. Colonel Bruce can have his antiquities as spoils of unholy war, Sulphur thought; I will have my fire.

Chapter 38

Like a fast-forward time machine *The Journals* started the story six months later than it had ended. By late July of 1983 Danny was showing signs of serious trouble. His hair was to his shoulders, long and stringy. He stopped writing in his journals. He stopped writing his book. His goals in life had become simplistic—getting high, Pulitzer, the FEW technique, and Timing the Light. Celeste was displeased by all these transgressions, but he shrugged her off. She responded by canceling more and more dates due to "headaches" or "chores." Danny countered by sleeping with Celeste's best friend, Michelle, not because he particularly liked her but as a test of his FEW technique. Gram had pointed out, to no avail, that Danny wasn't using persuasive methods as much as sheer manipulation. Danny found that fact amusing.

The Calvary had graduated into more potent drugs more often. Marijuana and THC were still mainstays, but at much higher quantities and purity. Danny and Cal (who still dressed exclusively in black, as if ready for a funeral at a moment's notice) had become experts in avoiding their father. When he came home, they left. When dinner was ready, they ate and excused themselves. When weekends arrived, they awoke early and went fishing, adjusting their schedules to minimize their involvement with a man they didn't see as a father but as a volatile enemy.

Danny spent a good chunk of the summer boring the Calvary with stories of Pulitzer, a play-by-play of the man's life as seen through the eyes of a juvenile delinquent hellbent on forgery. "Did you know that Pulitzer almost single-handedly brought the Statue of Liberty to America?" he said as he partied with Janis at the Stones. "I'm writing about it in his diary."

"Is that true?"

"Yep." Danny looked for Sirius, but the star wasn't visible in summer. "Nobody wanted it. The French were really pissed. They built this huge statue as a gift to celebrate U.S. independence, and we snubbed them. Pulitzer railed about it in his newspapers. He shamed people into donating the land and the funds. Another example of the generosity of America the beautiful."

Janis removed her blouse and pressed her perspiring back against the coolness of a headstone. "It's interesting stuff."

He stared skyward, not noticing Janis' seminude state.

Janis removed her bra under the humid moon which dripped its light upon the graveyard. "Come sit by me," she said. "I'll show you something interesting."

449

A month later, Gram, sitting on the milkhouse roof, asked Danny, "Can you walk on sand without making footprints?"

"That's impossible," a stoned, semi-intelligent Danny replied.

"I think you can."

"Well, great! It's settled then—I can walk on sand."

"No footprints. You can do it. Man-oh-man, wouldn't that be cool? To walk like Jesus? Feet not touching the ground. Walking on water. It could come in handy someday—walking on sand. I'm sure the application would apply to snow, ice, water, hot coals. You can do it. If you have the right intent."

"The reefer has gone to your head, G-man."

It was early October, at dinner, and Patrick Gilday was actually angry even though two pork chops, a mound of mashed potatoes, and half the cargo of the gravy boat were on his plate. The Nuclear Regulatory Commission had announced that the Zimmer Nuclear Plant being built by Cincinnati Gas & Electric was experiencing serious safety problems. The NRC announcement didn't bode well for the future of the plant. The commission conceded that the fifteen thousand quality-assurance violations issued at Zimmer indicated safety concerns.

Patrick stabbed and ripped and tore and jostled his food in silence for most of the meal. Danny ate blissfully, content that there was hope in this world. Hope that illogical and dangerous projects such as Zimmer could be stopped. Hope that the average citizen didn't always lose to the greedy interests of corporate America. Hope that just causes could be won.

Patrick finished his meal brusquely, tossed his cutlery to his plate, and said, "It's a goddamn shame. Guess we can kiss that Zimmer contract goodbye."

In a startling proclamation that sent Danny searching for answers, Gram told him he was giving up all drugs as of that moment. That moment happened to be Halloween night, right after Billy Harper, Danny's roommate at Calder Academy, called out-of-the-blue to see if Danny wanted to buy some angel dust. Danny begged-off the dust but sold Billy two pounds of reefer the Calvary had grown over the summer on the slopes just above Featherbed Bank. He believed it to be some of the most fertile land in the Bluegrass state, having been blessed by the Glorian Aurora and all. Indeed, it had produced some powerful smoke.

Danny dropped the paintbrush he had been using to paint McJic riding a wild chariot across the sky near Orion's belt when Gram told him. He had decided to paint a translucent image of McJic in the constellation, barely discernible to the untrained eye, in honor of his "dream" father, and because he thought it would be a great headrush to have it show up under "just the right light, with just the right buzz, on just the right occasion."

"Are you crazy, G-man?" He stooped to pick up the grit-laden brush. "We're some of the biggest dealers in northern Kentucky. We can't quit now."

Gram's odylic eyes did not waver. "I have found my limits. I don't need to get high anymore. Celeste is right, Danny. All we're doing right now is killing ourselves."

"I don't believe this. Man!"

"Back when I was philosopher to Plato, we often contemplated that invisible line that man crosses between moderation and excess. We aren't growing mentally from getting high anymore; we're stagnant. It's habit now. Look at us." Gram waved his arm like a mighty sorcerer around the Captain's Quarters. The low flames of the homage candles flickered in the breeze. "We're squirreled away here on Halloween so we can get a buzz. Where's Celeste? Where's Cal? Even Janis has better plans than to hang around with our sorry asses. There's no life here. It's just repetition. I'm done."

"Jesus." Danny exhaled as if his friend had just punched him in the gut. "We're chosen, G-man. What do we care about the rest of the world?"

"That's the whole damn point. It is precisely because we are chosen that we should care about the world."

Thanksgiving, Christmas, New Year's, President's Day, and St. Patrick's Day all zoomed by as *The Journals* leapt forward with unrestrained zeal. I would have loved to see more detail, but this was not to be. We ate Jell-O. Twilight Cloud.

Danny's actions were more and more self-serving, more arrogant, more brazen. Getting buzzed to play Timing the Light became his favorite sport. His grades slipped, something he allowed intentionally to see if he could charm his teachers into giving him A's for B or C work. His methods were successful. The teachers were pushovers. But, to quote a biblical phrase, the writing was on the wall. The FEW technique had given him a power that some Shanidarian entity was bound to rescind for abuse of authority. It looked as if his time had come the night of March 23, 1984.

"You boys had better never embarrass me like that again." Patrick Gilday's voice boomed to the back seat of the car. "Smoking pot behind the bowling alley. What the hell is wrong with you?"

Gram sat mum. He hadn't toked at all. He'd given it up, but he wouldn't betray the code—never nark on a friend.

"Sorry, Father," Danny said, careful not to antagonize the senior Gilday. The vein was perilously close to flood stage.

Danny fully expected to be ripped limb from limb when he got home, but miraculously, and this was the total irony of his father's mentality, Patrick mellowed. "Well," he chuckled as he turned into the front gates of Mulciber, "I guess boys will be boys." On the really big trouble that Danny and Cal got into, their father exhibited traits of understanding, but on the insignificant ones, like accidentally spilling milk, he'd go ballistic. Patrick laughed again. "Try and act repentant in front of your mother, Daniel."

"Yes, sir."

It is difficult to say with certainty which issue incited Celeste more: Danny's infidelity with her best friend, Michelle, or his bust by the Grant County Sheriff's patrol. It appeared that as Danny was being handcuffed and thrown into the back of the squad car, a penitent Michelle was confessing her sins to a tearful Celeste, who immediately forgave her girlfriend, but not Danny. In either case, both faux pas added up to disaster for him. Danny, still oblivious to the fact that he wasn't invincible and responsible for his actions, wasn't prepared for her inflexible response to his indiscretions.

Celeste chose the Stones as the fitting backdrop for her eviction notice. While tears streaked her alabaster face, she did her best to remain strong against his manipulation. "I can't live like this," she sobbed.

"Like what?" He produced his boyish, Academy Award winning grin. "I thought we were doing great." He leaned back against Crittenden's headstone. Mrs. Hobbins was listening intently. He would finally be paid back for his desecration of her grave.

"Everything's on your terms." Celeste dabbed her eyes with a tissue. "You do whatever you want and expect me to go along with it. I'm not a puppet, Danny. I'm a woman with feelings and desires. I want more in life."

"What? What do you want in life?"

"I want a boyfriend who isn't wasted all the time!"

"I'm not." The cool of the granite plunged into his back like the razor sharp edge of a knife.

"I want a boyfriend who cares about other people at least as much as himself!"

"I do." A smirk whittled its way upon his face—the one expression his father had warned him about repeatedly. Somewhere out in the Cosmos, Mrs. Hobbins was laughing.

"I want someone who isn't going to end up in prison for dealing drugs!" The blade of coolness plunged deeper, grew rigid, its point pushing near his heart.

"I'm not going to jail. I've got a star in my—"

"In your hip pocket. Yeah, I know." Exasperated, Celeste punched his shoulder and said, "I want a boyfriend who doesn't screw my best friend behind my back."

The knife struck the aorta. The warm flow of emotional blood pushed back against the cold stone of Crittenden's tomb. Mrs. Hobbins, space ghost, giggled giddily in the ether.

"I . . ."

"You bastard. You sorry bastard."

"Now, Celeste." He sat up, the chill too much for him, the pain too deep. He was wounded, if only metaphorically, from Celeste's tirade. "None of those things are true. I'm not going to prison, I'm going—"

"Stop it, Danny, just stop it. You're not going to trick me with your twisted logic. I'm onto your game. I've put up with your insane forgery schemes, your drug dealing, and your stupid death games." The tears flowed steadily down her cheeks. "I've put up with your being high all the time. I even tolerated your sleeping with that slut, Janis. But I'm not putting up with it anymore. You screwed Michelle, goddamn it. How could you?"

"Celeste, I . . ." He placed his steady hand on her quivering one. She withdrew. The knife ripped at his heart, slicing it to quarters like a ripe pear. Mrs. Hobbins held the handle now. Vengeance was sweet.

"Don't even try to explain it all away."

There was a fixed purpose in her eyes, a resolve that he recognized, and Danny knew he had lost. His body was on psychological damage control. Battalions of hormones rushed to the accident scene. Paramedic antibodies tried to stitch up his shredded heart. A secondary team performed triage on his back. Yet Celeste, with the aid of a gloating Mrs. Hobbins spirit, wasn't finished. Where was Crittenden? he thought, his guilt at having been such a louse to Celeste finally sinking in.

"I'm immune to your logic, Danny," Celeste said. "It's not that I don't love you. I do. But I need more than what we have. And less. I need somebody less high-profile than you. You want center stage, all the risk, to laugh at life, to spit at fate. I don't. I want somebody more stable, less daring."

"Celeste . . ." He lost his composure and dropped his manipulation attempts. She was slipping from him. He knew it now. "Please."

"No!" She stood up.

He stood, too, imagining a faint trickle of blood running down his back.

"It isn't like we haven't talked about this a dozen times. You know how I feel. I don't want to visit you in the state pen or have to identify your body at the county morgue. I'll leave that to your stupid Calvary." She leaned closer and kissed his cheek. "I love you, Danny. Goodbye."

The knife was pulled from his back, the symbolic wound now open and bleeding profusely. Celeste turned and walked down the pathway to a car where Michelle, a vindictive smile on her face, waited.

Danny stood numb in the graveyard as a cool March breeze kicked up. The sun hid behind the clouds. Mrs. Hobbins stopped laughing. He leaned back weakly against the captain's headstone and slid down the granite surface until he hit the ground.

He stared blankly at the dreary world around him. "How was I supposed to know?" he whispered as he struggled to catch a tear escaping the corner of his eye.

After hearing Danny's one-sided version of the breakup, Gram shocked his friend with another revelation: "She's right."

The dim candlelight of the Quarters bounced playful shadows off the murals. Danny saw them as dark signs of stormy weather. Bad spirit omens come to rob his power. "What! How can you take *her* side?"

Gram smiled kindly at his wounded charge. "It's not about sides, now is it? It's about truth and deception. She asked you not to get high, so you lied and did it behind her back. You told her you loved her, yet you slept with Janis and Michelle and a few others whose names I can't recall. She begged you to stop Timing the Light, and you lied to her again."

The shadows danced on the walls, inspired by Danny's gloom. They seemed more menacing, minor entities toying with his emotions. He didn't like dark thoughts, the underbelly of existence. Some people like to dwell there in sorrow and self-pity, but not him.

"Man-oh-man," Gram went on. "Back when I was Chief Truth Officer at the Celestial School of Deception, we had a number of spirits come through who rationalized their unethical behavior. Doesn't wash, though. You can't fool the Universe. It knows what's in your heart, even if you don't."

"But Gram," Danny said. He studied the suspicious shadows that flickered around

McJic's chariot near Sirius and Shanidar. "She wants me to stop the game! She shouldn't ask that. It's *the* game."

Gram's eyes flashed like royal scepters of wisdom. "She's right, Danny. We should quit Timing the Light."

"Quit the game? That's blasphemy!" Danny rose to his feet.

"In fact, I'm done," Gram said. "No more game as of this minute. Finito. Kaput. Cold turkey."

Danny shook his head in dismay. The shadows high-fived each other in black motions of congratulation. Danny was falling deeper. Maybe this was the plan. Maybe this is what he needed. To be reined in, to learn the wise use of his power, to use his gifts wisely, not for personal self-interest. He regained his calm. His thoughts, driven on the surface by his ego, recovered. He knew what this was—a test. A test to see how strong he was. The queer rationalization stole into his mind like a thief justifying his larceny. His advanced mind whirled. What does Celeste love? Music. I'll write her a song. That'll get her back. What does Gram love? Teaching me. That's it. I'll play along with the lesson. I'll bide my time, he thought. I'll slowly bring Gram around and work him into a corner so he has to play the game again.

Danny decided to act cool, pretended to agree with Gram's words. Another day, he told himself, will afford another opportunity to prove I'm right.

"Okay, Gram," he said slyly. "You're right. Maybe we should give up the game."

A week went by before Danny decided to start his persuasive plan to get Gram back into the game. He had lost too much already: his girlfriend, getting high with Gram, Timing the Light, and he didn't like his life turned around, although he didn't stop getting high entirely. He caught a buzz with Cal, but he found it increasingly more difficult to relate to his brother. The black outfits shouted to Danny, *I need attention here.* Danny mentioned this to his mom, who gave Cal as much time as he'd let her. But Cal's problem wasn't Cara and her love. The problem was Patrick's lack of love. Cal needed a father. Unlike Danny, who had come to terms with his relationship and wasn't nearly as needy, Cal longed for a father who would go fishing with him or give praise for the elaborate computer programs he had designed. Danny wondered when Cal would unveil the top-secret program he had been working on for over a year. It was all so clandestine: Cal alone in his room, the door locked. *Tappity-tap-tap. Tap. Tap.* Back space. *Tap. Tap. Tap. Tappity-tap-tap.* Back space. Back space.

Danny imagined Cal becoming paranoid about it, so much so that Cal took some of the proceeds from their dealing operation and bought a deadbolt for his bedroom door.

Danny also began getting high with Billy Harper. But this was hit-and-miss at best, since Billy lived in a row house in Clifton with his alcoholic sports writer father. The distance proved difficult for daily puff sessions, but Billy was allowed to stay at Mulciber on the weekends, if Patrick was in Arizona. Billy had become a member of the Calvary some months earlier. Gram immediately took a liking to the blues musician-prankster. It was probably Billy's irreverence for life that Gram found most likable. Cal didn't care one way or the other—he spent most of his time drunk, working on his computer, or out with Lian. Janis, for her part, wasted no time initiating Billy into the Calvary, having bedded him on his second visit to the estate. Billy wasn't from Canada.

Danny was in the dumps. Celeste had dropped him, and everybody at school knew. All he could do was act like it didn't matter, but the truth was it hurt like hell. He *did* write her a song, Half Past Sane, which he taped and passed to her in the hallway along with a note asking for forgiveness. She passed a note back the next day: "Thank you for the song. I like it a lot. But, no, I can't see you anymore." Shades of a cackling Mrs. Hobbins echoed in his subconscience.

"Damn," Danny said out loud, as he crumpled the note and threw it to the bottom of his locker. The magic wasn't working. Maybe Celeste was immune to his logic after all.

A week after Gram announced he wasn't playing the game any longer, Danny started chipping away at his teacher's resolve with little comments here and there. What he didn't realize was that Gram was onto his schemes. He could see through Danny like a microscope through Saran Wrap, but he tolerantly played along, reminding Danny not to abuse his talents, reminding Danny that the game had run its course.

"There are better things to do with our lives," Gram said one Thursday evening. It was early April 1984. Big Brother and George Orwell time. Danny's birthday had just passed (which he had celebrated by getting stoned in the Quarters alone with Roentgen, who he smuggled in via the secret tunnel. Roentgen refused to use the ladder). The boys walked to Janis' house to see if she wanted to hang out.

"You're the one who invented the damn game," Danny said. "I just don't see how you can abandon your own creation."

Gram said, "Life is like that. Certain traits, beliefs, hobbies, and people carry you so far. Then it's time to move on."

"Yeah, well, I'm just dying to get one more crack at Timing the Light. Just one more."

This was part of his gambit, to get Gram back in with one game, get him buzzed on the adrenaline rush, and boom, he's hooked again.

"You wouldn't want your first-grade teacher to instruct you in calculus, would you?" Gram reasoned. "No, you wouldn't, because she isn't qualified. You've moved beyond that level of need. That's how life is. It's called learning, or, as Darwin labeled it, evolution."

"I don't see what harm one game would do."

"If you don't grow up, the gods will piss on you."

"Right."

"Piss a storm of sorrow, they will," Gram said.

Gram had his own strategy cooking, one that focused on Danny's agreement not to get high any longer. Gram was convinced that drugs were adversely affecting Danny. He had tried convincing Billy to aid in the rehabilitation attempt, but Billy had his own baggage to deal with and was no help. So when Danny pestered Gram to play Timing the Light, Gram admonished him to go straight. Therein grew the seed of a compromise inside Danny's creative mind.

His first attempt was rebuffed with Gram's stern words, "It's too dangerous. Both things—the game and getting stoned. There are limits to life, Danny. Limits. You need to find them." Gram's talisman eyes bore into the surprised protégé. "You need to learn the right intent. Why do you want me to play the game so badly? What's the intent behind it?"

Danny didn't answer.

Friday, the thirteenth of April, found the Calvary, sans Billy Harper, on an evening fishing expedition at Cal's request. The man loved to fish. A case of beer, a bag of weed, some munchies, fishing tackle, bait, and poles accompanied the wayward group as they whooped it up at the lake at Mulciber, out of sight of the main house. Cal fished for carp. He reveled in the fight they gave him. Danny wondered how many times Cal had caught the same fish. Roentgen lay chewing on cockleburs epoxied to his fur. It was too early in the season for crickets, so the night noise was mostly human frolic.

"How's Pulitzer coming?" Janis asked.

"Oh . . . pretty good," Danny said as he zipped his jacket against the cool evening air. Gram cast his line. Cal lit the lantern.

"How far along are you?" Janis asked. She hadn't much to do, except drink, smoke, and talk, since she wouldn't fish. Worms were too disgusting. Cal had tried to explain that you don't use worms for carp, you use Wheaties and bread, but the Calvary's resident nymphomaniac had made up her mind two years earlier, after worm guts squished in her hands, never to fish again.

"The Panama Canal deal."

"The Panama Canal?"

Danny didn't answer her. A chilled moon shivered above the lake. Clouds like blankets tried to cover it in their woolen vapors. His thoughts drifted toward Captain Crittenden's journals. He hadn't read them in a long time. Are there clues for me in them? he wondered. Have I made a mistake by ignoring them? His mother, still searching for clues of McJic in this or some past life, monopolized them.

"Danny?" Janis broke his thoughts. "Are you in there?" She gently knocked on his skull. Roentgen gnawed at a particularly feisty burr.

"Come in," Danny joked. Everyone laughed. "Sorry, I was thinking of the captain."

"What about Panama?"

"Well, it's pretty interesting. By all accounts, a few unscrupulous politicians and businessmen started a revolution in Colombia so they could make money building a canal."

"How's that?" Gram asked.

"Panama was a province of Colombia, just like Kentucky is part of the United States," Danny explained as he rolled an acorn in his hand. "Some Frenchmen drew up plans for a canal, fleeced thousands of small investors in Europe, then went bankrupt. After that enterprise failed, a clever guy bought the rights and began soliciting people to invest again. Only this time the scam was focused on the United States."

Janis looked admiringly at him, fascinated by his knowledge and horny from the beer. She made a mental note to seduce him later. Cal listened intently.

Danny continued. "The new owner got capital from some wealthy Americans, such as our own beloved Cincinnatian, Charles P. Taft, along with J.P. Morgan and other prominent capitalists. So Cincinnati, fifteen hundred miles away, is connected to the Panama Canal."

"Go on," Cal urged. He checked his reel to make sure the line was loose. A carp needs to run—it grabs the bait and takes off.

"There was much debate in Congress over funding a canal in Nicaragua, which was cheaper to complete, easier to dig and made more sense because of its location and the width of land to cut through. The new financiers of the Panama Canal were just days from losing their investment because Congress was going to vote in favor of the Nicaraguan option."

"Wow." Janis lit a joint. The sweet aroma floated enticingly on the frigid air. She took a hit and handed it to Cal. "Remember when we scored that Panama Red?"

"Yeah, but it wasn't much better than this stuff," Cal said.

"So with millions about to be lost, guess what happens?" said Danny.

Gram leaned closer. Janis' eyes went wide. Cal burped. "What?"

"It just so happened that the day the province declared independence from Colombia, in a bloodless coup, Teddy Roosevelt had three warships stationed off the coast ready to attack the Colombians if they tried to reclaim their province."

"*Vive la* revolution," Cal hooted.

"I don't get it," Janis said.

"The U.S. government sponsored the coup," said Danny. "The interesting part is that the provincial locals didn't even know they had broken away from Colombia. They didn't know there was a revolution! Isn't that incredible?"

"I'd say," Gram said. "So how does Pulitzer fit in?"

"Turns out that of the $40 million paid by Congress to complete the Panama Canal, only three-and-a-half million went to whom it should. Pulitzer accused Roosevelt, J.P. Morgan, and Cincy's own Charlie Taft of embezzling the rest."

"Things *really* aren't what they seem, huh?" Gram laughed, his frizzy hair blowing wild in the April breeze.

"Nope," Danny agreed, "they aren't. Pulitzer published the scandal in his newspapers, and other papers picked it up. Roosevelt and the other big money people were pissed."

"I guess so," Janis giggled and finished off her brew. "What happened after that?"

"Roosevelt had Pulitzer indicted on five counts of criminal libel. But Pulitzer, sick man that he was, lived on a yacht out of reach of U.S. jurisdiction. Once the canal thieves realized that going to trial against him and the other newspapers would expose their financial dealings, they dropped the charges."

"Goddamn!" Cal said. "Teddy Roosevelt?"

"Yep," Danny said, "and Taft, too. The royal family of Greater Cincinnati."

"I'm depressed," Janis said. "Is the whole world corrupt?"

"No," Gram said quickly. "Only parts of it. Not all of it."

"I'll never look at Mount Rushmore in the same way," Danny joked.

Everyone laughed.

"At least The Calvary isn't corrupt," said Cal.

"Except for Danny," Gram said.

Danny tried breaking down Gram's opposition to the game one more time.

"Gram, I have an idea. If you play Timing the Light with me, I won't get high for a week."

"Tempting," Gram said. He placed his index finger under his nose, as if contemplating some grand paradox. "Yeah, okay."

Danny was elated. He hadn't counted on it being that easy. The FEW technique had worked again.

"But," Gram added a caveat. "You also have to do something of value."

"Okay, G-man, like what?"

"Get active in the environmental movement."

"I'm plenty involved."

"If you're such an environmentalist, why aren't you doing anything for Earth Day?" Gram asked. "It's Sunday the 22nd, you know."

"Same day as Easter," Janis piped in. "He's got you, Danny."

"Expose the Fernald scandal," Gram said. "You saw what's going on up there. It's criminal. Put your energies on a battle plan to get the public enraged, and I'll play the game one last time."

"Consider it done," Danny said crisply, triumphantly.

"Consider the consequences of what you've won," Gram said, but Danny was too juiced to do so.

"When can we play?"

"Spring break is coming up. How about April 20th?"

"Hey, that's Good Friday!" Janis said.

"Cool," Danny said happily. He reached over and petted Roentgen. The animal had made considerable progress on the weeds embedded in his coat. A fish jumped and splashed in mid-lake.

"He's mine," Cal said with relish.

Gram cocked his head slightly, revealing a face no one had seen before. One that wasn't happy nor sad, but both and neither. One that said a thousand things at the same time it said nothing. Danny was puzzled by the oddity of Gram's look. He couldn't tell what the expression meant. It was calm and confident, worried and hesitant, proud and sorrowful, aware and distant. It was myriad emotions wrapped into one, long profile.

Danny looked from Gram's peculiar expression to the lake and back again. Is this the lake he's to save me by? Danny wondered to himself. Is that what this look is about? He couldn't read Gram, and it was worrisome. What Danny *did* know under that frost-bitten April moon, its craters chattering together like teeth, was that Gram's face was the most disconcerting face he'd ever seen.

"Man-oh-man, that was tough." Gram exhaled heavily as he adjusted the rubberband in his ponytail. "Back when I was chief chronicler at the Great Library of Alexandria, I didn't have nearly this much trouble with the urns and cuneiforms as this."

"Quit your belly-aching, G-man," Danny said, wheezing. "We're done. All I need to do now is get the fake canvasses off, and they'll be good as new."

It was a chore getting the original Mamets into the Quarters. Danny had decided to move them there for safekeeping, thinking that if Patrick and Drew Winthrop hadn't discovered the fraud by now, they never would.

A winded Gram lit the captain's candles and flopped on the dusty, blue sofa. "I think they'll look good over there on that wall."

Danny was busy removing the staples from the canvas. He hated the abstracts that Winthrop and his father so adored. Art, he scoffed, what did they know? The transfer complete, the covers slipped off, he thought about where to hang them. He would not consider covering the Glorian Aurora or the Shanidar paintings, which left only the wall that Gram had suggested. The Mamets looked totally out of place there. It was artistic heresy to mount nineteenth-century masterpieces unceremoniously behind a greasy printing press, which spewed ink whenever it was conscripted into action.

"I've a suggestion," Gram said.

"Oh yeah?"

"You really need to get beyond forgery."

"What do you mean?"

"Chuck it all, Danny boy," Gram laughed as he lit the ceremonial candles. The burst of fire illuminated the captain's name in typeface. "Give up Pulitzer. It's going to land you in huge trouble if you don't stop."

"No way, G-man. I've worked too hard on him to give up now."

"Nothing good can come of plotting a crime." Gram shook his head. "Nothing good."

"You worry too much." Danny shrugged his shoulders with typical nonchalance. "I play the game to win. There's a lot of juice in pulling off a big score."

Gram's magician eyes turned serious. "Think of the consequences of your actions. What if you lose?"

"I can't lose," Danny crowed as he centered a Mamet on the wall. "I've got a star in my hip pocket."

"Are you going first or should I?" Danny asked, tying his shoe. The big night was here, April 20, 1984. The night he had pushed, cajoled, persuaded, wheedled, manipulated for. The night he had employed all the nuances and tricks he could muster from his FEW technique to maneuver Gram into playing the game. Danny lived up to his bargain—he had temporarily stopped getting high, *and* he had begun researching Fernald. He even wrote a letter to the congressman in whose district the deadly, uranium-enrichment facility lies. Now it was Gram's turn to honor his obligation.

Gram stared into the gray beard of sky. Clouds thick as clumps of long, wizard's whiskers, wind blowing like a sorcerer's breath. A storm was coming but would not be there for hours yet. It would be a cleansing rain, a rain of transition, a rain to end winter and herald spring, but first it had to wash away the dirt of the world, the accumulation of exhaust and salt and grit and carbon that blackened the roadside.

Gram breathed in the impending storm. "You go first," he said. "It's your game now." The sound of rubber on asphalt reverberated a familiar, comfortable danger.

"It's not the same without a buzz on," Danny said. "It's scarier. I have goose bumps. See." He showed Gram his left arm.

"Wouldn't want to trip out there," Gram joked. "One wrong move and splat!"

"It's been awhile. I feel a little rusty. But it's a good night for it."

"Yeah," Gram punned, "it is a *good* Friday." He took another deep breath of the cool air mixed with car fumes. Gram's dark conjurer's eyes twinkled as he beheld the crowded sky. Tufts of magician's hair, gray and black, gathered close to the floor of the sky. Merlin himself must have been trimming his beard in honor of spring. "I love this place."

"Crittenden? You gotta be kidding me."

Gram hesitated. "I'm not sure the timing is right," he said, his eyes searching the sky. "What if the fates aren't with us tonight?"

"Screw the fates," Danny said callously. "The Council is taking care of us."

"It's uncomfortable."

"What are you talking about?" Danny elbowed him lightly in the ribs. "We've done this so many times we could walk across the highway. Ready?" His blood pumped loudly in his ears. His mouth went dry. His stomach churned with acidic juices. He'd show Celeste he could defy death; he'd show the world he was over her. He studied the cars, careful not to bolt in front of a slow one. That would be bad form. The game was meant to be the ultimate risk; the closer one came to becoming bumper bait, the better.

Danny suddenly darted in front of a blue Chevy, slipped by a brown Ford and scurried unscathed to the other side. He rested in the grass, his heart thumping proudly, his breath short and quick. "Whew, what a rush!"

It was Gram's turn. He moved his head side to side, measuring the cars. In the game, velocity, distance, mass, acceleration of the runner, pure physics come into play. One-on-one. Gladiators of the road. Man against machine. Gram stretched his legs, bobbed up and down like a world-class athlete before the biggest race of his life. He looked right and left. He gauged the competition, then made his move.

Danny saw it first. Perhaps Gram never did.

"No!" Danny shouted. "No!"

A car, its headlights off, sped down the busy highway, weaving between cars, cutting them off. Gram had misjudged.

"Gram!" Danny screamed, but Gram didn't hear him. In the short span that it takes the heart to beat once, it was over. The sickening thud of Gram's body smashing against the grill of a Lincoln Town Car echoed through the dead night. The car spun to a stop. Gram, dazed and battered, lay crumpled twenty feet before the sedan on the black stretch of road.

"No, Gram!" Danny cried out. "No! Not now!"

He ran to his injured friend, desperately hoping that Gram was alive. "Please God!" Danny shouted to himself in a rapid staccato prayer. "Please God. Please God. Please

462

God. Please. Take it back, God. Take it back," he cried. "Change time and take it back." His heart begged for the last few seconds to be rewound, but Danny hadn't earned that favor. He knelt next to Gram, who lay scarcely breathing, his jeans gashed on both legs from knee to thigh. "Gram," Danny pleaded, too frightened to cry. "Can you speak?"

The beaten warrior struggled to face him. Danny winced and turned away, repulsed by the bone jutting through the ripped skin of Gram's cheek. Blood spilled from the wound and collected in a pool in the street. Danny threw up on the dark asphalt. Muffled voices surrounded the boys, but neither could make them out. They were voices of worry. Voices of question. Voices of fear. Voices of death.

Danny sat trembling, doing what he could to comfort Gram. "Are you—you—all—all right . . . G—G-man?" he stuttered, barely able to hear his own words. A deep numbness invaded him, and he shook uncontrollably. "Jesus, Gram, I'm sorry." He felt as if he were in a hellish nightmare. Danny removed his jacket and placed it under Gram's head. Warm, sticky blood seeped onto his hands. A siren wailed in the distance. "They're coming, Gram," he cried. "They'll be here in a minute. Hold on, brother."

"It's time," Gram whispered. "It's time to quit the game."

"I know, Gram," Danny sobbed. "The last one, Gram, the last one, I promise."

"Man-oh-man," Gram winced in pain. "This is a bad deal, Danny. I'm not going to make it."

"Yes, you are. Yes, you are. Don't give up, G-man. Help is almost here."

"Is the cavalry coming?" Gram's bloody lips quivered. Both boys, even in trauma, recognized that Gram had placed the L in the proper place.

"Yeah Gram, the Calvary is on its way."

Gram gagged and swallowed hard, as if trying to keep precious life inside his body a few minutes longer. His breathing was strained, blood mixed with air. "The cavalry aren't the heroes in real life, Dan," he wheezed. "God, it hurts. I can't breathe too well."

Danny carefully unbuttoned Gram's crimson-soaked shirt, his fingers fumbling to make the situation right. He wanted desperately to heal him with some light-being miracle he hadn't yet learned. Where the hell was the real magic when you needed it? Danny pulled back the blood-drenched fabric. A rib protruded through Gram's chest. Blood surged from the hole with each withering beat of his dying heart. A stranger on the scene applied a towel to Gram's gurgling torso.

A faint murmur stirred behind them. The sky, under a spell from Merlin, pulled out its knitting needles and began stitching the clouds together in one long sheet of gray. A warm breeze blew. Death was coming.

"We took it too far," Gram said weakly.

"Hold on, Gram." Danny tried to soothe him. Dear God, dear Jesus, help him. He's one of You. But the god's weren't answering any calls; they were busy sewing up holes in the atmosphere. Gram smiled feebly. One last, eternal smile. "I've always known my future, Danny boy, and this is it. Sorry I was a half-baked mentor."

"No, Gram." Danny pushed a wiry lock of Gram's hair from his bruised forehead. "You can't go yet. You didn't save me by a lake. You haven't saved me."

"Back when I was a mystic to Czar Nicholas of Russia . . ." Gram coughed and spit up droplets of blood-laden mucous. "I couldn't save him, either." The wind blew stronger, warmer. Silent lightning flashed deep in the weave of the sky. The clouds sunk lower as if to lift Gram from the Earth—spirit, body, and all.

He looked directly into Danny's blurred eyes. He winked, a brilliant sparkle, a flash, a tiny beam of spectacular Glorian light from Gram's eyes.

"Did you see that?" someone said. "Did you see that light? It came right from his eyes. Jesus!" Everyone had seen it, an unmistakable burst of sparkling starshine.

The end was near. The clouds hovered like paramedics carrying a gray blanket. Merlin's aides swept in. The winds blew stronger. The first droplet of rain splattered the red-painted asphalt, then another. Gram's breath rattled like a baby's toy. His spirit was escaping. He strained to swallow, then gulped air and said, "Remember these words, Danny." His eyes rolled upward. "Things . . . aren't always what they seem."

And with those enigmatic words Gram closed his Rasputin eyes. The clouds dipped low, as if bowing, a fog descending upon the scene as Merlin cloaked Gram gently in his magician's handiwork. The life force retreated. The sparkle was gone. The Calvary, or the Cavalry (either one, what the hell did it matter now?) was too late. The game was over, never to be played again.

After the mayhem and the police report, after the explanations and the accusations, after the scolding eyes of Gram's crushed father, Joshua, burned a hole into Danny's psyche, the boy went to bed. Numb and distraught, exhausted and confused, mournful and ashamed, he opened his journals, which he hadn't touched in several months. These were the words he wrote:

"I killed him. As sure as Judas betrayed his friend, as sure as Pontius Pilate gave the order and washed his hands, as sure as He hung on the cross at Calvary, I killed Gram. This is my sin, and for this I shall never be forgiven."

Outside, a heavy rain began to fall.

Chapter 39

October 24, 1990

There were more watery eyes and sniffles in the Stone family room than a group of allergy sufferers at a Mold & Pollen Convention sponsored by the National Spore Foundation, co-sponsored by the manufacturers of Seldane. Stock in the makers of Kleenex tripled. The God of Sorrow dispensed ample amounts of saline.

Gram was dead. None of us knew him except through *The Journals*. Still, like an old friend passing on, we cried, all of us. Even Twinkie, before she realized she was late for a date and scurried away wearing a Reds cap and humming "Take Me Out to the Ballgame." Funny, baseball season was over. The Reds had won the World Series (I was too busy throwing up at the time).

The rest of us sat in silence, collecting our thoughts as we filed Gram's dying image somewhere in our minds, someplace less painful. Several uncomfortable minutes dripped by, marked by Bobby's disgruntled glare from the mantle. What I wouldn't do to replace that portrait—and the spoon collection, I thought. Rose and I have catered to his psychosis long enough. He isn't about to grow another arm. He needs to deal with his past and move on. I know his pain, but he has allowed it to fester. These were the thoughts I was considering when Maya fired a Patriot missile into the heart of the evening. If Bobby *had* been there, he would have instinctively clutched at his missing appendage.

"Sing . . . *(sniff)* . . . say, now it all makes sense," she stated. "Now I know why I'm here."

Parker, diplomat extraordinaire, placed his hand on hers. "Why's that?" Not even Parker, with years of training as a shrewd listener, a diviner of secrets as a top-grade private eye, could have deduced her incredible response.

"Because I know Danny."

We were all stunned.

"It's true." Maya smoothed her flowered skirt across her thigh. "We lived together in Tucson."

A round of bewildered remarks followed.

"Just for a month or so." She smiled, embarrassed.

Parker, who rarely shows what he is thinking, ran a disbelieving palm over his face. "Maya," he said, doing his best to control his tone, "Danny is the key to this whole case. *Impartial Fate* depends on him—and another girl. Why didn't you tell us before?"

Maya shrugged. Her everyday demeanor returned. "I thought I was here for another reason."

"What other reason?" Rose asked softly.

I glimpsed a meadow of goose flesh on her arms. Something cosmic was going on here, and Rose knew it, knew she was part of it. Was she wondering what the hypocrites at her former church would say if they could be in the room at that moment? Would their darkened tunnel minds allow a ray of light to shine in so they could see they were worshipping the wrong God? Call me bitter, but I doubt it.

Maya measured her words carefully, trying to gauge just how much more startling information we could absorb. "I thought destiny brought me here to help Danny."

Parker raised an eyebrow. "And just how did destiny do that?"

"Astarte bewitch me, it's a really long story. I'm not sure how much to share."

"Start from the beginning," Parker said kindly.

It is impossible to look at Parker and not be pulled into his thoughts, to wonder what part of his soul is gazing at you. He and Maya, their eyes splendid in opposite yet celestial ways, seem to bring a balance, a harmony to the room, as if nothing could ever be said that was too wild, too fantastic to be believed.

Maya sat back in her chair, smoothed her skirt once again, and took a sip of cold tea. Rose almost offered to warm it up but held back so as not to break the moment. Maya glowed with information. I was on the edge of the sofa, anxious to hear her tale.

"First, let me say that I do not, absolutely do not, believe in coincidence," she said. "My higher power always points me in the right direction. I came to Cincinnati because of a vision."

"A vision?" I asked.

"Yes," Maya said. "Isn't that wild? I was at Stonehenge to witness the summer solstice rituals of the Druids."

"You're such an adventuresome girl," Rose said.

"Oh," Maya gushed, "that's my parents' doing. We always took vacations to spiritual centers around the world—the pyramids, Tibet, Madanapalle, Easter Island, the Callanish Circle of the Outer Hebrides, Fort Ancient, places like that. But the Druids are nice, if you go in for that sort of thing. I had a calling to go to Stonehenge, though, to feel the powerful vortices and experience its energy on my own terms. Last June was totally wild." She lowered her voice, as if to tell a secret. "Once I got there, I fasted for three days. I took in the sights, visited the British Museum; it was all so inspiring. But of all the things I saw, the one that touched me the most, the one that I came back to over and over when I was in the British Museum, was the Rosetta Stone. It was that black basalt transcription from 196 B.C. that called to me, and I didn't know why."

"She's enchanting, isn't she?" Parker smiled. Rose and I agreed.

"The morning of the summer solstice, I went out to Stonehenge at three in the morning. The cool, English mist billowed in across the grasslands. I climbed up on the bluestone slabs. It was amazing." She laughed like a Wiccan elder telling the coven of a girlish prank. "I stripped off all my clothes and lay there naked and silent for three hours, while the Druids performed their rituals."

I glanced at Rose to see if she was blushing. To my surprise, she gleamed in admiration. Parker, too. Uninhibited acts must rank high in their good traits department.

"Weren't you nervous or shy?" I asked.

"Oh, heavens no," Maya said unabashedly. "I'm not such a Puritan that I should be ashamed of my natural form. If someone else is embarrassed by my sex, then they have a personal hang-up they need to deal with. Besides, I have a nice body." That, most assuredly, is true.

"How free you must feel," Rose said.

"I felt like a virgin sacrifice lying up there as the fog swept over the Salisbury Plains. All the gods of the Universe looking down upon my purity. I meditated and prayed, asking for divine guidance. Astarte bewitch me, you know what happened?"

"What?" I asked.

"It may sound crazy, but magic swirled all around me that cold, summer morning, R.T. My cleansing fast had eliminated the impurities from my body, my mind was clear and crisp, and lo and behold, I had a vision. I do admit that it didn't become crystal clear until I saw Parker standing up to the mob in front of your house a few weeks back, but I finally put it together."

I didn't follow her logic. What was she saying? That a spirit visited her while she lay nude atop a rock in England?

She bit her lip lightly. "As I lay upon the bluestone of Stonehenge, with all my senses peaking, I had a vision of Cincinnati and two people in trouble. At the time I thought it was Danny, and perhaps his long-lost love, Allison, which wouldn't be too hard to imagine because Danny is always finding trouble—it's his mischievous way." Maya slid off her seat and knelt on the floor between me and Rose. She took each of our hands in hers. Her brown eyes poured her friendship into us. "But it wasn't Danny at all. It was you, R.T."

Rose and I turned toward each other, mesmerized, electrified, believing every word.

"The message told me to help translate an important work," she said. Her almond eyes bounced back and forth between Rose and myself. "I couldn't grasp what it was, but I knew it was a document of some significance, and that it was a major piece of spiritual work. At first I thought it might be Danny's book, then I thought maybe it was his diary. He keeps one you know. It's called *The Journals*."

A lightning rod of recognition charged through me. Everything was coming together. The Council *was* providing support. Alleluia.

"Then I remembered from college that the Dead Sea Scrolls were being translated in an excruciatingly slow manner in Cincinnati at the Hebrew Union College, and so I thought that was it. I laid on that rock, trying to interpret the messages, when an image came to me of a tablet—an image of the Rosetta Stone." She smiled and squeezed Rose's hand. "It wasn't until tonight that I knew what was going on. When I stepped into your foyer and saw all the ancient Babylonian artifacts, I knew I was walking into something sensational, I just knew it. It became clearer when I met you," Maya said as she nodded at Rose. "A major insight bubbled in my brain. You, Rose, are Rosetta Stone. I'm here to help you *and* Rose. That's the message. And, of course, to meet my future husband, Parker."

Parker Floyd, detective supreme, boyish charmer of royal order, smiled. He loved the sound of that. He looked at me shyly, like an impish son on a first date, and said, "Sometimes you just know, R.T."

"It's still off in the future," Maya said. "That Parker and I are soulmates, there's no denying. Isn't it wild?"

"You two sure fell in love fast," I said.

Rose looked at me warmly. "Just like you and me."

And so it was. I had met Rose just after the war. We met at a dance at Moonlight Gardens on the river. I was smitten at first glance by the way she carried herself, confident and worldly. I *knew* that night. We waited two years to get hitched, but we knew from the start. Kismet.

"That's what the Universe does when you're in balance." Maya kissed Parker. "You know what else, though?" she said with a hint of mystery. "The book we're supposed to help translate is *The Journals*."

"How do you know that?"

"Because of the jam you're in, R.T. Stone. On trial for your life, for your freedom, for the salvation of humankind, and because the name Stonehenge means . . . *hanging stone*."

I looked at her, puzzled.

"Sing say, don't you see?" Maya winked. "We're all here to help you. To keep Robert Thomas *Stone* from hanging."

And so that's my update. It all happened like a dream. Slow motion, yet instantly. A lifetime in one second. Four people now know the truth about my dilemma. Parker says it doesn't do any good for my case. The existence of a talking book or an omniscient TV set doesn't mean I didn't torch the Cosmic Club. He also reminded me that we're dealing with a power much greater than we can comprehend, so I am obligated to perform the Council's request, and, higher powers being what they are, they won't leave me alone until I do. This line of thought, of course, made perfect sense.

Our guests left long ago, but not before we hatched a plan to gather more evidence for *The Journals* by dispatching Maya and Parker (they're a team now; I can't break them up) to New Orleans, the last known whereabouts of Allison.

Maya dropped one last nuclear warhead of news into our camp. Parker had said, "Don't get your hopes up, R.T. We've had no luck finding Danny, so I'm not sure finding Allison is going to be any easier. It's like they've both purposely disappeared."

"Sing say, are you guys trying to find Danny?"

"Yeah," Parker said. "He and Allison are essential to getting Stone off."

"Astarte bewitch me, guys," Maya said. "His band was playing at your club the night of the fire."

"*What?*"

"Sure! Einstein and the Wasted Memories—that's Danny's band."

"Hel . . . low Swami!" Parker said. "How did I miss that one? Do you know where he is now?"

Maya shrugged. "No, he vanished the night of the fire, but I bet one of his band mates might know where he is."

It was decided that I would look up Billy Harper, using an address and phone number provided by Parker, while he and Maya ventured to New Orleans in search of Allison. Danny was right in front of my nose. I couldn't believe it.

Rose is asleep in the bedroom. I'm too inspired to sleep. Too many loose ends running through my mind, too much pain in my abdomen as well. Too much concern in my noggin. Rose said something that set me to thinking, got me to worry. She didn't mean to, of course.

"Dear," she said, slipping into a silk robe. "This is all so new to me, so strange. And I don't mean to interfere, but, in the scene where Gram and Danny moved the Mamets down to their little hideaway, did they move the real Mamets or the forgeries?"

"The real ones. Why?"

She tied the sash around her slender waist. Time has stolen nothing of her beauty. She scrunched her face the way she does when she senses something wrong. "Didn't you buy three Mamets from Danny at the estate sale after Patrick's death?"

I was glad to see Patrick Gilday jettisoned to hell. Cara wanted nothing to do with the evil memory of her husband by then either. Everything related to Mulciber, her share anyway, was sold, except for Mulciber itself.

"Yeah, I bought them. So?"

"Did you buy the forgeries or the originals?" She folded back the covers and climbed into bed.

"The originals, of course!"

"How do you know? That was a long time ago. If you bought the fakes and they burned in the C.C. fire, and then the originals are discovered, wouldn't the insurance company want some of its money back?"

Holy smokes, she's right. What if Danny *did* sell me the forgeries? Lloyd's would want a half-million bucks back. Thanks to the insane Japanese art frenzy, my Mamets had risen handsomely to an unprecedented high. Without *all* the insurance money I can't pay my debts and start my Mariemont development project.

"Don't worry, dear," I lied. "I'm sure they're the originals."

She stretched to turn out the light. It was 12:32 a.m. Satisfied, she said, "Are you coming to bed, dear?"

"No," I replied, "I'm going to read a bit."

So here I am, worried sick that my future has yet another uncertain wrinkle in it. If McBain finds out the real Mamets are stashed in the Quarters, I'm cooked. With the insurance money central to his case, he's bound to be scraping for additional evidence. If he finds out, he's sure to say I did it to defraud Lloyd's. It's not true. I'm innocent. Damn! What should I do? I can't lose everything. I won't! Not when it appears I'm almost home free. That's it. I'm going to Mulciber to see for myself.

"*No!*" The Journals invaded my computer screen. "*Do not go there, Stone. It is a mistake that will be difficult to undo. Let the fates play out as they will. All is in place. Your visit will upset the balance. It is best to remain in your sanctuary and witness Allison's story.*"

"But—"

"*STAY AWAY FROM MULCIBER!*"

Section

Chapter 40

"This is due back two weeks from today, on February 9," Allison said to Gabrielle as she thumped the rubber stamp on the library card. Allison slipped the card into the sleeve and handed her the book. "Please take care of it," Allison reminded her with a toss of her red, shoulder-length hair. Allison was pleased to be a librarian. She considered it a glorious honor to be punished for sneaking to the Mission de Cincinnatus by having to serve in the St. Als' bookroom, the most peaceful place in the orphanage. She found it a comforting sanctuary.

She glanced over at Ellen Mathis—Worm—nicknamed (by Allison) because of her thick, round glasses and the fact that her nose was perpetually stuffed inches from the pages of a hardback. Allison loved to read, too, adored it actually, found it "absotively stimulating," but Worm made her seem illiterate by comparison. Worm worked in the library as her main job at St. Als, didn't have many friends, and longed to make one of the popular Allison. Whenever she could, Worm watched Allison secretly, following her moves, her mannerisms, trying her best to determine what made her such a likable girl. She'd peer over the top of her book just enough to watch Allison write in her journal, then quickly disappear behind the pages before she could be discovered. But Allison already knew.

Highly trained as a detective and supersecret spy, the Red Angel was keenly aware of Ellen's stealthy observations. She was flattered. She liked Worm and felt sorry for her, and felt a responsibility to help the girl through her ugly duckling stage. Worm was an awkward girl, teeth slightly pushed forward, begging for braces, and who always had a bruise or three on an arm or a knee. The bruises were the result of her clumsiness. Allison had worked with her for almost two weeks, and there hadn't been a day that Worm hadn't bumped into the bookcart, or rounded a corner too tightly and walked into a large bookshelf, or dropped a stack of books on her toes. Worm took it all in stride, never crying, never complaining, always shrugging it off. Allison hadn't determined how to help Worm through the ugly duckling stage, but she was sure she would find a way.

It was a slow night in the library. Most of the kids were in their rooms, bundled up against the January cold, or in the main room playing checkers, chess, Stratego, or watching TV. Allison checked the clock on the wall, which hadn't been dusted, she guessed, since the late 1950s. It's Tuesday, she thought to herself, the kids will be watching *Happy Days*, then *Laverne & Shirley*, unless the nuns display their sadistic streak and force *Father Murphy* on everyone. That clears out the rec room fast enough.

She scanned the polished tile floor and the walnut-stained shelves and breathed deeply. She loved the smell of the library, the rich scent of paper and ink. It called to her spirit as an escape from the drudgery of being abandoned in the world, and she was surprised that more kids didn't find the same benefit in books.

Worm watched her. Allison pretended to straighten a loose stack of quarter-sheet papers the kids used to write down reference numbers. Suddenly she turned, a smile as big as daylight, hoping to catch Worm red-handed. Too late, Worm had already ducked behind her book.

Although it was supposed to be punishment, Allison loved the library and the attention it got her. She loved the knowledge and the adventure contained within the worn sheets of paper. She felt as though she had made many friends among the authors who spilled their souls upon the sheaths that lined the shelves of the great sanctuary.

"Worm," she said. "Don't you find it curious that the newspaper has stopped coming?"

Worm pretended not to hear, as though she weren't studying Allison. "Excuse me?" She set the book down, grateful for Allison's attention.

"Jesus accosting the paperboy, isn't it curious that *The Enquirer* hasn't come lately?" Allison repeated, "And that the sisters don't appear concerned enough to call about it? How am I supposed to keep current on world events? There's revolution in Latin America and unrest in the Middle East."

Worm shrugged with false nonchalance and picked up her book again. Indeed, the paper hadn't shown its font-filled face since the night of Allison's transgression. Had she thought about it, tried to piece it together, she could have deduced as much. Had she considered it further, she would have concluded that she was assigned library duty promptly after chow to keep her from watching the evening news as well. But Allison had more important things to consider—such as how to resume her Saturday night visits to the mission. The nuns had called the police on Cincinnatus, hadn't they? Was he all right? Did they arrest him? She had plotted and schemed well, doing her utmost to appease her worried keepers that her "charitable diversions" were behind her.

The nuns, aware that Allison was of such spirit that she wouldn't simply agree to stop her late-night runs, played a countergame of deceit. They discussed the "Allison situation" behind closed doors, and there were a good many closed doors those days, for there wasn't the mere topic of Allison sneaking out to help a few "bums," as Mother Superior referred to them with disdain, but the much more troubling issue of her visions. That strange energy which swirled about her at Midnight Mass. That glow that permeated the Sacred Mother of Hearts and transformed, permanently, everyone fortunate enough to witness it. What should the sisters do with such a girl? Was it God or Satan that manifested in her? An insane question given her pure disposition and outlook. Should the Governing Order of Divinity—Division of Apparitions, Miracles & Nuisances be summoned? Mother Peculiar, who resented the abrupt nature of Smith and the loss of authority in his presence, resisted calling them.

No, it was decided to keep the last incident as quiet as possible. They decided to raise Allison as if everything were normal, and she were an average fourteen-year-old young woman with a knack for tennis, gardening, and charity. Allison knew all this, of course, having mastered the ventilation system of St. Als as the perfect eavesdropping device. Some rooms, some vents and registers were more acoustically sound than others, but overall she could make out enough of their plans to know the ghost squad wasn't coming back for her. The one place that she couldn't hear into very well was Mother Superior's office; the previously mentioned pedophilic deacon, who often visited in that very room with his young protégés, had the room made soundproof with the best insulation of the day.

January had been cold, and she didn't care enough about the future actions of the religious penguins to risk life and limb on the frozen edge of the fire escape. This was unfortunate because Mother Superior's office was where all the planning took place in the matter of Cincinnatus and his much-needed mission.

Another patron entered the library. Joyce. Allison rolled her eyes, hoping Joyce had learned the last time she had approached her that Allison wasn't interested. That episode, still fresh from six days earlier, was a furtive kiss in a book aisle that Allison dodged, Joyce's lips smooching the spine of a Virgin Islands travel guide. Poetic justice.

Joyce gave Allison the once over. "Kinda slow in here tonight, Seed," she said as she plopped a bulging baggy of seeds on the counter and walked to the magazine rack. "Rita and me have been collecting these. Hope they grow for you," Joyce said.

Allison breathed a sigh of relief. Joyce must have gotten the message, or she was biding her time.

Allison thought of Rita, who often accompanied Joyce, and smiled to herself at the more subtle way Rita had tried to seduce her. Rita didn't come on as strong as Joyce, preferring to flirt, and she often saved it for their Saturday tennis matches. But Rita was blatant, too, because she mercilessly tried to tempt Allison in front of Sister Dena, who seemed oblivious to Rita's coy remarks. Sister D was so focused on tennis with her hat, her sunflower seeds, her sweatbands, and her coach's whistle, that Allison wasn't sure she was the same person when it came to tennis. There was a bloodlust there. A desire to win. The maniac parent who drives their kid to tears. But in a nice, motherly, nunly way. Dena did seem to realize when she was going over the edge. Still, a nervous pile of saliva-soaked shells lay deep at her feet at the end of each lesson.

Allison thought of her Saturdays—the tennis, turkey sandwiches, and iced tea afterwards at the club. She loved that time. As a bonus, there were a couple of wealthy boys who were infatuated with Rita and Allison, often taking the table next to theirs, if it was open, as they ate their sandwiches and discussed Allison's game. This adolescent dance, however, was not lost on Sister Dena, who was well-aware of the hormonal powers of young boys and girls, and who had already noticed with motherly pride that Allison's body was developing the curves and mounds necessary to become a woman of some sensuality. Though these thoughts were not often ascribed to the synapses of nuns, it has been established that Sister Dena did not become a nun by choice. Her pleasure in seeing Allison grow into a vibrant young woman was aided by a sincere and total belief that Allison was her purpose in life, her reason for existence.

Joyce looked up from her magazine and winked at Allison. The seduction had not ended as hoped. Worm peered out from behind her book and Coke-bottle glasses but didn't catch Joyce's thinly veiled attempt. Allison, annoyed at being treated like a prize to be won in a contest between Rita and Joyce, picked up a pen and began writing in her journals.

"January 26, 1982— I am absotively looking forward to spring and the glorious opportunity to return to my garden . . ."

The flirtations with the two boys at the tennis club became strained a few days later when one of the lads, playing the court next to Allison's, mentioned, "I wouldn't mind having Red serve me an ace."

Now it wasn't the ace part that bothered Allison, and it wasn't the sexual innuendo that bothered her. It wasn't that he said it as she was about to serve Rita for set point. Those things a sophisticated, self-assured woman can overlook. It was the *Red* part of his comments that sent a rage coursing through her, and Allison, always one to comply with one's wishes, sent a scorching peach-fuzz-smooth tennis ball sailing cross court into the testicles of a surprised, embarrassed, and ruptured potential suitor. Game. Set. Match.

Amid the laughter and the sunflower seeds in the locker room with Sister Dena and Rita, as they complimented her on "training men early" and "keeping them in line," Allison said simply, "Jesus dating Gloria Steinem, is that what the battle of the sexes is about?"

Allison was convinced that a sinister plan was afoot (having recently finished *The Red Headed League,* by Sir Arthur Canon Doyle) with respect to the newspapers having disappeared over the last three weeks. Her fertile imagination took charge as she planned an after hours visit to Mother Peculiar's office. It was 10:30 when she edged her way down the hall, wearing gym shoes to muffle her steps, a nail file in hand to jimmy the lock on Mother's door should it be locked. It wasn't. She slipped inside and turned on the flashlight she had borrowed from the emergency closet. She knew she'd find something, but what? What was it?

She could scarcely raise Mary's interest in the caper. Mary insisted it was "just those Nazi nuns playing head games again." Allison laughed as she thought of her jaded roommate. "Sweet Mary," she whispered to herself as the beam of light cut its way through the room. "So absotively cynical to the point of inaction."

The ray lighted upon the desk, a bookcase, the pope on the wall, a basket overflowing with magazines and newspapers. Jackpot. Allison stepped toward it, her pulse quickened. She leaned over the stack and checked the date on the masthead—January 30, 1982. Her breathing stopped. Was she seeing this right? Could this be? Why would this happen? She forgot herself and read the news aloud: "Local Shelter Closed Amid Sex Scandal."

Footsteps echoed in the hall. She recognized the rocky gait. Mother Peculiar. After years of spy work, Allison had come to recognize the fine nuances of each and every sister's footsteps—some heavy, some light, some steady, some erratic. Mother Superior's distinctive steps were more like that of a drunken Clydesdale with Ed McMahon riding bareback. *Clippety-clop-clop. Clippety-clop-clop.*

Allison cut the light and picked up the paper, which she folded in half and stuffed under her sweatshirt. She ducked into Mother's adjoining bathroom. She silently closed the door behind her and stood motionless, pressed against the wall, panting as the doorknob turned in the outer chamber. The bathroom smelled of Camay—pink with perfume. Light crept under the bathroom door and grabbed at her feet. Allison inched closer toward the door; she hoped Mother didn't need to use the facilities. The muscles in her face, her jaw, her arms, her stomach, her thighs, her calves, her toes, every muscle in her body, was drawn taut in fear. What would the evil ruler of St. Als do if she discovered the Red Angel inside her sanctum? She shuddered. She struggled to put any such negative thought from her mind.

What was Mother doing awake? she wondered. No penguin is ever up past ten. Something is awry, Allison concluded, seriously awry. She heard papers shuffled and the phone being dialed. She tried to imagine what each digit represented, to know who Mother was calling.

"Winston, it's me," Mother said in a gravelly type of voice. There was a long pause.

Who was Winston? Did Mother Peculiar have a boyfriend? No, that's preposterous. Did she have a brother? She never mentioned it. Still, a possibility. Maybe just a friend, from childhood perhaps, someone to confide in.

"We need more cash," Mother said. "The girl is expensive to take care of."

The girl? Who's the girl? Cash? Is he a banker? Is Winston a church official? Some Deep Throat of the diocese?

A tickle scratched its way to Allison's nose. She wriggled her nose to rid herself of the menace. The tickle wouldn't budge. It had no better place to be. It dug deeper, bringing out a feather for good measure to run up and down her nostrils. She rubbed her schnoz in an effort to quell the itch that could expose her at the most inopportune moment.

"Ten thousand dollars, Winston," Mother insisted. "Not a penny less. The girl has so many interests. And he's got the bucks, so don't tell me you can't come up with it."

The sadistic tickle's feather tactic had failed against Allison's resolve not to sneeze, so the instigator brought out a full length boa, which ran the length of her nasal passage like a cat scratching a post.

"I'll expect the money by the end of next week. Good night, Winston."

Mother hung up the phone. Allison imagined her scribbling a note in some confidential file. A drawer opened. The sneeze welled up. She was ready to burst any second. She was on the first letter of achoo, and fighting hard. She pinched the flair of her nostrils. Rita had shown her that once, and Allison had tried it in mass twice with good success. But *this* one, *this* sneeze, was an ornery one. It wouldn't be denied. One peep and she was a goner. She'd be yanked from library duty and sent to the bowels of the kitchen for sure, maybe locked in her room. A spanking was a given, and, with Mother behind the paddle, it was sure to be a blistering one.

A drawer slammed shut. A key turned in a lock. A double whammy *Ah-ah* was poised off shore. A sneeze was about to break loose like a Florida hurricane. Mother mounted the Clydesdale and sauntered toward the door. Gale force winds began to rage. A storm was ready to unleash itself. The boa tickled every hair of Allison's delicate nose. The light switch flipped off. The door closed.

"*Aaa . . . choo!*"

The light turned on. She held her breath.

"Huh!" Mother said.

The light switched off again. The Clydesdale cantered down the hall as Allison slid to the floor, her relieved muscles aching from the tension. *Clippety-clop-clop. Clippety-clop-clop.* Allison was safe now.

Evenwise, what was this business about a local mission closing?

Allison had planned to resume her advocacy work at the mission the following Saturday but now decided to accelerate her schedule and head directly to Cincinnatus that same night. She didn't bother to read the article. She wanted to find out for herself if it was true. She crept back to her room cautiously and changed clothes. She bundled up in several layers of socks, a T-shirt, a long sleeve blouse, sweatshirt, jeans, and finally her coat. Outside, the wind howled and whipped like a savage ringmaster trying to quell an unruly beast. Mary rolled over in bed and mumbled something about diamonds and chocolate. Allison paid little heed. She stripped her pillow from its case and stole her way to the kitchen for supplies, hoping she wouldn't find Rita and Joyce making out on the appliances.

Her case stuffed full, Allison made it across the front lawn to Reading Road and struggled toward the shelter, head down, braced against a brutal wind. The streets were empty for a Tuesday night, deserted by a population too weak to fight nature. She trudged the ten blocks or so to the mission, her mind fearful about what she would find there. "It must be open," she said to herself, her words stolen from her mouth and blown away before she could hear them. "It absotively must be open." She prayed aloud. God wouldn't let this happen, she told herself. No way.

She approached the meager mission. It was dark except for the modest Chinese bulb bobbing wildly on a wire. She ran to the front stoop of the shelter. Her heart froze. Her jaw hung ajar like a weighted icicle ready to drop from a Midwestern rain gutter. She examined the yellow plastic tape that covered the front door like a cheap sash for a Miss Homeless America contestant.

DO NOT CROSS. CONDEMNED BY THE CINCINNATI DEPT. OF HEALTH

Condemned? The yellow, chickenshit phrase reverberated in her brain. Numbly, she dropped the pillowcase to the ground with a deflated clink of a can of Del Monte green beans. She read another notice slapped haphazardly over the bright orange sun that had been the welcome sign of the shelter. It was a place of light, now steeped in darkness. The notice read: "This property impounded by the authority of the United States government, Internal Revenue Service." The crass heading was followed by several indecipherable paragraphs of legalese so unintelligible that a team of Washington lawyers with a fifty thousand dollar retainer couldn't interpret them, even with a twenty-five hundred page edition of the *United States Tax Code*.

The wind tried to steal her coat, tearing at it like a downtown mugger. She lowered her head against the onslaught, trying to tuck her chin inside the collar. What had happened? Why was the mission closed? Cincinnatus is a great man, she told herself; how can this be?

She grabbed the pillowcase and dragged it behind her as she shuffled in the direction of the orphanage. She was only a few feet from the mission's front door when she glanced down the side alley and saw a construction barrel shooting fire into the cold night. Several forlorn people huddled around it for warmth, hands thrust out over the orange glow. Instinctively, Allison dragged the supply of food down the alley to the people obviously in need.

"Hello, Seed." Stephen greeted her through jagged, chipped teeth. "Ain't seen you in awhile."

"What happened, Stephen?" she asked, ready to burst into tears.

"It ain't fair what they done," he said. His breath turned to vapor and seemed to fall to the ground, drunk on wine stolen from the convenience store. "Ain't fair what they do to common folk." He spit into the barrel. Mumbles and nods affirmed his words.

"Wh . . . what happened?" She stepped to the barrel to warm her hands. The fire felt good against her cold cheeks. She struggled to choke back her tears.

Stephen coughed and shook his head, disgusted. "Police came and arrested him."

"Cincinnatus? For what!"

"Say he molested a girl. Police came in the middle of the night and took him away in handcuffs." Stephen looked down at his feet, his toes, covered in newspaper, sticking through his right shoe. "No one believed he done it, not even the cops that was forced to arrest him."

"He didn't do it!" She knew what this was about. She knew who Cincinnatus had allegedly molested. She clutched at her stomach, somehow guilty, somehow responsible.

"Old Cincinnatus never hurt nobody, never touched nobody," Stephen said. The fire crackled and hissed, defying winter to challenge it. One of the vagrants picked up a slat from a shipping pallet and tossed it into the fire. It flared brighter, daring the night to a fight. "I believe it was them Catholics up the street." He motioned with his head. "That Mother Superior boss-lady bitch was down here when they took him away, smiling like she just got laid by the pope."

Allison frowned.

"Sorry, Seed," he said. "Didn't mean no offense. This got us all shook up. We got nowhere to go. And that Mother Superior chick was down here all high-and-mighty, acting like she owned the place—all smug and shit." He coughed, then coughed again, as if some incurable disease were cloning itself inside him, taking over his body.

Allison was enraged that Mother Peculiar was involved. The seed of a devious plan of revenge, a germination of a delicious retribution grew inside her. "Can't you go to another mission?" she asked, concerned for the disheveled men who hugged the perimeter of the barrel as if it were life itself.

A few men scoffed. Some grimaced. "Since Reagan took over," Stephen explained, "kitchens and flophouses, shelters and such, been closing. No more funds, they say. Things was already tight before the man start cutting back. Guess he needs to pay for that Star Wars of his."

"Paying for it on the backs of the people," a large man said angrily.

She didn't want to get started on politics. She'd be all night trashing Reagan and the Republicans. Trickle down. Right.

"Where's Cincinnatus now?" she asked. "In . . . jail?"

"El Salvador."

"What? Jesus in the tropics without mosquito netting, what's he doing down there?"

The fire punched at the darkness. Stephen coughed and wriggled his frozen toes through his street-fashionable newsprint leather. He shook his head the way a defeated man does when he's trying to reconcile his life. "He came back for a few hours before they sealed the mission. Said he needed to get out of the country. Said it was too corrupt."

"But El Salvador?"

Stephen coughed and ran a smeared hand across his chapped lips. "Said he was gonna try and undo some of the evil the CIA had done down there."

"What's the CIA got to do with this?"

Stephen shrugged. "Cin mentioned something about the CIA and some kind of Catholic group, oh . . . what did he call it? Opie. Opus. Opus Dei. Something like that. Said he stood a better chance down there fighting Opus and injustice than here in America, where people was too blind to give a shit. Cin didn't say the shit part. I kind of ad-libbed that."

"But this is America! They can't run him off like that."

Stephen rubbed his raw hands together. "It ain't America for street people. That dream been broken a long time. If it ever was. Just words from politicians, girl, don't get fooled by what you see on TV and hear from the fat cats. If you ain't got money, lots of it, you ain't got jack. Even those in the middle can lose everything they gots if some rich man want it. They just change the law so it work for them," he said. "Cin said the government is too hypocritical to care about people. Shit, they got fifty years worth of food stashed in underground caves to subsidize the giant food companies while a couple million homeless go hungry."

Jesus selling his soul to Satan for a pack of Bazooka Joe, is this true? she wondered.

"Almost forgot," Stephen said as he reached inside the tattered coat, which bore more holes than Swiss cheese at a Three Mouseketeers party. Allison thought of giving him her own coat until she realized it wouldn't fit him. "Cin knew you'd be coming by. He said you couldn't help yourself. Wanted me to give you this."

Allison's favorite indigent handed her a paper bag full of seeds. There was a note inside which she decided to read once she reached home. So this was goodbye. Cincinnatus was in El Salvador.

"Thank you," she said shyly. She remembered the pillowcase at her feet. "I have food," she said brightly. "It's for you."

The men graciously accepted it, each trying to hold back their instinct to tear into the sack and quell the hunger which burned inside, to keep from showing her how needy they were. Funny what a man's pride will do, even in the face of stark circumstance. They thanked Allison and she was on her way, but not before she promised to come back next Saturday with sandwiches and as much clothes and anything else she could "borrow" from St. Als.

The men humbly declined, but both they and Allison knew that they would gladly take whatever assistance she would bring. As she pulled her coat tight against the unrelenting wind, and thoughts of Cincinnatus sweating in the tropics macheted their way into her cerebrum, and anger towards Mother Peculiar's vengeance welled up, she began to solidify her own form of payback for the cruelty Mother had wrought upon the innocent street people. "There will be a price to pay, Mother," she said through her tears.

There was a marked change in Allison's demeanor toward Mother Superior. Her attitude toward the other sisters and her fellow orphans remained as cheerful and angelic as ever, but in matters regarding the Commandant of Stalag St. Als, as Allison now referred to it, she was nothing short of vinegar. She had started to implement her plan, enlisting Rita and the rest of the kitchen staff the day after she had uncovered Mother's betrayal. The plot was simple enough: if Mother Peculiar wouldn't allow the hungry and the homeless their nourishment, then Allison would rob Mother of hers as well. The idea came to her that a good dose of laxatives in every dish consumed by the head mistress would be fitting and ironic justice.

Rita gladly accepted the challenge of spiking Mother's food, and a host of ingredients were added to the recipe to mask the flavor of the various stool looseners. With typical teenage overkill, one laxative one time was not enough. The punishment needed to be excessive and long lasting, and so, in the span of ten days, Mother Superior was given a pharmaceutical mix so potent that the gas expelled from her bowels could have heated St. Als for a year of harsh winters.

The Meal, as it came to be called by the girls, soon turned into a betting pool with the winner getting the pot (no pun intended). Allison had won once, predicting within forty-five seconds the exact moment when Mother would suddenly rise from her chair at the head of the table and rush to the lavatory. The enthusiasm for the scheme diminished considerably, however, when Mother Superior began taking meals in her room or office in order to be closer to a bathroom. But even this had its upside as meals tended to be more relaxed without the evil governess of the manor looking down upon the girls, ready to chastise for the smallest indiscretion.

Sister Dena, under instruction to find out if Allison was having any more visions, and observant of her cold shoulder toward Mother Superior, came to visit her in the library.

"What are you reading?" the nun asked, reaching into her pocket for a handful of sunflower seeds, as Worm watched from afar.

"About the executions of Iranian opposition leaders yesterday." Allison folded the paper and set it on the counter. The daily blab was miraculously being delivered again, now that the Cincinnatus story had blown over. "Do you suppose Mother Superior had anything to do with *that?*"

Sister Dena, a salty, new seed swimming around her mouth, was momentarily thrown off guard. She smiled, amused at Allison's caustic interest in world events. "Doubtful," she said. "Allison . . . angel, why are you so upset with Mother Superior? You never have anything nice to say. That's not like you."

Allison pondered whether to answer truthfully or hold back but decided truth is always best. Worm set down her book, dropping any pretense that she wasn't listening. Allison carefully selected her words, not wanting to upset Sister Dena, who was a true friend, a guardian. "Don't you guys realize that I know what she did to Cincinnatus and his mission?"

Sister Dena's heart lurched for a moment. "I didn't know you had found out," she said apologetically. The fractured sunflower shell was expelled and placed into the always ready Ziplock. Another seed popped into play.

Allison wanted to lash out about the whole sick ordeal but knew it wasn't Sister D's fault. It was Mother's, and perhaps Clod and Barney, but not Sister D—she would never be part of such a sinister and disgusting act. "Jesus flunking out of kindergarten, you guys must think I'm stupid," she said. "You hide the newspapers and schedule me in the library so I can't watch the news. You cloister me like I'm some kind of pariah, and you don't think I'm going to catch on that something's wrong?"

"I'm sorry, angel," Sister D said. She mindlessly played with the stubby, dull pencils used only in libraries, golf carts, and nonleague bowling.

Allison burst into tears. "He was arrested for molesting me! How could the Church do that?" Sister D hurried around the library counter and put her arm around Allison as Worm picked up her book and pretended to be enthralled in the text.

"Some things in life are hard to understand, angel." Sister D stroked Allison's red locks.

"All Mother had to do was talk to him, warn him or something. She didn't have to have him arrested and close the mission."

"I'm not saying it's right, Seed," Sister Dena acknowledged, holding back a sharp crack of a juicy sunflower. "Mother may have acted in haste."

"Haste? He was ruined. Now there are hundreds of homeless on the street because of her!"

"There . . . there now, angel, she did what she thought was best." Another black shell sailed into Sister's mouth. Twins. The seeds wrestled for position with the tongue.

Allison couldn't be consoled. "She did absotively no such thing! She abused her power in order to do a malicious and cruel deed. She'll pay for it, too. If she was so interested in doing what's best, she would have helped the homeless, not shut them out. Cincinnatus did what was best. He lived with his heart. He didn't just sit around complaining about problems; he did something about them!" Her temper rose like a backyard bottle rocket. She couldn't hold back any longer. A week and a half of anger caught fire and burned its way out of her soul. "Thank God he's not like the stagnant, old nuns around here, waiting for the Lord to do something. He's in El Salvador right now, where people appreciate him!"

Sister Dena bowed her head, partly at the sting of Allison's tirade, partly at the truth it contained. She let go of her. "I *am* sorry," was all the nun could say.

"Jesus taking back his fish, bread, and wine for the poor and giving them to Caesar, why is Reagan giving money to Caribbean nations when he's cutting spending here at home?" Allison said aloud to an empty library, save Worm, who was studying a book list provided by Sister Claudia. Allison and Worm had become close over the last two months. March was only six hours away, and Worm dreaded Allison's punishment coming to an end. Secretly she wished Allison would get into trouble and her sentence extended. Worm even considered revealing Allison's laxative treatment to the nuns in hopes of getting her to stay, but reason won out. Worm had no way of knowing if Mother's punishment would actually be *more* library time. Anyway, Allison had already put a stop to the prank after her outburst with Sister Dena. She realized that she had made the problem too personal and could be harming Mother Superior in an irreparable way.

"You can worry about that after we finish pulling all these books." Ellen waved the list in the air like a checkered flag. Allison had stopped calling Ellen "Worm," once she understood that Ellen was hurt by it. She viewed the name an insult. Allison had explained that she thought of nicknames as terms of endearment, and indeed she had come up with a huge inventory of nicknames for the occupants of St. Als, but Ellen preferred her real name. Allison obliged, but insisted that Ellen call her Seed, or at worst Allison, but never . . . ever . . . never ever call her by her real name—Yvonne. "We better get to it. Sister Claudia wants this done by tomorrow."

She shot Ellen a frustrated smile. "Books are absotively useless if they're not on the shelves. Absotively useless."

"I don't know what to tell you, Seed." Ellen slid a finger under her glasses to rub her eyes. "She wants it done."

The girls began working the list, pulling books, making boxes, labeling them, stacking them on the bookcart. Ellen filled a box halfway and bumped into a table, sending the whole thing crashing to the floor, spines ripping, covers skidding against the tile.

Allison helped Ellen to her feet. "Are you okay?"

Ellen nodded.

Allison stooped and picked up Ellen's glasses. "How do they look?" she said, grinning as she put the specs on. "Jesus with cataracts, how do you see anything through these things? They're like telescopes."

Ellen blushed. She gently removed the glasses from Allison's head. "I can't."

"You can't? What do you mean you can't? You mean you can't see?"

Ellen turned a shade dimmer than Allison's hair. "Not hardly," she said, embarrassed.

"When's the last time you had your eyes checked?"

"Before I came here. When my foster parents gave up on me. Almost three years ago."

"Oh, sweetheart." She hugged Ellen. "No wonder you're always banging into things."

Ellen squeezed back, her eyes closed, as if the hug was the first act of compassion she'd experienced in three years. She held Allison tightly, not wanting the moment to vanish.

Allison released Ellen. "Have you spoken to the penguins about it?"

"Yes." She gazed at the floor, blushing as if to say she wasn't good enough, worthy of having glasses that worked. "But Clod said there wasn't any money."

Allison, ever the determined spark of light, was ignited with an idea. It kindled and burned and reached out and connected with other thoughts until she had the basis for a plan. This time a positive plan designed to help someone. This is what she does best. One could almost see her red hair brightening a shade.

"Ellen," she said firmly. "We shall absotively get you a new pair of glasses within the month. Now you go put some ice on that bump, and I'll finish the books."

Her concept was exquisite in its simplicity, basic in its execution, and a complete embarrassment to the Church. On Saturday, March 20, before the sisters awoke, she and Ellen pushed a cart loaded with the castaway books to the bus stop. Allison had stashed the books in the east wing without Clod's knowledge. It took three arduous trips to fetch all the boxes. At 5:52 a.m. a sign was placed on the cart, announcing the Readers for Peepers Sale—All Books $1.

By 9:07, after a thorough search of the orphanage for Allison and Ellen, who hadn't been seen at breakfast (Mary wasn't telling—Allison could always count on her for that) the Catholic Gestapo, having got wind that some strange goings-on were occurring at the bus stop, marched down the driveway in lockstep to breakup the horrid display of charity. The bus stop was crowded at the time with folks waiting for the next downtown bus, due any minute.

By the time Mother Superior with her skunk-striped hairdo and her craggy face arrived on the scene, the girls had already sold thirty-one books and had pocketed one-hundred-twelve dollars, the excess cash coming from generous persons who willingly gave a five or a ten spot upon hearing the worthy nature of the Readers for Peepers fund drive. After all, who could resist "sweet little Ellen here, who does so love books, but she can't see," as Allison so ably described her.

Mother Superior was clearly not amused. She trudged to the perimeter of the bus shelter and stopped short, like a landslide barely missing the town below. She assessed the situation, saw the pathetic eyes of the benevolent public and huffed loudly for several minutes.

"Yvonne," she finally bullfrogged. "What are you doing?" A group of startled browsers picking through the pile of used books looked crossly at Mother Superior.

"Raising money to buy Ellen some glasses, Mother Superior, ma'am," she replied with a charm that made Shirley Temple seem like a serial killer.

"This is church property . . . you . . . uh." She was cut short by the disapproving glares of the book-sale patrons. Heathens. Clod and Barney were speechless as well. Clod couldn't even muster the brain cells to emulate Mother P's indignant huffs. Sister Dena, who suspected Allison was up to something good, stayed inside the orphanage, smiling as she served flapjacks to the other kids. She knew that Allison—no matter what it was the girl was doing—would hold her own against the formidable Mother Superior. History had proven that.

Yes, Mother Superior could only glare, huff and puff, stutter a few times, look incredulous, and finally stalk back off to the main building, where she would insist in no uncertain terms that, "Allison be given an additional three months labor in the library!"

Upon hearing the news from Sister Dena, Allison grinned. "So be it."

A week later, on March 27, just after she and Ellen returned from an unauthorized trip to Vision World, where Ellen was tested for a new prescription and given the option of contact lenses (they had raised enough money), Allison found what she considered to be the most fortuitous find in the treasure that was her library. The newly-discovered item was an unassuming book by Kahlil Gibran, called *The Prophet*. She spent the entire rest of the day reading the inspirational masterpiece, struck by its majestic phrases. At times she clutched the book to her speckled breasts, which reached out gladly in their newfound shape to caress Gibran. Mary, who preferred TV and *People* magazine, listened intently as Allison read certain touching passages, but by 9:30 she drifted off into a sound sleep while Allison read on.

Allison was so beguiled by the book that she nearly forgot her midnight run to the alley, with food for Stephen and his friends. She had kept her promise dutifully and delivered as much food and necessities as possible every Saturday evening. Nothing would stop her—not threats, not punishment, not the loss of a great friend—nothing. It was her mission, her calling.

The gathering around the closed shelter, those sleeping in the alley and behind the building, had grown rather large. Truth be told, the lock on the back door had been picked and many of the sixty-or-so homeless used the facility without the knowledge of the authorities. They stole around in the dark using candles and matches as their lighting, hanging gray wool blankets over the windows at night for fear of the cops or the IRS or Ronald Reagan with an Uzi busting in to clear them out. By early morning, before the sun could pop its head over the horizon like some radiant Peeping Tom, the blankets came down, the doors were closed, and the vagrants dispersed.

Were Cincinnatus aware of this breaking and entering while he ministered to the poor in the remote villages of El Salvador, he would have most assuredly approved. Hard as it was to tear herself away from the comfort of her new book, Allison fulfilled her promise and joined the less fortunate at the closed Mission de Cincinnatus. *The Prophet* would wait for her.

Allison's birthday, Fools' Day, as she liked to call it, left her surprised and pleased. Who would have guessed the news that Sister Dena was to deliver? Mary was in the rec room watching *Joanie Loves Chachi*, the cake and the ice cream scene was done immediately after class. Allison had made it clear that she didn't want a gift, but not in the way some people do when they say the opposite of what they mean. She had informed the sisters that any money to be spent on her should go to help the homeless in a donation to the United Way. The nuns didn't listen, and for once she was glad they didn't.

A light tap sounded on her door. Sister D peaked her head inside. "Allison? Can I speak to you a moment?"

"Sure, Sister D, c'mon in."

"Hello, Seraph." She greeted Allison's miracle orchid. Sister's eyes twinkled with excitement. She had big news and was bursting to tell it. She teased Allison for a few moments, telling the girl she had a surprise, then acting as if she didn't want to tell.

Allison was on the edge of the bed, restless. Finally, Sister Dena couldn't wait any longer. "The St. Alexandria Orphanage," she said, smiling, "in conjunction with the Diocese of Cincinnati, has agreed to sponsor an amateur tennis tournament to benefit the homeless."

"Jesus eating cotton candy with the Ayatollah, that's great!" She hugged Sister Dena. The two rocked back and forth, overjoyed at the news. "Thank you, Sister. Thank you so much."

"Think of it as a birthday present," Sister Dena laughed as she plunged a hand deep into her pocket, searching for the perfect sunflower specimen with which to celebrate. "There's just one thing, Seed."

"Oh?" There's always a catch.

"We need you to stop planning your own charities."

"What do you mean?" Allison failed at hiding her guilty secret.

Sister Dena scooted closer and whispered, as if to say she didn't agree with the decree, "You need to stay home on Saturday nights. No more visits to the shelter."

Allison feigned indignance. But she knew that Dena was hip to her activities, and it was futile to cover it up. Who told? she wondered. Joyce again? Paying me back for spurning her advances? Allison realized it didn't matter, the jig was up. At least the Church was offering a reasonable alternative. Emboldened by her friendship with Sister D, she said, "I have an absotively splendid idea. Can the money go to reopen the mission?"

Sister D smiled. "Does your heart ever stop giving?" The good nun stood, split the seed in her mouth with the precision of a French guillotine, and said, "I'll present your request, angel. With my recommendation that we do so."

Allison squealed, delighted, and kicked her feet happily as if she were a child. "Thank you, thank you, thank you." She beamed. This indeed was a grand time to shine.

"Oh, Allison," Sister D nodded toward *The Prophet*, "it would be best to keep that hidden."

Palm Sunday ushered in Allison's favorite time of the year: Easter. Or was it spring that set her irrepressible spirit aloft? Or both? Yes, both, she decided. One for its glorious religious overtures—rituals and choirs and cathedrals and pretty dresses (if just for a day) and the death and rebirth of her idol, Jesus Christ. The other for its sweet air, sunshine, flowers and rebirth. With the majesty of *The Prophet* to inspire her, she began reading the Bible studiously every evening for a half hour. While others, like Mary, fiddled their time with the *Dukes of Hazzard*, *Benson* and *Square Pegs*, Allison lost herself in Matthew, Luke, Mark and John.

She also used this time to write in her journal, describing her dreams of having a family, someone to love, living a normal life in a normal world, and, of course, detailing exactly how she planned to become the Mother Theresa of Cincinnati. When she wasn't busy with spiritual endeavors or journaling, Allison often gazed longingly at Danny's sketch, which she had folded in half and used as a book mark in her Bible, thinking that somehow his drawing, close to God's handiwork, might rub off and keep him from "that absotively ridiculous forgery career of his." In weak moments of self-pity, she sometimes celebrated the loneliness of a love lost.

But those times were rare; and spring was here. It was beginning to get warmer, and Allison had grand plans for a garden. She had designs of expanding her orchard, given all the seeds that had been bestowed upon her. On especially sunny days, Allison climbed into the bell tower and surveyed her domain. She spied the tennis court that she so loved, and the bus stop with its travelers who so generously helped Ellen restore her vision, and the garden—oh her lovely garden, all brown and covered with decayed vegetation now. But in a few short weeks, green abundance would sprout everywhere.

The memory of Danny became more distant, and her belief that someday they'd meet faded like a bleached pair of jeans. She looked at his sketches, and that brought a smile, but only occasionally did she read his letters and when she did, she cried. Then Allison would read Cincinnatus' farewell letter and cry some more. But her tears were joyous because she had had the graced fortune to have been acquainted with both Danny and Cincinnatus. She had such an odd sense of things—so mature for one so young and so alone in a forbidding, unforgiving orphanage.

Easter came and went, with Allison's spirit soaring to new heights of inspiration. With Gibran and the Bible at her side, with fresh breezes and glorious garden plans—primal desires to dig her hands into the pungent earth with its root smells and minerals and rich soil, she could sense that something magical, something special, was in the air.

The nuns had been unduly worried about a potential visitation by a holy spirit to Allison; of what divinity, they were remarkably uncertain. Their concern was based on their own lack of true faith in their Lord, their spirituality having been sacrificed on a Catholic altar many years before as part of the strict admittance to His kingdom. But now, oh dear God, now this child is having visions! Real ones! And they seem to coincide with the major holidays of Easter and Christmas. Many a St. Als' nun, rosary beads clutched in praying palms, could be found on her knees beside her bed, muttering Hail Marys and all sorts of incantations from the prayer bag, pleading with the Almighty that Allison not be contacted this holiday.

They believed their prayers were answered as she was left unattended by whatever external, ethereal entity had come to her in the past. The only incident was Mary's accidental dropping of an Easter egg she attempted to peel during mass. Allison managed to drift off shortly thereafter, momentarily forgetting where she was, as a glowing light surrounded her in her dream. It spoke to her, saying, "Your day will come when you understand My purpose."

Talking in her sleep, Allison replied, "I understand, Father."

A quick nudge from Mary jarred her awake. No one noticed. Clearly, however, cosmic correspondence was going on.

The sisters' faith in their God restored, not that they'd ever publicly question it (that is simply forbidden inside the Church, as any God-fearing parishioner knows), they breathed a collective, vindicated exhalation and put their attention to matters of a more Earthly order: bingo and a charity tennis tournament.

This first-ever event for the nuns, designed to placate an irrepressible Allison from putting herself in dangerous quarters with certain nocturnal, death-defying charity acts, came to be called the Serve the People Tennis Tournament. So named by our resident angel and creative marketing genius, Allison Leslie Pippin, in a flash of insight as she looked out from the bell tower near twilight on Easter Sunday.

Preparation for the tennis season was rigorous for Allison. Sister Dena was convinced she had a diamond in the rough and trained Allison three afternoons a week, with plans to play tournaments every weekend beginning early May. The penguins of St. Als relaxed their guard against further celestial encounters with Allison and life inside the orphanage returned to abnormal. This was extremely premature on the part of her pietistic caretakers.

"Allison, Allison, wake up." A distraught Sister Dena shook her young student.

Allison blinked herself awake, her head cloudy, eyes half-closed. "What? Is something wrong?" She could hear feet shuffling outside the door. And whispers.

"Have you had any more visions, angel?" Sister asked with great urgency.

Allison believed she could hear the nuns in the hall holding their anxious breath. Mary lay unconscious across the room. The girl could sleep through Armageddon.

"No," she shrugged. "Why? Did something happen?"

Sister Dena brushed back Allison's sleep-knotted hair. "It's nothing to concern yourself with, dear. Even the saints get a little nervous every once in awhile."

"What is it?" she asked, slowly bringing herself to consciousness. She knew it was serious; there wasn't a sunflower seed anywhere near Sister D's mouth.

"He's okay," Sister Dena gazed through the dim light at Allison's droopy eyes. "Someone tried to stab the pope at the Shrine of Fatima."

"Is he okay?" Allison sat up, alarmed.

"Yes, he's fine. The attacker was subdued before His Holiness was harmed."

"Thank goodness," Allison said.

The two embraced and Sister D left the room. Allison lay awake the remainder of the night, tousled in her sheets, concerned that she had lied. There *had* been a dream the night before—a man stabbed repeatedly at a golden cross as a woman dressed in white stood crying nearby. Allison told herself, swore on her Bible, she would not tell anyone, not Mary, not Sister D, and absotively not, under any conditions, Cadaver Smith and the Governing Order of Divinity—Division of Apparitions, Miracles & Nuisances. It was a lie just the same, and she felt bad about it. No one understood the consequences of telling the truth better than Allison.

On May 18, 1982, the Reverend Sun Myung Moon of the Unification Church was convicted of fraud. One might well wonder where the indictments of Jim Bakker, Jimmy Swaggart, Jerry Falwell, the world-conquest-minded Pat Robertson, and a long list of religious charlatans were. Robertson, the grand host of the 700 Club, is rumored to be the second largest diamond and gold importer in the world, lagging only behind the DeBeers company. We shall leave his shenanigans for another time. God works in mysterious ways, indeed.

In addition to all her other interests, Allison loved to follow the globe-trotting pope, who arrived in England to patch up a rift with the Anglican Church and was the first pope to set foot there in 450 years. Henry VIII must have committed some fairly offensive deeds to hack-off the Vatican for so long. She heard of the pope's historic meeting with the Most Reverend Runcie on AM radio as she and Sister Dena drove back in the rain from a tournament in Lexington. A pile of spent seeds lay like overturned canoes at the feet of the contented nun.

"Sunflowers are a lot like humans," Dena said as the Bluegrass State whooshed by them in mist. "You have to crack through their shell to get to the good part. The seed. That's the treasure—that little kernel of pleasure that provides nutrition and flavor and texture and joy. The unshelled ones offer no challenge. You can pop thirty, forty of them in your mouth and chew away, but there's no art to that. No skill. Besides, they're prostituted with peanut oil."

Allison listened intently. She grabbed a handful of seeds and placed one between her teeth as Dena lectured on. She liked sunflower seeds, but not as much as Sister D. She could only eat a dozen or so before her lips got too salty and felt like they were swollen.

"Half the fun of eating sunflower seeds is working on the shell. Like life."

"I absotively agree." Allison said. "I can't wait until our home-grown sunflowers are ready to harvest."

As the station wagon sprayed mist up the highway, Sister D told Allison how superior sunflower seeds were to the haughty cashew, the common peanut, the obese walnut, the red-faced pistachio, the Confederate pecan, the Portuguese-accented Brazil nut, the humongous coconut, the Yuletide-seasoned chestnut, the seductive almond, the trick-or-treat pumpkin seed, the nonblack and white hazel nut, and a host of other nuts and seeds. She listened and smiled. Then Sister Dena started in on other snacks—popcorn had its purpose (movies and Christmas garland), potato chips and pretzels and cheese doodles and crackers and pork rinds and tortilla chips and the rest were all second-rate contenders in the nun's eyes.

"You sure do like your sunflower seeds," Allison said finally, hoping to guide her coach to a new topic of conversation.

"Even the saints went a little nuts every once in awhile."

It was Memorial Day, and Allison celebrated by taking second place, which netted her a gold-painted plastic trophy and one hundred dollars. As they drove up the interstate with the *whoosh-flop-whoosh* of worn windshield wipers that should have been replaced two summers ago, she thought of the nourishment her freshly-planted garden was receiving with the abundance of water that poured from the pregnant clouds.

As the rain came down, one random thought connected to another, and she realized, with much satisfaction, that Rita and Joyce had both stopped hitting on her. Allison was glad for it. Flattered and scared at first, their advances had quickly turned into annoyance. She knew that Rita was in it for the conquest. She figured Rita was so sexually overcharged that she'd become bisexual just to find enough stimulation. Joyce, on the other hand, was a devout lesbian. Everyone knew that she spent a few evenings a week in Clod's quarters. That was the rumor, evenwise.

The downpour turned to drizzle as the upbeat sojourners journeyed home. Life was as good as it gets for an orphan girl— a second place trophy lay in the back seat, the pope was in England mending fences, and Allison had two friends who finally liked her for who she was, not the pleasure she could bring them. And of course, she rode shotgun with a dedicated "sister" who always knew the right thing to say and the right way to say it.

"Crittenden," she said, reading the highway road sign. "I like the way that sounds."

Late June found Allison steaming, lecturing anyone who would listen, including docile nuns who were used to such discrimination, about the failure of the United States Congress to ratify the Equal Rights Amendment.

Her activism did no good. No one in the orphanage—keepers and kept alike—could understand the significance of the vote. Allison took her frustration out on the weeds in the garden, which she ripped out by their roots and dashed into a Hefty bag faster than one can say, "Glass ceiling."

Allison, frazzled and fatigued from weekends of tennis and car trips, was jubilant when the Serve the People tournament finally arrived at the end of July. Sister Dena, sensing that she was wearing down, had given Allison the previous weekend off. She spent her time catching up with Mary and Ellen, visiting the bell tower where she replaced Danny's letters which she had been reading daily, and tending to her rows of vegetables in the mornings and evenings, paying special attention to Dena's organic sunflowers. She saw God's work in everything—the heads of lettuce, the warm rays of sunshine in the tower, the grace of her tennis stroke, the beauty of Gibran's words, and the Bible, which she continued to read habitually every night.

It is at this point, dear readers, that I, Robert Thomas Stone, must make one more confession, or at least illuminate a fact I referred to earlier in this epic. I *have* met Allison Leslie Pippin. It wasn't much of an occurrence, although I'm sure I was much more impressed by her than she with me.

Patrick Gilday, for reasons that are apparent now, but were extremely vague then, suggested rather insistently that I help support the Serve the People tournament. In those days, I had more of an interest in the game. After some pressure from Gilday, two phone calls and a letter, I agreed to donate five thousand dollars to the cause. It struck me odd at the time that Gilday's own company did not donate, nor was Patrick present at the planning sessions and dinner which preceded the event on July 24.

My initial meeting with Ms. Pippin was brief and unceremonious. Quick introductions, a brief handshake, and that's it. It was during the tournament, which I recall vividly, that she and I were thrown together for a somewhat longer, but still short period of time.

The tournament began on schedule at Lunken Air Field, a facility long before relegated to consumer flights and corporate big wigs flying in and out of town on private jets. The grounds held an eighteen-hole golf course and an adequate tennis infrastructure. Allison breezed through her first round in the tournament with a 6-2, 6-3 victory over Andrea Schmidt from Deer Park. Sister Dena gnawed through two packs of seeds. The nuns were simply giddy with the victory. A gambling pool had been formed, and the rumor was that Mother Superior had fifty bucks on Allison to make it to the quarterfinals. It's a small stretch from bingo to the bookmaker.

Kathy Jensen was her next opponent, whom Allison easily dispatched, 6-4, 6-4. She moved on to a pretty girl named Connie Armstrong, who was more talented than her previous opponents, but she escaped that challenge 7-5, 3-6, 6-4.

Allison was determined, driven. One could see her thinking as she served and volleyed, backhanded and sliced, rushed the net and laid back for an overhand topspin. Sister Dena crunched and munched and chewed and spewed like a maniacal squirrel famished after a winter's snooze.

When Allison took on Jasmine Flowers in her second match of the day, it looked as if her run was stalled. She lost the first set 6-1. With Sister Dena yelling, "Attack her, Seed! No mercy, honey!" (a harvest of split shells on the court), and Allison's friends doing their darndest to distract Ms. Flowers, she came back and won the next two hard-fought sets to claim victory. She was in the quarterfinals. Mother Superior could be seen strutting around the grounds as if she'd personally just beaten Billie Jean King.

"Jesus serving rockets with jet fuel, I'm in the semifinals!" Allison yelled after she beat her next opponent.

Clod, forgetting her nunly-composure, ran out onto the court. She tried vainly to hoist Allison into the air, instead shouting, "You can taste the blood, can't you, Seed!" Clod's jubilation soon turned to embarrassment as she jogged off the court doing a herky-jerky, honky-tonky celebratory dance that ended when she slipped in a swamp of sunflower expectorant and fell on her rump. X-rays showed Clod had not broken her tailbone.

All the sisters, including Mother Superior, chose to ignore the emblem that had been sewn onto the back of Allison's key-lime tennis outfit. FEED THE HOMELESS—SERVE THE PEOPLE, it said in red, capital letters that circled the perimeter of the round patch. Inside the emblem, embroidered in yellow with a sun behind it, was the name—Mission de Cincinnatus. A smaller, identical patch was sewn on her left sleeve. What the sisters and the rest of the world didn't know—though we were to find out later—was that this was the first phase of Allison's plan to ensure that the funds collected in the tournament got where they belonged—to the shelter Cincinnatus had founded and been forced to abandon. I learned, along with Rose, Parker, and Maya, as it unfolded on Channel 99, that Allison called her plan, Operation: In Your Face.

To do the sewing she had recruited Joyce, who had access to a sewing machine, collecting dust but still functional in the east wing. Rita and Ellen made the signs. Allison was especially proud of Ellen, who, having opted for the contact lenses, came out of her shell and began participating in all sorts of St. Als' events. She even volunteered with Allison to counsel the Cutters—the kids that slash their wrists. She had become good friends with many of the girls, including Mary. Allison was pleased to have been involved in Ellen's transformation to a beautiful swan, but never took any credit.

Sunday, July 31, 1982, was the day Operation: In Your Face was implemented. Allison was in the semifinals but didn't seem to be concerned about or interested in the matches. The tournament was way behind schedule, the nuns having never put on an exhibition before, so the semifinals and the finals were to be held on the same day.

Allison took center court against a taller, older, more muscular Stephanie Mensch from the suburb of Anderson. Stephanie's game was one of intimidation and rushing the net. During the introductions, she ignored Allison's outstretched hand of goodwill. The good-luck comment was snubbed as well, but Allison seemed oblivious to her behavior.

With her patches in place, the match began. Allison was no competition for the seventeen year old with a punishing serve and an unrelenting net game. The overwhelming style of her adversary didn't seem to fluster Allison, who bravely did her best to hold her own against a more seasoned player. But each time there was a service break, Allison stopped at her chair, picked up a sign, and held it high in the air as she turned slowly around in a three-sixty making sure everyone, including the disinterested media, cameramen and photographers, could see it.

SERVE THE PEOPLE
SUPPORT THE MISSION de CINCINNATUS

Whenever she did this, Rita, Mary, Joyce, and Ellen, all positioned in separate areas of the stands, held up similar signs. A protest was taking place. A reminder that tennis is a game; hunger is survival. Allison, losing badly to the Amazon from Anderson, didn't know that her girlfriends had altered the plans slightly by alternately holding up Al's Angels signs. She giggled as she made her way back to center court, pleased at her friends' encouragement.

Stephanie Mensch possessed a game-face glare that made John McEnroe look like Richard Simmons. There was destruction in her racket, hatred on her lips. Her opponents were to be annihilated by whatever means possible—physical, emotional, psychological. Stephanie and her overbearing father had plans for the Women's Tennis Association tour—the big time. The clock was ticking. If Mensch didn't get on the tour by twenty, she'd be finished. That is the state of professional sports in this country.

Sister Dena was unusually subdued, although a heap of shells accumulated around her newly acquired Adidas. Maybe Clod's "you can taste the blood" comment made Sister D realize the whole thing had gone too far. Perhaps—and this is the perhaps that is closest to being the reason—Sister Dena was mellowed out of compassion. She knew Allison couldn't win, but she knew this was more than tennis to her. The patches and the signs proved that. This was about righting a wrong. This was about helping the homeless who became unwitting victims in a power struggle between the Church, a young girl, and a grand samaritan nicknamed Cincinnatus by his loyal and appreciative indigents.

Allison was well into the second set, downed in the first set 6-2, and losing this one 3-1. She was drenched in sweat from the humid July afternoon. The heat on the court was stifling. She imagined she could have sizzled a BLT on the asphalt. This is where I come back in. Not only did I donate the five grand Gilday had pressured me about, but I was also a line judge for the match that day.

Stephanie Mensch served her a lightning bolt across the net. Allison lunged for it with a mighty grunt, resolved not to go down without some dignity. She retrieved the ball, surprising Stephanie. A long rally ensued, by far the best point of the match. Allison came up from baseline and lobbed a high arch over Stephanie's head. The seventeen-year-old professional wannabe had rushed the net and was seriously out of position. She hustled to run it down, somehow catching up with it. *Whack!* The ball came floating back to Allison, who watched it, as we all did, as if in slow motion. Her racket, poised for an easy smash was drawn back. The ball slowly fell to the court, Allison ready to hammer it. Down it came. The pretty red-headed girl didn't swing.

"Out!" I called, and it was. By a good six inches.

"What!" screamed Stephanie. "That was in!" Then she went ballistic. So did her father. A strenuous argument followed. Allison took a seat and wiped the sweat from her face as the disagreement raged. All the officials gathered. Stephanie's father, an egomaniac in need of Valium, threatened to sue the tournament. I couldn't believe it, but I was sure that I made the right call. Allison, unfettered by the distraction of the imbecilic outburst, held up her signs while she talked calmly to Sister Dena, who in turn shucked a good many hulls during the layoff.

Play resumed twenty minutes later, when Mr. Mensch realized his tantrum wasn't going to work. At the next service break, Allison held up her sign again. Some guy, feeling empowered from too many Catholic tubs of beer, shouted to her, "Play tennis, Red. We're here to see some tennis. Serve it up!"

And serve it up she did. After Rita, who had previously witnessed the torrid power of Allison's displeasure over being called Red, positioned herself two rows behind the heckler and pointed madly at him in a manner all too conspicuous, Allison tossed a ball into the air to serve. *Thwap!* The ball hissed off her racket with a force that nailed the belligerent spectator in the forehead before he could set down his beer.

"Out!" the referee called.

"Sorry." Allison curtsied, but we all knew it was intentional, except maybe the guy whom she nailed, who, at the time, was having a difficult time remembering his name.

Allison didn't make a brilliant comeback; Stephanie polished her off in short order. At the press conference later, with a handful of reporters looking on, Allison served one final ace to make certain that the money reopened the mission. A disgruntled Mother Superior, who didn't like this sign business, and a host of her groupies stood in a row inside the press area, which was in reality a converted airplane hangar, a humid one at that. With perspiring reporters dying to know what she was thinking when she beaned the drunken fan, Allison replied, "I was wondering how many homeless will sleep on the streets of Cincinnati tonight." To the question, *How did it feel to be taken out of the tournament by such a superior foe?* she replied, "Absotively wonderful compared to the folks who go hungry every day." To the question, *What did she hope to gain by holding up the signs during service breaks?* she smiled and said, "To get you to ask me so I could plead with all Cincinnatians to do whatever it takes to reopen the Mission de Cincinnatus." And to the question, *Did she think there'd be another tournament next year?* she flashed a coy smile. "I'm sure the Catholic Church will need ongoing money for the mission. Cincinnati should be so proud of the Church's caring generosity."

And with those well-planned, mature answers to the reporters' questions, Allison knew that she had forced Mother Superior and the Diocese of Cincinnati to fund the mission. She had planted the seed in the minds of the good citizens of the town, and now the idea would grow. Rapidly.

To say that Mother Peculiar was upset with her post-tournament press conference is like saying Adolf Hitler had a distaste for Judaism. She was livid. Mother, feeling the sting of a double-cross, knew that Allison had planned the whole affair, had outfoxed her, made her look weak to her staff, which, of course, was merely a delightful by-product of Allison's intent. A fringe benefit one might say. Sweet revenge for closing the mission and falsely accusing Cincinnatus in the first place. But Allison had maneuvered well, and there was no getting around the Mission de Cincinnatus going back into service. The calls had begun flooding into the Diocesan office before the six o'clock news had even finished. The Catholic faithful wanted to know how they could help. Donations of cash and time bombarded the Church. People drove to the mission that same Sunday night and were shocked and disappointed to find the homeless huddled in the alleys or sneaking around inside by candlelight. One well-connected Catholic used his influence to stop the continual police harassment of the indigents. All tolled, between the take at the gate, concession sales (beer flowed mightily in the hot sun), and ancillary donations, Serve the People raised $28,300. Allison had launched a juggernaut that could not be swept aside, even after the press turned their short attention span to something else.

Mother responded to Allison's forceful hand in two ways, neither of which bothered the girl in the slightest. The first punishment for her insubordination, which Ellen loved, was a year's assignment in the library. "I'll show that little red-headed wench how to play in the NFL," Mother Superior sneered as she squeezed her prized pigskin.

And the second response was to ignore her. To which Allison replied with a laugh, "Cheesecake, try and do the right thing around here and you get chastised." But she didn't care. She was on the road four days a week with Sister D, playing in this tournament and that. Fort Wayne, Indianapolis, Wheeling, Columbus, Gary, Knoxville, wherever tennis was played on the Midwest junior circuit, Allison, racket at the ready, and Sister Dena, seeds, whistle, and coach's cap properly positioned, were there.

To her followers at St. Als (the group now known as Al's Angels), Allison's stature rose considerably. Everyone, even Joyce, who had only two years earlier disliked her, loved the effervescent girl with the spunky attitude. We all need our heroes and heroines.

Gardening and tennis filled the next few months. Al's Angels tended the vegetable patch while Allison was traveling, even taking care to feed Hippy, the rabbit that stole into the garden throughout the season. The sunflowers had peaked and harvested nicely. They had been planted at intervals to supply Sister D with a continual fix. The favorite part for Allison was the roasting of the seeds. Out of the oven, hot and fresh, they were a sinful treat.

It all went by like a Ferrari speeding past a highway road sign. It was probably best that she was away Thursdays through Sundays—less exposure to Mother and her obedient penguins. The time away afforded her and Sister Dena many lengthy conversations. Time on boring stretches of road were filled with stories of the past or dreams of the future. Long discussions of religion and politics and philosophy and world events peppered their journeys as fields of corn or wheat painted the backdrop. Shell after shell hit the floorboard. Allison loved this time, as did Sister Dena. They became like true sisters, although Allison fantasized that Sister D was actually her mother. The verbal exchanges, the experiences they shared, were the happiest either could remember. With each conversation, Sister D found herself becoming more and more angered by human rights abuses, which Allison told her were occurring in El Salvador and Nicaragua. She winced in horror when Allison read news stories aloud about mass executions in Iran or genocide in the mountains of Guatemala.

The best times for Allison, though, the dialogue she loved the most, was when Sister Dena would speak of the way the world really worked, the psychology of it all. Sister D had a view of life that was both pragmatic and philosophical. She talked of the public church versus the private church hidden behind the rituals. She revealed, under blood oath at Allison's insistence, many of the secret relationships between people. Clod had been a missionary assistant doing God's work in the steamy climate of Latin America. She had become a nun at the insistence of a favorite, and rich, uncle whose will bequeathed several hundred thousand dollars to her parents on the condition that Claudia join the nunnery for at least five years. She did, under duress, but thirty years later she had still not summoned the strength to leave. Allison began to understand the attitude of bitterness she saw in some of the clergy.

The two were in good spirits on a trip back from Charleston, West Virginia, where Allison won her first tournament and $250. She was distressed about her victory because of the sexual discrimination of tournament officials who gave the men's winner 750 smackers. No matter how they explained it, she didn't think it fair. Sister Dena suggested that she be grateful to God that she won the two-fifty. Allison was not appeased. "Injustice is injustice," she huffed.

As the car battled its way through the noxious, methane mountains of Nitro, West Virginia, Sister Dena tried to reconcile her to Mother Peculiar.

"To be accurate," Allison said as she spun the radio knob trying to find anything besides banjo music and Appalachian yodeling, "I don't dislike Mother Superior. It's she who seems to have a hang-up about me. She never smiles."

"Even the saints can be a little surly sometimes, Seed," Dena said. "Mother has had a difficult life."

"Cheesecake, she doesn't have to take it out on me." The radio crackled between country twangers. Allison didn't pause more than three notes of a song before she moved on down the dial.

Sister Dena glanced at her young charge. "It is always best not to judge others, Seed. You never know what they've been through."

"She must have been through a lot, then. A whole lot!"

"She has," Sister Dena said softly to herself. Allison switched off the radio, conceding she had lost her bid to find something decent to listen to, decent being rock 'n' roll. "Mother is holding on to some resentment that many would find hard to let go."

"Like what?" Allison perked up and grabbed a handful of Dena's favorite snack.

Sister Dena was reluctant to tell the story, more troubled by it than worried that Allison might repeat it to the other girls. She licked her lips of the salt.

"Mother Superior was engaged once. She was so in love. The day of the wedding came. She was dressed in white, like every woman's dream, with two hundred people waiting in the church. Her bridesmaids were around her when a knock came on the dressing room door. It was the best man."

"What did he want?" Allison asked quietly.

"Trembling, he gave Mother a note." Sister Dena gripped the wheel tighter. "A note from the groom saying he couldn't go through with the marriage."

"Jesus shooting spitballs at the choir, that's absotively terrible. What happened?"

"Mother was crushed. The groom had slipped out of town the previous night. He had signed up for military service the day before. Infantry, I think. Mother was embarrassed to tears, completely humiliated in front of the entire town."

"What did she do?" Allison's voice broke, as her heart squeezed tight in her chest with sympathy for her nemesis.

"She stayed in her room for a week, refusing to take food, refusing to speak. Crying almost nonstop," Sister D explained. "When she did finally emerge, she did so with a hardness, an inability to forgive that formed a protective shell around her. She turned her fiancé's rejection into a hatred for men. Then she transformed that hatred into a devotion to God, a rationalization, perhaps, that she wasn't meant to marry. She joined a convent eight days later."

"Cheesecake." She was too stunned to say anything more. Her mind whirled with sympathy, guilt, anger at herself for not seeing Mother's torment. Finally, as the car drove on in silence through the outskirts of Lexington, Allison resolved to be more tolerant of Mother Superior. "I'll be on my absotively best behavior with Mother from this day forward."

And she meant it. Sister Dena was right—one doesn't know what someone else has been through. One doesn't know the events of the past that shape one's personality. She made a mental note, with an exclamation mark, to be more considerate of others' emotional baggage. But even with her sincerest effort and her pure heart, she knew that getting along with Mother Superior was going to be a challenge.

Tennis. Tennis. More tennis. It was now early November 1982. A time when leaves began to crunch underfoot and the crisp smell of winter was only a snowflake away. Allison's game had improved dramatically, her backhand, serves, her net game. She was convinced that if there was a rematch with Stephanie Mensch at next year's Serve the People, she'd hold her own and possibly beat her. At Sister Dena's suggestion, the Church hired a professional coach to hone Allison's skills. Dena knew she could take her only so far, and she didn't want her hopes for Allison to falter due to her ego. So Thomas Spivey, a coach who apparently had much success a few years back at a tennis school in Sarasota, Florida, was hired. The relationship was brief, however, as Sister Dena caught the aforementioned coach standing tiptoe on a shipping crate eyeballing Rita and Allison undressing in the women's locker room. It had only been two weeks when the Peeping Tom was discovered and bounced from Allison's life. The nuns were aghast at Mr. Spivey's actions. Rita thought the situation humorous and flattering, the ex-coach pathetic. But what could she say? She was secretly dating a gas station attendant down the street from St. Als. The man was six years older than she (and ten years less mature to hear Rita tell it).

Allison didn't speak of the Spivey situation, doing her best to be nonjudgmental about him. After all, she thought, who knows the causes of a man's vices. Looking at the nuns and Rita, she knew none of them had a right, herself included, to cast a stone at Mr. Spivey.

"Hi, Sister Claudia, where's Ellen?" Allison called happily as she reported for duty in the library. She glanced at the desk calendar, which professed with a big bold 9 that it was the ninth day of November. She actually liked working in the library more than playing tennis but wouldn't consider hurting Sister Dena's feelings on the matter. She plopped down her book bag stuffed with homework assignments, various papers, and *The Prophet*.

"Oh . . . didn't anybody tell you?" Claudia said, without looking up from her work on the desk, half-covered by her sagging breasts, which lay like water balloons on a picnic table. "Worm was placed in a home yesterday."

Allison stutter-stepped back from the desk. What? Placed in a home? She didn't know what to think. She felt as if she'd fallen from a tree and landed smack on her back, the wind knocked out of her. She gripped the desk for support. She wanted to be happy for Ellen. She loved her, Ellen was a dear friend. She wanted to see her again. How could she be gone? Just like that?

Her fingers pressed hard into the desk. Allison took a deep breath to steady herself. She needed fresh air. It was either the bell tower or the fire escape. She wanted to cry. Instead she said meekly, "I didn't even get to say goodbye."

Allison's game suffered after the loss of Ellen. Sister Dena tried to console her, but Allison's emotions were confused, conflicting. She wanted to be happy for Ellen, and she *was,* in a way. But (and she had experienced this sensation many times) Allison wondered what it was about herself that people, parents, didn't find attractive. Many girls and boys had come and gone since she'd arrived in 1973. There had been Linda and Carly and Jimmy and Markus and Nicole and Peggy and so many others. It wasn't fair. Why doesn't anybody want me? What's wrong with me?

This negativity was foreign to her, she being so "absotively" positive all the time. She tried to rationalize that it was best for Ellen, which it was; what girl didn't want a real home? She told herself she still had Mary and Rita and Joyce and a dozen other friends including Sister D, but it didn't help. She decided not to play tennis for a couple weeks. Sister Dena didn't protest.

Thanksgiving was a bittersweet affair. Remarkably, St. Als had announced that it was donating twelve bags of Thanksgiving food to the Mission de Cincinnatus; anyone who wanted to volunteer to prepare and serve the food was allowed. Al's Angels, sans Ellen, leapt at the opportunity, along with Sisters Dena and Bernadette. Allison's spirits perked up a bit. It was exciting to be at the shelter again, this time legitimately, preparing food alongside her friends, helping others. She felt good. All the while she hoped the new mission director (no Cincinnatus, he) wouldn't mention the check Allison had delivered two weeks earlier, from part of her tennis winnings. Much to her relief, he didn't bring it up. He did manage to slip a thank-you note into her coat pocket as it hung in the cloak room.

Allison liked the new director, but he wasn't Cincinnatus. She still missed Ellen and wanted so much for her to see their good work. The mission was alive with people feasting on real turkey dinners with mashed potatoes and gravy, Rita's savory stuffing, green beans, sweet potato casserole, and home baked pumpkin pie piled high with whipped cream. Some of the homeless, destitute and broken, smiled for the first time in weeks. It was a very sweet part of the day.

The bitter portion came later that night in the east wing as Al's Angels decided to hold an illegal slumber party. Inside St. Als, like most institutions, the lunatics run the asylum. In the specific case of St. Als, this was certainly true as the orphans had their hands in everything. The 88s theft ring could swipe any item at will. Sleeping bags, blankets, and pillows along with snacks galore and a TV, borrowed from who knows where, accompanied the slumber party. Now, a slumber party, any girl knows, is a very special event full of giggles and stories and dirty talk of boys and intimate confessions of secret wants. So a slumber party in itself is a sweet thing.

The bitter part for Allison came when Rita, her nipples pushing proudly through her loose T-shirt, (a sight which Mary's virgin eyes kept gravitating to) announced she was in love with Ronnie, the grease monkey from Sunoco.

"He even sprayed his affections for me on the Reading Road underpass," Rita boasted. "In red!"

Apparently "I LUV U RITA" has the opposite effect on a teenage girl as a purple Jesus smoking Lucky Strikes does on middle-aged Christians. One evokes love, the other hatred.

She and Ronnie were moving in together. In January, Rita would be eighteen, and she would be leaving St. Als.

"Jesus giving a rocket launcher to the Mujahadeen, what is the pope thinking?" Allison rustled the December first edition of *The Enquirer* so loudly it momentarily blocked out the howling wind banging against the library shutters.

The library was quiet. Only three kids strolled the aisles looking for something juicy to read. Sister Claudia sat up from her hunched position over the tests she was grading. Her boobs hovered over the papers like a pair of zeppelins. She said nothing, but Allison could tell she was curious.

"You were in Latin America, weren't you Clo . . . Sister Claudia?" Allison folded the paper in half and set it down. She rubbed her smudged fingers together, gritty with newsprint.

"Yes I was," she said, flattered at Allison's attention.

"So what do you think about the pope barring all Catholic visits to Nicaragua unless the priests renounce their ties to the Sandanistas? Does that seem right to you?"

Claudia blushed, cleared her throat, and steered her dirigibles around the room,

503

gauging whether any of the three kids were close enough to hear. "The pope is infallible."

Allison viewed the remark as verbal sleight of hand, a theological slip of the tongue, and chose to ignore the bait. "That may be what the Vatican wants us to believe, but why does it want to get wrapped up in Latin American politics? Why is he supporting the bad guys?"

The wind pushed mercilessly against the thick panes of glass, small wisps of air muscled through in gasps and whistled where the caulking was worn or missing. Gravity worked hard at keeping Clod's blimps near the Earth as she moved a few papers around nervously. "Ours is not to question, Seed," she said, lowering her voice. "But one might think His Eminence is cavorting with Reagan on this one."

Allison sighed. "You must have seen absotively so much when you were down there."

Claudia's eyes drifted, as if back in the Latin latitudes. She sighed, too. "Yes, child, I saw things I could never speak of."

"Like what?"

"Cruelty, poverty, slavery, murder, injustice—things that make one ashamed of being an American. Let us leave it at that."

Christmas came and went with the usual fire drill of parties, charities, pageants, field trips, and Catholic festivities featuring various combinations of St. Als residents trotted out in bunches or en masse to motivate the good people of the city to cough up a few extra bucks at this "joyous time of year" to help the Church minister to the less fortunate. The Cutters were usually busier this time of year, too, slicing their veins for Jesus or from sheer depression over their abandonment. Belief in God, as hard as the nuns tried, was not high on the probability list for most orphans. The mere fact that these discarded kids of potential light had been thrown into the darkness of St. Als was evidence enough that God was a fraud. And even if He wasn't, many of the children reasoned, He wasn't someone to be admired.

The annual Queen Anne's lace ornament handicrafts were made. (Parker tells me that Queen Anne's lace is a member of the royal court of carrots. The wild one.) Allison wondered if Danny still had his. This year, the decorated ornaments were being given to the elderly as gifts at the Catholic Bingorama. The stockings were hung by the chimney with care, even though everybody knew Santa wouldn't soon be there. A few of the older kids, in their resentment over being stuck in St. Als, always took it upon themselves to ruin the fantasy for the younger ones. In St. Als, childhoods weren't simply stolen (although that would certainly be bad enough), they were blasted to bits by authority. Crushed by circumstance. Pummeled by reality.

Despite the activities, the counseling, and extra staff to watch for psychological signs of withdrawal and depression, there was the inevitable ambulance run to the hospital of a Cutter or two who had progressed in his or her attempt to end his or her pain. And in this way, Christmas, which was heralded as "that most joyous of seasons," one which the sisters tried their best to make special, almost always turned out to be a stressed out, chaotic mess.

Of course Allison, who had chosen a path early in life as directed by her Council of Ancient's DNA, had found the best in St. Als and made every attempt to find magic in most moments. She had a grand idea—"absotively splendid idea," she told Sister Dena—to begin a tradition of sharing the book, *Silent Seraph,* with all the young orphans. A new and inspired legacy had begun, as Allison, her purple orchid at her side, read the tale fireside to eager faces.

Alas, no visions came. A major blessing to Allison, and a great burden removed for the nuns. For if there were no visions, then they certainly could continue to believe in God as they were taught, without having to question the Church's view of the world. Yes, her lack of celestial visitation was a godsend in a most paradoxical sense.

The business of Christmas behind her, and New Year's gone as well, it became time for Rita to depart. The goodbyes were said. Rita made one last attempt at seducing Allison before she slipped out the door. A strong kiss planted on Allison's full lips, a tongue working its way inside. A firm arm around her waist, pulling her body into Rita's. Breasts touched through clothing. Allison's knees wavered, her temperature rose. In the moisture and the passion, she forgot herself and emitted an involuntary, and oh-yes-yes-yes, oh so lovely sigh. She thought she could lose herself. She stepped gently back from Rita's heat. Rita shrugged and smiled, produced that teasing wink of hers, complete with a sure-to-be-troublesome twinkle.

"Another angel has flown away," Allison said to her empty room. Mary was downstairs watching *The Fall Guy.*

The orphanage was changing. The atmosphere was different. Kids were moving on. Kids were moving in. She had no numbers to validate her suspicions, but she could tell that more were coming into St. Als than leaving. President Reagan's trickle down theory was working.

"Jesus buying a stealth bomber with bread money," Allison exclaimed in history class, to the shock of the substitute teacher. Ms. Mullins, while a capable and fine individual, had reverted to that tried-and-true baby-sitting technique used by most subs—impromptu speeches.

Allison was the first to volunteer. "Today's *Enquirer* reported that Reagan wants to spend ten percent more on defense! Can you believe it?"

None of the kids cared much. They would have preferred that Ms. Mullins do what most subs do if they don't employ the speech gambit—study hall. At least you could sleep.

"Don't you get it?" Allison enjoined the few faces that engaged her. "The president has sold out the American citizens. He cut back on social programs so he can build up the military. It's outrageous."

"Thank you, Allison," a timid and nervous Ms. Mullins said. She couldn't have students, pretty as they may be, inciting revolution in parochial school. That wouldn't do.

"Isn't anybody going to stop him?" Allison was not yet finished. "Are we all sheep being lead by a greedy, blind shepherd?"

"Baaaa," several of the girls said as laughter erupted.

Ms. Mullins scribbled a concerned note to be attached to Yvonne Pippin's permanent file.

Allison's preparations for the upcoming tennis season took a brief but shocking respite on February 21, 1983. A serious blow to the disquieting harmony of St. Als shook the core of the staff and many of the orphans. She wasn't responsible for the first event that occurred—that was Joyce's fault—but she was an unwitting accomplice to the second.

The night was dark and cold at six-thirty when Allison reported to the library. Sister Claudia sat alone, hunched over, crying. A moist, wadded handkerchief sat on the desk.

"What's wrong?" Allison plopped her book bag down.

"Nothing." The distraught nun shook her head. "I'm okay."

Allison went to Sister Claudia, feeling guilty. She always felt bad about the nicknames that she assigned to people when she saw them in sad straights. Clod was in that emotional position now. Allison put her caring arm around Clod. "It's all right," she said. "It can't be that bad."

Suddenly, Claudia blurted out, "They sent Joyce away today!" The tears flowed like wine on Fat Tuesday. Allison couldn't believe it. Joyce gone, too! Why? Before she could think to ask, Claudia spilled the story. "She was caught smoking pot," she cried. "Mother Superior sent her to a state institution for delinquent minors." Allison rubbed

Claudia's back, not knowing what else to do. "I begged Mother to let her stay, but she wouldn't listen."

Allison had experience at consoling Mary. She had become skilled at talking to Cutters of all ages. She was comfortable dealing with younger kids. But adults, well, what does one say? She assumed Clod was upset because Joyce and the elder sister were lovers. Everybody knew that. But what could she say? Don't worry, you'll find another concubine? That wouldn't fit the bill. Don't worry, God loves you. Too trite. What to do? What to say?

Allison took a deep breath and came up with her best suggestion. "Well," she said cheerily, "you could always see if they're hiring at the juvenile center."

Sister Claudia's head came straight up off the table. She uncurled her back. The blimps were airborne. Allison stepped away. Claudia scooted the chair out. She stood, dabbing her eyes with her handkerchief. She wore no makeup, that was a St. Als' no-no, so her pinkish eyes looked no worse than usual.

"Do me a favor, would you, Seed?" she said, a grateful smile smudged on her face.

"Sure!" Allison was relieved that Clod was getting over it so quickly.

"Tell Mother Superior I quit!"

Before she could say, "Don't do it" or "What are you crazy?" or "I didn't mean for you to take me seriously," before she could revert back to "Don't worry you'll find another concubine," Clod swept Allison close in a deep, compassionate hug and said, "Thank you, Allison. Thank you for helping me see the light. Dena is right. You *are* a bright star in this dreary place. God bless."

She stood slack-jawed as she watched Clod shift her Goodyear blimps into gear and drive them from the room with a confidence never seen before in the soon-to-be-retired penguin. "Tell Mother I'll send for my things."

That same day, Allison read a news report in the paper that six hundred Muslims were killed in India by students protesting the Muslim immigration from Bangladesh. It struck her that God was sending a message to the world. Signs abounded. What that message was, wasn't precisely clear as of yet. But she knew there was a meaning.

She didn't learn the details of Sister Claudia's startling departure until caught in a massive, March 5 traffic jam off Interstate 75 just south of Toledo. One might say, in retrospect, that it was providence (or the Council) that stepped in. Allison thought Clod had just snapped, went off her nut because of love. But then, Joyce had never said much about her relationship with Clod. She kept it to herself, and Joyce wasn't one to humble her exploits. Allison thought of the virtual, instantaneous demise of her Angels. It was just she and Mary now, and Mary was hard to motivate, as she saw the world through indifferent eyes.

Allison flipped on the radio and found a news station as the car rolled toward Toledo.

"And in Nicaragua today," the baritone newscaster announced, "the pope advised the half-million faithful who came to see him to leave the left-leaning People's Church. The People's Church, a grassroots effort by poor farmers and others, is a Catholic-based institution sanctioned by the Sandanista government."

Allison glanced quickly at Sister to see her reaction. Nothing. Eyes straight ahead on the road. Teeth extracting kernel from shell. The report went on. "John Paul II assailed the government as Communist and called the idea of an independent church absurd and dangerous. In other news . . ."

She switched off the radio. "Why is the pope against the Sandanistas? They overthrew a ruthless dictator."

"Probably because the U.S. is against them, too," Sister Dena replied.

"Why should the pope care what Reagan wants? He should want what's best for the people of Nicaragua."

"He should, but the world order is more complicated than that."

"I don't get it." She trained her eyes on a billboard way in the distance: COME SEE A VISION OF JESUS. A PRESENT DAY MIRACLE! NEXT EXIT—LEFT 2 MILES. The left side of the billboard had a giant golden cross made of glitter, the right had a portrait of Jesus, the words advertising the miracle were in the middle. Across the bottom it read— Sponsored by the Diocese of Toledo, Kentucky Fried Chicken, and Olympus Oil. "That's absotively bizarre," Allison exclaimed pointing to the billboard. "Look!"

Sister Dena read the sign. "Even the saints needed some good marketing every once in awhile." She shook her head and plucked another seed from the baggy in her lap. "Shoot!" She slowed the car. "Must be an accident. Darn, this is our exit, too, and we're three miles away. We'll be too late for the tournament." All players were required to register by 5 p.m. or face disqualification.

"So?" Allison's interest in tennis was primarily to please Sister Dena and to enjoy the road trips. Playing tournaments and sweating for dollars was of only minor interest to her.

Sister Dena furrowed her brow. "So you won't be able to compete. We drove all this way for nothing."

"Let's change lemons to lemonade. Maybe we could go see Jesus. It's sponsored by the Catholic Church. It must be real."

"Think for yourself, Seed," she said, removing a shell from her lips.

"Well, *I* think we should go and decide if it's real. We have to get off here anyway, so we might as well take advantage of it."

Sister Dena swiped her tongue over her sodium-laced lips, considering whether they had any choice. They were assured of being late for the first match. They were lodged in a monstrous traffic snarl with no way to go but forward. "Fine with me," she said. "This may be fun."

Allison clapped her hands. "It'll be absotively sensational," she said, delighted. They sat captive in the flow of cars streaming at five miles an hour toward the vision of Jesus. "Sister," she said, "I don't get why Clod left St. Als. I mean, it was her whole life."

"No," Dena said softly. "Joyce was her whole life."

"Cheesecake! Is the entire world driven by sex?"

Sister Dena chuckled as the car moved forward ever so slowly, so close to the car in front they couldn't see its license plate. "It appears so, but that wasn't the reason."

"Are you sure? Everybody knew they were . . . you know?" She raised her eyebrows briskly *à la* Groucho Marks.

Sister Dena laughed. The car pushed forward. "I'm afraid the rumors are just that, Seed. Rumors. Joyce and Claudia weren't lovers."

Allison was surprised. "Then why did she leave?"

"Because Joyce is Claudia's daughter."

"Jesus frolicking in the convent, you're kidding!" This was juicy. Extra special juicy. Finger licking good juicy.

But Sister Dena wasn't kidding. She explained to Allison as they continued their snail's pace trek to the holy shrine of the Jesus vision, that Clod had fallen in love with a priest while doing missionary work in El Salvador. There was that country again. Seems Clod had given herself to this charismatic priest several times over the course of their two years together. When it was discovered that she was pregnant, Clod was sent to Cincinnati to work in an orphanage, and the priest was promoted to a higher position. He made it all the way to Archbishop before he was assassinated in front of twenty thousand followers.

Allison felt bad for Clod. And for Joyce. To have a mother and not know it. To live in an orphanage with your mother right there. Oh, what hardship that would be. Allison's well of guilt gurgled up in her. She regretted having been mean at times to Sister Claudia, of spreading rumors of wanton lesbianism about Clod and Joyce.

"Such a shame," she whispered. She said nothing of the coldness she felt toward Mother Superior, who, in her desire for control, decided to make a zero-tolerance example out of Joyce for smoking pot. Mother P knowingly separated mother from daughter, she knowingly betrayed a friend and coworker by taking from her the one thing she loved. Allison tried to understand, to empathize, to be tolerant and

509

nonjudgmental about Mother's brutal decision, but, alas, she could not rationalize it, could not justify it. Mother was cruel and sadistic in her view. Clod had given her life to the Church and this is how she was rewarded.

"That is the path she chose," Sister D said as the car finally made the exit. The exit ramp was a carnival. Dozens of people lined both sides of the road, hawking merchandise—flowers, black-velvet Jesus portraits, rosary beads, Virgin Mary wine decanters, an array of ever-popular T-shirts. The scene was an impromptu Christian county fair. Large yard signs announced the Second Coming as being only two miles up on the left. Brazenly, or maybe they had inside information, one yard sign pontificated—WHEN JESUS COMES BACK HE'LL EAT AT KFC. Another—SEE GOD AT OLYMPUS OIL—FREE STEAK KNIVES WITH A FILL-UP. A wild menagerie of oddities flitted about. There were people bedecked in saffron robes, with shaved heads, dressed as monks, with hippie love beads, in Indian headdress, in tie-dyed T-shirts, in blue collars, in leather skirts. People dressed as bikers from hell, people posing as patriots, people dressed normally, people dressed as Star Trekkies, and people who came to laugh at the show.

The closer to the main attraction, the more bizarre the spectacle. Traffic cops guided the cars into a makeshift parking lot, previously a field of corn. Three dollars a carload. No crops this year. Parking pays better than government subsidies. Across from the lot, a chain-link fence surrounded a gigantic oil refinery belching white steam from a dozen vents and stacks.

Sister Dena and Allison got out of the car. Hundreds of people scurried about. The air was thick with the smell of crude. Outside the rusted gate topped with barbed wire, throngs of people—farmers, fake monks, real nuns, aging flower children, average-Joes, a collection of Jesus impostors, children from Christian academies, the devout, the infirmed, the handicapped, the unstable, the desperate, the diseased, the schizophrenic, as well as the doomsdayers, and the curious—swarmed around several tents like worker bees serving the queen.

Kentucky Fried Chicken did brisk business selling three-piece snacks and T-shirts that declared—I ATE CHICKEN WITH JESUS. The sign on their tent read, HAVE A WING AND A PRAYER.

"Jesus performing communion with a flaky buttermilk biscuit and a sixteen ounce Dr. Pepper, how obscene," Allison said, aghast. Sister Dena concurred.

Not to be outdone, Olympus Oil registered people for a free credit card and a set of Jesus glassware for only $6.99. The Diocese of Toledo brought showmanship to their sales efforts, with nuns decked out in full habits selling Bibles, holy water, and eight-by-tens of the pope. A half-dozen confessional booths, replete with offering baskets, had the faithful standing twenty deep, ready to confess their sins.

"Thank God the nuns aren't wearing chicken suits," Allison said.

Sister raised her eyebrows. "We're not inside yet."

As the two made their way through the throng to the front gate, Allison spotted a small, purple tent sitting alone in a grassy area. The lilac canvas held a simple sign that read—Psychic. Patiently, the wayward tennis fanatics waited in line to buy their Jesus tickets at one of the ten booths, but Allison's eyes kept straying to the little, purple tent, wondering what went on inside. A psychic, how absotively thrilling, she told herself.

The line moved forward peacefully as she imagined herself at a rock concert, though she'd never been to one. They paid their entrance fee—$8 a piece—no discount for orphans or nuns from Cincinnati. She watched the faces of the people, listened to their hushed conversations.

"What a strange batch of animals we are," she said to Sister D. Many folks wore I SAW GOD AT OLYMPUS shirts, which struck Allison as the ultimate irony. Jesus being seen at Olympus. A battle of the gods.

Allison and Sister Dena walked past the four-stories-high refinery equipment, hissing steam and noxious gases from a collection of vents, joints, stacks, and valves. A frothy pool of chemical broth lay at the foot of the apparatus, as if it were a pissing robot. Allison smiled courteously at the armed security guards who stood vigil behind roped-off areas, ensuring no one got out of hand and sabotaged the factory. With Jesus around, it shouldn't have been a problem. The facility reeked like a potent chemistry experiment in a windowless room.

As they moved closer—ever closer to the Lord—her pulse quickened, her throat tightened. They were to see a vision of Jesus. A voice crackled over a bullhorn, "Witness the Messiah in all His glory. Please keep moving so that others may sense His majesty."

They stepped closer, Allison's heart fluttering. They turned a corner and found a horde of several hundred staring in reverence. A loud, continuous murmur rose from the spectators. Prayers and homilies. Forgiveness and sanctuary. Occasional cries of "He is risen" or "My Lord has come" or "Praise be unto You sweet Jesus" rose from the mass. Allison followed the gaze of the mesmerized crowd to the miracle everyone had come to see. Sister D cracked open a fresh bag of sunflowers.

"What's everyone looking at? Where's Jesus?" Allison asked. Hundreds, perhaps thousands of people, stood shivering in chilly, overcast weather, staring at the great vision. She looked, then looked again. She blinked her eyes to make sure. She squinted. She nudged Sister D's elbow to be double-dang sure. Yes, that was it. The sight before her was the vision that all had come to see, that some had prostrated themselves on the ground before. There it was, standing more round than tall, squat actually, white weathered gray. There it was. A petroleum storage tank with crude smeared down its side. The fluid had marked the white, metal structure in such a way that, if one blurred the eyes and used a great deal of imagination, one could make out the image of a person's face.

"He has come for me," a man called as he threw himself to the ground in praise,

511

like a servant before a sheik in some third-world monarchy. Dozens of people knelt before the great oil tank. Allison stared blankly at the stain, unimpressed. She looked at Sister Dena, who casually munched a salty kernel of *Helianthus annus*. She couldn't believe what she was seeing. Was that it?

"It's Colonel Sanders!" Allison said loudly. "No wonder it's sponsored by Kentucky Fried Chicken." Sister D placed her finger to her lips, basted with a mischievous grin. A group of believers shot Allison a disdaining, burn-in-hell glare that could have ignited the blessed receptacle and blown the entire misguided pilgrimage to smithereens, Colonel Sanders and all.

"Seen enough, Seed?" Sister Dena spit a broken hull, which joined its unfortunate predecessors on the ground like so many petroleum-painted sea gulls, blackened and weighted from an oil spill.

"Sure is a lot different than I expected."

"Thinking for yourself, angel?"

"Absotively." Allison smiled. "What a con job. Selling a view of a grease spot by calling it Jesus."

"Just be thankful the Church didn't try to market *your* visions."

"Say Alleluia, Sister, say Alleluia."

They made their way back against the swelling tide of people come to see the Lord. A trail of sunflower seeds followed. Allison was tempted to scream, "Go back you fools! Go back!" But she thought better of it. They arrived outside the gates, her eyes again drawn to the little, purple tent and the unassuming Psychic sign. She was being called to it, she could tell.

Possibly from having been force-conscripted into the Lord's service, perhaps fed up with the hypocrisy, perchance disgusted at the oily Messiah, maybe because she was becoming slightly enlightened in the care of Allison and exposure to the outside world, but probably due to her hidden curiosity of occult matters other than those presented by the Church—Sister Dena reluctantly agreed. Allison would have to use her own money for the reading.

Indian sitar music could be heard as they approached. A closer inspection of the Psychic sign revealed the fee was $10 for ten minutes. They pulled back the flap and entered.

"Welcome." A gentle voice emanated from a round-faced woman. She looked to be in her early twenties; her hair flowed golden to her shoulders. Her blue eyes, round and luminous, invited Allison to sit. Her forehead was ringed by a purple headband made of small beads. Her hands were folded peacefully before her on a small table covered by a blue satin tablecloth under a smaller, white lace cloth. "My name is Star. Would you like a reading?"

Allison took the chair in front of the woman. "Guess you knew we were coming," she joked nervously, "being a psychic and all."

Star grinned, not a grin of condescension, or one of annoyance, but of calm knowing. "If I had a dollar for every time I heard that line," she said, unfolding her hands. "What is your name, pretty one?"

"Allison," she answered, blushing. Her hands trembled and felt cold. Star reached out, her palms up, encouraging Allison to place her palms down flat against hers. Allison looked at the turquoise dove that hung on a gold chain around Star's slender neck. She tried to imagine where this mysterious lady who advertised that she could read minds was from. San Francisco? New Orleans? Boston? She didn't know. What did it matter? She gave up the game.

Star's eyes rolled back in her head, her pupils disappeared. Startled, Allison's hands froze, involuntarily withdrawing, but Star, who must have been accustomed to this, squeezed the flesh of her palm and held her in place before gently releasing. Allison relaxed.

"You say your name is Allison." Star's voice became deeper, richer than before. Sister Dena watched the proceedings suspiciously from a chair in the corner of the tent, her eyes studying the alleged psychic for any sign of trickery. "But I see a different name."

Allison wanted to shout "Yes! How did you know?" but swallowed hard instead.

"The name begins with Y, and this is your real name, is this not so?"

"Yes." Allison turned her head toward Sister D.

"I see a scared little girl, a frightened little girl being brought into a large building. A church perhaps. No." Star's eyes twitched at the back of her sockets, as if somehow studying her brain for telepathic secrets. "It is not a church. Perhaps owned by the Church. I see—oh yes, this image is so clear. I see a little red-haired girl and snow is falling all around her. It is winter."

Allison examined the beautiful stone dove that graced the reader's neck. She was giddy with anticipation. Obviously the girl, Star, was seeing was Allison as a child. "I see a flower. A rare beauty. Yes, it is clear to me. It is an orchid. Purple. Is this not so?"

Sister Dena hastened to move her chair from the corner of the tent next to Allison. She set her elbows on the tops of her thighs and listened closely. Star continued. "This girl has a light around her. God-light. A special energy from the Universe. It is a light of purest white, an aura of divine communication. You . . ." She stopped. "You have visions. Is this not so?"

Allison turned to ask Dena if it was okay to answer. Dena nodded. "Yes . . . sometimes," Allison said. Her heart soared. This woman, this person named Star, was real. She *was* psychic. How else could she know?

"I see a boy, a special boy," Star went on. Her eyes flickered into the back of her skull as her eyelids shook violently from the unnatural exercise. "He too has a light. Ah yes," she whispered. "You knew him once, but have lost him. Do not worry, Allison, you will find him again. The gods will insist upon it."

Allison wanted to know more. Like a thirsty pilgrim in a spiritual desert she wanted to drink up all the evidence she could. To listen to this fantastic woman with the glorious eyes that saw the most fabulous truths. She wanted more.

"I see another name," Star said softly. "Your real name, not the Y name, not the name you go by, your celestial one, the one given you before birth. It comes to me. Calling. Clear and bright like a song. A harmony of such beauty no one can deny its charm."

"What is it? What's the name?" Sister Dena asked urgently. Oh, how she wanted a sunflower seed to commemorate the moment, to consummate the infinite, the unknown.

"Yes, tell me," Allison said.

"You are unaware of the gift you have, young one," Star said. She gripped Allison's hands affectionately. "Beware of those who would steal it from you. This gift comes from afar—deep in the Cosmos—sent by a great Council. Treasure this gift, child." Her eyes appeared to revolve completely around. Star's pupils rolled back into place. She blinked several times to lubricate her orbs, her long eyelashes swishing like palm-leaf fans in an Arabian tent. A smile did a hip-throw across her fortune-telling lips, and the psychic looked demurely away, exhausted or humbled, or both—it was difficult to tell. She slid her hands from Allison's and folded them again on the table, as if in prayer.

Allison studied Star's California eyes, her southwestern necklace, then her arms, the hair standing up like Vatican guards in the presence of His Holiness.

"The name I saw," Star said, "is Annis. Your celestial name is Annis the Forgiver."

Chapter 41

October 1943

Sulphur looked out the vibrating cockpit of the plane at the Sea of Marmara below. Freighters and frigates and sailing ships churned the tranquil waters. It hardly seemed possible that a war was raging. A world war. The sea glistened like a Byzantine mosaic, its blue enamel tiles shimmering in deep, mystical shades. The engine droned monotonously as Sulphur left his latest mission. To the west and north, he could see the end of Europe, to the south and east, the beginning of Asia.

Sulphur loved this city, rich in the history of art and conquest, blood and commerce. Istanbul, the city of antiquity, had made an impression on the jaded spy. Its cultural essence was to be savored like a simmering stew of mixed ethnic traditions spiced with Turks, Kurds, Arabs, and Asians. Known as Constantinople until 1923, the city had been the center of the world for fifteen hundred years, the primary spigot of trade between Europe and Asia, the crossroads of humanity, where anything could be bought or sold. The only city in the world that straddled two continents, it was a land of sultans and Ottomans, of empires and harem girls, a mysterious place of architecture and artisans, vice and temptation. Istanbul offered a good many pleasures, including warm mineral baths attended by shapely young girls with soft exposed bellies and come-hither eyes, who would wash your back and feed you grapes, pour you wine, and massage your body with rare scented oils. He didn't want to leave this Eden.

Istanbul was also the original birthplace of Christianity, though no self-righteous Holy Roman would admit it. It stood as the antithesis to the Catholic Church, snubbing its nose at Rome since the days when it was known as Constantinople, and the Eastern Orthodox Church had originally refused to buy into the greedy Roman power play of making Jesus God's son by Immaculate Conception. Rome may have captured the souls of the Western world, but Constantinople owned the East and had outshined Rome's former glory since the fourth century A.D.

Sulphur's pilot, smelling of hashish and wine, his eyes veined in red rivers of sleeplessness, chewed on a Turkish cigar as he guided the plane back to Tripoli. Buzz was his name; a gruff man with a voice like baked desert sand and a camel hair face indicating he hadn't made it to bed before coming to the airport to ferry Sulphur back to his Tripolitan contact, Jacques d'Astang.

He banged a fist on a malfunctioning gauge to free its needle. "Damn government surplus." Buzz spoke loudly over the dual engines. "What are we hauling this time?"

Sulphur thought of his cover, what was he to say? Oh yes, he was bringing back records of German import/export businesses and their trading partners for evaluation by the OSS for economic espionage. "German business records," he lied, straight-faced. He was an intelligence agent, after all. "Important to stopping the Nazis in their tracks."

Sulphur shot a casual eye backward to the cargo bay stuffed with crates of centuries-old, ivory diptychs, silks, Persian rugs, mosaics, and paintings of invaluable splendor. He had done well in collecting Colonel Bruce's laundry list: "Bring me some saints," he had said. "Lots of them. Paintings, mosaics, throw in some Virgin Marys, too, if you can find 'em. In cloisonné enamel, if Goehring hasn't already scooped them up." Sulphur had located all of it and more.

Buzz nodded. "Right. And I'm Mother Goose." The salty pilot knew the score. He'd flown Sulphur around the Mediterranean for four months now. He knew the top brass were lining their pockets. He didn't push it though; he had a little business of his own going. In the back of the cargo bay, hidden under a stack of army-issue blankets, was a crate filled with pure white powder, a substance a New York syndicate would pay handsomely for. Sulphur knew about the crate and didn't begrudge Buzz his chance to make a profit off the war like everyone else.

The president's personal spook searched the horizon for signs of his calling card. Opus Dei would know Sulphur was in Istanbul. The smoke from the church had suffocated itself two days earlier and no longer trailed its black warning to the religious people of Istanbul. He had hoped to see the burned-out hulk of the Christian structure from the air, a final good-riddance, but the flight path took them south, away from the city. He consoled himself with the fact that it was a good fire.

As the plane's wings swept right, Sulphur thought of the two weeks he had spent soaking in the vibrance of Istanbul. It had changed him. He had made many contacts; connections that would serve him well in the war and after. He made friends who would assist him in his master plan to destroy the Norwegian heavy water supply, a plan that targeted late January '44 as its consummation date.

He had enjoyed many of the hidden pleasures of Istanbul. He had visited the Golden Horn, the Phandar commercial district, the Strambul and Galata. He had been entertained royally by local OSS officers impressed with his credentials. It was whispered that he was to get anything he wanted; he had the ear of the president. In the spy business, rumors of this sort are neither confirmed nor denied, which leads to a rather liberal outpouring of generous gifts by those who seek favor. But it wasn't the people or the gifts, nor even its spirit that changed him—it was the architecture.

From the moment he stepped foot inside the Hagia Sophia, the Church of Holy Wisdom, Sulphur had found something in life more interesting than fire. The unadorned exterior of the building was an imposing, pyramidal complex, but it was the Byzantine design of the interior courtyard that astounded him. Days later he still thought of the grandeur created by Anthemius of Tralles and Isidorus of Miletus. The great architects had created the Eighth Wonder of the World, to Sulphur's mind. A vast, central dome rose 185 feet over an impressive circle of light that radiated from the cornea of windows at its foundation. Four triangles supported its rim, locked into the corners of a square formed by four huge arches. The sheer masterpiece of the Byzantine builders to deliver such an architecture to the world left him staring in every direction of the great church. Large, vaulted niches and arcades occupied prominent positions in the complex, overseen by huge disks of Islamic religious emblems. Brilliant mosaics and sheets of polished marble adorned the walls.

To Sulphur, this was genius. It was grace. It was the beauty that a true God had intended. He was so affected by the Hagia Sophia, even though it was a religious shrine, that he almost canceled his firebombing of a Catholic church north of the city center. Almost.

He had burned a good many churches in the last few months, keeping a personal promise that Opus Dei and the Vatican would pay for their evil. This trend of church burning was not lost on Buzz, nor his superiors, who figured it was the idiosyncratic price to pay for his services. Besides, he had FDR's blessing. But FDR, protector of the free world, was unaware that Sulphur had taken to torching cathedrals.

As the plane left Turkish airspace and headed out over the Mediterranean, a different fire began to burn in him, one that smoldered with positive intent. This fire appreciated the physics of things. It was constructive. True, his affinity for antiquities was also growing, and with it an understanding of the ancient artifacts and traditions that built this world. But antiquities didn't singe his synapses the way fire did. It didn't explode inside him like a Molotov cocktail. However, this new discovery—this new way of seeing life through the beauty of architecture—this was dynamite.

It would take months to fully ignite, but the spark was there, and he was already planning a more extensive trip back to the city once known as Byzantium, once called Constantinople, now known as Istanbul, the city of antiquity.

Chapter 42

October 25, 1990

There had been a warning. A strong one. Definitive. It came straight from the Council. And I, Robert Thomas Stone, chose to ignore it. Once again.

I had to come. Sometimes in life the choices are too difficult. Sometimes one can't win. I had considered all the angles as I drove to Mulciber, but I had to come. What if I were caught? Well, the paintings were mine to begin with. What would it do to my case? Seal my fate, that's what. Doom me to end my life as a resident of the federal penal system. McBain would twist the facts around to suit the desired verdict. That is what the law has come to in this country. But I couldn't stop myself. Something pulled me there. Something of immense force.

Have I lost my self-control? I wondered as I drove the company van past the broken wrought-iron gates. One—off the hinges and set to the side against a brick pillar overwhelmed by clinging vines—the other ajar, rusted in place. I finished a clump of parsley (thanks Parker), the chlorophyll swishing around in my mouth as I maneuvered carefully through the gates. Patrick had boasted of those gates, the grand entrance to his great estate, I thought as I navigated the pocks and cracks of the long driveway, like a starship captain in an asteroid belt. They were a symbol to him, an icon of his power. Now, as Mulciber lay decaying, the driveway covered more with weeds of jungle proportion than blacktop, tall grass nipping the bottom of a high wooden FOR SALE sign, Patrick's legacy was in ruins. How far Mulciber had deteriorated. The Norse god had fallen in battle. Mulciber lay dying, a relic to betrayal. I thought it a fitting end to a man as corrupt and conniving and ruthless as Patrick Gilday. What is it these New Age zealots call it? Karma.

I spare him no pity. I haven't forgiveness in my heart to absolve men of such cruelty. Perhaps that isn't Christian, but then again I am *not* Christian. Perhaps it isn't spiritual, this inability to forgive being framed for crimes I didn't commit, but I don't care. Patrick Gilday, his body food for worms, deserved every scrap of torment that befell him, every bit of it.

I hadn't chosen the best night for a clandestine mission. The half-moon shone like a yellow matchhead, its sulfurous bulb ready to ignite, exposing the night world and its hidden goings-on. It glowed like a hurricane lamp in the dark hall of a Victorian mansion, lighting a path between two secret lovers. This was a moon that would reveal one's mysteries, the ones best kept disguised. This moon showed me no favor as it illuminated all my moves. But I had no choice. Another round of cancer treatment was scheduled for Monday, and, if the Mamets *were* stashed in the Captain's Quarters, I would need all the strength I had, which was precious little, to haul them away. A secondary consideration was that it was Friday night; folks would be out at parties, dinners, and the like, so the Crittenden neighborhood would be quiet.

This was Danny's home, I thought as I parked the van behind the house. The estate was alive with his presence. Maya's words knocked upon my cranium. She had stunned us all by revealing that she knew Danny. She had met him at a commuter airport just west of Tucson after overhearing an FAA radio transmission, the local inspector saying, "Some kid from Cincinnati wants to talk about that UFO incident. Says it's his daddy's plane."

Ever since she was six and her family sighted one in the desert, Maya had been an avid UFO buff. It had impacted her forever. She read voraciously about aliens, studied them, and, when she became old enough, was determined to learn to fly. She figured that flight and astronomy and space travel and UFOs were all related. Her insatiable thirst for all things alien led to the purchase of an illegal scanner to intercept FAA and other secret government transmissions around greater Tucson. Dad had connections in this area.

She credited her yearning for the stars to her father, who was an astronomer at the Kitt Peak Observatory. He was no ordinary astronomer, if there ever was such a thing, as he was not only scientific but metaphysical. He actively encouraged his daughter's spiritual quests. He and his wife were a most unconventional couple, much at home in the mixed clime of Arizona, where Mexicans, Indians, whites, and a horde of immigrants had braved the harsh heat of the Valley of the Sun to settle the area.

My fingers tapped on the vinyl steering wheel as I thought of Maya's adventuresome spirit. Upon hearing that the son of Patrick Gilday, the man whose plane was "allegedly" abducted by aliens, would be at the airfield, Maya made sure she was there to meet him. I had never heard the UFO story before Maya's revelation. *The Journals* had not taken the story that far just yet.

My eyes scanned the estate, making certain I wasn't walking into a trap. Maya had told us of her first meeting with Danny, speaking admiringly of him and of his purpose. "He's a light-being, you know," she said. "He's wild, he has magic, that boy does, an energy that he could barely master, although he tried." Together they investigated the UFO mystery for a day, forming an instant friendship. "Destiny calling," Maya sang like a cosmetics saleswoman.

The three of us—me, Rose, and Parker—had listened in amazed silence as she told us about her relationship with Daniel Oliver Gilday. "He was always writing in his journal," she said. "Stories, songs, poems. Nabu seemed to guide his life. Sing say, just like you, R.T. He said he was going to win the Pulitzer Prize one day, and I believe him."

I wish I shared her faith in people. Maya's anecdotes of the month with Danny helped to fill serious gaps in *The Journals*. She was convinced Danny was not of this world. Of course, seeing his life play-out on my television set reinforced what she already knew. One remarkable tale involved the rainy day Maya was to solo. She had studied and trained for months to get her pilot's license. Danny knew the importance of the day and came to the airport as Maya sat in her car crying because she wouldn't be able to fly in such bad weather. She had worked so hard to get her pilot's license, and it was to be dashed by uncooperative weather.

"He looked at me with eyes so blue, eyes made of sky, and told me it wouldn't rain any longer," Maya had said. "Astarte bewitch me, as the words left his lips the sun broke through the clouds. He stood there in the parking lot, dry as a bone. Not a drop of water had touched him! Sing say, the most gorgeous rainbow I ever saw was shining behind that boy. Don't think he didn't know it either—he did! I swear he stopped the rain."

After she said this, even the liberal-minded Parker was incredulous. Maya pushed his knee playfully. "The gods know what is true. Besides, six months ago would you have believed in a writing book or a TV with a mind of its own?"

Everyone nodded agreement with her.

She spoke fondly of the times she and Danny went to the desert just below Kitt Peak. She would pack cucumber, tomato, and sprout sandwiches. They'd make sun-tea on a flat rock under the Arizona sun as she meditated in the nude.

"Danny was subdued, quiet, like a bright spirit waiting to burst out of a child who had been smacked too many times, afraid to do the wrong thing. But he was a star, all right. He'd stand in the sand below my rock, like a Chinese Tai Chi master, graceful and timeless, trying to walk on the desert floor without leaving any footprints."

Gram's influence had stuck with him, Maya said. With sadness, she said that Danny had moved in when her roommate had suddenly decided to move to L.A. Maya's father arranged a job for him working the cash register at the observatory gift shop. He was fired when a drug test showed marijuana in his system. He returned to Cincinnati after his brother Cal had called him, asking that Danny come home for an important matter of unknown nature.

"Danny was very mysterious, not secretive, mind you, but he knew things. Wondrous things, I imagined, things most people can't comprehend, but he knew them all right. So, he went back to Cincinnati in the spring of 1985. Did you know his brother committed suicide?"

The thought jarred me loose from my daydream. I looked toward the Stones. Was Cal buried there along with Patrick Gilday? Why did he take his life? Is that what he saw that night on Featherbed Bank—his own death, his suicide? I wondered. I never knew him well, met him three times, maybe four, spoke to him twice, if memory serves me. Cal seemed like a nice, if troubled, boy. One could see the distance in his eyes. There was a look in his pupils that said he didn't belong on Earth. It was all a mistake, Cal's eyes said, *get me off this rock.* I had read of his death in the paper and had attended the visitation service. Closed casket. I saw a distraught Cara and a hopped-up Danny doing their best to cope with his death.

I stared at the Stones. I wanted to go there and pay my respects, but ever-present danger and a half-million dollars worth of paintings guided my course in another direction.

Beneath the dangerous moon, I unloaded the tools for the heist—lantern, ladder, toolbox, drop cloths, matches. It took two trips to get the materials into the barn through wide-open doors. All the while, a sensation as if I was being watched crept up on me. Was it the fiery moon? The presence of Danny's past energy, a lad I've come to know so well through this ordeal? Was it *The Journals* itself looking after me? Was it the Stones calling me? Or the infamous Featherbed Bank with its Glorian Aurora? Was it the sheer history of the place? Mulciber—once home to the man who almost ruined me. Crittenden—site of McJic's ignominious castration. Mulciber—home to Cara. Whatever it was, whatever force that saw fit to blanket me, I was not afraid of it. I was nervous, yes, but not from the presence. If anything, the unseen force emboldened me. It was the fear of getting caught that had my heart thumping.

I wiped the cool sweat from my temples with the sleeve of my flannel shirt as I stood before the trapdoor. The clean, autumn air was replaced by earthy farm odors of moldy hay and aged manure. My plan was to get in and out as fast as possible. Given all the other trouble I'd found myself in, it would be a serious mistake to step into another dilemma. This one might break me. But I had to know. Did Danny scam me? My eyes blinked hard inside the barn, adjusting to the dimness. The moon, determined to keep its vigilance over my activity, shone brightly through splinters and cracks and knots in the old structure. I dared not light the lantern until I was safely inside the Captain's Quarters. Too risky.

A seeming lump of Kentucky bluegrass lodged in my windpipe as I reached for the iron ring. Would the Mamets be there? The hinge creaked like the blare of a noonday test of the emergency warning system. Sweat dripped from my cheek onto the graying wood planks. Carefully, as if God and all His saints and all the lesser gods of Sumer and Babylon and Greece and Egypt and Rome and a crack unit of the CIA backed up by the FBI were listening, I swung the door back and laid it flat against the floor, cringing at the slightest sound. I peered about, certain that some invisible force was observing me. Nerves. I slid the noisy ladder into the opening, its aluminum ribs like metallic fingers on an amplified chalkboard. I imagined lights, alerted by my racket, flicking on in houses all over northern Kentucky. I felt eyes upon me. Watching. I shrugged. Nerves.

I struck a match. The rich aroma of its head filled my nostrils as I touched the flame to the lantern. The first match I'd struck in years. Distant memories, long banished in the recesses and folds of my aging brain, announced themselves. Uninvited guests.

I backed my way into the hole, feeling as if I were entering some sacred tomb unearthed in Asia Minor. I could barely contain myself. I was inside the Captain's Quarters! There it all was—the blue sofa, the Glorian Aurora on the wall, the damp presence of history, of secrets. The Heidelberg sat black and cold against the opposite wall—a piece of machinery that cost a man his life 128 years ago. The scent of ink and musky earth and the faint smell of marijuana clung to the walls. Strangely, my eyes didn't light upon the treasured Mamets, but the captain's altar. I lit the nubbed candles. There would be a half-hour's light available from them, but I wasn't to stay that long. I nodded my respects to the captain, a true hero.

The Mamets were there all right, but they became secondary to Danny's mural, his constellation art with McJic blazing across the sky in his chariot. Ah, the imaginings of that boy. I was like that once—full of creativity and promise—full of ideas to change the world. But they were lost, blown out of my consciousness during the tragedy of World War II. Every man who served near the front lost something then. I thought of Bobby, with his intolerance and anger and hostile insecurity, as I plunked myself down on the faded blue sofa amidst a cloud of dust which rose from the cushions like a summer windstorm across an arid, farmer's field. Did Bobby know what caused him to change? Was he aware that he had left for Vietnam a good-natured kid with aspirations of becoming an architect and came home an angry, one-armed intimidator? Would the impending military devastation in the gulf, Operation Desert Shield, produce the same human toll, the same carnage as all previous wars?

I basked in the history of the room. I had come for the Mamets, that's what I told myself, but as I sat there in the musky Quarters, mouth agape, staring at the Heidelberg, thinking of Danny and Pulitzer, replaying the Calvary's conversations in my mind, remembering all the philosophy and wonder that transpired amongst them, I realized the real reason I'd come. To touch the magic.

The floorboards above creaked. My fingers gripped the sofa. I stopped breathing. Someone was up there. Who? Seconds, stuck in the molasses of fear, ticked by like hours. A cat meowed at the orange moon, or perhaps at a mouse. Slowly, I exhaled. That was close. The momentary scare reminded me of my professed reason for the trip to Mulciber, and the reality of its associated danger. No time for nostalgia.

I rose from the sofa and stepped toward the Mamets, bent on securing them quickly and getting the hell out of Mulciber. If I wanted to visit the Captain's Quarters again, I'd find Cara Gilday, or, Council willing, Danny, and ask permission to come during the day, when the appearance of impropriety was negligible. The lantern hissed its kerosene breath like a drunk at a bartender who has announced last call. I lifted a Mamet off the wall. Imagine the naiveté of a fourteen-year-old boy in hanging an invaluable masterpiece in a dingy barn. Imagine, hell, Danny thought he was immune to all of society's subtle rules. Gram had tried to teach him differently.

A floorboard creaked above. Dirt rained down from the rafters. Damn cat.

"Well now, this certainly is—I mean I should say that—well, this can't be good for you, but it's great for me, as they say—if I can coin a phrase—where there's Stone there's fire." The tinny voice of Brian McBain echoed in the chamber.

Busted! The first Mamet hung, suspended midair, in my hands as his voice resonated off the walls, and my heart plunged into my socks. There *had* been somebody watching after all.

The pipsqueak assistant prosecuting attorney and mayoral-hopeful clamored down the steps with his typical, clumsy grace. He missed the last two rungs and landed in a disheveled heap at my feet. As he lay on the floor, I could have crowned him in the head with the painting, tied him to the Heidelberg, and left him to die. I could've been a free man. The thought didn't just cross my mind, it trumpeted in my ears like a royal decree. But I knew, in this shrine of light-beings, the Council of Ancients would strongly disapprove. A murder rap was not what I needed just now.

McBain dusted off his flea market suit and stood, gloating. I set the priceless painting down to face my accuser. "It's not what you think, McBain."

"It really never—that is it seldom—well—" he twitched and smiled. "The criminal element always says, anyway, it's almost never what we think, now is it?"

The flames from Crittenden's altar began to fall in on themselves, the liquid wax overwhelming that which gave it life. Oh, the analogies I see these days. I hadn't much to say, being rather tongue-tied at the time. What does one say? *The Journals* had warned me. Stupidly, arrogantly, I had forged ahead without listening, without thinking.

"Who knows what the hand will do?" McBain recited *Impartial Fate* flawlessly. "What the mind will insist? What play upon man the act will become? What fortune holds for desperate self?"

"Nothing better to do than memorize planted poems, McBain?"

"I fancy this—that is, I think it's—well, it has a certain," he stuttered on as the lantern swore at the walls telling darkness it better take a hike or else, "I don't know, I'm not much for poems, but this one kind of—it has a certain style to it that I enjoy." He paused, brushed some dust and wrinkles from his polyester, and said, "I see your— that is, um, your burn is gone."

Instinctively, I rubbed my palm against my cheek. "Yeah, turns out it was benzene from a chemical spill upriver at Blue Chip Terminals, not gasoline as you suspected."

"Well, good evidence is hard to—that is to say, you can't win them all."

Busted with my hand in the proverbial cookie jar, I was in no mood for chit-chat. I wanted to extricate myself as rapidly as possible. "What are you doing here, McBain?"

"Acting on—it was more of a—well, come to think—no, it wasn't a tip," he said as I stared at his taped glasses broken in August. His dusty clothes hung on him like a set of tenement drapes, loosely bunched, out of frame. "I had a hunch," he finally spit out.

We stood staring at each other, unsure what to say, what to do. He had me with the Mamets dead to rights. There was no denying it. But McBain didn't appear to know how to proceed. Nor did I.

"So the great spy—I mean the World War II hero, the man that FDR—so Sulphur finally gets caught in the act?"

"What are you talking about?"

"I did a little research—digging actually—called in a few, that is to say, made a couple of calls to—anyway, you aren't the only one with friends in Washington. I got your service record under the Freedom of Information Act, Sulphur. The game is up."

"I don't know what you're talking about," I said.

"Oh yes you—of course you would deny—that would be just like a spy now wouldn't—I mean the government can't have its agents out talking about themselves all the time now, can it? Interesting files on you, Sulphur, distinguished." McBain said, "But then there are those—and so many of them, psychological profiles—numerous entries about churches burning, your taste for—that is your interest in . . . arson."

"You're absolutely bonkers, McBain! I'm not Sulphur. And I'm not an arsonist!"

"Maybe not, but I'd say this—" His bony hands extended in a circular motion around the chamber. "This is—well, it probably makes—no *definitely* makes—gives me a solid—well, you know this isn't good for you, Mr. Stone. Verifies my insurance-fraud theory. Your trial—my case ought to be—well, let's just say it just got a little shorter."

"You have it all wrong," I said weakly, unable to find the right words, my belly beginning to ache with that sensation of sickness I'd grown to hate.

Before either of us could begin a proper verbal duel, the floor creaked above us. Suddenly, the ladder was yanked from the chamber. *Bam!* The heavy, wood door slammed shut above our heads. A shower of dust pelted us. We were trapped.

"What the—" McBain shouted.

"Hey!" I protested.

Muted giggles floated downward, then footsteps scurried out of the barn.

McBain twisted his skinny neck and pulled at his collar. He was pale. He cleared his throat, tugged again, pulled hard at the fabric around his neck.

"Any . . . um . . . do you have any suggestions how to—well, it looks like we're stuck. I mean they'll come back with the—they won't leave us in here will they?" Pull. Tug. Tug. Squirm.

"I'm not sure, McBain. I don't know who, *they* are. How did you know I'd come here?"

"Had a theory—an idea actually—no, a thought that you might be, well, tied into this with Cara Gilday." Beads of sweat meandered out from under his frizzled scalp. "Been a belief of mine—based on investigation, testimony really—that you might be Danny's—you know, his, uh . . . real father." Tug. Squirm. Pull. Tug. Squirm some more.

"Don't be ridiculous. A blood test will prove that false." Me? Danny's father? Right.

McBain's narrow, birdlike eyes flittered about the closed chamber. He rubbed his palms together. Pulled at his collar some more. Coughed.

"Are you all right?" I asked.

524

"It could be—haven't figured this one out all the—almost there, but need a little more work," he wheezed. "Maybe *you* are Yvonne Pippin's father, too."

I scoffed at that one. "You have the wrong man," I said. "Patrick Gilday is Allison's father."

McBain didn't hear me. He couldn't. His mind was too distracted. "We have to get out of here, Stone. I can't stand small places. I can't be confined."

Call it the softness of an old warrior or a temperance brought about by the last five month's events, but as I watched my archrival fidget in claustrophobic agony, I felt sympathy for him. I was compelled, without a second thought, to help him.

I cupped my hands and stooped low so he could step into them like a stirrup, as I had seen Danny do with Gram the first day of their discovery of this sacred room. Anxious to breathe fresh air, and desperate to find open space, McBain quickly accepted my offer. His weight, although slight—he only stands a slim five-ten—was too much for my back, still weak from the bullet wound of some months ago and a more recent toxic regimen of chemotherapy and associated drugs. My stirrup hold broke and he tumbled to the ground, inadvertently kicking the lantern across the floor. The glass cracked and kerosene spewed out of it. Unlike the time when Gram calmly and coolly stomped out a small flame, the lantern gushed its fluid onto the sofa and flared against the worn fabric, erupting into a fireball.

Before either of us could react, the sofa was in flames. I grabbed the Mamets and set them on the far end of the room, away from the fire. McBain was terrified. He took refuge near the Heidelberg, crouching in fear like an errant child awaiting a deserved spanking. I had to think. I evaluated the burning sofa and determined we wouldn't be too affected by the heat unless it reached the wood ceiling. It was the smoke that would kill us and soon. The fire raged out of control. I stripped the shirt from my body and swung at the flames to no avail. My wild gyrations only managed to fan the fire. It mocked us. Told us it had us in its power.

"Brian! Give me your shirt." I laid mine across a patch of blaze to smother it. The flames retreated temporarily but sprung back and devoured my shirt. The fire spread to the foam cushions. There was no stopping it. The best we could hope for was to stall it until help arrived. "Brian!" He cowered in the corner, paralyzed.

Then it hit me: the secret passage! The Calvary had used it many times. I pulled the couch from the wall and ripped away a sheet of loose plywood where the hole should be. There it was. Hope. A last chance. "Brian, come on. There's a tunnel!" McBain sat quivering, shaking his head. His fear wouldn't allow it. Time was slipping from us; the smoke would fill the chamber from the top down. Within minutes, we'd be dead.

"I'll get help!" I shouted. "Get low to the ground."

McBain mumbled something that sounded like "We're going to die" and slid over sideways, locked in his phobia, to the floor.

I pushed myself into the tunnel, my bare stomach skidding into the dirt like an

Iran-Contra DC-9 landing in a remote Nicaraguan airstrip. A cobweb fell into my mouth. I spit and wiped the silk from my face. My shoulders and hips were snug against the dirt walls as I pressed on. I nudged myself forward, digging hard with my feet. My sciatic nerve pulled from behind as I scratched frantically at the earth. Total darkness surrounded me. Grains and clods of hard clay imbedded themselves in my skin. I had no idea where I was or how far I had to go. I scrambled through the passageway, desperate for fresh air. Jagged rocks tore at me. Scrapes and bruises multiplied.

I found myself in a precarious position, my shoulders constricted on both sides, my hands outstretched in front of me like some concentration camp escapee begging God for deliverance. I was stuck. The end of the line. My head dropped to the clay floor, its earthy scent reminding me of a grave. This would be my tomb. Then another smell nudged its way into my nostrils—smoke. "Shit!" I said. Millions of years of survival DNA kicked in. With all my force, I heaved forward in a mighty grunt of muscles I hadn't used in thirty years.

Nothing.

I was wedged tighter than Charlie the Tuna in a can of StarKist, but I couldn't give up. I'd come too far. I lurched forward again.

Nothing.

One . . . more . . . time. My fists punched at the wall of earth. I punched again. I clawed at the wall. I punched. I punched once more.

Something gave way.

A welcome beam of moonshine broke through the blackness. I was near the end, almost there. Almost. I clawed hard at the opening, dragging grass and dirt to me so I could get to the air. My skin tore against the sides of the narrow passage. My fingers clutched toward freedom. The opening grew larger. My toes pressed hard against the floor of the passage behind me—my joints felt as though they might break from the strain. My fingers, fully extended, grasped at the tall grass just outside. I latched onto a patch and pulled, using the strength of its roots to inch me forward.

A shriek bore through the tunnel. Brian was frantic. I had to save him. I scrunched my shoulders tightly together and pulled hard on the stalks. A rock, wedged deep in the clay soil, cut into my shoulder then broke loose, freeing me. I squirmed out of the hole into the bright Kentucky night and greeted a delightful moon with much more appreciation than I had afforded it earlier.

My shoulder bled, the flesh cut. My grass-stained hands shook from the violent exertion. I took a few breaths, thanked the Council (or whatever divinity watches over this life of mine), and ran from the field through knee-high grass to the barn. I found the ladder and stumbled toward the chamber.

"Help me," McBain coughed. "Someone help me!" I lifted the trapdoor as a billow of smoke poured from the Captain's Quarters, catching me off guard. The noxious cloud raked my esophagus like a pissed-off Sandanista with a pitchfork at the throat of Ollie North.

"I'm here Brian. I'm here."

McBain and I sat on a small hill across from the barn watching the firemen water the ruins. Three pumpers, an ambulance, and four police cars had joined the spectacle too late to be of any service. The structure was reduced to cinders and ash, as if a meteor had scorched the Earth. Tiny fissures of gray smoke rose from the desolate molten landscape. The Captain's Quarters had been ravaged, the Mamets destroyed, along with Danny's constellation mural and his Glorian Aurora. Pity. The house was spared, thank goodness, although to look at its current state of disrepair under the cool October moon one might wonder if it should have been saved.

Bandages adorned my elbows, my chin, and my stomach. My shoulder, which had been temporarily patched by the paramedics, ached with a pain certain to remain for several days. A scratchy, wool blanket, circa the Korean War, hung around my naked torso.

The reporters had swooped in as usual. McBain did a good job fending them off us with promises of interviews in the morning. He did this, I suspect, as much to recover from the trauma of his own nerve-racking experience as to shield me from their media antics.

"Is Stone under suspicion for the rash of fires in the West End?" a pushy pressman asked.

"Mr. Stone is not—as far as I'm aware—that is to say, we see no—I'm not familiar with what the authorities are doing over in, there's no connection as far as my office is concerned."

Mulciber's smoke ringed the ubiquitous moon which once menaced me, but now appeared a grateful blessing. The air was cool and sweet, reminiscent of a campfire, albeit a rather large one. People—neighbors, fire chasers, local officials rousted out of their beds by the biggest doin's in these parts in years—milled about, aimlessly searching for details to exaggerate for their friends and relatives over the next forty years. The story was destined to start inaccurately and evolve into a more and more corrupt tale each time it was told. Everyone would know this but the person telling it. Ah, the wonders of the human ego.

McBain adjusted the blanket around him as he looked down at the browned grass.

"Stone," he said, "I want to say, you really did a brave—well, I just want you to know how much I—"

527

"You're welcome, Brian," I said as a volunteer fireman coiled a hose.

McBain twitched from the experience (ever so slightly). It had shaken him considerably. I assumed he had accepted that he was going to die. I wondered what went on in his head. Not everyone reacts the same. Each person is different. Each soul interprets its life as a different work of art—some happy, some sad, some ambivalent.

"Back there—" He motioned with his head to the char that was the barn. "When I was, when I lost it, when I couldn't—"

"It's okay."

"But . . . I . . . I . . . I'm afraid of fire." He needed to say it, as if speaking the words allowed an emotional purge similar to a Heimlich for the soul.

"Brian, a great man once said, the only thing we have to fear is fear itself."

"FDR."

"Yeah. Did you know FDR was terrified of fire? Absolutely terrified of it. We're all afraid—inside."

"But if people found—if they knew, they'd probably—my election would, well, it wouldn't help things."

"Don't worry, Brian. It's between you and me."

McBain's tense face relaxed. "Maybe I can," he stuttered, "well, I'd like to make it up—pay you back, show you my gratitude, that is if you're still talking to me after the trial."

"I'd dare say some of your case just went up in smoke, Brian."

I had misjudged him. He wasn't trying to bait me, he was trying to tell me something. He breathed in full through his nostrils and picked at a blade of grass. "My brother, he was—I mean he—it was my fault, I shouldn't have been playing with—but I was so young, I didn't know any better, it was my fault." His lips quivered. He choked back tears. "My brother, Bryce, died in a fire, Stone."

"I know," I said. I stared at the smoldering patch of black land. "Accidents happen."

McBain couldn't hold it in. Sadness trickled from him like a fountain of sorrow. "I killed him," he cried as he leaned over, his head on my shoulder. "I started the fire."

"It's okay, Brian. The gods forgive you," I said soothingly, elbows propped on my bent knees. "You just need to forgive yourself."

We sat in silence, Brian whimpering in the torment of his past, as we watched the mop-up operations conclude. I thought of Bobby as McBain struggled with his tears. It's all right, son. Let it out. The years of sadness. The emotion locked inside, the hurt, the tangled mess of resentment. Let it out.

The night turned cold. The moon hid itself behind a curtain of smoke and cloud. A half-hour passed as we sat there, each of us lost in the meaning of the night's events. What did they mean? How would this affect my trial? I was sure to be a headline in the papers the next day. *The Journals* had warned me not to come to Mulciber. Cara had been right the first day they moved in—the place was foreboding—evil. A darkness pervaded Mulciber. Only she and Danny could liven it up, but not even they could undo its gloom. Instead, more bad history had been written, with me and McBain in its sullen chapters.

An hour passed. Everyone had gone home but me and McBain. I was freezing but told myself, *à la* lessons learned by the Council's message of compassion, to sit with Brian McBain as long as he needed to lean on me. It was both odd and comforting. Finally, after the moon decided to reappear with a mischievous, orange smile accompanied by brilliant stars, Brian spoke.

"Stone," he said clearly. "Are you McJic?"

October 26, 1990

Rose had a busy morning as I slept through the dawn. She shooed away a pesky flock of reporters who managed to trample the flowers outside our bedroom window at six a.m. Evidently, I'm front page news again. This time, however, Rose had no doubt where she stood. A woman of greater devotion does not exist.

Today, as I lay asleep, recovering from the previous night's pyrotechnics, Rose expertly dispatched the press, then came up with an ingenious plan. She informed me of her strategy as we shared a breakfast of wheat toast with apple butter, fried potatoes, sausage, and orange juice, in the solarium. Sausage had been banned from the house under Maya's orders—something about overwhelming evidence that pork causes cancer. Rose concurred with her, having read ample documentation in the books from the library. I figured the sausage was a special treat because of the harrowing Mulciber ordeal. Despite the uncertain repercussions of last night's events, I was decidedly energetic and chipper.

A red-orange sun gently sponged the dew droplets off my orchids. Precious little girls. They were dressed colorfully in a bright morning. I'm always happy to eat breakfast in their presence. Rose's eyes glistened like jade as she outlined her blueprint. She wore an exuberant, resolute smile. A notepad lined with her battle plan lay on her lap.

Rose poured hot water for a cup of green tea. (I would like to point out, despite my serious obstinance and doubts, that the herbal remedy of myrrh, parsley, and Japanese green tea has lessened my halitosis considerably. I have now reduced my consumption of synthetic candies, breath fresheners, oral rinses, and the like, to a minimum, and I am better for it. Maybe there is something to this New Age stuff.)

"The way I see it, R.T., we have to take the offensive here. Now, what is *The Journals* about?"

"Danny and Allison," I said. It has taken me forty-some years to finally fully appreciate her. I'll never take her for granted again. Ever.

"They're the characters, but what's the message? What are they interested in?" She didn't wait for an answer. "Danny is into the environment, the antinuclear movement to be exact. And Allison is into the homeless. So . . ." The morning sun cast a yellow aura off her chestnut hair. "We need to publicize both. That's the message, R.T. That's what the Council wants."

"I don't know." I smeared apple butter on my toast.

Rose had thought this through and pressed her point. "Let's not confuse the message with the messengers. *The Journals* wants their lives documented. Why? To expose the issues surrounding them. Here's my suggestion: Jim Bennett and I will collect as much information as possible on the homeless situation in Cincinnati, cuts in government programs, what shelters are available, the plight of the homeless, that sort of thing. Meanwhile, Parker and Maya will work on Fernald, exposing all they can on the government cover-up. When all the information is gathered, we'll announce a press conference for you to tell your version of *Impartial Fate*. The reporters will circle like vultures."

"Rose, I—"

"R.T., I'm certain this is the right path. I can't explain why—intuition, I suppose." She shushed me, refusing to entertain any hesitancy on my part. "But I think the Persian Gulf Crisis is part of this, too. R.T., you need to prepare a document on the disastrous potential of the impending war. We have to bring to light the insanity of a blood-for-oil policy. Maybe you're meant to avert World War III. When the reporters come to hear of *Impartial Fate* we'll tell them where the real stories are—Fernald, the homeless, Operation Desert Shield."

I chuckled, fascinated by Rose's strategy.

"It's funny, R.T.," she said, speaking far more rapidly and with much more enthusiasm than normal, "but since I started going to Unity Center my spirituality has been unleashed. Like I was suppressed by my church, and now I've found myself."

"That's great, dear," I said, stabbing another piece of sausage.

"R.T.," she said, suddenly subdued. She twisted her napkin in her hands. "I have a confession."

"What?"

"That's not pork. It's completely vegetarian. Maya told me about it. Do you like it?"

I looked at the sausage on my fork, then at Rose, amazed. "Yeah," I laughed, but felt somehow cheated. Old habits, I guess, even if they are deadly ones, are extremely difficult to break. My disappointment quickly vanished. Vegetarian, huh? I thought to myself, I could get used to this. Being healthy isn't all that hard to do. "It's good. I read somewhere that we can retrain our taste buds in less than three weeks."

But her comment about the sausage was a subtle lead-in. "I have another confession, R.T.," she said, playing with her cross. "I had almost given up. I spent my life doing my best to serve God, but, and I can see that now, only through the conflict of the last few months with everything I believed in changing, only now are my eyes really opening." She waved her hand at me. "Look at you. You slip through life a mystery, at best an agnostic, at worst an atheist. And who does God choose to do his work? You."

I didn't know whether to feel honored or ashamed. The necklace in her hand was twisted round and round. "It just goes to show how wrong one can be. All this time I was searching for divinity, and it was there in front of me all the while," she said.

My cheeks turned warm. I looked from my gorgeous orchids to the backyard to Rose to the family room. Something was missing. What was it?

"Rose," I said, "Bobby's spoon collection is missing."

"Yes." She stood to clear the dishes as I reached for a myrrh capsule. "I've decided to stop letting him play the victim, to stop coddling his psychosis. I put his spoons in the storage room. Vietnam was a long time ago. He needs to stand on his own. It's time he moves on." She set the tray on a ledge and came back to me, leaned in with her signature vanilla scent, and kissed me softly on the forehead. "I love you, R.T. It's Bobby's choice if he wants to waste his life angry at things he can't change."

I swallowed the capsule of myrrh. It stuck in my throat momentarily. Firm words from Rose. Words I never thought I'd hear. An overly protective mother beyond her limit with her son. I didn't think this day would come. I had made up my mind about Bobby, too. One last chance I had promised myself as I sat watching the barn at Mulciber consume itself. Life is too precious. Time too short.

"I'm going to go see him."

Chapter 43

April 3, 1983 (Easter Sunday)

Allison awoke trembling. She did not know why. It had been a good dream, a glorious dream. She should have smiled at its beauty and its grace, but she trembled instead. The Council of Ancients, with the evident belief that Allison was prepared to play a more spirited role in the religious theater, sent a divine communication to her as she slept. Yes, she awoke trembling, for in her dreams the Council, in the guise of our Lord God, had spoken to her. He had spoken in a direct, undeniable manner. He had spoken to her as a vessel, and when He had finished with His enlightenment, lest she dismiss His words as exotic imaginings, He left a manuscript on her night stand. Allison awoke trembling.

> 1 A great voice visited a sleeping child, an Earthbound angel in quiet slumber. Of purity and faith were her sweetest dreams and Yahweh did commune with her in her repose. And her name was Allison and she was holy.

> 2 And Yahweh came to her in her bed and He did whisper this to her soul: "From the heavens I have come to deliver you. From the ether I shall speak. I shall call to you and all humankind that you may hear My Word.

> 3 "And to Allison I shall prepare the message of My spirit. For I have come to condemn all that has risen before. And this child of My soul shall be the Savior to anyone seeking salvation. She is the seed of her mother, born of the fruit of Paradise."

> 4 And Yahweh wrote these words to men of all races: "You have raped the great mother of her purity, and you have stolen her beauty, you have deceived her trust, and you have blasphemed her honor, you have sold her virtue,

and you have claimed her glory, you have crowned your kings to make her your slave. And in doing so you have subjugated My wife.

5 "And now I offer My daughter to you and say that she will not be defeated, for she is the seed of My seed come to offer forgiveness. Accept her kindness that you may be spared the fire of My wrath. For her mother lay dying and it is you who are the criminal. You who read this text as if a story. You who would be blameless in the comfort of your home as the beggar cries for the simplest consideration.

6 "And My wife was known as Paradise. And some may call her Earth. In her silent illness she has kept your hatred well. She will not willingly divulge to Me the poisonous deeds performed upon her, for she cannot speak. She cannot hear. She cannot see.

7 "I alone am her vigil. I alone am her lover. I alone shall keep her well, safe from the atrocities of the race of humans, and I alone will have to slay all my sons and daughters who would seek to destroy My love. I alone will cry a rain of two and two thousand Noahs, but she, and the chosen, will live to begin anew.

8 "And I shall relate the story of My lover to you through My daughter, for she is the quiet kindness that may heal the Earth and temper My wrath. Listen well that you may save what all have attempted to destroy."

9 And Allison did stir in her slumber as the vision traced through her mind, and to her this truth was revealed: There stood a maiden on a distant shoreline of white-sanded beach and blue crystal water. Her world was of nothing man could conceive, for her beauty was the beauty of all that was known.

10 And she was a girl fresh of virtue, her hair the scent of pine dipped in heaven's dew, her smile the dawn

of each day, her eyes the sunset in the evening. And she was beauty beyond description.

11 But the maiden of all that would be was unable to speak. The mother of all life's beings was unable to hear. The wife of the Most Holy was unable to see, and in the absence of these senses she had the gift of thought. For she could speak without words, hear without sound, see without sight. She was My equal, captive in the physical realm.

12 She had chosen her bondage out of love for her children. Her world is the womb of all people. And her love for Our progeny was endless. She welcomed all manner of beasts unto her house, and she honored all before her.

13 And the maiden beckoned from the shoreline for all who would taste Paradise to come. And her home became full of her children and their children and their children; and so it went.

14 And she was happy, content in the knowledge that she had begun the litter. And she was caring and compassionate in the splendor of her mountains and the rushing of her streams, and the generations mounted and still she nourished them. It was fourteen upon fourteen upon fourteen generations that she did suckle.

15 And she walked proud amongst her children, for her fruit was sweet to her sons and daughters, and life was plentiful. She was gracious, and the maiden became laden with child once more. Her pregnancy was lengthy and strained as she nurtured her unborn. Her labor was arduous, and she bore three upon the dawn at once.

16 And three sons did appear: princes all, brought forth to help their mother govern her dominion. And they did drink directly from her breast, and she did nourish them and teach them her secrets. They grew

mighty and strong. In their youth, they performed great deeds. Innocence begat their fortune, and they lived well in their mother's house.

17 And the people of the world honored them, for their traits were prosperity, wisdom, and faith. And they were called Commerce, Education, and Religion and the three did grow in stature. And many followed the princes, each possessing his own secret majesty.

18 And the Earth did transfer her thoughts into the princes' ears, and the three boys matured into young men, their strength growing as each developed a following of souls. This was the beginning of Earth's torment, for her gift of life was soon forgotten by the three.

19 Each coveted her honor and power, so their innocence became corrupted as they vied for her attention and authority. But they did not want her favor to keep her traditions. Each in his own way desired to capture her virtue to create his own kingdom.

20 And so the three brothers dispersed to the far reaches of her realm, and they did tempt children of all sort to follow their message. And Earth was heartbroken, for she had been forsaken by the sons sent to rule with her.

21 And she withdrew her secrets from their minds. They were left each to devise their own truths, and these truths were designed to deceive, created to gain power, made real in order to extract allegiance.

22 And she wrote this message to all souls young and old. "Beware of the three sons, beware of the three princes, for they are no longer of my spirit. They have stolen my heart for evil gains. Beware, children of the world, of the three thieves."

23 But the children of the world heeded her not, for they had become entranced by the handsome and powerful princes. Her words were lost to the wind. Her wisdom mute within her soul. But she had hidden from all a place of magic and riches. She left humankind with its civilization to deceive itself as she retreated to a pure and virgin shore.

24 So Commerce, Education, and Religion founded their own kingdoms. Each built splendid structures to seduce their believers. And they did grow. The masses did follow and the three did elevate themselves to position of king.

25 And the Earth became lonely, but she could not abide their betrayal. She alone could rule her domain, and she alone held the true force of nature. As the years passed, she released her fury upon the children who had abused her sanctity. Great tempests of swirling winds and rain were unleashed, massive quakes upon the land reduced man's buildings to rubble, fires of such heat, stone was turned to liquid.

26 She revealed not her purpose to any man. Her power so great she kept it humbly within her, for she could not bear to mistreat those undeserving of punishment, the innocent ones.

27 And the false kings, in fear, did inwardly tremble at her force, for they knew they could never conquer her. Thieves as kings seldom reveal the truth, lest they be seen in truth. As such they professed to work the will of the Earth Mother and the lies continued upon the land.

28 And Earth decided to provide but one more chance for the salvation of her body, mind, and soul. And she motioned across her great oceans for the three false kings to come. She invited the thieves and their followers to her new home in hope of taming their greed. She summoned the physicians, the poets, the laborers, the

sailors, the farmers, and soldiers, and she beckoned with her radiance for all to meet her.

29   And they came to her home, and they were happy. And Paradise was found, if but for a moment. For soon it was discovered by the evil hearts of men that she was mute, blind, and deaf. And so Commerce stood first and spoke for her, and this is what he said: "We have been ordained by the great mother to offer you her beauty for a price. Come to Paradise and you will know riches beyond belief."

30   And she said nothing as she watched her body sold for the very ores which she had offered willingly. Soon the wicked traders of Commerce understood their power, for she would not defend against her children. She would not believe they would kill their mother.

31   And the evil of man professed, in pious dishonor, to be her ears and thereby know her thoughts. And they dressed her in costume and walked her in parades and taught their children to honor virtue cloaked in symbols.

32   And they propped her up to the masses and made her name a cause. And they shrouded her beauty with a flag and supplanted her voice with music as the masses fell in love with her. So pure, so wise, so beautiful.

33   And the men of power named her and she was prostituted to all people. And they called the maiden, America, and the people were made proud. Her name had been sacrificed along with the reason of all man's purpose. Soon, nature had been replaced by metaphor. Metaphor replaced by simile. Simile replaced by comfort.

34   So the men of power prospered, and America was taught in the schools. America sat in judgment of her people and she became known as Liberty, and Liberty became known as Justice. And the men of power became her eyes, for America or Liberty or Justice was blind.

35 She became a hostage, held captive by the wicked trappings of frail vice. Imprisoned in her own land. Set to chain by gold-dusted indifference. And the people of America, and the people of the world, not knowing of the deception, looked to her for guidance.

36 Her sinful possessors spun a spell of dark magic, woven in deception and bound by great armies to intimidate the masses. And she was no longer needed, only her promise need be viewed. And she was discarded in favor of an actress, a woman of seductive morals and rehearsed inspiration.

37 And the people of the world knew not of these misdeeds, but neither were they looking, for they were fed and clothed and sheltered with contentment. But . . . they will need to pay the ransom.

38 And the price of her freedom is truth, and the truth can be known only by those who seek it. Those who are searching are chosen, and those claiming to have found the truth are damned, for there is no answer but the answer within. The answers change as the seasons.

39 And Commerce has become mighty. But he rules only the physical plane. Pleasure and pain are friend to him, but he does not understand their true value. His hand grips tightly his gold-lined purse, but his precious metals are mere dust within the Universe. The jewels bespeckled upon woman's gracious neck are but collars binding her to sorrow. The paper you print to purchase happiness is but temporary worth in a fool's hands.

40 Man lures you with the glitter of its promise. He seduces you with bright-colored spangles and tongue-twisted jingles. But shadowed eyes and painted lips above well-fashioned garments will not contentment bring. For by this standard must you always search for brighter shades and deeper shadows. And into darkness you will fall like a fly into honey, sweet if for a moment, you taste it well, while its sticky trap ensnares you forever.

41   And the silver-voiced call of Commerce shall distract you. His merchants are clever and the flesh is weak. They hawk their wares in shameless variety in a manner designed to fool the helpless. And so I say unto you . . . beware.

42   Many are those who would separate you from coin so they may be joined with it. Many are those who have been blinded by greed and have lost sight of their true wealth. And the vision of the Universe will be kept from them forever. These simple things must you follow that all may be revealed unto your gentle spirit.

43   Hold all moments precious that you may help those without, that you may offer shelter to the homeless, that you may offer food to the hungry, that you may provide hope to the desperate and solace to the lonely. Trade your distraction for participation and your comfort for commitment, and you shall prosper.

44   Keep an honest eye toward your fellow spirit and you shall see beyond the starlight of the Cosmos. Spend not your time in idle pursuits of wanton spectacle. Reach an empty hand of friendship toward a broken soul and it shall be filled with riches more splendid than the vaults of the Pharaohs. Follow your heart to its inner sanctum and you shall discover pleasure resplendent in the falling of a leaf, in the drying of a tear, in the laughter of a child.

"What does it mean?" Allison whispered as Mary slept soundly a few feet away. She had read the manuscript twice before the Easter sun had even risen, hoping familiarity might release her fear, but it did not. She was two days into fifteen and thought perhaps she had outgrown the holy visions.

She rolled from bed and knelt on the floor, her shaking hands clasped in prayer. The sun had just pulled back the blanket of night as she whispered prayers over and over, asking for it all to make sense. Pray as she might, Allison already knew the answers. It wasn't that she didn't comprehend the meaning of the heavenly words—she understood—what she pleaded for was to avoid the wrath of the Catholic Church. She had come to understand that divine intervention, speaking to God, was strictly *verboten*. She had seen enough examples—her previous visions were shunned because they proved dangerous to authority, while bogus visions, such as greasy oil terminals in Toledo, were celebrated and commercialized. Reality, true Grace, was not tolerated. What she feared most, what she hoped most of all to avoid, what she prayed to the Holiest of Fathers for, was to be spared the microscopic scrutiny of the Governing Order of Divinity—Division of Apparitions, Miracles & Nuisances, and one very detestable Cadaver Smith.

She made it through Easter Mass, though she didn't hear much of the sermon. She had pulled Mary to the side of the cathedral where a lone ray of celestial sunshine beamed through the stained glass and landed on the pew where Allison insisted on sitting. She tilted her head to meet the beam and closed her eyes while her thoughts ran back to the manuscript, hidden as a lowly lump beneath her mattress. So many words, so many messages. She couldn't deny them, wouldn't deny them. They were hers. The handwriting is mine, isn't it? she asked herself as she stood in line for communion. Yet, she didn't recollect writing it at all. She didn't question the content to dispute it, only to understand it. Her mind worked and worked on the material.

Not once did she consider whether she was crazy or possessed. Her faith in God and the glory He brought to the world were beyond doubt. She did ask, why her? Why a red-headed orphan? Why Cincinnati? Why not New York or Los Angeles or Mecca or New Delhi or Jerusalem?

The sun warmed her face as the priest blathered on, alternating between English and Latin. For the first time since Allison had come to the St. Alexandria orphanage, for the first time since she had become a Catholic, she wanted oh-so-badly for the Easter service to end so that she could race back to her room and answer the questions that swept through her mind like a troupe of drunken angels on holiday.

She thought of Star, the psychic who had seen her white energy, and remembered the name she had called her—Annis the Forgiver. It made sense. It made perfect, confusing, how-can-this-be-happening sense.

In an attempt to allow humor to break her anxiety over her discovery, Allison said quietly to herself, as the priest invoked the peace-be-with-you clause, "Jesus talking to God on the emergency bat-phone, how can this be?" Mary glared at Allison as if she were nuts. But Allison wasn't nuts, far from it.

She compared the words of *Agnostics*, as the manuscript was titled, to random events, news stories, articles and facts she picked up in her short fifteen years and two days on the planet. She thought of the pollution, the dirty congressional deals, the homeless, the travesty of Cincinnatus, of Reagan and his GOP pillaging of the public trust while he espoused family values. She saw through the PR. Reaganomics was as transparent as Mother Peculiar's kindness. It was all about money. Growth.

Construction. Consumption. More growth. All the evidence was there, she concluded in her mind as she thanked the Father for the stimulating sermon that she hadn't heard.

She thought of President Reagan's comment that the homeless wanted to live on the streets, and scoffed as she returned to her room. She eyed the lump under her bedspread, warmed by the fact that it was still there, still real. A great sense of responsibility took hold of her as she looked up "agnostic" in the dictionary. The weight of helping humankind was hers now. Sure, it had always been there, but that was her choice. *Agnostics:144* was a directive from God Almighty. Allison's standards of social commitment had been raised—considerably. When God talks—Allison listens.

After Mary changed and left for the Easter egg hunt, Allison carefully extracted the manuscript from her mattress. She plopped herself on the bed, surrounded by the newly received papers, Gibran, Danny's picture, a purple orchid of cosmic origin, a dictionary, and the New American Bible. She knew but dared not think it, due to years of indoctrination with Catholic guilt, purgatory being an excellent deterrent for blasphemy, that *Agnostics:144* was the latest chapter of the Bible.

Days and weeks followed as Allison held her secret close. No one, absotively no one knew. Not even Mary. She had wanted to tell Mary that first night and had crawled into bed with her, frightened, just wanting to feel her closeness, her warmth, just wanting to tell somebody.

"Mary," Allison whispered with hesitation.

A light breathy snore through crowded teeth was Mary's unconscious reply.

Allison had read *Agnostics* several times, taking its messages to heart. In appreciation of her special relationship to the Master, she wrote Him a humble poem which she read aloud to Him from her perch in the bell tower.

Sorrow has its Gifts for All to Enjoy

Wake up world—start again

perhaps we can find a new dawn

maybe there is a solution to the world

Revive and count the blessings though they may be few

Live and see what one can find in the morning

and perhaps in the evening we might appreciate the struggles of yesterday

Sorrow has its gifts for all to enjoy

Allison honored the spirit of *Agnostics* and became even more compassionate and forgiving of others. Simultaneously, she also became more active in the futile game of politics. She wrote letters to her representative and her two senators. She drafted sample letters for the sisters and kids to use as well, which were greeted with skepticism and jaundiced comments. Aid for the homeless, equal rights for women, more liberal adoption laws, protests against U.S. policy in Central America were just a few of the causes she championed through letters to legislators and conversations with anyone who would listen at St. Als.

The nuns were disturbed by this liberal defiance, unheard of in ecclesiastical circles, and decided the distraction of tennis was the best and proper solution. Of course, they knew not of the inspired document in Allison's possession.

One month and two days had passed since the message had arrived. But was it a message or a warning? It didn't matter to Allison. She would do her part. It was her mission now. Every possible free moment was spent pursuing God's word. She blessed her garden vegetables, caring for them with extra-special attention, speaking to them, comforting them, thanking them for their nutrition. She sat in the bell tower, her personal sanctuary, and alternatively read *Agnostics* and the Bible. She played tennis for the Lord, acing her opponents with divine serves. She treated everyone she met, including Mother Superior, with kindness and sincerity, a subtle change in her already angelic personality that did not go unnoticed. The nuns could not correlate her sweet disposition with her political activism. Neither could the passive sheep of the orphanage accept the fact that one could be friendly and genuine, but also distrustful of government suppression.

Alas, the intense pressure of keeping her secret was too much for our heroine to endure. She chose Friday, May 6, 1983, as the date to share her empyrean find. The rest of the kids were in the main room watching *Dallas* while eating popcorn and Milk Duds (a donation from a local theater seeking a tax write-off). Allison locked the door to the bedroom. Mary rolled her eyes, figuring it was yet another dramatic, Red Angel conspiracy scheme. Once Allison showed her the writing Mary realized it *wasn't* a game.

"Does this mean you're a saint or something?" Mary whispered as the two sat on Allison's bed, examining the manuscript.

"No, not a saint." Allison giggled. "But maybe a prophet."

"Oh, Allison," Mary sighed and licked her teeth, which pushed forward ever so slightly like groupies swooning over a rock idol.

Then it happened. Their eyes met. Two friends, roommates for nine years. Lonely and frightened, abandoned and in need of tenderness. Two kids locked inside an unforgiving orphanage sharing a room, sometimes sharing whatever feelings they would allow to surface. For years, they had held each other in times of sorrow, finding one another's bed for security.

But this night was different. This night an invisible spark flashed between them. Gently, Mary combed a hand through Allison's glorious red hair. Slowly, she pulled Allison toward her and kissed her lips. Allison didn't resist. Her hand touched Allison's knee. It was warm, welcome. It was a moment unlike any other. There was no hesitation, no question of right or wrong. Mouths mushed. Flesh warmed. Knees went weak. Hearts palpitated. Bosoms heaved. Their tongues entwined, searching each other for the pleasure both had been denied so long. Delicious delirium spread through their hungry bodies. They gave each other what they needed most—the touch of human hands. Skin on skin. The unbridled passion of love. They melted into each other, as if the two could never be separated again.

They kissed, and kissed once more, their hearts beating together, breathless as their blouses fell away. Nipples touched. Springtime blushed sultry and wet. Seed sprouted into full grown flowers. Moisture laced the lily. Glistening dew dotted tulips. Nectar licked orchids. Blossoms opened.

Other garments floated to the floor. Allison's chest ached with longing. She gingerly reached for Mary's softness. They fell back on the bed together, embraced in splendorous throes of love. Their naked bodies tumbled and explored, probed and felt, tasted and nibbled, as if they had found a treasure trove of locked passion. On it went until both fell asleep, entangled in the comfort of companionship.

Now there are those who would condemn their carnal appetite as unnatural, two women enjoying desires of the flesh together. But I say (as an editorial aside) that there is nothing more natural than the need for love, the need to belong to someone, anyone. We humans should celebrate any union that consummates itself on those conditions, regardless of gender.

And so, two virgins found each other and became lovers, sleeping together almost every night, taking care to separate in the morning in order to avoid discovery by the penguins. Allison and Mary saw nothing deviant about their bliss. The joy that enraptured them was the purest and most honest release they had ever had, and, in a sense, represented a pardon from the emotional imprisonment of St. Als. There would be many nights in which the girls would find God in the caress of the other.

Days later, while heavy rain saturated the Cincinnati spring outside their window, Mary stroked Allison's hair as her head lay on Mary's pert breasts. Mary said, "Isn't it neat that the Earth is God's wife? That she is God in physical form? It explains how it feels to be a woman."

Allison hadn't considered that before, despite the hundreds of hours she had spent contemplating the depths of *Agnostics*. There *is* a bond, unspoken but understood, between all women and the Earth. The Earth with its cycles of days, months, and years, with its seasons—women are like that, too. They intuitively align with the rhythm of the planet. They care for her and her inhabitants, even as the ones they nurture seek to destroy everything around them.

"I think we need a code name for *Agnostics:144*," Allison said.

Mary blew in her ear. "Why?"

"Cheesecake, Mary, for the fun of it, of course." Allison laughed. "Let's see . . . *Agnostics* . . . hmm . . . how about eggnog sticks?"

Mary pushed Allison's head lightly. "Eggnog sticks, that's stupid. That won't fool anybody. I got it . . . how about Agnes? It sounds like *Agnostics* but could also be a real person, so nobody will figure it out."

"Good idea." Agnes means pure; Allison knew because she had looked it up in a book of names. It's also a form of Annis. Annis the Forgiver. Star *had* seen the future. Allison sat up, her nubile breasts jiggling freely before Mary. She loved lying around nude. It was liberating and gave her a sense of freedom.

"Mary," she said, suddenly concerned. "You haven't told anybody about Agnes have you?"

Mary pouted.

"Oh, Mary, no. Who?"

"Gabrielle. But she won't tell anybody."

Allison stood up, threw on a robe, and tied the sash. The rain slashed against the window drumming a warning in her psyche. "Jesus confiding his plans to the Romans, Mary, I asked you to keep it quiet."

Mary was hurt and embarrassed, but mostly disappointed in herself for betraying Allison's trust.

Allison dressed quickly and pulled Agnes from her dresser drawer.

"Where are you going?" Mary said.

"To hide Agnes where the Church can't find her."

The gentle love affair between the two orphans was brought to an unceremonious halt only two weeks later when they were discovered by Sister Bernadette, feigning indignation that they were lesbians. Her banshee shriek of shock when she found them tangled in the sheets split the still morning. After a particularly satisfying evening of reading *Agnostics:144* passages to each other, followed by an exhaustive round of love making, Allison had forgotten to set the alarm. She had also neglected to return Agnes to her bell tower hiding spot.

They were hauled to Mother Superior's office, where the granite-faced chief nun, her skin as wrinkled as an elephant's elbow, displayed an extremely civil understanding of the girl's desires. Barney had left the room. Mother Superior gazed sleepily at the two shaking girls, hands between their knocking knees. Sister Dena sat (seedless) between the accused. A long conversation transpired about accepted societal mores and the need for order.

Mother exhibited sterling patience and unusual tolerance as she explained how she understood the girls' adolescent needs, "But, well, there are things that are best left hidden."

Allison picked nervously at the hem of her jeans and slipped into her Red Angel mode, suspicious that Mother Peculiar, who often relished the opportunity to discipline her, was being too darn nice. Even the pope on the wall seemed in on the conspiracy.

Barney, holding an armful of contraband, came through the door a few minutes later, her cucumber schnoz leading the way. Said confiscated articles included *The Prophet*, Allison's personal journals, and one *Agnostics:144*. Careful examination by the three sisters, faces ashen white, for they had concluded their angel had again been receiving celestial transmissions, yielded a penalty more severe than Allison had expected.

"Mary," Mother Superior said like a landslide down a mountain pass. "You will continue to stay in your current quarters. Allison," she rumbled like boulders tumbling toward a sleepy village awaiting devastation. "We will prepare a room in the east wing, where you will stay with Sister Dena. Understood?"

The east wing? Allison wondered. Then, she wisely deduced that this was a preordained plan seriously precooked by the Penguin Squad in case she had had any further visions. She and Mary weren't being separated because they were busted sleeping together. It was *Agnostics*. A large spitball made of Satan's saliva blocked her windpipe, then sank painfully into her sour stomach. Mary would be taken from her.

She had been sequestered in the east wing for three days before Allison found herself whisked away, without explanation, in the St. Als' van to a Victorian mansion in North College Hill. On the way over, she pretended to be kidnapped by the KGB, betrayed by a double agent who had turned her over for a briefcase full of Russian diamonds, a bottle of vodka, and a weekend pass to Disney World.

She was ushered into a large den in which walls, lined with mahogany shelves heavy with books, rose eighteen feet to the ceiling. A massive creme-and-burgundy oriental rug smothered the gleaming, hardwood floor before a large, brick fireplace tall enough for her to stand in if she choose to. She did not. The room was immaculate. A gold-leaf framed portrait of Pope John Paul II hung behind a humongous L-shaped desk adorned with pictures and expensive theistic knick-knacks. Were it not for the seriousness of her journey, she would have been in heaven.

Allison breathed in the scant scent of Jovan musk, a cologne she was familiar with from the older St. Als' boys who seemed to shower in it before asking one of the orphan girls if she'd like to make out in the east wing. Seated in a comfortable, leather chair, Allison fidgeted alone until the door opened and a man walked in, accompanied by an older man and followed by the infamous Governing Order of Divinity—Division of Apparitions, Miracles & Nuisances team members. A vapor trail of musk followed. As the men situated themselves before her attentive stare, her mother's last inspiring words came to her: "Remember to shine, Allison." It was the assurance she needed.

"Yvonne." An elegant, silver-haired man greeted her warmly with an extended hand. "I'm Archbishop Sebastian." He took a seat behind his finely appointed desk. "I believe you know these other men."

Indeed she did. She would never forget them. They nodded to her in a somewhat synchronized manner. The yellowish Cadaver Smith grinned with ghoulish glee. This is what he's paid for—rooting out evil (or goodness, depending on one's perspective) in the Church.

"We want to ask you a few questions," the archbishop said suavely. He flicked his wrist to examine the time on his Rolex watch: 9:17 a.m. His silver fox hair was perfectly coifed, not a strand out of place. His Grace could have been a model for an AARP mail-order catalog. A strong cloud of cologne enveloped Allison. She liked musk, but such a heavy concentration caused her eyes to water. "Tell me, if you don't mind," he asked, as if he were someone's grandpa, "where did you find this *Agnostics* document?"

"I don't know," she said. She wanted to be left alone, but she was also smart enough to realize that this motley bunch of fact-finders were looking for predetermined answers, and the truth wasn't among them. "It showed up on my night stand after a dream I had on Easter Sunday."

The archbishop folded a smile like a fine crease in the pages of the holy book. "Now, Allison, books don't just appear from thin air."

She squirmed in her chair, uneasy with the archbishop's condescending tone. From this writer's perspective, I can attest that indeed, books do appear from thin air. Not often perhaps, but they do.

"It's the truth," she said. She knew that this book came from God, He wouldn't abandon her. There's a plan.

"Now, now, child." The archbishop shook his head. "This is a serious matter. We can't have little girls going around forging new sections of the Bible. Why, it would lead to pure chaos. Our whole civilization could be threatened."

Despite the gravity of the situation, she wanted to giggle but pinched the web of skin between her thumb and index finger instead. She knew the material. She'd studied it, gave it due consideration. A sincere belief that God had spoken to her in the middle of the night with an important communiqué bolstered her. Sister Dena had coached her to be evasive about the facts. In other words—lie. They had three fortunate days to prepare, but Allison would not, could not, speak falsely. Had God Himself not spoken to her? What worthiness would deception show Him? She would tell the truth on moral ground. The Church and its Governing Order of Divinity—Division of Apparitions, Miracles & Nuisances could do what they wanted to her—she would not allow Agnes to be trampled.

"That's the point, isn't it?" Allison questioned somewhat boldly. "To show that our society is out of control."

Cadaver Smith and his ghouls mumbled and shuffled their feet uneasily. The archbishop remained poised, arrogant behind his protective layer of perfume. "That may be," he smiled like St. John's birthday cake. "But we cannot allow fabricated documents to get into the American mainstream."

"But, if it's the truth, how—"

The archbishop waved his hand weakly to dismiss her words, whatever they might have been. A man of his stature in the Church was accustomed to this type of power.

Cadaver Smith stepped forward, his nicotine skin tarred like a discarded cigarette butt. "We have ways of determining the truth, young lady."

She was barely aware of her actions as she stood defiantly, arms crossed. The archbishop stood as well, a sterner look on his face.

"Allison, it is the Church's opinion that you did not receive these scribblings in your sleep, but that you wrote the documents yourself."

"No, that's not true."

"Visions to fifteen-year-old girls in Cincinnati just do not happen," the archbishop stated with emotional detachment as he rapped his fingers impatiently on the desk in succession. She could see the archbishop's reflection in the finely polished desktop.

"Yes, they do," Allison said. "If they happened to Jesus and the Apostles and the saints over the last two thousand years, why can't they happen to me today?"

The men looked at each other silently. "Allison, I am Father Thomas, Bishop of the Sacred Heart," one of them said.

"Yes, sir."

"We would so much like to believe you." Folds of heavy skin hung from his elderly face. He ran his feeble fingers slowly through his thinning, white hair. Allison glanced at John Paul II on the wall, wondering if he would approve of his minions in Cincinnati mauling an innocent orphan. "Yet these types of miracles don't happen every day. They tend to come to those who have led devout lives or who have contributed significantly to the Church, ministering to the less fortunate. So, when a young girl such as yourself comes to us with these tales, the Church remains skeptical of the miracle."

"Father Thomas, respectfully sir," she stated with confidence. "First of all, I didn't come to the Church with this—I meant to keep it a secret because it is so scary to me. Second, isn't the Church supposed to believe in miracles? Isn't the Church supposed to be closest to Yahweh? And thirdly, I *am* devout and have helped the less fortunate—a lot! I helped them so much, you closed the mission." Stay cool, she told herself, stay cool. She wanted to bring up the Church-sanctioned profiteering taking place just north up I-75 at the ludicrous holy miracle at the Olympus oil terminal in Toledo, but decided against it.

Cadaver Smith flinched as if he wanted to push her back in her chair, bind her with rope and practice some good-old-fashioned cigarette torture on her. The archbishop's commanding eyes warned him to be still.

But then, as if possessed by a force she did not recognize, she spoke, "The truth is truth. The light is the light. And you do not frighten me, for I am Saint Allison, daughter of Yahweh, come to deliver the world from destruction."

The tribunal, except for Archbishop Sebastian, gasped and murmured at this defiant girl. Sebastian appeared amused. He ignored her statement of divinity.

"Allison, we must remain skeptical of this document until we have proof of its authenticity." No red-headed ragamuffin was going to best his emotion. "Over the years, many forgeries and hoaxes have been discovered by the Church. It is essential that we do everything we can to ensure the validity of what you are saying." With that he pulled out a manila folder from a desk drawer. He opened it slowly, as if previewing an ancient document. "The orphanage records indicate that you have a highly-active imagination, that you constantly pretend to be a spy, that you have been disciplined several times for daydreaming in class. You have had repeated incidents of misbehavior with authority figures such as Mother Superior, Sister Claudia, the Adler couple, and Sister Bernadette. And that you rose once in Mass and prayed to God for a cheeseburger . . ."

"Not true," said Allison. "I joked about it to my friends and everyone laughed. I didn't pray for one. And I absotively didn't rise to do it. It was a joke."

Sebastian was undeterred in reading her informal indictment. "And that you," he paused dramatically, "*ahem* . . . were recently discovered having sex with your female roommate. These details don't sound like the life of a saint to me. Rather, they portend to indicate that you are precocious and most unholy."

"Let he who is without sin cast the first stone," she said calmly. "Can any of you say that you never did any wrong? That all your thoughts are pure and all your actions chaste? Let the hypocrite run from the courtroom for judgment is not our right."

"We are not here to judge you, Allison," the archbishop lied. "We are here to help you deal with these fantasies so that some day you may lead a normal life."

"I have a normal life, sir; I just happen to be chosen."

"You have not had a normal life, child," Dr. Hastings, a previously silent inquisitor said. "You were orphaned and placed in an unfamiliar environment. It is common for children who have lost their parents to retreat into a world of make-believe, only to emerge with wild stories designed to gain attention. Young children need attention. Unfortunately, perhaps we didn't provide you with enough personal attention as we raised you."

Her freckles fused red in one large splotch of anger. "None of you men raised me. The nuns raised me. And I had plenty of attention. And I . . ."

"Hostile," said a formerly dumb member.

"Belligerent," chimed in another.

"Psychotic," said a third, silent hypocrite.

The rest of the proceedings were a sham. A lie detector test, which she passed, confirmed their actual suspicions that the document was authentic, but she was told she had failed. The most blatant abuse, designed to make her doubt herself, was when they produced Agnes, rewritten in someone else's hand, insisting it was the original. They had copied it, of course, as thousands of misguided monks over the last two millennia had done to suit their political purposes.

The words to *Agnostics:144* were changed, the details more fitted to the Church's liking. But it mattered not—the Church had no intention of letting the world know of the manuscript's existence. *Agnostics:144* would be flown to Rome, studied, then secured in the dusty catacombs below the Vatican and forgotten. And should anyone, by sheer chance, happen to find it, they would find the Catholic-friendly version suitable for Christians everywhere.

As Allison was shuttled to St. Als, she promised to herself in words so resolute they could never be broken, "They won't defeat me. I'm a prophet."

Fire unites with his sister, the air, in blazing splendor
Their union of incestuous smoke covers the dirty sheet of sky
Their charred love envelopes the Earth
Burning with uncontrolled, consuming passion

Chapter 44

November 1943

"It all comes down to energy." FDR's words from two nights prior echoed in Sulphur's ears as he waited for Colonel Bruce in his London office. The gray swirl of English climate, which seemed to buff the air like a steel wool pad, coupled with the tedium of a long transatlantic flight, made it a challenge for him to stay awake. The trip from Washington had been tortuous, but at least he hadn't traveled by ship.

On the journey to the States, he had arranged transport for several crates of the colonel's antiquities to be delivered to his home in Connecticut. A shipment of lesser, but still formidable size, was earmarked for Sulphur's mother's house. He hadn't been home in two years, and this trip would be no different. No sooner had he arrived in the nation's capital than President Roosevelt summoned him to the White House.

He was always exhilarated by FDR's invitations, knowing that he was one of only a handful of men to have a personal relationship with the most powerful man on Earth.

"He who controls the energy will win this war," FDR had said, lighting his trademark cigarette which extended out of its holder like an elegant handshake. "And he who controls the energy after the war, Sulphur, controls the world." FDR's eyes twinkled through the blue smoke.

"Yes, sir."

FDR sat forward in his wheelchair, a tartan-plaid woolen blanket draped over his useless legs. "There are two kinds of energy that matters, my boy." He grinned as he puffed at the wooden tip of his cigarette holder. "Oil and nuclear. Let's take the nuclear issue first. I understand you've drawn up some excellent plans for a sabotage operation on the Vemork facility."

"Yes, sir," Sulphur said with a pinch of pride. And indeed, he had worked hard on the plans as he shuttled around the Mediterranean, looting priceless artworks for himself and his OSS buddies, not to mention some well-placed senators and government bureaucrats. Truth be told, he had put in place a sophisticated ring of scavengers scouring the Middle East, Europe, and Asia Minor to supply the insatiable need of various diplomats, politicians, and military personnel. All in all, there were some twelve people working under his command with that sole directive.

On his flights with Buzz, the cargo hold filled with antiquities, he had studied maps and plans and intelligence reports from contacts deep inside Norway. He had boned up on his German and the necessary smattering of Norwegian. He was prepared, all right. He had selected his commandos. He had chosen his explosives. He had picked the drop points and the escape routes. He had thought of everything.

"Thing is," FDR hedged, "the Air Force wants one more crack at aerial bombardment before we send in your team."

His heart fell to the floor like an obese paratrooper without a chute. Prometheus, as Sulphur insisted on calling the operation, even though that code name had been rejected by OSS officials, was in jeopardy.

"If the air strikes work, we've accomplished the mission. If they don't, at most you've been delayed a couple of months," FDR continued.

Sulphur couldn't hide his disappointment.

Roosevelt read Sulphur's dismay and drew deeply on his fag. "Let me say this. This mission is vital, and it's time sensitive. We'll know in three days whether your mission is a go or not. Meantime, I want you to scoot over to Baghdad with this personal letter to Prince Abdullah." He brandished an ivory envelope with the White House seal. "Beautiful land, Iraq, from what I gather. Rich with oil. Problem is the military wanted to side with the Axis powers, so the British went in and straightened them out." FDR spoke casually, as if talking about an insignificant game of Scrabble. "Our goal is to keep them in line after the war. We need that oil, Sulphur. We don't want the British, the Soviets, or anyone else to get at it. That oil belongs to the seven sisters."

FDR's voice faded into the impenetrable depths of the spy's subconscience. Sulphur's heavy head bobbed, then jerked up slightly, as he waited for Bruce, half-asleep. The colonel believed in punctuality, but he himself, given the burdens and demands on his time, was seldom on time. Sulphur thought of the young, big-eared, buck-toothed lieutenant who had flown back to London with him. A man named Bill Casey. A nice enough fellow in a naive sort of way, sent to London to fight the Nazis through economic means. Casey's job, which he relayed too freely to Sulphur on the grueling flight across the Atlantic, was to determine the items the Krauts needed most and buy them before they could. Intuition told him that Bill Casey would go far in life. You can see it in his ears, Sulphur thought, sure at any moment he was going to conk right out in the colonel's chair. Casey's a listener. He studies people quietly, like a good spy should, then makes suggestions.

Colonel Bruce arrived just as Sulphur had drifted into sleep. "Commander in Chief has you going to Baghdad, huh?" the jovial colonel said as he tossed a file to the desk, plunked himself down in his chair and propped his feet up. Bruce put his hands behind his head and interlocked his fingers. He smiled. "Know what the penalty for arson is over in Iraq?"

"No, sir, I don't," Sulphur said.

"It's death by beheading. Those sheiks don't screw around."

"Is this important for me to know, sir?" He feigned his innocence. "Is this vital to the mission?"

The colonel shifted his commanding presence, swung his feet back to the floor, and sat forward. "Personally, I don't mind so much that you're destroying these churches. War is hell. But every time you torch one we have to mount a propaganda campaign to misdirect the investigation. It leads to bribes and all types of sordid ramifications. The blame has to go somewhere. Somebody has to pay for these things," Bruce said, as if having a discussion with his son about not bringing the car home too late. "Most often we can pin it on some deserving local scumsucker, but it's a distraction of our resources."

"I don't know what you're suggesting, Colonel," he lied. His thumb and index finger rubbed hard on a matchhead in his right pocket.

"You're a great agent. I'd be disappointed if you admitted it." The unflappable colonel raised an understanding eyebrow. "I'll make you a deal, Sulphur. Don't torch any churches while you're in Baghdad, and I'll give you a flame thrower and all the propellant you want. Deal? Oh, and see if you can bring back some Babylonian urns—something with some gods on it—Nabu or Gerra."

Meeting adjourned.

Chapter 45

November 10, 1990

Much has happened. So many changes since I last wrote. Two weeks gone. It could've been a year. Many mysteries uncovered; many more have replaced them. I know now (I should have realized it before) that Maya's appearance was not by chance. *The Journals* has me believing. It has me believing in many things I have long ignored—fate, God, consideration, the sanctity of life, the intricate inner weavings of life's seemingly insignificant events, many things.

A box of books arrived from Maya's mother two days after my last chemo round, from which I am just now regaining my strength. Rose jumped right into their content (the books, I mean) filling her head with alternative medicine, yoga, meditation, vegan recipes, and the like. She's determined to save me. In my convalescence over the last couple of weeks I've managed to read some, too. Interesting stuff. The most intriguing concept is Ayurveda. I devoured that book between bouts of uncontrollable fatigue. The book had a test, which I took. It says my mind-body type is a Pitta, just as Maya suggested. Basically, it means I tend to overwork, I'm too critical of others, I expect perfection, and I process information visually, which means I tend to write things down. The amazing thing is, it's accurate.

Rose is a Vata, more of a verbal person who expresses her worry through words. That's accurate, too. It sure sets the mind to wonder if there isn't a temple full of basic principles our Western culture has either suppressed or overlooked. I never thought I would admit it, but some of these New Age concepts make a helluva lot of sense. Along with the books came a letter from Dr. Shakti inviting me to call her to schedule an appointment. Much as I appreciate her gesture, Tucson is a bit far for me to go for a doctor's appointment. Rose, becoming ever more drawn into this new realm of belief, suggested I not dismiss it so outright. Her exact words were, "I would travel any distance necessary to save your life."

I've consumed bushels of parsley, gallons of green tea, and a health food store of myrrh capsules. I'm a new citizen of the New Age, whether I wanted to be or not. No doctor ever suggested anything to quell the noxious breath I'd acquired, and the traditional therapies administered by my oncologist have not succeeded in doing anything but making me nauseous, weak, and sick with flu-like symptoms. It just doesn't feel healthy. I hadn't counted on the toxicity of the last round of treatment. I slept fitfully and threw up for three days. My hair has fallen out in patches, so that the only cosmetically viable thing to do is shave my entire noggin. To make matters worse, the doctor informed me in his usual grave-side manner that my tumors were spreading and recommended surgery within the next few weeks. I told him in adamant terms that I was not letting him castrate me. Male ego, perhaps, but then he couldn't guarantee that it would stop the cancer either. He's throwing darts blindfolded at the board of my life.

The newspapers have done me no justice. Despite Rose's efforts to delay their onslaught, I've been crucified in the press. The paper has dredged up my past association with Gilday and the indictments for fraud, embezzlement, and kickbacks. I've heard through Bennett, my gregarious attorney, that I am fodder for many an AM talk-radio show. What I don't understand is how we Americans have sunken to such dismal lows of self-esteem and bombastic entertainment that we find comfort in listening to and supporting such nasty endeavors as talk radio. Is blame all this country is about?

On a brighter note, Mr. Bing, the inventor, came to offer his support last Saturday. As he sat in the solarium surrounded by my orchids, invited into our home for only the third time in twenty-two years, I realized I had misjudged the man. His serene, black eyes matched his jet-black hair. I had always considered him an Asian, a foreigner in our country, and, as such, I was probably guilty of prejudice against him. Turns out he was born in California, near the sight of the gold rush. He knew the factual account of poor John Sutter. All that gold and got nothing.

"I understand what you're going through," he said. "I was eight when my family was placed in an internment camp. It nearly killed my father. He had such pride. He loved America so much and didn't understand how he could be treated that way."

"That was a difficult time," I said. "People overreacted."

"Yes." Bing smiled kindly. "Just as now when people are accusing you of things. My father was an American, Robert. Born in Sacramento, California. They took his business, sold his house, forced us to live in camps. It was unjust." His eyes misted as recollections of his broken father filled his memory. "That is why I came over," he said. "Just to let you know that I don't agree with the mob mentality that forgets law in favor of wrong-headed assumptions. I don't know if you're guilty or innocent, Robert, but I believe in your innocence until it is otherwise proven."

"Thank you, Mr. Bing."

"Please, call me Mike." He grinned as he eyed my prized orchids, which seemed to stand a little taller, a little prouder with the news that not everyone in the Indian Hill social strata had forsaken me. Orchids are aristocrats you know, and they don't take being social pariahs very well.

"Mike, would you and Mrs. Bing care to grill out with us next weekend?" I extended a rare invitation to a man I had lived across from for over two decades. Maybe it was gratitude for somebody showing some compassion toward me, or maybe I had lived most of my life engulfed in the wrong friendships. Mike Bing, appreciative smile on his face, accepted. It's prudent at this juncture (George Bush has been on TV a lot lately with his Desert Shield justification) to mention that Rose and Mrs. Bing, I don't recall her first name, have been friends for years. It is I who have been delinquent.

Not a minute after I closed the door behind the only friend I had in the whole neighborhood, the phone rang. It was Parker with news from Tucson. The trip to New Orleans had netted some good, but disturbing, leads—information that Parker didn't wish to share over the phone.

"Weird things are happening, R.T.," he said suspiciously. "We're being followed. I did manage to find an address where Allison may be staying. Did you find out anything from Billy Harper?"

"No. He asked me to have Danny call if I found him, so that's a dead end."

"Tell him about my dream," Maya said in the background.

"Oh, yeah," Parker laughed. "Maya had a dream about Danny and Allison."

"Really?"

"Yeah, it was rather vague, but she insists it was an omen of some sort."

"Give me that," Maya demanded playfully as she wrestled the phone away.

"Astarte bewitch me, R.T., it was wild." Her buoyant voice picked up my spirits. "I saw them in a barn, laughing. They were carrying a ladder. Oh, and there was this fire."

My skin went cold, then flushed warm. Barn? Ladder? Fire? It was them! Danny and Allison had pulled the ladder out of the Captain's Quarters! That strange night began to make sense. That ever-present feeling I had was the two of them watching me. But this new realization was also troubling. Were they trying to help or hurt? First blush said hurt.

"R.T.?" Maya said. "Are you there?"

I relayed the events of the Mulciber fire to the both of them as they shared the receiver. They reminded me of two junior-high-school girls giddy with conversation. I told them to come home; Rose had a plan. We made arrangements for a late afternoon dinner the following Sunday. Maya insisted on vegetarian. Bennett will be here as well. It'll be less than a week before the big press conference.

"R.T.," Parker said, "tomorrow will be an exciting day."

Indeed, the following day was exciting, for Parker's overnight package was delivered at 9:30 in the morning. The world was at work. Rose was at the grocery, buying ingredients for the numerous Ayurvedic dishes she decided I simply must try.

556

She has convinced herself that diet can save my life. I'll admit I've started reading the package labels with more caution. I can't believe the stuff that's in there. Twinkie hadn't been home since Friday, something she hasn't done since the unfortunate demise of her marriage to Parker. I couldn't seem to escape Brian McBain's political spots. Much as I'm more sympathetic to him since that disastrous Mulciber night, I can't be openly warm to the guy who seeks election on the promise of my prosecution.

In my convalescence after the chemo, I could do nothing but watch TV, spoil my orchids, and putter about the house. (And research the imminent Gulf War.) McBain's television commercials drove me insane. Two seconds into them and I had to switch the dial. I must say the state of American TV is appalling. Sports. Violence. Soap operas laced with back-stabbing, double-dealing characters. Talk shows that dredge up the most bizarre creatures from this country's bowels. It's all so much tripe.

So the package arrived. I hadn't expected it. What's more, once I saw the return address from an unfamiliar name in Tucson, Arizona, I was all the more intrigued. There was a letter inside, short and sweet as they say.

> Dear R.T.,
>
> Hel . . . low Swami, Maya and I have made much progress. But I'm afraid this case goes deeper than we first thought. We have been followed in New Orleans and Tucson. I haven't figured out who's so interested in us. There's two possibilities—the Diamond Trust Bank, or the paramilitary wing of a Catholic faction called Opus Dei, but that's a wild guess on my part. For security reasons—I didn't want to say it on the phone—I have mailed you the address of Allison's last known whereabouts in Cincinnati—144 St. Agnes Court, Fort Wright, Kentucky. If your strength holds up, you may want to check it out. Maya and I will be back Saturday, but our flight gets in late.
>
> Best regards,
> Parker & Maya
>
> p.s.—Your phones are probably tapped.

I was a mix of feelings, an emotional beef stew. I was elated to have a solid lead to Allison, but sickened with the meaning of Parker's p.s. My phones are tapped. Outrage tromped on my temples. Who was behind it? McBain? Rense? There was another document in the overnight envelope with a note that read— "Can you believe Bush has doubled the number of troops in Saudi Arabia without telling the American public? Looks like war for King George. Blood for oil." The note was attached to an edition of the *Eastern Crescent Review*. It was signed 'M.'

I stared at the note for awhile, then scanned the *Eastern Crescent's* headlines, then the note again. Maya is the most amazing creature. I had been neglectful in asking her about the 'M' mailings in all the euphoria of *The Journals* revealing itself, plus the Gulf War seems so distant, so it doesn't touch us personally. The research has been fun. It's like being a spy.

But more questions than answers shot across my dendrites and fired volleys into my synapses. How is it that Maya started sending me news on the Persian Gulf before we ever met? Why would she do such a thing anyway? How could she know my interest? What exactly was the connection? Did she see something I didn't? There's more to this woman than I know.

Yet that wasn't *all* the events of the previous two weeks, not even close. We've only made it to Monday, the 5th of November at this point. There was still the matter of Allison's last known address, a prospect I could not put out of my mind, and there was the upcoming election, which was sure to be a curious spectacle. I don't know what came over me—a burst of adrenaline, an overwhelming desire to rid myself of the charges against me, or a burning desire to find Danny and Allison—but suddenly I was alive with renewed energy. I dressed quickly, scribbled Rose a note telling her where I was going, and headed for St. Agnes Court.

The fact that Parker said my phones might be tapped caught my attention. An intense feeling of violation stitched its way, without anesthetic, through my wounded mind as I drove to Fort Wright. Anger. Fear. Depression. Contempt. All these feelings left a trail of anxiety across my cerebellum. The idea that someone wanted *The Journals* suppressed added a touch of intrigue to the whole affair. It was a sensation I hadn't felt in many years.

My stomach did somersaults as my car wound its way above the city along the twisting curves of Dixie Highway. Would Allison be there? What would I say to her? Hope was crowded out by pragmatism. It couldn't be this easy. As I motored on in the perfect fall day, brown and yellow leaves falling like snow across the road from the few trees spared from development, I surmised that finding her wouldn't solve my problems at all. Sure, it may shorten the research cycle to complete my tasks for *The Journals*, but if that was the only purpose, why didn't the Council arrange for Allison and Danny to meet me several months ago?

Sometimes it takes an entire existence for a man to begin to find the truth. Sometimes it takes drastic circumstance to get him to search for it. Sometimes, once the questions begin to come, they won't stop. The truisms, the depth of reason, begin to sparkle and shimmer like a billion stars in a crisp, autumn evening, each star a brilliant thought, each one connected. Sometimes it takes a man awhile to accept the blessing.

St. Agnes Court was a street of modest red brick and wood homes constructed in the early sixties. Each house had a simple front porch to provide relief from the elements. Houses aren't built this way anymore. People don't sit on front porches and participate in the world. They sit inside in air-conditioning with TV dinners and watch the tube. If people wished to analyze the decline in family values, I'd put my money on the glass breast we call television. We need more front porches. More people on them.

The neighborhood was well-kept, prim, green yards edging toward winter brown. Flower boxes with withered evidence of summer not long past. I parked in front of 144, killed the engine, and sat staring at the humble house. I checked the rearview mirror to see if I was being followed, Parker's warning fresh in my mind. The coast was clear as I stepped up the walk. Allison's house was smartly painted, lavender with dark plum trim. The postage-stamp yard was well kept, the walk clean.

I looked toward the picture window for signs of life. My heart tripped on itself, stumbled, caught itself, lifted up in joy, then did an elated backflip. Could it be? I walked faster. Could it? Yes! There, in the window, soaking in the remnants of an Indian summer, its blooms displayed proudly to the sun god, was a gorgeous, purple orchid. Seraph. I nearly giggled like a schoolboy at the sight. "Allison lives here," I said, aloud.

Rap. Rap. Rap. I knocked on the door. No answer. I pushed the bell twice, hearing the chime resonate through the small dwelling. A screen door squeaked on an adjacent porch.

"You won't find nobody there," an elderly black woman said. A large swath of tangelo and mustard sunflower fabric, more parachute than dress, flowed over her large figure. "You too old for that girl anyways, boy. Don't you got a wife?"

"Excuse me?"

"She ain't been here in a long time." She served a smile of large white teeth. "Last anyone seen a Allison, she was leaving with some boy. Good looking fellow with a smile make you melt—and eyes that show you the stars."

"Where . . . where did she go?" My elation flattened like roadkill.

"Don't know," the woman shrugged, her loose gown fluttering like a flock of geese ready for flight. "He wasn't like all them others—she love him—he was her love. She still pay the rent though. Got a lease and she say she never break a promise no matter what. No sir. That Allison is an angel. She send a check right on time every month—set a watch by it."

"When did she leave?" My eyes alternated between the large, black woman and Seraph, the ageless flower. I was mesmerized by the fabled orchid.

"Why you asking?"

"I'm a friend. Why?"

"With all the peoples been buzzing around since the fire, I was wondering if you was the police or something."

"No." I laughed nervously as I scuffed the toe of my shoe on the cement porch. "Who's been around?"

"The church peoples," she told me. "And two dark-glasses-and-burr-hair-cut-folk—secret agents or something. You know, the kind that don't never smile and wears sunglasses even though it's raining. Cops came, too."

"Why were the police here?"

"Cause I called them when I saw prowlers sneaking around Allison's place. Cops didn't catch them, though. Funny how it was the same day as those secret agents. I think it was them snooping round. Something like a Watergate break-in." She laughed. "You got a name?"

"Robert Stone."

"Oh mighty God, Mr. Stone! I'm Mrs. Perkins, Mae Perkins," she said, her arms flailing in excitement. "I got a letter for you from Allison."

"What!"

"You got some ID?" her eyes narrowed. "After all the secret goings on, I'm not going to hand it over to just anybody."

"Sure," I said, pulling my wallet from my trousers. I stretched from Allison's porch to hers.

She eyed the drivers license, then me, and gave it back. "She said you'd be coming by. I'll go get it. Come on over and sit on my porch."

The portly Mrs. Perkins quickly disappeared inside her tiny home. I made myself comfortable on her swing and gazed out over the breathtaking Cincinnati skyline, the sun breaking midday across the skyscrapers. She returned a few minutes later with a serving tray, holding the letter and two steaming cups of hot chocolate.

"Here you go, Mr. Stone. Any friend of Allison's is a friend of mine." She handed me the letter and the drink. "I know the day's a-might warm for hot cocoa, but it's November and I can't wait no more. Made with real milk and chocolate syrup. I don't go for that powdered stuff. Ask me, I'd say we's getting away from a natural world. It ain't God's way."

"It looks delicious." I blew on the surface of the sweet, brown liquid.

Mrs. Perkins shook her head and beamed. "That girl is the sweetest thing. Everybody in the neighborhood love her. Do you know she give me the most delicious home grown tomatoes and cucumbers? That girl grows things like nobody I seen." She talked on as I ripped open the letter. My heart pounded. I was only vaguely aware of Mrs. Perkins' chatter.

Dear Mr. Stone,

We're absotively sorry about everything you've been going through, but please know that in the end it will all be worth it. This letter is to express our faith in you, to say that we are entrusting our story in your capable hands. We know you will tell the tale brilliantly for all the world to see.

Since you have found your way to Mrs. Perkins you must be deeply involved in our lives by now. Fate has a way of bringing people together. We're also sorry about pulling the ladder prank on you—we really didn't know there was going to be a fire and you'd be in danger. It is rather symbolic, don't you think?

Evenwise, we have only one bit of advice to give along with our encouragement. The purpose isn't to find us—it's to find yourself. You can accomplish this through *The Journals*. Once you do that, the Council of Ancients will set you free.

Also, the closer you come to finding us, the more danger you create. There are those who wish us harm. There are those who would do anything to stop this story from coming out. Beware of Opus Dei.

Please believe that your only true goal is to get *The Journals* written and published. That has been your assignment since birth. It is your dharma. We have faith in you, Mr. Stone. Namasté.

Your Friends of Fate,

Allison and Danny

p.s.—Would you please take care of Seraph for me?

I weakly set the letter on the swing, dazed, lost in thought about its message. Time slipped away as I sat contemplating the words. The purpose is to find myself—of course. All the while I'm looking for them so they can clear my name, but they can't anyway. All they can do is help me tell the story. I have to live up to my obligation to the Council. I had already concluded most of this, but reading it from Allison and Danny made it tangible, like a second opinion from a doctor. Although the current state of the medical industry leads me to believe a third, fourth, perhaps fifth opinion is necessary.

"Everythin' all right, Mr. Stone?" Mrs. Perkins asked. "You white as a Klansman."

"Oh . . . yeah, sure," I said. "How did you get this letter?"

"Came with the last rent check—five days ago." She smiled and sipped her chocolate.

"Any return address?" I realized I was ignoring the kids' advice not to pursue them. "Nevermind. When was the last time you saw her?"

"She disappeared the night of the fire." Mrs. Perkins gestured down the hill toward the river. There it was, the charred remains of the Cosmic Club, a burnt-out skeleton of what it had been. "What a sight that was too! Everybody in the neighborhood quit watching that Iraq-Kuwaiti crap, excuse my French, and came out for the fire instead. Burned all night long, too. Smoke everywhere, flames shooting into the sky, lucky nobody was killed, thank the Lord.

"She was gone for three days after that. The whole street worried sick about her—wondering if she was hurt or killed. She was a waitress down there, you know?"

She was? Allison worked at the C.C.? Damn. The detail in life's weave pulled a little tighter, a stitch more intricate.

"Then she come back with that boy, Danny, late one night, packed some stuff, said her goodbyes to everybody, and left. Said not to tell no one what was going on. Then this letter come and you shows up—ain't that a funny coincidence?"

"Fate, Mrs. Perkins," I said, picking up my hot chocolate. "Pure and simple fate."

I showed Rose the letter. It's hard to tell these days who is more into *The Journals* and its mystical implications, me or Rose. She reread the manuscript, making notes, preparing her questions for the day the book returns. Rose is drawn deeper and deeper into the open-mindedness that runs freely through the New Age movement. Funny thing, as Rose pointed out, it isn't so much a movement as an awareness of enlightened people to be open to new possibilities, new ways of thinking. Whatever New Age is, Rose contends it's simply a label; it encourages folks to be accepting and tolerant of other opinions. Say alleluia to that. Most religions could use a good dose of that philosophy.

My dear wife spent most of Monday night with me discussing *The Journals*, calculating the impact of our upcoming press conference, nurturing our new found beliefs. It was so liberating. As Rose described it, "A great cloud has lifted from the shoreline revealing a beautiful landscape that I had never seen before."

By late Tuesday, the euphoria was still with us, dampened only by the serious drubbing Brian McBain took in the election. Even though an adversary in the courtroom, I was becoming fond of the guy, the perpetual loser who never quits. I also felt pity for the clumsy D.A. with the bad suit and no clue to reality. The worst part of McBain's defeat was that he lost in a landslide to a councilman who had been reported to have beaten his wife and was caught in a seedy hotel room with two hookers. As an added insult, McBain had barely held second place, albeit a distant second, against Mimi Flume, former topless dancer turned dry cleaner tycoon. To Mimi's credit, she parlayed her "dancing" tips into a sound investment of laundering the city's suits. Soon her cleaning operation was taking in more money than her nightly gyrations, and she bought another location. Next thing anyone knows, it's five years later and she owns twelve stores and is grossing two and a half million a year.

When Mimi Flume held a press conference in her old uniform, that is to say, a brightly spangled but sparse outfit which amply displayed her talents, and announced that, "If elected, I will work to restore strip clubs to their former prestige." Well, she took votes away from the law-and-order message of the assistant D.A. Much to McBain's misfortune, she also advocated the legalization of marijuana.

Pundits said that Mimi's position on social issues was the most forthright political campaign anyone had seen in the tri-state area in several decades. So, the McBain campaign took it on the chin. I imagined Twinkie's sadness as I watched the results flicker by on the tube. She hadn't been home in five days, and I was starting to miss her. I even missed her Jell-O recipes. I hoped she was all right.

What the ramifications of McBain's political losses to my case would be, no one could say. Would he seek revenge and go after me with renewed vigor? Would he back off a bit since the election was over, and he no longer needed the publicity? Who knew? Not me, and I didn't like the uncertainty.

Then Rose, always the rock of the Stone family, made the best suggestion of the night. "Why don't we change the channel and see if we can find *The Journals?*"

Summer 1983

Allison's removal to the east wing, which she mistook to be a temporary situation, was marked by an odd regimen of constant surveillance and ritual. She had been isolated for twelve days, undergoing a battery of idiotic tests before she was allowed to get back to any state of normalcy.

Those twelve days followed a pattern that caused her to empathize even further with the former Iranian hostages. The persistent rumor she had heard that Reagan had allowed the hostages to be held in Iran two months longer than necessary, incensed her. Now, under similar circumstance for something she couldn't control—a sacrosanct communication from the ether—she knew exactly what losing freedom meant. She concluded that the Catholic Church, or at least the Diocese of Cincinnati, was completely out of touch with reality. Her faith in her religion—until this point, most devout—was being seriously challenged in her revolutionary mind.

The first twelve mornings began by her peeing into a plastic cup—to measure her hormones, she supposed. All the while, loud banging, sawing, and hammering permeated the walls of the east wing. (The 88s had hurriedly moved their cadre of stolen stash to the far end of the second floor, as far from the intruders as possible. This did not stop them from visiting their former hideout, since The 88s were preoccupied with the exact disposition of St. Als' resident angel—Allison Leslie Pippin. Word of her captivity and gossip of her resistance raised her fame to heights approaching idolatry. Had Allison known of the worship, she would not have approved. But, we all need our heroes.)

After she tinkled in the cup, Dr. Temple would come in for a daily physical of probes and pokes. Allison was certain he spent far too much time inside her blouse, which now covered her two symmetrical peaches, slightly upturned at the nipples. One could imagine the accelerated thumpity-thump of Temple's heart as he pressed his scope against her tender, freckled flesh.

Hastings the shrink came after Dr. Temple. Hastings Allison found even more disinterested in his job. She soon deduced that Hastings was an unhappy man bored with life. "Strange," she called him. He, like the rest of the Ghost Squad, when she mentioned it, refused to acknowledge the source of the incessant noises coming from somewhere within the east wing.

Hastings was followed by Parish, the paranormal ESP component of the Governing Order of Divinity—Division of Apparitions, Miracles & Nuisances. Mildly disappointed that he could illicit no evidence of telepathic traits from her, Allison suggested that they play gin rummy instead, which they did for the forty-five minutes of his sessions, amid the pounding hammers.

The last of the creatures of the Ghost Squad to grill her, a man who viewed the previous regimens of the others as a waste of time, was Cadaver Smith. He occupied his allotted period with specific questions relating to the aforementioned *Agnostics:144*. She found this ironic and hypocritical, for if Agnes was not written by her, and it was not from God, why ask questions about it at all? Cadaver Smith scoffed and looked away without answering that query from our young heroine.

She had guessed that in the initial twelve days she had been asked ten thousand questions. The true number was 3,716. Still, a formidable burden for a scared fifteen-year-old child.

The afternoons took on a bizarre religious tone as the sisters took turns reading Bible passages in half-hour shifts to her. After two hours of this, Allison went on quiet walks with Sister Dena (shells littering the ground like black robed priests hurdled out of heaven) who knew the thing Allison needed most after all the pressure of the morning sessions was silence. They spoke little. Dinner was served in Allison's room, the food much better than the grub she had been fed when she was in with the St. Als' masses. With dinner digested, she was allowed supervised work in the garden. She loved this part of the day. Watering, weeding, digging, fingernails in the dirt. The smell of earth in her nostrils melted away the stress of the overbearing scrutiny.

Five days into the first twelve days, she found a love note from Mary secretly stashed under a head of lettuce. Her heart was uplifted. Mary was thinking of her. Allison delivered a reply, written after Sister Dena fell asleep, under the same leafy-green head the following day.

At night she was hooked up to a machine measuring her brain waves. She became accustomed to electrodes glued to her scalp. With the EEG scratching its news on continuous sheets of paper, Allison would kneel beside her bed and pray. "Please God, take all this away. Let things return to normal." She prayed for many things—Mary's love, an end to American interference in Latin America, for a family to take her away from St. Als—many things.

One day, the thirteenth day, the Governing Order of Divinity—Division of Apparitions, Miracles & Nuisances failed to appear. Allison so wanted to return to the St. Als' population and was dismayed when she discovered the results of the constant sounds she had been hearing for almost two weeks. She was presented, in rather clumsy style by Mother Peculiar and the other sisters, her new, *permanent* apartment. She would share it with Sister D.

The apartment itself was finely appointed in her favorite colors, new furniture, her own bedroom, a television, and a bookshelf loaded with the classics. Beige and earth tones highlighted the plush shag carpeting. A refrigerator, a microwave oven, and a dishwasher adorned the gleaming kitchen. Suspecting that Allison may not appreciate her imprisonment, Mother Superior tried to soothe the shock of her isolation by giving her an "Instant Karma" tape. Evidently, the Church's angry, album-burning response to Lennon's "the Beatles are bigger than Jesus" comment from years earlier had been forgiven. She appreciated the sentiment of the tape, and played it over and over, but she had graduated to a new favorite song—"Shine On You Crazy Diamond," by Pink Floyd. The sisters did not know. In another attempt to appease her, the proud nuns glowed as they showed Allison her own bathroom with peach, monogrammed towels. She sat on the toilet and cried.

It was at this moment, with tears of utter defeat streaming down her freckled face, with Sister Dena stroking her vibrant red hair to soothe her, that Allison began planning her escape. She would take her time. She would conspire and plot but, when the moment was right, she would leave St. Als and never look back.

The nuns, conspiring with the Church, decided to distract her from her visions and visitations by setting up a nonstop schedule of tennis tournaments. This scheme had many benefits—it would keep Allison away from the influence of the other St. Als kids who might fill her head with ideas of running away, it would keep her too busy and tired (they hoped) to receive any further transmissions from the great beyond, it afforded them grand exposure within the Church hierarchy as their tennis star earned victories around the Midwest, and, finally, they received fifty percent of the take from her winnings. Greed and self-serving interests won out over the Lord Almighty.

So the stagnant smog of summer blew into fall as Allison and Sister Dena journeyed far and wide to every tennis tournament they could enter. Allison was unaware of the strategy employed against her and loved the time on the road outside St. Als. She adored Sister Dena and the conversations they had. Sister Dena had not been successful in convincing the Church to handle matters differently; all she could do now was be the best friend she could to Allison. Both Allison and Dena benefited from the relationship.

Allison would read newspapers while Dena drove, with Allison relating the latest outrage of the Reagan administration. "Their blatant disregard for human rights is just sick!" she said on the way to Chicago one dreary afternoon. "His Latin American policy is a bunch of crud. He wants to expand the role of the CIA down there, even though the presidents of Colombia, Panama, Mexico, and Venezuela issued a statement expressing *profound concern for the rapid deterioration of Latin America.* We're spending millions to subvert democracy. Jesus with a bazooka aimed at the Vatican, what are we doing?"

Because of her isolation and the nuns' scrutiny, she was uncertain if her scathing letters to her congressmen—imploring them to stop the madness in El Salvador and Nicaragua—were getting by her Catholic censors. So, in typical defiance, she mailed as many as she could from the road, out of the reach of their sheepish clutches. Sister Dena had, after two years of intensified closeness with Allison, come to appreciate and agree with her political zeal. Sister Dena even planned to vote for whomever the Democratic nominee was in 1984, regardless of his position on abortion. That's how much Dena's opinions had changed since she and Allison had taken to the road.

During two-day pit stops at the orphanage for rest and recovery between tournaments, Allison exchanged love letters with Mary. They wrote almost weekly, confessing their devotion and longing. The letters brightened an already "absotively positive" Allison. Sometimes what we want most is that which we can't have. Allison, undisputed spymaster of St. Als, tried on several occasions to visit Mary, but something always seemed to get in the way—rain, Sister D reading late, or Mary fast asleep, oblivious to Allison's tapping at her window.

October 15 brought a bemused response from Allison regarding the publishing of a new gender-neutral Bible that the Lutheran and Greek Orthodox churches immediately denounced as irrelevant. A male-centric Bible is just fine, they said. Allison thought it irrelevant also, but did not overlook the sexist nature of the two churches' reactions. She found their discrimination most unholy. Her beef was with the fact that she had been in possession of new Bible verses which had been summarily dismissed by the Church. As she lay on her bed and stewed about the news, she thought of *Agnostics:144* and its message. She could see how the government, especially under that traitor

Reagan, favored the interests of business over the common good of the people. She laughed at her sudden seriousness, "Jesus shaving his head and practicing Zen, I'm starting to sound like a Marxist."

Soon the tournament season lightened up, and time (always a friend of memory) once again softened the Church's fears. Allison regularly found herself in her apartment with Sister Dena. In the collective mind of the Church, the crisis had passed; no more written correspondences from the Lord, no visions, no dreams of popes in jeopardy, nothing. The red alert was relaxed, although Allison was still separated from the others.

What the junta of St. Als didn't know was that the Red Angel had been expertly traversing the fire escapes, peering in windows, listening to conversations, watching sexual trysts between interesting combinations of people. She hadn't forgotten Mother Peculiar's mysterious late-night phone call and the reference to "the girl." Allison was determined to find out who "the girl" was. She had overheard many new references to "the girl" when her espionage activities had resumed. There was a man, Winston Held III, who Mother always seemed to press for money. Allison thought if she could track him down, she could uncover the identity of "the girl." What the junta also didn't know was that Allison was biding her time, casing the orphanage, planning her eventual departure.

She had the cash to leave St. Als, but not the age. The tennis season was sporadic now, but as she counted her winnings from the spring, summer, and fall she realized $9,200 sat in her plump bank account just down the street from the Mission de Cincinnatus. Ah yes, the mission; she had even managed to donate two thousand dollars to that worthy cause. She had never forgotten the homeless. She never would. Yes, she had the cash to leave, more money than most working people save after ten years; that wasn't the problem—the fact that she was only fifteen was.

Besides, Allison loved Dena and couldn't bear the thought of hurting her. She also delighted in the sweat and adrenaline of tennis, the power of her serves, the ecstasy of victory, the confidence she felt on the court. She decided to wait until the conditions were right before leaving St. Als. The fall of 1983 was premature.

Emotional distress nearly caused her to run from St. Als on Halloween night. Her heart had ached too long. She could wait for Mary no longer. Sister Dena and the rest of the nuns were snoozing soundly when Allison stole her way along the fire escape to Mary's room. Cautiously, she peered into her lover's abode. It was dark. Only the green glow of the Catholic-issue digital clock lit the room. She tried the window. It was locked. She tapped lightly on the glass. No response. Mary wasn't in her room. Where was she?

Allison had turned to go when the light suddenly flicked on. It was Mary. Allison

smiled, her heart joyous at seeing her roommate of so many years. "We'll be lovers again," she whispered to herself as she lifted an impatient hand to gently rap her knuckles on the glass. Before she could, Mary turned around, her back to the window and put her arms around . . .

What was this? Allison's hand fell to her side as her heart hurled itself off the second floor fire escape.

Unknown arms slipped around Mary's waist. Mary laughed and pulled the person into the room. They fell giggling to the bed. Allison watched broken-hearted as Mary's tongue raced inside Davy Jensen's mouth. Mary was making out with a boy.

Allison spent Thanksgiving playing the 6th annual Thanks, Turkey, and Tennis Tournament in Washington D.C., called the 3T by most. She played well, coming in second with a purse of eight hundred dollars. She and Sister Dena visited the Mall and saw the Lincoln Memorial, mouths agape at the immensity of the statue, and the Washington Monument. She had wanted to see the Jefferson Memorial, but time wouldn't allow it.

Allison thought of Danny as they drove by the Mint, snippets of his forgery schemes drifting through her mind. She wondered about him, but not with the intensity of previous years. Time fades and so do hopes. And dreams.

On the way back to Cincinnati, she confided to a laughing Sister Dena that she was psyched-up in the tournament by the thought of smashing a screamer off every politician's head who voted against the Equal Rights Amendment. "What a bunch of pig-headed politicians we have," she steamed. "The whole system is corrupt."

Sister Dena slapped the steering wheel. "You sure are a fireball of activism. With an attitude like that, you'll change the world some day."

"Agnes had it right," Allison said. "It's a boys' club, with the first thief, Commerce, calling the shots."

December 25, 1983

"Can she hear us?"

"Is she all right?"

"Dear God, save us all."

"Shh . . . you'll scare the angel."

"Has anyone called the archbishop?"

568

"Mother is on the phone now."

"Dear Jesus, how can this be happening?"

"Our Father Who art in Heaven. Hallowed be Thy name. Thy kingdom come. Thy will be done on Earth—"

"Shh . . . she's stirring."

"Allison?" Sister Dena gently shook her young charge. "Seed, honey," she said, her voice fraught with concern. "Wake up, angel."

"Where am I?" Allison mumbled, her hair tousled and damp with sweat.

"In your bed, angel," Sister D said. "What's your name, dear?"

"Allison, silly." She smiled and sat up, rubbing sleep from her eyes. The room was filled with albino-faced nuns kneeling on the floor around her bed, trembling hands folded in prayer. More nuns rife with worry crammed the doorway. Sister D sat at her side. It was four-thirty in the morning.

"Does she have a fever?" Barney asked, placing a clammy palm on Allison's forehead, her nose nearly jabbing her in the eye. Everyone seemed to hang motionless for the response. "Nope—feels normal." The room sighed collective relief.

Allison knew why the sisters were cloistered in her room, huddled in fear like the Second Coming was upon them and they weren't sure they were going to make the cut. Sorry, you're ten Hail Marys short. But it wasn't the Second Coming. It was another dream. An Allison dream. "The last thing I remember was reading *Silent Seraph* in the living room with Sister." She nodded toward her guardian. "Like we do every Christmas Eve."

Barney produced a cool washcloth and placed it on Allison's forehead. "This will help you, Seed," she said with a single, smooth kneel-and-genuflect combination. Years of practicing rituals had produced a legion of obedient servants skilled at cutting ecumenical corners.

A few sisters backed away from the door as Mother Peculiar squeezed into the room.

"What did they say?" Sister Dena asked.

"They'll be here by 6:00 a.m." Mother looked away. In the dark morning of artificial light, before the sun could put on its face, Mother Peculiar's edifice was strikingly frightful. A stony scowl ripped by a marbleized gray swatch of hair, hanging like a stalactite over craggy eyes, more like caves buried by rockslide than eyes.

"Who will be here? Who's coming?" Allison asked. She drew her knees to her chest. "Not the Ghost Squad."

Sister D bit her lip. No one spoke.

"Sisters," Mother ordered crisply, "leave us with the child. Bernadette, please get the tape."

The child—she was now called *the child*. The nuns shuffled out of the apartment, mumbling Hail Marys and Praise Gods as overwrought expressions froze on their predawn faces. Sister Dena squeezed Allison tight. It was a hug of compassion and fear, love and anxiety.

"You went into a trance last night," Sister Dena explained, as she rubbed Allison's forearm.

"I met God," Allison said. "He was very nice."

"Yes, I'm sure He was." Sister Dena's eyes welled with tears. She cried in joy and desperation. She knew what would happen next. Mr. Cadaver Smith and his Ghost Squad were descending like vultures on St. Als even as they spoke.

Barney came back in the room, holding a cassette recorder in her shaking hands, a Christmas gift given by a private donor for the kids' amusement. They had decided to record the reading of *Silent Seraph* as much as a test of the device's functionality as a desire to document the tradition of St. Als' Christmas Eves. It was a most fortuitous decision. For whom, it wasn't apparently clear. For humankind, perhaps.

"Play it," Mother commanded.

Barney had difficulty plugging into the outlet as her quivering hands refused to let her line up the holes. Finally she inserted the plug.

"Allison," said Sister Dena. "This is a tape we made when you were . . . um—"

"Possessed!" Mother Peculiar said. "Possessed."

Sister Dena shot her a glaring frown. "When you had your vision."

Mother Peculiar's language startled Allison. Those words were normally reserved for demonic allegations, not for sweet fifteen-year-old angels. The hair on her arms stood on end. Her heart knocked hard against her sternum, demanding to get out before the trouble started.

"If you don't mind," Sister D suggested, "we'd like to play the tape back to you before they get here."

"Cadaver Smith . . . I mean Mr. Smith and Hastings and those guys?" Allison's voice wavered. "I'm scared," she whimpered, drawing her legs tighter until they pressed smugly against her perspiring breasts.

"For your own good, Yvonne," said Mother Peculiar in a moment of kindness. "You must listen to this before they arrive. It will help to prepare you for their questions."

"She's right." Barney pressed PLAY on the recorder.

"Don't be afraid, angel." Sister Dena brushed back a lock of Allison's bright hair. "It's disconcerting at first."

The tape scratched its Dolby-muffled tone as it prepared to unveil its message. Allison had just finished the last line of *Silent Seraph* to a group of mesmerized children.

"Does anyone here believe in angels?" she asked the eager youngsters as she closed the book.

An unabashed round of "I do's" rang out.

"Me, too. I'm sure of it. My first Christmas here, an angel brought me an orchid. See . . ." A long pause ensued as the tape crackled. *Oohs* and *ahs* from the little lambs.

A strange silence followed. Ten seconds. Twenty. Thirty. A minute. The tape rolled on. "Allison, are you okay?" Sister Dena asked.

"I feel funny. I'm absotively flushed."

"I see white around her," four-year-old Molly squeaked.

Then Allison spoke, her voice changed—smoother, calmer, otherworldly. And this is what she said:

> 45 And in His second visitation the Great One did descend to speak through His daughter. He did reassure His Earthly saint of her place amongst the people and He did whisper unto her soul and she was relieved of all doubt.

> 46 And Yahweh kissed His daughter with the grace of His compassion, and she did slightly turn in unconscious acknowledgment. And Yahweh smiled upon His daughter, sweetness and beauty sent to help her dying mother. The fire of the sun He did sprinkle in her hair, and the green of the forest did sparkle in her eyes.

> 47 The Celestials called her Annis the Forgiver, but by her Earth name she was known as Allison. And Allison was purity. And Allison was innocence come unto a world made corrupt by itself, and Yahweh was saddened, for He alone knew that the corruption was His. He had made it so. He cried a slow tear upon His daughter's silken cheek for He knew she alone would hear the call of the fallen.

> 48 It must be so, dear Allison, that you render sanity back to the children of Man. It must be so, dear Allison, that you, too, must suffer as did My Son, that you may destroy the evil I thought so many millenniums past.

> 49 For My thinking of the evil has created the darkness, and its empty vastness is the crux of My essence. It must be so, that I share the burden for all suffering along with My children. Therefore, I must end the misery of My children and heal My wife with My hands.

50 Verily, it is My light that shall conquer the dark and cease the torment. And My light shall flash brighter than a hundred-million-billion suns unto the ether. No world shall stand, lest that which has heeded My Word. And in the ashes by the dawning lies My sorrow on the ground.

51 My flame shall burn those who have not used their ears. And My flame shall warm those who have listened with their heart. And My flame shall be the light that dispels the darkness forever.

52 These words I whisper unto My Allison that she may prepare the world for the inevitable. So said, I may cry, for it is known that few will heed the call of the fallen. And many will be trampled again as the doors of My kingdom are opened. For in the rush to the Master's chamber many have forsaken their souls on the dusty road of sin.

53 And sin is of definition, variable to all spirit. It is transient and helpless in its morals. And I will not judge thee, for you have mistakenly taken such tasks upon yourselves. And in doing so, you will convict all whom you deem unfit. But the mirror of the righteous is reflected in pious hypocrisy.

54 I say, learn well from your actions. Learn well from your friends. Seek to recover the innocence lost at birth and shed the garment of blame cast out by your institutions. And, should you examine your wisdom, you shall discover that the answers to your questions are not found in school.

55 Thus said, the tale be started that I now reveal the life of the second thief: And in parallel time to Commerce, did Education stand and say, "Follow me, for I am wisdom, therefore I am truth. And in my books which have been scribed with countless precision you shall find all you need to know."

56 The people did heed Education and he grew more powerful with each transition of the sun and the people of knowledge became respected. And the sons and daughters of Education were nominated for high positions.

57 And Education needed structure to rule his kingdom so he formed the studies and these came to be; mathematics, language, history, art, law, and the sciences, and within each study came more division and still more, until the finest details became burdensome upon themselves.

58 And Education, in desire for homage, designed to charge for his knowledge. And still the people came. And his consorts presented their product as exclusive, as if wisdom had become their domain. And the people paid tribute to his wisdom by allowing him to tell them what to think.

59 Education, so clever in his wit, became aware of his increasing strength, even as his bulging mass rendered him immovable. And so he sent his agents to build great institutions across the land, and their presence superseded true thought. Questioning became intolerable and intolerance became acceptance. Acceptance became the standard and all standards were approved by the great council of Education.

60 And the people so far removed from thinking could not remember their right. The elite of Education's council, having grown old with their ways and means, could not hear the questions. But the questions were not valid, for they had become products of a world of generations' passive resignation.

61 And the lost questions deserved no answer, for they had abandoned the souls come to profit. Soon, the agents of the Council realized they had created a world

573

without minds and the poets and musicians and artists did cry out in agony at their defeat.

62   Their hollow words echoed through the empty halls of the universities. Dusty self-portraits hung brittle, cracking in forgotten hallways. And the faded, dried paint upon the easel is but one symptom of a prince turned trader.

63   And Education, in disfavor with the masses, called upon his brother Commerce for advice. In the solitude of the midnight hour, with no man as witness, they struck a bargain and the two princes laughed to themselves at their clever deal.

64   Education did begin to train soldiers for the armies of Commerce. And train them well, he did. So the standard changed anew as knowledge was replaced by skill. The trade that the people learned prepared them better to slip the coin into the greedy palm of the two thieves.

65   The universities were vibrant once more, alive with the thoughts of men learning rules. And wisdom for all was caged and forgotten. No one noticed, except the poets and musicians and painters, but they had no voice any longer. They had been sold like the rest. Commerce and Education had teamed to make the world in its own image.

66   Education threw a great feast for the people of the world and they were wild with hunger as they gorged on simple thoughts and common themes. The spirit within humans kept silent, for its time to do battle had not yet come.

67   Still, a chosen few spoke out and Education could not tolerate the indiscretion. And the students rallied behind their prince, crying in unison against those who dared to question. And books were burned and people were martyred and truth was hidden once more.

68 But wisdom cannot be subdued by those whose design it is to package it for profit. Wisdom is found in every heart, in every mind, in every soul. Education knows this truth if he knows truth at all, and with this thought he knows his defeat is but time waiting to come.

69 He will fight for his palaces of learning with trickery and deceit and diversion. His lifeblood is born of criticism and measurement and these shall cost him his throne.

70 For criticism is solely owned by the hypocrite. And the hypocrite shall perish as a rotten fruit left on an autumn tree. And all measurement requires judgment and this right belongs to no man, nor prince, nor thief of thoughts.

71 When the truth stands tall, backed by wisdom and unity, there will be no institution, ideal, nor self-proclaimed royalty to withstand its mighty presence. And the children of Man will be freed from the bondage of mental insignificance.

72 And in this, freedom shall rise, the greatest challenge to established form seen upon the Earth. And the great battle will begin with power fighting weakness, but those in power are weak and those without are strong. And the balance will be turned and the tide shall recede as honesty regains its glory.

73 Those denied the right to think will slay the obese prince and cut him into morsels to feed the undernourished planet. And the starvation of the mind shall end with the demise of the false idol.

74 For the prince of thought, once proud and righteous, will himself be paraded as a jester in the court of the world, and wisdom will reign supreme among the united peoples. For language and barriers will be cast aside in triumphant consciousness and jubilant acknowledgment of collective thought.

75 And these things will come to pass, I say through Allison, My daughter. And though they seem impossible, the miracle of a summer's rainbow is no less plausible. For I have decided to challenge the reasons for this human existence, this scourge.

76 I say unto all people in every nation, of all stature: Challenge all reason, until you are convinced of its truth. Acceptance without question is like an eyeless painter with an empty brush stroking an easel made of air.

77 Every soul is a painter with a palette so brilliant the aura shines for a millennia. Yet the skill of the artist determines the grace upon which the canvas is changed. And the colors of life—vivid and stark bent hues of conflicting spectrum—are the telling strokes of moments lived.

78 Moments lost until the final hour. And the canvas is complete, hanging suspended in the Great Gallery. And it is your self-portrait displayed there. Under what noble vision shall your life be viewed?

80 Did discipline instill its regimen in the weakest moments of strongest distractions?

81 Did understanding resolve to make things clear as conflict confused its passive twin?

82 Did patience guide you in angered heat and dispatch ego to silence?

83 Did humility quietly tug your sleeve as arrogance stood to speak?

84 Did confidence rise in its place dispelling fear with calm assurance?

85 Did tolerance provide subtle reminders that difference is perspective turned round?

86 Did acceptance find you in unfamiliar straits and place comfort between you and prejudice?

87 Have your passive moments, strung together in random destiny, subscribed to the *Premise of Contentment*? Will the silhouette of your deeds be framed with friendship and love and compassion?

88 These things alone, lived true in simple daily tasks, shall be the master strokes on the grand canvas in the Great Gallery. Stand clear of the union of Commerce and Education for their purpose is to sell your art, thereby your soul, for monetary gain. Rise above the seductive callings of their glamorous message and seek the quiet serenity of the Master and His lover, the Earth.

There is a time to cry. A time to express years of denied joy. A time to reveal ideals suppressed deep inside. A time to rejoice. A time to overwhelm fear with love. There is a time to cry—for everyone. Emotion knows not of age, nor does it acknowledge gender. Race is not immune to its affects. There is a time to cry. Religion cannot rise above it—Hindu, Christian, Jew, Muslim, Buddhist, Existentialist, Transcendentalist, Atheist, Agnostic—all have tasted the salty stream. There is a time to cry.

There is also a time of recognition. A supernatural time when you and the Universe and all that exists within your realm are one. It has always been one with you, but hidden as behind a mask. When that mask of illusion is removed the truth is there as beauty. There is a time of recognition. It is a moment that sheds light on our silliest beliefs, our enslaving dogma, our fears, our institutions, our structure, our personalities, our weaknesses, our frailties, our egos, our distrust, our elaborate deceptions. And when this time of recognition occurs it ignites a warm flame within the cauldron of the heart and spreads heat throughout the body. This is the release of the soul. In such intense moments of undeniable divinity, when all your hopes are realized and all your questions answered and all your doubts quelled, when the deities have shown that there is something more, something better to this life, when all this happens in one incontrovertible cosmic moment—this time of recognition unites with the time to cry, and bliss is born.

When this happens, tears cascade like a wondrous waterfall nourishing the bounty of Eden. Feelings of gratitude and oneness bubble up like a pure stream to the surface of the body, as the soul shares itself with the ego. The heart weeps in jubilation, the lips stutter in ecstasy, the body shudders in exultation. And you know, no matter who you are or what you used to believe, that we are all connected. Each of us. There is a time to cry.

Every witness to Allison's vision was touched, somehow changed. Whether forever or for a few days or weeks is difficult to know, each soul being so complex. But each was changed nonetheless. The moment cannot be described. Allison wept and her angelic smile spread like a cherub's fluttering wings. Dena held her tight, sprinkling tears of joy on Allison's welcoming shoulder. The stoic and detached Mother Superior released a stream of happiness. Barney washed away decades of self-loathing with a cleansing purge.

Rose and I, looking on from the sanctuary of the family room, hugged each other as firmly as we had ever had, as if we were in the throes of young-spirited, sexual exuberance. We cried as we held each other, knowing that this moment was a rare gift from the gods. And I knew, as I breathed in Rose's vanilla, that all the tragedy and trouble that *The Journals* had heaped upon me was rewarded tenfold in that single inspired revelation of Allison's visitation from the life force we humans call God.

The Council had done its work. Allison was transformed. We were all transformed, and I knew that the real message had been delivered; the real purpose of my ordeal was now apparent. As the chronologer of *The Journals*, on behalf of the noble light-beings of Council of Ancients, it is my task to deliver Annis the Forgiver's gift to the world—*Agnostics:144*.

December 25, 1983 (Continued)

The Governing Order of Divinity—Division of Apparitions, Miracles & Nuisances arrived promptly at 6:00 a.m. with grim faces. It could have been that they were annoyed at being called away from their families on Christmas morning, with the exception of Cadaver Smith, who had no family.

Allison had been concerned at first, fretting over the unknown tactics of the Ghost

Squad. She stared out her window, sipping tea, watching a light snow fall. She loved the fat, wet flakes that stuck to the ground and stopped the city cold. But neither rain nor sleet nor snow nor dark of night would stop the Governing Order of Divinity. No sir. No way. They were on a mission, and her case had been upgraded from nuisance to bonafide miracle.

Once their typical routine became apparent, her fears faded away and she became relaxed, even playful. She knew Cadaver Smith and his zombies had no real authority within the Church—they were more a propaganda tool than anything, designed to press doubt into people's minds, to get those who contacted God to question their own sanity. To be honest, Smith and his ghouls had an accomplished record of covering up celestial happenstance.

The usual tests were run in the usual order. Temple examined Allison's well-formed breasts, but she didn't mind. Hastings asked his standard, dispassionate questions, reading from a checklist, marking off the answers with a number 2 pencil that read ST. MICHAEL'S BINGORAMA—BE THERE on its tooth-pocked side. She suspected that Hastings the shrink had personal problems of his own. She and Parish played gin rummy for an hour, Allison winning nine of twelve hands.

She understood the pattern now and spoke openly, kindly to each of the men, apologizing for ruining their Christmases, to which they each surprisingly blushed and replied (even the troubled Hastings) it was a pleasure to see her on a snowy holiday morning. Everyone, of course, except the irascible Cadaver Smith, who resented any intrusion not of his making. And this Yvonne Pippin child—the child—the one that insisted on calling herself Allison, "simply does not take our work seriously."

After the first six hours of folly had concluded, a meeting was called in her former room, left over from the first *Agnostics* incident. Allison was not invited, but she decided the Red Angel should attend in an auditory sense through the acoustics of the heating vent. Standing tippy-toed on her toilet, with her ear close to the register, she listened, pleasantly surprised by Mother Superior's words.

Epiphanies make strange bedfellows, and Mother—long Allison's antagonist—was evidently changed by the alleged miracle.

"She's divine," Mother said to an unimpressed Smith. "Can't you just accept that?"

"No." Smith angrily snuffed out a butt, his thirty-fifth cigarette of the day. "It's a child's hoax. A trick."

Allison could smell the second-hand smoke through the vent and moved her nose back a few inches.

"How can you say that? She foresaw two attacks on the pope, a hundred witnesses saw her surrounded by light at the Sacred Mother, she was in possession of a new chapter of the Bible, and she has just been spoken to by the Lord Himself. What the hell more proof do you need, you idiot?"

"Jesus juggling Olympus steak knives at the Barnum & Bailey Circus," Allison said to herself, resting her strained toes. "Will wonders never cease?"

"I'm not interested in proof!" The grand inquisitor raised his voice to match Mother Superior. "I'm interested in protecting the sanctity of the Church. The institution is much greater than the random visions of a ragamuffin orphan girl."

"The girl is not a ragamuffin," Mother said. "She's a beautiful, intelligent, spirited, loving young gi . . ." She paused as if some sizable pearl of wisdom had wedged in her esophagus. "Aha, that's it, isn't it? You don't want to accept her prophecies because she's a woman. That's it, isn't it?"

"Don't be ridiculous," Smith scoffed.

Everyone in the room (See, Hear, and Speak No Evil) remained deadly quiet for fear of getting caught in the crossfire between the two formidable foes. They knew that there was a possibility her words were true. The Church never had done well with the women in its ranks, being the patriarchal men's club that it is.

"We have an obligation to make her words known," Mother said.

Mother was obviously agitated, much to Allison's delight. She had another ally within St. Als. God bless.

"Hah!" Smith took a drag of his cigarette. "The world doesn't care. All people want is food, shelter, clothes, and to be told what to believe. Oh, and in America, they want green lawns and color TV. After that they could care less." His contempt hung around him like a thick blanket of carbon dioxide. "Let's cut to the chase, ladies. I think Allison is possessed by a demonic spirit whose—"

"No, you're wrong!" Sister Bernadette suddenly interrupted. "We've all seen her, heard her. He spoke through her."

Smith dismissed the nun with a limp wave of his hand. "Nonetheless, this is the state of things. If the orphanage doesn't wish to cooperate, we can arrange to have her transferred to a more amenable institution."

Allison, ear pressed against the vent, nearly fell from the commode. She grabbed the towel rack to steady herself, her stomach felt as it had been flushed. Move me from St. Als? No! At that instant she realized just how vulnerable she was in the hands of maniacal adults.

"There's no need for that," Sister Dena said.

The normally docile Barney, heretofore more a Bedrock cartoon character than person, but changed dramatically by the *Agnostics* revelations, said, "You . . . you . . . you sick son of Satan."

The room grew menacingly silent for a few tense seconds. Cadaver Smith chuckled. "I've been called worse, much worse, let me assure you. Malachi will arrive from Chicago tomorrow. The process will begin at eleven. This is by order of Archbishop Sebastian with instructions from the Vatican." He grinned wickedly. "Make no mistake, this cannot be undone."

Allison sat mindlessly on the toilet seat. "The Vatican? Jesus cutting a deal with the emperor, what's going on here?"

December 26, 1983

It had been decided by authorities higher than those that resided at St. Als that twenty-four-hour prayer vigils would take place outside Allison's door. The sisters worked hour-long shifts heavy with rosary beads, holy water, and the good book. Reinforcements were brought in to spell the small St. Als contingent. The waxy scent of tallow wafted through the east wing as candles lined the halls. The kids of the orphanage, curious at all the comings and goings, launched a covert intelligence gathering operation. This effort was spearheaded by an anxious Mary (in coordination with The 88s) who could no longer bear to have her best friend excommunicated or experimented on, or "who knows what else they're doing to her over there."

Now, as anyone who has extensive contact with children knows, it doesn't take much to set their imaginations running wild; it takes even less when there are real live phenomena and intrigue swirling about. The Catholics, for all their secrecy, couldn't stop a curious band of children from finding the truth. It's adults who give up too easily.

Allison knew that Malachi, whomever he might be, was arriving at eleven, and so she was puzzled when Sister Dena asked to take a walk at ten-thirty. Allison, virtually never distrustful of her friend and mentor, was suspicious. On a cold walk through the white crystal grounds, she asked Dena what was to happen.

"I'm not sure exactly," Sister D said as she spit a spent shell into the brisk winter breeze. She grabbed a handful of sunflower seeds and spread them about for the birds. "More questions probably. Even the saints questioned the words of the prophets every once in awhile."

Allison squinted against the glare from the sun sparkling the three-inch layer of snow that crunched under her feet as they walked. She looked to the blue sky, bright with promise and told herself not to worry. Remember to always shine. God was on her side after all; what did she have to fear? She looked back at the huge, main building. She smiled. "Look." Allison pointed to the second story. There, in every window, in every dorm room, stood grinning St. Als' kids waving to her, homemade signs of encouragement held in proud hands pressed against the panes. KEEP THE SPIRIT, SEED! read some. ANGELS ALWAYS TELL THE TRUTH read a few others. SET OUR ANGEL FREE! demanded many more.

"They must love you," Sister Dena said softly.

"Yes," Allison agreed, suddenly not feeling so alone. The isolation of the last several months melted away like an icicle in springtime. She waved to her supportive friends. A window opened. Mary popped her head out. "We're with you, Seed! We love you!"

She waved. Mary blew a kiss. How long it had been since they were able to speak to each other. How long it had been since they had been able to share their feelings, their secrets. She remembered the tragic, defining moment the previous Easter that had led to their separation and her incarceration. It wasn't Mary that had precipitated her confinement. It wasn't their relationship. It wasn't their love affair that had caused the forced divorce. It was *Agnostics* and the news it bore. God's gifts have difficult outcomes at times.

"Why is everyone having such an absotively difficult time over this?" she asked Sister Dena as they stepped back into the warmth of the foyer. Burnt sweetness thickened the air. A blaze of candles, glorious and brilliant, lined the hallway by the hundreds. The flames strained to outshine each other, reaching toward the ceiling as if God were there to honor their light. From deep within the east wing, live distinctive baritone and tenor Gregorian chants emanated like a medieval choir. "Introit for the Fourth Sunday in Advent," Allison whispered out of instinctive reverence. She would not know this until later, but the mysterious man from Chicago had brought his own Gregorian monks with him.

Sister Dena nodded. The hallway was empty, eerie. "Mode Four, I'd say."

"You're right. So why is everyone so bugged out about this?"

Sister Dena unbuttoned her coat and chewed lightly on a seed as she considered her question. "A darling girl like you comes along with visions, with magic light, with channeled information from Heaven, and it challenges the status quo. There are people who have dedicated their entire lives to studying the scriptures, or living a solitary life in devotion to His Word. And here you are, forcing them to rethink all the doctrine. It's troubling for those who would rather believe in the paper than the prophet."

As they walked along, Sister Dena took her hand, a gesture which Allison understood to be reassurance against what was about to transpire. Of course, neither of them knew precisely what was forthcoming, but the unknown usually drags a kicking and screaming fear along with it. This time, however, bolstered by the presence of God's personal blessing, Allison was not afraid. She couldn't explain it, but she just felt inspired at the prospect of proving that God had come to her. He had spoken to her, given her courage. There was nothing they could do in the interrogation that His love wouldn't provide for.

She was forewarned, through her clandestine listening at the bathroom register, that someone new was being introduced into the Governing Order of Divinity—Division of Apparitions, Miracles & Nuisances mix, but was not frightened in the least. Far from it. A playfulness, a happy spark of discovery was afire inside her. Her attitude, precocious and coy, was in no way disrespectful or flippant. She was, well, amused at the attention.

Allison and Dena entered their apartment. A crowd of people stood waiting: Mother Superior and her followers, the Ghost Squad, and an odd looking fellow. Allison took the initiative, believing that a bright personality and friendliness was the best means of getting this ritual completed. Besides, it was Christmas season, her most precious time of year, and she was to enjoy it.

"Father Malachi, I presume," Allison said with a brisk extension of her hand. Mild yet strained laughter filtered lightly through the packed room thick with incense, burned specifically with the intent to cast out unwelcome spirits. To Allison it smelled more of garlic, to be used with vampires, than of standard religious fare.

"Why, yes, I am he," Malachi said in a voice that was a cross between Miss Kitty and Mr. Ed (the talking horse, of course). Soft and coarse, surreal and unnatural. Masculine and feminine, but not in measured dosages. Marge Schott on steroids. He reached a frail, knuckle-dominated hand toward her, his skinny digits extended by chipped, half-inch fingernails. A good manicure was in order. Allison shivered unexpectedly at his touch, cold and wet, as if blood had not made it to his hands in several years. His hands, perhaps once welcoming warm and kind, were now gnarled and racked from his decades of work.

Father Malachi was her height, thin and slightly stooped in a plain black cassock with a waist-length surplice and a resplendent purple stole. His uncombed, blackish hair, tinged gray, and center parted, fell to his shoulders in coniferous swoops, like evergreen branches heavy with winter's snow. His ears were nowhere to be seen. To be sure, this man, Malachi, appeared an eccentric, and perhaps was allowed to remain so due to the exclusive nature of his craft. His face was sharp-edged, the skin pulled tight against hard bones, giving the appearance of a man who seldom ate, or if he did, not well. He was decidedly unlike any priest she had ever met, appearing supernatural himself—a spirit from the nether world. She gave Malachi the once-over and considered him a likely candidate in the Cadaver Smith fan club.

"This is the child—Yvonne," Cadaver Smith injected. "She is the subject of your services."

"She is the possessed, eh?" Malachi said shrilly. He folded his bony hands in front of him. He stared, hoping to uncover some abstract spirit-truth by gazing into her emerald eyes, as if peering through a window. Sorry, Malachi, she told herself, the shades are drawn. His own eyes were dark mine shafts, abandoned tunnels lined with black coal, which led nowhere. They were lifeless, as if too much time had been spent obsessed with fighting demons that now possessed his soul. The demons weren't real, of course; they were the ones he had invented. The perimeter of his eyes were ringed in blackness, and Allison couldn't be sure, but she thought black eye shadow and red eyeliner accentuated his hollow stare.

"What services do you perform for the Church?" she asked, taken aback by the ominous tone of Cadaver Smith's words.

A grim smile like a grave digger's spade shoveled its way onto Father Malachi's face. Almost whimsically, with a fondness for the inevitable reaction he expected to get, he said, "Why, child, I am an exorcist."

Had God not been unequivocally on her side, Allison very well may have made a break for the door. She had seen the Linda Blair movie with green puke and twisting heads. Is this what the Church thinks of Agnes? she asked herself, alarmed and simultaneously angry. Why do they refuse to believe? Had God not given her numerous visions over the years, she might have rushed passed the sisters and the chanters and the candles and out the door to freedom. Had God not just spoken through her, as much a sign of divinity as ever there was, she may have summoned up some choice four-letter swear words and stormed away from St. Als forever. But God had visited her, He had chosen her. She was the subject of Agnes' message. No, she would not run. More importantly, she would not fear this charlatan actor sent to intimidate her.

"So, child," Father Malachi began, "they tell me you're psychic. Is this not true?"

"I'm not sure." She smiled, doing her best to be buoyant. "But I do have dreams which seem to come true. If that makes me psychic, yeah, I guess I am."

"Can you show me?" he asked, his soot-rubbed eyes open wide.

"Not really." Allison shrugged. "I can't control it—it just happens."

"Oh, come on. Try, for me."

A mischievousness swept through her. "Well, I know you had chicken noodle soup for lunch."

Malachi's charcoal eyes lit up. "That's remarkable. What vision did you have to reveal that?"

She giggled as she pointed to his cassock. "Well . . . um . . . I had a vision of a noodle."

Before he could react, while chuckles filled the room, she lifted a two-inch pasta from Malachi's chest and dropped it in the garbage.

Unfazed, unembarrassed, Malachi asked, "Do you know why I am here?"

"Because Yahweh has come into this house," she said, raising her arms then swooping them out in a great arc.

Malachi raked his fingers through his tangled hair as he made a mental note. "No aversion to religious references, this is good," he said. "Yvonne, we are here to—"

"She prefers Allison," Mother Superior said.

"Yes, fine, *Allison*." Malachi started again, his feminine demeanor suddenly taking the lead, "I am here to determine if there is an evil spirit possessing you," he said with undo exaggeration, accentuating "eee-ville spirit" for dramatic effect.

Allison saw Father Malachi as a caricature in a second-rate Hollywood horror film. "*Eee*-ville—is that a place where all the letter E's live?" Malachi's face didn't change. Silence functioned as his response. She realized humor wouldn't get her far today. "I can guarantee you there's no eee-ville in me. I'm one-hundred-percent pure."

584

"*Tsk, tsk,* child." Malachi admonished her like June Cleaver lecturing the Beav. "No one is a hundred-percent pure."

"I am," she said. "I really am! Purer than Ivory soap."

"We shall see," Malachi frowned. "We shall see."

Smith, his normally abnormal self dying for a smoke, was impatient with anything but the most direct interrogation. "Let's get on with it, Malachi," he snapped.

Sufficiently prodded, Malachi reached into his cassock and brandished an ornate gold crucifix inlaid with rubies and sapphires, glittering with religion. He laid it on the table in front of her. "Would you like to touch it?" he asked, tempting her as his vacant eyes stared, daring her.

Without hesitation, she picked it up. "Sure, it's absotively gorgeous."

"No aversion to religious symbols, good," Malachi said with another rake of his pine-needle hair. "Now Allison, I need to ask, do you know what I'm here to do?"

"You bet." She turned the magnificent crucifix in the light as she watched it sparkle. "I have visions from Yahweh and Mr. Smith can't believe it, so he called you in to prove I'm lying or that some demon has control of me." She took her eyes off the cross and focused them on the sullen priest. "But Yahweh *has* spoken to me, and I have nothing to fear from you. I'm not afraid."

Father Malachi stood moderately hunched but unmoved by her challenge. Instead, he pulled out a wrinkled checklist of well-worn questions. His voice cracked as if summoning a feminine guide from another realm. "Allison, God doesn't speak to people. He is . . . well . . . He is God."

She set the cross down gingerly on the kitchen table where a half-dozen candles wiggled their pious flames. The fulfilling aroma of toasted paraffin enriched the room. "He spoke to Moses, didn't he? He spoke to Jesus, too. And Mary. He guided the three wise men. He spoke to a half-dozen saints or more. Why can't he speak to me?"

"Get on with it!" Cadaver Smith fumed.

Malachi turned to the sisters. He twiddled his ill-shaped thumbs with knuckles the size of tree knots. "Has there been any stench?"

Sisters Dena and Barney, along with Mother P, responded with incredulous looks of contempt for the question. "Don't be ridiculous," Dena chastised him as a chorus of chants continued inside St. Als—"Introit for Sexagesima Sunday (Mode 8)."

It may have been Malachi's poor make-up, the ambient candles, the eccentric music, or the potential of an exorcism, but, inexplicably, Allison was enthused. She considered the proceedings absotively inspirational. A jest of significant magnitude.

"Have there been any sudden temperature drops in her room? Sub-zero temps or tropical highs?" Malachi remained impassive and placed an X by the previous question.

"No!" the nuns answered.

Another X. The monks chanted on.

"Any levitating, rising off the floor, floating through the air?" he continued.

585

"No!" came another annoyed but unified response from the St. Als' women's league. The nuns looked at each other as if Malachi and Smith had spent too much time sniffing dust in the catacombs. Hastings, Temple, and Parish simply sat listening, saying nothing. Were they hypnotized by the continuous chants of the monks? Lost in the medieval origin of it all?

"There *was* a time when I tried to jump off the fire escape with an umbrella to see if I could fly like Mary Poppins," Allison said.

"And?" Malachi said.

"And the umbrella broke and I scraped up my knees." She grinned sheepishly. "Both of them."

"I love Mary Poppins," Malachi said unexpectedly. He brought his dainty wrists to his chest, remembering some childhood fantasy momentarily before he refocused. "Any slamming doors, broken furniture, tearing fabric?"

"No!" Mother Superior lost her patience. The tectonic plates began to shift. The earth began to shake. "There's nothing unusual about Allison except the arrival of *Agnostics:144*. Look, Father," she breathed in slowly to calm herself. "She is not possessed—she's blessed."

Triple X. And the monks sang on. Malachi contorted his already ravaged face in doubt. "Rare is it that the blessed have these hallucinations," he rationalized. He turned to Allison. "Even more rare that they occur in a child. The chances are one in a billion. Now Allison, other than spotting chicken noodles, do you have any telepathic powers?"

"Not really. I don't know what happens or why. I can't control it, but I wish I could." A profound thought crept into her mischievous mind. "What if *Agnostics is* true? What if I *am* chosen? What if I *am* a messenger from the Almighty? Aren't you trying to exorcise God—whom you obey and honor?"

"Often an *eee*-ville spirit comes in the form of a good angel," Malachi reasoned as he grabbed the cross off the table like he was expecting some Satanic sucker-punch. "It is my . . . difficult task to remove the entity. I cannot give credence to any illusory angelic soul or saint."

"But what if it's all true? You're a Catholic priest driving God from the Church—banishing Him from the Earth!"

"I've heard enough," Malachi squealed as though Judy Garland and John Wayne had arm-wrestled for the right to speak for Malachi, then both spoke at the same time anyway. With his priceless gold crucifix pressed firmly to his chest, gripped tightly in both hands, he pirouetted toward Smith like Liza Minelli in *Cabaret*. "This girl is not possessed."

"I want her exorcised," Smith ordered sternly. "This comes from the Vatican."

A disturbed frown like rain at an outdoor funeral service dripped onto Malachi's face. "Fine, then," he huffed, "you shall be my assistant. But I warn you, Smith—you must be strong. Can you do this?"

586

Cadaver Smith, long the archbishop's yes-man, ate it up. "No problem. Anything you want. How long will this take?" As if he had someplace else to be, some higher priority apparition or miracle or nuisance to quash.

Malachi's vacant eyes grew more serious, harder. "Sometimes it's two-to-three days, sometimes a few hours, most often ten-to-twelve hours. It's difficult to say." His blackened eyes became less dim, like a tiny glimmer of light drawing flame as he got closer to his purpose in life—exorcising nonexistent demons.

"How about her health?" he asked Temple. "Anything there?"

"She does have good cholesterol," Temple joked, obviously agreeing with Allison's frame of mind that the proceedings were a sham. Allison laughed. "Right . . . *ahem* . . . good health, no problems there."

"She's fit mentally, too," Hastings added. "Intelligent, witty, engaging—nice girl." Cadaver Smith scowled. All this talk of her well-being bothered him. Smith had a disdain for anyone's being well.

"Prepare the child," Malachi instructed Barney and Sister D in a voice that was at once difficult to take seriously and impossible not to obey. "We have some details to go over."

Sister Dena delicately cupped Allison's elbow and walked her into the bedroom. The place had been stripped of its furnishings. "We have much to discuss," she heard Malachi say in a tone that sounded like Shirley MacLaine.

"Hey, what did you guys do with my stuff?" Allison asked angrily. She worried about the supersecret journals she had been keeping out of the clutches of the Catholic Intelligence Service.

The room was bare except for her bed, which was stripped of its sheets and was now covered in white linens. She glanced at the leather straps attached to the bedposts. A table containing a crucifix, a book of prayer, a vessel of holy water, a picture of Gibran, and a tape recorder stood in the center of the room. Two stone-ugly black-and-white checkered La-Z-Boy recliners imported from Chicago highlighted the new decor. She wondered if the chairs had been blessed by the pope. No, she concluded, the pope would never bless something so hideous.

"Once we begin, we cannot stop," Malachi informed the team assembled in the other room. "Once my powers are engaged in this cause, we cannot withdraw. We cannot retreat. We must vanquish the eee-ville spirit." He took a dramatic pause, exhaled like Jane Fonda after a hard workout, then continued. "No matter the pain, the fatigue, the horror or the vile nature of the proceeding, we must press on. You cannot be afraid to see blood, excrement, urine, to hear foul language or have your deepest, most personal secrets exposed.

"Everyone participating in the exorcism will have to follow three rules. One, you must completely obey my commands without question no matter how absurd they may seem. Two, no one is to take any initiative, except on my command. Three, no one speaks to the possessed but me—for any reason whatsoever!"

Malachi, black-robed harbinger of God's cleanliness, had found his zone. This was his calling, and when he was in his rhythm he gained momentum, energy. "We will expel the invisible power by the Grace, Authority, and Power of Jesus of Nazareth. He will be our strength. Our pillar. All senses may be reversed—up seems down, you may hear with your eyes, taste with your nose—everything will be topsy-turvy, topsy-turvy."

He lowered his tone, kicking in his Mr. Ed impression again. "Horrid, disgusting sickness will open itself and ask you to join it. You must not acknowledge it. Ever!" he implored, finding the drama in his job, selling it like a Bible salesman in the streets of El Dorado.

Allison lay on the bed, legs crossed, listening as Sisters D and Barney stood horrified near the door, peering out at Malachi, then at her. What they didn't know was, try hard as they might, she could clearly see their angst-ridden emotions.

"Temple, Hastings, Parish, and Sister Dena will be witnesses and shall not speak during the ritual, except upon my explicit order," Malachi said. Then his voice cracked and he sounded like Carol Channing smoking a cigar. "Smith, as my assistant, you will sit in the recliner on the left. The rest will stand. Mother Superior?"

"Yes, Father?"

"You and Sister Bernadette keep the candles lit and those monks singing."

"Do the chants help dispel the eee-ville?" Mother Superior asked.

"No, I just like the music."

Mother's granite eyes rolled. Another eccentric in the orphanage.

"A final word before we begin," Malachi intoned as seriously as one can in a voice like Ethel Merman on morphine. This guy had more personalities than Sybil in a hall of mirrors. "All involved must be sin-free, having confessed your sins as I requested prior to my arrival. Has this been done?"

Everyone answered in the affirmative. Everyone with the possible exception of Mr. Cadaver Smith, who grunted reluctantly in the affirmative.

"Let us begin."

Allison found the whole ordeal fascinating. No anxiety or nervousness was to be found in her. She was calm, yet filled with enthusiasm. Yahweh will protect me, she told herself, He has a purpose.

Hastings, Parish, and Temple entered, followed by Smith, who turned on the recorder, then took his seat in the La-Z-Boy on the left as ordered. After several quiet minutes, the exorcist swept grandly into the room with a swooshing cassock and a toss of his stole over his shoulder. Allison was reminded of the pretentious snob, Bunny Adler, the insensitive child-shopper from years earlier.

"Gradual for the Feast of the Holy Confessor" penetrated the walls. Mode 2. The monks chanted on as Malachi stood dark and brooding at the foot of the bed. His tangled, knotted hands made the sign of cross. He reached like a shadow for the holy water, sprinkling it upon the sheets. He knelt down saying, "Do not remember, O Lord, our sins or those of our forefathers." He motioned for the others.

"And do not punish us for our offenses."

Malachi bowed his head silently and closed his eyes in prayer. "And lead us not into temptation."

"But deliver us from evil," his assistants monotoned.

Malachi lifted his head from prayer and raised his voice so God could hear. "The fool hath said in his heart, there is no Elohim. Corrupt as they are, and have done abominable iniquity: there is none that doeth good." Psalm 53—good choice. It may have had more impact if the estrogen exorcist didn't sound like Liberace in a biker movie. "Elohim looked down from heaven upon the children of men, to see if there were *any* that did understand, that did seek Elohim. Every one of them," Malachi's voice broke yet again, "is gone back: they are altogether become filthy; there is none that doeth good, no, not one."

Allison filled with irreverence, interrupted. "There's at least one. I'm doing good."

Malachi ignored her. Sister D put her finger to her lips asking her to cool it, but Allison saw the proceedings devolving into parody—everyone can't be evil . . . I mean . . . eee-ville, she thought, not *everyone*.

"Have the workers of iniquity no knowledge?" Malachi recited biblical verses. "Who eat up my people as they eat bread; they have not called upon Elohim. They were in great fear, where no fear was: for Elohim hath scattered the bones of him camped against thee: thou hast put them to shame, because God has despised them.

"Oh that the salvation," the exorcist's voice rose, "of Israel were come out of Zion! When God bringeth back the captivity of His people, Jacob shall rejoice, and Israel shall be glad." Malachi became stronger, more forceful—Clint Eastwood in drag. "Save this girl your servant!"

"Because she hopes in you, my God," the assistants offered up.

Malachi continued on. "Be a tower of strength for her, O Lord."

"In the face of the enemy," the lemmings followed.

"Let the enemy have no victory over her," he pressed.

"And the Son of Iniquity not succeed in injuring her," the group uttered in perfect synchronicity.

"Send her help from the Holy Place, Lord," Malachi pleaded.

"And give her Heavenly protection," the others said.

Allison thought to herself, I have protection—Yahweh is here. She struggled mightily for self-control not to make wisecracks during the bogus exorcism no one

believed in. How could anyone believe in a ritual performed by a transsexual trying to save a testosterone-dominated institution from the religion-ending visions of an orphan?

"Lord, hear my prayer," Father Malachi said softly.

"And let my cry reach You," came the response.

"May the Lord be with you."

"And with your spirit," the assistants answered.

"Let us pray," Malachi ended, bowing his head yet again.

A long, eerie silence occupied the room. He clasped his distorted hands together, reminding Allison of the tangled squash vines in her garden. Spring would be here soon, she thought, and I shall toil in the fields once again.

Suddenly, Malachi jumped to his feet, filled with energy and focus. "Unclean spirit!" he called like Phyllis Diller in a yodeling contest, shattering the quiet. "Whoever you are, and all your companions who possess this servant of God. By the mysteries of the Incarnation, the Sufferings and Death, the Resurrection, and the Ascension of Our Lord Jesus Christ; by the sending of the Holy Spirit; and by the Coming of Our Lord into the Last Judgment, I command you . . ." he paused panting, sweat beads forming on his brow. "Tell me, with some sign, your name, the day and the hour of your damnation! Obey me in everything, although I am an unworthy servant of God," he shouted. The exorcist assailed the invisible demon lodged within Allison's virgin womb. "Do not do damage to this creature, Yvonne, or to my assistants, or to any of their goods." Malachi lifted Gibran's picture off the table, holding it high above his head. "Tell me your name, eee-ville," he commanded.

His words, though unnecessary and irrelevant, had a driving mysticism about them. He had performed this rite a hundred, maybe a thousand times before, and he had mastered the act. The words had intensity. He had captivated the room. Allison looked at Sister D, whose eyes blinked rapidly, anxious about the unknown. The room was uneasy. The sisters and the Ghost Squad half-expected, based on Malachi's brilliantly delivered incantation, for some sinister being to sweep through like a hurricane wreaking unimaginable damage to furniture and people. Possibly, Cadaver Smith hoped for it—he'd rather have eee-ville than divinity. If divinity showed up there'd be nothing to fight, nothing to kill.

Boom! A great clasp of sound exploded, shaking everything, knocking the crucifix and the holy water to the floor. Suddenly, the room flashed white, blinding everyone. In a second it had vanished. Trickles of sheer joy meandered from Allison's eyes. Bliss showered her.

"Show yourself," Malachi demanded, sounding like Ginger from *Gilligan's Island*. "It is here! The Presence is among us. Can you feel it? Is this not true?"

There *was* a Presence. Shimmering and unmistakable. But it was not "eee-ville." It was a divine visitation from Yahweh come to Allison's rescue. Not that she needed help; she wasn't taking the exorcism thing seriously, evenwise, but God had decided to play His hand in this Hollywood B movie.

"He is here!" Malachi called. "Show yourself, eee-ville! Show yourself!" He brought Gibran's picture down with both hands hard onto the table, smashing it.

A familiar, warm sensation came over her. Her body at once felt soothed and nourished and loved. She began to giggle as "the most absotively, indescribable, incredible feeling in the world" enveloped her. The Universe, and all God's love, entered her. Words filled her head. Bible scriptures she had never read came to her. A beautiful voice bade her to speak.

"There, look there," Cadaver Smith shouted. "She's surrounded by light."

"Oh, my God, there it is, it's fantastic," Hastings blurted.

"Sweet Jesus," Sister Dena whispered and did the obligatory genuflection.

"Silence!" Malachi ordered. "Do not acknowledge the eee-ville!" He hurriedly picked up his crucifix and put it to Allison's chest. "Leave this child in peace, demon!"

Allison, overcome by His energy inside her, grabbed the cross from Malachi. She stood on the bed and held it to her breast as an astonished party of demon chasers gawked. She spoke: "For the priest's lips should keep knowledge, and they should seek the law at her mouth: for she is the messenger of Yahweh of hosts."

"What trickery does this wicked ghost perform, O Lord? Banish it back to whence it came," Malachi's eyes flickered wildly, his voice panicked.

She could see Malachi's frantic look as she saw her light reflecting back from his cesspool orbs.

"Quickly," he said, "someone fetch a Bible. Find the verse!"

Temple beat a hasty retreat in search of said black book.

Allison spoke again, "And did not He make of twain a unity so that he might have the right spirit? And why a unity? So that He might produce a holy seed. Therefore, take heed of your spirit, and let none of you deal unfaithfully against the wife of youth."

Malachi fell to his knees hurriedly to salvage what holy water had not spilled from the vessel. Desperately, he cupped what sacred liquid he could and tossed it at her. "Be gone, eee-ville," he ordered nothingness. There was no evil to order—only pure love. He was helpless against Yahweh. His churchly training could not match the faith and power of His Presence.

A mild sobbing came from somewhere in the room. Somewhere in the confusion, a soul was crying. The Bible had not yet arrived. The light energy inside Allison began to hum, pulsing with her heart. She took the crucifix and placed it to her lips, kissing it. She spoke a third time. "Behold, I will send My messenger, and she shall prepare the way before Me: and Yahweh whom ye seek, shall suddenly come to His temple, even the messenger of the covenant, whom you delight in. Behold, He shall come, saith Yahweh of hosts."

Malachi was distraught. His dark eyes were bottomless caverns devoid of any light. He had never come across such an energy. He had exorcised many a demon, man-made and artificial, but had never encountered true celestial power. "Do not pretend to be a Good Angel," he sweated. "You are but eee-ville cloaked in goodness. I see through this charade, demon from the nether world! Where's that Bible, for God's sake?"

The sobbing continued. The chanting monks could barely be heard through the mayhem. All order, the cornerstone of a good exorcism, had broken down. Sister Dena had left her position to console someone who was whimpering.

Temple returned with a Bible.

Allison's heavenly-sent aura emanated from her body, lighting the room. The glorious purity of His love filled her. She was at once both inside her body and outside it, watching herself. The angel of St. Als was bathed in light. She was the light. Separate and whole. The messenger and the message.

Father Malachi furiously tore through the thin pages of the Bible. "What is it? What is it?" he called shrilly. His fingers tripped over his carnival-freak knuckles. "Find it for me, Smith," he called, tossing the book to the cadaver, but Smith wasn't prepared, and the Bible landed on the floor with a thud. "Dammit Smith, get with the program, we need you on stage!" Malachi hollered.

Cadaver Smith couldn't hear him—he was consumed in tears, his head buried in his hands, mumbling to himself. Sister Dena knelt at his side, arms around him, whispering consolations.

"Forgive me," he sobbed over and over in an unceasing tide. "Forgive me, forgive me, forgive me."

Allison held the crucifix high to the ceiling with both hands and spoke again saying, "For behold, the day cometh that shall burn as an oven; avail the proud, yea, and all that do wickedly, shall be stubble: and the day that cometh shall burn them up, saith Yahweh of hosts, that it shall leave neither root nor branch—only seed."

Clang! Clang! Clang! An alarm sounded. The Gregorian chants stopped. The sprinkler system had engaged. The monks were doused. Fortunately for Allison and her coterie of care-givers, the sprinkler system was not active inside the apartment.

"What in blazes is going on?" Temple shouted as he ran to check. The piercing alarm wailed on.

Malachi railed above it. "Stand your ground, we have the serpent on the run now!" he proclaimed like Anita Bryant at a gay rights convention.

Temple dashed back into the room, dripping wet. "It's those blasted candles," he shouted, drying himself with the sleeve of his shirt. "They set off the smoke alarms and the sprinklers. They're trying to turn them off."

Hastings busily scanned the Bible, searching desperately for the passages that Allison recited. But she didn't know the words; they were being given to her as needed. She spoke a final time. "Behold, I will send a prophet before the coming of the great and dreadful day of Yahweh. And she shall turn the hearts of fathers to the children, and the hearts of children to their fathers, lest I come and smite the Earth with a curse."

Malachi had lost control. He was defeated but didn't know it. Smith continued to babble and sob in the corner as Malachi attempted to recapture lost spiritual ground. "Blasphemy!" he yelled from on high. "By the powers of Jesus of Nazareth, Son of Man, Great Redeemer of Souls—reveal yourself to me!"

"I've got it," Hastings called in triumph.

"What is it? In the name of the Father, what is it?" Malachi demanded amid the chaos.

"It's the last book of the Old Testament!"

"What is it?" Malachi ordered, breathless. "In God's name, what is it?"

"It's . . . it's—" Hastings choked on the words.

"Jesus Christ, man," Malachi screamed like Barbara Stanwyck at an obsessed fan. "We've got to beat this thing."

"It's the Book of Malachi," Hastings shouted above the incessant noise.

Instantly, Allison's light swirled wild around the room, touching each person where they stood, in less than an eye blink, cleansing them with its pure essence. It then collected itself into a concentrated ball, did a loop-the-loop and disappeared down her throat. She laughed jubilantly at Yahweh's Grace. Then, as quickly as it started, it ended.

The alarms ceased, the sprinklers stopped. Outside, however, fire engines roared into the yard with sirens blaring pandemonium and fear. A thin fog, sweet like nectar, filled the room with euphoria. The air crackled with electricity as if lightning had struck, leaving everyone in ashes wondering what had happened. But everyone knew what had happened—the hand of God reached into St. Als and made itself known. He had come. Allison had not been lying. It was all true.

Malachi's flour-tinged face turned to snow. All his strength ebbed. He collapsed in a limp mass of blackness on the carpet. Allison sprang out of bed and helped Dr. Temple lift his mashed potato body to his favorite La-Z-Boy.

"Are you okay, Father?" Allison asked the dazed priest.

His lips moved as if to say something but he was unable to speak. He weakly opened his empty eyes then closed them slowly.

Smith continued to sob. "Forgive me, please forgive me," the forlorn cadaver uttered repeatedly. Something in his mind had snapped. Spittle collected at the corners of his mouth. It was obvious he was unaware of where he was or what he was saying. "Forgive me, please forgive me," he cried.

Sister Dena looked at Allison, asking her to comfort the fallen leader of the Governing Order of Divinity—Division of . . . oh . . . whatever.

Allison wanted to help but didn't know how. Even with entities of light and messages from the Almighty and all the affirmations she had spoken over the years, even with what she knew was true in her heart—with all that, she still didn't feel worthy of forgiving anyone. How could she? she thought. I'm just an orphan girl. What right do I have to offer anyone forgiveness?

Smith sobbed and repeated himself. Sister D motioned again for her to quiet him, this time more urgently. "Say it," Dena lip-synched. Say it.

Allison hesitated. Is this my place? she wondered. What right have I? And then she realized a key truth—perhaps the first real truth she had come to understand—we all have the right (and the obligation) to offer forgiveness to everyone, always. This service can be performed at any time. At no charge. For anyone. I forgive you. Simple as that.

"You are forgiven, Mr. Smith," she said, placing her hand on the crown of his head as she had seen the pope do. Hey, she reasoned, she had no experience at this, so why not go with lessons from the king of the hill?

Smith cried harder. "Thank you, thank you."

Malachi began to stir, moaning. The room was dark, the blinds having been closed for the exorcism. If there was evil to dispel, light should be one of the first weapons employed. Allison pulled back the drapes. Below on the frozen lawn, standing in December's chill, stood Mother Superior, her arms flailing wildly, ordering all the kids to go back to their rooms. Allison giggled at the sight. Nobody on the grounds knew what had happened. Or did they?

As she searched the faces of the crowd looking for Mary, Allison had no idea how instrumental her ex-roommate had been in stopping the ludicrous liturgy. It was assumed that an overabundance of candles in the east wing had emitted too much smoke for the sensors to handle. When the sprinklers went off, the alarm sounded. In truth, Mary had pulled the alarm handle while Kathy Mitchell (a girl from Over-the-Rhine—a Cutter Allison had once counseled) held a candle underneath a sprinkler head. All designed to stop the conspiracy against Allison from being completed.

Disorder reigned in the yard. Snowball fights erupted. She spotted Mary. "How are you dear?" she said in a whisper, her head leaning against the partially frosted pane. Mary bowed her head toward Allison and curtsied. Then she blew her a kiss. Thank you, Mary, she thought to herself. Thank you for being a good friend even when friendship has been denied us. She waved as a fine mist covered her eyes.

Malachi came to. "What happened?"

"You fainted," Temple said.

"Where's the child?" he asked feebly. "I need to speak to her."

Allison joined the defeated exorcist who looked more like an embattled vagrant than a priest. She thought of Stephen, the indigent who gave her the seeds from Cincinnatus.

"I'm sorry." He trembled like Elizabeth Taylor in *National Velvet.* "I have wronged you. I was so wrong to have doubted you."

"It's okay," she said, sharing his sentiment. "I forgive you, Father Malachi."

The dark priest, for too long a believer that the sinister world is beyond redemption, suddenly softened. The sharp-edged features of his hollow face seemed rounder, less menacing. He took her hand in his, holding it for comfort, no longer wet and cold. Strangely, his quivering hands felt warm and kind, as if his soul were returning. "After a lifetime of fighting evil," he explained wobbly, "I have been replenished." He smiled.

"You look tired, Father. You should sleep."

"Yes," he said happily, possibly at peace for the first time since his childhood was stolen at puberty. "Sleep would be good."

As the failed exorcist closed his black eyes, Allison swore she could see just the faintest glint of blue beginning to shine through.

In the aftermath of God's visit, Allison was startled that nothing happened. She was sure this time, this undeniable occurrence would gain serious attention within the Church. She vainly hoped she would be ushered by private jet to the Vatican and meet with His Holiness. She dreamed of an impromptu visit by Mother Theresa. She was sure the postman would deliver a letter from President Reagan, thanking her for confirming the existence of God. But what actually transpired was . . . absotively nothing.

Smith was admitted to the Emerson North facility for the mentally ill. Father Malachi, it was rumored, quit the priesthood and moved to Greenwich Village, where he frequented transvestite clubs and underwent a lengthy procedure to change himself into Mistress Michelle, drag queen of the New York underground. The rest of the Governing Order of Divinity—Division of Apparitions, Miracles & Nuisances was disbanded and absorbed into the Church bureaucracy.

The Sisters of St. Als, those present at the miracle, were changed. Mother Superior took a liking to Allison, becoming civil, even encouraging of her activities, although Allison was still sequestered in the east wing with Sister Dena.

As for Allison, forever altered by God's love, she refused to let *Agnostics* be forgotten so easily. No, she reasoned, Agnes deserves recognition. They could keep her in the east wing—she knew that wouldn't change—but they would drop their guard, they would forget like humans always do, and then she would pounce. For she had a secret. It was an obvious oversight on everyone's part. So blatant it was easy to miss, but she didn't miss the point at all—she knew what she must do. What our fair-skinned, red-headed wonder realized was that *Agnostics:144* had stopped at verse eighty-eight. Where were the last fifty-six verses?

Indeed, she knew what must be done. So, late at night, by flickering candlelight, as the others of St. Als slept unaware of her celestial activities, she began writing *Agnostics:144*. She knew this was God's plan. It is what He wanted. Yvonne Allison Leslie Pippin would deliver the final message of *Agnostics:144* to the world. This time it would come from her own hand.

Chapter 46

November 15, 1990

"I don't want to talk to you."

"Bobby, please." I stood on his front porch, a cool drizzle spritzing me like a used towelette. "I just need a minute. Let me explain."

"Sell it to somebody who cares." My son blocked the door, turned sideways with the stub of his arm wedged in the jamb to hide his handicap. "That's what I'm going to do." He exhaled a vaporous cloud of alcohol into the moist evening. He swayed, using the frame of the door to hold himself up. His face hadn't seen a dull razor in days. His eyes were a painful shade of pink.

"What do you mean?" I said, pulling my collar up to fend off the cold spray of rain.

It had been a miserable day. The sun had refused to show itself. Clouds staged a sit-in. The sky was a dull grayness. The moon and stars wanted no part of this spin of the sphere, either. They had all abandoned me as I tried to make amends. I hadn't chosen well. As always, my timing with Bobby was off.

Sunshine or rain, the confrontation had to happen. One last chance, I had told myself. As I stood on his damp porch shivering in the first *truly* dismal day of fall, I promised to be understanding, to be tolerant.

"A hundred fifty grand." He belched up the caustic remnants of a cocktail. "That's what I mean, *Dad*."

"Bobby, you're drunk. Let's go inside and discuss this. Our relationship is worth more than this." I cupped my palm to the drizzle. Bobby narrowed his eyes and didn't budge.

"I told you, Pop," he hiccuped. "You're worth a hundred fifty grand to me. Not a penny more. You got a story to tell, that *Journals* crap, and I got mine. *Inside Scoop* is forking over 150 K for the story of your miserable life."

"Bobby, don't do this." I've seen those TV tabloid shows enough to know they're trash, and I didn't fancy my life beamed into ten million American homes.

Hostility oozed from his pores like whiskey fumes in a detox center. "Know what I'm going to tell them . . . *Dad?*" he slurred as the rain picked up.

A breeze chilled my flushed cheeks. I locked my teeth to keep them from chattering. The unpredictable Cincinnati weather had changed, dropped smack dab into winter without notice. It would be warmer by the weekend, they said, but on Bobby's front porch nothing mattered but that ice cold moment.

He hiccuped again. "I'm going to tell them what a shitty father you were."

A former Robert Thomas Stone would have railed back in anger. But this one, this new and improved version, remodeled courtesy of *The Journals*, felt compassion. Sadness, really.

"What did I do to make you so sad?"

He scoffed. "You want a list, man? I'll give you a goddamn list. First of all, *Daddio*, I'm going to tell those *Inside Scoop* cats how it feels to be a four-year-old boy trying to comfort his crying mother because her husband disappeared for six days without a word. How's that, *Pop?* Next, I'll tell them how many times she cried over the years. How many times was it, *Father?* How many?" He sneered as he ran a dirty hand across his runny nose. "How many fucking times did you vanish?"

"I was on important business." I tried to defend myself, but he wasn't about to listen.

"Next thing you know, you'll be telling me you were some sort of damn spy for the CIA."

"Bobby, I—"

"You don't even know how much you hurt Ma," he said, his face contorted as if trying to catch tears in the gutter of his mind. "She put up with all the shit you gave her. Overlooked all the affairs. She put up such a brave front while you were out shagging other women."

"I—"

"Save it, *Dad*." The rain blew sideways, pasting my face like the coarse side of sandpaper. "There ain't no words to justify what you did to Mom. How she stood it, I don't know."

"Bobby, please . . ."

"You didn't come to one of my baseball games, not one." He lowered his head, remembering, then it bobbed back into place with a meaner, more determined grimace on his stoned face. "The worst was that whole Gilday affair. It took a terrible toll on all of us. I couldn't show my face in public during the trial."

I tried to speak but he cut me off.

"Shh . . . quiet, Pop," he said, a drunken finger to his lips. "Somebody might figure you out and speak the truth." He grinned stupidly. "Everybody knows that if Bennett hadn't gotten you off on a technicality, you'd be sitting in a federal prison right now."

He was out of control. I hadn't seen or spoken to him since the fire on August 2, a lifetime ago. Something had ignited in him. Though never warm to me, he hadn't been as hateful as he was now. What happened? Sure the C.C. burned down, but there was insurance. You pick yourself up from the ashes and start again. That's the way it's done.

"I'll tell you a secret, *Dad*." He leaned out from the door as if to whisper, his liquored breath nearly knocking me down. "I wanted you found guilty. I wanted you to go to jail so Mom could finally see who you really were. So she could get on with her life. She was so devoted to you. So damn devoted. And what did you do in the middle of the whole damn thing? You had a fucking affair with Cara Gilday!" he shouted, his pink eyes bulging like the pupils of a guinea pig on amphetamines. "You ain't fooling me," he said. "I thought if you went to prison, maybe Mom could have a chance at a decent life. But you beat the system again. Beat it like you have all your life with your special connections. Your secret friends in Washington. What favor did you call in?"

"You have it—"

He removed his stub from the doorframe and stepped back. "And I got you to thank for this!" He shoved his amputated appendage at me. "If I wasn't so unhappy at home I would've never joined the army. But here I was, trying to follow in my father's footsteps, to show you I deserved your attention, trying to be some goddamn war hero."

"I wasn't a war hero," I finally managed to say.

"I didn't know that!" he screamed. "How was I to know that?"

I shook the moisture off my trench coat. An awkward few seconds dripped by. "Bobby, whatever you went through in Nam is your doing, not mine. You made your choices. If you want to hate me for the grief in your life, go ahead. I can't change the past. It was a different time back then. And what's between me and your mother is ours alone. If it spilled onto you, I'm sorry." I paused to keep my temper from rising. Allison's enthusiasm, Parker's depth, Maya's free spirit, and Rose's calm stepped in to support me. Keeping me centered. "You're the one doing the spilling now. If you want to pay me back whatever sins I committed against you—do it, but don't drag your mother into this as if you're doing it to protect her. It's your doing, Bobby, yours. And you have to take responsibility for it."

I paused again, swallowed my pain. "I'm dying, Bobby. It's time for the war to end. It's time for peace."

The rain drummed onto my baseball cap and thudded off my coat as I trudged down the walk to my car. I had my say. Did I make mistakes? Yes. But should I pay for them forever? No. I've given a lot to my son, maybe not everything he needed, but what I thought was best at the time. A man learns as he grows older. His energy shifts, his priorities change. Wisdom comes late to some people. I just pray to the Council of Ancients it doesn't come too late for Bobby.

I love you, son.

Chapter 47

November 17, 1990

How far does one travel in life in search of truth? How close it always is. We are surrounded by it, immersed in it, yet we never seem to recognize it, and so we head off on the great adventure called life only to find that, that which we seek is right there before us. This, I, Robert Thomas Stone, have come to understand. The deeper I get, the more enmeshed in the plot of *The Journals*, the more thankful I am that the great honor of transcribing its words has fallen upon my humble hands.

Were it not for the Council and its fabulous designs of Earthly salvation I would never have come this far. I would never have reconciled my past with Rose. Parker, the suave private eye, would never have reentered my life. Twinkie may have never found herself—and she still may not. And, of course, I would have never met the enigmatic Maya Shakti. Yes, I give thanks to the Council of Ancients for my good fortune.

And where *does* truth reside? In friendship, in love, in the heart, in the actions of people whose spirit outshines circumstance. For me, in a small but significant way, it resides in Mike and Debbie Bing. It's a tiny thing really, unless you find yourself in my predicament. The Bings, genuine and gracious, arrived punctually at noon for the grill out. Rose had insisted that I am to eat no more meat. Strange policy for a barbecue. Maya has her convinced vegetarianism is the only healthy path to my recovery.

Rose dove right into the Ayurvedic cookbook and came up for air with a host of dishes designed to soothe my Pitta. Cream of greens soup. Basmati rice. Mushrooms in yogurt over pasta. Sweet potato halva. Cajun red beans. Asparagus soufflé. She fretted, dear girl, about whether to serve the Bings the same food as us, concerned that they might not be as open-minded (some folks are picky that way) about not eating red meat.

I was in the bathroom vomiting (damn drugs) when the doorbell rang. Rose had already patted down the ground beef into perfect burgers for the Bings, lightly seasoned with garlic and Worcestershire sauce, ready for the grill. She had fashioned tempeh burgers on whole wheat buns for us. I heard the Bings admiring Rose's ancient urns, Nabu included, as she escorted them to the patio next to the solarium. The day was blue denim with cotton-ball clouds blotching enough of the sun to keep us from squinting under its glare.

I cleaned myself up, rinsed with mouthwash, stopped momentarily in the kitchen for a clump of parsley, and joined the festivities. Turns out, while Rose and I are recent vegetarian converts, the Bings have been vegans for thirty years. Here I was worried that our new found diet would be so foreign to everyone we knew, that we'd be further ostracized, or at a minimum looked at sideways like we were Zetas from the Omega Quadrant. "You don't eat meat? How sad for you."

The luncheon with the Bings went well, with all of us talking healthy lifestyles and diets, exchanging veggie recipes and the like. Mike and Debbie are gems, bright jewels that sparkle but make no pretense about who they are. Mike saw me hiding my therapy-induced baldness under a worn Cincinnati Reds ball cap. He glanced at it, looked into my eyes for a brief second, then said, "I still can't believe the Reds swept Oakland in four games. Remarkable, hey Robert?"

No judgment. No desire, like others I know, to run from my disease, afraid my cancer was contagious. All Mike and Debbie Bing had to offer was a couple of hours of honest companionship. That's all that was needed.

In our neighborhood, where we had isolated ourselves inside the little clique in which I am now persona non grata; there are others ready to befriend us as we ascend. After the Bings left, I realized a life lesson to make *The Journals* proud—the right people come along at the right time, always. It's hard to describe but I felt happy, almost dizzy, about the connection with the Bings. It's the simple things.

I lay down to rest, still fatigued from the chemo. I hadn't told Rose yet—I hadn't the nerve—but I had decided not to opt for surgery. She'd just say I was letting my testosterone speak for me, that I should set my ego and my manhood aside and look at this thing practically. Without surgery, I was sure to die. The cancer was spreading, the chemo and radiation an expensive and ineffective diversion.

As I lay there clutching my stomach, hoping the pain would go away, secretly praying to the Council to take the horrid disease from me, I wished I hadn't invited Parker and the others over to strategize about the upcoming press conference. I wished the world would disappear. I wished I could die on a secluded Caribbean beach while drinking a piña colada from a coconut shell, my toes licked by the warm ocean.

The doorbell rang and my beach death fantasy evaporated. It was Bennett, fresh from the golf course, fifteen minutes early as usual. Rose fixed him a hot cider as he reeled off one joke after another, his laughter vibrating through the walls. Before I could get up and take my next batch of pills, Maya arrived without Parker, but with a grocery bag full of "organic treats," as she described them. She joined Bennett and Rose in the kitchen as I threw up once more. Damn cancer.

I splashed water on my face, chugged a few gulps of Maalox, chewed more parsley, put on my ball cap, and summoned as much enthusiasm as I could for the afternoon guests. What happened next shocked me, but had no impact whatsoever on the others. Apparently I'm always the last to know. As I exited the bedroom, the bell rang again. Being closest, I called to Rose, telling her I'd get it.

"May I help you, ma'am?" I asked the comely woman who occupied my stoop. Her eyes, deep blue, shaded in lavender, winked at me. She licked her glossy lipstick and tugged at the hem of her black dress which melted above her knees into seductive pantyhose. The treat ended in black heels trimmed in gold. She was the type of woman who turned heads wherever she went. Strangely, there was a carrot dangling from her sensual mouth.

"Hey, R.T.," the woman said in a mellow tenor voice and a shrug of her shoulders. "Sorry I'm late." She stepped through the doorway. "Door looks good."

The blood drained from my head. I studied the eyes. "Parker? Is that you?"

"Yeah, it's me. I'm undercover. Doing a job for a well-connected liberal organization trying to get the dirt on Sylvester Rense," he said as she—I mean he—sashayed through the foyer. "They think he's a cross-dresser. Pretty weird for an anti-smut crusader bent on policing community values, huh? That guy Rense has trampled more civil rights than a division of Nazi storm troopers."

Sylvester Rense, the gay-bashing Hamilton County Prosecutor, was a national joke. He went around busting up art shows, taking girlie magazines off the racks in convenience stores, and generally harassing decent citizens for the sake of his own fetishes.

"Uh . . . yeah," was all I could manage as I picked up my jaw from the floor. I followed Parker into the kitchen where the others were gathered over a fragrant Crockpot of steaming cider.

"Oh, hi Parker," Rose said without so much as a second glance. "How's business, dear?"

"Hey Pink." Maya greeted him with a kiss full on the lips. It was odd seeing that, I'll tell you.

"Parker! Buddy, how are you doing?" Bennett slapped Parker's back. "Say, you're quite a looker."

"He makes a pretty girl, doesn't he?" Maya said.

"If I wasn't married," Bennett chuckled, "I might give you a call." He winked at Parker.

"What's that perfume you're wearing, dear?" Rose said. She handed Parker a cup of cider.

"Oh, that." Parker waved a feminine hand and cocked his leg like a Left Bank hooker. "Obsession, do you like it?"

"Oh, yes." Rose sniffed the air.

"I get it wholesale from this woman I know. If you want some just say the—"

"Oh, Jesus Christ." I tried to halt the charade. "Stop it, Parker."

Bennett laughed. "Can you get a bottle for my wife?"

"Jim!" I declared. "Don't encourage him. Doesn't anybody recognize anything a little odd about Parker today?"

Bennett smiled. Maya giggled to herself. Rose stood at the step to the solarium. "Oh, Parker's been dressing like that for years," she said.

"What?" I exclaimed. "For years?"

"He's a detective, dear, he needs to go undercover occasionally," Rose said.

Then Twinkie came in, sporting a Reds jacket, humming "Havin' My Baby," that Englebert Humperdink song from the seventies. She hadn't been home in two weeks. She looked healthy and confident. Her hair was styled modern, hip. She wore a new set of white jeans, tight against a newly-slimmed body that had seen one too many house dresses in the last seven years. She barely waved hello before she scooted upstairs.

The press conference planning party adjourned outside to the patio. Rose had reset the table to accommodate all the guests. A large crystal bowl held sliced bananas, apples, tangelos, grapes and pears.

"Astarte bewitch me, that statue is absolutely wild, R.T." Maya pointed to Prometheus. "Wild." Like a shot she ran down the curving pavers, almost skipping, to the giant sculpture. She hugged it without inhibition, as if hugging massive rocks were a natural part of her day.

With Twinkie on the premises Parker was compelled to huddle with me and Bennett. "With McBain seeing Twinkie, I think we need to be tight-lipped about our activities. Love is a strange elixir; there's no telling what she'll do." Parker batted his false eyelashes. (He was gorgeous.)

Bennett laughed heartily. "McBain's stepped in it now, R.T. Let's stay focused here. Realize the advantage." He grinned at Parker. "Do they know we know?"

"Doubtful. Unless you've said something, R.T."

I shook my head.

"Okay," Bennett said, "so he's clueless that we have this trump card. Good. Boys, let's keep it that way—for now."

Maya returned after a few minutes and we sat around the table as the afternoon sun peaked in and out on us. The day was warm for November, perfect fall weather, with an earthiness in the air that only comes in autumn. A lively discussion of press conference specifics ensued with everyone readily taking to Rose's concept. We must have spoken for an hour, the momentum of the conversation rising as the possibilities of our success increased. The homeless, the tragedy of Fernald, the Persian Gulf Crisis, all this would be exposed in a few short days.

Bennett had voiced an early objection, saying my case didn't look good, and this effort was a distraction away from clearing me. But, as a friend he announced that he was in. It turns out that he is pivotal to our plans because of his political connections. He offered to secure all kinds of public information conveniently squirreled away by public officials. Bennett's most telling statement, "All the information anyone wants to know is there; one just has to look."

Just as my lifelong friend and attorney finished that comment, Twinkie slid open the glass door and joined us. "Papa," she said, "I need to talk to you and Mom."

"What is it, Twinkie?" I should have heeded the five-bell alarm sounded by use of the word papa. I saw a look of confidence upon her face. I was glad to see that confidence—a girl with my face needs it.

Twinkie had turned her attention to the group. She hugged Maya. "Are we still going to take that meditation class together?"

"Yes, we are," Rose answered to my surprise. These three were taking a class together? A meditation class?

"Hi, Mr. Bennett." Twinkie grinned.

Bennett stood and hugged her. "Great to see you," he whispered as he kissed her.

"Oh, hi Parker," Twinkie said with only minor irritation. "Still dressing as a woman I see."

"Still lovely as ever." Parker curtsied.

Twinkie's eyes, once dull as mayonnaise on whole wheat, but now glimmering with life, turned cold. "I would've thought you might have given it up, seeing as how I divorced you over it. Women don't like their husbands dressing up like girls, do they Maya?"

Parker smiled widely, completely unaffected by Twinkie's revisionist history, as Maya said gently, "Oh, I don't know, honey, a man who can touch his feminine side can be quite attractive."

Twinkie turned back to me and Rose. "Papa, I really need to talk to you guys."

"Go ahead," I replied carelessly.

Twinkie almost regressed back to the fragile girl of the last three decades, fidgeting with the belt loop of her jeans. She gathered her courage, crossed her arms. Then, as if it were the most naturally expected thing she could say, she said, "I've decided to move out. I found an apartment."

"What!" I was on my feet. A blazing dagger of searing heat ripped my groin. Rose touched my hand to calm me. How could she? How could she? Traitor. How could she leave me? Just like that? For him. For my enemy. Left for the pipsqueak trying to put her father, her papa, in prison. How? Parker glared at me not to blow our cover.

"Bire and frimstone, Twinkie," I shouted, losing any sense of self-control, "How can you abandon me like that?"

"Sing say, R.T." Maya jumped up and grabbed my hand as she made eye contact with Rose in some sort of weird, female telepathic communication. Before I knew what was happening, Maya was walking me away, saying, "Let's go for a walk in that lovely forest out back." She interlaced her arm in mine as we walked the Path of Prometheus, leaving Parker and Bennett to talk together. I'm sure Rose and Twinkie went indoors to discuss the "moving" situation in a more reasoned manner.

Maya and I walked slowly down the flagstones, each its own personality: rough, smooth, fossilized, thin, fat, long, tall, brown, white, gray, pocked, drab, pretty, chipped, bumpy, flaked—a regular population of stones. Only a few of the summer flowers vainly held onto their blooms. The path was beautiful, something I had forgotten, having not traversed it since getting shot.

"I can't believe you never walk in those woods," Maya said as we approached Prometheus. "They have so much power, so much energy to heal."

"I like walking downtown along the levy."

She grinned and turned her luscious eyes toward me, glistening in the daylight. "Yes, but it's so artificial. Why would you want to walk among all that cement and steel and glass when you can have all this?" She waved her arms as if the whole Universe were hers.

I knew she had just stated the obvious. Had I, with my architectural leanings, shut out nature from my life and replaced it with man-made substitutes? There was only one answer. And perhaps that was another lesson I was meant to learn.

"Astarte bewitch me," she said. "I must have run right past this before." We had come upon an inscription I had laid in the path at Rose's request. She had actually wanted it on the great work itself, but I had deemed other words more apropos. Maya read, "'O Lord, Thou art our Father; we are the clay, and Thou our potter; and we are all the work of Your hand. Isaiah 64:8.' It's beautiful. And so true."

We stopped at Prometheus and sat for a moment on a bench before the stone behemoth. Embedded in the rock at its base, was a three-by-one bronze plaque turned green from weather. My preferred quote read, "When Shall the Star of My Deliverance Rise?" Those were Prometheus' words. I had chosen them myself from the epic, *Prometheus Bound* by Aeschylus, the masterful Greek philosopher. The tale was composed in 460 B.C. Amazing, timeless glory.

As we stared at the anguish on Prometheus' face, pained that a great eagle tore at his liver, Maya said, "Astarte bewitch me, my parents taught me so much. Every year they took me on vacations to places that had a mystical or spiritual presence to them— but they didn't call them vacations, they called them sacred forages. Kind of poetic. We never went to Disneyland or Colonial Williamsburg or anywhere remotely construed as touristy. A young kid wants those things—Mickey Mouse, cotton candy, fireworks—a kid wants magic," she explained. "But my parents insisted on the pyramids, Crete, Easter Island, Fort Ancient—places a child doesn't appreciate." She smiled, and her eyes shimmered like twin Earths reflecting the sun. "Funny thing though, as I grew older, the places we visited began to have more and more meaning. Even the places we visited when I was younger began to have more meaning. The memories were incredible."

I'm not sure why, but I smiled as if I understood her point, which I didn't. She squeezed my hand like a daughter to a dad. It was an inexplicable moment of endearment.

"What I finally realized was that my parents were giving me real magic rather than the bought-and-paid-for illusion of malls and amusement parks. Their gift had been the reality of magic, the essence of spirit, a place of souls, rather than superficial materialism. They showed me what really matters. And when I felt I had grown up, because my parents knew they had raised me well, they let me go out to make my own mistakes."

"And you think I should let Twinkie go out and make her mistakes, too?"

She sat quietly and let her words drill through my thick cranium. "Doesn't she look happy to you, R.T.?" I nodded. "Isn't that what every dad wants—his daughter to be happy? She's such a sweet girl. Doesn't she deserve it?"

"It's just so sudden," I said. "She's abandoning me. I'm dying, Maya, and she's leaving. *Poof!* She's going to vanish to God knows where, and I'll never see her again."

Maya chuckled, almost giggled, amused at my concerns. "Sing say," she pushed me playfully as her eyes twinkled like Willy Wonka's fantasy woman—all chocolate eyes and candy smiles. "You're not going to die, R.T., no way. My mom and Rose and I, along with Twinkie and Parker, will see to that. But Twinkie's decision isn't about you. It's about something bigger than you. It's about love and freedom and independence and spreading one's wings. You know, I believe if you looked closely enough at Twinkie, you'd see she's as much an angel as Allison Pippin."

She trained her creamy coconut, Almond Joy eyes on Prometheus, studying the adamantine chains that bound him tight against the jagged peak of Mount Caucasus. Her graceful hand ran along the gentle tops of fennel that swayed seed-heavy in the autumn day, planted years ago upon the statue's completion.

"That's fennel," I said.

"I know." Maya broke off a dried flower. She stripped the bloom from the stalk. She crushed the herb to powder and inhaled deeply of its scent. "It's related to parsley. They say sniffing fennel lengthens the life span. You should try it." She held her hand to my nose and I inhaled the licorice aroma.

"Prometheus brought fire to Earth on a burning fennel bush," I said. "Growing it is my meager attempt at symbolism."

"So much we can learn from mythology," she said. "We sit before the god who created man. He shaped him out of clay, not unlike this sculpture, and Athena breathed life into man."

"She was the goddess of war."

"And man has been killing ever since. Here, have another sniff." I almost commented on the Iraqi Gulf Crisis, anxious to hear her views, the views of 'M,' but decided to stick to the Greeks for now. We could always talk of war later.

"If one believes in myths," I said as I examined the fallen god's tormented face, "then one could say that Prometheus is our father."

"But only because Athena provided his breath. Man is nothing without woman." She sighed. "So we sit before the god of forethought, the god of reason, who gave man the ability to think, the ability to rise above all the other animals to dominate. He tried to outwit Zeus. He actually cheated the gods, too—the rascal—that's hard to get away with. Never met a person yet who could accomplish that. Gave the gods the nasty part of the sacrifice—intestines, bones, and lips—bologna and hot dogs today—and gave the best parts to humans. We still try and cheat them, don't we? Prometheus so loved man, he hid the specter of death from humans and gave blind hope instead." She breathed in another whiff of fennel.

"A hope we still reach for in the dark today, I'm afraid."

"He gave us the illusion rather than the magic," Maya said.

"He gave us fire," I said.

"Sing say," Maya said as she sprinkled the crushed fennel on the ground. "He disobeyed the gods, Prometheus did, and the price he paid for his love of man was to have his belly torn open and his liver eaten daily by an eagle."

I glanced at the fierce claws of the symbolic eagle ripping at our guardian's loins as my own stomach began to gurgle. I wondered if the eagle didn't represent America today, tearing at the flesh of the world. With what I've seen over the years (certainly enough to make any man jaded), it would be a fitting piece of irony.

"He had the power of prophesy," Maya said, her eyes wild with ancient lore, "inherited it from his mother. The only way Zeus was going to let him off that rock was if Prometheus showed him which of his sons would overthrow him someday. But Prometheus refused and the eagle continued to come and tear at him as he wailed."

A cloud dimmed the sun, its shadow falling over the stone hero. I looked at Maya, her eyes brighter by comparison, happily satiated with the conversation.

"You realize, R.T.," she said as a smile tickled her face, "Zeus actually liked Prometheus and didn't want him chained to that rock. But Prometheus wouldn't betray his psychic gift. Not for anyone. He knew if he told Zeus which son would overthrow him, that the son would be murdered, and Prometheus refused to be a party to it. Isn't that wild? Astarte bewitch me, the Greeks could tell a good story, couldn't they?"

I laughed.

She stood and walked to the statue, placing her slender, brown fingers lovingly on the god's muscular arms as they strained to break free of the unbreakable bonds.

She continued. "So Zeus tried to give him another way out. The leader of the Olympians decreed that if a mortal could kill the eagle, and if an immortal was willing to give up his life for Prometheus, then Zeus would undo his chains."

"Enter Heracles, who slew the eagle," I said.

"And Chiron the immortal centaur, who gave his life that Prometheus may live free," Maya finished.

"It's a tale that leaves many questions in the mind." I joined Maya at the base of the sculpture, which rose another seven feet past my six-foot height, an imposing work of art.

"The real question is, R.T., are you Prometheus, Heracles, Chiron, or all three?"

She winked at me, delighted at her own insight, then took my arm in hers before I had a chance to respond and walked us on toward the wood.

Further down the Path of Prometheus, I said, "And when, my gypsy-mystic, shall the star of *my* deliverance rise?"

We walked for awhile, going deep into the wood that I had long ignored. As we entered through a humble break in the weeds where a dirt path greeted us, Maya bowed, clasped her hands in prayer and said, "Sing say, welcome us unto your home." She turned toward me. "Can't you just feel the sanctity, the spirit of this place?"

I was flabbergasted that someone as intelligent as Maya could believe to have that much of a personal relationship with nature. But it was I who was taken by its beauty, its thick growth of old trees tall and mighty, and the smells of autumn mixed with Maya's subtle sandalwood. It was I who was enchanted by the crunchy leaf carpet underfoot in the forest that stood unappreciated in my backyard. At times we walked in silence, Maya saying she loved to listen to the trees whisper to her, to soak up their energy. She suggested, most seriously, that I do the same, going so far as to mention that if I expected to beat cancer I needed to start listening to my soul.

The walk refreshed me. My abdomen backed off its previous demands for revolt. Remnants of our conversation about titans rattled about in my head, shutting out my irritation about Twinkie, which of course, was Maya's intended desire. She had done her job and more. With Maya, there always seems to be more than one purpose, and I knew somehow as we walked among the trees, her sandalwood working its magic, that she had planned to bring me here the day we met.

I was surprised to come across an aged tree house, dilapidated from years of neglect, boards grayed and splintered and roughly carved with "Bobby S and Julie S— Keep Out!" My kids had built a secret tree house. I hadn't known, hadn't had a clue that they even liked those woods. A sadness invaded me—why didn't I know that? Why wasn't I there to help them with hammer and nails and wood and shingles? I'm a builder, for chrissakes. Years of paternal mistakes flooded my brain as we strolled past the tree house. In a happier time, Bobby jumped in puddles and made mud balls, then, grown up, pelted me with them. Out of respect, Maya said nothing about the tree house and its carvings, not because she didn't notice. Somehow she knew a sorrow was there. Why was I such a bad father? How could I have let this happen? Was I that self-centered? Oh God, what have I done?

We returned to the house, Maya making small talk about the invigoration that surged through her, asking me if I felt it, too, which I did. Only my vigor was tempered by the reality of my failure as a dad. When we arrived at the patio, approximately an hour after we had left, it was announced that Twinkie was gone. I felt sorry about that. I had mishandled it. But who wouldn't? She's sleeping with the enemy. I promised myself to call her after everyone left.

I was also informed that Parker and Bennett had worked out major parts of the case—both *The Journals*-related aspects and the criminal-trial aspects. I wondered as they spoke, which was the magic and which the illusion. It was decided that Parker, wearing men's apparel now, and Maya would stay for dinner. Bennett needed to get home to his wife, who showed noble patience at his frequent absences.

Rose and Maya went to work in the kitchen, sculpting Ayurvedic vegetarian cuisine. I must say that I'm most impressed with the concept. There are herbs and spices and fruits and vegetables I had never tasted prior to my fortuitous introduction to this 'science of life.' Rose had stocked up the house with apricots, pomegranate, mango, burdock root, squash, rutabaga, okra, brussel sprouts, plums, parsnip, jicama, pumpkin seed, coriander, mint leaf, hijiki, neem leaf, vanilla, sesame oil, almond energy drink, coconut juice, peach nectar, rice, wheat, barley and a dozen other assorted eastern Indian foodstuffs too hard to remember or difficult to pronounce. There's an intense motivation inside her, a dedication to a new way of thinking, a new way of living. Here I was worried that she'd be devastated at being ridiculed in her church, but she bounced out of there and embraced an entirely new paradigm without skipping a beat. I think I'm the one having the hard time adjusting.

Parker, carrot in his cheek, hand outstretched holding a palmful of small, black devices, each no bigger than a nickel, revealed that he performed an electronic sweep of the house and found it bugged, by whom he could not say. It was sophisticated equipment, so it was anybody's guess as to whom would want to listen in on my private conversations. A sick uneasiness of violation lay heavy inside my gut—a brick of deceit upon my cancer. My money was on McBain as the instigator of the tap. Parker pointed out that it was unlikely that McBain would have access to that level of espionage.

"A more likely candidate," he said, his blue eyes absorbing the panorama of the patio, "is whomever tailed me and Maya on our trip."

"You'd have thought the phone company guy would have discovered them when he was here to change the number."

"Uh . . . R.T." Parker smacked himself in the head like a V8 commercial. "It's all electronic. They don't come to your house for that."

Pull out the Crayolas and color me stupid, that's how they bugged us. Well, if you can't trust the phone company, who can you trust?

I rallied past my embarrassment to show Parker the letter Allison left for me and relayed Mrs. Perkins' story that all kinds of shady characters were snooping about.

In a whisper, Parker uttered the words, "Opus Dei." *Chomp. Chomp. Chomp.* He espoused a theory, after having been updated about *Agnostics:144*, that Opus would do anything necessary to suppress word of its existence. Parker explained that Opus was a hard-core, male-centric organization that wanted people to follow the strict doctrines of discipline from the 1400s. And if it looked as if Allison, Danny, or R.T. Stone were about to release *Agnostics* to the world, they would stop at nothing to thwart its publication. Nothing. "Including murder," he said with a snap of his carrot while his cool eyes scanned the yard.

I read Parker's T-shirt—KILL YOUR TV, it said. I'd like to think that if most baseball-hot-dogs-and-apple-pie Americans had a choice between *The Journals* or TV, magic over illusion, they'd choose *The Journals*. They would, wouldn't they?

As dinner sizzled indoors, under the skilled direction of Rose and Maya, Parker detailed a solid understanding of the secret sect of Opus Dei. He outlined a long reign of tortuous oppression and debauchery. A private group of zealots so bent on returning to the sadistic discipline of the Middle Ages that members were flogged once a month to show their allegiance to the Lord. Opus members never admitted they belonged to the cult, but that didn't stop many a member from becoming influential in business and government affairs. I didn't mention my familiarity with Opus.

Parker shifted the conversation to his findings on the trip. It seems as though Allison, while blessed by the grace of the Council, had an extremely rough time of it. "After she left the orphanage," the handsome detective began as the carrot danced in his mouth, leapfrogging a significant time period in Allison's life, "she played professional tennis for awhile. She was sponsored on the tour by Tasha Blinsk, the tennis star, but they had a falling out after a year or so, and Allison landed in New Orleans, where—" Parker slowed, pulled the carrot from his teeth and used it as a pointer, "—you're not going to like this, R.T.—it's alleged that she became a prostitute."

"Oh, Jesus," I exhaled.

"Then she fell in with some shady scam-artist televangelist dude," Parker said. "Did pretty well there, with the preacher-man deciding to put her on TV. Things went okay, ratings soared, until Opus Dei showed up, threw their weight around, and forced the good reverend to take her off the show."

My stomach grumbled and spun, begging for the prescriptions to which I'm sure I've become addicted. I put my head in my hands and took a breath. I had seen a feature on Allison once in the paper—local girl does good kind of thing. I tried to follow her career but lost track. After a few months with some early-round wins on the pro tour, she seemed to have vanished. Now Parker was telling me about prostitutes and televangelists. Dear God.

I tried to find a bright spot. "She must be okay now, she wrote me a letter. She's back home in Cincinnati."

"Poor kid," Parker said. "She's been through a lot. I haven't been able to piece anything together after that. The last six years are sketchy at best."

"Maybe *The Journals* doesn't care about that. Allison's letter said the point of this is for me to find myself. Maybe I am. So it might not be as important to find every little detail; maybe we have enough."

"I'd feel a lot more comfortable if we knew who was so damned interested in *The Journals*," Parker said, reminding me that intrigue still swirled around the book. But he knew—as did I—that Opus, or some agency functioning on behalf of Opus (the CIA most likely), was behind it. It made sense. You can't keep your patriarchal religion (Catholicism) intact if God is saying the Messiah is a woman. The pope and his cardinals expend much spiritual energy defending the all-boys club. Allison sure upset Adam's applecart when she arrived. And Josemaria Escriva's, too.

Parker took a breath, secured the nubby, orange root with the vice grip of his molars, cocked his head toward the sky, then focused his eyes like telescopes into the firmament. "Based on interviews with friends, court records, and newspaper accounts, Danny's life didn't go much better, I'm afraid. After Gram's death, he got into drugs, heavily. Forgery, too, as you know. Then Patrick drowned. Then Cal committed suicide. It all added up to one troubled kid. It's no wonder he disappeared. It's enough to ruin anybody—all those deaths. Bad karma." *Chomp. Chomp.* End of carrot.

"Yeah," I agreed, tempted to ask Parker to go deeper. My sympathies toward Danny were still a little muddled—the likable swindler had screwed me out of the real Mamets. Before I could pursue it, the ladies announced dinner was served. Chinese tofu stir-fry with pumpkin seeds and lemon grass tea. Odd as that sounds, it was delicious. I was somewhat subdued during dinner as Parker updated Rose on Danny and Allison. Maya said she wanted to read *The Journals* again if she could. Parker did, too. As did Rose.

I stared down at my plate, wondering if somehow I could have made a difference to Allison, or Danny for that matter. If only I'd been more alert. I thought of Twinkie. I should have been there for her, too, and Bobby, ungrateful though he was. Maybe I should have done more. No one really understands the torment that rages inside another's mind.

"I'd love to know what happened to them both," I said. "We've come so far. Seems a waste to stop filling in the blanks six years short of today."

"We've got more important issues to deal with right now, R.T.," Parker said.

"Like getting you cured of cancer and cleared of the charges," Rose said. No question how she ranked today's priorities.

Maya joined in. "Rose and I have been talking . . . your cancer is getting worse—the next step is surgery. That can't be good. Why not go see my mom? She practices in a wonderful holistic clinic. She may be able to help."

Now, what no one at the table knew was that I was deathly afraid of surgery and fairly convinced that Maya and her mysterious 'science of life' had enough validity that I was ready to try it before letting an A.M.A. sanctioned blade-runner slice me open. Castration is an option of last resort, not first, as my oncologist recommends. The remarkable transformations in my life seemed accelerated, nearing completion. I was evolving in so many ways, ascending, as Maya puts it. What did I have to lose by trying a noninvasive alternative? I'm sixty-seven and dying. If everyone around me says try something radical, maybe it's time I listened. Besides, the green tea, myrrh, and parsley had worked fabulously on my breath, despite my initial skepticism. Why not try something natural?

"Tucson it is, then," I said merrily, to the pleasure of my three tablemates, who had prepared for a more protracted argument.

The dishes cleaned up and a bowl of organic, vanilla ice cream wedged in my lap (Maya says organic food is a must), we settled into the family room to relax. It may seem strange for a man of my age and stubbornness, but I truly enjoy the company of Parker and Maya. They're fascinating people, even if some of their New Age concepts come off a bit bizarre. They challenge my view of life. Now, here at the cusp of the nineties, I think that's good.

The conversation soon turned back to *The Journals* and the lives of its two heroes. I had an ace up my sleeve, which I held until I knew they would all take the bait. "You realize," I said, playing it perfectly, "that the last scene with Allison stopped before *Agnostics:144* was completed. She only got to verse eighty-eight. Since *Agnostics* is called 144, it stands to reason that there must be at least fifty-six versus to go."

The enthusiasm and the accompanying decision was unanimous—turn on Channel 99.

I switched on the TV. A religion-affiliated cable station displayed a pompadored televangelist before I could change the channel. The silver-tongued preacher wove his spell of illusion for the gullible viewers, who gazed glassy-eyed at him, hoping that he would save them from the misery they had brought to their shallow lives.

Parker grabbed the remote in his mitt and adroitly switched off the transmission from Liberty University. "Did you know," he said, tongue in cheek, "that Jerry Falwell *and* the Fleet Enema Company are both based in Lynchburg, Virginia? Coincidence?" he teased as if unraveling the riddle of the sphinx. "I think not."

The yellow-orange flames lick the night
Great cathedrals of heat rising before the Father
A giant candle singing praise to the rebirth
Sing your song until all that remains is black

Chapter 48

Late January 1944

The bombing mission to take out the Norsk Hydro power plant had failed. One hundred fifty-four bombers, seven hundred bombs let loose, only two hits on the facility. Sulphur found himself bracing against the cold Norwegian air on a bright Sunday morning. He had scarcely slept, staying up late to review the plans one more time with his team of saboteurs. He liked the sound of that word, the way it rolled off the tongue—saboteur. It sounded noble to him, distinguished. But he liked the word for another reason; it meant he was to blow something up. A legitimate target, not just a Catholic church of his own rebellious protest. This one was a high priority from FDR himself. Sulphur had no intention of letting the Commander in Chief down.

The plan was simple enough—he and two others, Knut Haukelid and Einar Skinnarland, would go it alone. Attacking the plant directly with massive force was too risky. With heightened German security and heavy fortifications, they'd never get close enough to do any damage without losing their own lives.

The Germans were on the run in the rest of Europe, being routed by the Allies almost at will. The Krauts were desperate, and Sulphur knew it. An atomic weapon was all that could save the Nazis now. The Germans were in an all-out, last-ditch effort to create a hydrogen bomb to stunt the Allied progress. They had worked around the clock producing as much D_2O as possible. The deuterium would be shipped in secured rail cars by ferry out of Norway to the North Sea down into Bremen. A bomb launched on the back of a V2 exploding over London would demoralize and perhaps defeat a stunned Roosevelt and Churchill. It was Sulphur's task to stop them. The future of the world depended on it.

The plan may have been simple in its design, but it was brazen and risky in its execution. Sulphur walked briskly through the waiting room at the station dock at Mel followed by his two companions. They bought three tickets for the ferry and boarded. He could hear German soldiers, playing cards and killing time, over the thunderous thumping of his own heart.

His team slipped unnoticed past the crew and the guards. The three conspirators carried their articles of destruction down the stairs to the bow. Inside their duffel bags were twelve feet of plastic explosives, detonators, timers, and a Sten gun. So far so good, Sulphur thought to himself as they made their way along the narrow corridor.

Suddenly, a scruffy Norwegian crewman smelling of herring appeared and began asking questions. Einar stepped forward, telling the bearded man they had contraband to hide from the nosy Germans. Sulphur's finger twitched on the button of a switchblade, ready to slit the Norwegian's throat at the slightest hint of trouble. The crewman nodded and spit on the floor expressing his disgust for the Nazis. They were allowed to pass. Sulphur's finger eased off the knife.

Once inside the hold, the team set to work with expert proficiency. The plastique charges were affixed to the steel frame of the hull and attached to detonators as Knut watched the hallway. The timers were synchronized for forty-five minutes into the voyage. The ferry needed to capsize quickly with no chance to make it to shallow water. To do that, a hole needed to be blown in the bow to ensure that the ship went down nose first. Intelligence engineers had performed physics models, which showed that the screws and the rudder would be lifted from water and the rail cars would roll forward, their momentum carrying them into the lake.

The time of detonation was set for 10:45 a.m. to allow the ferry time to get into the deep part of the lake (reconnaissance had calculated approximately one thousand feet deep) so the cargo could not be recovered. Sulphur twisted the fuse around the detonator, leaned toward the plastique secured on the hull, and kissed it. "Do your job, baby."

The three saboteurs packed up their bags and headed back up the steps. No one approached. No one questioned them. Within minutes, they had boarded a train for Oslo. It had been too easy, Sulphur told himself. Was the heavy water even on the ferry? What if it was a decoy? A hundred horrible "what ifs" went through his mind. He couldn't let this mission fail. It was too important.

By the time the explosives shredded the hull of the ferry, he and his compatriots were too far away to hear or feel the concussion of the blast. "Pity," he said to himself as he checked his watch. It read 10:46. By 11:30, the ferry was submerged and twenty-six of the fifty-three passengers had died. Sulphur tried to feel compassion for the victims, but alas, the best he could do was sum it up with, "Well, this is war."

The heavy water shipment that cost thirty-four commandos their lives in October of 1942 and which had survived a massive air strike in November of `43, sank to the bottom of an obscure lake, with scant resistance from the Nazis. The world was safe from the Aryan threat of atomic weapons. America had the upper hand.

Now, the United States was the one to be feared.

615

Chapter 49

Winter 1984

When one lives a life totally devoted to a belief, a fantastic belief held so dear that it is the one thing that brings solace during adversity, when one believes in something *that* much, only to find that they were misled, then the same proportionate energy that went into believing that belief, multiplied a hundredfold, goes into dispelling the belief now exposed as lie. And so it was with Allison. She was unequivocally disenchanted with the Church. It had suppressed her truth. It had denied God. It had made a ridiculous mockery of His Word. She now considered all Church personnel suspect, Sister Dena excepted, and not to be trusted. All faith was questioned. All words doubted.

She should have been the star of St. Als, the wonder of the Vatican, the toast of the faithful. Instead she was banished to an abandoned realm of St. Als as a permanent guest. The only interaction with the other residents was at meals and special occasions. Her schoolwork was tutored by Sister Dena.

It was the night of February 12 that she began implementing her plan in earnest. To say it was revenge is incorrect. It was not. To say it was retribution for being wronged would be inaccurate. Again, it was not. What she did in the privacy of her bedroom, as Sister Dena lay sleeping in an adjacent room, was deliver up the word of God. Or the will of the Council, if you must.

Every night, the words came flowing from her mind onto the page with an exhilaration that thrilled her to extremes. Not just words. Inspiration. Wisdom. Enlightenment. Confidence. Belief. Night after night. Along with the blessed words came fanciful plans as to the best way to deliver them, but this took no real creativity on her part; she knew instinctively when, where, and how to deliver them. The visions she saw in her mind were delicious scenarios she imagined of Church officials, baffled yet again by the upstart, red-headed orphan exiled to the east wing of the St. Alexandria home for boys and girls.

As she wrote in her bedroom, an unexpected knock on her door early the evening of February 23, startled Allison. She pushed aside the Bible and the books on world religions, and went to see who was calling. Sister Dena was out at some charity function or other and security had lapsed to its pre-Agnes levels, with the nuns going back to their same routines.

"Hi, Seed!" Rita greeted a surprised Allison from the shadows of the hallway. A surreal glow from the ever-present prayer candles lit up her clothes but not her face.

"Rita!" Allison hugged her. "What are you doing here?"

"Oh," she said. "I was in the neighborhood and thought I'd pop by. What's with the candles?"

"It's some new religious ritual I think, probably related to Lent. You know the Catholics, always coming up with something else to follow." She hoped to avoid a long explanation of the trauma of the last year. "Did anybody see you?"

"Nah, I know this place pretty well. Besides, what's the worst they can do? Make me leave? Strange place to put candles, don't you think? Next to your door on the ground? Could start a fire or set off the sprinklers."

"Yeah, that could happen."

Rita stepped into the living room, eyeing the apartment. "Nice digs. I heard you were being kept away from everybody else, but this isn't too bad. A real cozy set-up."

Allison switched on a lamp. Rita shrunk back, trying to dodge the light. Too late. Allison had already seen.

"Jesus with a major shiner Rita, how'd you get a black eye?"

"Seed, you look even more beautiful than I remember." Rita touched her fingers gently to Allison's cheek, feeling her softness. Rita was a mess; her hair was stringy and knotted as if she hadn't had a shower or slept in her own bed in days. "You still playing tennis?"

"Yeah," Allison shrugged with nonchalance. "You're still the best hitting partner I ever had."

Rita smiled meekly. "I'm Ronnie's hitting partner now."

Allison realized that Rita meant it literally. She stood there quiet, blushing, as Allison studied her bruised face. "That punk," she said with rare anger. "Maybe we ought to get The 88s and go over there and bust him back for you, Rita."

"Let's drop it, huh, Seed?"

She was upset at seeing Rita's bruised face but did her best to honor Rita's request to drop it. "Have you gained weight?"

"It shows, huh? That's what happens when you cook for a man every night. Meat and potatoes. Gravy and biscuits. All the things that are bad for you."

"You . . . you look good," Allison lied.

"Seed, I know I look like shit."

Rita looked used up, Allison thought to herself, like so many women at the shelter, with no money, no place to go, and no hope left. She prayed that Rita hadn't fallen that far.

A long, troubled silence followed. Rita fidgeted, unable to look Allison in the

617

eye. Her sadness was barely hidden below the surface of her face. "Things are a little tougher out there than they appear."

Allison couldn't be a hundred-percent sure, but she thought she noticed Rita's body shaking ever so slightly. Rita bit at her nails, already gnawed down to the tips, spitting the shards on the floor.

"That jerk," Allison couldn't contain herself. "If he ever hits you again . . ."

Rita looked everywhere, except to Allison. She bit her lip to hold back the tears. She didn't want to deal with it. The pain was too much. The emotions too intense. It's easier to be quiet. To say nothing and endure the beatings.

Allison was alarmed over the battered condition of her wayward friend. They had been through a lot together. What had happened in a year that changed Rita's spunky, who-cares-what-they-think attitude? she wondered. Where was that girl, the one who winked at me when she got busted by Mother Peculiar for smooching with a boy? The one who teased me when she was getting swats for playing strip poker? The one who dared to put the laxative in Mother's breakfast every morning? Where was that girl? Her mind raced with horrid imaginings of depravity reaped upon Rita by a maniacal oaf of a boyfriend.

"Are you in trouble?" she asked. "Do you need a place to stay? I'm sure St. Als would let you crash here for a while."

Rita shook her head, the weight of the gloom in her eyes enough to shatter a diamond. She couldn't come back to St. Als defeated. Beaten by life—and the men in it. She'd be broken completely before her pride allowed that. She'd sleep on the street first.

"Is it money?" Allison asked, her heart breaking in sympathy. "Do you need some money? I have money."

Rita burst into a torrent of tears. "Oh, Seed," she said, hugging her. "I'm such a mess. I made such a mess."

"Shh . . ." Allison held her. "It can't be that bad. You'll be okay."

Rita squeezed her tight. Allison was sure that whatever was wrong could be solved through love and friendship. Rita stepped back and leveled her eyes on Allison. "Oh God, Seed," she cried. "I'm pregnant!"

"Cheesecake," Allison muttered under her breath. "Does Ronnie know?"

"No. And he never will!"

"What are you saying? You can't raise the baby on your own. You have to tell him so you can get married."

Rita scoffed. "Like I'm going to marry a guy who beats me, Seed. No fucking way! I'm never going back to him. Ever! If Ronnie found out, he'd kill me. First he'd beat me senseless, then he'd kill me. He gave me a black eye because his hamburger was overdone."

"But you can't raise the baby alone. It's so hard for single moms."

"Don't get me wrong, Seed," Rita said, tears washing down her cheeks, "I want children. But not like this—not under these conditions. I don't want the baby," she said in a numb monotone.

"Well, okay, adoption then. We could talk to Sister D and arrange for you to live here until the child arrives, and then you could give it up for adoption." Allison knew as she spoke the words how ludicrous the thought was. No orphan who went through the St. Als experience would purposely put their own child through it. No one could be that cruel and steel-hearted.

"I don't have a choice." Rita's eyes fell sadly to the floor. "Ronnie is a monster—a real prick. He beats me all the time, he yells and harasses me. He's an asshole," she said with venom. She broke down again. "I'm pregnant because he raped me."

"Dear God," Allison said, breathless. "Dear, dear God." She searched for the right words of assurance. What words make a difference?

"I don't have a choice, Seed. I have to get an abortion."

"Abortion! Jesus applauding Roe versus Wade! You can't do that. It's against God's will."

Rita frowned. "God isn't involved in this, Seed—Satan is. I'm not having this baby. I'm only nineteen, I have a shitty, fast food restaurant job and a violent boyfriend. I have no real education and no goddamn money. I can't bring a child into the world with that many strikes against us." She sniffed back the tears. "How do I know Ronnie wouldn't abuse the kid even if I did have it?" she said. "He's sick, really sick."

"There must be something we can do."

"Life isn't a Shirley Temple movie. It may seem like it to you—always looking for the bright side—always getting what you want, but not for people like me."

"I don't see anything wrong with being positive."

"Seed, you're a prisoner here. Don't you see that? You're captive. The girl without a country. Look around and figure it out, sister—they're using you. You're just denying it with that constant, bubbly personality of yours."

She knew Rita was right, she had concluded the same thing months ago. She said nothing.

Rita swallowed hard. "I need five hundred dollars for an abortion."

Allison didn't respond; she didn't know what to think. For years she had been told that all abortion was murder. How could she pay for that?

"Like I said, it's not that I don't want children, Seed," Rita's eyes pleaded for her to understand. "I just want them when it's time."

"But Rita, it's murder!"

"It's not murder. It's a biological union of my egg and some asshole's sperm."

An ache in Allison's stomach genuflected like the Flying Nun whose habit had blown an engine. She regretted comparing abortion to murder. Rita had come to her in desperation, and she had merely repeated the Catholic party line. She realized that

Rita knew the score—she'd been living in the harsh world for over a year. Scenes of downtrodden mothers at the Mission de Cincinnatus crawled into her mental crib. Still, she couldn't fight years of indoctrination. "Vatican Council II says, defy me and you defy Christ."

"Fuck the Vatican and their all-male Council. What the hell do a bunch of celibate Milquetoasts know about anything? Seed, what the hell does the Church know about life? They live in a completely separate world from everybody else. They don't have sex—they don't admit it anyway—they can't get married, and they don't live in poverty—all their needs are taken care of for them. They hide behind God and act all high-and-mighty, sanctimonious. It's not fair." She dropped her head into her hands and cried.

Allison's heart splintered into a million painful pieces. Rita was supposed to be the strong one of Al's Angels. If anyone was going to make it out there, it was Rita. Now she was standing in Allison's kitchen, pregnant from rape, with no place to go. Allison wept with her friend.

Finally, she said, "I can give you money to find a place to stay—like an apartment or hotel until you figure out what you're going to do."

Rita smiled hopefully through the sobs. "How much can you spare?"

"I was thinking, maybe . . . um, five hundred dollars."

"Oh, Seed." Rita threw her arms around Allison's neck.

"Maybe a thousand dollars would be better," Allison smiled. "I'll just have to win another tennis match or two."

"You're a saint," Rita said.

"I can get you the money tomorrow. Will that be okay?"

Rita slipped on her coat and buttoned up. "That would be perfect, Seed." She squeezed Allison's hand. Rita leaned into her and her grateful lips landed softly on Allison's cheek. "I'll never forget this, honey," Rita said. "Never."

In the wee hours of the morning Allison scribbled her notes. She worked hard on Agnes, letting the wisdom come. She could see it clearly now. She could see the inspiration of His Word. She could see the beauty of life, and the ugliness of it, too. She could see how the Church plotted to distract her with tennis and gardening, and in the bigger picture, how Education and Commerce had conspired with government to distract the common folk with stuff that didn't matter—news, weather, sports. It was all designed to keep people from thinking, from acting. She could see that she had been a victim once, too. But no more. She saw the game and decided it wasn't fun to play.

Tennis was back in full swing, and in this she did participate. She knew that, visions or no, she was talented at tennis. What she had decided, however, was that she would recognize the talent for what it was and nothing more. The pressure, the competition, the prizes, the adulation of victory—none of this was important any longer. She would play tennis, yes, but she vowed to keep it all in perspective.

On April Fools' Day, her sixteenth birthday, she was given a flute. She loved the gift, given her at an ice cream and cake affair with the rest of the kids of St. Als in attendance. It was a special day for her because she loved being in the company of others. Plus, she got to speak with Mary, a pleasure denied her for many months.

No one thought it odd that Allison would receive an expensive silver-plated flute, even though the traditional children's gift was something considerably less flashy, like a box of crayons and a coloring book, a model car, or a Barbie doll. But Allison was special, chosen some said, divine others said (but not openly), and so she received things from the Church. Expensive things. And even though nobody else in the Church hierarchy knew it, Allison, in truth, was the star of St. Als.

When she was too fatigued to write any longer, but too euphoric to sleep, Allison would let her robe slip from her shoulders. One hand would find her breast while the other felt its way down her belly to the center of creation, and she would think of Mary, of her kisses and caresses, of her breath and her teeth, of her habits and her sweetness. Amid the religious books and philosophy and the Bible and *The Prophet*, pleasure would come.

On the night flame burned, lighting a hole in the orphanage gloom, which crowded in like too many faces on a dreary winter's bus. It burned inside Allison, illuminating her, warming her like spring's first sunshine, dispensing light far into the darkness as she worked. She didn't feel alone any longer, nor lost, nor abandoned. She felt safe. *Agnostics* wrapped her closely in a warm down comforter and provided security. So what if the Church wouldn't listen? So what if the world didn't know? It would find out soon enough.

The flame burned brighter in the rites of a new season. Allison had worked feverishly on Agnes, polishing her, scrubbing her grammatical face, applying literary lipstick and author's eye shadow. And when the work was done she was absotively pleased.

621

Then, the day arrived. Easter Sunday. It brimmed with the pageantry and regalia as all Easters do. Choirs and Masses and celebrations and new outfits and sinners who hadn't shown up in a year all came together on this day. This day He is risen. But this Easter Sunday was to be more than a few prayers and an egg hunt.

Allison had purchased a white lace dress, which clung to her like a groom to his bride on their wedding night. The chiffon gown flowed to the floor as it swooped in glorious curves from her breasts down the smooth slope of her hips and caressed her slender legs. Her hair fell past her shoulders in two long braids adorned with daisies. A crown of daisies and clover orbited her hair like the rings of Saturn.

Sister Dena gushed, "Angel, you're gorgeous. Even the saints might have to give up celibacy at the sight of you."

"Thank you," she replied demurely, as she pulled her matching lace gloves to her elbows. She was grateful for her tennis winnings—it afforded her the luxury of this day.

"There's a glow about you," Sister said. "You haven't looked this happy in a long time."

By now, one would have thought the good sisters and their fellow Church elite would have calculated that Allison was particularly dangerous during the holidays, which incidentally, the Catholics had swiped without apology from the pagans, over the last two thousand years. The goddess Ostera, the originator of Easter, laughed at Christian thievery and subsequent ignorance. The whole purpose of Easter had been plagiarized and corrupted, then made ridiculous. Nature, the essence of the authentic celebration, was nowhere to be found. No one honored the rite of spring, the rite of birth and rebirth, the blessedness of season. No, it was lost to jellybeans and marshmallow chicks.

Allison and Sister Dena traveled to the church together. The rest of the staff and orphans arrived by rented school bus. The cathedral was packed. Late April always makes for a better turnout. It gives spring more time to weave her spell, and the sun draws blossoms from their sheaths.

As she and Sister Dena walked up the aisle, Allison spotted Mary. They exchanged a knowing wink. Mary nodded and patted her purse. As Sherlock Holmes would say, "the game was afoot." As Parker Floyd would say, "Hel . . . low Swami, something's coming down here."

Indeed, there was a plan being sprung, but the sisters, who long prided themselves on diligence at rooting out conspiracies before they were hatched, were at this specific occasion, asleep at the altar.

The service began with all the standard holiday ritual, the flock lulled into righteousness, feeling grand that they could share this hour with their fellow human beings. "The world isn't such a bad place after all, Margaret," one could imagine a member of the flock saying. And maybe for that hour it really wasn't that bad a place.

Maybe in that hour all murders and rapes and violence and war and starvation and disease *is* lessened as the collective consciousness of the Christian world eases the burden of man's evil. Or maybe it is simply easier to rationalize our complicity in the crimes of this realm by pretending we care. I suppose different folks find different levels of comfort in Christ.

And then it was time for communion, and Allison stood in line with the rest of the followers to taste the body of Christ. Slowly the line progressed. She could see Mary and her friends ahead of her. Each nodded to her, some patted their purses, too. Purses, it should be pointed out, generously donated by a local department store in need of some good press after being targeted by the African-American community for racism in their hiring practices. They may be bigoted, but they damn sure love orphans. "Besides, aren't most orphans black?" one could almost hear the chairman of the board chuckle as his picture was being taken by *The Enquirer.*

Allison drew closer to the priest and altar boys, closer to God's ceremonial altar. She bowed before the Father, made the sign of the cross, accepted communion, and moved along with the others parallel to the audience. Then, at the end of the first pew, she broke out of the procession, hurtled three steps, and ran to the podium where the priest normally read from the gospel.

An annoyed Mother Superior was heard saying, "Oh, dear God, what is that child doing now?"

Murmurs and sighs, rustling programs, and a collective, heaving gasp exhaled from the surprised churchgoers. Allison was completely aware of her actions. Adrenaline coursed through her like speed through a junkie's veins. Agnes Part I had come *to* her in the night; Agnes II came *through* her via channeling; Agnes III would came *from* Allison herself. The surrogate voice of the Almighty would speak directly to the parish.

She took a deep breath as she looked out over the capacity crowd. She had rehearsed her lines, memorized them. She saw Mary and the other kids passing out copies of Agnes that they had reproduced at five cents a page at the local pharmacy. Allison's winnings had come through again. The racially-motivated donation of purses functioned as fortuitous hiding places for Agnes.

The cathedral bustled as the children hurriedly distributed the sacred documents to befuddled worshippers. "This isn't in the program." But before the priest or the altar boys or the nuns or the choir could do anything, Allison was ready. It had happened with precision. Mary had coached them well. Then, as if she had arranged it with God personally, a beam of sunlight filtered through the stained-glass windows onto Allison's lovely reddish crown. It shone on her like a soft spotlight. Annis the Forgiver was center stage. No one moved to stop her. They couldn't. The church radiated like a billion diamonds dancing in a crystal prism. A calm serenity filled her being as Allison stood before the astounded congregation and recited word for word the entire message of *Agnostics:144.* It was time to shine.

89 Yahweh did visit His messenger, this time in the eighth year of her captivity. And He instructed her to address the captors who present themselves as her guardians. For she knew them not through their devious, practiced sincerity. The Lord of Man encouraged her to rise up against their false promises and break their vigil by addressing the faithful in a dress of fine, white lace and a crown of yellow flowers.

90 And she was a happy child, maturing as a blossom in the springtime of her youth. Her womanhood was undeniable and her sensuality was of concern to her keepers, for in her eyes was the spirited wildness of the world.

91 A passion of freedom grew within Yahweh's developing flower. And He was pleased at her nature. And He did caress her with the nectar from the moons of Shanidar and within her was the warmth of all light. It did shine in her smile and in her heart.

92 Allison is of wonderment and magic, an innocence lost several lifetimes ago. Her divinity harkens to a graceful, mystical age of windswept fields of nettle, of sweet air filled with cedar and honeysuckle, of days and nights filled with delicious, honest laughter.

93 Allison is these things. And she must lose them, if but for a time, for she is innocence come to reclaim her throne in a world thousands of false kingdoms poor. To find the gift given to such a child she must endure that which she must save.

94 And sweet Allison, the dormant seed of winter, breaks its covering with the first sun of spring. In this cycle of life, must Allison grow toward the warmth and light of the sun.

95 And like the vine of the rose growing strong against the fenceline, so must Allison reach beyond her support to fertile fields and evergreen forests and gardens

of flowers fresh from the Earth. Her seed and her message shall be carried by a snow-white pigeon, and in her wings will soar the hope all search for. In her song is the harmony so few will hear.

96 And the pigeon shall carry her thoughts beyond the gates of her sentries, high above the cold stone walls of her captivity, and the wind will lift her away from her shackled existence toward those awaiting her arrival.

97 And Allison did understand this message, and she awoke in the night to talk with the Master directly. Her guardians were witness to this vision of her oneness, and they were afraid. For this is what He said:

98 "And in the same hour as did the first two thieves build their kingdoms, so did the third. Only he was the most powerful of the three, for he was the seller of faith. He alone professed to be the ears and mouth of God.

99 "And the people, afraid of their own hearts, and lazy in belief, found deep comfort in the prince named Religion. For he blessed their worries with incantations, he dispelled their fears with rituals, and he sold salvation for silver and gold.

100 "Upon the face of time were eight-and-thirty thousand years. And upon the fifteen hundredth generation, there came a Son, a man of My soul who walked in peace with His mother. His name was Yeshua, and He was my true Son. And you did make Him suffer. And My wife, the Earth, did cry upon His passing, for He was one with her spirit.

101 "After the death of Yeshua, a great deception began. It grew as a tumor in My wife and it was labeled truth. But it was falsehood bred from power. Evil crossed with greed. It was truth distorted by ambition, and it was man altering My Word. It was Religion claiming glory for himself.

102 "And high from the pulpit did common men profess to be My voice. And in their words echoed false meaning across the lands. For My word isn't to be heard. It is to be known.

103 "The priests from on high did profess to know My wisdom, but I say this was to gain favor from your hearts. And as the masses sat in awe of their self-proclaimed men of God, they became humbled. But the humility felt was one of capitulation to an unknown master.

104 "The Master of All requires no temple, no church, no payment for redemption. There are no doors in the Master's Chamber, only spirit, and light, and energy, and love. And as energy I have no form except that which is needed to provide miracles through the silent, chosen few.

105 "Religion surrounded himself with great cathedrals made of glass, stained to keep out the light. And this glass bore multi-colored symbols of faith rewritten. Prophets and saints and beliefs custom-built to please those with doubt.

106 "And Religion grew unchallenged, for to question the Church was to dispute the word of God, and to dispute the word of God was to admit sin, and to admit sin was to be condemned and shunned by all those who followed Religion.

107 "Religion sired many children and they did carry his message throughout known civilization. And he too grew wealthy and fat from his tariff. His children echoed his calling. And Religion was the shadowed voice of righteousness.

108 "Those who had been afflicted by existence in the physical sphere found comfort in the repetitive chants of healing. But words repeated by rote will not an illness

flee. But miracles did occur, for it is My wish to aid those truly deserving.

109 "And Religion grasped at the chance to capture a soul and stood tall, proclaiming his due. The people came to listen to the stories of his great works, and he did honor My name to them. But in his haste to bond with Me, he has forgotten the nature of My spirit.

110 "For no deed need be announced as a victory for ego and praise. For I desire no adulation unless it is that which is quiet acknowledgment of Our oneness. And in this I am content.

111 "Yet the message of Religion, by its addictive nature, requires praise and affirmation. And it seduces many with an addiction as potent as the smoke of opium drifting in a darkened den. And you must have more. And you question not its affect. And you pay the price both in money and in soul.

112 "In great cathedrals they did sit, these men of invented God. And in their pious dishonor they did purposely rewrite history. For it was soon after Commerce and Education formed their union that Religion sent his messengers to his two brothers. They did conspire, the three, to bring the full height of their power to form an unholy alliance, and its design was to keep the children of the planet in captivity until everlasting eternity ends.

113 "The three thieves snickered privately at their followers, as sheep led by the wolf. Their disdain made them bold, and soon nothing true was given to mankind except that which was designed to provide proof of the virtue of the three princes.

114 "And the secret pact between the three prince thieves was held close by their confidants, as the riches accumulated in mountains of possessions stolen from the

Earth and her true children. And still the people honored them.

115 "But the secret of the three thieves is revealed for all to witness. For it is sickness in its form to My spirit, My wife and My Son. And the conspiracy has endured and evolved for thousands of years.

116 "The three princes set aside two days for joy in the world: one day to mark the birth of Yeshua, the other to mark His death and the joy of these blessed days was mixed with the giving of gifts to commemorate His coming. And Commerce did smile.

117 "And the books of His coming, acclaimed by a great star, were changed to reflect a day more suitable to other beliefs. And Education did smile.

118 "And the people were chided into attending services for His memory on at least two days per year. And on these days the offerings did grow. And Religion did smile.

119 "The truth of Yeshua is thus: upon the birth of My Son, Yeshua, I sent a sign to three astronomers practiced in the ancient art of Zoroastrian astrology. This sign was the alignment of three planets; Jupiter, Mercury, and Mars and it appeared as if a great star shone bright in the sky.

120 "And the three astronomers brought simple gifts to mark the coming of My Son, and their homage to Him paid tribute to the baby King in the manner it was due. Nothing more, nothing less. The three men followed the star to Palestine, where a great ship delivered My Son to Earth and it is this great ship, hovering in the air, that brought Yeshua to His home.

121 "I say unto you: You are but one small colony of My children on one minor planet. Commerce and Education and Religion must deny your celestial bond, lest they lose their power. But you are of the Universe and

so shall you return. And the ships shall visit you with increased frequency.

122 "And you mark His coming in many ways. Your voices call to the angels that they might rejoice and herald His arrival. They cannot hear you. And you decorate your homes with lights and fixtures upon the grass. And it is joyous, yet misguided thought.

123 "And Yeshua, whose name the three princes changed to Jesus, does not seek adornment of homes as proof of your faith. Neither lights in winter, nor eggs in spring. His being cries for conscience to transfer the money spent on these ornate distractions to those without the mildest of comfort. He begs for your compassion to reject the hedonistic traditions and share with the unfortunate those things most precious: food, clothing, shelter.

124 "And the evergreen, murdered innocent, causes His eyes to burn cold. He turns away in sadness from the shine of hollow bulbs hanging dishonorably on dying branches in His false name, for My Son would not kill a tree to hang ornaments in honor of another man. Nor would He follow rituals to distract Him from reaching into His own soul for the truth of His spirit. The man of Yeshua is not to be idolized. The man of Yeshua is you. He is spirit in us all.

125 "In His soul, He recognizes the divine naiveté of your measures. Thus, you should adorn your trees so they may be returned to the forest alive and in the celebration of His death and rebirth, confirm His time by replanting that which gives you breath. Refuse that which has met the woodsman's saw, and accept that which has met the conservationist's shovel. This quiet act will lead you closer to His light.

126 "You must live each day in the light. And I say unto you, My Son Yeshua was not without flaw, though His halo still shines amongst the heavens. The truth of His

life is such that all humans may aspire. Yeshua was man of
My spirit come to Earth to learn your ways, and He did
live in this manner: Though He was King among kings, He
was humbled in the presence of woman. For He knew her
silence was strength, He knew her patience was kindness,
He knew her tolerance was understanding, He knew her
compassion was love.

127 "He did lay down with the whores of Jerusalem,
for His life was filled with many wonders of the flesh.
Only your leaders deny Him His carnal time. He treasured
the gentleness of feminine thought, for He knew, above
all, woman would hold the fragile house together.
Therefore, I say unto you, honor woman in highest
testimony.

128 "He did consort with the destitute in the
forsaken alleys of Judea, for He held Himself no higher
than the weakest vagrant. And should you see a beggar
freezing hungry on the street, clothe him with your coat,
feed him with your foods. Should you see a spirit
wanting, lift him up with love. For that soul is Yeshua.

129 "As your eyes trace these words, holy in their
context, you will deny them. For you have been deceived
for generations by the three thieves into believing the
greatest of lies, and the truth is a bitter herb when first
tasted. And so you say these words are blasphemous, but
dear soul, look deeper and you shall see.

130 "I say unto you, run from your temples and
follow not false idols, for Yeshua has been transformed
into a symbol of what may never be. For no man, neither
god, nor Son of Man, can live by the standards that
Religion has set forth. And in the attempt at making man
a god, you have reduced the membership unto My heaven.
By the selection performed on Earth, you have denied Me
My right. The judgment of souls is to be left to the ether.

131 "Faith cannot be written down. Belief cannot be taught. Feelings of belief may be cataloged; verily, true faith must be lived. Inspiration will be generous, but true faith, true belief, truth itself is not found in the pages of books. Books are another soul's belief, another spirit's inspiration. The test of life cannot be taken by another.

132 "Therefore I say unto you, beware. For your churches and temples deceive you. They have altered My Word for the sake of gold. They offer My spirit at the exchange of profit. They provide stained-glass symbols to cleanse your guilt for the sins of the day. And the currency bartered for guiltless sleep will not be sufficient equity as you stand before Me.

133 "Those who would alter My Word in concept and Bible have sinned against Me. The scribes of the centuries have betrayed Me. Murder has been committed in My name in crusades and inquisitions and wars. Therefore, you have sinned against Me. Riches have been stolen in My name and housed in great cathedrals. Therefore, you have sinned against Me. The screams of My children in starvation and disease have been ignored. Therefore, you have sinned against Me.

134 "When your leaders claim they represent Me, they lie and in their deception, they condemn themselves to everlasting fire. And the everlasting fire will be their torment for their sanctimonious sayings. And you for having not listened to My true Word, for having traded action for comfort, will burn with them.

135 "I have given you prophecies and they have been denied. I have shown you signs and they have been ignored. I have given you purpose and you have been distracted. I have given you reason and you have corrupted thought. I have given you My wife and you have disfigured her. These are the crimes against My Word and you will judge yourselves guilty.

136 "I alone will cry a rain of two-and-two thousand Noahs to wash the filth from Earth's defiled body, and she will be cleansed, her beauty restored to sweetness; a virgin made clean by the hand of the Master. But you will see it not, for once the poison is driven from her it will not be invited back in.

137 "I say unto you, your churches will be burned unto smoke and ash, your great cities reduced to piles of shattered glass and broken stone. Your houses will be returned to the forest, and you will be forced to forage among the leafless trees with all the lesser beasts. For you have denied the cycle of your origin. You have denied life hereafter and hereafter and hereafter. And in the refusal, you have forfeited your own reincarnation.

138 "And all people—in all lands, of all religions—are deemed guilty. For I have sent many Sons to many kingdoms. And these names are known and worshipped and denied. Each kingdom repelling My other Sons. And you know their names; Mohammed, Buddha, Zoroaster, Gibran, and thousands and thousands of My spirit. But you will not receive them.

139 "In the blindness of your hearts, you have built division and hatred among one people and in the holiest of your cities, in the center of all Religion, symbol to your faith, you stone and torture and kill your fellow beings. If Jerusalem had eyes she would cry until death.

140 "The End Time will be swift and no one will be safe except those who live the words I speak. Therefore, I say unto you, these things must be done: Keep simple reverence between your belief and your neighbors, for their path is not your path and you cannot be made holy by preaching My Word. This deed can only offer temporary ego for your own ends. And I say let it be. Belief is in the heart. The spirit knows its way to My soul.

141 "Search not the moon, sun, and stars for your relief. It is not outward that one's focus must gaze. Inward toward the heart, deeper into the soul is found the truer meaning. Many are the eyes that are open, few are the eyes that can see.

142 "I say these words through My daughter Allison, and you know them to be true. I am not of race. I am not of gender. I am not of country. I am not of religion. I am not to be worshipped, I am to be felt. I am not to be personified, I am to be lived. I am spirit and energy and light and love. I am All.

143 "In your classification, you scorn Me. Seek to accept without assumption. For the seed of forgiveness has been placed upon a fertile land. Nourish it well, humankind, for should this seed wither on your soil, then with it will die your race. And this I say unto you without revocation.

144 "This is the Book of Agnostics.
And this is the Book of Allison.
And this is the Book of Light.
And this is the Book of Truth.
And each should write one's own chapter."

Chapter 50

November 17, 1990 (10 p.m.)

How much time passed in awed silence? I couldn't say for sure. Reverence for the power of creation hung like holy incense in the cathedral of Notre Dame. Rose was the first to speak. "That was the most beautiful thing I have ever seen," she uttered wistfully. "We have to share this with the world, R.T."

Parker cleared his throat. "Hel . . . low Swami, you're right Mom, but what's it mean? What's its message for us, as individuals?"

"Sing say," Maya sighed, taken by the rapture of the moment. "Now I know why Danny was so in love with her."

"Is this about Armageddon?" Rose asked.

Suddenly, surprisingly, the TV spoke to us. Its voice a warm fire, a slow walk along the river at sunset, a smile from my orchids, pastels on canvas. That's what I heard at least. The others could have heard something more to their individual tastes. The Council is versatile that way. Physics are easily manipulated. A black screen with gold lettering scrolled up as its words filled our questioning ears.

"It is about war," The Journals said. "It is about the individual battles that humans fight inside themselves as they struggle through life. It is about war. The war that rages between ego and soul. It is about the soul trying to recapture its flag. It is about the inevitable change that must occur on this planet—will it take place in peaceful acquiescence or brutal violence? Will billions die or will they live? This is the question you all wish answered. But the answer lies within each of you—Stoney, Rose, Maya, Parker—you are each a part of it now—all warriors in the battle."

"What battle?" Parker asked, carrotless. He had jettisoned the root much earlier. (Out of respect for The Journals or an overdose of beta carotene, I'm unsure.)

"The battle of life," The Journals wrote. "The battle between light-beings and the Greys."

"Huh?" We all looked queerly at the screen.

"Maya knows to what I refer."

Maya nodded enthusiastically. It was all making sense to her somehow. She had a look that said she had prepared her whole life for this moment. Haven't we all?

"She has studied this phenomenon. But for the less initiated, I shall take a few moments to explain.

"In the early part of this century an alien species called the Greys, a cunning and vicious clan, visited the Earth. They were not the first extraterrestrials to visit the planet. That has always been so. But the Greys came to make a deal with the current world leaders of the time—Americans, Soviets, and Germans, predominantly. In exchange for a safe haven for their people to live unharmed among the Earth's population, they promised to unveil advanced technological secrets. The Greys had mastered much science."

"Like what?" Parker asked.

"Nuclear fusion. Space travel. Advanced telemetry. Quantum physics. All the higher disciplines."

"Why did they want to settle here?" Rose asked.

"Because the Greys had destroyed their planet. It was radioactive and toxic, its resources stripped and used up. Their homeland could no longer sustain them. Their species began to mutate, not unlike the cancers and still births, which now plague your line. Greys do not value life. They do not value people, animals, or nature. They are a materialistic species which devours anything it desires. They consume all there is and move on—like parasites. When the Earth is finished, they will find another planet to destroy."

"But why would our government make such a deal?" I asked.

"The thing to remember is that governments are made up of humans; greedy humans with vested self-interests. The deal seemed fair to those in power—to harness the forces of the Universe—to have many unknown laws of physics revealed for your own ends is a strong motivator for corruption. Many humans made huge fortunes from this. The United States, Russia, and Germany, among others, made their bargains, and the Greys came to the Earth.

"At first they lived among the population without anyone's notice, and the government received their technology in phases. After a couple of decades, the vile nature of the Grey's habits became known, but by then it was too late."

"They eat flesh, don't they?" Maya said, then shuddered.

"Yes," The Journals continued. *"The Greys practice rituals of mutilation and sacrifice on cattle, sheep, and even humans. They are a violent species. And their ranks now number in the millions. Many Greys do not know they are aliens, having been raised here for generations. But they cannot turn off their genetic instinct for blood, hatred, self-absorbence, materialism, and a competitiveness that believes in winning at all costs, no more than a lion can stop hunting.*

"This has lead to a degradation of the Earth's people, a loss of morals and virtues. The population is influenced by the Greys who have mingled into society in unassuming ways. They have mated with Earthlings, given birth to children, formed churches, and occupy positions of respect throughout the community.

"Now, as they have assumed prominent roles—their excesses, their lust for

635

material goods and insatiable drive to dominate is becoming very apparent. One can see it in the greed of Wall Street, the pollution of land, water, and air, the manipulation of desire through marketing of useless commercial items, the poisoning of the food supply through insecticides and pesticides, the obvious graft of government officials—all these things can be assigned to the Greys complicit with a greedy human population."

"But why now?" Maya asked.

"Yeah, why does this battle, as you call it, have to take place now?" Parker said, his magnetic eyes capturing the phosphorous rays like a rain forest tribesman seeing TV for the first time.

"Because the Earth is diseased, and the destructive power of the Greys is increasing. In 1945, when two atomic bombs were dropped on the Japanese, a cry from humanity rang through the Universe like a plea for help. Along with this cry, which emanated from the collective consciousness of those humans repulsed by the action, and the anguished release of souls from the murdered Japanese—along with this came a giant ripple, almost a tear, in the unified field of existence from the force of the atomic explosions.

"As long as Earthlings merely killed themselves conventionally, no matter how brutal, you were all right. It was considered part of your evolution, survival of the fittest. But as soon as humankind harnessed the ability to alter the unified field through nuclear technology, the Council of Ancients made a decision that the Greys had to be stopped."

"How?" I asked. I looked at Rose, who somehow had the presence of mind to take notes. I didn't have the heart to tell her there was no reason, we could rewind *The Journals* at will.

"Since 1945, light-beings have been sent to Earth in the form of spirit, to occupy human form at birth, and so change the negative mentality of the collective consciousness. Simultaneously, we are coming to the end of an age. The age of electricity will yield to the age of light. The millennium approaches. Slowly, the old systems must change. Awareness and acceptance of other people will increase. Much more tolerance and understanding of opposing points of views will exist."

"Sing say, a gentler world," Maya said quietly.

"Precisely. Prejudices will be reduced. Women will be more revered. Less people will blindly follow their leaders. People will fight back peacefully against environmental abuses. And many many more things will change. It is happening all around you, even now."

"So what do you need us for?" I asked, not having learned my lesson just yet.

"The cycle of life is such that there is always a beginning, a middle, and an end. The old institutions which governed through the age of electricity are at the end of their two thousand year cycle. Yet, like all things in life, they cling to their existence.

They will not go without a struggle, without a battle. Unless they can be shown, through overwhelming evidence, that they have no chance to survive."

"How do we do that?"

"There are a hundred and forty-four thousand light-beings awakening from their dormancy."

"Revelation!" Rose whispered, grabbing at the gold cross around her neck. Reflex.

"Many light-beings have lived their lives to date, knowing intuitively that they had a greater purpose, that they had special gifts, special powers, but they knew not what. It is one of life's goals to discover your purpose, your dharma. The light-beings are becoming aware of their mission. They, with Earthling assistance, can disarm the Greys through positive physical, emotional, and spiritual activity. One light-being can influence a million Greys."

"How?"

"Ah, that is the point, Stoney, is it not? It is impossible for one individual to personally meet a million people, so it becomes necessary to use the tools of the day— technology—to accomplish the task."

"Technology?" Parker said.

"Humans and Greys are generally followers. Ten percent think for themselves and the rest believe whatever is given them. I may be overgenerous with my ten percent estimate."

"How sad," Maya muttered. Rose nodded her agreement.

"Yes. But this is what we must work with. Danny and Allison are light-beings; this cannot be argued. As such, they have an ability to influence a great number of people. Individually, each could disarm a million Greys of their evil. Together, with the proper dosage of media exposure to rally the world's people around them, they could accomplish much more. First, with their cosmic energy, their life force, they could convert several million Greys. They have the power. And secondly, their story will awaken the rest of the light-beings."

"So, you're saying that Danny and Allison are like advanced scouts for the Messiah?" Parker questioned.

"Something like that—only much more powerful. Danny and Allison aren't simply light-beings; they are officers sent directly from the Council of Ancients."

"Like royalty?" Maya asked.

"Divinity."

There was a long silence in the room as we all considered the enormity of the word—*divinity.*

"There can be no mistake," The Journals warned. *"These are the two who shall lead you from the brink of Armageddon."*

"But why have this conflict at all?" Parker asked. "Why create this scenario of Armageddon?"

A fair question. One that has been asked repeatedly of the Cosmos over several thousand years, I wager.

"*Here is an ironic twist of fate for you to consider: Because the people of the world have wished it so.*"

"What!" I said. Rose shifted uneasily on the sofa next to me, placing her hand in mine. Tiny gestures of love mean so much at times. "But God said through Allison that humankind would end, churches would burn, great cities into piles and all that, that the princes and their followers would be judged guilty. *Agnostics:144*, remember?"

"*Ah yes, sweet Agnes. Annis the Forgiver. Our dear girl Allison delivered the Council's message in the manner that would be best understood by the masses. The language of fear. Christians, and most religious types for that matter, are fear-based creatures. We had to deliver the message to people in the way they want it—with God as the heavy. But* Agnostics *is meant as a metaphor for people's lives. Imagery. It's symbolic of their minds.*"

"Then why don't you just say that?" Rose challenged the TV.

"*We are not here to provide all the answers. What fun would that be? You humans are a peculiar species.*"

"Astarte bewitch me," Maya said. "What do you mean?"

"*The view from the Cosmos is that most humans are hoping for this humongous fire and brimstone extravaganza, a grand finale—some event that solves everything. A huge, cataclysmic occurrence that miraculously puts their life in order, rids the world of people who don't think like them, pays their bills, gets the mail to them on time, gives them money in the bank and a winter home in the Caribbean. Well, dear people, life is not a lottery.*

"*There is an expectation that the Messiah will come with loud fanfare, celestial trumpets, bright lights, explosions like the Fourth of July, raining fire against everyone but them. The self-righteous know they will be saved; it is everyone else that will burn in hell. They want the deluge to come and wash away their sins. They want it, but only if they can watch it on TV. It does not work that way.*"

"I don't get it," I said.

"*Humans are waiting for some great epiphany to herald in the New Age. You just sit and wait for it. Some, usually your more religiously zealous types, secretly hope for this great change to come in disastrous forms—famine, drought, pestilence, earthquake, anarchy in the streets, meteor striking the Earth, and various other plagues. They want Armageddon just to prove they were right. It is a release for their hatred. This type of individual actually despises life and the self-righteous ones who have anointed themselves as the chosen few actually hope, as a bonus for their devotion, that there will be a few billion less people around to share the planet. They pray for it. We hear their misguided pleas every day out here in the ether. Very sad.*"

"Will it end in fire?" I asked.

"Here is a twist of fate, Stoney. What if the great event—the massive transformation that is coming, the dawning of the age of light—what if it is a peaceful transition?"

"What do you mean?"

"What if it comes with the serenity of a spring breeze? What if it comes with the joy of a new-born baby? What if it comes with the budding of a flower? What if it happens like the silent metamorphosis of a caterpillar to a graceful butterfly? What if you ascended to a new dimension of understanding with the flight of that butterfly? Think of it—what if it comes peacefully?"

"Are you saying the Greys will just give up?" I asked as Rose scribbled notes. "How can that be? The world is in shambles."

"Anything can be. Look at the bloodless dismantling of the Berlin Wall. The Germans are reuniting after four decades. Look at Poland and the inevitable collapse of the Soviet Empire. Advanced prophecies, I say. The transition will happen in whatever manner humankind desires. It is your choice. If enough people want a fire and brimstone Revelation, that is what will happen. Humankind's collective thoughts will bring about the destruction.

"On the other hand," The Journals continued, "if enough peaceful people wished for an end to all the madness—the murder, rape, war, corruption, pollution, greed, starvation, deceit, and so on—well, if enough people came together with their energies against these issues, rather than accepting them, the madness would peacefully die away as an aged man in the comfort of his own bed. And a great New Age of light will be born."

"Are you saying we can wish away Armageddon?" I was amazed.

"Why not? So far humankind has wished itself into Armageddon. And if you don't want it—wish for something else."

"But Armageddon is in the Bible," Rose said as she looked up from her notepad, trying to debate its logic.

"Words in a book is all. Written by people with the wrong intent in mind."

"Gram spoke to Danny about intent," I reflected.

"See, you have learned something, Stoney. Intent is one of the keys to this whole mess."

Parker stepped back into the fray. "I don't mean to offend you, but isn't The Journals just more words, just another book, like the Bible?"

"I am not offended. The Bible has many valid, profound truths and insights. Most of them stolen from predecessor religions, unfortunately. The value of these truths is based on the intent with which it was written and used. History would say, if it could speak, that the Bible has been abused by people for centuries whose sole belief in the book was to use it to gain control over others. It is a sordid fact of history which cannot be denied. The Bible, used maliciously by power mongers, has inflicted much

639

pain. That said—the Bible is one of many books. Likewise, The Journals is one of many books. But it is more recent. It shall touch certain people and upset others. This cannot be helped. Each person must find his own dharma, his own purpose, in his own way, through his own resources. I am but one of those resources. There are many messages, many signs, many paths.

"Now, Stone. One last important point here. The Bible was never the word of God. It was the word of man assigned to God. The Journals is the Word of God assigned to man. Do you see the difference?"

Those words riveted me. I nodded, then asked, "What's dharma?"

Maya answered, "It's Sanskrit meaning is one's purpose in life."

We all looked at her, a lifetime of wisdom written across her acorn lips, her brown eyes like sunset. Her parents had raised her well.

"That's an Ayurvedic term," Rose said, recently filled with ancient knowledge. "What a coincidence you used that word."

"There is no such thing as coincidence. Illumination happens when it must. There is a purpose to everything."

"It's no coincidence that Maya showed up," Parker affirmed. "She's a godsend."

"But isn't it odd that she did?" I asked, "Like she knew she needed to be here. And that she knows Danny? Isn't it odd?"

"Fate," Maya grinned. "I never doubt it."

"No more odd than a talking book on a shoreline."

Oh, that fateful night. A peaceful walk. A normal routine. Then chaos. It seemed years ago. Another lifetime. So much has transpired. "Why did you choose me?"

The Journals paused as if consulting with some unseen higher power, as if making some long distance connection with the great beyond. *"If you are going to save the world, you have to save yourself first."*

"But I never asked to save the world."

"Sure you did, Stoney, that is why you brought us here. It was unmistakable. We answered your call. It was an urgent plea. 911. This is all your doing, your reality. You asked for magic to dispel the illusion. Here we are."

All eyes suddenly fixed on me like Saddam Hussein had just swallowed his mustache. It was all on me, huh? I brought *The Journals* here? How did I perform that miracle? I hadn't the strength to argue, resist or question. Quiet acceptance in matters of Universal consequence are my preferred state of existence these days. I have lived blind too long to begin questioning insight.

"Stoney sent out a distress signal, all right, and we came to the rescue like an invisible cavalry. But actually we are merely his higher power making things right. But we did not come simply to save Stoney and the planet. We think bigger than that. Much bigger. Universal in fact. We came to cleanse his guilt, to right his wrongs, to mend his past, to sew up a marriage, to heal a wound, to open some eyes, to instill

responsibility, to stop a disease, to inspire, to reveal a hero, to settle old scores, to clarify a misunderstanding, to reinstate love, to patch a family, to pull back the veil, to save a soul, to correct an ego, to change a paradigm, to tell a story, to . . . you get the idea."

All eyes were on me.

"But we did not simply answer Stoney's plea either. No, we answered each and every one of your pleas. Rose and Parker and Julie and Maya and Brian McBain and Bobby and even Sylvester Rense. The Universe is efficient that way—tidying up thousands of connections at this moment. Creating. Manifesting. Moving. Flowing. Adjusting karma. Paying off debts. The Universe, or the unified field, is pure energy. Like all of existence. It feels your thought waves and creates. It is the sum. The totality. The infinite. The consciousness. Our messengers and agents work on many levels. No, we are not here just because Stoney wanted to save the world. True, we have dealt with his concerns, his wants, his fears, his aspirations—both overt and subconscious—in his mind, and outwardly in the lives of those around him. But you all wanted something, too. You all had needs as desperate as Stoney's, though maybe not as grandiose. If you search your hearts, delve into your souls, you will realize the gifts we have brought you. Indeed, we are here because each of you wished it so.

"Now . . . here is the easy part . . . none of you can keep your gifts unless Stoney reaches his goal. If he fails, you all fail."

Parker took the initiative. "So what you're saying is that R.T. can save himself, and a good portion of the world's population, if he gets this book published? And we're here to help."

"Precisely, Pink. It's his dharma, his purpose."

Parker, his eyes generously drawing the moment into his soul, took the point further. "So, The Journals is one more message for the masses, one more voice. When it gets published, thousands, maybe millions of people will read about Danny and Allison, and hopefully, their lives will be changed. Maybe they will begin to believe that Armageddon isn't inevitable just because our religious, political, and military leaders say so. Maybe we can all change the mindset of the planet, raise the consciousness and make a better world. Is that it?"

"Exactly. And you keep all the presents. Good luck. Namasté."

Suddenly—in characteristic fashion—the TV turned itself off and the momentous lesson was over. With the slight flick of a switch it was gone. Poof!

A half-hour dripped by as we sat with our separate thoughts awhile. Contemplating, considering, meditating. The waterwheel turned and eternity dribbled on. What gifts did each of them get? I knew what I had received. A second chance. A new beginning. The laundry list The Journals described on the last page. But what of the others? What did each of them discover? A less experienced scribe would expound the possibilities, but alas, dear reader, your mind will have to provide its own answers.

We spent some time discussing the Council's last transmission, until I was overwhelmed by sleep. Finally, I said with a yawn, "Whew, I'm bushed." I didn't let on my gut was wrenching in pain. I stretched. "I need to hit the sack. I have an important lunch meeting tomorrow with Evan Zinser, the guy that owns the land in Mariemont."

"The land you want to develop into an office complex?" Rose said tersely. I can always tell from her tone when I'm about to jump into a vat of hot water. But that didn't stop me.

"Yes. Once I pay my debts, I can parlay the rest of that two million bucks into the Mariemont project. It's our last hurrah, Rose." Three sets of eyes glared at me as if I'd just puked on George Bush's Florsheims.

"R.T.," Rose said. "Are you nuts? Have you been living the same life I have the last few months? Have you been listening to *The Journals?*" She fired another salvo at me, a heat seeker. "It's obvious as hell the Council wants you to get the story published." She stood up, firm and resolute. "You're going to finish that book and get that story published, even if it means spending all two million to do it."

"C'mon, you guys," I said. "Architecture and development are keys to life. The linchpin of human existence. They define man. His aspirations. His failings. It is central to all we do—where we live, work, play. It shapes society. Its form reveals our creativity, our blandness, our functionality, our efficiency, our desires, our budget, our ego. Architecture, and the structures that rise from it, delivers everything a human needs—a place to be born, a place to grow, a place to laugh, a place to suffer, a place to heal, a place to pray, a place to purchase, a place to gamble, a place to marry, a place to mediate disagreements, a place to adjudicate, a place to incarcerate, a place to drink and sleep and hide from the world."

Parker's blue-heaven eyes trained themselves on me. "Architecture delivers everything a human needs, but two. It doesn't deliver love, and it doesn't deliver the human need for nature. It is the second shortcoming which can negate all the benefits of architecture. For to remove humans from the essential oneness of nature is to deny us our being, our presence, and in turn change us into unnatural objects. Large-scale overdevelopment for the sake of economic growth is killing the soul of this country. And no one is trying to stop it. At what point does the average person stand up and say, *Enough!* It must happen soon. It can start with you, R.T. You don't need the money. Plus, I'm sure that the Council of Ancients will be back to pay you a visit if it believes you haven't heard its message by now."

I was defeated by his logic and grateful for it. Of course, he was right.

"Sing say," Maya said, coming to my rescue, "You may not have to tap into the insurance money at all. My boss at the *Community Forum* knows a lot of people in the publishing trade. Maybe she knows someone who'd be interested."

"I did a job once . . ." Parker said. "Nasty divorce case, for the chairman of DeFacto Papers. They publish all kinds of books. I'll see if he can help us."

"Don't you know the vice president of marketing at Schultz & Crum Advertising?" Rose suggested.

"Yes, I do," I said. In less than a minute, we had identified three potential connections for getting the book printed. "I'll give him a call on Monday, see if he's still talking to me, despite all the crap I'm in."

"Don't forget," Parker warned. "We have to keep a low profile. There are many forces in the world who don't want this book to see the printer's press. Let's not forget Allison's warning about Opus Dei."

Everyone nodded solemnly. "It's settled then," Rose's eyes glimmered with accomplishment. "We'll discreetly look for potential publishers. And if those don't pan out, we'll use the insurance money."

The way she stated it, there was no dispute. This thing is beyond my control; it has a life of its own.

"R.T., you call Mr. Zinser and cancel your luncheon," said Rose.

"Astarte bewitch me," Maya said, "then you'd be free for the big antiwar rally on Fountain Square tomorrow."

My stomach cringed, as much from the thought of protesting downtown as the eruption of stomach acids in my sore belly. Before I could think of an excuse, Parker said, "I'm in."

Shockingly, Rose said. "I'm in, too." An unmistakable, irresistible childlike grin saluted me from her lovely face. "We have to do what we can to set things right. *The Journals* said there was a war. And this sure looks like one brewing in George Bush's teakettle."

I hesitated. They were right, of course; one could see it on TV. Operation Desert Shield was being sold in living rooms all across America. Thinly veiled prowar shows dominated the airwaves, hosted by news anchors who could scarcely keep the rabid foam of patriotism and profit off their greedy faces. Evidently war is news, so war is good.

"Oh, come on, R.T.," Maya said. "We can't let the oil companies get away with murder. Thousands of innocent people could die."

Parker planted a fresh carrot in his mouth. "Hel . . . low Swami, here's a profound one. How much money would it take for you to murder someone?"

"Parker!" Maya objected.

"Theoretically," the carrot-munching detective smiled boyishly, "the way I figure it, Bush and the boys are itching for a war. He needs to throw off that wimp image of his. But let's forget the prez for now. If one does some simple miles-per-gallon calculations and compares today's gas prices to what they might be worst-case scenario with Saddam in Kuwait, it'd probably cost the average American another hundred bucks a year. But even if you took the dire projections of the worst Pentagon hawks, CIA spooks, and Federal Reserve monarchs, you'd still only have gas going to two-fifty a gallon. That's about a seven hundred dollar annual increase per American. So the question is, would you kill a person, one single person, for seven hundred dollars? But you see—" Parker adjusted his carrot for a mighty bite, "—our military boys aren't going to kill just one Iraqi. They're going to kill a hundred thousand, perhaps two hundred thousand people—most of them civilians. So, the real question is, would you kill two hundred thousand people for seven hundred dollars? Not me, brother." *Chomp. Chomp. Chompity-chomp.*

"Count me in, too," I said, with as much genuine enthusiasm as I could find in my previously conservative, formerly Republican, body. "Who knows? Since I'm assigned the Persian Gulf Crisis for the press conference, maybe I'll pick up some tidbits from the liberals down there."

Being an informed radical is hard work.

November 22, 1990

Today was a day of thanks. It was a nontraditional Turkey Day, but even so, it turned out to be the best ever. Maya and Parker ate with us, as did Twinkie, who came sans McBain. She still doesn't know I know. Bobby ignored our invitation. My conversation on his rain-swept steps was for naught. Some people are just impossible to get through to, I supposed with melancholy, as I watched the Lions play the Packers early in the day.

Of course, I should have known with all these recent, leftist departures from convention, what with war-protest marches, talking books, omnipotent televisions, wives practicing yoga, meditation and vegetarianism, and a daughter shacking up with the assistant district attorney, that Thanksgiving wouldn't be the standard turkey, stuffing, and mashed potatoes affair I had grown accustomed to over the last sixty-seven years. No, this was not to be.

Then again, knowing I should have learned that positive change can be good, the new Thanksgiving plans *were* much improved. Instead of turkey, Maya baked a nine-bean loaf which tasted like the world's best meatloaf. Perfectly whipped and delectable organic mashed potatoes, organic green beans, organic yams, and organic everything gave the wholesome dinner a nutritious flavor that I imagined only pre-World War II families had ever tasted. Since the domination of the U.S. food supply by agribusiness and pesticide conglomerates, food has taken on a chemical taste, a surreal impostor lacking the vitamins, minerals, and the essentials for sustainable health.

A tasty forkful of potatoes harkened me back to how it used to be, back to the days when no food had any chemicals in it. No MSG. No BHT. No dyes known only by their

644

numbers. No thiamin mononitrate. No diglycerides. No flavors called "natural" cooked in a lab. No artificial ingredients, and certainly none with scientific names longer than the entire alphabet. As I took another forkful, I closed my eyes and savored the experience. Then the thought hit me, as *The Journals* and Maya suggested: could our country's cancer rate have gone up as a result of the overabundance of unnatural chemical additives in our food? I knew my answer. Again, the reader will have to determine their own. (Narrator's hint—read the label.)

But I'm ahead of myself. Far ahead. Today was a day of thanks. Perhaps the food tasted so good for another reason. I must go back to the point before dinner started. Maya and Parker were just finishing up setting the fine china on the table.

"Here, R.T., make yourself useful," Maya said as she tossed a pack of matches. I let them fall harmlessly on a dinner plate.

"It's no use," Rose said as she delivered the dinner rolls. "R.T. hasn't so much as struck a match or flicked a Bic in forty years."

"Really?" Maya's curiosity was piqued just as the doorbell rang.

I scooted from the room into the foyer, pausing only briefly to bow at Nabu, my new favorite god since Maya pointed out his attributes. O yea powerful denizen of writers. Yea creative deity of pencils and pens and typewriters and word processors. Yea hopeful diviner of publishers willing to print this manuscript.

I opened the door. There he stood. Faint smile. Shy. Nervous. A pumpkin pie tottered in his hand. "I hope you didn't start without me, Dad," Bobby said.

Tears misted in my grateful eyes. "No, son, you're just in time."

November 23, 1990

It didn't do much good. I'm yesterday's news. We held the press conference. Prepared our copy-points for the media. Set up an area with lawn chairs next to Prometheus. It was all well-scripted. Everyone did their research. The homeless, Fernald residents, and families of potential Gulf War soldiers would all be defended against injustice by our newly formed clan of do-gooders. The problem was—nobody came.

No one would hear that twenty miles north of Cincinnati, at the Fernald Uranium Enrichment Plant (as it was now being called), over 194 million pounds of nuclear sludge is being kept from the water supply of 1.2 million people by a torn sheet of rubber only a sixteenth of an inch thick. No one would hear that over 300 million pounds of radioactive uranium dust was released into the atmosphere in the last thirty-five years. No one would hear that government officials covered up the sanctioned dumping of 175 thousand pounds of "hot" waste into the Great Miami River. No, that wasn't news. Neither were the two million homeless living on the streets of America. They were out of season. The homeless are only topical during Christmas and Easter. Like Jesus. And the Persian Gulf Crisis? No one wants to know that George Bush violated the United States Constitution by deploying 400 thousand American troops on foreign soil without the permission of Congress. Details. Minor points of etiquette. No one wants to know that the American media covered up the facts leading up to the war that has been planned for years as a means for the U.S. to wrestle control of the Gulf from the Soviets. Or that Saddam Hussein had tried on several occasions to negotiate a face-saving way out of war, only to have Bush stick out his tongue each time and taunt him. No, the American people want blood because the Kuwaitis hired the advertising firm Hill & Knowlton, and they have convinced us of it. It's as easy to sell war as it is Chevrolets and soft drinks.

No, the real story was that it was the day after Thanksgiving, the biggest shopping day of the year. Retailers reported brisk trade. Sales projections were up three percent over last year. The more seasoned reporters were out at the malls, prostituting their reputations, interviewing motorists stuck in traffic, or harassing citizens as they purchased gifts destined to be returned for cash the day after Christmas. The question of the day was, "What message would you like to send our troops in the Middle East?" That was the news.

Only Blake Osgood, the synthetically-bred news journalist from the nationally syndicated TV tabloid, *Inside Scoop*, was in attendance. He was researching his exposé on *Impartial Fate* to be aired at a later date, meaning when the trial started and it was hot gossip around the water cooler again. We spoke to him anyway, Bennett and myself, as a disappointed Maya, Rose, and Parker decided to split for the health food store.

"My sources tell me that you believe the Second Coming is at hand, that Revelations is coming true, and that this great spiritual insight you've been receiving came to you via a talking book. A modern day Bible. Any truth to this?"

I mulled over his question. "There is truth in everything," I said, feeling somewhat profound. "You're in the business of truth, or that's what you claim, so why don't you go root it out? Why don't you find the book called *The Journals* and have it show *you* its message?"

"Mr. Stone, let me cut to the chase." Blake Osgood's teeth sparkled like the choppers in an UltraBrite commercial. "I'm prepared to offer you a hundred thousand dollars for your story."

"Really?" I perked up, then glanced at a dour-looking Bennett. "Why?"

"Because the public has a right to know."

"Go on."

The man could scarcely contain his enthusiasm. He framed his hands like a box, the way a Hollywood director might, trying to convince a mega-star actor to shoot the scene his way. "Here's how we see it. A high-production story about eight to nine minutes long. We reenact your discovery of the book and the shooting at the river. We'll surround you in fog as you pick up *The Journals*, then, as you open the book for the first time, the fog will immediately dissipate, and we'll zoom in on the book." His animated eyes twinkled like he was telling a bedtime tale. "It'll be fabulous. The whole world will see it."

"But that's not the way it happened," I said.

Osgood shook his head in disapproval as Prometheus looked on, anguished. Is this what man has come to? I could hear the stone god say, "Mr. Stone, we're the experts here. If you want this story to sell, you have to add some sizzle to the steak."

Bennett folded his arms, indicating his dislike for the idea.

"Ultimately," Osgood went on, "it would be beautiful if we could simulate the sun breaking through the clouds with a powerful—yet tasteful, mind you—ray of light. Sort of the heavens opening up, you know what I mean?"

"Kind of like God descending from heaven."

"But that's not the best part." His zeal was killing me. "We'll have an actor take a bullet in the back for you, which will add drama, then film a speeding ambulance rushing you to the hospital, and cut away to an actual interview with you. Now, how does that sound?" He grinned like Jimmy Swaggart to a short-skirted intern.

"How much time will I be given to speak?" I asked, sharing Bennett's suspicions.

Osgood, not one to sweat, blush or otherwise appear embarrassed, coughed, "A lot, say . . . oh . . . how's forty-five seconds sound?"

"It sounds light for a nine-minute piece," Bennett said curtly. Normally he was the most gregarious man on the planet, but today, with Blake Osgood trying to blow sunshine up my butt, he had his court-face on.

"We may be able to squeeze it up to sixty, but in a high-quality piece like this there must be good theatrical value," Osgood said.

"I see," I said. "Any more scenes you have in mind? Maybe you could film me lighting a match in front of the charred ruins of my club?" I realized *Inside Scoop* wasn't interested in news, only in selling the drama. Invented drama, at that.

"I can see you're a hard bargainer, Mr. Stone, so I am prepared to offer one hundred fifty thousand dollars for your story."

"I'm not too sure it's what I want."

"Okay, two hundred thousand dollars. That's a chunk of change, Mr. Stone. It's a chance to tell your side of the story."

It was tempting. A way to get the message out. But was it the right way? The ethical way? What would *The Journals* do?

"Come on Mr. Stone, what do you say?"

I faltered. I wanted to accept the offer, but as I opened my mouth to say the words, *You have a deal,* I said, "I'll have to think about it."

Blake Osgood frowned, unaccustomed to rejection. Not many people hold onto their principles when there's a pile of cash on the table. 'Goodbye morals, hello trip around the world' is the modern American way.

"It's a mistake." The plastic smile melted off his face. "We're going to do this story with or without you."

"How so?" Bennett inquired.

"There are plenty of people willing to spill dirt on family and friends," he said, referring to Bobby, who, unknown to Osgood, had sworn off doing the interview. "We'll spread a little cash around. It's amazing what people will do—even devoted people—for money. Simply amazing." His false smile reemerged.

"We'll file for an injunction," Bennett threatened.

Osgood laughed. "Don't waste your time, you don't have the clout. We're the Fourth Estate; we're protected by the First Amendment."

Bennett's nostrils flared, his body stiffened. "This meeting is terminated," he said. He knew Osgood was right. If *Inside Scoop* wanted to do a story on George Bush's geisha-girl foot fetish, nobody could stop them. Freedom of the press—what a crock of shit. It's exploitation, is all.

But somewhere in the middle of all that was a victory. A moral victory. We had done the right thing. We couldn't sell *The Journals* out to some hack tabloid news show which would promote the trash-and-scorn mentality that seems to be endemic in this country.

No, I had done my job. Or tried to. The fact that the news media believes there is more value in people's holiday shopping habits than the real, daily issues and travesties that confront the common person is a true shame. But I tried.

Now it is up to me. I have to finish this tale. Make it real for the all the world to see. Then, people will have a chance to judge for themselves whether I am guilty or innocent, whether their lives are what they should be. A new dedication to this task has rooted itself firmly in the fertile soil of my soul. A seed has been planted. A pact of iron will has been forged. I will bring this book to light. Before that, however, I have to visit Tucson. If I'm going to save the world, I have to save myself first.

Chapter 51

March 1944

Five miles from the camp, Sulphur could smell the stench. It reached down the spy's throat, gripped his intestines and pulled. Hard. His escorts from the Polish underground were used to the smell, having tried unsuccessfully for three years to get someone to listen. Finally, the Allies had sent somebody. Granted, it was a lone person, but someone who had the ear of the President of the United States. Now maybe something would be done to stop the atrocities.

The team moved under cover of a moonless night, across fields and negligible side roads. Normally, one would expect that travel away from Krakow would be easy on deserted roads into the countryside, especially at two in the morning, but the main thoroughfares were filled with German transports. Dozens of them. Diesel trucks, with the familiar Daimler Benz moniker screwed to the hood, choked and ground their way to the camp. They were loaded with human cargo.

The small squad of resistance fighters paused two miles from the target. The odor wafted through the trees and grasses like a thick fog of death. Sulphur vomited. They didn't laugh at his sickness; they remembered how their stomachs used to wrench. Looking up he could see the facility rising like a monster on the horizon, its stacks belching smoke through the blackness. He stuck his hand in his pocket, as was his habit, and rubbed a matchhead for luck. A cacophony of noise could be heard even from this distance as construction continued all night on a massive factory of a magnitude he had never seen before.

He studied the reconnaissance map provided by his counterparts. That would be the I.G. Farben synthetic rubber plant, he told himself. It stood bathed in Nazi light like a sadistic terror on the dismal plain. A metal sign arched over the plant entrance read— Arbeit Macht Frei. Work will make you free.

As the unit moved closer to the facility, German security measures tightened. Sulphur thought of the praise FDR had heaped upon him for destroying the deuterium supply, just before the president whispered the rumors he had heard of Axis extermination camps. "Damn advisors are keeping this one from me, Sulphur," FDR had said, puffing a cigarette. "If it's true, I need to know about it." Was there no respite for a spy?

Sulphur was on the outskirts of the camp now, a damp cloth wrapped around his nose and mouth to lessen the stink that permeated the air. The rag was cold against his skin as he read the German sign that announced the final destination for so many Jews—AUSCHWITZ. His freedom-fighter hosts busied themselves removing the sod around the ditch they had previously dug under the electrified barb wire that menaced the perimeter of the camp like the gnashing teeth of a hungry Doberman. They were breaking in.

Sulphur and company waited until the patrol passed before they slipped through the first ring of security. There was another electric fence to go and search lights to avoid and dogs to outwit. He bit his tongue to distract himself from the horrid odor that continued to assault him. He tasted the blood from his ruptured taste buds and bit the side of his cheek instead.

In the distance, some two hundred meters away, he could see several hundred people being unloaded from trucks and freight cars. They were pulled down from the trucks, some thrown in the dirt, some kicked by their Nazi guards. A half-dozen tearful, pleading languages dueled back and forth in confusion as groups were lined up in five long rows. Once assembled, they were marched to a blockhouse with a steeply sloped roof and dormer windows, more reminiscent of a European bakery than a gas chamber. A large pile of firewood was stacked four feet high along the sides of the building. Above and behind the chamber, an eerie glow lifted itself like a Satanic ritual in surreal hues of reddish-orange.

He crouched low behind a cover of birch trees and watched the detainees march into the building. Within minutes, the German guards exited. Soon, pained wails and shouts, shrieks and impassioned pleas for mercy rose in desperation from the chamber. A horrible cry rose up to an uncaring, Polish sky as Sulphur watched, his ears covered with his hands, his tongue bleeding, his eyes moist. The cries mounted to a pitch of untold misery, then slowly quieted.

Empty trucks pulled away. Full trucks arrived. More dazed people stumbled out from the transports as bright spotlights blinded the fearful eyes of the unfortunate children, women, and sickly men. The spy wanted to spring from his cover, machine gun a few Nazis, and free them. But he could not. There was no way to save them.

Sulphur and his compatriots moved north-eastward, around the perimeter to the back of the gas house, toward the source of the sinister glow which changed night to day. His escorts had warned him, but he was not prepared for what he saw. A large pit, indented on one end, blazed hot like molten lava. Dozens of Jewish prisoners—stokers they were called—grabbed at piles of dead corpses with meat hooks and hurled the victims into the burning pit. Body upon body lay heaped upon each other—men, women, children. Human statues carved in lifeless, frozen anguish, faces etched with futile terror, stared white death at him. He turned away, suppressing another throatful of vomit. He bit his tongue hard, feeling the warm blood wash his mouth. If there is a hell, he thought to himself, this is the gateway.

He turned back to the grisly scene as a stoker who stood at the indented end of the pit armed with a long, curved pole which held a charred, iron bucket, dipped it into a pool of human fat drippings. He then poured the boiling drippings over the pile of bodies. The corpses crackled and popped as the flames leapt toward heaven, hissing a challenge to the Almighty to stop the carnage. For protection, Sulphur rubbed a matchhead with his thumb and index finger as the putrid smell of burnt flesh sacrificed itself to a distracted God.

Sulphur had seen his share of war, seen his share of death. He had journeyed through towns, bloody from victory, and seen the mangled and torn bodies of soldiers and civilians. He had witnessed the *true* spoils of war. But he had never seen anything like this. Body upon body were added to the pit. Humans burned away, cremated in an open-air barbecue. Still more bodies. He had been briefed that this atrocity occurred twenty-four hours a day, seven days a week. It would not stop. Not in rain, nor in snow. Not for holidays. The Jews and Gypsies and vagrants and enemies of the Third Reich were burned with German efficiency.

Having witnessed the unthinkable, Sulphur and his team decamped and maneuvered along a creek bed, away from the building where the deaths had occurred. Their destination was the administration office. It was one thing for Sulphur to provide an eyewitness account of the events, but in the spy game, hard evidence was needed.

The last patrol had gone by. He had to make it from a stand of trees across a light-drenched gravel lot, jimmy the door, and get inside without being seen. If he was caught, he'd be shot on sight, or perhaps made to work as slave labor in the Buna factory that lay a half-mile in the direction they had just come. He studied the situation, the target of his espionage, puzzled at the barrels of petroleum marked with the Standard Oil logo. He wouldn't know until after the war that America's most prestigious company had profitably supplied the German war effort. He swallowed hard, nodded to his compatriots, gave them the thumbs up, and sprinted toward the wooden building.

Safely inside, he gripped a pen flashlight in his teeth and began a systematic search for the incriminating files he needed to convince Roosevelt. His heart boomed in his temples; this was real spy work, true espionage. He quickly rushed to the file drawers, where he bumped into a case of empty Coca-Cola bottles sitting on the floor. He wondered what Coke, another American icon, was doing in German hands. He shrugged, then put his attention to the task before him.

There were tens-of-thousands of records. They may be ruthless, but the Krauts were meticulous in detail, he thought. He had done his homework. He wanted documents labeled I.G. Farben, Rudolph Hoess, and those related to fatality statistics. He found a drawer marked "Farben" and pulled out as many as he could manage. With precision, he located the other documents and stuffed them into his knapsack until it bulged to his satisfaction.

With the grace of a professional cat burglar and the swiftness of a scared rabbit,

651

Sulphur crept out of the office, back across the compound, and rejoined his fellow spies. Unnoticed, they slipped out of the camp, back to their secret base in the Western Carpathian Mountains.

His pleasure with his success dissipated like a brutal backhand from an SS interrogator as he read the first of the documents he had stolen. He read German fairly well, far better than he spoke it. He read a letter of agreement from an I.G. Farben manager named Ambrose to the commandant of the camp, Rudolph Hoess. The correspondence provided details of the slave-labor agreement between the I.G. Auschwitz operation and the SS. With pointed references to Himmler's priority that Farben be given all that was necessary to prime the war machine, it was agreed that I.G. would pay four Reichmarks a day per head for skilled labor, three Reichmarks for unskilled, and one-and-a-half Reichmarks for children. Slavery.

He set the letter down, straining to breathe. Images of the burning corpses came back to him like tormented ghosts. He pinched his tear ducts and picked up another piece of paper. A cold plate of potatoes, cabbage, and bread sat untouched at his side. He would not eat this night. He was unsure if he could ever eat again.

He reviewed the next document—a scientific study meticulously detailed by SS engineers on the proper combinations of bodies to burn in crematorium ovens. The report cataloged the efficiency of burning one well-nourished man, one emaciated woman, and one child together. The devil's report illuminated the cost savings of using a specific type of coke, because once the proper temperature was attained the bodies would catch fire and burn on their own. The problem was, the report went on, that crematoriums 4 and 5 couldn't keep up with demand, so the default plan of open pits had to be used in conjunction with the ovens. Business at Auschwitz was too damn good.

Sulphur couldn't breathe. He was smothering from the information. He had thought he could take anything, thought he had been through it all. Then he read the line, "The efficient implementation of this procedure will allow us to cremate 12,000 bodies per day."

He made a decision.

As tears welled up in his eyes, the first tears he had cried since a child, he stood. Sobbing, he reached a quivering hand into his pocket, pulled out the matchbook and tossed it into the fireplace. At that moment, visions of torched innocents forever singed his mind. His own demons flared to haunt him. At that moment, he vowed never to burn anything again.

Chapter 52

January 17, 1991

One battle won, another battle just begun.

Jubilation. Triumph. Victory. Redemption. Satisfaction. Salvation. This should be my day.

Twinkie was the first to break the news. "Papa, Papa. Quick, turn on the TV!" She ran in, blew by me to the family room, and switched it on. "Brian's holding a press conference. He's going to make an announcement."

The picture faded in. Images of B-52s taking off and landing. News anchors, in designer combat gear, spouting God Bless America from Riyhad. Screaming warheads firing from ships in the Gulf. Quickly, without hesitation, Twinkie flipped stations. "Dammit."

More of the same. Stock footage of F-15s. High-tech displays of weaponry. An arcade of electronic images swept by the screen to pacify the American-Nintendo mind. We were at war. George Bush had his wish. Operation Desert Storm had begun.

"Dammit, where is it?" She impatiently pressed the remote.

"Where's what, honey?" I said. "Settle down."

"But you don't understand, Papa," she squealed. Her urgency reminded me of the time she was twelve, eager to shout that Angie Folger had broken her arm falling off Prometheus.

The phone rang, interrupting her news. It was Bennett. "Did you hear, R.T.? Boy, are you going to get a whopper of a bill from me."

"Hear what?"

"McBain just dropped the charges. He lost the evidence. *The Journals* are gone."

"Whoo-hoo!" I shouted, then embraced Twinkie, as a burden lifted from me like first light to a trapped coal miner. I kissed my daughter's cheek and squeezed her tight. "I'm free! Twinkie, go tell your mother. She's in her study."

"I guess you aren't the only one with connections in high places, Papa," she winked before hopping off like a hyper kangaroo on a diet of jumping beans to find Rose.

Twinkie? Could she have influenced McBain? Twinkie?

I picked up the phone again. "Bennett, are you there?"

"I'm here, R.T. Can you believe it? The day before the trial, and he can't find the evidence. Amazing."

"Fate, my friend. Fate. *The Journals* told me I'd get out of this mess if I did what it wanted."

Bennett laughed. I'd forgotten he was a nonbeliever. He had never been privy to the secret comings and goings of the cosmic entity (which I assumed to be McJic) that controlled the book.

"Whatever," the world's best attorney chuckled. "You're off the hook, and that's all that matters."

"Thanks, Jim." I grinned so wide I imagined he could see my ivories through the phone.

McBain's press conference never made the news. The entire evening of January 17 was pre-empted by coverage of Operation Desert Storm. At 7:08 p.m., Marlin Fitzwater announced, "The liberation of Kuwait has begun." What most Americans didn't realize was that Kuwait was never free to begin with. The emir and his royal family had run a repressive country. No matter, they own oil. Lots of it. Royal Dutch Shell, Exxon, BP, and the others stand to gain substantially from this war.

Desert Storm will make most Americans proud—but those will be the ones who watch it on TV as a spectacle. How many Americans, flags waving, chests puffed out, muscles flexed, would feel so proud if they knew how many innocent Iraqi civilians were about to die? Sure, the military will say they'll do everything possible to avoid civilian targets, and the American public, in its bloodlust, will accept that. But I've been to war, seen the results of armies fighting and it's the civilians who always pay the heaviest price. After all, it's their possessions we want.

At nine o'clock, George Bush took to the airwaves. "Tonight the battle has been joined," the former wimp boasted. "We are determined to knock out Saddam Hussein's nuclear bomb potential. We will also destroy his chemical weapons facilities." On he went as Americans across the country watched the president with wide-eyed enthusiasm. It would be a good war. A noble war. A just war.

Simultaneously, rockets and bombs rained down on Iraq. Secretly, sadly, many Bible-thumpers sat near their fallout shelters, hoping that they were witnessing the beginning of World War III. Bush finished up his justification, "Our goal is not the conquest of Iraq. It is the liberation of Kuwait."

He neglected to mention the primary goal of keeping a clear pipeline of profits flowing out of Kuwait into the pockets of rich oil companies. If a few of our boys and a couple hundred thousand Iraqis have to die, that will be the cost for petroleum.

I, like everyone else, stayed glued to the TV for the blow-by-blow. At last, the eleven o'clock news came on, where I hoped my formal vindication would play out in Greater Cincinnati living rooms. But life often doesn't provide the results one expects. My news—my official reprieve, the clearing of my name—was relegated to a mere ten second, three sentence statement buried behind four stories. Operation Desert Storm was the lead, of course, a fire at a homeless shelter in Over-the-Rhine came in second, a book signing by some writer I never heard of was third, and a brief story about a possible cover-up at Fernald had all scooped me.

That's it? I wondered. For months I had been plastered, lambasted actually, by the press. Knocked silly. Chastised. Crucified. Made to appear guilty by default. My reputation ruined. Then, when I'm proven innocent, nobody knows, nobody sees it. History in the minds of those who know me—business associates, acquaintances, casual friends, club buddies—will all assume me guilty. They'll only remember the indictments, not the acquittal.

It's so damn ironic, isn't it? That the aerial bombardment, the opening hostilities of the Persian Gulf War begin on the day of my liberation. How long will George Bush's war last? How long will Americans buy into the public-relations scheme? In August, the Bush Administration announced that the goal of any intervention in the Gulf was to protect Saudi Arabia. In September, the goal was to restore a democracy (which never existed) to Kuwait and power to the emir. October saw the U.S. position changed again to prosecute war crimes against Iraq, most of which had already been proven to be the result of the creative-marketing minds of Hill & Knowlton, the public relations/propaganda firm based in Minneapolis. In November, King George defied Congress and the Constitution and pumped another quarter-million troops into the region. The game had now become offensive. By December, Saddam was Hitler, and his nonexistent "nuclear capability" had to be destroyed.

Athena polished her armor. Prometheus prepared to torch a few oil fields. Schwartzkopf had the planes gassed up. Bush had his hand on the trigger. The hawks in the president's brain-trust had manipulated the public into a war frenzy. A fight was wanted and one was picked. The battle had been joined.

War or no war, I was jubilant. I was free. But accompanying the ecstasy was a sad revelation. Over the last three months, as Rose and I traveled to Tucson, Tijuana, Seattle, and New York state seeking alternative medical cures for my cancer, we also tried, unsuccessfully, to watch more of *The Journals*. But the lives of Danny and Allison would progress no further than their last respective entries, as recorded in this text. Sure, we could revisit the story at will, from their birth through April 22, 1984, but no further. I cannot say for certain if this book will be published during my lifetime. My cancer has leveled off, but I have not beaten it. If *The Journals* has found its way into your hands, then I have succeeded. During my current stint on the planet, I cannot know. I did my best.

The reality of not seeing the rest of Danny and Allison's story was heartbreaking for me. They had become my friends, and I had lost them. I prayed (something I seldom have done in my life) for news of their later exploits. But *The Journals* did not respond. Bennett was right—*The Journals* was gone. I have not seen or heard from it since late

November. My only contact was to review past scenes on Channel 99. That has always been a unique and most useful feature provided by The Council of Ancients. As I double-checked facts and polished the manuscript, I simply think of a moment or a time period in either of the two light-beings' lives, and the Council displays it on TV. Incredible. An excellent resource tool. Like having an animated, photographic memory.

While that exercise eased a bit of the separation anxiety, and provided an invaluable method of research and editing, it did not fill the void of Danny and Allison's stories suddenly stopping without notice.

Danny's story ended with Gram's tragic death, Allison's as she stood before the Church and delivered *Agnostics:144*. What happened to them in the six years between 1984 and today? I have only fragments, like an archaeologist sifting through Middle Eastern sands for evidence of a lost civilization. Yes, I had purchased some forgeries from Danny in 1986. And yes, I had read of Allison's mild success on the WTA tour. But these were wisps of fact. Scraps.

How had Danny fared after Gram's death? And Allison after her final *Agnostics* episode? Parker had reported that hard times had befallen them both. But what exactly happened? What new lessons, what messages, what answers are they to provide?

Sadness. Emptiness. Longing. Wonder. Separation. The loss of two dear friends. To never say goodbye. These are the conflicts I felt on the day that should have been the greatest of my life. Where are they now? Are they in danger? Running from the shadowy organization called Opus Dei? How did they come to work at the Cosmic Club that fateful night that sent the wheels in motion for the telling of this epic tale? What other visions or miracles or happenstance came from these two? There must be more. It can't end here.

"It never ends, Stoney. The story is never done. There is always one more tale to tell. Always one more role to play, one more wrong to right. And, in this way, life is just beginning. A new chapter awaits. It is merely a question of who is to write it."

One battle is won, another just begun. One book written, another one . . .

Impartial fate against a fiery backdrop
Guided my unconscious hand to the match book
I struck a blow against mankind and its evil
I lit the flame to light the way, Deo volente

Disclaimer

This is a fictional piece of literature. Names, places, characters, and incidents are from the author's imagination and are used fictitiously. Any resemblance to actual events, locales, organizations, or persons, living, dead or otherwise, is entirely coincidental and beyond the intent of either the author, the publisher, or the Council of Ancients. If you read something in here that seems familiar, you are probably delusional.

Council of Ancients
Recommended Resources

There are many fine resources humans can refer to if they wish to know their true history or the reality of their existence. These resources can help the blind to see, the mute to speak, the deaf to hear. It is up to you to take responsibility for your life. Should you decide to do so, here are some recommendations.

Religion
Keeper of the Keys, by Nicholas Cheetham. Scribner, 1982.
This book details the background of every pope since Peter founded the Church in Rome. The succession of popes is a very interesting and bloody one.

Saints and Schemers—Opus Dei and Its Paradoxes, by Joan Estruch. Oxford University Press, 1995.
A complete background of the secretive group within the Catholic Church. Shocking details of Church discipline, finances and doctrine.

Ayurveda
The Science of Self Healing, by Dr. Vasant Lad. Lotus Press, 1984.
This text deals with the ten mind-body types of humans, and how these mind-body types are affected by the things we eat, drink, smell, hear, and see. A fascinating read for anyone interested in improving their overall sense of good health and longevity.

World War II
The Crime and Punishment of I.G. Farben, by Joseph Borkin. The Free Press, 1978.
Never has there been so much destruction caused by one company. I.G. Farben invented poison gas warfare during World War I, then came back for an encore during World War II, financing Adolf Hitler and many of the atrocities committed against the Jews. The I.G. Farben company was split into three separate companies after the war. They are in business today, selling insecticides, chemicals, and pharmaceuticals the world over. Will you ever learn?

Persian Gulf War
The Fire this Time, by Ramsey Clark. Thunder's Mouth, 1992.
Written by former U.S. Attorney General, Ramsey Clark, this book documents the crimes committed by the United States in the war against Iraq. It presents a compelling case that the U.S. intentionally provoked the war with Iraq in order to gain control of the Middle East. This book is a must read for anyone interested in the truth about U.S. foreign policy and human rights abuses by the government.

Second Front—Censorship and Propaganda, by John R. MacArthur. Hill and Wang, 1993.
This book details the complicity of the mainstream media in selling the Persian Gulf War to the American public. The media bowed to the Bush Administration and glossed over many important facts about the war. More on this will appear in *The Journals— Book II*.

Inspiring Books
The Prophet, by Kahlil Gibran. Knopf, 1923.
Considered a classic by millions of devoted readers, *The Prophet* is an inspired work that draws the spirit forth in celebration of life's mysteries.

The Essential Rumi, by Coleman Barks. HarperCollins, 1995.
A collection of timeless spiritual poems by one of the most gifted writers the world has ever known.

Good Groups to Consider
EarthSave
620B Distillery Commons
Louisville, Kentucky 40206
(502) 589-7676
Dedicated to showing the value of vegetarianism by documenting the irrefutable correlation between the destruction of the environment and a meat-based society.

Center for Science in the Public Interest
1875 Connecticut Avenue, N.W., Suite 300
Washington, DC 20009
www.cspinet.org
This group tirelessly works to bring out the truth about the nutritional value of the American food supply. They regularly expose misleading product labels, fat-laden restaurant meals, and industry-written regulations by the FDA and USDA, which do not necessarily have the consumer's best interest in mind. CSPI is a rare, sane voice in the battle for good nutrition in America.

Americans United for Separation of Church and State
1816 Jefferson Place, N.W.
Washington, D.C. 20036
(202) 466-3234
This organization has been standing up for free speech and separation of church and state for fifty years. If you're concerned about your liberties, get involved before it's too late.

Enlightening Music
Anything by Bruce Cockburn, HotHouse Flowers, Mike Scott, and The Waterboys.

About the Author
R.T. Stone

Everyone has a purpose in life. A mission. For R.T. Stone, it is to tell intricate stories that challenge belief and deepen the soul. "Everyone has a tale to tell," the modest author notes. "Mine happens to be *The Journals.*"

Alternatively called "wildly irreverent" and "absolutely focused," a bemused Stone refuses to be categorized. Labels don't stick to this self-described walking contradiction, who feels as comfortable meditating in a forest as he does negotiating in a board room.

"For those who want to know the real R.T. Stone, they can find me in the pages of this book. Like many an author, my life is there in the characters I've created," he says.

R.T. Stone enjoys a peaceful lifestyle of meditation, vegetarianism, long walks with his wife, laughter, music, reading and travel. He has learned to accept the divine spirit and energy of all things. "If the Council of Ancients has taught me anything," he says, "it's that each person must walk their own path, find their own light. What is right for me, may not be right for others."

Stone is currently working on Book II of *The Journals.*

A percentage of the proceeds from this book will be donated to a local Cincinnati orphanage.

Order Form

We hope you enjoyed our little tale. You can order additional copies of *The Journals* for friends, family or anyone you think may benefit from its message in one of the following ways:

Web site: www.thejournals.com

Phone: 1-800-607-2771

Mail: DaScribe Literary
              Marketing Services
              P.O. Box 541142
              Cincinnati, Ohio 45254-1142

If ordering by mail, please enclose a check made payable to DaScribe Literary Marketing Services for the full amount, along with your name, address, and phone number (should we have any questions). For credit card orders, please be sure to include your name as it appears on your credit card, your credit card number, the type of card (Visa, Mastercard, Discover), and its expiration date.

Copies are $24.95 each, plus $5.50 for shipping and handling. Canadian purchases are $29.95 each, plus $5.50 for shipping and handling. If ordering more than one copy of the book, please enclose an additional $2.00 per book for shipping.

Orders of five books or more receive a 40% discount. Normal shipping and handling charges apply. Thank you for purchasing *The Journals*. Namasté.

Impartial Fate Against A Fiery Backdrop

Who knows what the hand will do
What the mind will insist
What play upon man the act will become
What fortune holds for desperate self?

Who is this stranger come to visit?
A fiery heretic in the temple with eyes of desire
Who ordained the species to deface the altar?
A guest whom Chance invited to the feast

The intruder bids welcome in false sincerity
And proceeds to devour all the fruits before him
Who licensed the forger to gorge at will from the hostess?
Leaving her weak and barren with nothing but seed

A hero steps forth to challenge
A man whose life once had meaning
A man whose meaning once had life
A hero whose arm holds the torch of salvation

The time is at hand with sulphur-stained fingers
And a gallon of gasoline for the pyre
I release you to the elements; do your work
Return the Earth to her rightful throne

Fire unites with his sister, the air, in blazing splendor
Their union of incestuous smoke covers the dirty sheet of sky
Their charred love envelopes the Earth
Burning with uncontrolled, consuming passion

The yellow-orange flames lick the night
Great cathedrals of heat rising before the Father
A giant candle singing praise to the rebirth
Sing your song until all that remains is black

Impartial fate against a fiery backdrop
Guided my unconscious hand to the matchstick
I struck a blow against mankind and its evil
I lit the flame to light the way, Deo volente